Lilly's Dream

Lilly's Dream

Lilly's Dream
BY PEGGY DARTY

Kelly's Chance
BY WANDA E. BRUNSTETTER

Surrendered Heart
BY JERI ODELL

Some Trust in Horses
BY SALLY KRUEGER

HeavenSent
FROM
Crossings

This edition was especially created in 2007 for Crossings by arrangement with Barbour Publishing, Inc.

Published by Crossings Book Club, 401 Franklin Avenue, Garden City, New York 11530.

ISBN: 978-1-58288-289-5

Printed in the United States of America

Lilly's Dream

Lilly's Dream

by Peggy Darty

$\mathscr{P}$ROLOGUE

On a beautiful spring morning in May of 1882, Lilly Brown was certain that her dream had finally come true. The answer to her prayers appeared in the form of a strange little Frenchman named Simon Dupree who arrived at St. Paul's orphanage bearing a small chest of rich mahogany, slightly scarred, and inscribed with the initials M M.

Seated at her desk in the main office, Lilly was balancing the records for the past year when Sister Ophelia swept into the room and stood staring at Lilly as though she were a stranger, rather than a lifelong resident at St. Paul's. Lilly stared back, wondering what was wrong with the older nun who rarely lost her composure.

Then she saw the man lingering quietly in the open doorway. He was only a few inches over five feet, with a handlebar mustache of pale brown. Thinning brown hair receded from his high forehead, and his small eyes glittered like black gems against his olive skin. He had not seen Lilly, and she studied him curiously, as he fidgeted from one foot to the other. When his gaze met Lilly's, he gasped and stared at her as though he had just seen a ghost.

"Monsieur Dupree, please come in and take a seat," Sister Ophelia said.

Lilly continued to watch the little man whose clothing seemed to date back to another era, yet his speech and his manner indicated that he had once been a man of class.

He glanced at the wooden armchair opposite Lilly, dropped to the edge of the seat, and stared at her as though he were in a trance.

"Monsieur Dupree, this is Lilly Brown. Lilly, this is Monsieur Simon

Dupree who has come here with . . . well, an unusual story, but one that you must hear since it concerns you."

Lilly sat up straighter, looking from Sister Ophelia to the strange man and the small chest that he clutched in his lap.

"It seems . . ." Sister paused, cleared her throat, then began again. "Monsieur Dupree was asked to present this chest to the child . . . to the one . . . who was placed on the doorstep of St. Paul's on the morning of December 13, 1862."

"My birthday," Lilly gasped, her eyes drawn to the box.

"Yes. I didn't recall another baby being placed on our doorstep that year, and only one child the following year. Nevertheless, I have searched through our records to be certain there was no mistake."

"There is no mistake," Simon exclaimed. "All I have to do is look into the face of this lovely young woman to know she is the daughter of Megan McCoy."

Lilly caught her breath. Automatically, her eyes lifted to the gold-framed mirror over the fireplace, and she met her reflection.

Her hair looked like burnished copper in the sunlight from the open window. Seeing herself anew, she realized her wide-set hazel eyes, slim nose, and full lips completed the face that must bear a striking resemblance to Megan McCoy—her mother.

She looked back at the man seated nearby, and her heart began to race in her chest as the words he had spoken settled into her mind.

"You know my mother?" Lilly asked. "She sent you here?"

Sister Ophelia was standing beside her now, her hand resting gently on Lilly's arm. "Wait, Dear. There is . . . sad news, I fear."

"Sad?" Lilly swung around, glaring at the nun beside her whom she had always considered her friend. "How could finding my mother ever be sad? Oh, Sister Ophelia, it's the most wonderful thing that could happen!"

"But Lilly . . ." Tears were pooling in the older woman's eyes.

Lilly whirled and looked back at Simon Dupree and saw that his head was bowed, and tears were slipping down his thin cheeks.

Throughout her life, she had fought the voice that screamed in her mind, *It isn't fair, it isn't fair. . . .* But at nineteen years of age, she had already learned there were many things in life that did not seem fair. And so she sat back down, silent and waiting, staring at the small mahogany chest.

Her mother hadn't cared about her after all; she had dispatched this poor, suffering man to bring to her . . . whatever was in the chest.

"Lilly, your mother is dead." Sister Ophelia made the announcement gently.

Lilly whirled, jolted again by this news. Was there no end to shocks the morning held?

"Her last wish was that you should know the truth about your heritage and why you were brought here."

Lilly lifted her gaze from the box and stared into the tearstained face of the man who had known her mother, who had gone to the trouble to honor a deathbed wish. But for the present, she had only one question.

"Why didn't she come to me sooner? Why did she wait until she was dying? There's nothing in there that interests me now!" Bitterness accented her outburst, and she didn't bother to conceal her feelings.

Then another thought struck her, and hope surged back. Maybe her mother hadn't cared enough to come for her, but what about her father? She tried to squelch the rising tide of hope, but already she was caught up in the image of a father who might want to know her.

"Please, I must tell you." Monsieur Dupree stood up, and Lilly sensed it was a gesture of respect. "Your mother, Megan McCoy . . ." He paused, allowing the name to drift through the air like a beam of sunlight. "She was a woman of courage and dignity. Life was hard for her, she had no family, no one to help her. And for many years she has been ill. I think she did not want you to see her that way."

"But I would have cared for her," Lilly cried. "I would have been at her side, helping her . . ."

Sister Ophelia's grip tightened on her arm. "I'm sure she knew that, Lilly. And perhaps she did not want to burden you. In any case, she has written you a letter. It's in the chest."

As though he were offering Lilly a gift of gold, the man stepped forward with the chest and placed it in her open hands.

"Perhaps the letter will help you," he spoke softly. Then he looked at Sister Ophelia. "It has been a great pleasure to look upon Megan's lovely girl."

He turned to leave the room.

"Wait!" Lilly cried. "I want to know more about her."

He shook his head. "I know very little." He paused, as though choosing his words carefully. "She had a lovely voice. When she was young, she sang Irish ballads in coffeehouses around the Vieux Carré—that is, the French Quarter. But then . . ." He shook his head again. "She stopped singing. I must go," he said, turning quickly. "I only knew her for a short time. She never talked about herself. I am sorry."

Then he was out the door, gently closing it behind him. Lilly turned to Sister Ophelia.

"Aren't you going to open the box, Dear?" Sister asked.

"I'm afraid of what I may find," Lilly whispered, clutching it against her.

"Poor child, I shouldn't wonder," Sister Ophelia said.

Taking a deep breath, Lilly reached down to unfasten the tiny gold clasp on the chest. Slowly, she opened the lid. The letter lay on top. Black ink, in a neat, slightly slanted scroll, was spaced evenly over the white parchment.

To the child placed on the steps at St. Paul's on the morning of Wednesday, December 13, 1862.

You have a right to know your heritage. Your father was Leon Bordeaux. We met on the third day of March in 1862 while he was on furlough. We married at St. John's on the 30th day of March. We were man and wife for only three days when he was called back to Fort Jackson. After he returned to duty, I discovered I was pregnant. Soon after, I learned that Leon had been killed in battle. I went to the home of his family, but his mother was cold and cruel, and she refused to believe me. She wanted nothing to do with an uneducated Irish girl. After that, I went back to being Megan Mc-Coy. I did not want their name.

I have no family and have been in poor health most of my life. I

wanted a better life for you, and with the war going on, life was dif-
ficult for everyone. So I did the best I could for you and placed you
at St. Paul's where I knew you would be cared for. But I am dying
now, and before I pass on to a better world, I feel I owe you the
truth. You should go to these people, try to convince them of who
you are, and demand what is rightfully yours. I am enclosing the
record of our marriage and a picture of Leon. I wish you well. I
pray your life will be a happy one.

Love,
Megan McCoy

Lilly stared at the signature to a letter obviously well thought-out,
but quite formal to be sending to one's daughter. And never a mention
of love from a woman who had carried her in her womb, given birth
to her, and placed her on the doorsteps of a church orphanage. But,
she reminded herself, her letter had mentioned prayer and the fact
that she was passing on to a better world. Knowing her mother may
have been a Christian helped Lilly to a certain extent.

Taking a deep breath, Lilly picked up the faded marriage certificate, scanned it, then focused her attention on the daguerreotype of
the man Megan McCoy claimed was her father. Leon Bordeaux.

She studied him carefully.

Her first impression was that he in no way resembled her. Her
next thought was that he was not particularly handsome. He had dark
hair and eyes, with thick dark brows and a full dark beard. He was
wearing the Confederate uniform. She wondered when the picture
was taken.

"I just feel as though I am looking at a stranger," she said. "I feel
no connection whatsoever."

"Of course you would feel that way, for you never knew him. And
while he was a distinguished-looking gentleman, he does not resemble you."

Lilly nodded in agreement and continued to search his face, as
though she might find some important clue there. *Bordeaux.* She turned
the name over in her mind. It was not unfamiliar to her, for while Summerville was ten miles out of New Orleans, she had, on occasion, been

into the city. And she felt sure she had seen the name on signs, or perhaps heard it spoken somewhere.

"The Bordeaux family started a cotton brokerage firm in New Orleans many years ago. It is now one of the largest in the South," Sister Ophelia informed her. "I assume Leon was a member of this family, but I will look into it immediately."

Lilly listened and nodded. But she wanted to say it didn't matter. Both her parents were dead. All she felt was a dull ache in her heart.

"At least now I know something about my background."

"Lilly, you must go to these people! You must tell them who you are."

"I don't know. . . ."

"But you must!" Sister Ophelia insisted. "You owe it to them. And you owe it to yourself."

"I suppose so." Lilly looked down at the intricate carving on the chest and traced the initials with her finger. "Megan McCoy," she said, trying to hold back the tears. "How I wish I could have known her."

"Your future has taken a mysterious turn. Maybe you will someday learn about Megan McCoy through the memories of others."

Lilly opened the box and stared again at the letter. "Yes, maybe I will come to know Megan McCoy, after all."

$\mathcal{L}$illy was a bundle of nerves as the hansom cab rolled over the cobblestone streets of New Orleans, bearing her to the address of the Bordeaux estate in the Vieux Carré. She had taken time and care in dressing for this day. She had done her hair in a popular style, upswept on the sides, then pulled back to a bun that sat securely beneath her navy hat. As a farewell present, her friends at St. Paul's had bought her a navy linen suit and kid slippers and gloves. She felt happy and confident.

She glanced down at the small mahogany chest in her lap and instinctively clutched it tighter, knowing her link to the Bordeaux family lay within.

It had been her mother's wish that Lilly come to this family. *Demand what is rightfully yours,* she had said. Lilly had no interest in trying to latch onto wealth the easy way; she simply wanted a family, someone to belong to, and someone to love. For a moment, the dream was so vivid in her mind that all sense of logic seemed to desert her. Oh, how she longed to have a real home and someone to love.

Sister Ophelia had learned that Marie, Leon Bordeaux's sister, lived alone. Her parents were deceased, and Leon had been her only brother. Marie was a spinster and was rarely seen in society. While Marie's mother had been cruel to Megan McCoy, Lilly believed that her aunt would want to know her only living relative. Of course, she would be suspicious at first, but once Lilly showed her the documents in the chest, certainly Marie would accept her. Lilly had toyed with the idea of first writing a letter to her but, in the end, had decided to meet with her personally.

Lilly prayed that her aunt was a kind woman, a Christian, for she believed this would make everything easier for both of them.

She closed her eyes for a moment, silently praying. *Dear God, please direct me. Put Your words in my mouth rather than my own.*

Lilly knew her own words could come out all wrong, and it meant everything to her to make the right impression. A spring breeze drifted through the window of the cab, bearing the sweet aroma of flower gardens in bloom. She turned and gazed through the window. White-pillared mansions with wide galleries and lush front lawns stretched before her. Huge oak trees spread brawny limbs over the homes, offering a thick shade of protection. In the center of the yards, stately magnolia trees boasted the ivory blossoms that decorated wreaths, mantles, and dining tables with their sweet perfume.

The driver called to the horse, then the cab slowed down and rocked to a halt. Lilly's heart rocked in a different rhythm. The mansion before her was the grandest on the street. It was a huge, three-story brick manor with a wide front gallery framed in scrolled wrought iron. The house had a flower garden and a huge magnolia tree on one side and a brick wall on the other. In the center of the brick wall, an iron gate secured the rear of the house, but she could see the gabled roof of a carriage house beyond the wall.

The driver had opened the door, prompting Lilly to get on with her business. Tucking the chest under her arm, she stepped down and paid her fare. Taking a deep breath, she hurried up the flagstone walk and climbed the steps to the wide gallery. Long panels of glass flanked the front door with a brass knocker in the center. She lifted the brass knocker, let it fall in place, then waited.

A curtain fluttered at the long window nearest the door, and soon she could hear footsteps approaching. The door swung back, and Lilly faced a tall, slender man dressed in navy trousers, coat, and vest over a white linen shirt with a neatly tied navy necktie. His dark brown eyes were the exact shade of his hair; he had a slim nose over full lips and a square chin. Unlike many men, he had neither a beard nor a mustache. Lilly found that appealing.

"Good morning," he said, in a smooth, cultured voice.

Staring into his handsome face could result in losing her poise, she realized, as her experience with men was limited. Her gaze moved above his head to the chandelier in the foyer.

"Good morning," Lilly responded. "Is Mademoiselle Bordeaux at home?"

He hesitated. "May I ask your name?"

"My name is Lilly Brown. She has never met me, but I am her niece."

There! She had said it, and now she looked back at him with a sigh of relief.

The friendly smile disappeared and was replaced by a look of suspicion.

"There must be some mistake! Mademoiselle Bordeaux has no living relatives."

"Then I would appreciate the opportunity to meet her and explain why she doesn't know me."

His gaze locked with hers as a frown settled over his forehead. She looked him squarely in the eye, never wavering.

"Excuse me," he said, turning away.

He had left the door ajar, and she had a clear view of the foyer. The polished marble floor reflected the glow of the chandelier. A massive, ornate table held a crystal vase filled with a lush bouquet of roses—pink, white, and yellow—fresh from the garden, no doubt. Her gaze moved on to a gold-framed painting of a European city, occupying a large portion of the end wall. Lilly could not imagine living in such luxury, and her stomach tightened as she thought of her father being raised in this environment.

She shifted her weight from one foot to the other, rustling her full petticoats. She forced herself to stand tall and hold her chin up with dignity, but the *tip-tap* of heels on the foyer put her nerves on edge. She took a deep breath and prepared herself to face Marie Bordeaux.

A middle-aged woman appeared—with a look of irritation that indicated she was in no mood to be fooled.

The woman was short and plump, wearing a tan faille dress with twin gold buttons down the front of the bodice. The dress was the latest in fashion, yet the tight bodice did not compliment Marie's round figure. Her hair was jet-black, parted in the center, and pulled back to a tight chignon. Her dark, close-set eyes were small, and her gaze seemed to pierce Lilly.

"I am Marie Bordeaux," she snapped in a shrill voice. "And this is my attorney, Andrew Desmond." She indicated the handsome man who had reappeared at the door. "I have no living relatives. I do not know what kind of deception you are attempting, young lady, but I am not gullible, nor is Mr. Desmond."

Lilly cleared her throat, trying not to take offense.

"It must be quite a shock for someone to arrive on your doorstep claiming to be a long-lost niece," Lilly said gently. How she wished she had not blurted out her mission at the front door. There was no taking back what she had said, however, and now she must prepare herself to finish the story. "If you'll allow me to relate the news that I learned only last week . . ." Her voice trailed off, silenced momentarily by the coldness in Marie's sullen expression. Only the trill of a mockingbird in the magnolia tree broke the tense silence.

"Maybe you should hear what Miss Brown has to say, Marie," Andrew Desmond calmly suggested.

Lilly took a closer look at him, wondering if he were more to Marie than her attorney. He looked to be in his late twenties, while Marie appeared to be in her forties. However, it was money and bloodline, rather than age that determined one's relationship in New Orleans society. Or so she had heard.

"You may come in," Marie said, opening the door.

"Thank you."

Forcing her thoughts back to the story she had come to tell, Lilly held the chest close to her heart and stepped inside the foyer. She was telling the truth, or as much of the truth as she knew, and surely they would see that she was an honest person, once they got to know her.

She followed Marie through an arched doorway into a large, sunlit parlor while Andrew Desmond lingered behind. She could feel his gaze boring into the back of her head, but she held herself erect and refused to be intimidated.

I am a child of the King, she told herself. *I do not need their money or their identity or anything other than the hope of a family.* But her hopes had already been dashed by her aunt's sharp tone and haughty attitude.

Lilly looked around the room where beige brocade walls and green velvet drapes gave an air of luxury, enhanced by the elaborate rococo styling of the sofas, armchairs, and gold-framed art.

She took a seat in the nearest armchair and watched as Andrew sat down on the sofa seat next to Marie.

"So, what is this startling bit of news you received?" Marie asked, her gaze narrowing as she studied Lilly.

Lilly removed her gloves, placed them in her lap beside the chest, and faced the two strangers whose faces mirrored only suspicion and distrust. "I was reared at St. Paul's orphanage in Summerville," she said, beginning the story she had rehearsed a dozen times in her mind. "I have always been told that I was placed on their doorstep when I was a newborn."

She did not want to sound melodramatic or allow the sadness she felt to creep into her tone. Reminding herself not to stray from the main subject, she looked Marie straight in the eye.

"I was at work in the office of St. Paul's last week when Sister Ophelia brought a gentleman to see me. His name was Simon Dupree. He brought news that a woman claiming to be my mother had died," she continued, keeping her voice calm. "Her dying wish, he said, was that he deliver this chest to St. Paul's. It contained a handwritten letter from her and a daguerreotype of Leon Bordeaux, whom she said was my father."

"That's ridiculous!" Marie lashed out. "My brother was never married. He had joined the Confederate troops and was killed at Fort Jackson."

Lilly drew a breath, knowing this was the most difficult part. Still, she had to press on, hoping that Marie would believe her when she heard the rest of the story.

"He and my mother had a brief courtship when he was on furlough in early March 1862, and they married at St. John's in late March. He was called back to duty at Fort Jackson soon after and, as you said, was killed in battle."

Marie gasped, staring at her in dismay. She cleared her throat and began to speak in a slow, deliberate tone. "Anyone living in New Orleans knew about the fall of Fort Jackson. And many people know that Leon died there. What you have told me is a convenient lie, devised to take advantage of this family. Knowing my brother could not dispute her claim, this woman concocted a ridiculous story about a courtship. If Leon had been on furlough at that time, he would have come here to visit us."

Marie paused to catch a breath, her gaze darting to Andrew. "It's not the first time someone has tried to take advantage of my family. But this is the most ludicrous of all the schemes I have ever heard."

Her gaze was sharp as daggers and, like her words, pierced straight through Lilly's heart. She took a deep breath, trying to recover from the pain. Once Marie saw the marriage certificate, perhaps her attitude would change.

"My mother asked Monsieur Dupree to deliver this chest to me. It contains proof of who I am."

Andrew was on his feet, stepping over to get the chest as she opened it. When she placed it in his hand, her gaze met his. An expression of intense scrutiny passed over his features as he examined the daguerreotype then stared into her face for several seconds. He returned to his seat and scanned the record of marriage. His dark brows were drawn in concentration as he read the letter. He glanced at her again. This time Lilly was certain there was something different in his gaze.

"Let me see what she has brought," Marie snapped, and he passed the chest to her.

Silence filled the room while Marie read the letter whose message Lilly knew by heart. She watched Marie as she read the letter, studied the record of marriage, then lingered over the daguerreotype. Finally, she looked back at Lilly.

"Is that man . . . Leon Bordeaux?" Lilly asked, then held her breath.

Marie shrugged. "Possibly. But even so, the fact that you have in your possession a picture of my brother is no proof that you are related. As for the woman, I never heard of her. And this . . ." She paused, waving the faded certificate of marriage. "This could have been falsified. Why, the print is so worn it's not even legible. As for her coming to our home and meeting with my mother, that, too, is preposterous. If this woman had come with such an astounding story, I would have seen or overheard something as I was always at my mother's side."

"Perhaps you were too young to remember," Lilly offered tactfully. "Perhaps you were asleep—"

"No! I was old enough to recall all the details of that atrocious war, and the guests who came and went during that time."

Marie stood, indicating the interview was over. "Young lady, I'm afraid I cannot accept this absurd story."

Lilly's mind reeled with shock. She had come here with proof of her heritage, or so she believed. Yet, her aunt had scoffed at her evidence and destroyed Lilly's dream. Although her heart ached, she reached deep inside for strength and forced herself to stand and look Marie in the eye. When she spoke, her voice was soft yet firm.

"May I have my chest?"

For a moment, Marie hesitated, her eyes widening in surprise, as though wondering what Lilly was about to do. Then she turned to Andrew and shoved the chest into his hands.

"As I said, Miss Brown, Andrew is my attorney," she said. "In the future, if you have anything to say, please consult him."

"There is nothing more to say," Lilly replied, as Andrew handed the chest to her. "My visit has not been in vain, for I now believe what Megan McCoy wrote about the way she was treated when she came to your mother for help. I will harbor no bitterness, only pity for the Bordeaux family. Because I am a Christian, I will ask God's forgiveness for you all. Good day, Mademoiselle Bordeaux, Mr. Desmond."

Gripping the mahogany chest, Lilly turned and started for the door.

"Wait!" It was Andrew, not Marie, who called to her.

She paused, glancing back over her shoulder.

"You can hardly expect Mademoiselle Bordeaux to naively accept what you have told her as absolute proof that you are related. What else do you know about your mother?"

When she looked at him, she thought she read concern, perhaps even compassion when she would have expected arrogance or a semblance of the contempt Marie had shown. But she did not see that in his eyes.

"I know nothing of my mother, only that she sang Irish ballads at a coffeehouse in the Vieux Carré when she met . . ." She bit off the words *my father*. "Monsieur Dupree told me she had been in poor health for quite some time. . . ."

She hesitated, then decided to say what had been troubling her from the beginning. "Why would a dying woman have these items delivered to me if her story were not true? How would she know the date I was left on the doorstep at St. Paul's orphanage?" Then she saw the cynical twist of Marie's lips, and she spoke what she believed was on Marie's mind. "Of course, I could have made up the entire story, and that's what you believe, because you do not know me."

She sighed. "I have done what I was asked to do. I have no reason to trouble either of you again."

She turned and walked out of the house and down the front steps. Despite the ache in her heart, she felt a sense of peace for she had completed her mission. How foolish she had been to think the heartless woman inside this house would accept her, or even believe her. She was not going to waste time going back over in her mind what she should or should not have said. Perhaps the hope of finding a relative and at last having a family had overtaken her good judgment. Even Sister Ophelia had been caught up in the dream and had encouraged her to visit Marie. But it was done now, and she must get on with her life, whatever it was to be.

Lilly began to walk toward the heart of Jackson Square. She could make her own way in the world. And she would. She had a Father, she reminded herself, a heavenly Father, who would guide her in finding employment and a place to live. She liked the city, and she was determined to make a life for herself here, and she didn't need Marie Bordeaux to do that.

At the corner, Lilly spotted a coffeehouse, and she peered through the glass window. Within, white linen cloths topped round tables where men and women smiled and chatted. There was a look of happiness about the place, and it beckoned to her. She turned and pressed the latch to enter.

She found a small table in a quiet corner and ignored the growl of her stomach, ordering only coffee with cream.

She had worked in the office at St. Paul's for the past two years and had received a small wage for her services. But her meager savings would not last long here in the city, and she must pay for her lodging until she obtained a job. She could always return to the orphanage, but she hadn't the heart to go back just yet. She had been instructed to write to them immediately, and she would. But she wasn't ready to do that, either. She sensed Sister Ophelia would be almost as disappointed as Lilly when she heard the outcome of her meeting with the disdainful Marie. Well, she would write with news of a job and a place to live, then no one would feel sorry for her.

As she placed the chest on the table, she thought, again, of the man whom Megan McCoy had claimed was her father.

The waiter delivered her coffee, and as she sipped it, she opened the chest and removed the daguerreotype. Placing it on the crisp linen cloth, she studied the man's intense dark eyes, but they revealed nothing. She wondered if he had been a coldhearted man who would not have wanted her, even if he were still alive.

"I don't remember him." The man's words were spoken softly.

When she raised her eyes, Andrew Desmond was standing before her, his hat in his hands. "I was very young when he went to war. May I speak with you for a moment, Miss Brown?"

She swallowed and lifted her chin. "I will not make trouble, if that concerns you, Mr. Desmond." Lilly replaced the picture in the chest and snapped the clasp. "I have no desire to ever see Marie Bordeaux again."

There was a strange expression on his face as she spoke, and if she had not known better, she would have thought he was sympathetic toward her. No doubt, he was merely pretending to be nice so he could see what she planned to do. She felt certain they had watched her from the parlor window when she left, and he had followed her to the coffeehouse.

"If you will allow me to sit down for a minute," he said, "I would like to tell you something about Marie Bordeaux."

His request sparked her curiosity, and although she did not verbalize a response, she inclined her head toward the seat opposite her.

Slowly, he sat down, his gaze searching her face all the while. Her gaze locked on him, waiting for him to tell her more about the cruelest woman she had ever met.

$$2$$

*M*iss Bordeaux has had a sad life," he began, then broke off as if pondering how to proceed discreetly.

"I realize your life has not been easy," he amended, "but clearly, your spirit has not been broken."

Lilly weighed his words, grateful he had acknowledged that she was a woman of spirit and determination. But she owed her strength to the hand of God upon her, giving her the resolve to go on in the face of hardship.

"Marie and Leon's father also went to war," he began again, speaking the name carefully. "He was killed early on, and their mother took to her bed and never recovered. They lost most of their fortune, which was sizable. Perhaps you're wondering how she kept the house and grounds, when so many in the South lost everything. It is common knowledge that Marie's father was a good businessman, and he was wise enough to place his dwindling funds in a bank in the Bahamas. After Leon died, an attorney for the estate was able to reclaim those funds to pay taxes on the house and care for Marie and her mother. They were alone, with only two servants. Marie cared for her mother for the next four years until her death. The only bright spot in her life was a short engagement to a man she described as handsome and dashing, until he broke the engagement and left New Orleans with another woman. While it is perhaps indiscreet for me to say so, he did not leave town with empty pockets—he took advantage of Marie's naïveté."

After he had finished the story, he remained silent, waiting for a reply.

"And you think I should forgive her?" Lilly asked quietly, remembering the woman who regarded her as an impostor. "I understand why she would be distrustful or suspicious of me, Mr. Desmond. But the fact that she could be so unkind toward my mother's memory and toward me . . ." Lilly took a deep breath to steady her voice. "Forgiving Marie makes her scorn no less painful. She might at least have offered to investigate my story or contact someone at St. Paul's to confirm what I told her."

"What makes you think I won't do that?"

She stared at him. "Did she ask you to?"

Again he lowered his eyes, and she respected him for not lying to her.

"Then if you intend to verify my story, you can save yourself the trouble. As I told you earlier, I have no desire to trouble Marie Bordeaux ever again."

He said nothing for several seconds, studying her as though trying to figure her out. Then he leaned back in the chair and sighed. "My parents and grandparents were friends of the Bordeaux family. Both Marie and I are descendants of the French who were exiled because of their loyalties to Napoleon Bonaparte. The Desmonds and Bordeaux were among several families who sailed together from Philadelphia to Mobile in 1816. Most of the others went north to Demopolis, Alabama, to organize the Vine and Olive colony. But the Desmonds and Bordeaux settled in New Orleans and were lifelong friends. They were courageous people who built a new life here, and they did well for many years. Then the war came, and for the Bordeaux family . . ." His voice trailed off, then he shrugged. "It was difficult for the women to cope."

"The war ended years ago! New Orleans has been rebuilt, and its citizens now live a different life. Surely some of the bitterness must have passed by now."

"Yes, the war ended, and New Orleans has been rebuilt. But its citizens have suffered greatly as a result. Those who lost loved ones in the war and suffered the hardships afterward are not likely to forget those painful memories.

"I lost a father and grandfather to the war. My grandfather was killed the first year. My father returned home but died within the year as a result of an injury sustained in the war. My mother tried to be strong, but the next year her heart just gave out. They were devoted to one another."

Lilly felt her heart soften as he spoke, and as she looked into his eyes she felt the weight of sadness. "I am sorry that happened to your parents. And to you. So that's one reason you share a friendship with Marie."

He nodded. "We have much in common. Unlike Marie, I have an older sister—Julia. She lives in Mobile. Julia is happily married to a banker, and they have five children."

"Five?" She smiled, glad the conversation had taken a happier turn.

"Julia always wanted a large family, and she is a wonderful mother." He smiled for the first time in several minutes, and it seemed to light his brown eyes.

As Lilly looked at him and thought about his loss, she felt a strange yearning, one she had not experienced with any other man. But she had to keep her emotions in check. He had admitted his loyalty to Marie, and she must not allow her feelings to cloud her better judgment.

"Why are you being so nice to me?" she asked.

"I admired the way you spoke of your faith in God," he replied. "I, too, am a Christian, and I must admit that too often I shrink away from telling people about my faith. But you spoke boldly, despite the fact that Marie . . ." He caught himself.

"Has faith in nothing?" she asked.

He nodded. "I believe one reason the Bordeaux have lived such a tragic life is because they thought they were invincible and did not need a God or even believe there was a God. It is sad that Marie never accepted Christ into her heart, for her life could have been so different."

"It is never too late," Lilly replied.

She looked into Andrew's eyes, and they were both silent for several seconds. Then she drew a shaky breath and allowed a tiny smile to settle over her face.

"You've been very kind. Thank you, Mr. Desmond." She thought about the French family he had been a part of, and she wondered what sort of life he led here in New Orleans.

"What do you plan to do now?" he asked.

She took a sip of her coffee, considering the question. Then she shook her head. "I'm not entirely sure, but don't trouble yourself. I'm perfectly capable of taking care of myself."

His gaze held hers for a moment, then he nodded in agreement. "I feel certain that you are. Nevertheless . . ." He reached into his pocket. "I would like to leave my calling card with you." He stood, hesitating for a moment. "If I can be of service, Miss Brown, I hope you will get in touch with me. Good day."

Lilly registered every word, noticed every movement. He was tall and slim, and when he moved, he did so with the utmost grace. He seemed to be a kind and compassionate man, and she believed what he had said about being a Christian.

"Thank you, and good day, Mr. Desmond," she said, looking up at him, allowing the attraction she felt for him to creep into her smile.

His gaze rested on her face for another second, then he turned and circled the tables to reach the front door. Lilly watched him as he pressed coins into the hand of a waiter who glanced toward her table. Her gaze was still upon him as he opened the front door. Placing the top hat on his head, he stepped out into the surge of pedestrians and disappeared.

Lilly stared after him, amazed that a total stranger had shown her more kindness than the woman she believed to be her aunt. She picked up the calling card and as she read the name and address, she found herself wishing she could have met him under different circumstances.

$$3$$

*L*illy turned the corner on Chartres Street, feeling the bite of her tight shoes. Her feet were swollen and blistered, and the muscles in her legs pinched with each step. She had spent the past week walking around Jackson Square seeking employment— and having no luck.

At the door of the market, an older woman stepped onto the banquette and headed toward the residential district. She was dressed in the clothes of a domestic—gray muslin dress and white cap—and Lilly imagined she was employed as a housekeeper or cook.

Lilly would have applied for such work herself, if she had the experience. But because she was good in arithmetic, the nuns had trained her for working in the office. Still, if she could not obtain work as a clerk in one of the shops, she would take any job she could find.

She was exhausted from a futile job search and sluggish from hunger. The humidity of the warm afternoon wrapped around her like a cape she had outgrown, adding to her discomfort.

In the background, she could hear the lilt and flow of voices, the rich vowels of New Orleans' residents flowing over the staccato tones of out of town visitors.

How strange, she thought, *to be surrounded by people and yet feel desperately alone.* During the years she had spent at the orphanage, she had often longed to escape the noise and crowded quarters at St. Paul's. Today, however, she missed the familiar faces, the opportunity to stop and chat with someone who knew and cared about her. Depression settled deeper, like a gray fog around her, and a wave of nostalgia for St. Paul's hit her hard.

I am not alone, she reminded herself. *God walks with me every step of the way.*

As she reached the hotel, she felt one last surge of strength as she climbed the steps and entered the lobby. Averting her gaze from the people milling about, she headed straight for the stairway. She lifted her cotton skirt with one hand and reached for the oak banister with the other. Lilly began to trudge up the stairs to the second floor. The ache in her legs spread throughout her body, and yet the ache of disappointment hurt worse. What was she going to do? She was tired, hungry, and almost broke, except for the meager funds she had tied in a lace handkerchief in her trunk for her return to St. Paul's, if necessary. No matter what happened, she could not use that money. It was the only security she had left.

At the landing, she paused to take a deep breath. As she did, she suddenly felt light-headed, and she clutched the crown of the banister. At the end of the hall, the afternoon sunlight streamed through a large window. She frowned as tiny dark things wiggled around in the light, growing and growing, until the darkness overtook the light. A sour taste rose in her throat, then a weakening nausea gripped her. *I'm about to faint!* She tried to draw oxygen into her lungs. A door closed somewhere down the hall, and she heard distant voices. Taking another deep breath, she focused her energy on putting one foot in front of the other until she reached her room. But her body would not obey the command, and slowly the whirling dizziness surrounded her, buckling her knees. Something hard smacked her left cheek.

"Wally, look!" a woman screamed. "That pretty lil' woman has fallen."

"Well, don't stand there with your mouth open. Go see what's wrong with 'er," a male voice shouted.

Lilly wanted to answer the voices and tell them nothing was wrong . . . but she couldn't get the words to come out.

The smell of a strong perfume drifted over her, and she heard the rustle of skirts. Then a gentle hand pressed her shoulder, and the voice of a man penetrated her gray world.

"Hey, little lady. You all right?"

"Wally, are you daft?" the woman snapped. "Would she be

sprawled out here in the floor like a rag doll if she was all right? We hafta get a doctor."

A doctor. The words jolted Lilly to move. A doctor meant money, and she had none. "No," she croaked. "I'll . . . be okay. Just a weak spell . . . I have them . . . occasionally."

A moment of silence.

"Are you in the family way, Dearie?" the woman asked.

Lilly's eyes snapped open. "No!" she answered, horrified. For a moment, she only stared at the odd couple kneeling beside her. The woman had a large floppy hat with feathers dangling over her blond hair. Her cheeks and lips were rouged, and she wore a low-cut, pink satin dress. The man looked even more bizarre. He had a handlebar mustache that reached almost to his ears on each side, bushy brows, and a jaunty, gray felt hat cocked low over his right brow. Was she dreaming?

"Don't let us give you a scare," the woman said, patting Lilly's shoulder. "We're on our way to Fifth Street Theater. We're actors."

"Oh." Lilly blinked, and her head began to clear. Their attire seemed to make more sense to Lilly, now that their work had registered in her mind.

"Missus, which room is yours? We'll give you a hand," the man offered.

She pushed up on her elbow and faced the couple who were so eager to help. She had never seen them before, for she certainly would have remembered. A smile wobbled on her lips. "Thank you."

"I'm Dolly Sampson," the woman said, as her red lips stretched in a friendly smile. "And this is Wally. We're Wally and Dolly, at the theater, so you can call us that too. Our real names are Eudora and Walter Ray, but we've nearly forgotten. Here, give us your hands, and we'll help you up."

Despite their rather blunt approach, they gently wrapped their arms around her as they lifted Lilly to her feet and guided her toward her room.

"My key . . ." She lifted her arm, and the drawstring purse swung from her wrist.

"Get her key, Dolly."

"You had to tell me! 'Course I'll get her key; she won't want your big, clumsy hand in that fancy little purse. You're a pretty little thing, especially with that red hair. Ever thought about being in the theater?"

"No," Lilly replied, smiling at the absurd idea.

"Here, I'll get your key." Dolly fished inside Lilly's purse and soon the key rattled in the lock of the door, then they were entering her room.

"To the bed we shall go," Dolly trilled as they walked her across the room and settled her on the bed. Lilly wanted to sink down into the depths of the feather mattress and never move again.

Pillows cushioned her head and shoulders, and her ankles were gently swung up to the bed, while Dolly unlaced her boots.

"Missus," Wally said, his strong voice filling the room, "it's no wonder you fainted, walkin' around in them fancy little boots. Makes my toes turn under just lookin' at 'em."

"That's 'cause you're flatfooted, Wally. And don't be going on about her boots. You scoot down to the dining room and fetch her some tea."

"I wouldn't care for any tea," Lilly said. While her stomach still ached from hunger, she didn't want to impose.

"If we had more time, we'd bring you some hot soup. But we gotta get to the theater."

"I'll be fine, thank you."

"Are you sure you don't want us to get a doctor, young lady?" Wally asked.

"No, I feel fine now. And my name is Lilly Brown."

Lilly's eyelids were pressing down while she struggled to stay awake. She was vaguely aware of the couple stepping back from her bed, whispering to one another. From the corner of her eye, she saw the woman place Lilly's purse on the dresser.

They were whispering again. Dolly picked something up from the dresser and showed it to Wally. He nodded. It was Andrew Desmond's business card. She had opened her mouth to speak, but Dolly had put the card down, and they were moving toward the door.

"We gotta go, Hon. I'll look in on you later," Dolly said.

"You just rest," Wally called, as they hurried out the door.

"Thank you," Lilly responded, as the soft curtain of sleep settled over her.

Lilly was not sure how long she had slept when the faint knocking on her door penetrated her consciousness. She sat up on her elbow, relieved that she was no longer dizzy. She reached over and lit the lamp as the soft tapping continued.

"Lilly, it's Dolly Sampson," a voice called from the other side of the door. "Can I come in?"

The memory of Dolly and Wally brought a smile to her face. "Sure, just a minute, please."

She was careful to move slowly, in case the dizziness returned, but fortunately, it had left her. She lowered her feet to the floor and stood, glancing toward the window. It was dark outside, and she could no longer hear noise from the street below. It must be quite late. She walked slowly to the door, pushing her tousled hair back into her hairnet.

When she opened the door, the rich aroma of chicken broth drifted in from the hallway, and her mouth watered.

Dolly Sampson was holding a white bowl of soup and smiling at her.

"Me and Wally just got in from work, and we always like a snack. I know you were probably sleepin', but I thought this would do you good. Mama always told me chicken soup would cure anything."

"You're so kind," Lilly said, opening the door wide and stepping aside for the woman to enter.

Dolly was still in stage dress and makeup, a bit smeared, and Lilly felt a rush of tenderness toward the kind woman as she carefully placed the soup on the small table near the bed. Then she reached in her pocket and removed a linen napkin and soup spoon.

"Here, Hon. Now you sit down and eat this. It'll make you feel better."

"Thank you so much. How was the theater tonight?" She hardly knew what to ask, for she had never been to the theater.

"Packed and noisy," Dolly replied, rolling her eyes. Without the floppy feather hat, she looked prettier with her blond hair pulled back from her face and twisted into a knot on the back of her neck.

"Me and Wally just love performing," she continued pleasantly. "We make a good team with our silly jokes and such."

Lilly smiled. "I'd like to come watch you perform sometime."

Dolly's thinly arched brows lifted, and she smiled. "I'll get you tickets, Hon. We'd love to have you sittin' there on the front row. One night soon, we're planning a magician act. Wally's going to saw me in half." She burst into laughter when Lilly's mouth dropped open. "It's just an act. Well, get busy with your soup and sweet dreams."

Her satin skirts rustled as she swung around and headed to the door.

"I appreciate your thoughtfulness," Lilly said, following her to the door.

Dolly whirled, patting her hand. "We never had children. Guess it just wasn't in the cards, as they say. So it's kinda fun getting to mother you a bit. Now you take care." She winked, then hurried out the door.

Lilly turned the key in the lock, then she closed her eyes to offer a prayer of thanks. But before the words formed in her mind, a verse she had learned as a child came to mind.

I will be with thee . . . I will not fail thee nor forsake thee. . . .

The verse was true. God had not failed her. She had been hungry and lonely, and He had provided food and friends. She opened her eyes and smiled as she hurried over to sample the chicken soup.

$\mathscr{L}$ illy opened her eyes slowly and looked toward the window. Daylight seeped through a crack in the drapes. From the street below, she could hear the *clip-clop* of horses' hooves and a man's voice raised in greeting. She sank deeper into the pillows, not ready to face another long day in her search for employment. She closed her eyes and pulled the soft quilt to her chin, longing to remain in bed. But the harsh hand of reality shook her, bringing back the memory of yesterday, and her eyes flew open.

She had fainted at the top of the stairs. She thought about her funny yet kind neighbors, the Sampsons, who had helped her to her room. She rolled over and looked across at the table where the empty soup bowl sat. The tasty soup had warmed her empty stomach. Afterward, she had slept like a baby.

Lilly tossed back the covers and swung her legs around to place her feet on the rug. Her body answered back with an ache of weariness. She took a deep breath, blinked, and studied the clock on the dresser. She gasped. It was five minutes past ten! She could not loll in bed another second. *Today, I will find work,* she promised herself. She had lost count of the number of shops she had visited the past week while looking for work. To her surprise, shopkeepers seemed reluctant to hire her; in retrospect, she thought they seemed almost suspicious of her, and she couldn't understand why.

She stood up, reaching for her wrapper and house slippers, then she hobbled across to the pitcher of water. Her feet were still sore, bringing to mind Wally's remark about her boots and Dolly's lighthearted retort about his flat feet. She smiled as she dipped her hands in the water, cupping it in her palms to splash the drowsiness from her face.

During her devotion time yesterday morning, her prayer had been for friends, and before the day had ended, her prayer had been answered with the wonderful Sampsons. Again she would pray for a job, and she must believe that this prayer would be answered as well.

With new hope and strength, her movements quickened and soon she had bathed and dressed. She was tying the small satin bow under her lace collar when someone tapped on the door.

Lilly hurried to the door, wondering what Dolly had brought her this morning. When the door swung back, she caught her breath.

Andrew Desmond stood before her, looking incredibly handsome in a tan coat, white shirt, and brown trousers.

"Good morning. I wonder if I might speak with you for a moment."

Dolly was standing behind him, clasping and unclasping her hands.

"Lilly, please don't be mad at Wally and me. We ran into Mr. Desmond, and well—we saw his business card on your dresser. And . . . we mentioned that you were feeling poorly."

Lilly felt a rush of blood to her cheeks, and as she stood there blushing, she had no idea what to say or how to react. At the same time, she knew she must not take offense. The couple meant well, and they had shown her nothing but kindness.

"I must apologize for intruding," Mr. Desmond said. "When the Sampsons mentioned their acquaintance with you, I became quite bold. I've been looking for you, and I took the liberty of coming to call. May I take you to brunch? I have some business to discuss with you, and since I haven't eaten, I would be pleased to have you join me."

Lilly felt inclined to refuse, yet Andrew Desmond was so polite that it was difficult for her to say no. *Business.* The word locked into the center of her thoughts, and she suspected that Marie had sent him over with some type of proposition. Or perhaps he had information about her mother.

"Just give me a minute," she replied.

"Wally is waiting on me to get to rehearsal," Dolly said, peering around Andrew Desmond's shoulder. Today she looked more normal without her stage makeup. She was wearing a plain dark dress, with her blond hair pulled back into a hairnet.

"Thank you, Dolly. Have a good day."

"You too, Honey," she replied, looking embarrassed as she whirled and set off down the hall.

"Miss Brown, don't rush. I'm in no hurry."

Lilly nodded and closed the door, leaving him alone in the hall.

She hurried to the dresser and looked into the mirror, inspecting her reflection. Her red hair was as stubborn as ever, poking out in all directions from her hairnet. She decided to dispense with the net, and yanking out the pins, she shook her head and sent waves of fire around her face. With a few strokes of the hairbrush, she had subdued the long ends into soft swirls about her shoulders.

She studied her simple dark dress which seemed appropriate for going out. But her eyes—seeming rounder than ever—held something of a startled expression, thanks to the strange turn of events.

She paused, taking a slow, deep breath and told herself to put the day in God's hands.

Setting the mirror aside, she opened the armoire and reached for her white knit shawl. Moments later, she opened the door, then locked it and dropped the key into her purse.

Andrew offered his arm. "Shall we go?"

She tucked her hand into the crook of his arm, and they walked quietly down the stairs.

He began to speak casually of the day's events; a carriage had almost run him down this morning, then he related an amusing story the shoeshine boy had told him.

Lilly glanced down at his patent leather shoes and could just about see her reflection there.

As they alighted the stairs and crossed the lobby, Mr. Desmond nodded to someone in passing and spoke to another. A smile formed on her lips, as well, and she began to feel relaxed and at ease with him. His casual, lighthearted manner helped to evoke this mood, and for a little while, it was easy to forget there was business to discuss.

Even though her dress was not as fine or as fashionable as those of the other ladies she had seen around the hotel and in the shops, she didn't feel embarrassed or uncomfortable. She was who she was, and most of the time she was happy with herself.

As they stepped out onto the banquette, New Orleans bustled with morning shoppers. The street vendors had already lined up with fresh flowers, and the shoeshine boys waited at their stands, their eyes seeking a dusty pair of boots.

The lively energy of New Orleans was contagious, and the sadness and disappointment of days past were suddenly forgotten.

"It's a beautiful morning, isn't it?" he asked, smiling down at her.

"Yes, it is. And I do like to walk. I've walked so much the past week that I have blisters on my feet." It occurred to her that the sisters would consider that remark inappropriate, and yet it felt so good to be relaxed—for the first time in days—and to enjoy herself.

"I like to walk too," he was saying. "Many evenings, if I'm wrestling with a legal matter for a client, I go out and walk for hours."

She looked up at him, curious for the first time about his work. "What type of law do you practice?"

"Mainly I work with businesses who need representation. I do have private clients, as well. The Sampsons, for example." He grinned down at her. "Don't take offense at their telling me you were their neighbor. They have good hearts, Miss Brown."

She nodded. "I know they do. And you may call me Lilly," she added with a smile.

"And I'm Andrew."

A wonderful mood had settled over her by the time they arrived at the restaurant. As Andrew pressed the latch on the lace-curtained door, the enticing aroma of fresh coffee and yeasty bread wafted to greet them. Hunger began to claw at Lilly's stomach again.

A waiter hurried up, grinning at Andrew as though he were a favorite customer.

"Could we have a seat in the garden?" Andrew asked.

"I have the perfect table." The waiter's grin spread to his ears. He led them through an arched door that opened onto a courtyard, complete with a fountain. Wrought iron tables were spaced about, and each table held a crystal vase with fresh flowers.

"Perfect," Andrew said, pulling back her chair.

Lilly took a seat and glanced around, enjoying the ambiance, while the waiter placed menus before them.

When Lilly opened the menu and looked at the selections, a growl rose up in her stomach. She had forgotten how hungry she had been the past days, and now she was overwhelmed by the delectable choices. She had no idea what she wanted. Actually, she wanted one of everything on the menu.

She closed the menu and looked across at Andrew. "Why don't you order for me?"

"I'll be happy to. What about a tray of fresh fruit? Some muffins. And how does an omelet sound?"

She swallowed. "Wonderful."

"Do you like coffee, or would you prefer tea?"

"Coffee at breakfast, tea or coffee in the evenings."

He nodded in agreement. "My sentiments, exactly."

The waiter swept away with the menus, but neither seemed to notice for they sat staring at one another, saying nothing for a moment. Lilly had begun to dread getting down to the *business* he had mentioned earlier. She felt if he had brought good news, he would already have shared it with her.

"A woman who likes to walk, who isn't finicky about food, and who will drink strong coffee," he remarked, tilting his head to study her. "You're an interesting lady."

She raised an eyebrow. "Those things just sound healthy to me."

He nodded. "I agree. I suppose what I'm trying to say is that you have a wholesome attitude about so many things. I find that very refreshing."

He seemed to notice everything about her, and now she longed to know more about him. She loved hearing him talk, and it didn't seem to matter what the subject was. She liked the way his dark brown eyes lit up when he was amused or when he spoke with passion about something. All the while, there was such gentleness in his voice and in his smile. It was easy to forget that he and Marie were such good friends, and it jarred her each time she recalled that fact. She thrust that aside, for now, in her curiosity to learn more about him.

"Tell me about yourself."

"I've lived in New Orleans all of my life. I was educated at the university here, and for a short time, I entertained thoughts of going to some other city to practice law."

He paused, and he seemed to be reflecting on his life. "I had friends at school who lived in other parts of the country, and I often visited in their homes on weekends and summer breaks, but wherever I went, I was always glad to come back home."

"Why was that?" she asked. She had never been out of Louisiana, nor had she ever had the opportunity to venture very far beyond Summerville and the bayou.

"We have a unique city because of the Spanish and French influence and the Anglo-Saxons who came down the Mississippi, docked their boats, and never left," he replied. "As a result, we have a lot of interesting people. Here, everyone moves at a slower pace, and I like that."

He took a deep breath, glancing toward the street. "I like to hear the street musicians play their instruments, and I like to smell the flowers, especially the magnolia blossoms."

Lilly was fascinated as he described his life in New Orleans, and it was refreshing to hear a man go on about the smell of flowers and the sound of music. Everything he had said to her since the first day at the coffeehouse seemed to indicate that he was a kindhearted person who cared about everyone.

"And I like the history and tradition here," he continued. "One reason I became a lawyer was to help protect that history and tradition. When Julia and I were small, my family often came to Jackson Square on Sunday afternoons. Every time our carriage passed the equestrian statue of Andrew Jackson, my father would launch into stories of the Battle of New Orleans. He was a history professor at the university before the war."

Lilly nodded, imagining that his parents must have been very intelligent and cultured. Andrew seemed proof of that.

"Who was his favorite war hero?" Lilly asked, thinking back to her history classes.

"General Jackson! He loved to talk about the Battle of New Orleans, and how Old Hickory defeated the Redcoats with his own small army and the famous New Orleans militia. They were a ragtag army of frontiersmen, former pirates, and former Haitian slaves. I can recall, as a youngster, my father sitting with me on the carpet in the parlor. With his ink pen and parchment, he would sketch out the battle lines and patiently explain each skirmish." He paused, glancing back at Lilly. " 'The victory was sweet,' he would say with great pride."

"What an interesting man he must have been," she replied.

Andrew had described to her a family life that sounded so perfect, and her heart literally ached for those kinds of memories. Would having a family of her own ever be possible, or would it always be an elusive dream?

She realized he was staring at her so she shifted and tried to pick up the conversation again.

"I like what you say about this area of Louisiana. It makes me appreciate being born here."

For just a second, there was the possibility of an awkward moment in referring to her birth, and yet that was not the center of who she was. She had developed as a person long before Simon Dupree came with the mahogany chest and the news that had changed her life.

"I even like the muggy summers that stick like glue to your skin," Andrew spoke up, as though trying to change the subject.

"But that weather gives us these beautiful flowers," she said, reaching across to touch the petal of the pink camellia in the crystal vase.

The waiter had returned with their food—it was beautifully prepared and served on fine bone china. As he carefully set the plate before her, she forced herself to take her time with her linen napkin and the heavy silver fork, although she was ravenous. Then she remembered the One who had made this possible. She closed her eyes for moment, offering a brief prayer of thanks.

When she opened her eyes, she felt Andrew watching her. He merely smiled at her, then they both turned their attention to their food.

The omelet was a delicious blend of minced vegetables nestled in rich cheese and eggs prepared to perfection. The fruit tray held orange slices, strawberries, and melon, and the rich aroma of the chicory coffee drifted over everything.

For several minutes, they ate in contented silence, then Andrew looked across at her, touched the napkin to his mouth, and asked the first serious question of the day.

"Do you know where I might find Simon Dupree?"

The question took her by surprise. She hesitated, then began to shake her head. "No, I wish that I did. Sister Ophelia and I tried to locate him but had no luck. I'm still amazed that we let him leave without getting an address the day he came to St. Paul's."

"I'm sure you were both so shocked over the news he had brought you that neither of you were thinking logically."

"You're right. Sister Ophelia seemed as stunned as I was. And at the time, all I could think about was how frustrated I felt that Megan McCoy—my mother—had waited so long to get in touch with me. Waited until she was dying . . . It was like it all came too late, and there was nothing I could do. Of course, after he left, I thought of dozens of questions, but that was after I had adjusted to the shock." She sighed, shaking her head. "And yet that must sound like a poor excuse to anyone else, since Simon Dupree was the key to getting information about my mother."

He reached across and touched her hand. "Please understand something. I believed you from the beginning. And I believe you now."

She stared at him, at first not quite sure if he meant it, and yet she thought he seemed sincere. And, she reminded herself, he was a Christian. The fact that he did believe her, despite everything, touched her deeply, since Marie—who might be her only living relative— regarded her story as ludicrous. She would have expected it would be the very opposite of him, given the fact that he was an attorney, accustomed to sorting through facts.

"Let's not give up," Andrew said. "I feel certain there are people in New Orleans who know Simon Dupree, and maybe they knew Megan McCoy, as well."

Lilly considered his words, wondering if this was the extent of what he had come to tell her. She wanted to ask about Marie, but remembering her promise to herself not to let the woman hurt her again, she kept silent.

She noticed that Andrew was pushing back his plate, and feeling as though she couldn't hold another bite, she pressed the crisp linen napkin to her lips. "The meal was delicious, Andrew. Thank you."

"It was my pleasure. Thank you for joining me." His gaze lingered on her, and he appeared thoughtful for a few seconds. "How have you been spending your time?"

"Looking for employment."

"Oh? What kind of employment?"

"For the past two years, I've worked in the office at St. Paul's. I like working with figures, so I was handling all of their bookkeeping."

"That's impressive. So you're looking for employment as a book-keeper?"

"I was. But there seems to be a shortage of work for women. Most of the shops employ men."

He nodded. "Most of the women who do work are usually the shopkeepers' wives or family members. Let me ask around. Maybe I'll hear of something that would be suitable for you."

His offer startled her. "That's very generous of you, but you've already done more than you were sent to do."

He appeared confused. "What do you mean?"

She tilted her head and looked across at him, trying to remember what he had said when she opened the door this morning.

"Did Marie send you today? I mean, is that why you're asking where to find Simon Dupree?"

He hesitated for a moment, then shook his head. "No, Marie doesn't know I came."

Lilly stared at him for a moment, confused. "Then why did you come?"

He hesitated, obviously choosing his words. "Lilly, I came because I cared about you," he answered softly.

Cared about her? He mustn't care about her! What would Marie think and say? Or maybe he meant he cared about her as a friend. Either way, she felt embarrassed and uncomfortable and had no idea what to say to him now.

"Can't you think of me as a friend, rather than Marie's attorney?"

"I've already begun to think of you that way, but . . ." Her voice trailed off as her mind returned to that dreadful day at Marie's house.

And as the memory filled her mind, she saw him in a different light. He had appeared so loyal to Marie that day, and Marie was obviously dependent on him. She had even wondered if there was something more between Andrew and Marie than friendship.

"We don't have to make this so complicated," he said. "I confess I'm attracted to you. I want to get to know you better, and if I can help in any way, I would like to do that. I suppose you can't help feeling a little suspicious."

She took a deep breath. "No, I can't. You're Marie's attorney and friend. I can't express how much I have wanted to find my family. I was certain that once I took the papers to Marie, she would believe me and we could be family. Instead, she was cold and cynical. And now I feel cynical when I think about how I guarded my mother's mahogany chest with my life, holding it against me as though it were a family crest. I came to New Orleans with all the hopes and dreams of a lifetime. And in minutes, Marie stripped away all hopes of an identity. I was nobody again, just a baby left on a doorstep."

As she spoke, her anger outgrew the hurt, and she began to feel a stronger emotion: hate. As a Christian, she must not hate another human being, but she was finding it difficult not to hate all of the Bordeaux. And Andrew, who had grown up as a member of their elite circle, wanted to be friends with *her*? For the first time, she felt a twinge of distrust toward him.

Looking across the table to Andrew, so well dressed and comfortable with his lifestyle, so coddled and protected as a child, she felt an overpowering urge to lash out at him.

When she spoke, the bitterness she felt spilled over into her chilling words. "It may be hard for you to understand my way of thinking."

"Why? Because I'm Marie's friend? I had a comfortable upbringing, yes. But my parents died during my adolescence. True, I had the money for my education, but I had to do my own thinking, and believe me, I earned a law degree on my own."

"And went to work for friends of the family."

The words spilled out before she could stop them, and now she thought about the tragedy of losing his parents, and she felt ashamed of herself. She had never been a vindictive person. What was happening to her?

She lowered her eyes. "That was a cruel thing for me to say. I'm sorry, Andrew," she said, feeling utterly miserable. When she forced herself to meet his gaze, she could see that she had offended him—he was motioning for the waiter.

She pressed her lips together, wishing she could take back the words she had spoken in anger, but it was too late. So she kept silent as he paid their bill and left the restaurant. Once they had stepped out onto the banquette, she turned to him. "Andrew, I apologize for being rude. But you see, I would like to forget that visit to Marie's house. She hurt me deeply, and I am giving over to anger as a defense. I appreciate your kindness, and yes, I wish we could be friends, but I can't forget that she is your client and your lifelong friend. I'm sorry. I just had to speak my mind."

"And you do. I learned that soon after me met."

The words were not spoken in anger, but rather in a calm voice. She searched his face. There was no anger in his eyes now, only regret. She took a deep breath and turned her gaze toward the shops along the boulevard. "You needn't walk me back. I have an errand. Good day, Andrew."

She turned on her heel and began walking back toward the hotel. She shouldn't have gone into a tirade, but on the other hand, she had to keep her wits about her. She was a country girl who had never dealt with wealth and society, and she did not feel equipped to participate in the sophistication of Andrew's world. It would be so easy to let her attraction to him override her common sense, but her common sense had always been a gift—one that she must call upon now in order to survive.

5

$\mathcal{A}$ ndrew checked the address on the note in his hand: 7 Waterfront Street. He scanned the row of shotgun houses. None had numbers on them, and he began to suspect that the residents here did not want to advertise their address. He decided to count down the houses to the seventh one and hope and pray it was Simon Dupree's former address.

Obtaining the address had not been easy, but his persistence had paid off. It was not surprising that Lilly and the nuns had been unable to locate Simon Dupree; they had not gone to half the taverns in New Orleans, as he had. After being unable to locate Dupree through war records or government offices, he had gone to an older hotel where many of the French immigrants often gathered for tea or late supper. When he asked around for Simon Dupree, an older gentleman thought the name was vaguely familiar, that perhaps he had met him at a bar down on the waterfront.

Andrew had hurried off with high hopes, but after searching a dozen bars along the waterfront, he was ready to give up. Then, at his last stop, he met a bartender who nodded slowly as he heard the name.

"I have some money for Monsieur Dupree," Andrew added hopefully.

Indeed, he *would* have a sum of money for Mr. Dupree if he could learn more about Megan McCoy.

The promise of money had sent the bartender to a table in a dark corner. Andrew tried not to stare as the bartender spoke quietly with an older couple. Then he returned with an address. Thanking him and leaving a generous tip, Andrew had come directly to the waterfront.

He climbed the rickety steps of a paint-chipped, green house and tapped on the scarred door.

Beyond the door, footsteps boomed across a board floor, then the door flew open. A bald man, well over six feet tall and weighing at least three hundred pounds, glared down at him.

The man was dressed in a work shirt and dungarees, and his gaze crawled down Andrew's suit. Before the man could make any assumptions, Andrew quickly explained his business.

"Good day, Sir. Sorry to bother you," Andrew said. "I'm looking for Simon Dupree."

"He ain't here." The voice was as big as the man. "Packed up and left a week ago."

"Do you have a forwarding address on him, Sir?"

"Nope."

"That's too bad. I had some news for him," he said.

"What kind of news?"

"He had a friend, Megan McCoy, who passed away recently. It concerns her."

At the mention of her name, the steel glint faded from the big man's eyes, and his grim mouth relaxed. "Miss Megan," he said, heaving a sigh that came from deep in his chest. "Too bad about her."

Andrew nodded. "Yes, it was. Did you know her?"

"Met her once. She came to pick up some clothes that needed mending. Seemed like a good woman. Real quiet. I paid her more than she woulda charged. Looked like she needed a good meal." He shook his head. "That's all I know, 'cept ol' Simon fell crazy in love with her. On warm nights, they went to the park. Simon said she sang Irish songs to him. Said she sang with her soul. When she died, seemed like he died too. On the inside, I mean."

Andrew paused, thinking of what the man had said. "Do you know where she lived?"

"Thought you knew her."

"I'm an attorney representing Lilly Brown, Miss McCoy's daughter. Monsieur Dupree came to her with news that Miss McCoy had died."

The big man obviously recognized the truth in this statement, and he began to nod.

"Simon talked to me about that. Whether or not to find that gal Megan left on the church steps. But, you know, a promise being a promise, he kept his word to her."

Andrew was surprised that the man seemed to know as much as he did about the situation. Maybe he knew more.

"He did keep his promise. And the daughter, Lilly Brown, is sad and confused. She wants to know more about her mother. She's a very nice young lady," he added.

The man stared at him for a moment, then he shook his head. "Can't help you. All I know is what Simon told me. Just said Miss Mc-Coy'd had a hard life, mostly bad luck through it all. They met over in the park. She went there to feed the birds every day. She was sick, you know. Been sick a long time. Her lungs, I think."

Andrew listened carefully, making mental notes. "Do you, by chance, know where she was living before she died?"

The man hesitated. "Not far from here if she walked to the park. You might try Garner, three blocks behind us. There are some cheap boardinghouses over there. Most of 'em respectable, though. That'd be my best guess."

"Thank you, Sir. I appreciate the information." He turned to go, then hesitated. "Do you think Simon will be coming back to New Orleans?"

"Doubt it. Packed up his things, said he wouldn't be back. Too much sadness here, he said. Poor little guy . . . came from some uppity family in France, got over here, never could get enough work to keep him going."

"What kind of work did he do?"

"He had taught in some fancy school in Paris. Over here, he got odd jobs teaching French to rich folks' kids."

"I see." Andrew nodded, a clearer image of Simon Dupree taking shape in his mind.

"Thanks again, Sir." He turned and descended the rickety steps, deep in thought. Megan McCoy had been a silhouette on a moonlit night; but now the silhouette was coming into focus.

Glancing once more toward the waterfront, he watched a hawk dive down for a fish, while seabirds squawked and ran for cover. A feeling of gloom seemed to permeate the air, and it touched him, as well. He rarely gave over to such feelings, as he was a cheerful person, by nature. Today had been different.

With his hands in his pockets and his head lowered, he walked along thinking about a beautiful red-haired woman who fed the birds and loved Irish music and sang with her soul. Who befriended a lonely little Frenchman and took pains mending the burly landlord's clothing.

Once upon a time, she had been a romantic who, in the bloom of womanhood, had fallen in love with Leon Bordeaux—fallen quickly and deeply, marrying him after a three-week courtship. Then she had been faced with the devastating news that her husband was dead. He could not imagine the sorrow and loneliness that must have followed. And on the heels of that, she had discovered she was pregnant. She had been a courageous woman, searching out the Bordeaux family, telling them she carried Leon's child, only to be cruelly turned away.

With no family, the note had said. An unselfish woman, Megan had been, doing what she believed was best for the child, suffering greatly in the process, he imagined.

He turned the corner onto Garner and looked down the block. The first few houses were smaller ones, family residences, with children playing in the yard. At the far end of the block, older two-story homes wore the look of having seen better days. Andrew knew that homeowners occasionally rented out rooms to offset expenses on these older homes. Maybe Megan had rented a room in one of them.

He glanced at the graying skies above him, wondering if he would get rained on before he returned to his office. The sun had sneaked out from behind the clouds an hour ago to take a peek at the day; but now the clouds swallowed up the sun again. The curling fog trailed wisps of gray in his path. *Bad spirits,* the voodoo lady would say, but he did not believe in those spirits, only the Holy Spirit of a loving God to whom he prayed daily for guidance. Andrew truly believed he had been guided here today, in an effort to help Lilly.

Lilly. He was confused about his feelings for her. He prided himself on being sensible, looking at a situation objectively. He needed this in his profession. Yet, something different had taken place in his mind, or his heart, where Lilly Brown was concerned.

Perhaps it was the romantic French blood that flowed in his veins, the legacy of ancestors who had followed their hearts to the new world.

He had reached the boardinghouses, and he hesitated, looking from one to another, trying to choose which to approach. He decided to start with the first one, a faded, yellow frame house. Pots of pink and purple geraniums on the porch gave the place a happy look, and he turned into the brick walkway.

The woman who answered his knock was a round little dumpling of a woman, with friendly blue eyes and a nice smile. She was a pleasant contrast to the burly man who had sent him in this direction. A spicy aroma wafted out the door to greet him as she spoke a greeting and waited for him to state his business.

"Good day," he said, removing his hat. "I wonder if you might help me. I am trying to locate the boardinghouse where Megan McCoy lived."

Her expression changed, and the bright eyes seemed to grow sad. He sensed he had come to the right place.

"Oh yes, Megan lived here for a little while," she said, nodding. "Who might you be?"

He introduced himself and repeated his reason for searching for her.

She nodded thoughtfully and stepped onto the porch.

"She came here about a year ago, looking for a room to rent. She had lived in Mobile for many years. She had been married to a seaman who was much older than she. When he died, he left her a little money, enough so she could return to New Orleans. She was dying from a rare lung disease, she told me. She'd had years of treatment, but nothing else could be done."

Andrew listened intently, waiting and hoping for something concrete to take back to Lilly, perhaps even to Marie.

"Sad to say, she couldn't afford to stay here for long. My rooms rent for a few dollars more than the other two houses." She glanced down the street. "Because my rooms are nicer and my food is better. One day, Megan found me in the kitchen and said she'd be taking a room down at the widow Hamsley's house." She paused and shook her head. "A dreary woman and a dreary house, if I may say so. I knew it was because of money, and I even offered to drop my price just a bit in order to keep her. But she wouldn't agree to it." She paused again, looking out at the street.

"Never talked to her much again. I'd see her walking past, walking slow like she was heavy of heart. Then I didn't see her for awhile, and one day I met up with Mrs. Hamsley at the market, and I asked about Megan. She told me Megan was ill, that she stayed in her room most of the time. I tell you, Sir, I felt bad for Megan. She was a sweet woman for all the fiery red hair and even a look about her that made you think once upon a time she could have been a little spitfire, were she of a mind to be. Not anymore." She looked past him down the street. "You could go down and talk to Mrs. Hamsley." She pointed toward a weathered gray house at the end of the block. "But you won't find out much. Not many folks care to be friendly with Mrs. Hamsley."

"I'm grateful to you for telling me this," Andrew said. "Can you think of anything more I could tell her daughter?"

Her brows arched. "Didn't know she had a daughter. She told me she never had children with the older seaman. I do remember once her saying she was orphaned when she was about fourteen after her parents got yellow fever during that epidemic back in the early fifties. Megan said she'd had to work hard to survive after that."

As Andrew listened, he realized tragedy seemed to have been very much a part of Megan McCoy's life. If she had been forced to work hard to survive, he could understand why she would have wanted a better life for her child.

"Again, thank you," he said, placing his hat on his head and turning toward the house she had indicated. He had hoped to bring Lilly here to meet this woman, thinking it might lift her spirits. But the story she told added yet another dimension of sadness to Megan McCoy's life.

Mrs. Hamsley's drab gray house matched the gloomy skies. And when the woman came to the door, she was even worse than he had expected.

Tall, stringy, and rail-thin, she wore a soiled apron over a faded black dress. When she poked her head farther out the door, he was reminded of the hawk he had seen out in the bay. She had a hooked nose, angry eyes, and thin black hair that trailed from her bun and hung carelessly about her face.

"What d'ya want?" she asked bluntly.

He repeated his mission, but her reaction differed from that of the kind woman up the street. Even Simon's burly landlord had turned out to be helpful. He suspected this woman would offer as little as possible.

"Megan McCoy?" She rasped the question. "Don't know nothin' about 'er. She 'uz barely able to pay 'er rent, then got sick an' coughed all the time. Died awhile back."

Andrew stared at her, shocked by the lack of emotion in her voice.

He struggled to regain his composure.

"Did she leave anything behind? I'm sure her daughter—"

"Nothin' but some raggedy clothes, ol' books. Wadn't worth nothin', I got less'n a dollar for 'em."

"So . . . there's nothing left. . . ." He glanced across the old porch, where not even one chair was placed to catch a breeze in the afternoon.

"Lil' man who hung aroun' like a stray dog—he took a thin' or two. Listen, if tha's all you want, I got a back room to clean up."

He knew his expression had turned cold, and he didn't bother keeping his tone friendly or even polite.

"Then I won't keep you." He turned and walked away.

He had hoped he would have some good news for Lilly, something that would bring a smile to her lovely face. But the situation was worse than he could have imagined. As for Marie Bordeaux, hardhearted from the beginning, he had hoped to offer solid proof that Megan was her niece, for he honestly believed that Marie needed family even more than Lilly did.

But he had found nothing for Marie and very little for Lilly. What he had learned today about Megan McCoy was that she had died in poverty with only one friend to honor her deathbed request.

A chill ran down his spine as he thought of her. A slow drizzle began to fall and his spirits sank lower.

He suspected Lilly had thoughts similar to those surfacing in his mind now: If Frances Bordeaux had believed Megan McCoy many years ago, if she had taken her in, life would have been drastically different for her. And for Lilly.

It was possible that Lilly could have grown up as he had, among the wealth and culture of a prominent family. She could have had a life like other girls he knew: pretty clothes, a circle of friends, parties, and fun. And an education to benefit her intelligence. She might already be married to a man of prominence in that inner circle.

Would he have been the one she chose? Their families were friends, they would have been in the same social circle. They would have met and . . . things could have been so different for them. The feelings he had for her frightened him. He had never felt this way about any woman. If Frances Bordeaux had accepted Megan McCoy everything would be so different now.

He sighed. But who was he to question the hand of fate? And because he knew the Bordeaux family were not Christians, he could hardly accept that what had happened to Lilly in the past was God's will. Instead, he felt strongly that God had brought them together now.

He paused under the leafy branches of a live oak, hoping to wait out the rain. As he stood there, listening to the patter of the raindrops on thick leaves, he closed his eyes.

Dear God, please be kind and merciful to Lilly. Please bring into her life the happiness that she deserves. And please touch Marie's heart, as only You can do.

He opened his eyes, thinking that only God could change Marie. His attempts to tell her about a loving God had been met with cold rebukes. Marie wanted no part of what she called "fanatical religion." Whenever he tried to broach the subject, she seemed to know his intentions, and the sharp hike of her brow and thin set of her lips silenced the words before they were spoken.

The rain fell harder around him, and he decided there was no waiting it out. It was going to get worse. As he scanned the street in search of a hansom cab, he thought of something else, something very important.

His search today had not been in vain. He was more determined than ever to help Lilly Brown. Hadn't he just said a prayer for her? And he was certain of something else. Her story of Simon Dupree and the chest and the letter from Megan McCoy seemed authentic. He believed everything she had told him, but one fact still troubled him greatly. Why would Marie's mother have dismissed Megan? Why wouldn't she welcome Leon's widow and child, despite the difference in backgrounds?

He would continue to search for the truth. He would obtain solid proof that Lilly Brown was, in fact, the daughter of Leon Bordeaux so that she could finally be given what should have been hers from birth. No one could give back the years when her life might have been easier or happier, but he was determined to do everything he could to help her now. If only she would let him.

$$6$$

*L*illy sat in her room, toying with the bread, gazing intermittently at the morning sunshine, a welcome reprieve from yesterday's rain.

She couldn't stop thinking of Andrew. At first it felt good having Andrew as a friend. She had enjoyed their conversations, the laughter, and the good food. But the friendship had begun to escalate to something more. He had told her he was attracted to her, and from the look in his eyes, she wanted to believe him. But there was Marie, whose presence was like a thundercloud on the bayou, heavy and dark, a cloud that seemed to swell around her, obscuring all else.

She blinked, trying to separate Andrew from Marie. What if she had just met him here, at one of the coffeehouses, perhaps?

The thought was tantalizing, but her common sense reminded her that she was a country girl who had spent her life in an orphanage. She had nothing in common with him, other than the fact that they liked to walk and talk, eat good food, and drink strong coffee.

I, too, am a Christian, he had said.

The words he had spoken moved to the center of her thoughts, and she realized they had something very important in common, something on which to build a solid friendship. But Andrew would always be a link to the Bordeaux family—the family who had hurt her mother, and would hurt her, if she allowed it. No, she would not. She was determined to rise above the petty hate and anger that threatened her. That meant putting Andrew Desmond out of her mind.

She sighed, pushing aside the small china plate from the dining room, and the remnants of a huge biscuit. Despite the loneliness she felt when she returned to her hotel room, she knew the difference between the true loneliness and emptiness in one's soul. She always sensed the presence of God, and this brought great comfort to her as well as a peace that truly did surpass all understanding.

She had made a decision. She was going back to St. Paul's to ask for her job. She would settle into the small familiar room that had been hers for the past three years, the room she had shared with one of the nuns, and often a younger girl to accommodate the over-crowded orphanage.

It had been a pretty good life, she now realized. And she was grateful that she had wisely hoarded enough money to pay her fare back to Summerville.

A gentle knock sounded on her door, and she brushed her skirt and stood. She was wearing the same navy dress she had worn the past two days, but it didn't seem to matter. She was no longer on a job search, and she rarely went out.

Turning the key in the lock, she opened the door expecting to find Dolly Sampson with an account of last night's adventure at the theater. To her shock, she was looking straight into the dark eyes of the man who had been dominating her thoughts all morning.

Andrew stood before her, twirling his hat around in his hands. He wore a beige coat and vest, a white linen shirt with a brown satin necktie, and beige trousers. She imagined he was on his way to work, or had already been.

"Please don't close the door on me," he said. "I would like to talk with you, but first I admit that I have come of my own volition. No one sent me, and I haven't forgotten your wish not to see me—"

"I don't remember saying I didn't wish to see you," she interrupted. "What I believe I said was that because of your connection with . . ." Her voice trailed off, and she felt a sadness that she was certain had reached her eyes. "Well, you know what I mean."

He nodded. "And now I've turned up at your door once again. This time, however, I do have something important to tell you. I found Simon Dupree's landlord. And that led me to your mother's old neighborhood."

"You went there?" Lilly gasped, staring at him in dismay.

"Yes. Could we discuss this over coffee?"

She nodded, trying to collect her thoughts. "I'll get my purse," she said, closing the door. Hurrying to the armoire, she pulled out the matching navy hat and shaped it around her face.

Tucking her hair more securely into its net, she thrust the pearl hat pin through the back of the hat. Then she picked up her handbag and hurried to the door.

Barely aware of what she was doing, she locked the door and dropped the key into her purse. She was full of questions, but she forced herself to keep silent until they could find a quiet place to talk. He offered his arm, she took it, and they descended the steps to the lobby.

What had he discovered upon going to her mother's neighborhood? Anxiety twisted her stomach into a knot, and her nerves were so taut that she jumped as a door slammed behind her.

And what had he learned of her father? Perhaps Leon Bordeaux was not her father, after all.

Her thoughts flew in every direction as they stepped out on the banquette and walked the short distance to the Café du Monde. She had ventured here on her second day in New Orleans, relishing the rich coffee and a beignet. Food on this day was the last thing on her mind, however, as Andrew found a table and the waiter took their order and hurried away.

"Tell me what you found," she said, as soon as they were alone.

Andrew took a deep breath and began to tell her about locating Simon Dupree's landlord. Then he told her how the Frenchman had loved Megan McCoy, a woman who fed the birds and sang from her soul when they sat together in the park.

Lilly hardly noticed the waiter or the coffee being placed before her. She was caught up in Andrew's description of the neighborhood and the friendly landlady at the boardinghouse who remembered her mother with kind words. Then she felt a pang of sadness as he told her about the other woman who was all business and had not bothered getting to know Megan McCoy. Yet, the woman verified the fact that Megan had died in that house recently.

"What was wrong with her?" she asked finally, when Andrew had finished the story and they took a sip of their coffee.

"I gathered it was some sort of lung disease. The important thing, Lilly, is that so far everything Monsieur Dupree told you seems to be the truth." He was looking at her with that gentle kindness which seemed to be so much a part of him, and she was so grateful he had come into her life, despite the bizarre circumstances.

"Did Megan say anything to anyone, or was there anything to substantiate her claim that Leon Bordeaux was my father?"

He shook his head. "No, I'm afraid not."

They were silent again, drinking their coffee, each lost in thought. "I want to go there, Andrew. I want to meet these people."

"We can do that. However, there isn't much more to learn, I'm afraid."

"I'm sure you've told me everything, but I just want to, well, I want to see where she lived and try to get a better understanding of what her life was like."

He sighed. "I was afraid you would say that."

"What do you mean? Is there something else?"

"No, I've told you everything. I just think it may distress you to go there, but you certainly have the right to make up your own mind."

She sat back in her chair, thinking. Did she want to delve deeper into the puzzle?

"You're right. Why go any further with this? I'm only torturing myself, and it seems you've done a thorough investigation."

"Lilly," he said, reaching across to touch her hand, "thank you for being so trusting of me. I have told you the truth. And you know that I have no ulterior motive in this."

Tears rushed to her eyes before she could stop them, and she lowered her head. "No one has ever been more kind. Thank you." She swallowed hard, took a sip of coffee, and struggled to regain control of her emotions.

He gave her time and silence, and for a moment, there was only the rise and fall of voices around them and the clatter of silverware on china.

Lilly took a deep breath and looked up at him with clear eyes.

"Well," she said, trying to lighten her tone, "I am returning to

St. Paul's. I've more or less accomplished my mission, and there doesn't seem to be anything left to do."

A frown crossed his face. "You mean you're leaving New Orleans?"

She wondered why he looked so distressed by this news. After all, there was no chance of their friendship developing, given his connection to Marie. Did he think she disliked living in Summerville?

"St. Paul's is my home," she replied. "I still have a job there, and it is rewarding work. I feel needed and appreciated there."

She couldn't help the tinge of bitterness that crept into her words. She only wished that she could remove the resentment she felt toward the Bordeaux family, for she knew that ultimately she was hurting herself by hanging on to it.

Andrew was silent for a moment as he gazed into his coffee.

When he looked up at her, his lips pursed for a moment before he spoke. "Let me suggest another possibility. I was talking with a gentleman who owns a small art gallery over on Decatur this week. My firm is handling some business for him. His name is Carl Mercer. He's rather eccentric but well respected. I went over to pick up some paperwork, but he said his records were such a mess that he needed more time to get them together. He explained that his mother has kept books for him but was taken ill recently and is unable to return to work. If you're interested, I think it would be a pleasant job. It's a nice gallery. Since I know something about his business, I believe the job would be relatively straightforward once you get the records organized."

He paused, grinning. "Carl Mercer's interest is in the art he commissions, not in keeping the books straight. In fact, he reminds me of a professor I had in college who was always dropping books and misplacing tests."

They laughed, and as Lilly thought about the job, it did sound appealing. She had always taken pride in her ability to organize the records at St. Paul's, and Sister Ophelia had often remarked on how accurate she was in totaling large sums.

Lilly was amazed again at the lengths to which Andrew had gone in order to accommodate her. She had spent endless hours walking the streets, wearing herself out, day after day, searching for just this type of job. It sounded like the answer to her prayers if she chose to stay in New Orleans. She thought she had made up her mind to leave, but now she wasn't so sure.

She shook her head, feeling slightly dismayed. "I don't know what to say," she replied softly.

"Then let's go speak with Carl," Andrew answered lightly, as though it were a very simple decision. "After you talk with him, you can make up your mind about what you want to do."

"When should I speak with him?" she asked, feeling anxious about an interview.

"If you would like, we could go there as soon as we're finished."

Lilly caught her breath, then she glanced down at her dress, wondering if it were appropriate for a job interview.

"You look just fine," Andrew said.

She looked back at him, feeling a bit uncomfortable about the way he seemed to read her thoughts. Then she smiled.

"All right. If you're willing to go along with me to meet Mr. Mercer, I think I'd like to go now, so I can make a decision, one way or the other."

"Good. Carl Mercer is a very colorful character. You'll see what I mean. . . ."

Lilly stared at him, wondering about the man she was about to meet.

7

*T*he art gallery was situated in the middle of the block, surrounded by boutiques, coffeehouses, and a couple of antique shops. Through the glass window, she could see an impressive array of artwork in lovely frames. Andrew opened the door for her, and as they entered, the jingle of a sleigh bell announced their presence.

"Come in," a voice called from the rear of the gallery.

Lilly saw a small, blond man seated behind a beautiful antique desk covered with papers. He leaped to his feet, bumping a corner of the desk as he hurried to greet them. Papers sailed through the air and furled across the hardwood floor.

"Hello, Mr. Mercer." Andrew extended his hand.

"Hello, Andrew. And please call me Carl. I hate the formality of last names, don't you? When I hear 'Mr. Mercer' I start looking around for my grandfather."

Lilly smiled at his remark as Andrew turned to her. "I've brought a friend to meet you. May I present Miss Lilly Brown?"

"Miss Brown, a pleasure," Carl said, kissing her hand.

Lilly was taken by surprise at this dramatic gesture; yet, she was secretly amused by the man who managed to give the impression of moving in all directions while standing still. He seemed to be a bundle of energy, crossing and uncrossing his arms, and his bright blue eyes glanced from her to Andrew then back to her. He was only an inch or so taller than Lilly. His blond hair was worn long around his ears; he had a long angular face and a quick smile beneath a thin mustache. Lilly guessed him to be in his early thirties.

She tried not to stare at his clothing, a fascinating mix of a green coat, orange paisley tie, and tan slacks tailored in a loose-fitting fashion.

"Miss Brown has experience at keeping books," Andrew explained, "and I remember you mentioned needing a bookkeeper."

"Needing, did the man say? I am desperate!" He swung his arms toward Lilly, taking a closer look. "And you live here in New Orleans?" As he glanced back at Andrew, she sensed he was curious about the nature of their relationship.

"I just recently moved here from Summerville," she replied.

"I see. And how did you two meet?" he asked, crossing his arms tightly across his chest.

"A mutual friend," Andrew answered.

"Mmm," Carl mumbled, stroking his chin.

"I realize you have valuable artwork here and need to be careful in choosing your employees. But I can vouch for Miss Brown."

"Oh, of course," he replied quickly. "Do you know anyone else in New Orleans, Miss Brown?"

Lilly hesitated.

"She knows Marie Bordeaux," Andrew said, and it was as though the weight of the name loosened all caution from Carl's mind. His blond brows hiked up, and his quick smile appeared.

"Excellent. And you have experience at keeping books?" he asked, shifting his weight from one foot to the other.

"Yes, I do. For two years, I have been the principal bookkeeper at St. Paul's Church in Summerville. I enjoy working with figures."

He nodded, his gaze assessing her as she spoke.

"And you're pleasant and neat. I can see that you would do well in dealing with my customers. But, alas! I would be a monster not to show you the absolute horror of that desk!" He jabbed his finger in the direction of the scramble of papers on, under, and around the desk.

Lilly ventured toward the desk, automatically retrieving some papers from the floor. Carl began to explain his mother's system of keeping books, and Lilly breathed a quiet sigh of relief. It appeared to be an elementary system compared to what she had done at the orphanage and church.

She turned and looked back around the gallery, and as she did, she liked the feeling that came over her. She really would enjoy working here.

"I can manage this," she said, the confidence she felt ringing true in her tone of voice as she looked at him.

He clapped his hands over his heart and looked heavenward. "Thank You, dear Lord, for this angel of mercy."

Lilly and Andrew exchanged amused smiles. Then, like a human whirlwind, Carl was turning, charging ahead, and giving them a tour of the gallery. In the process, he spun tales of the artists he represented, going into great detail about their lives. Suddenly, he halted in mid-sentence, and his glance darted from Andrew to Lilly.

"Forgive me for babbling, but I do love my work. And, Miss Brown," he paused, giving meaning to his words, "I would be *delighted* to have you come to work for me."

"Thank you," she replied. Lilly smiled at Carl and considered her options as he stated the hours she would be expected to work and her wages. While it wasn't a large sum, she could manage without using her savings. It seemed a shame to go back to the life she had always known before she gave this new life a fair chance. And she did like New Orleans. She willed herself not to look at Andrew, but her heart made the argument that she would have an opportunity to be with Andrew if she stayed. And perhaps she should give God time to work out the complicated details of their relationship.

"I'll do my best. And since you don't stand on ceremony here, please call me Lilly."

He nodded. "A lovely name." He whirled to Andrew. "How can I ever thank you for bringing this remarkable woman to my door and saving me from going mad?"

He was such an amusing man that Lilly knew she was going to love working in his gallery. In less than five minutes, she had the perfect job. And it had happened with pleasure and ease, in contrast to the drudgery she had experienced in seeking work, only to be turned down.

"When would you like me to begin?" she asked.

"Today!" He laughed quickly, and Lilly was relieved to see that he was joking.

Glancing back at the desk, however, she knew there was no time to waste in restoring order. Lilly felt the sense of purpose which was so important to her in whatever she undertook. "What about tomorrow?" she asked.

His eyes lit up. "That would be wonderful." He extended his hand to Andrew. "Thank you, thank you, thank you."

"My pleasure," Andrew replied, as they shook hands and both men turned to Lilly.

"I'll see you in the morning," she said, as Andrew's hand touched her elbow and they began to walk toward the door.

"And I shall sleep in peace tonight," Carl called after them.

"Lilly, I'm so pleased you accepted the job," Andrew said as they stepped out onto the banquette.

"It seems to be exactly what I have searched for, and I have you to thank," she said, looking up at him.

"All I did was introduce you. You got the job yourself."

"Why?" she asked, as they began to walk. "I've been to so many other shops only to be turned down."

"I think I know why. Or at least I can give you my opinion. Seldom do we see ladies as young and lovely as you, out on their own, seeking employment as a bookkeeper. My guess is that a few suspicious minds thought you were too good to be true. I told you before, you're a rare combination of intelligence, honesty, and beauty, out looking to do a man's job."

"A man's job?" She tilted her head and looked up at him, irritated by that logic. And yet she sensed he was right. "So that's it?"

"That's *it* to my way of thinking. I believe this calls for a celebration. Unfortunately, I have to meet with a client in about fifteen minutes. And afterward, I'm scheduled to travel up to Baton Rouge for about a week on an important case." He sighed. "Too bad about that. But we can have that celebration when I return. I could stop by the gallery as soon as I get back in town, and we can plan something fun. What do you say to a carriage ride around the city, then dinner at Antoine's?"

Lilly's head was already in a whirl over her new job. Feeling lighthearted again, she quipped a familiar remark spoken merely in jest. "I'd say you know the way to a woman's heart."

His eyes darkened as he leaned closer to her and lowered his voice. "I'm only interested in one woman's heart, and her name is Lilly Brown."

8

*A*fter the first couple of days, Lilly felt completely at ease working for Carl Mercer. She was adjusting to his disorganization, his flamboyant style, and his nervous habits. His sense of humor kept her entertained, so there was never a dull moment. Her interest in the gallery grew, and Carl explained that his grandfather had opened it as a small shop for starving artists to display their work. His grandfather, John, was born with one leg a bit shorter than the other, which had been deemed a liability so he had not gone to war. As a result, he had become one of those starving artists who had combined talent with persistence to build a small business while becoming a modest success with his paintings. He had long since retired and lived with his wife in the garden district. Their only son, William, Carl's father, had died in the war, but Carl's mother had remained close to the family and had, for years, worked in the gallery.

Once Carl told her about the Mercer family, Lilly better understood the history of the business. One morning soon after, the door opened and an older gentleman with a slight limp appeared, a painting tucked under his arm.

"Come in, Pop!" Carl hurried across to greet him. "Come over and say hello to my new employee, Lilly Brown, who is an absolute angel delivered to save me from the demons of disorganization! Lilly, this is my grandfather, John Mercer."

Lilly and the older gentleman laughed at Carl's enthusiasm and exchanged hellos. Then John Mercer tilted his head and looked at her curiously.

"A very pretty face. I think I've seen you in my dreams," he teased.

He had lingered for a few minutes of pleasant conversation with Lilly before shuffling back to his storage closet to leave the painting and pick up a few supplies. As he was leaving, he turned at the door and glanced back at her with a twinkle in his gray eyes. Then shaking his head as though confused, he turned and headed out the door.

For one reckless moment, she fought an urge to ask him if he had ever met Megan McCoy. Simon Dupree had said there was a striking resemblance; was that why John Mercer had thought he had seen her in his dreams? She made a mental note to ask him the next time he came in. She liked him very much and saw that Carl, in some ways, was an exaggerated version of his grandfather. And yet Carl was like no one else, always in a flurry of activity, talking and rushing around and living his life in a most dramatic way.

Once she settled into a routine at the cluttered desk, she lost herself in the challenge of restoring order. It had taken several long, hard days of steady work, but she had made great headway, and Carl seemed immensely pleased.

"You are truly amazing," Carl said to her one morning, as they paused long enough to sip his favorite blend of tea from dainty china cups. He had just sold an expensive painting and was delirious over his commission.

"Not really," Lilly replied. "Your mother has done an excellent job of keeping the books. I simply caught you up on the paperwork."

The sleigh bell jingled as the door opened and both turned to face Marie Bordeaux.

For a moment, Lilly was frozen in shock at the sight of Marie, dressed in the latest Parisian fashion, every hair in place beneath the pale blue hat—a perfect match for the crisp, blue linen dress expertly tailored to flatter her plump figure.

"Mademoiselle Bordeaux, what a delight to see you," Carl trilled, hurrying to greet her.

Marie's dark eyes looked past him and directly into Lilly's face; her thin lips tightened in obvious disapproval.

"And look!" Carl whirled, pointing toward Lilly as though Marie had not already seen her. "Your friend Lilly Brown is my new bookkeeper, and what a saving grace she has been."

Marie's cheeks were mottled with red splotches as she sputtered out a reply. "She is not *my* friend!" She charged toward Lilly, obviously brimming with rage.

"How dare you misrepresent your connection to me! I'm going to speak to Andrew right away about starting a suit against you for fraud. That's what it is!" She whirled to Carl. "She is trying to pass herself off as a relative of mine, which is an outright lie. And, Carl," she spat, "I am horrified that you would hire anyone who used my name without first consulting me."

"But . . ." Carl, paling visibly beneath Marie's verbal assault, looked from Marie to Lilly. For the first time since Lilly had met him, he stood stock-still, paralyzed by dismay.

"I'll not be returning to this gallery as long as *that woman* works here," Marie said, thrusting her chin into the air and huffing out of the shop.

Lilly put her face in her hands, fighting tears of humiliation. She was too mortified to be angry now; that would come later. All she could think about was the way Marie kept shattering her hopes. And, as Lilly had feared, she was going to drag Andrew into this nightmare. Lilly had missed Andrew terribly the past week and was eagerly anticipating his return. Now, Marie had spoiled everything.

"Lilly?" Carl's voice sounded as though someone had his hands around his throat, squeezing the word out.

She opened her eyes and looked at him, wondering what to say, or whether she should even explain. It seemed pointless.

"I thought. . . ." Carl sank into the nearest chair. He cleared his throat. "You are Andrew's friend. I thought. . . ."

Lilly took a deep, long breath and tried to gather her dignity. "It isn't the way she made it sound, but I'm sorry her name was ever mentioned the day I came here with Andrew." She stood up. "I'll get my things."

She began tidying up the desk, her last act of affection for the job she had come to love.

"Why are you getting your things?" Carl asked, his expression blank.

Lilly looked up in surprise. "Because I can no longer work for you.

She has made it quite clear that she'll never return to your shop. And I can only imagine the things she will say about my working here. You can't afford to lose business over my problem with . . . her."

She couldn't bear to speak her name. She knew this time she would have to pray long and hard not to hate Marie—or the rest of the Bordeaux family for what they had done to Megan McCoy.

Carl was silent for a moment, then he came out of the chair, yanked a monogrammed handkerchief from his pocket, and began to mop his brow. "My dear Lilly, we're going to have a cup of tea," he said, rushing toward the enameled teapot, "and you're going to tell me your side of the story."

Lilly stared at him, amazed that he even wanted to hear her story. No one was going to believe her over Marie. And yet . . . She sat down again, trying to collect her thoughts as Carl refilled their teacups. The cups rattled in their saucers as Carl placed them on a corner of the desk, then wilted into the nearest chair. Then he turned to stare at her again, and she knew she owed him the truth, or what she believed to be the truth.

She began with the day Simon Dupree came to her door. She told him about the small mahogany chest, the papers, especially the letter from Megan McCoy.

"This is incredible," Carl interrupted. "Amazing, truly amazing."

Lilly nodded and picked up the story again, sparing no mercy in describing the way Marie had dismissed her that day. As she spoke about her friendship with Andrew, she noticed that Carl was looking at her a bit differently.

"You two are in love, aren't you?" he burst out.

Lilly stopped in mid-sentence, shocked by his words. And yet . . . her gaze lifted over his head to a painting on the wall that she often stopped to admire. A couple stood hand in hand before St. Louis Cathedral in Jackson Square. Their faces were turned toward one another, and the artist had created an aura of radiance around them as they gazed into one another's eyes. Each time she looked at the painting, she thought of Andrew.

She snapped her mind back to the moment and slowly shook her head. "We haven't a chance to be anything because of Marie."

"What do you mean?" Carl asked.

"She is Andrew's client."

"She's certainly not his only client. Although I am quite sure she's a very important one."

"Their families have been friends for three generations. He feels a great loyalty toward her."

Carl sighed and shook his head. "Poor Lilly."

She stared at him. "Poor Carl. Just look what a predicament I've put you in now."

"Yes, look! A perfect set of records, for the first time in my fifteen years here. No reflection on Mother, of course, but sweet Lilly, you are a genius with the bookkeeping. And my clients adore you. Furthermore, you know exactly how to deal with the temperament of an artist. I watched how cleverly you handled Jules when he came to vent his frustration over not having sold his painting—which is not up to the usual standards, if I may say so privately."

He paused to take a slurp of tea, and Lilly stared gloomily into her cup of tea, untouched. What could she do? Carl obviously wanted to keep her, and yet she knew Marie would give him no peace, would continue her threats, and would even berate poor Andrew, once he returned.

A friend of Carl's entered the gallery and immediately Carl was at his side, chatting, showing him the latest painting, which had just been delivered.

Lilly leaned back in her chair and sipped her now tepid tea, trying to collect her thoughts. Once again the idea of returning to St. Paul's entered her mind. There was no way she could avoid Marie; that was apparent to her now. And despite Carl's kindness, and Andrew's attentiveness, she was only going to complicate their lives by staying on. Marie's money and influence spread over New Orleans like an enormous umbrella. Perhaps she could go to another part of town to get a job and never, ever mention Marie's name.

Then she recalled how difficult it had been the past two weeks, trying to get suitable employment when no one would hire her. If she went to a remote area, the jobs would be even scarcer.

She finished her tea, then picked up their cups and went out to the small room that served as a makeshift kitchen. Rinsing out the cups and placing them on the draining board, she decided she had no choice but to return to Summerville. There. It was settled. Or so she believed.

Until she walked back into the main part of the gallery and saw Andrew waiting for her. She could tell by the happy smile on his face when she entered the room that he had no idea what had transpired between Carl and Marie.

A feeling of sadness choked her for a moment, and because the sadness in her heart must have been reflected on her face, his smile faded.

He walked over to her, extending his hand. "Has your work week gone badly? That's not the smile I was hoping for."

She shook her head. "I love working here. And Carl couldn't be a better employer."

He frowned, obviously puzzled.

Carl rushed up, looking from Andrew to Lilly. "Did you tell him?"

Lilly bit her lip, wishing the wonderful relationship could have continued, but now it was about to end.

"I can see that you have not. Andrew, Marie Bordeaux came in here today and threatened to have you start some sort of ridiculous suit against Lilly."

Andrew was astonished. "For what?"

Lilly placed her hand on his arm. "I'll explain it." She looked at Carl. "Since it's almost five o'clock, may I go?"

"You may go for the evening, but I will expect to see you at the usual time in the morning."

Lilly felt a rush of emotion for the man whom she had known such a short while, and yet he had become a dear friend. She leaned forward and gave him a quick hug, which caused him to blush and hastily bid Andrew good-bye, then dash off.

Andrew still looked thoroughly confused, and she could understand why.

"Do you feel like dinner?" he asked.

"No. Could we just find a quiet place to talk?"

"Of course. What about the little tea shop down the street?"

"Perfect. I'll just get my purse."

§

An hour later, they sat in a back corner of the little Victorian tea shop, and Lilly had told him everything.

He reached across the table and took her hand. "Let me put your mind at ease about any ridiculous threat of a lawsuit. Marie hasn't a leg to stand on when it comes to trying to sue you. All she can do is rant and rave. And as for using me and my firm as a weapon against you, she has no power there. Not anymore. After today, I will no longer represent her in any legal matter; nor do I have any intention of keeping up a friendship with her."

"Are you sure about what you're doing?" Lilly asked tentatively.

"Positive. So try to forget about Marie, and let's proceed with that celebration I've been counting on ever since I left Baton Rouge. Are you ready for the evening I promised?"

Lilly looked into his handsome face, admiring the way his dark eyes lit up when he spoke and the gentle features that were a reflection of his spirit. He was a dream come true, but if this were a dream, she never wanted to awaken from it.

"I've looked forward to it too. I'd like to change into a more suitable dress."

"You look just fine to me."

She smiled. "Thank you. But I have something else in mind."

He stood and offered his arm. "Shall we go?"

§

Andrew had seen her to her door, promising to return in one hour.

What she'd had in mind was the dress Dolly had brought her the evening before. Lilly hurried to bathe and dress, marveling at the perfect timing of Dolly's gift. It had been a stroke of good luck, according to Dolly, but to Lilly it was an answer to prayer.

One of the ladies in Dolly's theatrical group had ordered the gown from a New York catalog, but when it arrived, the dress was a disappointment to her. The other women in the group considered it a bit too mild for their tastes as well, but when Dolly saw it, she had thought it was perfect for Lilly.

It was a pale beige of the popular slipper satin fabric, with a long bodice ending in a vee at the waist. There were no lace insets or tucks, and while Dolly's friends might consider the dress plain, Lilly adored it.

When Lilly tried it on and whirled around, Dolly had clapped her hands together and let out a whoop.

"Just knew it, just knew it! That dress was nothing special on Betsy, but on you . . ." Her voice had trailed off as she led Lilly over to the mirror. "With that creamy skin and red hair, you're a sight to behold. Oh, Lilly Brown, you are a beauty!"

Lilly had stared, pleased at the way the flair of her hips and the fullness of her bust complimented the dress. It suited her figure as though it were made for her. And she saw what Dolly meant. Her hair had hung in wisps about her face, and she saw that if she wore her hair down, the beige satin was perfect for her. Her hazel eyes, which she had always considered too wide set, had seemed to glow above the sheen of the satin.

She had told Dolly, "When I get my wages next week—"

"You'll put them in your pocket," Dolly had said as she reached out, placed her hand over Lilly's and closed it, as though emphasizing her point. "Oh, my darlin', just the sight of you in that dress is the greatest pleasure I've had since Wally took me on a boat ride on the Mississippi."

"But, Dolly, it's too much," Lilly had protested, only to be shushed again.

"I already told you now, and don't be makin' me repeat it again. Me and Wally never had children, and secretly, I always wanted a daughter, but I hushed up about it, not wanting to make Wally feel worse, you know. I'm afraid I've taken a real motherly attitude toward you . . ." Tears had shimmered in her eyes. "It's I who should be thanking you for such happiness."

Lilly had become choked up as well, and she'd given Dolly a loving hug. "I'm honored that you would think of me as a daughter. All of my life I have wanted a family to love. It's been my dream."

"Mine too," Dolly had said between sniffs. "So we can sort of belong to each other.

"Now you wear that dress when Mr. Desmond gets back in town, and he'll fall head over heels once he sees you."

She now stood again before the mirror, admiring the dress. She owned no jewels, but having brushed her hair until it shone like burnished copper, she realized that she would pass inspection without adornments.

As she glanced at the clock, she noticed that Andrew was due to return any moment.

ॐ

When Andrew knocked on her door, she took only a drop of the Parisian perfume Dolly had loaned her. It had an enticing aroma but was almost too strong for her taste. By rubbing her wrists together, then making circles over her head with her fists, the effect was just right. She reached for her purse and went to the door.

When she opened the door and Andrew saw her, Lilly smiled at the expression of surprise, then admiration. Lilly felt a bit shy, and yet she felt beautiful for the first time in her life. And in a flash of insight, she knew why. She had always heard that beauty was in the eye of the beholder, and she sensed Andrew was thinking that tonight she was beautiful. The dress had a lot to do with it, she suspected, but it didn't matter. If she were Cinderella at the ball, she intended to enjoy the glass slipper until the stroke of midnight.

"All I can say is . . . you take my breath away." Andrew was grinning at her.

Lilly smiled. "It may be the perfume, which I suspect is a mite strong."

"The perfume is nice, but it's the lady that has my head spinning."

Lilly felt as though her head were spinning as well as she gazed at Andrew. He wore a navy coat and trousers—tailored from quality fabric—cut expertly to his lean frame. His dark hair and eyes and clean-shaven face fit the image of the distinguished attorney that he was.

When they reached the banquette, a fancy carriage with fine horses waited. The driver was also dressed up in a tailcoat and a black top hat. Lilly glanced at Andrew and smiled.

"You do make an impression, Mr. Desmond."

"I try," he said, helping her into the shiny carriage.

Andrew had many good characteristics, it seemed to Lilly, but one of the most important to her was his reliability. Lilly needed someone who was dependable, and he had given her no reason to believe otherwise.

It was a lovely June evening, and Lilly thought there must have been a million stars winking around a huge silver moon.

"Did you order a full moon for tonight?" Lilly teased.

"I did, along with a pretty lady to ride with me in my magic carriage."

Magic. It was exactly the word that had come to her mind earlier, when she thought of herself playing Cinderella.

"Imagine my luck," Andrew teased. "I was blessed with both."

Lilly laughed as the carriage passed under a huge magnolia tree, and she remembered that Andrew had told her the magnolia blossom was his favorite flower. She liked knowing those small yet endearing things about him. She liked magnolias, but her favorite was the night jasmine, now wafting around them on the evening breeze. It was perfect.

"May I ask what you are thinking? You have a lovely smile on your face."

She sighed and turned to him, rustling the silk of her dress as she moved. It felt so luxurious against her skin, and it seemed to her the most perfect night of her life.

"I feel like standing up and shouting, 'Thank You, Lord!'"

At his look of surprise, she laughed and touched his arm. "Don't worry, I'll try to restrain myself. It's just that I am constantly having to be reminded that my hope is in Him, and when I start letting my own stubborn will get in the way, I make a mess of things every time."

Her smiled faded, and she felt a twinge of sadness. "I still feel bad about being so short-tempered at brunch the other day. I've been praying to get over this anger toward the Bordeaux family; I've asked God to help me trust in His ways, rather than my own."

She swept her hand around her. "So just look at the beautiful evening," she said, turning back to him. "And the nice man He has kept in my life, even after I was rude and ungrateful."

Andrew was staring at her with a funny grin on his face. "You know, I just love your honesty and your openness about your faith. You are a remarkable woman. I knew it from the beginning, and you continue to prove me right."

"Mmm, and you are a special kind of man who likes flowers and music."

"And tonight we have both," he said, pointing toward the upstairs balcony of a garden home where a man was playing the violin.

The carriage moved slowly along, and the plaintive notes of the violin began to fade. Yet the night breeze swept the echo along with them.

"I reserved a table at Antoine's for seven, so it looks like we'll be right on time," Andrew said as the driver turned down Rue St. Louis. "Are you hungry?"

Lilly brushed a strand of hair back from her face and smiled. "I am always hungry."

The carriage pulled up before Antoine's, and Andrew stepped down and helped Lilly out of the carriage.

Lilly smoothed her skirts and glanced around her. Antoine's was considered the finest restaurant in New Orleans. She recalled that one of the sisters had attended a special celebration at Antoine's for her parents' thirty-fifth wedding anniversary. She had regaled everyone at St. Paul's with rich descriptions of Antoine's elegant dining room and marvelous food. Most of the children who heard her story dreamt of someday going to such a place, but many doubted they ever would. And yet Lilly was entering Antoine's on the arm of a special man who had hired a carriage and planned this event especially for her.

She glanced appreciatively at him as they walked under a twinkling chandelier, and he spoke to a host who quickly led them to a table overlooking Rue St. Louis.

As Lilly settled into the soft-cushioned chair and glanced around her, she noted that her dress seemed appropriate for the evening. The women seated at other tables, talking quietly with their companions, wore lovely dresses that were classical yet elegantly simple.

What a wonderful restaurant! She trailed a finger over the white brocade cloth that complimented silver-edged, white china and silver cutlery polished to a mirrored gleam.

"Would you like me to order?" Andrew asked politely, as the waiter placed thick menus before them.

"Please do," she answered, lifting a crystal goblet for a sip of water.

She loved the fact that Andrew possessed a sensitive nature and spared her the embarrassment of trying to figure out French names or choose from among the numerous entrées. Yet, he consulted her in making decisions, and when he took the lead, he did it in a polite and gentle manner.

"For starters, we'll have Canapé St. Antoine. As a soup . . ." He hesitated, glancing at her. "Would you like some gumbo? It's one of their specialties."

"Yes, please."

"We'll have Gumbo Creole," he continued, "then Chateaubriand. For a sauce, we'll take garlic butter." He looked at her. "Fresh asparagus?"

"Definitely."

"And we'll have your famous salad and iced tea."

The waiter appeared delighted with the choices as he accepted the menus and hurried off to fill their requests.

"Did that meet with your approval?" Andrew asked, leaning back in the chair and studying her thoughtfully.

"Absolutely. But what is Chateaubriand?" she asked, not embarrassed by the fact that she didn't know. She was always candid with him and never wanted to pretend to be someone other than Lilly Brown.

"Chateaubriand is a prime cut of tenderloin, served with a variety of sauces. I prefer the one I ordered. And Antoine's serves it with potatoes and—"

"Good evening," a familiar voice interrupted. Carl Mercer's grandfather stood near their table, smiling down at them.

John Mercer was dressed in a fashionable dark suit with a white shirt. His silver hair and beard added to his distinguished appearance as his keen gaze settled on Lilly.

Andrew stood. "Good evening, Sir. May I introduce Miss Lilly Brown?"

Before Lilly could explain they had previously met, he began to nod. "The girl of my dreams," he said, his gray eyes twinkling. "My grandson introduced us recently, and I have told him how fortunate he is to have her in his employ."

"Thank you," Lilly replied, as he continued to stare.

"Forgive me, but I keep trying to place you."

Lilly hesitated, glancing at Andrew. He seemed to read her thoughts.

"Sir, I remember that you were a friend of my father's. I wonder if you ever knew Leon Bordeaux?"

His white brows arched. "Of course. I was better acquainted with his father, however."

"Did you ever meet a young Irish woman by the name of Megan McCoy?" Lilly asked.

He pursed his lips, staring at the floor for a moment. When he looked back at Lilly, he shook his head. "I don't know that name. An Irish gal, you say?"

"Yes. She . . . she was my mother."

He stared at her for a moment, obviously trying to sort out a puzzle in his mind.

"We don't want to detain you," Andrew said, speaking slowly. "However, we are searching for anyone who knew Megan McCoy. We have been told that she was married to Leon Bordeaux shortly before his death."

At that, John seemed to make the connection he had been struggling toward, and he turned to Lilly. "Ah, I see! That does jog my aging memory."

He stroked his chin, looking from Andrew to Lilly. "Let me think about this. I may have something that will help you, but I don't want to speak out of turn. I seem to recall a young woman, a red-haired woman, who looked very much like you," he said, smiling down at Lilly. "Let me look into it." He glanced over his shoulder to a dainty woman with pure-white hair. She sat alone at a table for two. "My wife is waiting for me."

"Of course. Have a pleasant evening." Andrew shook his hand.

"And if you remember anything about Megan McCoy," Lilly added, "I would greatly appreciate your letting me know."

"There's just one thing," Andrew added, his tone cautious. "We would prefer that Marie Bordeaux not be involved in this. She has been . . . well, let's just say she has been less than cordial."

John Mercer rolled his eyes. "That's Marie. Not a very nice person, if I must say so—and I shouldn't." He turned to go, then looked back at them. "You're a nice young couple. Enjoy being young and happy," he said, winking at them before he turned and, limping slightly, rejoined his wife.

"He's such a kind man," Lilly said, watching him take his seat and pat his wife's hand.

Then the waiter began to deliver their meal and conversation was dispensed in favor of sampling the delectable food.

Later, as they sat contentedly over caramel custard and demitasse, Andrew looked across at her and smiled.

"Was everything to your liking?" he asked.

"Everything was perfect. I was just thinking about all of my friends at St. Paul's, wishing they could have this experience."

"Then perhaps sometime you can invite them to come visit you, and we can return to Antoine's. I'm always looking for an excuse to dine here."

She laughed softly. "Before you make such an offer, you should be prepared to spend a lot of money. You've learned what a hearty appetite I have. Some of my friends can outdo me."

"No, surely not!" he exclaimed with mock seriousness.

"Oh yes. And I'll remind you that my—what did you call it?—my hearty appetite is one of the things you like about me."

"Just *one* of the things I like about you," he responded, as the waiter handed him a message.

"It seems our driver is getting anxious," Andrew informed her. "Shall we go?"

"Of course." As they left Antoine's, she glanced back at the empty table where the Mercers had sat. Again, she wondered what had gone through the older gentleman's mind when he looked at her face.

Andrew helped her into the carriage, and the driver set the horses at a slow pace to take Lilly back to her hotel. She leaned against Andrew and let her thoughts drift.

"You're very quiet," Andrew said.

"I was thinking about John Mercer and wondering what he's going to tell me."

"I had the impression he wanted to be certain of his words, whatever they are. Let's hope he remembers something that will be helpful."

Lilly nodded, and yet she was afraid to hope.

"Sister Ophelia, the nun who was closest to me, used to say, 'You can have anything you want, if you know what to want.' It's good advice when you think about it." She looked over at Andrew.

"It is. But don't you think miracles can come when you least expect them—and exceed your greatest dreams?"

"Maybe so. *This* is a miracle."

"This?"

"This evening, this carriage, this man who arranged the carriage and the perfect dinner. My problem is, I'm always feeling a bit of sadness in the back of my mind, knowing it will soon end."

He reached out and touched her hand, enfolding it in his. "It doesn't have to end."

Lilly felt the warm pressure of his hand on hers, and when she looked into his eyes, her heart lurched. What was happening to her? Was it just the magic of the evening, or was it more?

"You can have a good life here, Lilly, and you'll make lots of friends. You already have me. And Carl. And the Sampsons." He nodded slowly, as his gaze moved over her face. "I want to introduce you to some of my friends. You don't need the Bordeaux money or the name. You'll be able to build a life of your own. And I'd like to help you."

His offer touched her deeply, and for a moment, she couldn't find the right response. "You are a kind and generous person," she said. "Why would you do all of this for me?"

He was silent for a moment, looking into her eyes. Lilly wondered what he was thinking, then he leaned forward and touched his lips to hers in a sweet, tentative kiss.

At first she held back, then as the kiss deepened, her arms reached out to him, and she gave herself up to the joy of his embrace. Then, slowly she forced herself to pull back from him, for what she had just experienced was unlike anything she had ever felt. What did this mean? What was this feeling?

"You asked me what I was thinking earlier. Now it's my turn to ask you." Her voice seemed too loud in her ears, and she tried to calm her nerves.

"I am thinking, Lilly Brown, that I'm falling in love with you. Before you say anything, let me tell you the rest of it. From that first day I saw you, I was impressed with your courage and honesty. Then I started to notice how pretty you were." He paused, lifting a strand of her hair, then winding it around his fingers. "In fact, that first day I sat with you in the coffeehouse, after you left Marie's house, I kept thinking how much I liked you. As we've spent time together, I've liked you more and more. When I was up at Baton Rouge, I couldn't wait to get back to you. And now I know—I'm sure, Lilly. I'm in love with you."

He sighed again, turning his eyes toward the night sky as he rested his head on the carriage cushion. "If you don't feel the same, just don't tell me tonight. It's been too perfect."

In one of those impulsive moments, when her Irish blood sent her into a passion before she could stop herself, she opened her mouth and told him the truth.

"I do feel the same, Andrew. I'm falling in love with you too."

The carriage slowed before her hotel, then stopped.

"End of the ride," the driver called over his shoulder.

"No." Andrew smiled at Lilly. "It's only the beginning."

છે

Lilly was engrossed in totaling one last column of figures before Andrew arrived to take her to lunch. The sleigh bell jingled, and she looked up to see John Mercer entering the gallery with what appeared to be a small painting, partially covered with brown paper.

His gaze went straight to her, and he quickened his uneven pace.

"Good morning, Mr. Mercer," she called pleasantly.

"And a good morning to you, my dear." He glanced around. "Where is Carl?"

"He's in the back room searching for an easel to mount a painting," she replied, noting the way his gray eyes were twinkling. He seemed to be very pleased about something, and she had a feeling he was eager to tell her about it.

"I have something to show you," he said as he reached her desk. He carefully began to remove the brown paper from the painting.

What she saw made her gasp. She was looking at a soldier in a Confederate uniform and a beautiful young woman with hair the color of burnished copper. The woman wore an emerald green dress with a scoop neck and cap sleeves that showed off her fair skin.

Lilly's throat constricted, and tears welled as she looked into the woman's hazel eyes—and saw a painted reflection of herself. The man's smile was restrained yet genuine; the woman's smile reflected a radiance that John Mercer had captured. Lilly pressed her fingers to her lips to choke back a sob.

"It's my mother!" she said, her voice breaking. "It has to be."

"Yes, young lady. I agree. I think she has to be your mother."

At that precise moment, the sleigh bell jingled, and Lilly turned and looked into a pair of dark eyes, glittering with anger. Marie Bordeaux stood in the doorway, glaring at her.

"I see you are still here," she shouted. "And I understand that you have been poisoning Andrew's mind against me."

Carl rushed in from the back, then froze in his steps as Marie cut her angry glance in his direction. "I warned you about what I would do if you continue to employ this conniving woman who is pretending to be my relative. Now I intend to make good my threat."

"Mademoiselle Bordeaux," John Mercer spoke up, his voice clear yet firm. "I have come to show this young lady a painting I did in March of 1862. I think you need to hear my story.

"As you know, my limp made me unacceptable for military duty during the war. It grieved me not to be able to serve my beloved South, so I threw myself into my art. Times were hard throughout the 1860s, and I spent many hours around Jackson Square begging to do portraits.

"One spring morning, your brother walked by with a beautiful young woman on his arm. The woman was very pleasant. She stopped to admire a portrait I had on display to advertise my work. She turned to Leon and asked if they could have their portrait painted. Leon seemed quite happy to be with her, and he said yes, if it could be done quickly. He was due to report back for duty the next day."

Silence lay heavy over the group as Mr. Mercer slowly told his story. Lilly had scarcely breathed, and she dared not look at Marie.

"Leon and the young woman posed for an hour," Mr. Mercer continued, "but then they had to leave. I agreed to have the portrait completed in a week. Leon paid me for my work, and the young woman promised to return to the same place a week from that day. She never came back, and that young couple, who looked so much in love, never saw the painting. I've kept it in a back closet, and over the years other unclaimed paintings joined it. I kept it, never certain why, other than the fact that I am a silly, old romantic. Maybe this painting is about to serve its most important purpose."

Slowly, he turned the painting around for Marie to view. She turned deathly pale, and her dark eyes seemed to bulge in her flushed face. "This is a trick. It's a conspiracy." She whirled on Lilly. "You! You are ruining my life. . . ." A spasm shook her, and she collapsed on the floor.

Lilly jumped up from the desk and ran over to kneel beside Marie's still body. The painting clattered to the floor behind them as John Mercer rushed out onto the banquette, yelling for someone to get a doctor.

9

*O*ne day melted into another as Lilly sat by Marie's bedside, first in the hospital, and then at her home. Marie had been comatose the first week, then slowly she began to regain consciousness. Relief turned to shock, however, when Marie tried to speak, but her words were garbled, making no sense. When she tried to move, her right side was partially paralyzed. Marie appeared to be in shock as well, but as the days wore on, shock turned to fear and fear to rage.

Since Andrew's firm still represented her, he had hired a full-time nurse for her care. Lilly, however, felt compelled to remain at her side, which constituted her first ongoing argument with Andrew.

"I cannot understand your sense of duty here, Lilly," Andrew said, as they sat out in the garden one afternoon in late June.

"Don't you understand, Andrew?" Lilly implored. "I feel responsible for Marie's stroke. If not for me—"

"If not for her own venomous rage," he interrupted, "which could have been vented on the gardener or the housekeeper or me. She brought this on herself, Lilly. Can't you see that?"

Lilly shook her head. "No. I agree that she could have become angry with someone else, but I don't think anyone else could have evoked the kind of rage that I brought to her. And it's more than that, Andrew."

She took a deep breath, glancing around the courtyard where the roses were in full bloom and songbirds darted about the branches of the oak trees. It should have been a beautiful setting, but a sense of gloom seemed to permeate the house and grounds.

"I know Marie is my aunt. It doesn't matter whether she accepts that or not. After seeing the painting of my mother and father, I know I am a Bordeaux."

He nodded thoughtfully. "Do you want me to initiate legal proceedings to prove that is your birthright?"

Lilly shook her head. "No. Unless Marie accepts me, I won't remain here after she recovers."

"*If* she recovers." Andrew's tone was gentle. "Dr. Bishop has made it quite clear that she could have another stroke, and the next time it would likely be fatal."

"I know. And that's why I don't want to leave her, Andrew."

"But, Lilly, what about your job? Do you think it's fair to Carl to abandon your job there and sit by the side of a woman who . . ." His voice faltered.

"Who obviously hates me." She shook her head and reached up to push a trailing strand of hair from her forehead, aware that she had neglected her appearance. "I hate doing this to Carl. But for now my loyalty is here, don't you see that?"

Andrew leaned back in his chair. "She has a nurse to attend her."

"*Had* a nurse to attend her," Lilly corrected. "The nurse resigned last night. She refused to work for Marie any longer. Apparently, Marie's left arm is strong enough to strike someone in the face."

Andrew stared in shock. Then finally he voiced his thoughts. "So what makes you think she will cooperate with you, Lilly?"

"I don't know but she does. Addie gives her liquids, since she cannot take solid foods yet. And I sit by her bedside reading the Bible to her."

She glanced at the gurgling fountain. "I'm not sure if she understands anything I read. But, Andrew, she calms down each time I read to her."

"Lilly, I agree it's good that you are reading the Bible to her and that she is not, by some miracle, striking out at you. But you don't have to spend all of your time with her. She has Addie to attend to her needs."

"Addie can't read."

Andrew sighed. "Lilly, what about me? You've given me twenty minutes at the most, here in the garden, and that's it. We haven't been to dinner, we can't go for a ride, or even walk up the street for coffee."

Lilly was torn with conflict, and she knotted her hands together in the lap of her apron. "I know, and I'm so sorry. It's just that I'm needed here. Oh, Andrew, you're strong and healthy, and your faith is equally strong. Marie is not a Christian, and if she should die . . . I want her to know the peace of God. I want her to accept Jesus as her Savior. If I can help to accomplish that . . ." Her voice trailed off.

Andrew stood and reached down to gather her up in his arms and hold her close. For several seconds, neither spoke, then Andrew broke the silence. "Lilly, you are such a wonderful person. You exemplify what a true Christian should be. I'm sorry for pressuring you."

She lifted her hands to each side of his face and gave him a tender kiss. "Thank you, Andrew. And I do love you."

The joy of her love for him overflowed her heart as she looked into his dark eyes and quietly thanked God for such a wonderful man.

"I love you too, Lilly Brown." He kissed her passionately until she slowly pulled back from him.

His shoulders slumped in a deep sigh as he stood. "Tomorrow I'm scheduled to return to Baton Rouge to try to rectify the legal problems of my client there. I have delayed the trip for a week because of Marie, but I can't wait another day. It isn't fair to my client."

"I know, and I don't want to detain you. You will be in my prayers and in my heart every moment."

He smiled and kissed her on the cheek. "Knowing I am in your heart and your prayers will keep me reasonably content until I return."

"God be with you," she said, hugging him again. Then she turned and hurried up the brick walk to the back door.

ಶ

Andrew let himself out the side gate and walked back to his office, his hands thrust deep in his pockets, his heart heavy. He had told Lilly he would be reasonably content, knowing he was in her heart and her prayers, but in all honestly, he felt quite the opposite. The past two weeks had been a nightmare for him. Marie had swept into his office that horrible day and confronted him.

"What have you done about that woman?" she had demanded. "I told you to start legal proceedings."

"Marie, I have no intentions of doing such a thing," he had replied firmly.

"Well, then *I* intend to do something!" she had yelled, then stormed out of his office.

Afterward, he had finished some paperwork and hurried to Carl's art gallery. He found Carl pacing the floor, wringing his hands. He had shown Andrew the painting and related the horrible scene that had resulted in Marie's collapse. And that was only the beginning of the nightmare.

Lilly had remained at Marie's side, exhibiting an emotion that was difficult for him to understand. At first, Andrew had thought this was simply a gesture of concern and thoughtfulness, but now it exceeded what he considered reasonable. He walked past the coffeehouse where Lilly had gone that first day, after Marie had so cruelly dismissed her. Glancing through the window to the corner table, now occupied by another couple, he recalled how he had followed Lilly there, feeling compelled to speak with her. Her strong faith and openness had first attracted him that day, and in the days that followed, he discovered many qualities about her that he admired. She was like no woman he had ever known, and he cherished every minute he spent with her.

During Marie's illness, Lilly had, he believed, developed a misplaced sense of loyalty toward Marie. He had known Marie all his life, and she had always been a selfish, coldhearted person. If Lilly believed that Marie was calmed by her presence or that she might be growing fond of her, Lilly was letting herself in for another heartache. He suspected Marie was using her as a nursemaid and caretaker and nothing more. Even worse, he imagined Marie would enjoy leading Lilly to believe that she might someday inherit the family home or be a part of the family. This could only happen if Marie signed papers to that effect or if Andrew somehow proved that Lilly was a rightful heir.

He thought of John Mercer's painting, which had stopped Andrew in his tracks. The resemblance was absolutely startling, and he had found himself stopping by the gallery on two other occasions, just to stare at the portrait of Megan McCoy and Leon Bordeaux. Finally, as an attorney striving to prove his point, he had taken the portrait to the boardinghouse where Simon Dupree had lived. The burly landlord was quick to agree that this was, indeed, a younger version of Megan McCoy.

The portrait was convincing, but the marriage certificate was not. As Marie had said, it was faded and the parchment worn thin. Another attorney might argue that it was a fake. He had already checked for a marriage record with the court and found none. There was absolutely no legal record of Megan McCoy ever marrying Leon Bordeaux.

When he returned from Baton Rouge, he planned to go to the parish where they were married and go over the church records. It was his only hope of proving that the marriage had taken place. Of course, the painting proved that Leon and Megan had been together, and the resemblance between Megan and Lilly offered credence that the two were mother and daughter. But was Megan really Leon's wife? And why hadn't Marie's mother believed her when she had gone to the Bordeaux estate with the certificate?

Then another thought occurred to him. Frances Bordeaux would have checked with the court for a record of the marriage, just as he had. Finding none, she could have chosen not to believe Megan. But Megan had written that she had gone there to visit only once, and Frances had immediately dismissed her. Each time he thought of the situation, he felt as though his mind had entered a maze.

His intense thoughts had stirred up a pounding headache. He had been walking for the past ten minutes, and now he stood before the equestrian statue of Andrew Jackson. This brought his own parents to mind, and for a moment, nostalgic tears filled his eyes. He found the nearest park bench and sat down.

Closing his eyes, he tried to pray, but he couldn't seem to find the right words. He hardly knew how to pray. Should he ask God to heal Marie? Should he ask God to show Lilly that she was not thinking rationally? More than likely, he needed to pray for himself, for he suspected he was the one acting selfishly now. He was in love with Lilly, and just when everything seemed to be going their way, life had dealt them a blow.

Normally, he could regain his senses after awhile and think clearly how best to pursue the challenge. It was different this time. He could not do Lilly's thinking for her, nor could he convince her that she shouldn't feel duty bound to Marie. He had hoped after the first couple of weeks that she would no longer feel compelled to stay by Marie's side every waking hour—because it was interfering with their relationship. He had tried to be patient, but he recalled what Dr. Bishop had told him: Marie could slowly improve, or she could have another stroke and die. It was also possible that Marie could remain like this for the rest of her life. If so, would Lilly continue this vigil? And if she did, how long could he remain understanding with her, when she had no time for him anymore? Thirty minutes in the garden. What kind of relationship could develop from that?

Andrew brushed his hand over his forehead, trying to massage away the headache.

God, please heal Marie, he finally prayed, *in body and in spirit.*

10

*L*illy sat by Marie's bedside reading Psalm 91, a favorite chapter in her King James Bible.

He that dwelleth in the secret place of the most High shall abide under the shadow of the Almighty. I will say of the LORD, He is my refuge and my fortress: my God; in him will I trust. Surely he shall deliver thee from the snare of the fowler, and from the noisome pestilence. He shall cover thee with his feathers, and under his wings shalt thou trust: his truth shall be thy shield and buckler. Thou shalt not be afraid for the terror by night; nor for the arrow that flieth by day; Nor for the pestilence that walketh in darkness; nor for the destruction that wasteth at noonday. A thousand shall fall at thy side, and ten thousand at thy right hand; but it shall not come nigh thee. Only with thine eyes shalt thou behold and see the reward of the wicked.

Because thou hast made the LORD, which is my refuge, even the most High, thy habitation; There shall no evil befall thee, neither shall any plague come nigh thy dwelling. For he shall give his angels charge over thee, to keep thee in all thy ways. They shall bear thee up in their hands, lest thou dash thy foot against a stone. Thou shalt tread upon the lion and adder: the young lion and the dragon shalt thou trample under feet. Because he hath set his love upon me, therefore will I deliver him: I will set him on high, because he hath known my name. He shall call upon me, and I will answer him: I will be with him in trouble; I will deliver him, and honour him. With long life will I satisfy him, and shew him my salvation.

Lilly had been reading slowly, carefully, thinking about each verse with her eyes lowered. When she finished the last verse and glanced up, she saw that Marie was staring oddly at her. The stroke had left her partially paralyzed on the right side, from head to toe, and when her lips moved it was difficult to tell if the expression was a smile or a smirk.

"I hope you don't mind that I read the Bible to you," Lilly said. "I find strength in the promises of the psalms. I was hoping this might help you feel better."

Marie began to nod, but there was still an expression in her eyes that Lilly couldn't define. At least Marie was not striking out at her as she had the nurse, and there was no rage in her eyes as witnessed at Carl's art gallery. Still, when she looked into Marie's eyes, she wasn't quite sure what she saw.

She continued to pray for a miracle, and in doing so, she constantly kept reminding herself that miracles did not always happen overnight.

Marie mumbled something that sounded like *more* to Lilly, so she turned back to the Twenty-third Psalm and began to read. By the time she had finished, Marie was asleep again.

Lilly closed the Bible and placed it on a table and stood up. Her back ached, and her legs were stiff from sitting for so long. She tiptoed across the carpeted floor and through the door to the hallway on the second floor.

The house was huge, although she had entered only a few of the rooms. She did not feel at liberty to look around. Addie, the housekeeper, admitted her at seven each morning, and she always went straight up to Marie's bedroom, where she spent most of her time. At noon, she went down to the kitchen for the lunch Addie prepared. Lilly had insisted on helping with the dishes, and afterward, Lilly usually ventured out to sit in the garden. When Andrew came they always went out to enjoy the beauty and peace of the garden.

Not once had she entered the front parlor where she had sat opposite Marie, her mahogany chest on her lap, her hopes high. These visits were entirely different. She sat with Marie because she felt an obligation, but she expected nothing in return.

Addie was just coming up the winding stairway with a silver service of tea. Lilly smiled and greeted her.

"Thought you'd be needing a cup of tea," Addie said, returning Lilly's smile.

Addie Castelow was a tall, strong woman who had been with Marie for many years. She managed a cleaning lady who came in twice a week for the heavy work, but for the rest of the time, she did all the cooking, shopping, and housework. Aside from being a hard worker, Addie possessed a dominant, no-nonsense manner about her. Marie would be reluctant to press this woman too hard or too far, Lilly suspected.

"Thank you, Addie, but I'll come down to the kitchen and prepare what I need," Lilly replied. "Marie is sleeping now; perhaps when she wakes up, some warm tea would taste good to her."

"Maybe. But the tea's for you," Addie replied. "There's a sitting room at the end of the hall. Shall we go in there?"

"All right." Lilly smiled and followed Addie into a cozy room with a wall of books on one side and windows overlooking the garden on the other. Two thickly cushioned sofas had been placed opposite each other with an ornate coffee table in between.

Addie placed the tea set on the table, poured Lilly a cup, and handed it to her.

"Thank you." Lilly accepted the dainty cup and took a seat on the sofa. A sigh escaped her as she settled deeper into the cushions.

"I believe she is doing better," Lilly said, then sipped her tea.

"Then you'll be to thank," replied Addie, settling down opposite her.

For a moment, Lilly merely studied the woman. She appeared to be in her mid-thirties and had a long, serious face and straight, brown hair.

"I can take no credit," Lilly replied. "We should thank God for the progress she has made."

Addie sniffed and said nothing more as she sipped her tea. There were many questions Lilly would like to have asked her about the Bordeaux family, but she feared Addie would suspect her of using Marie's illness as an opportunity to snoop around.

Lilly had expected Marie's housekeeper to treat her with the condescension that Marie had displayed. Surprisingly, Addie had been pleasant to her from the first day Lilly arrived. Lilly had explained that she would be assisting with Marie's care, and Addie obviously assumed Andrew had hired her as an aide to the nurse.

"Do you have a family, Addie? I believe I heard you mention a husband."

She nodded. "Wilbur. We have seven young 'uns, which is why Wilbur and I both work. My mother keeps the kids."

"Seven children? That's amazing. How many boys, how many girls?"

"Four girls, three boys."

"And how old are they?"

"Thirteen, eleven, eight, six, twins five years old, and a three year old."

Lilly gasped. "How are you able to do so much here, then go home and work? You must work very hard."

Addie nodded. "I do. The three oldest are girls so they can do housework and help in the kitchen. Catherine, the thirteen year old, does some of the cooking, with my mother lookin' on, of course."

Lilly smiled. "I always thought it would be wonderful to have a large family."

"How many's in your family?"

Lilly hesitated, surprised to realize that Addie didn't know anything about her. Then she remembered she hadn't seen Addie the day she came to meet Marie for the first time, so perhaps Addie had been out shopping. Marie probably hadn't even mentioned Lilly's visit.

Lilly sipped her tea, aware that Addie was looking at her and waiting for an answer. *Family. She asked about my family.*

"I was raised in an orphanage in Summerville," Lilly replied, "so I guess you could say I had many sisters and brothers, but none who were blood kin."

"You don't say?" Addie's mouth was hanging open. "Then how . . ." She stopped herself, glancing toward Marie's room.

Lilly could guess what she was thinking: How did Lilly get to know an aristocratic woman like Marie Bordeaux?

"Do you come from a large family?" she asked quickly, hoping to divert the subject.

"Eleven of us. So my ma's had plenty of experience. Listen, I don't mind sittin' with Mademoiselle Bordeaux some. You'll need someone to help you, now that the nurse is gone. I know you been comin' in early and stayin' late. I can make up the guest room for you, if you'd like me to, and I can sit with her till around ten tonight. I'd have to leave then, but I already told Wilbur and Ma I might be stayin' late, with the nurse leavin' and all."

"That's very kind of you, Addie." She glanced at the grandfather clock in the corner. It was only three o'clock, but she would welcome a long nap. "I think I'll take you up on that offer."

"Good idea. I've made up a pot of beef stew downstairs if you want a bite before you lie down."

"I'll have some later, thank you. For now, a nap sounds wonderful."

Thanking Addie again for the tea, she slipped down the hall to the room that Addie had pointed out. She was too tired to pay much attention to the elegant room. It was the thick-looking mattress on the cherrywood bed that interested her.

Removing the apron from her dress, then slipping out of her shoes, she pulled back the spread, a silken whisper against her fingers. When she slowly sat down and extended her legs onto the mattress, she seemed to sink for several inches into the depths of softness. She sighed. She could imagine that she drifted on a blue cloud—the room was painted a deep blue, the silk spread and cotton bedding a paler blue, like the sky at different times of the day. She was asleep in a matter of minutes.

She felt someone tapping her shoulder, and when she awoke, Addie was leaning over her.

"Sorry to wake you, Lilly, but Miss Marie is askin' for you. At least, I think that's what she's sayin'. Sounds like 'lil.'" Addie rolled the sound slowly over her tongue.

Lilly rubbed her eyes and sat up, glancing toward the window. Darkness prevailed beyond the blue curtain. Blinking, she looked around the room and saw that Addie had lit the lamp.

"I can't believe I slept so long. What time is it?"

"Five minutes past seven. And that's not so long for all the hours you been puttin' in. Listen, there's no need to be goin' back to your place. Well, I don't know where your place is, but you oughta stay right here till Miss Marie gets another nurse. It'll be easier on you."

"Maybe I'll do that."

She was conscious of a wonderful smell in the room, and she saw that again Addie had brought up a tray. This time there was a china bowl filled with beef stew and a huge fluffy biscuit on a small plate, along with more tea. She quickly got out of bed, pulled the apron back over her dress, and put on her slippers.

"Addie, you're so kind," Lilly said, feeling a silly rush of tears to her eyes. She hated these emotional moments when she couldn't seem to control her tears. Reaching out, she gave Addie a warm hug. When she released her, Addie seemed a bit startled by her sudden display of affection.

Lilly sat down in the nearest chair and took the tray from the table and began to eat.

"Mmm, Addie," she said between bites, "you are a divine cook."

"Thank you," she said, still standing in the center of the room, her hands folded over her apron. "You take your time now. I'll go back to Miss Marie."

She was halfway through her meal when she heard the bell ringing. The nurse had brought along a small bell for Marie to ring in case she was alone in the room and needed something. In her hasty departure after Marie struck her, the nurse had left the bell on the table.

Addie stuck her head around the door. "She's working herself up about something. You wanna come see what you think?"

Lilly jumped up from the chair and hurried down the hall to Marie's room.

Addie had lit the lamp by the bed and beneath the lamp's glow, Marie's skin looked pale and drawn. The wrinkles in her face seemed to have deepened, and the skin on her eyelids drooped lower over her dark eyes.

"M–m–m–m–m," Marie mumbled, then cried out in anger. She tried more sounds, only to become further agitated.

Addie was wringing her hands, clearly distressed. "Miss Marie, what is it? Are you hurtin' somewhere?"

As Marie gurgled out sounds that made no sense, Lilly felt a stab of anguish in her heart. How terrible it must be to try so hard to make a word, just one word, only to blurt a mishmash of consonants.

Addie had closed the Bible and laid it on a dresser. Lilly began to quote a familiar verse of Scripture as she went over to pick up the Bible.

"'I am the Lord your God who takes hold of your right hand and says, do not fear, I will help you. Do not be afraid.'" She had paraphrased the verse just a bit, to make it seem like a direct promise from God to her the first time she had heard it in chapel. She repeated the verse again as she found the book of Psalms and settled into the chair beside Marie.

Marie had been thrashing around on the bed, but as Lilly began to read, Marie became still. The lamplight shone on her damp face where tears had poured from her eyes, down her cheeks, wetting the lace collar of her nightgown.

"Why, look at that. Them verses settled her down!" Addie declared, her voice distinct in the background as the room became awkwardly silent.

Lilly continued to read, beginning with the first Psalm. When finally she reached the fifth chapter, a low snore filled the room. Lilly looked up. Marie was sound asleep.

Lilly leaned back in the chair and closed her eyes. Her throat was sore from so much reading the past few days, but she would gladly endure a sore throat if it was helping Marie.

Sometime later, she felt a warm presence beside her, and when she opened her eyes, she was looking into Andrew's face.

"You're back!" she whispered. "How was the trip?"

He glanced at the bed, noting that Marie was asleep. He reached out and grasped Lilly's hand. "Come with me," he whispered.

Addie stood behind them. "I'll sit with her," she said softly.

Hand in hand, Andrew and Lilly walked from Marie's bedroom out into the hallway. There, he stopped to tilt her chin and place a tender kiss on her lips.

"I've missed you," he said, looking deep into her eyes.

"I've missed you too. Oh, Andrew! I'm so glad you're back." She threw her arms around him and hugged him tight.

"I'll make a note to myself to leave every few days. I like this kind of greeting."

She turned her head toward his cheek as she pulled back, sending a swirl of hair around her face. She thought she saw the love in Andrew's eyes as he looked from her face to her hair, then reached out and cupped a thick strand in his palm.

"Your hair feels like a magnolia blossom, but it smells of roses."

For the first time in days, she laughed. "Some of the roses from the flower garden had withered, so I gathered the petals, crushed them, and made a rinse for my hair."

He titled his head and looked down at her, obviously amused. "Now how did you know to do that?"

She shrugged. "I didn't. Well, actually I remembered the sisters would use a cologne of rose water. It made sense to me that I could do something like that for my hair. And, Mr. Desmond, if you are trying to win my affection by comparing the texture of my hair to your favorite flower, you just moved up a notch on the ladder. Although I doubt you could rise much higher," she added, watching with fascination as he kissed the strand of hair he had been touching. He was breathtakingly romantic at times, and it did strange things to her senses.

"Come down to the kitchen," he said. "Addie has offered supper, and I have taken her up on it. I just got in from Baton Rouge."

"I'm glad you came by," she said, as they made their way down the winding staircase.

They followed the marble-tiled hall back to the huge kitchen at the rear of the house. This was Lilly's favorite room, or rather it was the only room in which she felt comfortable. She fought a curiosity about the people who had lived here, and more than once, she yearned to look around and see this as her father's home. Then her mind quickly clamped down on her thoughts, shutting the door to further speculation.

The long kitchen table was covered with a floral cotton cloth and set with plates of white bone china with matching soup bowls. Addie had made coffee, and as Lilly breathed deeply of the wonderful aroma, she felt a wonderful sensation flow through her. For a moment, she closed her eyes, delighting in the moment.

"What is it, sweet Lilly? What are you thinking?"

She opened her eyes and looked at Andrew and merely smiled, taking a seat opposite him. "Rabbit fur against my cheek."

"*What?*"

She laughed. "I often read stories to the younger children at St. Paul's, and one of them was about a little rabbit named Hip-Hop, and he felt very special when little people hugged him. But the little people felt special too, because there was nothing quite so wonderful as the brush of rabbit fur against their skin."

Her voice had taken on a dreamy sound, and she smiled at Andrew as she began to explain. "Hip-Hop found a home and he was happy. And in return, the little people in his world were happy too. That's how I feel right now, as though my dream has come true. I have a real home, although temporary, and I have the pleasure of being with good people here—like you and Addie."

She paused, noticing that he had put down his soup spoon and focused his attention entirely on her. She hoped he understood what she was trying to say to him.

"Have you ever had one of those special moments when you feel as though God has reached down and made every dream come true?" she asked.

He reached across the table and took her hand. "I feel that way each time I look at you."

Her heart tripped over a beat or two as they sat holding hands, staring dreamily into each other's eyes. The sound of the brass knocker on the front door broke through their reverie, and they sat up straighter in their chairs.

"I'm expecting someone," Andrew said, getting up from the table and hurrying to the door.

Puzzled, Lilly went over to the big coffeepot and filled two mugs with coffee. Then, on speculation, she reached up in the cupboard and took down two more mugs. She wondered if perhaps Carl and his grandfather were stopping by.

A tall, blond woman dressed in a white nurse's uniform walked into the kitchen, just ahead of Andrew.

"You must be Miss Brown," she said, her tone pleasant yet formal.

"Yes, I am." Lilly's gaze moved past the nurse to Andrew.

"Lilly, this is Mrs. Forrester. She will be Marie's night nurse. And she has recommended a friend for a day job."

Lilly forced a smile. "How do you do? I'll take you upstairs."

She hurried past Andrew and started up the steps, struggling to keep her temper in tow. Why had he hired this woman, *and her friend,* without first consulting her? Lilly's steps quickened as she nearly huffed up the stairs. It was unfair.

Addie was coming out of Marie's bedroom just as they reached the door. Lilly stopped and made the introductions.

"Just in time," Addie sighed. "She's getting agitated again. I hope you'll know what to do."

"I'm sure I will," the nurse replied.

Lilly didn't like her smooth confidence or her assumptions that she could walk in and immediately win Marie over. Then it occurred to her that she was standing alone in the hallway. Alone. She was no longer needed. This nurse was far more poised than the other one; no doubt, she would know exactly how to handle Marie.

Her anger now shared another emotion: wounded pride. She had been doing a good job here. *Marie seems to do better when I read psalms to her. This woman would not read to her or—*

"Lilly?" Andrew stood at the top of the stairs, looking down the hall to her.

Snatching her apron off, she started marching toward him, not even trying to control her temper. She shot an angry look at him as she brushed past, then flew down the stairs.

She entered the kitchen and headed toward the mug of coffee. Grabbing it up, she took a big swallow, scalding her lips, tongue, and throat in one gulp. Belatedly, she found the pitcher of cream and swirled a generous circle into the black coffee.

"Lilly, why are you so angry?"

"Why did you hire the nurse?"

"Do you remember our conversation before I left for Baton Rouge? I told you we had no time to spend together anymore, and you told me you felt responsible for Marie. You can still visit her as often as you like, or stay here to oversee the nurses if you feel you should. But Marie needs medically trained people."

She took another sip of coffee, eyeing him over the rim of the mug. "You had no right to go out and hire a nurse—two nurses—without discussing this with me."

"I have every right," he replied firmly. Thrusting his hands into his pockets, he circled the table to stand beside her. "As her attorney, I manage her business and her finances. Perhaps I neglected to tell you this, but I have power of attorney in her affairs. I have hired the nurses because it is my duty to do so."

"That's not the only reason," Lilly lashed out. "You're jealous that I'm spending so much time here with her."

"Jealous! That's ridiculous! Why would I be jealous of a woman as coldhearted as Marie?"

"That's not fair! Marie is very ill."

"Which is why she needs medical attention."

Lilly slammed the mug down on the counter, sloshing hot coffee onto her hand. She cried out and reached for a dish towel.

"Here," Andrew said, taking the towel from her trembling fingers and wrapping it gently around her red hand. "You've worn yourself out. I'm taking you back to the hotel."

She snatched her hand away. "You're not taking me anywhere! I'm staying in the guest room until I see how your very proper Mrs. Forrester gets along with Marie."

Because her skin burned with the heat of the coffee and her emotions were running riot over her common sense, she burst into tears.

"How can you say you love me when you don't even understand my feelings? Marie *needs* me, and I like *being* here. Maybe I don't belong here, or maybe I won't be staying long, but let me tell you something, Andrew Desmond. For the first time in my life, I have a home, a beautiful home, with a bed so soft that it feels like I'm sinking into a cloud. And look—real cream for coffee made from fresh roasted beans delivered from the best market in town. And food—delicious food made from fine beef and fresh vegetables. And even Addie likes me."

The sobs tumbled from her throat, but she couldn't stop them or keep her voice from breaking when she spoke.

"Marie calls for me. She can't say my name, she just says 'Lil' or something that sounds like Lilly. She *needs* me, Andrew. Do you have even the faintest idea what it means to me to think that my aunt—and I know she is my aunt—needs me by her side? That I am in the home where my father lived, where the man whose blood flows through my veins . . ." She paused, whirling to the cupboard to lift an old, cracked cup from the back of the shelf. "Maybe he drank from this very cup. This was his home. My grandparents' home." Her voice sounded as raw as her throat, and unable to hold back sobs, she covered her face with her palms and gave over to waves of anguish.

"No, I don't know how you feel, Lilly." Andrew gently pressed her head against his shoulder as he stroked her hair. "I'm sorry if I ever acted like I did. You are exhausted. Come on, I'll walk you up to your room."

Your room. There, he had said it. Lilly snuffed and wiped her cheeks with her apron and tried to calm herself down. Her room, it was hers, just as this was her home. And her dream. And no one was going to take it away from her. At least not tonight.

She lowered her eyes, for her anger had cooled and it was beginning to dawn on her that she had finally released the tempest of emotions that had been brewing in her for days—emotions she did not want to acknowledge, feel, or even hope for. But they were there, growing and growing, and once again, she felt like a little girl inside, lonely and confused, riding into town on holidays with the nuns, looking through the windows of nice homes where the lamps glowed and wreaths hung on the door. And families gathered together for Christmas dinner.

But she was not a child, she was an adult, and she must act like one. As she sniffed and looked toward the doorway, she saw Addie framed there, her eyes wide, her mouth agape.

11

$\mathcal{A}$fter Lilly had entered the guest bedroom and closed the door, Andrew stood in the hall for a moment, shaken to the core by the things Lilly had said to him. It was like watching a terrified little girl cry out for love.

Tears had filled his eyes then and filled them again now. What a tangled web of emotions for Lilly and for him. And even for Marie. Then, thinking of Marie, and hoping perhaps he was wrong about her, he sauntered down to her room and peered inside.

The nurse sat at her bedside, trying to coax her to take some medication. Marie's hand swept out, knocking the spoon from Mrs. Forrester's hand.

The nurse's voice was firm. "Mademoiselle Bordeaux, this will accomplish nothing. You will grow weaker and sicker if you do not take your medicine. You are not upsetting me, you are upsetting yourself. Now here, let's try again."

Andrew took a deep breath and knocked gently on the open door. Mrs. Forrester crossed the room to face him.

"How is everything going?" he asked pleasantly, as though he had not just witnessed a sample of Marie's temper.

"We're doing fine," Mrs. Forrester replied smoothly. "Would you like to come and visit with her for a few minutes? It might be best if you didn't stay long."

"I don't intend to," he said under his breath as he crossed the room and looked down at Marie's pale face.

"Hello, Marie," he said, keeping his voice pleasant. "You look better than the last time I saw you." He had intended this to be a compliment, but as he watched Marie's response, it was obvious he had said the wrong thing.

Her dark eyes glittered, her lips twitched, then struggled with sounds. He was shocked at the babble of syllables and consonants that hurtled from Marie's mouth, making no sense whatsoever. He had never seen anyone who had been the victim of a stroke, and now he felt sick to his stomach.

He sank into the chair by her bed and lowered his eyes. He was more disgusted with himself than he had been with Marie, moments before. Who wouldn't be frustrated by this condition? Who wouldn't want to strike out in frustration and anger? And yet Lilly said Marie had not behaved that way toward her.

Did Marie secretly believe that Lilly was her niece, and in her illness, was she reaching out to her only living relative? Perhaps he had misjudged her, after all.

The meaningless babble had ceased, and he raised his head and looked into Marie's face. Tears were flowing down her cheeks, and he gently laid his hand on her forearm.

"Marie, I'm so sorry this has happened to you," he said quietly. "I promise you, I will obtain the best specialist I can locate to help you with your speech. And if you can communicate to us what you want or need, I'll do my best to get it for you."

For a moment, her eyes were expressionless, and he wondered if she had understood anything he had said. Then she took a long quivering breath and began to nod her head.

"Th–h–n–k . . ."

Andrew nodded, patting her arm. "You're welcome. And I'll come back to see you tomorrow. Try to rest. And please take your medication. Dr. Bishop prescribed it for you, and you must trust him to do what is best for you. He's been your physician most of your life. You do trust him, don't you?"

The blank expression at first, then the slow nod.

"He'll be coming by to see you first thing in the morning. And I'll come back as well. I want to see what he thinks of your progress." He motioned for the nurse and stood. "Mrs. Forrester will get your medicine for you now. And I'll say good night."

Marie's gaze moved beyond him to the darkened corners of the bedroom. Then she looked back at him, a question in her eyes. But he was not sure what the question was. Perhaps tomorrow there would be answers. Tonight he had none.

ॐ

Lilly had gone to bed that evening, feeling sick at heart. She had prayed for Marie and for Andrew and for herself. She was conflicted with emotions, and after tossing and turning and wrestling with the problem, she decided that Andrew was right. She was exhausted and much too involved in the situation. And she even suspected that she was using Marie's illness as an opportunity to settle into a home that was not destined to belong to her. If it was not God's will for her to be a part of this family, she must accept it.

Lilly slept intermittently. Just after midnight, she got up to pad barefoot down the carpeted hallway, the soft gown she had borrowed from a drawer in the guest room, flowing about her.

Peeping around the bedroom door, she could see that Marie was threshing around on the bed, while Mrs. Forrester spoke to her in a low tone. She decided not to interfere.

Later, when she got up to check again, she met up with the nurse in the hallway. A deep scowl creased her forehead, and the friendly disposition she had displayed earlier was noticeably lacking.

"Is anything wrong?" Lilly asked, concerned.

"Is anything *right?*" Mrs. Forrester quipped. "When I finally got her to take the medication, she only slept a couple of hours. She has been rude and uncooperative the rest of the time. Go on back to bed. You need to rest while I'm on duty. You may be facing a difficult day tomorrow."

Lilly had taken her advice and returned to bed.

A cool summer morning broke on the horizon, and in the clear light of day, Lilly realized that she had behaved irrationally with Andrew. Her first order of business was to apologize to him for the things she had said.

Before her thoughts moved further, however, Marie's bell began to ring, and Lilly jumped out of bed. Hurrying down to Marie's room, Lilly found a distraught Marie and the nurse sound asleep in her chair.

"What is it, Marie?" Lilly asked, reaching out to her.

Marie stared at Lilly for a moment, saying nothing. Then she threw the bell down with a clang and nodded toward Mrs. Forrester.

Lilly turned to the snoring nurse. She reached over and tapped her gently on the shoulder. Mrs. Forrester came awake with a start, looking from Lilly to Marie.

"What is it?" she asked, smoothing down her hair and coming to her feet.

"Marie needed you, and you were sound asleep," Lilly admonished. "Mrs. Forrester, if you are to sit with her at night, you *must* be alert. I can relieve you through the day so that you can go home and rest, but you cannot sleep while on duty."

Mrs. Forrester tossed her head back and glared at Lilly. "I have been up and down with her all night long. And she has been less than cooperative, I might add. I'm not sure I want this job."

An object flew past Lilly and landed in the center of Mrs. Forrester's chest. Then, with a thud, it hit the carpet.

For a moment, both Lilly and Mrs. Forrester stared at the nurse's wet bodice, then Lilly reached down and picked up the water glass.

"Well, I never! I resign as of this moment," Mrs. Forrester snapped. "I do not have to take abuse from a patient." She whirled toward Lilly. "Good luck, young lady. You're going to need it."

At that moment, the knocker on the front door sounded. "Please wait just a minute. Dr. Bishop is scheduled to come by first thing, and he'll want to talk with you."

She hurried downstairs and opened the door. She was facing the older Dr. Bishop, as well as Andrew, and she smiled.

"Come in, both of you. We're having problems."

"What kind of problems?" Andrew asked.

She explained about the nurse as the three of them climbed the stairs. Mrs. Forrester met them in the hall.

"Mr. Desmond, I am resigning this case. I am a *nurse* not an animal, and I will not be treated like one. She has been abusive throughout the night, and now . . ." She paused, pointing to her wet clothes.

"She just threw a glass of water at me. I tell you, Sir, you'll be hard-pressed to find anyone who will work for *her*. And I certainly won't be recommending this job to my friend."

For a moment, Andrew and Dr. Bishop stared at the woman whose cheeks flamed with anger and whose confidence and poise had vanished overnight.

"I'll go see her," Dr. Bishop mumbled, looking embarrassed.

"Mrs. Forrester, I have your address," Andrew replied crisply. "I'll see that you are paid for your services."

"Very well," she said, brushing around him and bumping into Lilly in the process. With her head high, she stormed down the stairs and slammed the front door behind her.

"Lilly, if Marie will not permit nurses to attend her here, then she'll simply have to be placed where she can get twenty-four-hour care."

"Where?" Lilly asked, wide-eyed.

"The hospital," he answered. "Dr. Bishop was just telling me about a ward that specializes in caring for patients with needs too complicated for home care."

"Oh no, Andrew!"

"This is a nightmare," Andrew said, raking his hand through his dark hair. "Why isn't she throwing things at you?"

Lilly shook her head. "I don't know."

Andrew reached out to take her hand, then lifted it to his lips and kissed each finger. "I'm afraid I know, Lilly. While I don't like saying this to you, I have to be honest. I've told you that by nature she is a selfish person. The physical abuse she is dealing others is one thing; with you I believe she is using a different type of abuse."

"What do you mean?" Lilly asked, hoping his response wouldn't lead to another bitter argument. She hated arguing with him. This time, she had promised herself she was going to be more open to his suggestions and not so quick to lose her temper. After all, he had known Marie all his life, and she should pay attention to his instincts about her.

"I think she is taking advantage of your time and energy, allowing you to believe that she appreciates what you are doing and that she cares for you."

"Building my hopes up, you mean?"

He nodded sadly. "I may be wrong," he said.

"Or you may be right," Lilly said, considering that possibility.

Marie seemed to enjoy having the Bible read to her, but Lilly had looked up once and noticed that an odd tilt to her mouth, and she had been sure it was a smirk, not a smile.

If she were honest with herself, she felt more like a servant than a niece, but she didn't really mind. She loved living in the house, wandering from room to room and letting her imagination fill in the missing blanks as she gazed long and hard at Bordeaux portraits, never seeing a resemblance to herself in any of them. Nevertheless, she had known this was only a temporary situation and that the most important matter at hand was facing the truth about Marie's health.

"Andrew!" Dr. Bishop yelled.

Andrew and Lilly rushed into Marie's bedroom.

Dr. Bishop was standing at Marie's bedside, her wrist grasped in his hand. "Her pulse is racing, and I don't like the way she is behaving."

Marie tossed her head on the pillow, looking at the wall, ignoring all of them.

"Andrew, you have to consider placing her in the hospital on the ward I mentioned to you," Dr. Bishop said. "If she refuses her medication, she could have another stroke. Furthermore," he said as he lowered his voice and stepped closer to Andrew and Lilly, "I'm afraid her mind has been affected by the stroke. I know Marie is headstrong, but this violence . . ." He shook his head. "This is going to make it impossible for her to have adequate care here at home. I think you should commit her today and—"

"No, wait!" Lilly interrupted.

"Lilly, we discussed this."

She turned to Andrew. While his eyes reflected kindness, his tone was firm.

"Please," Lilly said, turning to the doctor. "Just let us keep her here a few more days," she pleaded, unable to keep her voice down. "Addie and I will care for her. I know Marie would rather be at home, and maybe we could try another nurse." She turned to Andrew, hoping he would understand, but his dark eyes flashed with anger, and there was no mistaking it in his voice when he spoke.

"Lilly, why are you defending her?" he asked, his voice raised. "She treats you like a servant, and I hate to tell you, but I doubt that she thinks of you in any other way. If Dr. Bishop wants her in that ward, I intend to admit her."

"N–n–o–o–o!" A shriek cut through the discussion, and everyone turned to see Marie struggling up in bed, tears streaming down her cheeks. Her left hand flailed out, reaching toward Lilly. "L–l–l," she cried.

Lilly hurried to her side, holding her hand. "Maybe she doesn't think of me as her niece," Lilly said, "but in my heart, I believe she is my aunt."

"But that's only in your heart, Lilly. We can't prove that you're blood kin—not yet."

"I *will* prove it, even if you don't help me," she snapped. She turned back to Dr. Bishop, who was clearly locked in confusion and conflict.

"I say we try her at home for two more days," she spoke firmly, keeping her attention focused on Dr. Bishop. She knew this was going to cause problems between her and Andrew, but this time she had to do what she felt was right. "If she won't take her medication and if she continues to act unruly, then I'll honor your wishes. I'm sorry. I don't want to be obstinate; I just believe that she will do better here."

She felt a soft pressure on her hand, and she looked down at Marie. The tears had dried on her cheeks, leaving only a soft film in her dark eyes. The eyes that were fixed on Lilly's face held a quiet pleading, and Lilly merely squeezed her hand in return.

This time Lilly was not seeing a smirk on Marie's face, she was seeing a pitiful smile.

12

*L*illy knew there was no point in walking to the door with Andrew. He had not bothered to conceal his anger. He had merely turned and walked out of the room, and after a few more instructions to both Marie and Lilly, Dr. Bishop had left.

Lilly sat down in the chair next to Marie's bed, and for a moment, the two women stared at one another. "Please cooperate with me," Lilly said, feeling an ache of weariness, physical and emotional. "I don't want you to have to go to that ward. Maybe I'm no more than a servant to you, but you are more than a sick person to me. I care about you, and even if you don't consider me family, I'm your best friend right now, Marie. And it's time for your medication."

She poured the liquid into a spoon and held it to Marie's mouth. Without a word of protest, Marie opened her mouth as Lilly tilted the spoon, and the liquid slid over Marie's coated tongue. When she lifted the water glass to Marie's lips, she sipped the water, then turned sad eyes to Lilly.

"Thank you," Lilly said, replacing the cap on the bottle. "As soon as Addie arrives, you must try to take more liquids. Will you do that?"

Marie nodded, and for the first time, Lilly thought she saw humility in her eyes. Perhaps now she was ready to hear the most important chapters in the Bible.

Lilly opened the Bible to the New Testament and began to read about the birth of Jesus, the star, and the wise men, and from the corner of her eye, she noticed Marie settling down into her pillows, staring thoughtfully at the ceiling as she read.

Sometime later, she heard footsteps in the hall and heard Addie calling.

"Good morning," she began cheerfully, as she entered the room and glanced around. "Where's the new nurse?"

Lilly hesitated. "Mrs. Forrester decided she didn't want to keep the job. You and I will be Marie's nurse for the next couple of days."

Addie looked from Lilly, to Marie, then back to Lilly. "I'll make coffee and start breakfast," she said, backing out the door.

Lilly could only imagine what Addie was thinking: another nurse gone and Lilly back in the chair, reading again. She stared at the page of Scripture, saying nothing for a moment, as her mind replayed the difficult morning.

Was she selfishly taking a stand because she wanted to stay here and make it her home? If she had overstepped her boundaries, she would apologize later when proven wrong. But she felt certain that keeping Marie in familiar surroundings was best. She knew how this might look and sound to Andrew and Dr. Bishop, but if the plan didn't work, they could always commit Marie to the ward. For now, Marie had been given a second chance.

Lilly began to read the Scriptures again, and she noticed that Marie was very still. Her eyes stared into space, but she had the look of one in deep concentration.

When Addie entered with coffee and juice and offered to relieve Lilly, she gratefully accepted the offer.

"I'm going out to the garden to get some fresh air," Lilly said, picking up her cup of coffee and glancing back at Marie. Again, the little half smile.

When Lilly stepped out onto the back gallery, a beautiful summer morning greeted her. The air was sweetly scented with flowers from the rose garden, and she inhaled deeply as she descended the back steps. Placing her coffee cup on the wrought iron table, Lilly went over to a rose bush and gingerly picked half a dozen in full bloom. Sunlight danced over the roses, and dewdrops twinkled like diamonds on the lush, red petals.

Lifting one to her face, she touched the velvety blossom against her cheek. Suddenly, she was remembering what Andrew had said about her hair smelling like roses and her explanation about the rose water.

She closed her eyes, breathing the scent of the rose, recalling the sweet ecstasy of love when Andrew held her in his arms. It seemed to her that each time she and Andrew grew closer, something happened to pull them apart. She wondered if their romance would parallel the ups and downs of her life—hope then disappointment. Whatever happened, she must commit her life and her plans to God, for she knew she couldn't trust her impetuous nature or her own limited knowledge of human beings.

"Oh, God, please don't let him be angry with me," she said on a plaintive sigh. "Even if we can't be together, at least let us remain friends. And let me cling to the verses that tell me You work miracles Your own way, in Your own time."

Feeling a sense of peace, she gathered the bouquet and returned to the kitchen. She rummaged through the cupboards, looking for a vase, then finally located one in the pantry. As she arranged the flowers and poured water into the vase, she began to hum to herself, feeling happiness despite the morning's difficulties.

"I think she's wantin' you again," Addie said, entering the kitchen with a tray of empty cups and glasses. "She was her best self this mornin', so I can't understand why the nurse up and quit."

Lilly gave Addie a wry grin. "She wasn't her best self last night. Addie, we're going to have to insist that she takes her medicine and gets plenty of liquids. If she doesn't improve, Andrew and Dr. Bishop are going to place her in a special ward at the hospital. I persuaded the doctor to give us two more days with her, and Marie understands she must cooperate. It's her last chance."

Addie set the tray down and thrust her hands on her narrow hips as she turned to face Lilly. "You've got the patience of a saint—or a niece."

Lilly noted that although Addie had overheard her conversation with Andrew, she had refrained from making any comment until now. "It's a long story, Addie. Maybe we'll talk about it another day. For now, I'll get back upstairs and see what I can do."

"And I'll be up to relieve you in a bit. You can't wear yourself out again."

Lilly nodded. "I know. But if only she will listen to the Scriptures . . ." She broke off, unsure what Addie thought about her reading the Bible to her. On the few occasions that Lilly had spoken of her faith, Addie had answered with a little sniff or with total silence. Then, as though reading her mind, Addie spoke up.

"I been listenin' to you read to her. I can't read, you know. And my folks weren't religious. I'm afraid I followed the same pattern. Now, I'm thinkin' maybe we'd all have been better off if we'd had us a Bible. Or found someone to read it to us."

Lilly reached out and touched her arm. "I'd be honored to read to you whenever you want."

With her spirits lifted, Lilly took the vase of flowers and climbed the stairs to pick up her reading where she had left off—the miracles that Jesus performed. She hoped Marie would be listening.

ڊ

"I will be so grateful for anything you can do," Andrew was saying to Helen Watkins, a middle-aged woman who taught reading to children who were slow in developing.

"Well, I don't know how much I can help, but I will certainly try."

Her clear voice rang through the air like a bell, and he thought she would be pleasant to listen to, whether one learned from her or not.

"I would think if you can teach children the correct sounds for speaking and reading that you can help Marie. At least, it's worth a try."

"Yes, it is. There is research underway in New York for people with speech problems, but nothing concrete has emerged. Dr. Bishop called me once before to try to help a patient of his. It was a slow and painful process, and ultimately, the patient learned on her own. I simply helped her find her way back to communicating with people. She still has problems but at least she is able to function in her environment."

"That's what I want for Marie. And she's slowly making progress physically."

He cleared his throat, thinking back to the previous day when finally he had swallowed his anger and pride and stopped by the house. Addie had answered the door, saying that Lilly was taking a much-needed nap. He had gone to Marie's bedroom, anticipating a show of temper. Instead, he discovered a calm woman who regarded him with a polite smile. He doubted that she had forgotten the recent conversation in which he insisted upon committing her to a ward. Yet, she had obviously made her mind up to try to cooperate.

The driver pulled up in front of Marie's home, and Andrew and Mrs. Watkins alighted from the carriage. Addie opened the door, and the smell of food and fresh coffee wafted past them. It was already ten o'clock, and Andrew had hurried into the day's activities with only one cup of coffee and nothing to eat.

"Good morning, Addie. This is Mrs. Watkins, and she will be working with Marie to try to help her speak clearly."

"Good morning, Ma'am, I do hope you can help," Addie said, as they entered the foyer.

Andrew led the way up the stairs and down the hall to Marie's room. Lilly sat by her bed, reading a chapter in the book of John. As they entered the room, Lilly turned and glanced over her shoulder, then came quickly to her feet.

"Good morning," she said, smiling warmly at Andrew.

He was relieved to see Lilly in good spirits and hoped this meant she had forgiven him.

"Good morning, Lilly," he said, returning her smile. Then he approached Marie. "You're looking even better today, Marie," he said, then introduced Mrs. Watkins to Marie and Lilly.

"Mrs. Watkins teaches reading and has made some progress in helping people with their speech," he explained. "Marie, Mrs. Watkins is willing to try to help you get your words right—with your permission, of course."

Marie focused on the woman, sweeping her gaze up and down, then slowly her lips tilted in a half smile.

Lilly closed the Bible and placed it on the bedside table. "That's wonderful, Mrs. Watkins. Here, please sit down." Lilly indicated the chair beside the bed.

"Thank you. It will be easier for Miss Bordeaux if we are informal. Please call me Helen." She opened the satchel on her arm and removed a tablet and ink pen. "First, I would like to get some information."

She asked about Marie's current condition. Lilly supplied what she knew, Andrew filled in, and finally, as Addie entered the room with a pot of coffee, she was drawn into the discussion. Eventually, Helen said she felt she had enough information to begin.

"I met with Dr. Bishop yesterday and made some notes from his medical records," Helen said, then turned to Marie. "Are you ready to get started?"

For a moment, she answered only with that blank expression that was becoming familiar to everyone. Then slowly she began to nod.

Meanwhile, Addie was pouring coffee and offering the sugar bowl and cream pitcher.

Encouraged by Marie's attempt to cooperate, Andrew turned to Lilly.

"Shall we take our coffee and walk out to the garden?" he asked.

She nodded. "Yes, let's do that."

He glanced back to see Helen Watkins settling into the chair, speaking to Marie about what she hoped they would accomplish.

As they walked down the hall, Lilly turned to Andrew. "I hope you have forgiven me," she said.

His hand slipped down her forearm to grasp her hand. "Apology accepted. And I offer one as well. You were right to defend your conviction that she would do better at home. She is much better; that's quite obvious. Now we must hope that Helen can help her with her speech."

"I want to hear more about her," Lilly said. "Are you hungry? Addie has left some buttered biscuits warming on the stove."

"Just what I need!" He reached forward to pluck a fat biscuit from the half dozen resting in a pan. Taking a bite, he breathed a grateful sigh and followed Lilly out to the garden.

They sat down at the wrought iron table, and as he munched his biscuit and sipped the coffee, he listened to Lilly's account of the past four days. He already knew that Dr. Bishop had stopped by and was pleased with Marie's progress.

She was silent for a moment, and Andrew saw that she was looking toward the fountain, where a cardinal was sailing down from the live oak toward the water. He closed his eyes for a moment, breathing the fragrance of the flower gardens. For a moment, his worried mind stilled.

"It's so pleasant here, isn't it?" Lilly's voice nudged him out of his sluggish state.

He had not slept well the past three nights. His mind knotted with problems once his head hit the pillow. The trip to Baton Rouge had been long and tiring, and he had worked hard to finish his business quickly. He had, however, left a satisfied client. He only wished he could find a solution for Marie—and for Lilly, as well.

"You look very tired, Andrew," Lilly said, placing her hand on his arm.

He sat up straighter and took another sip of coffee. Then he turned his bleary eyes toward Lilly, who looked remarkably fresh for having endured what sounded like a horrendous ordeal.

"I doubt that I'm as tired as you."

"Excuse me," Addie called from the kitchen door. "Mrs. Watkins is asking for you."

Placing his coffee mug on the table, Andrew came quickly to his feet and hurried up the walkway. He could hear Lilly's steps close behind.

By the time he reached Marie's bedroom, he had prepared himself for another ordeal. He was pleasantly surprised to find Marie looking reasonably content. Mrs. Watkins stood at the bedside, smiling at Marie.

"I'm so pleased. She's managed to get a couple of words right already. Marie, will you repeat the words for Mr. Desmond?"

Marie opened her mouth and with careful deliberation said, "More p–lease."

"Good work, Marie." He turned to Helen. "And good work on your part."

"I don't want to tire her, so I'll come back this afternoon for another session. I am very encouraged by her progress, Mr. Desmond." She turned back to Marie and patted her arm. "Marie, I believe you will be able to say what you intend in a matter of time. But time and patience are required. I'll return this afternoon, if that's all right with you."

Marie nodded her assent.

"Very well. Have a good day, Marie."

Marie smiled and nodded again, then looked at Lilly.

Andrew could see that Marie was becoming dependent upon Lilly, or at least she appeared to be. He only hoped that she was not acting upon selfish motives, and that ultimately, she would care about Lilly's feelings, as well as her own.

"Mr. Desmond," Helen was saying, "if you will be kind enough to take me home, I'll arrange my own transportation hereafter."

"I'll walk you out," Lilly said.

Once they reached the front hall, Helen went on out to the carriage, and Andrew turned back to Lilly. As they stood by the front door, it occurred to him that he had first met Lilly on this very spot. So much had happened since that day, good and bad. But for the moment, as he looked at her and felt a surge of love in his heart, he knew that for him the most important thing that had happened was their falling in love. That love had brought joy and happiness, along with pain and difficulty. But he knew there were no smooth or easy roads in matters of the heart. If he and Lilly could survive this ordeal, he felt they had an excellent chance for happiness in the future—one he hoped they would share.

He reached down to plant a kiss on her forehead, no longer caring who saw or what they thought. He was in love with Lilly, and he was determined to fight for their love. And that reminded him, he had scheduled a trip to St. John's Parish, just outside New Orleans. There, he hoped to find the marriage record that he needed to confirm her bloodline and establish her rightful claim to the Bordeaux name.

ટ✿

Lilly had asked Addie to sit with Marie while she returned to the hotel to pick up her belongings. She had decided to move into the guest room until Marie was stronger. The arrangement seemed to be working, and later on, she might try to locate a boardinghouse nearby where she could rent a room.

Once she returned to the hotel and crossed the lobby, she ran into the Sampsons. They were dressed like ordinary people today, rather than decked out in their stage clothes and makeup.

"Where have you been, Missus?" Wally asked. "Dolly's been worrying herself to death about you. But worrying is one of her favorite pastimes, so don't feel bad about it."

"It is not!" Dolly swatted playfully at his shoulder. "We've missed you, that's all. And before I forget, we have tickets for you to come to our magic show."

"Thank you! I've missed both of you as well. I've been staying with a sick friend. In fact, I'm moving into the guest room of her house today."

"And leaving us?" Dolly protested.

"No. In fact, I'll write down the address for you. Maybe you can come visit me when you have the time."

"We'll make the time," Dolly answered, giving her a hug.

"We can't dawdle," Wally spoke up. "We got rehearsal in ten minutes."

"Here." Dolly reached into her purse and pulled out two tickets. "There's one for you, and one for a guest. We'll be doing the eight o'clock show every night until they run us off. Be sure to wave to us from the front row."

"No, don't do that," Wally exclaimed. "Dolly'll get distracted and fall out of the box too quick."

Lilly laughed so hard her sore throat ached, but it felt good to laugh again. The Sampsons always brought laughter and joy to her, and she was grateful she had crossed their path that day.

"I'll look forward to your performance," Lilly said, hugging Dolly again before they rushed off.

She went upstairs and began to pack her things, glancing intermittently around the room. Her stay here had been bittersweet, but it helped to focus her thoughts on Andrew, and the Sampsons, rather than the sadness and loneliness which had, at times, been her companion here.

She wrote Marie's address on a note and pushed it under the door of the Sampsons' room. Then she hurried downstairs to settle her hotel bill.

When she got in the hansom cab, she decided, on an impulse, to stop by Carl's gallery. She felt guilty about leaving him so abruptly, but she had hoped he would understand. When the carriage pulled up in front of the art gallery, Carl was out the door to greet her before her feet were on the banquette.

"Lilly, dear Lilly!" he said, lifting her gloved hand to plant a kiss.

"Carl, I'm surprised you have a warm welcome for me after I deserted you."

Carl fidgeted from one foot to the other. "I would be a monster not to understand. Are you wanting your job back?" he asked, looking a bit worried.

She hesitated, sensing that he may have hired someone else. "No, I just came to see if I could take some work to the house to catch up."

"Actually, a friend of a friend stopped by. Her name is Miss Marion Manning, and she offered to help me out. Lilly, please don't think this is because of Marie's threats."

"I'm delighted someone has come to your rescue, Carl. Is Miss Manning working out?"

"Oh yes! But she doesn't do the job as well as you," he added quickly.

"I suspect that she does the job better. Carl, I'm so relieved to know you have someone to help you."

He nodded. "And Mother is feeling better. She's been coming by two afternoons a week to help Marion out."

"Miss, will you be wanting me to wait for you?" the driver called.

"Yes, I'm not staying," she replied, then turned back to Carl. "Marie is getting better."

Carl's brows shot up, then fell as he thrust his hands into his pockets, jingling coins. "I've been keeping up through Andrew." He glanced around and lowered his voice. "I'm shocked that the old bat has had a change of attitude toward you."

Lilly decided not to remark on his poor choice of words. "Yes, it seems she has. I'm moving into her guest room until the doctor feels she is out of danger." She paused, thinking there was no point in going into detail. "Carl, will you stop by for a visit sometime?"

"If I can enter by the side gate and meet you in the courtyard. I still have nightmares of that last screech from Marie."

"There's no need for nightmares, my friend. And you will be welcome anytime. Take care of yourself." She reached out to squeeze his hand. "I'll keep you in my prayers."

"Good day," he said.

Waving good-bye, she got back in the cab, and the driver clucked to the horse. She rested her head against the cushions and let her mind drift back over the past two months.

She had written to Sister Ophelia several times, relaying only good news in her letters. In the first letter, she had simply told her that Marie was a bit slow warming up to her, but that she hoped in time God would work things out. In the second letter, she had told of meeting Andrew, a wonderful Christian man. The next letter had explained her interesting job. Her last letter had detailed Marie's illness, omitting the unpleasant scene at the art gallery. She had asked her to pray for Marie, and as a postscript, she had given Marie's address.

As the carriage bore her there now, she closed her eyes and prayed for Marie's healing, both in spirit and body.

The coming days flowed smoothly, one into the other. Still, there was no permanent nurse, but Marie seemed to grow stronger each day and less dependent on nursing care. She was able to get out of bed, and using the walking cane Andrew had brought her, she hobbled about the house, never lingering long. Helen Watkins was working wonders with her, and her speech was improving dramatically. Although her words were slightly slurred, Addie and Lilly had no trouble understanding her.

On the Friday afternoon of the following week, a weary Andrew arrived, his business satchel in hand. Lilly greeted him warmly, trying to hide her disappointment over not seeing him. She knew he was busy and had neglected his other clients while helping Marie. She had missed him dreadfully and had made up her mind to spend more time with him.

"Andrew! I'm so happy to see you," she said, hugging him.

"You can't be happier than I am to see you," he replied, kissing her lightly on the lips.

As he pulled away, Lilly studied him carefully. "Either you're tired or worried. Which is it?"

"Maybe a little bit of both. I need to discuss some business with Marie. Do you think she's up to that?"

"I think so," Lilly said, leading the way up the stairs.

As they reached the top of the stairs, Andrew touched her shoulder, halting her. "How has she treated you?"

Lilly paused, considering the question. "She's treated me very well." She turned to face him. "Ever since I began reading the New Testament to her, she's been different, Andrew. I honestly believe she has had a change of heart. But Andrew . . ." She hesitated, wanting to ask the question that had been nagging her. "Andrew, none of her friends have been to visit her. Do they know she has been ill?"

He sighed. "Lilly, she has no friends. She has acquaintances through charity work or through long-standing associations with her family." He shrugged lightly. "She has no one to blame but herself. She's not a good friend to other people; or to put it bluntly, she's not even friendly to most people. Those who tolerate her do so out of obligation."

"How sad," Lilly said, as they walked hand in hand toward Marie's bedroom.

Once they reached the open door, Lilly removed her hand and let Andrew enter the room ahead of her. Marie was sitting in a chair by the window, staring down at the rose garden.

"Good morning, Marie," Andrew called pleasantly.

She turned in her chair. The left side of her face lifted in a half smile. "M—mornin' 'Drew."

"It's good to see you up and dressed. And Helen Watkins is very pleased with your progress."

Marie nodded. She looked down at the satchel he carried, then over his shoulder to Lilly.

"I'll leave you two to your business," Lilly called. "Would you like some coffee or tea?"

"No, thank you," Andrew replied.

Marie merely shook her head.

Her thoughts returned to Andrew, and she hurried to the kitchen to put a frosting on the chocolate cake she had baked earlier.

ã➤

"Marie, I'm leaving some reports for you to look over," Andrew said, as he removed papers from the satchel. "These show your profits on current investments, all of which are doing well, by the way."

She nodded, looking into his face and giving him the half smile. "Th–n–nks."

"And there's another matter I need to discuss with you. It's about Lilly."

He watched her carefully as he spoke the name, and to his regret, he saw a frown gathering on her forehead. Either she was not pleased by the idea of discussing Lilly, or she was apprehensive about what he wanted to discuss.

He had decided to be completely honest with her, for he still acted as her attorney, and he wanted to be fair. To do this, he knew he must put aside his feelings for Lilly until he had made the necessary explanations to Marie.

"I have taken it upon myself to make a more thorough investigation of Lilly's background. I hope you won't be upset about this, and I pray that you will hear me out." He paused, waiting for a reaction from her, but she merely stared at him, the frown digging deeper into her forehead.

"To come to the heart of the matter, I have been unable to locate a record of the marriage between Leon and Megan McCoy." He paused, expecting to see an expression of relief on her face, perhaps even a smirk. He still was not convinced that Marie really cared about Lilly; in fact, he maintained his suspicion that she was only using Lilly. Instead, the frown deepened.

"As I told you before, I located Simon Dupree's landlord, and he confirmed Megan McCoy's connection to Simon. And her landlady told me Megan had died at her boardinghouse. The point of that is to make sure the story, as it was told to you and me, is true. I hesitate to bring up the matter of the portrait, but you saw them together. Aside from that, I have no further proof. So what I am saying to you is that while I am convinced that Lilly may be your brother's daughter, I have no paperwork to back it up. You questioned the marriage certificate, and frankly, so did I. I could not locate a record of marriage either through the court or at St. John's. Their records were burned in a fire when the Union soldiers came through, torching many of the buildings in that parish."

He paused to draw a breath and took that opportunity to study Marie's face. She was staring out at the rose garden. He wondered what she was thinking. She had not smirked over the absence of a marriage certificate, as he had expected. Studying her carefully, he thought she appeared troubled, and yet he could not read her mind. He wanted to ask her how she felt about Lilly, but he reminded himself he had to maintain a professionalism as her attorney.

Slowly, she turned back to him. "P–arker. L–ike P–arker."

"Parker?" he repeated, trying to make a connection. Perhaps her mind had been affected more than anyone realized.

She nodded. "Th–he p–aper."

He stared at her, his mind drawing a blank for several seconds. Then a memory dawned, and he made the connection. "Are you referring to Jackson Parker, the butler?"

She nodded quickly.

"Oh." He thought back to his attempts to locate the butler who had absconded with Bordeaux money and silver. When the police had failed to locate him around New Orleans, Marie had produced a daguerreotype taken that Christmas when she hosted a dinner party and Parker had stood behind her chair. Andrew had taken the picture to the newspaper and the editor, a friend of the Bordeaux family, had placed the picture in the Sunday edition, requesting information from anyone who might have seen Parker. A former girlfriend had come forward to claim the reward and had led the police straight to Parker's hideaway.

"You want me to place a picture of Megan McCoy in the newspaper and offer a reward for information about her during the 1860s." It was a statement not a question, and Marie nodded emphatically.

Andrew thought it over. "That might work. It's certainly worth a try. I'll get an artist to do a daguerreotype of her face from Mr. Mercer's portrait." He reached forward to pat Marie's hand. "That's an excellent idea, Marie. I can see your mind is as sharp as ever, and I'm confident in time your body will be strong again and your speech will clear up as well."

She gave him a half smile again, and Andrew returned a warm smile. As he closed up his satchel and told her good-bye, one thought was uppermost in his mind. Lilly had managed to win Marie over, after all.

$$\textbf{13}$$

The picture appeared in the Sunday newspaper. Beneath the photograph, the caption read: MEGAN McCOY 1862. A short article had followed requesting anyone who knew her during this time to contact Andrew Desmond, attorney for her family.

"Lilly, don't get your hopes too high over the article," Andrew said as they sat at Café du Monde having coffee. "That was twenty years ago, and remember, there was a war going on then."

She nodded, reaching across to touch his hand. "I know that. I'm just so appreciative that you are making this effort."

"As I told you, Marie asked me to do it."

Lilly looked across at him and was silent for a moment, studying his handsome face, thinking how dearly she loved him. During their last argument, she had realized she did not want to lose Andrew, and she had accepted his invitations to dinner or coffee or the opera, whenever he asked. They were planning to attend Dolly and Wally's special act the following week.

"Well, I must get back to the office," he said. "I could sit and talk with you all day, but I have a client coming for an eleven o'clock appointment."

"And I promised Addie I would stop by the market."

As he paid their bill and they walked out, he looked down at her and grinned. "You seem to enjoy going to the market."

"I do. And I'll tell you another little secret, Mr. Desmond. I like to cook."

"No!" He pretended to be shocked. "You don't cook."

"I didn't cook very well when I came here, but now I'm taking lessons from Addie, and she's a wonderful teacher."

He arched his dark brows. "And when do I get to sample some of your cooking?"

"Very soon. But it won't be Chateaubriand! When I have a few dishes perfected, you can expect an invitation to dinner."

"I'll be anxiously waiting," he said, leaning forward to kiss her lightly on the cheek.

"Then I'd better get busy," she called over her shoulder, as she hurried off to the market.

ঌ

Lilly was surprised when Andrew knocked on the front door two hours later. Addie was upstairs, and Lilly was trying out a new recipe Addie had given her.

"Andrew! What a nice surprise," she said, opening the door for him. She was acutely aware of the flour on her apron and the wisps of hair trailing from her net.

"Let me guess." He put his hand to his chin in mock concentration. "From the flour smudge on your nose, I'd say you were practicing up on that meal you're planning for me."

She laughed. "Come in."

Then suddenly it occurred to her that he must have come for a reason, and in the midst of closing the door, she whirled and looked at him. "Have you heard anything?"

He paused, reaching into his pocket. "A message was just delivered from a woman by the name of Patty Monroe. She lives out at St. John's Parish, and she claims to have known Megan McCoy. She invited me to come out either this afternoon or tomorrow afternoon."

Lilly stared into his eyes, holding her breath for a moment. "Can we go this afternoon?"

"We?"

"Yes, *we*. You knew I'd want to go along."

He reached out for her hand. "Yes, I knew that. But again I need to caution you not to set your hopes too high."

"Oh, Andrew! You're always trying to protect me, but you needn't bother. I'm not the same person that floated into this house like a schoolgirl caught up in a dream."

He looked at her and smiled, but Lilly thought there was a hint of sadness there. "You were every inch the lady, not a dreaming school-girl. I took you seriously, and at last, Marie does too."

Lilly released his hand and turned toward the stairs. "I'm going to freshen up and change clothes. I'll be ready in five minutes."

"And I'll go up and speak to Marie. She'll want to know about this message from Patty Monroe."

As Lilly dashed into her room and flung open the door of the armoire, she was gripped with indecision. She thought of what she had just said to Andrew about feeling like a schoolgirl with her head full of dreams when first she came to this house. Now, as her gaze moved over the beautiful clothes before her, she realized that some of those dreams had come true.

Marie had told Andrew that she wanted Lilly to be paid for helping her, but Lilly refused. Then, Marie's seamstress had knocked on the front door and announced to Lilly that Marie had instructed her to measure Lilly for some new clothes.

"Just a few things," the pleasant little seamstress said as she winked at Lilly.

"A few things" had become an entire wardrobe of beautiful, fashionable clothes, and Lilly was overwhelmed with gratitude. She had gone to Marie's bedside and tried to convey her feelings.

"I appreciate the lovely clothes you have provided," she had said to Marie. "But I want you to understand that I don't expect anything from you, Marie. I am here because I want to be."

Marie had smiled and waved toward the Bible on the night table. "Th–an–k–s."

"Oh, Marie, you're more than welcome. And when you're ready, we can talk about the story of Jesus Christ and His miracles. I have been praying for a miracle for you," Lilly added softly. She half expected a frown or an outburst from Marie, but the expression on her face was one of quiet contemplation.

Soon she was dozing peacefully, and Lilly had slipped out of the room, encouraged by the change she had begun to witness in Marie.

She selected her favorite new dress, a blue silk with a matching bonnet. The fabric rustled beneath her fingers when she lifted it out and spread it on her bed. It thrilled Lilly to realize that this dress had been made just for her. The blessings in her life were almost too much to comprehend.

Then she thought of the trip they were about to make to St. John's Parish, where her mother had claimed to have married Leon Bordeaux. What would she find there? She fought a crazy impulse to dash downstairs and persuade Andrew to cancel their visit to the home of Patty Monroe. What if this stranger refuted her mother's letter? What if Leon was not really her father? Or if he were, what if they had never married?

Questions pounded through her thoughts until she pressed her fingertips to her temples and forced herself to calm down. If, in fact, this woman could tell her the truth she was seeking, she must be strong enough to accept it. She closed her eyes and prayed for strength.

ॐ

Lilly stared out the window of the carriage as it rolled into the sleepy little community of St. John's Parish.

"This reminds me of Summerville," she said, feeling a moment of nostalgia.

"It's very similar, I imagine. Summerville is northeast of New Orleans, and St. John's Parish is northwest, but as the crow flies, so to speak, the two communities are not that far apart. I imagine one of these back roads would lead us straight over there."

The carriage slowed down, and Lilly pressed closer to the window. A small picket fence enclosed a neat patch of grass and a one-story, white frame house. On the front porch, a rocking chair and a clay pot of geraniums conveyed a sense of home.

The driver opened the door, and Andrew stepped out, then helped Lilly down.

Smoothing her skirts, she followed Andrew up the rock walk. An old oak tree with bent branches held a small mockingbird that was trilling out its happy tune, and Lilly looked from the bird back to Andrew.

"This seems like a peaceful place," she said, as Andrew lifted the latch and the gate swung back.

"Yes, it does." He closed the gate behind them and secured the latch, then they walked up to the narrow porch.

As Andrew rapped on the front door, Lilly's heart seemed to echo the tapping while her nerves bunched in knots. Despite the warm afternoon, her hands felt cold inside the soft gloves, and her throat was as dry as the dust on the road they had traveled.

She glanced at the aged wood of the rocking chair and an image blazed in her mind: Megan in the chair; rocking back and forth, back and forth. She pressed her hand to her throat in an effort to stifle a gasp.

A creak sounded as the door opened. A tiny, dark-haired woman peered out, casting a glance toward Andrew, then settling her gaze on Lilly. A flash of recognition appeared in her eyes, and Lilly suspected that this woman was seeing a reflection of Megan McCoy.

Lilly licked her dry lips and smiled at her.

"Good morning," Andrew said. "We're looking for Mrs. Patty Monroe."

"I am she," Mrs. Monroe replied, looking from Lilly to Andrew.

Andrew introduced Lilly and himself. "You sent a message that you knew Megan McCoy in 1862."

She nodded quickly. "Yes, I knew Megan. But I sensed from the article that she . . ." Her voice faltered as she turned to Lilly.

"She passed away in May of this year," Andrew supplied. "Lilly never knew her mother, and we are trying to gather information about her."

A sad smile touched the little woman's face. "Won't you please come in?"

"Thank you," Lilly responded.

While her heart beat faster, the knot of tension in her chest began to dissolve. The woman's friendly manner had put her at ease, and now she could hardly restrain herself from bursting into a torrent of questions. Biding her time with her questions, she concentrated on the house.

The ceilings were low, and the rooms were small. The pine-board floor gleamed with wax, and on the hall table, a pitcher of lilacs breathed their sweet fragrance through the house. A sense of comfort wrapped around her like a soft cotton shawl. It was a feeling to cherish. Everything about the woman and her home offered a hearty welcome.

They followed Patty Monroe into a small living room. The upholstery was worn, the rug frayed, yet there was a wealth of peace here, from the cozy room to the kind woman motioning them to a seat.

Lilly sat down on the settee beside Andrew, and suddenly, she felt the prickle of gooseflesh rise on her skin. Although she knew it was impossible, she half expected her mother to emerge from another room and stand before them.

Lilly took a deep, quivering breath. Her mother had been to this house. She knew it; she could feel it. At long last, they had found someone who would tell her something about Megan McCoy.

"Could I offer you some iced tea?" Mrs. Monroe looked from Lilly to Andrew.

"No, thank you," Lilly replied, unable to resist the urge to stare at Patty Monroe.

Her dark hair, threaded with a few strands of gray, was pulled back from her face into a neat bun. Her skin was a smooth ivory creased with tiny wrinkles around her brown eyes. She seemed to Lilly a woman who would wear her years well, or perhaps it was the impression of gentleness and kindness that softened the lines in her face. Her dress was a simple, pale gray cotton, and she smelled like the lilacs in the pitcher.

Meeting her gaze, Mrs. Monroe smiled. "I adored Megan. And you are so very much like her. You're a bit taller, I believe. And prettier, if that's possible. Megan complained about her freckles. You don't have quite as many."

"Mrs. Monroe, how did you happen to know my mother?"

"I first met Megan when she came to my father's church to marry Leon Bordeaux—"

"Your father married them?" Andrew asked. "I came out to St. John's two weeks ago. I was told the only church in the community was burned during the war and that all the records were destroyed."

"That is true, about the church being burned. It was a terrible thing," she said, lowering her gaze to her lap. "It broke my father's heart. But not everything was burned," she said, looking up again. "My father kept his legal documents and business papers here at home. He had a fear of the church being burned, after hearing that the Union soldiers set fire to buildings. As it turned out, his nightmare came true."

She stood and crossed the narrow room to a writing desk in the corner. Lilly watched anxiously as Mrs. Monroe reached for the knob, opened the door of the secretary, and extracted an envelope. She turned and walked back toward Lilly and Andrew.

"I think you might want this," she said, extending the envelope to Lilly.

Lilly stared at the pristine parchment, but she could not bring herself to touch it. Not yet.

"Thank you," Andrew said, reaching for the envelope. Carefully, he opened it and gently removed a document. It was a duplicate of the marriage certificate Lilly had been given, only this one had been well preserved.

"My father made a trip into New Orleans every week or so to take care of business. He had planned a trip to the courthouse to record his documents, but we heard the soldiers had taken over the town and soon they were here in St. John's Parish."

"Your home was spared?" Lilly asked.

"Yes, thank the Lord. As you can see, it is a small house and the soldiers showed little interest in us." Mrs. Monroe glanced around the room. "I was born and raised in this house. When I married, Will was agreeable to living here, since it had always been my home. My parents died here."

Silence followed her words momentarily, then Andrew spoke up.

"We're grateful to you, Mrs. Monroe. This marriage certificate is vital to proving Lilly's birthright."

"I was there the day my father married them," she continued, her countenance brightening. "My mother and I had been cleaning the church. Will, my husband, had gone to war." She glanced at Lilly. "I know I'm fortunate that my husband survived the war and came home unharmed. We have enjoyed a happy life together. He works with our son in the general store just down the road. But I am straying from the subject, forgive me." She took a deep breath. "I later learned that Leon was killed in battle."

"That's right," Andrew replied. "And it is our understanding that Megan went to the home of the Bordeaux family and told them she was his wife. For some reason, Leon's mother did not believe her."

Mrs. Monroe nodded. "What a shame! Megan was a kind, sweet girl. I've never seen a happier couple than Megan and Leon. Megan asked if I would stand beside her while my father read the Bible and she and Leon exchanged their vows. I was delighted that she asked me. My father performed the ceremony, and afterward, they came back here for refreshments."

"My parents came here? After they were married?" Lilly stood, wandering toward the dining room. In her mind, she pictured the couple in the photograph standing in the dining room as newlyweds, enjoying refreshments, their hearts full of love and hope. They could not have imagined the tragedy that was about to unfold.

"Lilly." Mrs. Monroe stood beside her, gently touching her arm. "I have something for you, something that may ease your pain. But first I should explain. We took a liking to Megan, as she was such a delightful person. Leon was more reserved, but he was a nice man. Just a bit shy. We knew Leon was returning to Fort Jackson, and my mother invited Megan to visit us sometime. To our surprise and delight, she came to see us a week later and stayed on for three days. She told us about singing at a coffeehouse in the Vieux Carré, but she said she had quit her job when she agreed to marry Leon. I told her that she was welcome to stay here for as long as she wished, but she was planning to visit Leon's mother to tell her about their marriage."

She took a deep breath, lifting her gaze to the narrow window where a lace curtain fluttered in the breeze. "Megan was very nervous about going there, but we told her the Bordeaux would welcome her. She asked to leave her trunk here, just in case she was not invited to live with them."

She sighed. "Megan never returned. But she wrote to me, one letter in April, then another in December. I have kept the letters all these years, just as I kept her clothes and her trunk."

She indicated a battered black trunk that sat in the corner of the living room, and Lilly turned and stared at it, her thoughts spinning.

"I always hoped," the woman continued softly, "that Megan would come visit someday. She never did. But seeing you . . . well, it's almost as if Megan has returned."

Lilly turned to face her again. She could feel a smile wobbling on her lips, but it was impossible to keep her eyes focused on anything other than the trunk. For the past months, her mission had been to solve the mystery of Megan McCoy and Leon Bordeaux. She felt certain she had come close and that the trunk held the remaining answers for her. But every muscle in her body seemed to be locked in an odd paralysis.

"Perhaps the letters will explain everything in a way that I cannot." Mrs. Monroe stood, walked over to the trunk, and lifted the top.

Lilly's breath caught in her throat as she saw the beautiful green taffeta dress with beige lace insets at the collar, neatly folded. It was the same dress Megan had worn in the portrait! And underneath that dress was a rose taffeta with a beaded purse. Lilly jumped up, hurrying over to kneel beside the trunk.

"Megan told me she had never owned a beautiful dress before," Mrs. Monroe continued, "and that she sang Irish songs for hours on end to afford these two."

Lilly reached out, trailing her fingers over the soft folds of the green dress. In her mind, the portrait was as sharp and clear as it had been the day John Mercer had unwrapped it in the gallery. *This dress,* Lilly thought. Megan had worn this dress on that spring afternoon when her parents had been so much in love. John Mercer had captured that love, unaware that it would be reflected back to a startled group twenty years later.

The green taffeta felt cool against her fingertips as she stroked it lovingly. Then she opened the small beaded purse. Within, she found a crumpled lace handkerchief that smelled of wildflowers, and her breath caught in her throat.

"Here are the letters she wrote to me," Mrs. Monroe said, reaching into the trunk and bringing out two envelopes.

Lilly stared at the slightly slanted script on the front of the envelope, recognizing the same handwriting that she had read on that spring morning when her life had changed forever.

"I think you might like something cool to drink," she said, her hands clasped before her. "Excuse me."

"Thank you." Lilly swallowed hard as she looked at Patty Monroe and thought about what a kind and sensitive person she was, allowing her the privacy she needed as she stepped back in time, connecting at last with her mother.

She looked at Andrew. "If you don't mind, I'd like to go out and sit in the rocking chair to read these letters."

"Of course I don't mind. I'll be waiting here for you," he said, leaning forward to brush a kiss across her lips.

Lilly gripped the letters as tightly as she had held her mother's small mahogany chest. What would these letters reveal to her? Would she finally understand why her mother had placed her on the doorsteps of the orphanage that December morning?

She stepped onto the front porch and sat down in the rocking chair. The mockingbird was still singing, and for a moment, she let the birdsong flow over her as she quietly breathed a prayer.

Oh, God, please help me to understand. Please help me to feel what my mother felt, so that I can make peace with her at last.

Checking the date on the outside of the envelope, she first opened the letter written in April.

Dear Patty,

I want to thank you and your family for being so kind to me. How I wish there were more people like you. I have not heard from Leon, but I went to visit his mother. I will spare you the details, but she does not believe that I am his wife. Leon never went to visit her when he came home, as they did not get along. His father was killed at the beginning of the war, and I think this is why his mother acts so strange. She seems to be on strong medication, so I really would not want to live there until Leon is with me. I am waiting anxiously to hear from him. I may have some exciting news to tell him.

In the meantime, I am going to live with a couple who came to the coffeehouse and liked my Irish songs. The man was severely injured

*in battle and he can no longer be a soldier. But they are very kind
people who live near Summerville and need someone to help them
manage their home and children. As soon as this awful war is over,
Leon and I will make a home of our own—hopefully, away from his
family and all the horrors of this war.*

*Please keep my trunk in a closet out of your way, and I will
come for it when time permits.*

Your friend,
Megan McCoy Bordeaux

Lilly folded the letter and returned it to the envelope. She stared
into space, thinking. There was no mention of Marie. Obviously, her
mother never met her.

Taking a deep breath, she opened the other envelope and removed a two-page letter dated December 1, 1862.

Dear Patty,

*I am sorry I have not written to you sooner, but I have not been
well.*

*First, I must tell you that Leon was killed when the Yanks took
Fort Jackson.*

*My heart is broken. Never again will I love anyone as I have
loved Leon. No, perhaps there is someone I do love more. I am expecting a child any day now. I already love this baby more than
life, but there are problems.*

*Two months ago, I collapsed after a bout of coughing. The doc-
tor has told me I have a lung disease. He does not think the baby is
affected, but the hope of my recovery is not good. He says that I
may live several years or only one or two. Apparently, this is an
odd disease. He has told me about a special hospital for those who
cannot pay for medical care. It is located in Mobile. I have sold my
wedding ring, and I now have enough money to travel there after
my baby is born.*

*As you know, I have been on my own since I was fourteen. I
think there is nothing worse than being cold and hungry and having no one to look after you. Because of the uncertainties of this*

war, I have chosen to leave my baby in a safe place where it will always have food and clothes and people to care for it. I am leaving my baby at St. Paul's here in Summerville.

If, by some miracle, a cure can be found for this disease, I will come back for my baby. If not, my child will be better off without me. I have walked by St. Paul's many days now, and I have observed the children playing out in the yard. They look well and happy.

Tears blurred the words, and for a moment, Lilly laid the letter on her lap and sobbed quietly. Yes, the children *looked* well and happy, and perhaps not all of them had shared her desperate yearning for a real home, a real family.

And yet . . . She sniffed. What else could her mother do? There was a war going on. People were losing everything, no one knew what their future held.

Except Megan who believed she was dying from the lung disease. Perhaps the care she had received in Mobile had been better than she expected; obviously, it had prolonged her life. Lilly wiped her eyes and picked the letter up again.

If I get better, I will come back to New Orleans, for my heart is here. Then I will come visit you. If I do not return, please accept the trunk and the dresses as a small token of my affection for you.

I pray that your husband will come back to you safely. And please pray for me.

Your friend,
Megan McCoy

Lilly did not realize that she was sobbing openly until she felt Andrew's arms around her. She could feel the letter being taken from her trembling hands as she buried her face in his shoulder.

"Oh, Lilly, I wish I could ease the pain," he said, holding her tightly and rocking her back and forth in his arms.

14

*A*ndrew, I don't want to go back to that house," Lilly said as they sat together in the garden of a quaint little restaurant on the edge of New Orleans. "The woman who was my grandmother was a monster. I hate that house and everything in it!"

"Lilly." He held her hands in his, trying to offer all the comfort and love that he could possibly give her. "Your grandmother was a very sick woman. John Mercer recently told me something that may explain part of the mystery of why your grandmother did not accept Megan. Mr. Mercer said that after Frances Bordeaux lost her husband to the war, and fearing that her son would be killed as well, she became addicted to morphine. He was not surprised that Leon did not visit her on furlough, because apparently Frances Bordeaux had turned into a very different woman. She stayed in her room most of the time, refused to see friends, and became paranoid about everything. The Mercers called on her one afternoon, having heard she was ill. When they were taken to her bedroom, Mrs. Bordeaux screamed at them and ordered them out of her house."

Lilly stared at him, stunned by the information.

"As for Marie, from childhood she was cared for by servants, who handed her whatever she cried for, but never gave her what she needed: love. Unfortunately, Marie was not a pretty girl, and her temper tantrums ruined any possible friendships. Everyone she ever loved deserted her. Her father and brother were killed in battle, then a subtler enemy took her mother. I suppose it was inevitable that someone as conniving as George Lacy would cross Marie's path and swoop down like a vulture to take advantage of her wealth and her loneliness. After that, she never trusted anyone again."

"She trusted you," Lilly said, squeezing his hand. "Thank God, she could trust you."

He grimaced. "I realize, in telling you the Bordeaux history, that I have not always been as kind to her as I should have been." He lifted her hand to his lips and kissed each finger. "At the risk of sounding insensitive, I wonder if Marie's upbringing was sadder than yours."

Lilly took a deep breath and looked toward the western sky where the sun trailed scarlet ribbons across the horizon.

"I agree. I didn't have a mother, but I did not suffer the tragedies that Marie did," she said. "I was taught about the love of God, and my faith has been my mainstay. I'm sorry that Marie never had that."

"But now she does, thanks to you. God is working in her life, that's obvious to everyone who visits her now."

Lilly swallowed hard. "Are you going to tell her what we learned today?"

"Of course. And I've set a date for Mrs. Monroe to come into the city and speak with Marie. After that, it will be up to you whether you stay or leave. It's your home too, Lilly. Your mother wanted you to claim what was rightfully yours, and now you can legally do that."

"Perhaps I could, but it doesn't matter anymore." She felt the threat of tears, then she reminded herself how grateful she was for Andrew. "What matters most to me is being with you."

"Lilly," Andrew began, then hesitated. "I love you, you know that. And I would like to plan a future with you. But I want to give you time to heal, and I want you to be very sure of your feelings. In the meantime, please remember that for as long as you need me or want me, I'll be here for you."

৶

Exactly a week later, Andrew came to pick up Marie. He had told Lilly there were business matters to discuss and had left her in the kitchen with Addie. Lilly stood before various spices, inspecting first one, then the other, as she planned her chicken-and-dressing dinner, to which he had been invited. If the meal was successful, she planned to repeat it on Sunday with the Mercers and the Sampsons as guests.

"That's a diverse group," Andrew had teased.

"I have diverse friends," Lilly had reminded him.

He was recalling this conversation as the hansom cab pulled up before his office building.

He helped Marie out and watched her thoughtfully as she reached back for her cane. Although she walked with a slight limp, it seemed to Andrew that she was more attractive than she had been before her stroke. He kept glancing at her, wondering why. The right side of her face had been strengthened through facial exercises, and the only hint of a stroke was a slightly crooked smile. Most people scarcely noticed.

"Why–y–y are you . . . staring at me, Andrew–w–w?" she asked slowly.

"I was thinking, Marie, that you look quite well. It's amazing what you have accomplished. I must say, I admire the way you have conquered what could have been a debilitating illness."

Tears filled her eyes, the sight of which rendered Andrew speechless. "I've . . . h–ad h–elp," she replied humbly.

Andrew placed his arm around her shoulders. "I'm proud of you," he whispered.

Patty Monroe and her husband, Will, waited for them in the reception area, and he invited them back to his office.

As he made the introductions, Marie and Patty eyed each other warily, then Andrew cleared his throat and asked Mrs. Monroe to tell Marie exactly what she had told him and Lilly.

She cleared her throat and, in a gentle voice, repeated the account of her relationship with Megan McCoy, from beginning to end. Marie listened intently, saying nothing.

"Mademoiselle, I do not know what you have been told or what you believe," Mrs. Monroe said, upon finishing the story. "I can only tell you what I know for sure. Megan McCoy and Leon Bordeaux were very much in love. As I said, my father, who was the minister for St. John's Parish, married them. Her letters were filled with love for Leon and the baby they were expecting. She had no reason to lie to me, and she did not seem the type to make up such a story. She was a beautiful young woman who could have taken her pick of men in New Orleans, but her heart belonged to your brother."

As Marie listened, her eyes began to fill with tears, and soon she was weeping openly. She turned to Andrew. "L–illy is my . . . n–iece."

"Yes, Marie, she is your niece."

15

*L*illy's Sunday dinner was a huge success.

"Can you teach Dolly this recipe?" Wally yelled down the long dining table.

"I don't want to learn, thank you," Dolly yelled back. "The last time I cooked for Wally he accused me of serving shoe leather for meat loaf. I made him a promise he'd never have to eat my cookin' again. And I don't like to break promises!"

Everyone laughed heartily; even Marie chuckled. The couple was decked out in their colorful costumes and stage makeup, since they would be going directly to the theater as soon as they finished their meal.

"Lucille and I want to catch your act," John Mercer declared. "We haven't had this much fun in years."

"And we're just gettin' warmed up," Wally boasted.

Carl, however, had not warmed up to the Sampsons, Lilly decided. She watched as he fidgeted in his chair and stared at his water goblet. She caught Andrew's gaze and inclined her head toward Carl.

Andrew leaned forward. "Carl, the gallery seems to be doing well. When I stopped by this week, your assistant was tallying an impressive column of figures. She said you've commissioned some new artists."

Carl's eyes snapped wide, and a quick smile stretched his lips. "Yes, isn't it just wonderful? I'm absolutely thrilled."

"New . . . artists?" Marie inquired, pronouncing each of her words slowly and carefully. "L–illy, we need . . . some new . . . paintings."

"Oh, Marie," Carl gushed, "you're going to love these paintings."

The talk flowed on as Addie and her helper unobtrusively removed empty platters and dinner plates.

Addie exchanged a conspiratorial look with Lilly as she slipped out of her chair and followed Addie to the kitchen.

"What do you think?" Lilly asked Addie.

Addie studied the huge, round cake with its butter-cream frosting, then turned to Lilly. "Whoopey-tee-doo! You've done it!" she exclaimed.

"And it only took three gooey flops and ten pounds of butter and cream!" Lilly laughed, then something occurred to her, and she frowned. "Do you think she knows?"

"How would she know? Her birthday ain't till tomorrow."

"I want it to be a surprise," Lilly said, turning back to the cake. "Now follow me."

"You're gonna embarrass her."

"Maybe I will. But I don't think she'll mind."

Addie motioned to her helper and the procession entered the dining room, bearing the cake and wishing Marie a happy birthday in unison.

Marie's gaze widened at the sight of the cake, and a flush colored her cheeks. Then she bit her lip and seemed to be struggling to hold back tears.

As Lilly placed the cake before her and everyone chimed in with their birthday greetings, a thought struck Lilly. She belonged to a wonderful family. Her gaze moved around the table, taking in the delightful Sampsons, the kind Mercers, her wacky friend Carl and finally . . . her beloved Andrew. And Marie, her aunt. A lump that felt as big as the birthday cake wedged in her throat and tears stung her eyes.

Marie reached for her hand, and Lilly squeezed it.

જ

Later, after the crowd had dispersed and Andrew drew her out to the courtyard for a quiet cup of coffee, he reached for her hand. "I wonder if you know what a difference you have made in the lives of those around you."

"I know what a difference you people have made in my life."

"Addie is going to church for the first time in her life, and she vows she'll raise her children in a Christian home," Andrew reminded her. "John Mercer's painting of your parents is now on display in the gallery, and although he's had several offers, Marie declares she is buying the painting after Carl is through showing it. This has made John very proud of his work."

"But not as proud as I am," Lilly spoke softly, thinking of her parents.

"Marie is a different woman since you came into her life and read the Bible to her, teaching her something about real love," Andrew continued. "And last but not least—look at me."

She looked long and hard, admiring the handsome man whose dark eyes reflected the glow of the moonlight.

"No, Andrew, look at *me*. I harbored some bitterness in my heart, as well as a lot of confusion in my head. I know without a doubt that it was God who inspired my mother to send Simon Dupree to bring the little chest she had kept all these years to me. She thought it was being delivered to St. Paul's and that someone there would locate the girl she had loved and left. But God made it a simple task. The hard part was showing me that I have been truly blessed, after all. Why did I think my fate was so much worse than that of others? It was just a different fate."

"And yet, Lilly, you used your faith to build courage and character, not only in yourself but in all of us."

"Andrew, you give me too much credit. I'm just a poor country girl who trusted God to show her the way. And He led me to this house, this family, and to you."

"And I will be eternally grateful," Andrew said with a smile. "So will Marie. The happiness you've brought to her is amazing. She was genuinely touched by the cake, and by the fact that you shared her emotion."

"What do you mean?"

"When Marie was moved to tears, she saw that her tears affected you."

Lilly smiled, peering through the light of the full moon to the face of the man she loved. "I must confess. My tears were purely selfish."

"Oh?"

"Andrew, the most beautiful thing happened tonight. I realized . . . as we sat around the dinner table, laughing and talking, that . . . at last . . . I have a home and people to love."

"And people who love you, Lilly Brown. By the way, did you decide when you want me to draw up the papers for legally changing your name?"

She frowned. "I don't know. For some reason, the name Bordeaux just doesn't feel right."

He got out of the chair and smiled down at her. "Then how does the name Desmond feel?"

She watched in anticipation as Andrew dropped down on one knee, reached into his pocket, and withdrew a small velvet box. "Will you marry me?" he asked, handing the box to Lilly.

"Oh, Andrew!" She peered at the huge diamond, sparkling brilliantly in the moonlight. "Yes! Yes, of course I will marry you."

Tears were flowing down her cheeks as she reached out to him, pulling him into her arms and kissing his lips. As he embraced her and she tilted her head back to look at the sky, a thousand stars winked down at her—even the moon seemed to be smiling.

Lilly looked into the heavens and sighed. "Dreams really do come true," she whispered softly.

$\mathcal{K}$ELLY'S $\mathcal{C}$HANCE

BY WANDA E. BRUNSTETTER

To my husband, Richard, born and raised in
Easton, Pennsylvania, near the Lehigh Canal.
Thanks for your love, support, and research help.

To Char and Mim,
my brother-in-law and sister-in-law.
Thanks for your warm hospitality
as we researched this book.

1

Lehigh Valley, Pennsylvania
Spring 1891

$\mathcal{K}$ elly McGregor trudged wearily along the towpath, kicking up a cloud of dust with the tips of her worn work boots. A size too small and pinching her toes, they were still preferable to walking barefoot. Besides the fact that the path was dirty, water moccasins from the canal sometimes slithered across the trail. Kelly had been bitten once when she was twelve years old. She shuddered and groaned as the memory came back to her . . . Papa cutting her foot with a knife, then sucking the venom out. Mama following that up with a poultice of comfrey leaves to take the swelling down, then giving Kelly some willow bark tea for the pain. Ever since that day, Kelly had worn boots while she worked, and even though she could swim quite well, she rarely did so anymore.

As Kelly continued her walk, she glanced over her shoulder and smiled. Sure enough, Herman and Hector were dutifully following, and the rope connected to their harnesses was still held taut.

"Good boys," she called to the mules. "Keep on comin'."

Kelly knew most mule drivers walked behind their animals in order to keep them going, but Papa's mules were usually dependable and didn't need much prodding. Herman, the lead mule, was especially obedient and docile. So Kelly walked in front, or sometimes alongside the team, and they followed with rarely a problem.

Herman and Hector had been pulling Papa's canal boat since Kelly was eight years old, and she'd been leading them for the last nine years. Six days a week, nine months of the year, sometimes eighteen hours a day, they trudged up and down the towpath that ran alongside the Lehigh Navigation System. The waterway, which included the Lehigh Canal and parts of the Lehigh River, was owned by a Quaker named Josiah White. Due to his religious views, he would not allow anyone working for him to labor on the Sabbath. That was fine with Kelly. She needed at least one day of rest.

"If it weren't for the boatmen's children, the canal wouldn't run a day," she mumbled. "Little ones who can't wait to grow up so they can make their own way."

Until two years ago, Kelly's older sister Sarah had helped with the mules. Then she ran off with Sam Turner, one of the lock tenders' boys who had lived along their route. Sarah and Sam had been making eyes at each other for some time, and one day shortly after Sarah's eighteenth birthday, they ran away together. Several weeks later, Sarah sent the family a letter saying she and Sam were married and living in Phillipsburg, New Jersey. Sam had gotten a job at Warren Soapstone, and Sarah was still looking for work. Kelly and her folks hadn't seen or heard a word from either of them since that time. Such a shame! She sure did miss that sister of hers.

Kelly moaned as she glanced down at her long, gray cotton skirt, covered with a thick layer of dust. She supposed the sifting dirt was preferable to globs of gritty, slippery mud, which she often encountered in early spring. "Long skirts are such a bother. Sure wish Mama would allow me to wear pants like all the mule boys do."

Sometimes, when the wind was blowing real hard, Kelly's skirt would billow, and she hated that. She'd solved the problem when she got the bright idea to sew several small stones into the hemline, weighing it down so the wind couldn't lift her skirt anymore.

Kelly looked over her shoulder again, past the mules. Her gaze came to rest on her father's flat-roofed, nearly square, wooden boat. They were hauling another load of dark, dirty anthracite coal from the town of Mauch Chunk, the pickup spot, on down to Easton, where it would be delivered.

Kelly's thoughts returned to her sister, and a knot rose in her throat. She missed Sarah for more than just her help. Sometimes, when they'd walked the mules together, Kelly and Sarah had shared their deepest desires and secret thoughts. Sarah admitted how much she hated life on the canal. She'd made it clear that she would do about anything to get away from Papa and his harsh, stingy ways.

Kelly groaned inwardly. She understood why Sarah had taken off and was sure her older sister had only married Sam so she could get away from the mundane, difficult life on the Lehigh Navigation System. It didn't help any that Kelly and Sarah had been forced to work as mule drivers without earning one penny of their own. Some mule drivers earned as much as a dollar per day, but not Kelly and her sister. All the money they should have made went straight into Papa's pocket, even if Mama and the girls had done more than their share of the work.

In all fairness, Kelly had to admit that even though Papa yelled a lot, he did take pretty good care of them. He wasn't like some of the canal boatmen, who drank and gambled whenever they had the chance, wasting away their earnings before the month was half over.

Kelly was nearing her own eighteenth birthday, and even though she was forced to work without pay, there was nothing on earth that would make her marry someone simply so she could get away. In fact, the idea of marriage was like vinegar in her mouth. From what she'd seen in her own folks' lives, getting hitched wasn't so great anyway. All Mama ever did was work, and all Papa did was take charge of the boat and yell at her and Mama.

Tears burned in Kelly's eyes, but she held them in check. "Sure wish I could make enough money to support myself. And I don't give a hoot nor a holler 'bout findin' no man to call husband, neither."

Kelly lifted her chin and began to sing softly, "Hunks-a-go pudding and pieces of pie; my mother gave me when I was knee-high. . . . And if you don't believe it, just drop in and see—the hunks-a-go pudding my mother gave me."

The tension in Kelly's neck muscles eased as she began to relax. Singing the silly canaler's tune always made her feel a bit better. Especially when she was getting hungry and could have eaten at least three helpings of Mama's hunks-a-go pudding. The fried batter, made with eggs, milk, and flour, went right well with a slab of roast beef. Just thinking about how good it tasted made Kelly's mouth water.

Mama would serve supper when they stopped for the night, but that wouldn't be 'til sundown, several hours from now. When Papa hollered, "Hold up there, Girl!" and secured the boat to a tree or near one of the locks, Kelly would have to care for the mules. There was always currying and cleaning of the animals to do, in particular around Herman and Hector's collars where their sweaty hair often came loose. Kelly never took any chances with the mules, for she didn't want either of them to get sores or infections that would end up needing to be treated with medicine.

When the grooming was done each night, Kelly fed the animals and bedded them down in fresh straw spread along the floor in one of the lock stables or in their special compartment on the boat. Only when all that was done could Kelly climb on board, wash up, and sit down to Mama's hot meal of salt pork and beans or potato-and-onion soup. Roast beef and hunks-a-go pudding were reserved for a special Sunday dinner when there was more time for cooking.

After supper, when all the dishes had been washed, dried, and put away, Kelly would read, draw, or maybe play a game. Mama and Papa amused themselves with an occasional game of checkers, and sometimes they lined up a row of dominoes and competed to see who could acquire the most points. That was fine with Kelly. She much preferred to retire to her bunk in the deck below and draw by candlelight until her eyes became too heavy to focus. Most often she'd sketch something she'd seen along the canal, but many times her charcoal pictures were of things she'd never seen before. Things she'd read about and could only dream of seeing.

On days like today, when Kelly was dog-eared tired and covered from head to toe with dust, she wished for a couple of strong brothers to take her place as driver of the mules. It was unfortunate for both Kelly and her folks, but Mama wasn't capable of having any more children. She'd prayed for it; Kelly had heard her do so many times. The good Lord must have thought two daughters were all Amos and Dorrie McGregor needed. God must have decided Kelly could do the work of two sons. Maybe the Lord believed she should learn to be content with being poor.

Contentment. That was something Kelly didn't think she could ever manage. Not until she had money in her pockets. She couldn't help but wonder if God cared about her needs at all.

Herman nuzzled the back of Kelly's neck, interrupting her musings and nearly knocking her wide-brimmed straw hat to the ground. She shivered and giggled. "What do ya want, ol' boy? You think I have some carrots for you today? Is that what you're thinkin'?"

The mule answered with a loud bray, and Hector followed suit.

"All right, you two," Kelly said, reaching into her roomy apron pocket. "I'll give ya both a carrot, but you must show your appreciation by pullin' real good for a few more hours." She shook her finger. "And I want ya to do it without one word of complaint."

Another nuzzle with his wet nose, and Kelly knew Herman had agreed to her terms. Now she needed confirmation from Hector.

ॐ

Mike Cooper didn't have much use for some of the newfangled things he was being encouraged to sell in his general store, but this pure white soap that actually floated might be a real good seller. Especially to the boatmen, who seemed to have a way of losing bars of soap over the side of their vessels. If Mike offered them a product for cleaning that could easily be seen and would bob like a cork instead of sinking to the bottom of the murky canal, he could have a best-seller that would keep his customers coming back and placing orders for "the incredible soap that floats."

Becoming a successful businessman might help him pursue his goal of finding a suitable wife. Ever since Pa died, leaving him to run the store by himself, Mike had a terrible ache in his heart. Ma had gone to heaven a few years before Pa, and his two brothers, Alvin and John, had relocated a short time later, planning to start a fishing business off the coast of New Jersey. That left Mike to keep the store going, but it also left him alone, wishing for a helpmate and a brood of children. In fact, Mike prayed for this every day. He felt he was perfectly within God's will to make such a request. After all, in the Book of Genesis, God said it wasn't good for a man to be alone, so He created Eve to be a helper and to keep Adam company. At twenty-four years old, Mike thought it was past time he settled down with a mate.

Mike's biggest concern was the fact that there weren't too many unattached ladies living along the canal. Most of the women who shopped at his store were either married or adolescent girls. There was one young woman—Sarah McGregor—but word had it she'd up and run off with the son of a lock tender from up the canal a ways. Sarah had a younger sister, but the last time Mike saw Kelly, she was only a freckle-faced kid in pigtails.

Then there was Betsy Nelson, daughter of the minister who lived in nearby Walnutport and regularly traveled along the canal in hopes of winning folks to the Lord. Betsy wasn't beautiful, but she wasn't as ugly as the muddy waters in Lehigh Canal either. Of course, Mike wasn't nearly as concerned over a woman's looks as he was with her temperament. Betsy should have been sweet as apple pie, her being a pastor's daughter and all, but she could cut a body right in two with that sharp tongue of hers. Why, he'd never forget the day Betsy raked old Ross Spivey up one side and down the other for spitting out a wad of tobacco in the middle of one of her daddy's sermons. By the time she'd finished with Ross, the poor man was down on his knees, begging forgiveness for being so rude.

Mike grabbed a broom from the storage closet, shook his head, and muttered, "A fellow would have to be hard of hearin' or just plain dumb-witted to put up with the likes of Miss Betsy Nelson. It's no wonder she's not married yet."

He pushed the straw broom across the wooden floor, visualizing with each stroke a beautiful, sweet-spirited woman who'd be more than happy to become his wife. After a few seconds, Mike shook his head and murmured, "I'll have to wait, that's all. Wait and keep on prayin'."

Mike quoted Genesis 2:18, a verse of Scripture that had become one of his favorites since he'd decided he wanted a wife: "'And the LORD God said, It is not good that the man should be alone; I will make him an help meet for him.'"

"I know the perfect woman is out there somewhere, Lord," he whispered. "All I need is for You to send her my way, and I can take it from there."

2

$\mathcal{K}$elly awoke feeling tired and out of sorts. She'd stayed up late the night before, working on another charcoal drawing. It was an ocean scene, with lots of fishing boats on the water. Not that Kelly had ever seen the ocean. Her only experience with water involved the Lehigh, Morris, and Delaware Rivers and Canals. She'd only seen the ocean in her mind—from stories she'd read in books or from the tales of those who had personally been to the coast.

If she could ever figure out a way to earn enough money of her own, Kelly might like to take a trip to the shore. Maybe she would open an art gallery there, to show and sell some of her work. She had seen such a place in the town of Easton, although Papa would never let her go inside. Kelly wondered if her drawings were good enough to sell. If only she could afford to buy a store-bought tablet, along with some oil paints, watercolors, or sticks of charcoal. She was getting tired of making her own pieces of charcoal, using hunks left over in the cooking stove or from campfires that had been set along the canal. Kelly would let the chunks cool, and then whittle them down to the proper size. It wasn't what she would have liked, but at least it allowed her to draw.

Kelly swung her legs over the edge of the bunk and stretched her aching limbs. If a young woman of seventeen could hurt this much from long hours of walking and caring for mules, she could only imagine how older folks must feel. She knew Papa worked plenty hard steering the boat and helping load and unload the coal they hauled, which might account for his usual crabby attitude. Mama labored from sunup to sunset as well. Besides cooking and cleaning, there was always laundry and mending to do. At times, Mama even steered the boat while Papa rested or took care of chores only he could do. Kelly's mother also helped by watching up ahead and letting Papa know where to direct the boat.

Stifling a yawn, Kelly reached for a plain brown skirt and white long-sleeved blouse lying on a straight-backed chair near the bed. She glanced around the small cabin and studied her meager furnishings. The room wasn't much bigger than a storage closet, and it was several steps below the main deck. Her only pieces of furniture were the bunk, a small desk, a chair, and the trunk she kept at the foot of her bed.

I wonder what it would be like to have a roomy bedroom in a real house, Kelly mused. The canal boat had been her primary home as far back as she could remember. The only time they lived elsewhere was in the winter, when the canal was drained due to freezing temperatures and couldn't be navigated. It was during those days that Kelly's dad worked at one of the factories in the town of Easton. Leaving the few pieces of furniture they owned on their boat, the McGregor family settled into Flannigan's Boardinghouse until the spring thaw came and Papa could resume work on the canal. During the winter months, Kelly and her sister had gone to school when they were younger, but the rest of the year Mama taught them reading and sums whenever they had a free moment.

Kelly's nose twitched and her stomach rumbled, as the distinctive aroma of cooked oatmeal and cinnamon wafted down the stairs, calling her to breakfast. A new day was about to begin, and she would need a hearty meal to help get her started.

"We'll be stoppin' by Cooper's General Store this afternoon, 'cause we need some supplies," Papa announced when Kelly arrived at the breakfast table. He glanced over at Mama, then at Kelly, his green eyes looking ever so serious. "Don't know when we'll take time out for another supply stop, so if either of you needs anything, you'd better plan on gettin' it today." He slid his fingers across the auburn-colored handlebar mustache that filled the space between his nose and upper lip.

"I could use a few more bars of that newfangled soap I bought last time we came through," Mama spoke up. "It's a wonder to me the way that stuff floats!"

Kelly couldn't help but smile at her mother's enthusiasm over something as simple as a bar of white soap that floated when it was dropped in water. *I guess things like that are important to a woman with a family. Mama doesn't have much else to get excited about.*

Kelly ate a spoonful of oatmeal as she studied her mother, a large-boned woman of Italian descent. She had dark brown hair like Kelly's; only Mama didn't wear hers hanging down. She pulled it up into a tight bun at the back of her head. Mama's eyes, the color of chestnuts, were her best feature.

Mama could be real pretty if she was able to have nice, new clothes and keep herself fixed up. Instead, she's growing old before her time—slavin' over a hot stove and scrubbin' clothes in canal water, with only a washboard and a bar of soap that bobs like a cork—poor Mama!

Papa's chair scraped across the wooden planks as he pulled his wiry frame away from the table. "It's time to get rollin'." He nodded toward Kelly. "Better get them mules ready, Girl."

Kelly finished the rest of her breakfast and jumped up. When Papa said it was time to roll, he meant business. In fact, when Papa said anything at all, she knew she'd better listen.

&

It was noon when the McGregors tied their boat to a tree not far from the town of Walnutport and stopped for lunch. Normally they would have eaten a quick bite, then started back up the canal, but today they were heading to Cooper's General Store. After a bowl of vegetable soup and some of Mama's sweet cornbread, they would be shopping for needed supplies and more food staples.

Kelly welcomed the stop. Not only because she was hungry and needed to eat, but also because Papa had promised to buy her a new pair of boots. She'd been wearing the same ones for more than a year, and they were much too tight. Besides, the laces were missing, and the soles were nearly worn clear through. Kelly had thought by the time she turned sixteen her feet would have quit growing. But here she was only ten months from her eighteenth birthday, and her long toes were still stretching the boots she wore. At this rate she feared she'd be wearing a size nine when her feet finally stopped growing.

Kelly ate hurriedly, anxious to head over to the general store. She hadn't been inside Cooper's in well over a year because she usually chose to wait outside while her folks did the shopping. Today Kelly planned to check the mules over and offer them a bit of feed, then hurry into the store. If she found new boots in short order, there might even be enough time to sit on a log and draw awhile. There were always interesting things along the canal—other boats, people fishing, and plenty of waterfowl.

Too bad I can't buy some oil paints or a set of watercolors, Kelly thought as she hooked the mules to a post and began to check them over for harness sores, fly bites, or hornet stings. *Guess I should be happy Papa has agreed to buy me new boots, but I'd sure like to have somethin' just for fun once in awhile.*

Kelly released a groan and scratched Hector behind his ear. "If I ever make any money of my own, I might just buy you a big, juicy apple." She patted Herman's neck. "You too, Old Boy."

ಆ

Mike whistled a familiar hymn as he dusted off the candy counter, always a favorite with the children who stopped by his store. He was running low on horehound drops but still had plenty of licorice, lemon drops, and taffy chews. He knew he'd have to order more of everything soon, since summer was not far off, and there would be a lot more little ones coming by in hopes of finding something to satisfy their sweet tooth.

Many boats were being pulled up the Lehigh Navigation System already, and it was still early spring. Mike figured by this time next month his store would have even more customers. Last winter, when he'd had plenty of time on his hands, Mike had decided to order some Bibles to either sell or give away. If someone showed an interest and didn't have the money to buy one, he'd gladly offer it to them for free. Anything to see that folks learned about Jesus. Too many of the boatmen were uneducated in spiritual matters, and Mike wanted to do his part to teach them God's ways.

Mike leaned on the glass counter and let his mind wander back to when he was a boy of ten and had first heard about the Lord. Grandma Cooper, a proper Englishwoman, had told him about Jesus. Mike's family had lived with her and Grandpa for several years, when Mike's pa was helping out on the farm in upstate New York, where Mike had been born. Ellis Cooper had no mind to stay on the farm, though, and as soon as he had enough money, he moved his wife and three sons to Pennsylvania, where he'd opened the general store along the Lehigh Canal.

Mike's father didn't hold much to religious things. He used to say the Bible was a bunch of stories made up to help folks get through life with some measure of hope.

"There's hope, all right," Mike whispered as he brought his mind back to the present. "And thanks to Grandma's teachings, I'd like to help prove that hope never has to die."

When he heard a familiar creak, Mike glanced at the front door. Enough daydreaming and reflecting on the past. He had customers to satisfy, and as always, he'd do his best to see that their needs were met.

As he moved toward the front of the store, Mike's heart slammed into his chest. Coming through the doorway was the most beautiful young woman he'd ever laid eyes on. *Don't reckon I've seen her before. She must be new . . . just passing through. Maybe she's a passenger on one of the packet boats that hauls tourists. Maybe . . .*

Mike blinked a couple of times. He recognized the man and woman entering the store behind the young woman: Amos and Dorrie McGregor. It wasn't until Amos called her by name that Mike realized the little beauty was none other than the McGregors' youngest daughter, Kelly.

Mike shook his head as amazement swept though his body. It couldn't be. Kelly had pigtails, freckles, and was all arms and legs. This stunning creature had long brown hair that reached clear down to her waist, and from where he stood, there wasn't one freckle on her lovely face. She looked his way, and he gasped at the intensity of her dark brown eyes. *A man could lose himself in those eyes. A man could . . .*

"Howdy, Mike Cooper," Amos said, extending his hand. "How's business these days?"

Mike forced himself to breathe, and with even more resolve, he kept his focus on Amos and not the man's appealing daughter. "Business is fine, Sir." He shook Mr. McGregor's hand. "How are you and the family doing?"

Amos shrugged. "Fair to middlin'. I'd be a sight better if I hadn't hit one of the locks and put a hole in my boat the first week back to work." He gave his handlebar mustache a tug. "In order to get my repairs done, I had to use most of what I made this winter workin' at a shoe factory in Easton."

"Sorry to hear that," Mike said sincerely. He glanced back at Kelly, offering her what he hoped was a friendly smile. "Can this be the same Kelly McGregor who used to come runnin' in here begging her pa to buy a few lemon drops?"

Kelly's face turned slightly pink as she nodded. "Guess I've grown a bit since you last saw me."

"I'll say!" Mike felt a trickle of sweat roll down his forehead, and he quickly pulled a handkerchief out of his pant's pocket and wiped it away. Kelly McGregor was certainly no child. She was a desirable woman, even if she did have a few layers of dirt on her cotton skirt and wore a tattered straw hat and a pair of boots that looked like they were ready for burial. *Could she be the one I've been waiting for, Lord?*

Mike cleared his throat a few times. "So, what can I help you good folks with today?"

Amos gave his wife a little nudge. "Now don't be shy, Dorrie. Tell the man what you're needin'. I'll just poke around the store and see what I can find, while you and Kelly stock up on food items and the like."

Kelly cast her father a pleading look. "I'm still gettin' new boots, right, Papa?"

Her dad nodded and grunted. "Yeah, sure. See if Mike has somethin' that'll fit your big feet."

Mike felt sorry for Kelly, whose face was now red as a tomato. She shifted from one foot to the other, and never once did she look Mike right in the eye.

"I got a new shipment of boots in not long ago," he said quickly, hoping to help her feel a bit more at ease. "They're right over there." He pointed to a shelf across the room. "Would you like me to see if I have any your size?"

Dorrie McGregor spoke up for the first time. "Why don't you help my husband find what he's needin'? Me and Kelly can manage fine on our own."

Mike shrugged. "Whatever you think best." He offered Kelly the briefest of smiles, and then headed across the room to help her pa.

ॐ

Kelly didn't know why, but she felt as jittery as one of the mules when they were being forced to walk through standing water. Was it her imagination, or was Mike Cooper staring at her? Ever since they'd first entered the store, he seemed to be watching her, and now, while she was squatted down on the floor trying on a pair of size-nine boots, the man was actually gawking.

Maybe he's never seen a woman with such big feet. Probably thinks I should have been born a boy. Kelly swallowed hard and forced the threatening tears to stay put. *Truth be told, Papa probably wishes I was a boy.* Most boys were able to work longer and harder than she could. And a boy wasn't as apt to run off with the first person who offered him freedom from canal work, the way Sarah had.

Kelly glanced around the room, feeling an urgency to escape. She stood on shaky legs and forced herself to march around the store a few times in order to see if the boots were going to work out okay. When she was sure they were acceptable, she pulled the price tag off the laces and handed it to Mama. "If ya don't mind, I'd like to wait outside. It's kinda stuffy in here, and since it's such a nice day, maybe I can get in a bit of sketchin' while you and Papa finish your shopping."

Mama nodded, and Kelly scooted quickly out the front door. The sooner she got away from Mike Cooper and those funny looks he kept giving her, the better it would be!

3

*K*elly's heart was pounding like a hammer as she exited the store, but it nearly stopped beating altogether when Mike Cooper opened the door behind her and called, "Hey, Kelly, don't you want a bag of lemon drops?"

She skidded to a stop on the bottom step, heat flooding her face like it did whenever Mama lit the cook stove. She turned slowly to face him. *Why does he have to be so handsome?* Mike's medium-brown hair, parted on the side and cut just below his ears, curled around his neck like kitten fur. His neatly trimmed mustache jiggled up and down, as though he might be hiding a grin. The man's hazel-colored eyes seemed to bore right through her, and Kelly was forced to swallow several times before she could answer his question.

"I–uh–don't have money to spend on candy just now. New boots are more important than satisfyin' my sweet tooth." She turned away, withdrawing her homemade tablet and a piece of charcoal from the extra-large pocket of the apron covering her skirt.

Kelly was almost to the boat when she felt Mike's hand touch her shoulder. "Hold up there. What's your hurry?" His voice was deep, yet mellow and kind of soothing. Kelly thought she could find pleasure in listening to him talk awhile—if she had a mind to.

"I was plannin' to do a bit of drawing." She stared at the ground, her fingers kneading the folds in her skirt.

Mike moved so he was standing beside her. "You're an artist?"

She felt her face flush even more. "I like to draw, but that don't make me an artist."

"It does if you're any good. Can you draw something for me right now?"

She shrugged her shoulders. "I suppose I could, but don't you have customers to wait on?"

Mike chuckled. "You've got me there. How about if you draw something while I see what your folks might need? When they're done, I'll come back outside and you can show me what you've made. How's that sound?"

It sounded fair enough. There was only one problem. Kelly was feeling so flustered, she wasn't sure she could even write her own name, much less draw any kind of picture worthy to be shown.

"Guess I can try," she mumbled.

Unexpectedly, he reached out and patted her arm, and she felt a warm tingle shoot all the way up to her neck. Except for Papa's infrequent hugs, no man had ever touched her before. It felt kind of nice, in a funny sort of way. *Could this be why Sarah ran off with Sam Turner? Did Sam look at my sister in a manner that made her mouth go dry and her hands feel all sweaty?* If that's what happened to Sarah, then Kelly knew she had better run as far away from Mike Cooper as she possibly could, for he sure enough was making her feel giddy. She couldn't have that, no way!

Kelly took a few steps back, hoping the distance between them might get her thinking straight again. "See you later," she mumbled.

"Sure thing!" he called as he headed back to the store.

Kelly drew in a deep breath and flopped down on a nearby log. The few minutes she'd spent alone with Mike had rattled her so much, she wondered if she still knew how to draw.

In all the times they'd stopped by Cooper's General store, never once had Mike looked at her the way he had today—like she was someone special, maybe even pretty. *Of course*, she reminded herself, *I usually wait outside, so he hasn't seen me in awhile.* The time it took for her folks to shop was a good chance for Kelly to sketch, feed and water the mules, or simply rest her weary bones. Truth be told, it had probably been more than a year since she'd seen Mike face-to-face.

Forcing her thoughts off the handsome storekeeper, Kelly focused her attention on a pair of mallard ducks floating in the canal. The whisper of the wind sang softly as it played with the ends of Kelly's hair. A fat bullfrog was posed on the bank nearby. It seemed to be studying a dragonfly hovering above the water. It was a peaceful scene, and Kelly felt one with her surroundings. In no time, she'd filled several pages of the simple drawing pad she usually kept inside the pocket of either her skirt or apron.

Kelly was pulled from her reverie when Papa and Mama walked up, each carrying a wooden box. She rolled up her artwork and slipped it, along with the hunk of charcoal, inside her pocket. Then she wiped her messy hands on her dusty skirt and jumped to her feet. "Need some help?"

"I could probably use another pair of hands puttin' stuff away in the kitchen," Mama replied.

"Will we be leavin' soon?" Kelly asked, glancing at Cooper's General Store and wondering if Mike would come back to see her drawings as he'd promised.

"Soon as we get everything loaded," Papa mumbled. "Sure would help if we had a few more hands. Got things done a whole lot quicker when Sarah was here."

Kelly watched her dad climb on board his boat. She knew he'd been traveling the canal ever since he was a small boy. Except for times during winter when he worked in town, running the boat was Papa's whole life. Even though he had a fiery Irish temper, once in awhile she caught him whistling, singing some silly tune, or blowing on his mouth harp. Kelly figured he must really enjoy his life on the canal. Too bad he was so cheap and wouldn't hire another person to help out. Most of the canalers had a hired hand to steer the boat while the captain stood at the front and shouted directions.

I wish God had blessed Papa and Mama with a whole passel of boys. Sarah's gone, and I'm hoping to leave someday. Then what will Papa do? Kelly shrugged. *Guess he'll have to break down and hire a mule driver, 'cause Mama sure can't do everything she does now and drive the mules too.*

As Kelly followed her mother into the cabin, she set her thoughts aside. They had a long day ahead, with much to be done.

ॐ

Mike hoisted a box to his shoulders and started out the door. He had offered to help Amos McGregor haul his supplies on board the boat. It was the least he could do, considering the fact that Amos had no boys to help. Besides, it would give him a good excuse to talk to Kelly again and see what she'd drawn.

Mike met Amos as the older man was stepping off the boat. "Didn't realize you'd be bringing a box clean out here," Amos commented, tipping his head and offering Mike something akin to a smile.

"I said I'd help, and I thought it would save you a few steps." Mike nodded toward the boat. "Where shall I put this one?"

Amos extended his arms. "Just give it to me."

Taken aback by the man's abruptness, Mike shrugged and handed over the box. Amos turned, mumbled his thanks, and stepped onto the boat.

"Is Kelly on board?" Mike called, surprising himself at his sudden boldness. "I'd like to speak with her a moment."

Kelly's dad whirled around. "What business would ya have with my daughter?"

"She was planning to show me some of her artwork."

Amos shook his head. "Her and them stupid drawings! She's a hard enough worker when it comes to drivin' the mules, but for the life of me, I can't see why she wastes any time scratchin' away on a piece of paper with a stick of dirty, black charcoal."

"We all need an escape from our work, Mr. McGregor," Mike asserted. "Some read, fish, or hunt. Others, like me, choose to whittle." He smiled. "Some, such as your daughter, enjoy drawing."

"Humph! Makes no sense a'tall!" Amos spun around. "I'll tell Kelly you're out here waitin'. Don't take up too much of her time, though. We're about ready to shove off."

Mike smiled to himself. Maybe Amos wasn't such a tough fellow after all. He could have said Kelly wasn't receiving any visitors. Or he could have told Mike to take a leap right into the canal.

Mike waited on the dock, and a few minutes later Kelly showed up. She looked kind of flustered, and he hoped it wasn't on account of him. It could be that Kelly's pa had given her a lecture about wasting time with her sketches. Or maybe he'd made it clear he wanted no one calling on the only daughter he had left. It might be that Amos was afraid his youngest child would run off with some fellow, the way his eldest had done.

He needn't worry. While I'm clearly attracted to Kelly McGregor, I don't think she's given me more than a second thought today.

&

Kelly's legs were shaking as she lifted one foot over the side of the boat and stepped onto dry ground. She could hardly believe Mike Cooper had really come looking for her. She knew Papa was none too happy about it because he'd told her she wasn't to take much time talking to the young owner of the general store. Kelly figured it was probably because Papa was anxious to be on his way, but from the way her father had said Mike's name, she had to wonder if there might be more to his reason for telling her to hurry. Maybe Papa thought she had eyes for Mike Cooper. Maybe he was afraid Kelly would run off and get married, the way Sarah had done. Well, he needn't worry about that happening!

Mike smiled as Kelly moved toward him. "Did you bring your drawings?"

She averted his gaze. "I only have a few with me, and they're done up on scraps of paper sack so they're probably not so good." She blinked a couple of times. "I got some free newsprint from the *Sunday Call* while we were livin' in Easton, and some of my pictures have a white background. Those are in my room on the boat and might be some better."

"Why not let me be the judge of how good your pictures are? Can I take a peek at what you've got with you?"

Kelly reached inside her ample apron pocket and retrieved the tablet she'd put together from cutup pieces of paper sack the size of her Bible. She handed it to Mike and waited for his response.

He studied the drawings several seconds, flipping back and forth through the pages and murmuring an occasional "ah . . . so . . . hmm . . ."

She shifted her weight from one foot to the other, wondering what he thought. Did Mike like the sketches? Was he surprised to see her crude tablet? The papers were held in place by strings she'd pushed through with one of Mama's darning needles. Then she'd tied the strings in a knot to hold everything in place. Did Mike's opinion of her artwork and tablet even matter? After all, he was nothing to her—just a man who ran a general store along the Lehigh Navigation System.

"These are very good," Mike said. "I especially like the one of the bullfrog ready to pounce on the green dragonfly." He chuckled. "Who won, anyway?"

Kelly blinked. "What?"

"Did the bullfrog get his lunch, or did the dragonfly lure the old toad into the water, then flit away before the croaker knew what happened?"

She grinned. "The dragonfly won."

"That's what I expected."

Kelly pressed a hand to her chest, hoping to still a heart that was beating much too fast. If only Papa or Mama would call her back to the boat. As much as she was enjoying this little chat with Mike, she felt jittery and unsure of herself.

"Have you ever sold any of your work?" Mike asked.

She shook her head. "I doubt anyone would buy a plain old charcoal drawing."

He touched her arm. "There's nothin' *plain* about these, Kelly. I have an inkling some of the folks who travel our canal or live in the nearby communities might be willing to pay a fair price for one of your pictures."

Her face heated with embarrassment. She got so few compliments and didn't know how to respond. "You . . . you really think so?"

He nodded. "In fact, the other day there was a packet boat that came through, transporting a group of people up to Allentown. Two of the men were authors, and they seemed real interested in the landscape and natural beauty growing along our canal."

Kelly sucked in her lower lip as she thought about the prospect. This might be the chance she'd been hoping for. If she could make some money selling a few of her charcoal drawings, maybe she'd have enough to purchase a store-bought writing tablet, a good set of watercolors, or perchance some oil paints. Then she could do up some *real* pictures, and if she could sell those . . .

"How about I take two or three of these sketches and see if I can sell them in my store?" Mike asked. "I would keep ten percent and give you the rest. How's that sound?"

Ten percent of the profits for him? Had she heard Mike right? That meant she'd get ninety percent. The offer was more than generous, and it seemed too good to be true.

"Sounds fair, but since I've never sold anything before, I don't know how much of a price to put on the drawings," Kelly said.

"Why not leave that up to me?" Mike winked at her, and she felt like his gentle gaze had caught and held her in a trap. "I've been selling things for several years now, so I think I can figure out a fair price," he said with the voice of assurance.

She nodded. "All right, we have us a deal, but since these pictures aren't really my best, I'll have to go back on the boat and get ya three other pictures."

"That's fine," Mike said as he handed her the drawings.

"The next time we come by your store, I'll ask Papa to stop; then I can check and see if you've sold anything."

Mike reached out his hand. "Partners?"

They shook on it. "Partners."

$$4$$

*S*haking hands with Mike Cooper had almost been Kelly's undoing. When Mike released her hand, she was trembling and had to clench her fists at her sides in order to keep him from seeing how much his touch affected her.

Mike opened his mouth, as if to say something, but he was cut off by a woman's shrill voice.

"Yoo-hoo! Mr. Cooper, I need you!"

Kelly and Mike both turned around. Betsy Nelson, the local preacher's daughter, was heading their way, her long, green skirt swishing this way and that.

Kelly cringed, remembering how overbearing Betsy could be. She didn't simply share the good news, the way Rev. Nelson did. No, Betsy tried to cram it down folks' throats by insisting they come to Sunday school at the little church in Walnutport, where her father served as pastor.

One time, when Kelly was about seven years old, Betsy had actually told Kelly and her sister, Sarah, that they were going to the devil if they didn't come to Sunday school and learn about Jesus. Papa overheard the conversation and blew up, telling sixteen-year-old Betsy what he thought of her pushy ways. He'd sent her home in tears and told Kelly and Sarah there was no need for either of them to go to church. He said he'd gotten along fine all these years without God, so he didn't think his daughters needed religion.

Mama thought otherwise, and while the girls were young, she often read them a Bible story before going to bed. When Kelly turned twelve, Mama gave her an old Bible that had belonged to Grandma Minnotti, who'd died and gone to heaven. It was during the reading of the Bible story about Jesus' death on the cross that Kelly confessed her sins in the quiet of her room one night. She'd felt a sense of hope, realizing Jesus was her personal Savior and would walk with her wherever she went—even up and down the dirty towpath.

What had happened to her childlike faith since then? Had she become discouraged after Sarah ran away with Sam, leaving her with the responsibility of leading the mules? Or had her faith in God slipped because Papa was so mean and wouldn't give Kelly any money for the hard work she did every day?

Kelly's thoughts came to a halt when Betsy Nelson stepped between her and Mike and announced, "I need to buy material for some new kitchen curtains I plan to make."

"Go on up to the store and choose what you want. I'll be there in a minute," Mike answered with a nod.

Betsy stood grounded to her spot, and Mike motioned toward Kelly. "Betsy, in case you didn't recognize her, this is Kelly McGregor, all grown up."

Kelly felt her face flame, and she opened her mouth to offer a greeting, but Betsy interrupted.

"Sure, I remember you—the skinny little girl in pigtails who refused to go to Sunday school."

Kelly knew that wasn't entirely true, as it had been Papa's decision, not hers. She figured it would be best not to say anything in her own defense, however.

Betsy squinted her gray blue eyes and reached up to pat the tight bun she wore at the back of her head. Kelly wondered if the young woman ever allowed her dingy blond hair to hang down her back. Or did the prim and proper preacher's daughter even sleep with her hair pulled back so tightly her cheeks looked drawn?

"I was hoping you would help me choose the material," Betsy said, offering Mike a pinched-looking smile.

Mike fingered his mustache and rocked back on his heels. Kelly thought he looked uncomfortable. "I'm kinda busy right now," he said, nodding at Kelly.

"It's all right," she was quick to say. "Papa's about ready to go, and I think we've finished with our business."

"But you haven't given me any pictures," Mike reminded her.

"Oh . . . oh, you're right." Kelly's voice wavered when she spoke. She was feeling more flustered by the minute.

"Kelly, you got them mules ready yet?" Papa shouted from the bow of the boat.

Kelly turned to her father and called, "In a minute, Papa." She faced Mike again. "I'll be right back with the drawings." She whirled around, sprinted toward the boat, and leaped over the side, nearly catching her long skirt in the process.

A few minutes later, Kelly came back, carrying three drawings done on newsprint and neatly pressed between two pieces of cardboard. Two were of children fishing along the canal, and the third was a picture of Hector and Herman standing in the middle of the towpath. She handed them to Mike. "I'll have more to show you the next time we stop by."

Mike lifted the top piece of cardboard and studied the drawings. "Nicely done, Kelly. Very nice."

Heat rushed to Kelly's face, but she appreciated his compliment. "Thanks. I hope the others will be as good."

"I don't see why they wouldn't be." Mike held up the picture of Kelly's mules. "Look, Betsy. See what Kelly's drawn."

"Uh-huh. Nice." Betsy barely took notice as she grabbed hold of Mike's arm. "Can we go see about that material now?"

"I guess so." Mike turned to Kelly. "See you in a few days."

She nodded. "If Papa decides to stop. If not, then soon, I hope."

"Kelly McGregor!" Papa's voice had grown even louder, and Kelly knew he was running out of patience.

"Ready in a minute," she hollered back. "See you, Mike. See you, Betsy." Kelly grabbed hold of the towline and then hurried off toward the mules waiting patiently under a maple tree. A few minutes later she was trudging up the towpath, wishing she could have visited with Mike a bit longer.

Kelly glanced over her shoulder and saw Betsy hanging onto Mike's arm. A pang of jealousy stabbed her heart, but she couldn't explain it. She had no claims on Mike Cooper, nor did she wish to have any. Betsy Nelson was more than welcome to the storekeeper.

❧

Mike headed for the store, wishing it were Kelly and not Betsy clinging to his arm. As he reached the front door, he glanced over his shoulder and saw the McGregors' canal boat disappear around the bend. He'd wanted to spend more time with Kelly, but Betsy's interruption had stolen what precious moments they might have had.

As he stepped into the store, Mike shot a quick prayer heavenward. *Is Kelly the one, Lord? Might she make me a good wife?*

"Mr. Cooper, are you listening to me?" Betsy gave his shirtsleeve a good tug.

Mike refocused his thoughts and turned to look at Betsy, still clinging to his arm.

"The material's on that shelf, and please feel free to call me Mike." He pulled his arm free and pointed to the wall along the left side of his store. "Give me a minute to put Kelly's drawings in a safe place, and I'll join you over there."

Mike could see by the pucker of Betsy's lips that she wasn't happy, but she headed in the direction he had pointed.

Did Betsy think he would drop everything just because she wanted his opinion on the material she wished to buy? Mike doubted his advice counted for much. Truth of the matter, he knew little about kitchen curtains. His mother had decorated the house he lived in, which was connected to the back of the store. Since Ma's death, he hadn't given much thought to her choice of colors, fabric, or even furniture. If it had been good enough for Ma and Pa, then it was good enough for him.

Mike placed Kelly's drawings on a shelf under the counter and headed across the room to where Betsy stood holding a bolt of yellow-and-white calico material.

She smiled at him. "What do you think of this color?"

He shrugged. "Guess it would work fine."

For the next half hour, Mike looked at bolts of material, nodded his head, and tried to show an interest in Betsy's curtain-making project. He felt a sense of relief when another customer entered the store, but much to his disappointment, Betsy was still looking at material when he finished up with Hank Summers' order.

"Have you made a decision yet?" Mike called to Betsy from where he stood behind the counter.

"I suppose the yellow-and-white calico will work best." Betsy marched across the room and plunked the bolt of material on the wooden counter. "I'll take ten yards."

Ten yards? Mike thought Betsy was only making curtains for the kitchen, not every window in the house. *Guess women are prone to changing their minds.*

Betsy grinned at him and fluttered her pale eyelashes. "I'm thinking of making a dress from the leftover material, and I want to be sure I have plenty. Do you think this color will look good on me?"

Mike groaned inwardly. He didn't want to offend the preacher's daughter, so he merely smiled and nodded in response.

As soon as Betsy left the store, Mike withdrew Kelly's pictures from under the counter, took a seat on his wooden stool, and studied the charcoal drawings.

Kelly McGregor had talent; there was no doubt about it. The question was, would he be able to sell her artwork?

5

*O*ver the next couple days, Kelly daydreamed a lot while she walked the towpath. Was it possible that Mike Cooper might be able to sell some of her drawings? Were they as good as he'd said, or had Mike been trying to be polite when he told Kelly she had talent?

"Sure wish he wasn't so handsome," Kelly muttered as she neared the changing bridge where she and the mules would cross to the other side of the canal. A vision of Mike's face crept into her mind, and she began to sing her favorite canal song, hoping to block out all thoughts of the storekeeper.

"Hunks-a-go pudding and pieces of pie; my mother gave me when I was knee-high. . . . And if you don't believe it, just drop in and see—the hunks-a-go pudding my mother gave me."

Kelly found herself thinking about food and how good supper would taste when they stopped for the night. Mama had bought a hunk of dried beef at Mike Cooper's store, so they would be having savory stew later on.

Up ahead was the changing bridge, and Kelly knew it was time to get the mules ready to cross over to the towpath on the other side of the canal. Soon they were going up and over the bridge, as Kelly lifted the towrope over the railing. Obediently, Hector and Herman followed. In no time they were on the other side, and Papa was able to steer his boat farther down the canal.

Kelly was relieved it had gone well and that the towline hadn't become snagged. Whenever that happened, they were held up while Papa fixed things again. Then he was angry the rest of the day because they'd lost precious time. Every load of anthracite coal was important, and payment was made only when it was delivered to the city of Easton, where it was weighed and unloaded. The trip back up the navigation system to Mauch Chunk was with an empty boat, and Papa never wanted to waste a single moment.

Today they were heading to Easton and would arrive by late afternoon if all went well. Kelly knew there was no way Papa would agree to stop by Cooper's General Store on the way to deliver their coal, but coming back again, he might.

Maybe we'll get there early enough so I'll have time to get some drawing done, Kelly told herself. If there was any possibility of Mike selling her artwork, she needed to have more pictures ready to give him.

Kelly didn't realize she'd stopped walking until she felt Hector's wet nose nudge the back of her neck. She whirled around. "Hey there, Boy. Are ya that anxious to get to Easton?"

The mule snorted in response, and she laughed and reached out to stroke him behind the ear. Not to be left out, Herman bumped her hand.

"All right, Herman the Determined, I'll give you some attention too." Kelly stroked the other mule's ear for a few seconds, and then she clicked her tongue. "Now giddy-up, you two. There's no more time to dawdle. Papa will be worse than a snappin' turtle if we make him late tonight."

The day wore on, and every few miles they came to another lock where they would wait while it filled with water to match the level of the canal. Then their boat entered the lock, and the gates enclosed the boat in a damp, wooden receptacle. Right ahead, the water came sizzling and streaming down from above, and gradually the boat would rise again, finally coming to a respectable elevation. The gates swung open, Kelly hooked the mules back to the towrope, and they resumed their voyage.

Ahead was another lock, and Papa blew on his conch shell, letting the lock tender know he was coming. When they approached the lock, Kelly saw another boat ahead of them. They would have to wait their turn.

Suddenly, a third boat came alongside Papa's. "Move outta my way!" the captain shouted. "I'm runnin' behind schedule and should've had this load delivered by now."

"I was here first," Papa hollered in response. "You'll have to wait your turn."

"Oh, yeah? Who's gonna make me?" The burly looking man with a long, full beard shook his fist at Papa.

Standing on the bank next to the mules, Kelly watched as Mama stepped up beside Papa. She touched his arm and leaned close to Papa's ear. Kelly was sure Mama was trying to get Papa calmed down, like she always did whenever he got riled.

Kelly took a few steps closer to the canal and strained to hear what Mama was saying.

"Don't tell me what to do, Woman!" Papa yelled as he leaned over the side of his boat. The other craft was right alongside him, and the driver of the mules pulling that boat stood next to Kelly.

The young boy, not much more than twelve or thirteen years old, gave Kelly a wide grin. His teeth were yellow and stained. Probably from smoking or chewing tobacco, Kelly figured. "Looks like my pa is gonna beat the stuffin's outa your old man," he taunted.

Kelly glanced back at the two boat captains. They were face-to-face, each leaning as far over the rails as possible. She sent up a quick prayer. *Not this time, Lord. Please help Papa calm down.*

"Move aside, or I'm comin' over there to clean your clock," the burly man bellowed.

"Amos, please!" Mama begged as she gripped Papa's arm again. "Just let the man pass through the lock first. This ain't worth gettin' into a skirmish over."

Papa shot the man a look of contempt and grabbed hold of the tiller in order to steer the boat. "I'll let it go this time, but you'd better never try to ace me out again."

Kelly breathed a sigh of relief as Papa steered the boat aside and the other vessel passed through the lock. She'd seen her hot-tempered father use his fists to settle many disagreements in the past. It was always humiliating, and what did it prove—that Papa was tougher, meaner, or more aggressive than someone else? As far as Kelly could tell, nothing good had ever come from any of Papa's fistfights. He was a hotheaded Irishman, who'd grown up on the water. His dad had been one of the men who'd helped dig the Lehigh Canal, and Papa had said many times that he'd seen or been part of a good many fights throughout his growing-up days. If only he would give his heart to Jesus and confess his sins, the way Kelly and Mama had done.

Herman nuzzled Kelly's shoulder, and she turned to face her mule friends. *If God really loves me, then why doesn't He change Papa's heart?*

ॐ

Mike had been busier than usual the last couple days, and that was good. It kept him from thinking too much about Kelly McGregor. How soon would she and her family stop at his store again? Could he manage to sell any of her drawings before they came? Was Kelly the least bit interested in him? All these thoughts tumbled around in Mike's head whenever he had a free moment to look at Kelly's artwork, which he'd displayed on one wall of the store. The young woman had been gifted with a talent so great that even a simple, homemade charcoal drawing looked like an intricate work of art. At least Mike thought it did. He just hoped some of his customers would agree and decide to buy one of Kelly's pictures.

As Mike wiped off the glass on the candy counter, where little children had left fingerprint smudges, a vision of Kelly came to mind. With her long, dark hair hanging freely down her back, and those huge brown eyes reminding him of a baby deer, she was sure easy to look at. Nothing like Betsy Nelson, the preacher's daughter, who had a bird-like nose, squinty gray blue eyes, and a prim-and-proper bun for her dingy blond hair.

Kelly's personality seemed different too. She wasn't pushy and opinionated, the way Betsy was. Kelly, though a bit shy, seemed to have a zest for life that showed itself in her drawings. She was a hard worker too—trudging up and down the towpath six days a week, from sunup to sunset. Mike was well aware of the way the canal boatmen pushed to get their loads picked up and delivered. The responsibility put upon the mule drivers was heavy, yet it was often delegated to women and children.

I wonder if Amos McGregor appreciates his daughter and pays her well enough. Mike doubted it, seeing the way the man barked orders at

Kelly. And why, if she was paid a decent wage, would Kelly be using crude sticks of charcoal instead of store-bought paints or pencils, not to mention her homemade tablet?

Mike's thoughts were halted when the front door of his store opened and banged shut.

"Good morning, Mike Cooper," Preacher Nelson said as he sauntered into the room.

"Mornin'," Mike answered with a smile and a nod.

"How's business?"

"Been kind of busy the last couple of days. Now that the weather's warmed and the canal is full of water again, the boatmen are back in full swing."

The preacher raked his long fingers through the ends of his curly, dark hair. His gray blue eyes were small and beady, like his daughter's. "You still keeping the same hours?" the man questioned.

Mike nodded. "Yep . . . Monday to Saturday, nine o'clock in the morning 'til six at night."

Hiram Nelson smiled, revealing a prominent dimple in his clean-shaven chin. "Sure glad to hear you're still closing the store on Sundays."

Mike moved over to the wooden counter where he waited on customers. "Sunday's a day of rest."

"That's how God wants it, but there's sure a lot of folks who think otherwise."

Not knowing what else to say, Mike merely shrugged. "Anything I can help you with, Reverend Nelson?"

The older man leaned on the edge of the counter. "Actually, there is."

"What are you in need of?"

"You."

"Me?"

The preacher's head bobbed up and down. "This Friday's my daughter's twenty-sixth birthday, and I thought it would be nice for Betsy if someone her age joined us for supper." He chuckled. "She sees enough of her old papa, and since her mama died a few years ago, Betsy's been kind of lonely."

Mike was tempted to remind the preacher that his daughter was two years older than he but decided not to mention their age difference—or the fact that most women Betsy's age were already married and raising a family. "Isn't there someone from your church you could invite?" he asked.

Pastor Nelson's face turned slightly red. "It's you Betsy thought of when she said she'd like to have a guest on her birthday." He tapped the edge of the counter.

Mike wasn't sure how to respond. Was it possible that Betsy Nelson was romantically interested in him? If so, he had to figure out a way to discourage her.

"So, what do you say, Son? Will you come to supper on Friday evening?"

Remembering that the Nelsons' home was next to the church and several miles away, Mike knew he would have to close the store early in order to make it in time for supper. This would be the excuse he needed to decline the invitation. Besides, what if the McGregors came by while he was gone? He didn't want to miss an opportunity to see Kelly again.

"I–I'm afraid I can't make it," Mike said.

The preacher pursed his lips. "Why not? You got other plans?"

Mike shook his head. "Not exactly, but I'd have to close the store early."

Rev. Nelson held up his hand. "No need for that, Son. We'll have a late supper. How's seven o'clock sound?"

"Well, I—"

"I won't take no for an answer, so you may as well say you'll come. Betsy would be impossible to live with if I came home and told her you'd turned down my invitation."

Mike didn't want to hurt Betsy's feelings, and the thought of eating someone else's cooking did have some appeal. "Okay," he finally conceded. "Tell Betsy I'll be there."

6

$\mathcal{K}$elly hummed to herself as she kicked the stones beneath her feet. They had made it to Easton by six o'clock last night, and after they dropped off their load of coal and had eaten supper, she'd had a few hours to spend in her room, working on her drawings.

Now it was the following day, and they were heading back to Mauch Chunk for another load. By five or six o'clock they should be passing Mike Cooper's store. Kelly hoped she could talk Papa into stopping, for she had three more drawings she wanted to give Mike. One was of a canal boat going through the locks, another of an elderly boatman standing at the bow of his boat playing a fiddle, and the third picture was the skyline of Easton, with its many tall buildings.

Kelly was pretty sure her pictures were well-done, although she knew they could have been better if they'd been drawn on better paper, in color instead of black and white.

She stopped humming. *Someday I hope to have enough money to buy all kinds of paints and fancy paper.* Even as the words popped into her mind, Kelly wondered if they could ever come true. Unless Papa changed his mind about paying her wages, she might never earn any money of her own. Maybe her dream of owning an art gallery wasn't even possible.

"At least I can keep on drawing," she mumbled. "Nobody can take that away from me."

Kelly's stomach rumbled, reminding her it was almost noon. Since they had no load, they would be stopping to eat soon. If Papa was hurrying to get to Easton with a boatload of coal, Kelly might be forced to eat a hunk of bread or some fruit and keep on walking. Today, Mama was fixing a pot of vegetable and bean soup. Kelly could smell the delicious aroma as it wafted across the space between the boat and towpath.

A short while later, Kelly was on board the boat, sitting at the small wooden table. A bowl of steaming soup had been placed in front of her, a chunk of rye bread to her left, and her drawing pad was on the right. She'd decided to sketch a bit while her soup cooled.

Kelly had just picked up her piece of charcoal to begin drawing when Papa sat down across from her. "You ain't got time to dawdle. Get your lunch eaten and go tend to the mules."

Tears stung the backs of Kelly's eyes. She should be used to the way her dad shot orders, but his harsh tone and angry scowl always upset her.

"My soup's too hot to eat yet," she said. "I thought I might get some drawin' done while I wait for it to cool."

Papa snorted. "Humph! Fiddlin' with a dirty stick of charcoal is a waste of time!" He grabbed the loaf of bread from the wooden bowl in the center of the table and tore off a piece. Then he dipped the bread into his bowl of soup and popped it into his mouth.

Kelly wasn't sure how she should respond to his grumbling, so she leaned over and blew on her soup instead of saying anything.

Mama, who was dishing up her own bowl of soup at the stove, spoke up. "I don't see what harm there'd be in the girl drawin' while her soup cools, Amos."

Papa slammed his fist down on the table so hard, Kelly's piece of bread flew up and landed on the floor. "If I want your opinion, Dorrie, I'll ask for it!"

Kelly gulped. She hated it when Papa yelled at Mama. It wasn't right, but she didn't know what she could do about it. Only God could change Papa's heart, and she was growing weary of praying for such.

"Well, what are ya sittin' there lollygaggin' for?" Papa bellowed. "Start eatin', or I'm gonna pitch your writing tablet into the stove."

Kelly grabbed her spoon. No way could she let her dad carry through with his threat. She'd eat all her soup in a hurry, even if she burned her tongue in the process.

Awhile later, she was back on the towpath. She'd given the mules some oats in their feedbags, and they were munching away as they plodded dutifully along. Kelly knew they were making good time, and they'd probably pass Mike Cooper's sometime early this evening. She'd hoped to ask Papa about stopping by the store, but he'd been so cross during lunch, she'd lost her nerve.

Besides, what reason would she give for stopping? She sure couldn't tell her dad she wanted to make a few more drawings so Mike could try to sell them in his store. Papa had made it clear the way he felt about Kelly wasting time on her artwork. If she told him her plans, Papa might make good on his threat and pitch her tablet into the stove.

"If he ever does that, I'll make another one or find some old pieces of cardboard to draw on," Kelly fumed.

A young boy about eight years old crossed Kelly's path. He carried a fishing pole in one hand and a metal bucket in the other. The child stopped on the path and looked at Kelly as though she was daft. Had he overhead her talking to herself?

Kelly stopped walking. "Goin' fishin'?" *What a dumb question. Of course he's goin' fishin'. Why else would he be carryin' a pole?*

The freckle-faced, red-haired lad offered Kelly a huge grin, revealing a missing front tooth. "Thought I'd try to catch myself a few catfish. They was bitin' real good yesterday afternoon."

"You live around here?" Kelly questioned.

"Yep. Up the canal a ways."

Kelly's forehead wrinkled. She didn't remember seeing the boy before, and she wondered why he wasn't in school. The youngster's overalls were torn and dirty, and when Kelly glanced down at his bare feet, she shuddered. It was too cold yet to be going without shoes. Maybe the child was so poor his folks couldn't afford to buy him any decent footwear.

"My pap's workin' up at Mauch Chunk, loadin' coal," the boy said before Kelly could voice any questions.

"But I thought you said you lived nearby."

He nodded. "For the last couple months we've been livin' in an old shanty halfway up the canal." He frowned. "Don't see Pap much these days."

"Do you live with your mother?" Kelly asked.

The boy offered her another toothless grin. "Me, Ma, and little Ted. He's my baby brother. Pap was outa work for a spell, but things will be better now that he's got a job loadin' dirty coal."

Kelly's heart went out to the young child, since she could relate to being poor. Of course, Papa had always worked, and they'd never done without the basic necessities. Still, she had no money of her own, and that bothered Kelly a lot.

"Kelly McGregor, why have you stopped?"

Kelly whirled around at the sound of her dad's angry-sounding voice. He was leaning over the side of the boat, shaking his fist at her.

"Sorry, Papa," she hollered back. "Nice chattin' with you," Kelly said to the child. "Hope you catch plenty of fish today." She gave the boy a quick wave and started off.

As Kelly led her mules down the rutted path, she found herself envying the freckle-faced boy with the holes in his britches. At least he wasn't being forced to work all day.

ह✦

Mike pulled a pocket watch from his pant's pocket. It was almost six o'clock. He needed to close up the store and head on over to the preacher's place for supper. All day long he'd hoped the McGregors would stop by, but they hadn't, and he'd seen no sign of their boat. Of course, they could have gone by without him seeing, as there were many times throughout the day when he'd been busy with customers. As tempting as it had been, Mike knew he couldn't stand at the window all day and watch for Amos McGregor's canal boat. He had a store to run, and that took precedence over daydreaming about Kelly or watching for her dad's boat to come around the bend.

Mike put the "closed" sign in the store window and grabbed his jacket from a wall peg near the door. He was almost ready to leave when he remembered that tonight was Betsy's birthday and he should take her a gift.

He glanced around the store, looking for something appropriate. Mike noticed the stack of Bibles he had displayed on a shelf near the front of his store. He'd given plenty of them away, but he guessed Betsy, being a preacher's daughter, probably had at least one Bible in her possession.

As he continued to survey his goods, Mike's gaze came to rest on Kelly's drawings, tacked up on one wall. What better gift to give someone than something made by one of the locals? He chose the picture that showed two children fishing along the canal. He thought Betsy would like it. This would be Kelly's first sale, and he would give her the money she had coming as soon as he saw her again.

Since it was a pleasant spring evening with no sign of rain, Mike decided to walk to the Nelsons' rather than ride his horse or hitch up the buggy. He scanned the canal, looking for any sign of the McGregors' boat, but the only movement on the water was a pair of mallard ducks.

Mike filled his lungs with fresh air as he trudged off toward Walnutport. Sometime later, he arrived at the Nelsons' front door.

Betsy greeted him, looking prim and proper in a crisp white blouse and long blue skirt. Her hair was pulled into its usual tight bun at the back of her head.

"Come in, Mr. Cooper—I mean, Mike," she said sweetly. "Supper is ready, so let me take your coat."

Mike stepped inside the small, cozy parsonage and slipped off his jacket. He was about to hand it to Betsy when he remembered the picture he'd rolled up and put inside his pocket. He retrieved it and handed the drawing to Betsy. "Happy birthday."

Betsy smiled and unrolled the picture. She studied it a few seconds, and her forehead creased as she squinted her eyes. "This isn't one of those drawings young Kelly McGregor drew, is it?"

Mike nodded. "I thought you might like it, seeing as how there are children in the picture."

Her frown deepened. "What makes you think I have a fondness for children?"

"Well, I . . . that is, doesn't everyone have a soft spot for little ones?" Mike thought about his desire to have a large family, and he remembered reading how Jesus had taken time to visit with children. It only seemed natural for a preacher's daughter to like kids.

Betsy scrunched up her nose, as though some foul odor had permeated the room. "Children are sometimes hard to handle, and I don't envy anyone who's a parent." She batted her eyelashes a few times. "I get along better with adults."

Mike wondered if there was something in Betsy's eye. Or maybe she had trouble seeing and needed a pair of spectacles.

"Do you like Kelly's charcoal drawing or not?" he asked.

Betsy glanced at the picture in her hand. "I'll find a place for it, since you were thoughtful enough to bring me a present."

Mike drew in a deep breath and followed Betsy into the next room, where a table was set for three. Preacher Nelson stood in front of the fireplace, and he smiled at Mike.

"Good to see you, Son. Glad you could make it tonight."

Mike nodded and forced a smile in return. He had a feeling it was going to be a long evening, and he could hardly wait for it to come to an end.

7

*K*elly plodded along the towpath, tired from another long day, and feeling frustrated because they'd passed Mike's store without stopping. It was getting dark by the time they got to that section of the navigation system, and she hadn't seen any lights in the store windows. Maybe Mike was closed for the day.

It had been less than a week since Kelly had left three of her drawings with him. Chances were none of them had sold yet. By the time they did stop at Cooper's General Store, Kelly thought she would have a few more drawings to give Mike, and hopefully he'd have good news about the ones he was trying to sell. In the meantime, Kelly knew she needed to be patient.

"Patient and determined," she muttered into the night air. The moon was full this evening, and Kelly could see some distance ahead. They were coming to another lock, and Papa was already blowing on his conch shell to announce their arrival to the lock tender.

Kelly looked forward to each lock they went through. It gave her a chance to rest, tend to the mules, or draw.

She patted her apron pocket. *That's why I keep my tablet and a hunk of charcoal with me most of the time.*

Tonight, however, there were no boats ahead of them, and they went through the lock rather quickly. Kelly wasn't disappointed. It was too dark to draw anyway, and getting through the lock meant they would soon be on their way.

Kelly was hungry and tired. She could hardly wait to stop for the night. She didn't smell the usual aroma of cooking food coming from the boat, however. It made her wonder if Mama was tired and had decided to serve a cold meal. Maybe cheese and bread, with a piece of fruit or some carrot sticks. At this moment, anything would have tasted good.

When Kelly thought she'd die of hunger and couldn't take another step, Papa hollered for her to stop. With her dad's help, Kelly loaded the mules onto the boat, where they would be bedded down in the enclosed area reserved for them. If they'd been at a place where they could have stabled the mules, they wouldn't have to go through this procedure.

Kelly stretched her limbs with a weary sigh. "What's Mama got planned for supper, do ya know?"

Papa shook his head. "Your mama ain't feelin' well, and she's taken to her bed. You'll have to see about supper tonight."

Kelly felt immediate concern. "Mama's sick? What's wrong, and why didn't you tell me sooner?"

Papa shrugged. "Saw no need."

"But I could've come aboard and started supper. Maybe seen if there was somethin' I could do to make Mama more comfortable."

Papa grunted. "It's best you kept on walkin'. I don't wanna be late picking up my load of coal in Mauch Chunk tomorrow."

Kelly stared down at her clenched hands as anger churned in her stomach. All Papa cared about was hauling coal and making money he never shared. Didn't he give a hoot that Mama was sick in bed?

Feeling as though she carried the weight of the world on her shoulders, Kelly headed for their small kitchen. She would get some soup heating on the stove, then go below to see how Mama was doing.

A short time later, Kelly and her dad sat at the kitchen table, eating soup and bread—leftovers from their afternoon meal. Kelly had checked on her mother awhile ago, and she'd found her sleeping. She didn't have the heart to wake her, so she tiptoed out of her parents' cubicle with the intention of offering Mama a bowl of soup later on.

"You'd better get to sleep right after ya clean up the dishes," Papa said. "I'm planning to head out at the first light of day tomorrow mornin'." He wiped his mouth on the edge of his shirtsleeve. "If your mama's still feelin' poorly, you'll need to get breakfast made before we go."

Kelly watched the flame flicker from the candle in the center of the table. More chores to do. Just what she didn't need. She'd better pray extra hard for Mama tonight.

ॐ

Mike was never so glad to see his humble home as he was tonight. The time he'd spent at the Nelsons' place had left him feeling irritable and exhausted. Didn't Betsy ever stop talking or batting her eyelashes? Reverend Nelson had acted a bit strange all evening too. He kept dropping hints about his daughter needing a God-fearing husband, and he'd even asked Mike to sit on the sofa beside Betsy as they drank their coffee after dinner. Maybe the preacher was trying to link Mike up with his daughter, but it wasn't going to work. Mike had other ideas about who was the right woman for him.

Mike hung his jacket on a wall peg near the door, sank into an overstuffed chair by the stone fireplace, and looked around the room. He really did need someone to help fill his lonely evening hours. He'd been praying for a wife for some time now, but surely Betsy Nelson wasn't the one God had in mind for him. The woman got on his nerves, with her constant jabbering and opinionated remarks.

"It doesn't seem as if she likes children either," Mike murmured. He didn't see any way he could be happily married to a woman who didn't share his desire for a family. Mike saw children as a gift from God, not a nuisance, the way some folks did. He'd had customers come into his store who'd done nothing but yell at their kids, shouting orders or scolding them for every little thing.

Mike's thoughts went immediately to Kelly McGregor. Did she like children? Would Kelly make a good wife? Was she a believer in Christ? Mike knew so little about the young woman. The only thing he was sure of was that he was attracted to her.

I need to figure out some way for us to become better acquainted. With the McGregors' canal boat coming by every few days, there ought to be a chance to see Kelly more and get to know her.

Mike closed his eyes, and a few minutes later he fell asleep, dreaming about Kelly McGregor.

ॐ

Kelly stretched her aching limbs and forced herself to sit up. Inky darkness enveloped her room, but Papa was hollering at her to get up. She needed to see if Mama was still ailing, and if so, fix some breakfast. Then she'd have to feed the mules, lead them off the boat, and get ready to head for Mauch Chunk. She hadn't slept well the night before, and she'd had several dreams—one that involved Mike Cooper.

Why do I think about him so often? Kelly fumed. *Probably because he has my drawings, and I'm anxious to see if he's sold any. Yep, that's all there is to it—nothin' more.*

After Kelly washed up and got dressed, she rolled up her finished drawings and placed them inside her apron pocket, just in case they made a stop at Cooper's store today. Then she tiptoed over to her folks' room to check on Mama.

Her mother was awake, but she looked terrible. Dark circles lay beneath her eyes, her skin was pasty white, and her forehead glistened with sweat.

"How are ya feelin' this mornin'?" Kelly whispered.

Mama lifted her head off the pillow and offered Kelly a weak smile. "I'll be back on my feet in no time a'tall. It's just a sore throat, and my body aches some too."

Kelly adjusted the patchwork quilt covering her mother's bed. "I'll bring you a cup of hot tea and a bowl of cornmeal mush as soon as I get Papa fed. He might be less crabby if his belly is full."

Mama nodded, coughed, and relaxed against the pillow. "I'm sorry you're havin' to do more chores than usual. If Sarah were still here, your load would be a bit lighter."

Kelly shrugged. She didn't want to think about her runaway sister. "I'll manage. You just get well." She patted the quilt where Mama's feet were hidden. "I'll be back soon."

A short while later, Kelly was in the kitchen preparing breakfast.

"What about lunch and supper?" she asked her dad when she handed him a bowl of mush.

His forehead wrinkled. "What about it?"

"If I'm gonna be leadin' the mules all day, Mama's still sick in bed—"

Papa grunted and pulled on the end of his mustache. "Guess that means I'll be stuck with the cookin'."

"But how will you do that, watch up ahead, and steer the boat too?" she questioned.

"I'll manage somehow. Don't guess I've got much other choice." He snorted. "If that renegade sister of yours hadn't run off with Sam Turner, we wouldn't be shorthanded right now."

Kelly drew in a deep breath, feeling a bit put out with her sister too.

Things seemed to go from bad to worse as the day progressed. Kelly kept an eye on the boat, and a couple times she spotted her dad racing back and forth between the woodstove sitting on the open deck and the stern of the boat. He would lift the pot lid and take a look at the beans she knew he was cooking, run back to the stern and give the tiller a twist, and do it all over again. Kelly wondered if he might collapse or run the boat aground from all that rushing around.

When it came time for lunch, Papa gulped down a hasty meal, leaped from the boat to the towpath, and took over leading the mules so Kelly could eat. She did all right getting into the boat, but when she jumped over the side again, she missed her mark and landed in the canal with a splash.

Now she was walking the towpath in a sopping wet skirt that stuck to her legs like a tick on a mule. She'd been forced to remove her boots because they were waterlogged, and she sure hoped no snakes came slithering across the path and nailed her bare feet.

To make matters worse, the drawings she'd put in her pocket that morning had gotten ruined when she fell in the water. Now she had nothing to give Mike if she saw him today.

The only bright spot in Kelly's day was when Papa told her they would be stopping by Cooper's General Store later on. He wanted to see if Mike had any cough syrup in stock. Papa thought it might make Mama sleep better if they could get her cough calmed down. Stopping at the store would be good for Mama as well as Kelly. She only hoped her dress would be dry by the time they got there.

8

For the past couple of days Mike had tried unsuccessfully to sell some of Kelly's drawings. "Isn't there anyone in the area who can see her talent and needs something special to give as a gift?" he muttered as he studied the two remaining pictures displayed on the wall of his store. Was it possible that Kelly wasn't as talented as Mike thought? Maybe folks were put off by the simplicity of the paper she used. Maybe he was too caught up in his unexplained feelings for the young woman. He might have been thinking with his heart instead of his head when he'd agreed to try to sell some of her artwork.

Mike clicked his tongue against the roof of his mouth. Now he was going to have to face Kelly when she stopped by the store again and tell her nothing had sold.

That's not entirely true, he reminded himself. *I took one of her pictures to give Betsy Nelson, and I plan to pay Kelly her share for it. Maybe I should buy a second picture, then frame and hang it in my house.* Mike smiled, feeling a sense of satisfaction because of his idea. Kelly wouldn't have to know who'd bought the drawings. She'd probably be happy just getting the money.

With that decided, Mike removed the picture of Kelly's two mules and stuck it under the front counter. He would take it home when he was done for the day.

Mike pulled an envelope out of a drawer underneath the counter and wrote Kelly's name on the front. Then he withdrew some money from the cash box and tucked it inside. Hopefully he'd be able to sell her other drawing before Kelly came by the store again.

"I need to get busy and quit thinking about Kelly McGregor,"

Mike muttered as he grabbed a broom and started sweeping the floor. Thoughts of the young woman with dark brown eyes and long, coffee-colored hair were consuming too much of his time.

Mike had just put the broom away in the storage closet when the front door opened. He pivoted, and his heartbeat quickened. Kelly McGregor stood there, her straw hat askew, and her long, gray skirt, wrinkled, dirty, and damp. She looked a mess, yet he thought she was beautiful.

Mike swallowed hard and moved toward her. "Kelly. It's good to see you again."

è•

"Hello, Mike Cooper," Kelly said, feeling timid and unsure of herself.

He smiled, and the dimple in his chin seemed to be winking at her.

She took a tentative step forward. "Mama's sick and needs some cough syrup. Have ya got any on hand?"

"I think there's still several bottles on the back shelf." Mike pointed to the other end of the store. "Would you like me to get one for you?"

She nodded. "If ya don't mind."

"Not at all." Mike headed in the direction he'd pointed, and Kelly turned her attention to the wall nearest the door. One of her drawings of children playing along the canal was there, but the other two were nowhere in sight. A feeling of excitement coursed through her veins. Had Mike sold them? Did she have some money coming now? Dare she ask?

When Mike returned a few minutes later, she was still studying her drawing. She glanced over at him. He held a bottle of cough syrup and stood so close she could smell the aroma of soap, which indicated that he at least was wearing clean clothes. Mike's hair was nicely combed too. She, on the other hand, looked terrible. He probably thought she was a filthy pig. Should she explain about falling into the canal? Would he even care?

"You're quite talented," Mike said, bringing Kelly's thoughts to a halt. "Have you done any more pictures lately?"

"I did have three more ready, but Mama's been sick, so Papa and me have had to share all the chores." She glanced down at her soiled skirt and frowned. "As you can probably see, I fell in the canal earlier today, trying to jump from the boat back to the towpath. My drawings were in my pocket, and they got ruined."

Mike shook his head slowly. "Sorry to hear that. I did wonder why your skirt was so rumpled and wet." He moved toward the counter, and Kelly followed. "Sorry you're having to do double duty, but maybe this will make you feel better." He set the cough syrup down, pulled open a drawer beneath the counter, withdrew an envelope, and handed it to Kelly.

She took the envelope and studied it a few seconds. Her name was written on the front. "What's this?"

"It's your share of the money for two of the drawings you left with me."

She smiled up at him. "You really sold two of my pictures?"

Mike's ears turned slightly red, and he looked a little flustered. Was he embarrassed because he hadn't sold all three?

"I—uh—found someone who really appreciates your talent," he said, staring down at the wooden counter.

Kelly's smile widened. "I'm so glad. Once Mama gets better, I'll have a bit more time to draw, and maybe when we stop by here again I'll have a few more pictures to give you."

Mike's smile seemed to be forced, and his face had turned red like his ears. Something seemed to be troubling him, and Kelly aimed to find out what it was.

"Is everything all right? You look kinda upset."

Mike lifted his gaze. "Everything's fine. Feel free to bring me as many drawings as you like."

Kelly felt a sense of relief wash over her. If she could get Mama back on her feet, she'd have more time to draw. Mike wanted her to bring more pictures, she'd already sold two, and things were looking hopeful. She slipped the envelope into her apron pocket and turned toward the door.

"Aren't you forgetting something?" Mike called after her.

Kelly whirled around and felt the heat of a blush spread over her face when Mike held up the bottle of cough syrup. She giggled self-consciously and fished in her pocket for the coins to pay for her purchase.

Mike's fingers brushed hers as she dropped the money into his hand, and Kelly felt an unexpected shiver tickle her spine. What was there about Mike Cooper that made her feel so giddy and out of breath? Was it the crooked smile beneath his perfectly shaped moustache? Those hazel-colored eyes that seemed capable of looking into her soul? The lock of sandy brown hair that fell across his forehead?

Kelly snatched up the bottle of cough syrup, mumbled a quick thanks, and fled from the store.

ह&

Mike couldn't believe the way Kelly had run out of the store. Had he said or done something to upset her? He'd thought they were getting along pretty well, and Kelly had seemed pleased about her drawings being sold.

Maybe she suspects I'm the one who bought the pictures. But how could she know that? He'd been careful not to give her too much information, so she couldn't have guessed he was the one. He hadn't actually lied to her, but he didn't see the need to tell Kelly he was the one either. She might have taken it the wrong way.

Seeing Kelly again had only reinforced the strong feelings Mike was having for her. When their hands touched briefly during the money exchange, he had felt as though he'd been struck by a bolt of lightning. Had Kelly felt it too? Could that have been the reason for her sudden departure? Or maybe she just needed to get back to work. The canal boaters always seemed to be in a hurry to get to and from their pickup and delivery points. That was probably all it was. Kelly's dad had no doubt told her to hurry, and she was only complying with his wishes.

How am I going to get to know Kelly better if she only stops by the store once in awhile, then stays just long enough to buy something and hurries off again? Mike closed his eyes, folded his hands, and placed them on the counter. *Lord, would You please work it out so Kelly and I can spend more time together?*

Mike was still standing behind the counter, mulling things over, when Amos McGregor entered the store.

"Mr. McGregor, your daughter was just here buying some cough syrup for your wife."

"Don'tcha think I know that?" the boatman snapped. His bright red hair stuck out at odd angles, like he hadn't combed it in a couple of days, and there were dark circles under both eyes.

Mike's only response to Amos's comment was a shrug of his shoulders. It was obvious by the scowl on the man's face that he wasn't in a good mood, and there was no point in saying anything that might rile him further.

"The wife's been sick for a couple of days," Amos mumbled. "That left me stuck doin' most of her chores." He stuffed his hands inside the pocket of his dark blue jacket and started for the back of the store.

"Can I help you find something?" Mike called after him.

"Need some of that newfangled soap that floats," came the muffled reply. "I told Kelly to get some, but as usual, she had her head in the clouds and forgot."

Mike skirted around the counter and went straight to the shelf where he kept the cleaning supplies and personal toiletries. "Here's what you're looking for, Sir," he said, lifting a bar of soap for the man's inspection.

"Yep. That's it, all right." Amos shook his head slowly. "I dropped our last bar overboard by mistake and didn't wanna take the time to stop and fish it outa the canal." He grabbed another bar of soap off the shelf and marched back to the counter. "Better to have a spare," he muttered.

Mike nodded and slipped the cakes of soap into a paper sack. "Good idea." He handed the bag to Amos. "Need anything else?"

"Nope." Amos plunked some coins on the counter and started for the front door.

"Feel free to stop by anytime," Mike called after him. "And if you ever need a place to spend the night, I'll gladly let you stable your mules in my barn."

The boatman mumbled something under his breath and shut the door.

Mike shook his head. "I wonder why that man's such a grouch? No wonder Kelly acts like a scared rabbit much of the time. Guess I'd better pray for the both of them."

On Saturday evening, much to Mike's surprise, Kelly and her mother stopped by the store.

"That cough syrup you sold Kelly a few days ago sure helped me sleep," Dorrie said as she stepped up beside Mike, who'd been stocking some shelves near the front of the store.

Mike smiled. "I'm glad to hear that, Mrs. McGregor. Are you feeling better?"

She nodded. "I'm back to doin' most of my own chores now too."

Mike glanced at Kelly out of the corner of his eye. She was standing by the candy counter, eyeing something she was obviously interested in. He started to move toward the young woman, but Dorrie's next words stopped him.

"Amos is feelin' poorly now, so we need more medicine." Her forehead wrinkled, and she blinked a couple of times. "Sure hope you've got some, 'cause I used up the bottle of cough syrup Kelly bought."

Mike nodded toward the back of the store. "There's a couple bottles on the second shelf to the right. Want me to get one for you?"

Dorrie glanced over at Kelly, still peering inside the candy counter, and she shook her head. "Why don'tcha see what kind of sweet treat my daughter would like, while I fetch the medicine?"

Mike didn't have to be asked twice. He'd been holding a tin of canned peaches, which he promptly set on the shelf, and then he hurried over to Kelly.

"How are you?" he asked. "Sure hope you're not gettin' sick too."

"Nope. I'm healthy as a mule."

"Glad to hear it, but I'm sorry about your dad. Is he able to keep on working?"

"He made it through the day, even with his fits of coughing and fever. I think he's plannin' to tie up here and spend the night. We'll stay all day Sunday, so he can rest." Kelly's gaze went to her mother, who was at the back of the store. "Mama doesn't have all her strength back yet either, so a good day's rest should do 'em both some good."

And you, Kelly, Mike thought as he studied her face. There were dark circles under her eyes, which gave evidence to the fact that she too was tired and probably needed a break.

"The last time your dad was in the store, I told him I'd be glad to stable your mules in my barn anytime he wanted to dock here for the night."

"That's right nice of you." Kelly gazed at the candy counter with a look of longing on her face.

Mike wondered how long it had been since she had eaten any candy. Without hesitation, he opened the hinged lid on the glass case. "Help yourself to whatever you like—my treat."

Kelly stiffened. "Oh, no. I couldn't let you do that. Thanks to you sellin' a couple of my charcoal drawings, I've got money of my own now." She shrugged. "Although, it's safely hidden in my room on the boat, and I'd have to go back and get it."

"Wouldn't you rather spend it on something more useful than candy?"

She pursed her lips. "Probably should be savin' my money, but I've sure got a hankerin' for some lemon drops."

Mike reached down and grabbed the glass jar filled with sugar-coated lemon drops. "Take as many as you like, and please consider it a present from me to you."

Kelly tipped her head to one side, and he knew she was contemplating his offer. Finally with a nervous giggle, she agreed.

He filled a small paper bag half full of candy and handed it to her, hoping she wouldn't change her mind.

She took the sack and stuffed it in her apron pocket. "Thank you."

"You're welcome."

Kelly shuffled her feet, and her boots scraped nosily against the wooden planks. Why did she seem so nervous? Was it because her mother was nearby and might be listening in on their conversation?

Hoping to put her at ease, Mike reached out and touched Kelly's arm. She recoiled like she'd been bitten by a snake, and he quickly withdrew his hand.

"Sorry, I didn't mean to startle you."

Kelly's only reply was a slight shrug of her shoulders. What was wrong? They'd had such a pleasant visit the last time she'd come by the store.

"Did you bring me any more drawings?" Mike asked, hoping the change of subject might ease the tension he felt filling up the space between them.

She shook her head. "I'm out of charcoal, and for the last couple days Papa's been burnin' coal instead of wood in our cook stove. I haven't come across any cold campfires along the canal lately neither."

So that was the problem. Kelly was feeling bad because she hadn't been able to draw, and she'd promised Mike she would have more pictures the next time she came by.

Mike had a brand new set of sketching pencils for sale, along with some tubes of oil paints. He would have gladly given them to her but was sure she would say no. It had taken some persuasion to get her to take a few lemon drops, and they weren't worth half as much as the art supplies. Since Kelly did have some money of her own, she could probably purchase a box of pencils, but she might be saving up for something more important.

Suddenly, Mike had an idea. "I've got some burned charcoal chips in my home fireplace at the back of the store," he announced. "How 'bout I run in there and get them for you?"

Kelly hesitated a moment but finally nodded. "That would be right nice."

Before she had a chance to change her mind, Mike hurried to the back of the store. He passed Kelly's mother on his way to the door leading to his attached house.

"I'll be right back, Mrs. McGregor. Take your time looking around for anything you might need."

Kelly watched Mike's retreating form as he disappeared behind the door at the back of his store. He seemed like such a caring young man. Probably would make someone a mighty fine husband. Maybe he and the preacher's daughter would link up. Betsy had seemed pretty friendly to him the last time Kelly saw the two of them together.

She frowned. Why did the idea of Mike and Betsy Nelson together make her feel so squeamish? She reached into the sack inside her pocket and withdrew a lemon drop, then popped the piece of candy into her mouth.

"We'll head on back to the boat as soon as the storekeeper returns and I pay for the cough syrup and a few other things I found," Mama said, driving Kelly's thoughts to the back of her mind.

Kelly's response was a slow nod of her head.

"Mike Cooper seems like a nice young man," Mama remarked.

Kelly nodded again. "He offered to let us stable Herman and Hector in his barn for the night."

Mama's dark eyebrows lifted. "For free?"

"I think so. He never said a word about money."

"Hmm . . . guess as soon as we leave the store, you should get the mules fed and ready to bed down then."

"I'd be happy to," Kelly readily agreed. "I'm sure Hector and Herman will be right glad to have a bigger place to stay tonight than they have on board our boat."

"You're probably right." Mama smiled. "Say, I was thinkin'—since tomorrow's Sunday, and we won't be movin' on 'til early Monday morning, why don't the two of us head into town and go to church?"

Kelly opened her mouth to respond, but Mama rushed on. "It's been a good while since I've sat inside a real church and worshiped God with other Christian folks."

"Well, I . . . uh . . . ." Kelly swallowed against the urge to say what was really on her mind. Being in church would make her feel uncomfortable—like others were looking down their noses at the poor boatman's daughter who wore men's boots and smelled like a dirty mule. Kelly had seen the way Betsy Nelson turned her nose up whenever the two of them met along the towpath. She wasn't good enough to sit inside a pretty church building; it was just that simple.

"I'm waitin' for your answer," Mama said, giving Kelly's shoulder a gentle tap.

"I was kinda hoping to get rested up tomorrow. Maybe do a bit of drawin'."

Mama's squinted eyes and furrowed brow revealed her obvious concern. "You ain't feelin' poorly too, I hope."

Kelly shook her head. "Just tired is all."

"And well you should be," Mama agreed. "The last few days, you and your dad have been workin' real hard trying to do all my chores plus keeping up with your own jobs as well." She gave Kelly a hug. "I think you're right. It might be good for us all to spend the day restin'."

Kelly felt bad about not being willing to attend church with her mother. She could tell by Mama's wistful expression that she really did miss Sunday services inside a church building. Reading the Bible every night after supper was a good thing, but it wasn't the same as being in fellowship with other believers.

She and her mother moved away from the candy counter and went to wait for Mike by the wooden counter where customers paid for their purchases.

A few seconds later, Mike entered the store, carrying a large paper sack. He handed it to Kelly and grinned. "This should get you by for awhile."

She peered inside the bag. Several large clumps of charcoal, as well as some smaller ones, completely filled it. Mike was right. These would last a good while, and tonight she planned to start putting them to use. "Thanks," she murmured.

He winked at her. "You're more than welcome."

Kelly cleared her throat, feeling kind of warm and jittery inside. Maybe she was coming down with whatever had been ailing her folks. A day of rest might do her more good than she realized.

10

*S*unday morning dawned with a blue, cloudless sky. It would be the perfect day for Kelly to enjoy the warm sun and draw. She hurried through her breakfast and morning chores, anxious for some time alone. Mama would be tending to Papa's needs for the next little while, and after that, she would probably take a rest herself.

Papa had taken to his bed last night and not even shown his face at the breakfast table. Kelly figured he must be pretty sick if he wasn't interested in food, for her dad usually had a ravenous appetite. She had taken him a tray with a cup of tea and bowl of oatmeal a little while ago, but Papa turned his nose up at both and said he wanted to be left alone—needed some sleep, that was all.

It seemed strange for Kelly to see her dad, who was usually up early and raring to go, curled up in a fetal position with a patchwork quilt pulled up to his ears. His breathing sounded labored, and he wheezed and coughed like the steam train that ran beside the canal, despite the medicine Mama had been spoon-feeding him since their visit to Mike's store last evening.

Thinking about Mike Cooper made Kelly remember their mules had been sleeping in his barn all night. She needed to feed and groom the animals, then take them outdoors for some fresh air and exercise. Wouldn't do for the mules to get lazy because they'd stopped for a bit. As soon as she was finished tending the critters, Kelly hoped to finally have some free time.

As she headed for the barn, which sat directly behind Mike's house, Kelly hummed her favorite song—"Hunks-a-go Pudding." Would Mama feel up to fixing a big meal today? Would it include a roast with some yummy hunks-a-go pudding? Kelly sure hoped so. It had been a good long while since she'd enjoyed the succulent taste of roast with beef and hunks-a-go pudding, where the batter was put in the fat left over from the meat and then fried in a pan on top of the stove.

Forcing thoughts of food to the back of her mind, Kelly opened the barn door and peered inside. Except for the gentle braying of the mules, all was quiet. The sweet smell of hay wafted up to her nose, and she sniffed deeply. She stepped inside and was almost to the stall where Hector and Herman were stabled when she heard another sound. Someone was singing.

"Sweet hour of prayer, sweet hour of prayer, that calls me from a world of care."

Kelly plodded across the dirt floor, and the sound of the clear, masculine voice grew closer. She recognized it as belonging to Mike Cooper.

"And bids me at my Father's throne, make all my wants and wishes known."

Kelly halted, feeling like an intruder on Mike's quiet time alone with God. He must be deeply religious, for not only was he kind-hearted, but he sang praises to God. Whenever Kelly sang, it was some silly canaler's song like "Hunks-a-go Pudding" or "You Rusty Canaler, You'll Never Get Rich." As a young child she would often sing "Jesus Loves Me," but she'd been a lot happier back then. Sarah was still living with them, helping share the burden of walking the mules and visiting with Kelly for hours on end. Papa expected twice as much from Kelly now that Sarah was gone. But was that any excuse to quit worshiping the Lord in song?

Kelly knew the answer deep in her soul. She was angry with God for not changing Papa's heart. She was angry with Papa for being so stubborn and hot-tempered and angry with Sarah for running off and leaving her to face Papa's temper while she did all the work.

I'll show them. I'll show everyone that Kelly McGregor doesn't need anyone to get along in this world. I'm gonna make it on my own someday.

When Mike's song ended, Kelly moved forward again. She could see him sitting on a small wooden stool, milking a fat brown-and-white cow.

She cleared her throat real loud to make her presence known and stepped into the stall where Herman and Hector had bedded down for the night.

"Good morning," Mike called to her.

"Mornin'," she responded.

"Looks like it's gonna be a beautiful day."

"Yep. Right nice."

"What plans have you made for this Lord's Day?" he asked.

Kelly patted Herman's flank and leaned into the sturdy mule. "As soon as I get these two ready, I plan to take 'em outside for some exercise and fresh air."

Mike didn't say anything in reply, and Kelly could hear the steady *plunk, plink, plunk,* as the cow's milk dropped into the bucket. It was a soothing sound, and she found herself wishing she had a real, honest-to-goodness home with a barn, chicken coop, and maybe a bit of land. For nine months out of the year, her home was the inside of a canal boat, and then during the winter, it was a cramped, dingy flat at a boardinghouse in Easton. Papa seemed to like their vagabond life, but Kelly hated it—more and more the older she got. Someday she hoped to leave it all behind. Oh, for the chance to fulfill her dreams.

ॐ

Mike grabbed the bucket of milk and headed for the stall where Kelly's mules had been stabled. He was finally being given the chance to spend a few minutes alone with Kelly, and he aimed to take full advantage. If things went as he hoped, he would have the pleasure of her company for several hours today.

Mike leaned against the wooden beam outside the mules' stall and watched Kelly as she fed and groomed her beasts of burden. She wasn't wearing her usual straw hat this morning, and her lustrous brown hair hung down her back in long, loose waves. His fingers itched to reach out and touch those silky tresses.

"You're good with the mules," he murmured.

Kelly jumped, apparently startled and unaware that he'd been watching her. "Hector and Herman are easy to work with."

Mike drew in a deep breath. *May as well get this over with.* "I . . . uh . . . was wondering if you'd like to go on a picnic with me later today."

Kelly turned her head to look directly at him, and she blinked a couple of times. "A picnic? You and me?"

He nodded, then chuckled. "That's what I had in mind."

"Well, I was plannin' to spend some time drawin', and—"

"No reason you can't draw after we share our picnic lunch."

She hesitated a few seconds. "Mama may need my help with somethin', and my folks might not approve of me goin' on a picnic."

Mike smiled. At least she hadn't said no. He took that as a good sign. "While you finish up with the mules, how about I go talk to your parents?"

Kelly's forehead wrinkled. "I don't know if that's such a good idea."

"If they say it's all right, would you be willing to eat a picnic lunch with me?"

She nodded, but made no verbal reply. It was enough affirmation for Mike, and he grinned at her. "Great! I'll take this milk into the house, get cleaned up a bit, and run down to the boat to speak with your folks."

"Papa's still in bed," Kelly said. "He ain't feelin' much better today than he was last night."

"Sorry to hear it. I'll ask your mother." Mike hurried out of the barn before Kelly had a chance to say anything more, and he hummed "Sweet Hour of Prayer" all the way. God was already answering his prayer for the day, and he felt like he was ten feet tall.

᳂

Kelly couldn't believe her mother had actually given permission for Mike Cooper to take her on a picnic. Maybe she felt bad because Kelly worked so hard and rarely got a day off. Or it might be that Mama needed some quiet time by herself today, so she thought it would be good if Kelly were gone awhile.

The idea of a picnic did seem kind of nice. It would be a chance for Kelly to relax and enjoy Mike's company, as well as the good food he'd promised to prepare. On the other hand, spending time alone with the fine-looking storekeeper might not be such a good thing. What if he got the notion she was interested in him? Would Mike expect her to do more things with him when she was in the area? In some ways, she hoped they could. Life along the canal was lonely, especially for Kelly, whose only companions were a pair of mules.

Kelly stood in her tiny room below the boat's main deck and studied her reflection in the mirror that she kept in the trunk at the foot of her bed. Did she look presentable enough to accompany Mike Cooper on a picnic? Mike always smelled so clean, and he wore crisp trousers and shirts without holes or wrinkles. It was hard to believe he had no mother or wife caring for his needs. He must be very capable, she decided.

Mike had said he would meet Kelly out in front of his store, a little before noon. This gave her plenty of time to get ready, and she'd even taken a bath in the galvanized tub and washed her hair, using that new floating soap Mama liked so well.

Kelly grabbed a lock of hair, swung it over her shoulder, and sniffed deeply. "Smells clean enough to me." She glanced down at her dark green skirt and long-sleeved white blouse with puffy sleeves. Both were plain and unfashionable, but Kelly didn't care a hoot about fashion, only comfort and looking presentable enough to be seen in public. Her clothes were clean; Mama had washed them yesterday. At least today she wasn't likely to offend Mike by smelling like one of her mules.

Kelly took out her drawing tablet and a piece of charcoal and stuffed them in her oversized skirt pocket. Then she grabbed her straw hat and one of Mama's old quilts. At least they would have something soft to sit on during their picnic lunch. She left the room and tiptoed quietly past her parents' bedroom. It wouldn't be good to wake Papa. He'd probably be furious if he knew she was taking the day off to go on a picnic—especially with a man. If Papa got wind of her spending time with Mike Cooper, he might think she was going to up and run off, the way Sarah had. Well, that would never happen!

As Kelly stepped off the boat, she caught a glimpse of Reverend

Nelson and his daughter, Betsy. They were standing in front of Mike's store, and several boatmen and their families had gathered around.

It made no sense to Kelly. Shouldn't the preacher have been at his church, pounding the wooden pulpit and shouting at the congregation to repent and turn from their wicked ways? Instead, he was leading the group of people in song, and his daughter was playing along with her zither.

Kelly hoped to avoid the throng entirely, but Mike, who stood on the fringes, motioned her to join him. He was holding a wicker basket, and Kelly figured he was probably ready to head out on their picnic. If she hung back until the church service was over, it would mean they would lose some of their time together. If she joined Mike, he might say he was ready to go now.

Mike crooked his finger at Kelly again, and she inched her way forward. *Guess I may as well see what he's plannin' to do.*

*M*ike smiled at Kelly when she stepped up beside him.

"What's goin' on?" she whispered.

"Reverend Nelson finished his worship service early today, so he and Betsy decided to bring a bit of revival to the boatmen and their families who stayed in the area for the night."

"Do you attend their church in town?" Kelly asked.

Mike shrugged his shoulders. "Sometimes." The truth was, he used to go every Sunday, but here of late he'd been feeling mighty uncomfortable around Betsy Nelson. He'd stayed home the last couple weeks, praying and reading his Bible in solitude. He knew he shouldn't be using Betsy's overbearing, flirtatious ways as an excuse to stay away from church, but it was getting harder to deal with his troubling emotions where she was concerned. Especially since Kelly McGregor had come into his life.

He stared down at her, small and delicate, yet strong and reliable. Where did Kelly stand as far as spiritual things were concerned? He needed to find out soon, before he lost his heart to the beautiful young woman.

"Ready to head out on our picnic?" Kelly questioned.

Now was as good a time as any to see how interested she was in church.

"I thought maybe we'd stick around until Rev. Nelson is done preaching," Mike said. "It's been awhile since I've heard a good sermon." He studied Kelly's face to gauge her reaction. She looked a bit hesitant, but agreeably she nodded. He breathed a sigh of relief.

"Should we take a seat on the grass?" he asked, motioning to a spot a few feet away.

She followed him there and spread out the quilt she'd been holding so tightly.

Mike set the picnic basket down, and they both took a seat on the blanket. Leaning back on his elbows, Mike joined the group singing "Amazing Grace." His spirits soared as the music washed over him like gentle waves lapping against the shore. He loved to sing praises to God, and when the mood hit, he enjoyed blowing on the old mouth harp that had belonged to Grandpa Cooper.

He glanced over at Kelly. She wasn't singing, but her eyes were closed, and her face was lifted toward the sun. *She must be praying. That's a good indication that she knows the Lord personally.*

He smiled to himself. The day had started out even better than he'd expected.

ॐ

Kelly opened her eyes and looked around. A couple dozen people were seated on the ground. Some were singing, some lifted their hands in praise, and others quietly listened. She couldn't believe she'd let Mike talk her into staying around for this outdoor church service. It was a beautiful spring day, and she wanted to be away from the crowd, where she could listen to the sounds of nature and draw to her heart's content. When she'd agreed to accompany Mike on a picnic, the plan hadn't included church.

Kelly knew her attitude was wrong. She'd asked Jesus to forgive her sins several years ago. She should take pleasure in worshiping God. Besides, out here among the other boatmen and their families, Kelly didn't stick out like a sore thumb. Nobody but the preacher and his daughter were dressed in fine clothes, so Kelly blended right in with her unfashionable long cotton skirt and plain white blouse.

The singing was over now, and the Reverend had begun to preach. Kelly's gaze wandered until she noticed a young boy who sat several feet away. He had bright red hair, and his face and arms were covered with freckles. The child's looks weren't what captured Kelly's attention, though. It was the small green toad he was holding in his grubby hands. He stroked the critter's head as though it were a pet.

He's probably poor and doesn't own many toys. If his papa's a boatman, they travel up and down the canal most of the year, so the little guy can't have any real pets.

Kelly knew that wasn't entirely true. Many canalers owned dogs that either walked along the towpath or rode in the boat. She figured the little red-haired boy's dad was probably too cranky or too stingy to let his son own a dog or a cat. *Kind of like my dad. He'd never allow me to have a pet.*

Kelly's thoughts were halted as Preacher Nelson shouted, "God wants you to turn from your sins and repent!"

She sat up a little straighter and tried to look attentive when she noticed Mike look over at her. Had he caught her daydreaming? Did he think she was a sinner who needed to repent?

After the pastor's final prayer, he announced, "My daughter, Betsy, will now close our service with a solo."

Betsy stood up and began to strum her zither as she belted out the first verse of "Sweet By and By." As the young woman came to the last note, her voice cracked, and her faced turned redder than a radish.

Kelly stifled a chuckle behind her hand. *Serves the snooty woman right for thinkin' she's better'n me.*

"He that is without sin among you, let him cast a stone at her." Kelly gulped as she remembered that verse of Scripture from the Book of John. Mama had quoted it many times over the years.

The preacher's daughter might be uppity and kind of pushy at times, but truth be told, Kelly knew she was no better in God's eyes. Fact of the matter, Kelly felt that she was probably worse, for she often harbored resentment in her heart toward Papa. She resolved to try to do better.

When the service was over, Mike stood and grabbed their picnic basket. Kelly gathered up her quilt and tucked it under one arm. She'd thought they would head right off for their picnic, but Mike moved toward Preacher Nelson. Not knowing what else to do, Kelly followed.

"That was a fine sermon you preached," Mike said, shaking Reverend Nelson's hand.

The older man beamed. "Thank you, Mike. I'm glad you enjoyed it."

Betsy, who stood next to her father, smiled at Mike and fluttered her eyelashes. "How about the singing? Did you enjoy that too?"

Mike nodded. It was downright sickening the way Betsy kept eyeing him, as though she wanted to kiss the man, of all things.

Kelly nudged Mike in the ribs with her elbow. "Are we goin' on that picnic or not?"

"Yes . . . yes, of course," he stammered.

Why was Mike acting so nervous all of a sudden? Did being around Betsy Nelson do this to him? Kelly opened her mouth to say something, but Betsy cut her right off.

"You're going on a picnic, Mike?" Her eyelids fluttered again. "It's such a beautiful day, and I haven't been on a picnic since early last fall. Would you mind if I tag along?"

"Well, uh . . ." Mike turned to Kelly, as though he expected her to say something.

When she made no response, Betsy said, "You wouldn't mind if I joined you and Mike, would you, Kelly?"

Kelly's irritation flared up like fireflies buzzing on a muggy summer day. She didn't want to make an issue, so she merely shrugged her shoulders and made circles in the dirt with the toe of her boot.

"Great! It's all settled then." Betsy grinned like an eager child. "Have you got enough food for three, Mike?"

"Sure, I made plenty of fried chicken and biscuits."

Betsy turned to her father then. "I won't be gone long, Papa."

He smiled. "You go on with the young people and have yourself a good time. I want to visit with several folks, and if I'm fortunate enough to be invited to join one of the families for a meal, I probably won't be home until evening."

"Everything is perfect then. I'll see you at home later on." Betsy handed her father the zither and slipped her hand through the crook of Mike's arm. "So, where should we have this picnic?"

"Guess we'll look for a nice spot up the canal a bit." When Mike looked at Kelly, she noticed his face was a deep shade of red. Was he wondering why he'd invited her on a picnic? Did he wish he could spend time alone with Betsy Nelson? Should Kelly make up some excuse as to why she couldn't go? Maybe it would be best if she went off by herself for the day.

She had made up her mind to do just that, when Mike pulled away from Betsy and grabbed hold of Kelly's hand. "Let's be off," he announced. "I'm hungry as a bear!"

$$12$$

*K*elly, Mike, and Betsy sat in silence on the quilt. The picnic basket was empty now, and everyone admitted to being full. There had been plenty of food to go around.

Kelly leaned back on her elbows, soaking up the sun's warming rays and listening to the canal waters lapping against the bank. She felt relaxed and content and had almost forgotten her irritation over the preacher's daughter joining their picnic.

Seeing a couple of ducks on the water reminded Kelly that she'd brought along her drawing tablet and a piece of charcoal. She sat up and withdrew both from her skirt pocket and then quickly began to sketch. A flash of green on the mallard's head made her once again wish she could work with colored paints. Folks might be apt to buy a picture with color, as it looked more like the real thing.

"In another month or so the canal will be filled with swimmers," Betsy said, her high-pitched voice cutting into the serenely quiet moment.

"You're right about that," Mike agreed. "It scares me the way some youngsters swim so close to the canal boats. It's a wonder one of them doesn't get killed."

"I hear there's plenty of accidents on the canal," Betsy put in.

"Kelly could probably tell us a lot of stories in that regard," Mike said.

Kelly's mind took her back to a couple years ago, when she'd witnessed one of the lock tender's children fall between a boat and the lock. The little boy had been killed instantly—crushed to death. It was a pitiful sight to see the child's mother weeping and wailing for all she was worth.

Kelly had seen a few small children fall overboard and drown. Most folks who had little ones kept them tied to a rope so that wouldn't happen, but some who'd been careless paid the price with the loss of a child.

"Yep," Kelly murmured, "there's been quite a few deaths on the Lehigh Navigation System."

Mike groaned. "I was afraid of the water when I was a boy, so I never learned to swim as well as I probably should have. That means I don't often go in the canal except to wade or do a couple of dives off the locks now and then."

"If you can't swim too good, aren't you afraid to dive?" Kelly asked.

He shrugged his shoulders. "I can manage to kick my way to the surface of the water, then paddle like a dog back to the lock."

"Hmm . . . I see."

"What about you?" Betsy asked, looking directly at Kelly. "As dirty as you get trudging up and down the dusty towpath, I imagine you must jump into the canal quite frequently in order to get cleaned off."

Kelly sniffed deeply, feeling a sudden need to defend herself. "I learned to swim when I was a little girl, so I have no fear of drowning." *Just scared to death of water snakes*, her inner voice reminded. She saw no need to reveal her reservations about swimming in the canal, however. No use giving the preacher's daughter one more thing to look down her nose about.

Mike shifted on the quilt and leaned closer to Kelly. She could feel his warm breath against her neck and found it to be a distraction.

"That's a nice picture you're making," Mike whispered. "Is the charcoal I gave you working out okay?"

"It's fine," she answered as she kept on drawing.

"Maybe you can get a few pictures done today so I can take them back to the store and try to sell them."

She nodded. "Maybe so."

"How about you and me going for a walk, Mike?" Betsy asked, cutting into their conversation.

Mike moved away from Kelly, and she felt a keen sense of disappointment, which made no sense, since she wasn't the least bit interested in the storekeeper. She'd already decided Betsy Nelson would make a better match for Mike than someone like herself.

"Kelly, would you like to walk with me and Betsy?" Mike asked.

She shook her head. "I'd rather stay here with my tablet and charcoal. You two go ahead. I'll be fine."

Betsy stood up and held her hand out to Mike. "I'm ready if you are."

He made a grunting sound as he clambered to his feet. "We'll be back soon, Kelly."

Keeping her focus on the ducks swimming directly in front of her, Kelly mumbled, "Sure, okay."

ॐ

Mike wasn't the least bit happy about leaving Kelly alone while he and Betsy went for a walk. This was supposed to be his and Kelly's picnic—a chance for them to get better acquainted. It should have been Kelly he was walking with, not the preacher's daughter.

Betsy clung to his arm like they were a courting couple, and she chattered a mile a minute. If only he could figure out some way to discourage her without being rude. Mike didn't want to hurt Betsy's feelings, but he didn't want to lead her on either.

"Maybe we should head back," he said, when Betsy stopped talking long enough for him to get in a word.

She squeezed his arm a little tighter and kept on walking. "Why would you want to head back? It's a beautiful day, and the fresh air and exercise will do us both some good."

Mike opened his mouth to reply, but she cut him right off.

"I missed seeing you in church this morning."

He cleared his throat a few times, feeling like a little boy who was about to be reprimanded for being naughty. "Well, I—"

"Papa says we need young men like yourself as active members in the church," Betsy said, chopping him off again.

Mike shrugged as a feeling of guilt slid over him. He knew what the Bible said about men being the spiritual leaders. He also was aware that he needed to take a more active part in evangelizing the world. Maybe he would speak to Reverend Nelson about holding regular church services along the canal. Mike could donate some of his Bibles for people who didn't have one of their own. As far as attending the Nelsons' church, Mike wasn't sure that was such a good idea. It would mean spending more time with Betsy. It wasn't that he disliked the woman, but her chattering and pushiness got on his nerves.

"Mike, are you listening to me?"

He pushed his thoughts aside and focused on the woman who was tugging on his shirtsleeve. "What were you saying?"

"I was talking about mission work," Betsy replied in an exasperated tone. "I said we have a mission opportunity right here along the canal."

He nodded. "I agree. In fact, I was just thinking that if your father wanted to hold regular Sunday services out in front of my store, I'd be happy to furnish folks with Bibles."

Betsy's thin lips curled into a smile. "That sounds like a wonderful idea. I'll speak to Papa about it this evening."

Mike was amazed at Betsy's exuberance. She either shared his desire to tell others about Jesus or was merely looking forward to spending more time with him.

He grimaced. *I shouldn't be thinking the worst.* Mike knew he was going to have to work on his attitude. Especially where the preacher's daughter was concerned. She did have some good points, but she wasn't the kind of woman Mike was looking for.

A vision of Kelly flashed into his mind. Dark eyes that bore right through him; long dark hair cascading down her back; a smile that could light up any room. But it was more than Kelly's good looks and winning smile that had captured Mike's attention. There was a tenderness and vulnerability about Kelly McGregor that drew Mike to her like a thirsty horse heads for water. Sometimes she seemed like an innocent child needing to be rescued from something that was causing her pain. Other times Kelly appeared confident and self-assured. She was like a jigsaw puzzle, and he wanted to put all the complicated pieces of her together.

"Mike, you're not listening to me again."

He turned his head in Betsy's direction. "What were you saying?"

"I was wondering if you would like to come over for supper one night next week."

He groped for words that wouldn't be a lie. "I . . . uh . . . am expecting a shipment of goods soon, and I need to clean off some shelves and get the place organized before the load arrives."

Betsy's lower lip jutted out. "Surely you won't be working every evening."

Mike nodded. "I could be."

Her eyebrows drew together, nearly meeting at the middle. "I was hoping to tempt you with my chicken and dumplings. Papa says they're the best he's ever tasted."

"I'm sure they are." Mike gave Betsy's arm a gentle pat. "Maybe some other time."

"I hope so," she replied.

Should I be frank and tell her I'm not interested in pursuing a personal relationship? Mike stopped walking and swung around, taking Betsy with him, since she still held onto his arm. "We'd better head back now."

"Why so soon?"

"We left Kelly alone, and I don't feel right about that."

"I'm sure she's fine. She's not a little girl, you know."

Mike knew all right. Every time Kelly smiled at him or tipped her head to one side as she spoke his name, he was fully aware that she was a desirable young woman, not the child who used to drop by his store with her parents. He was anxious to get back to their picnic spot and see what Kelly had drawn.

"Mike, please slow down. I can barely keep up with you," Betsy panted.

"Sorry, but I invited Kelly to join me for a picnic today, and she probably thinks I've abandoned her."

Betsy moaned. "I didn't realize you two were courting. Why didn't you say so? If I'd known, I certainly would not have intruded on your time together."

Mike's ears were burning, and he knew they had probably turned bright red, the way they always did whenever he felt nervous or got flustered about something.

"Kelly and I are not officially courting," he mumbled. *Though I sure wish we were.*

Betsy opened her mouth as if to say something, but he spoke first.

"Even though we're not courting, I did invite her on a picnic. So, it's only right that I spend some time with her, don't you think?"

Betsy let out a deep sigh, but she nodded her head. "Far be it from me to keep you from your Christian duty."

"Thanks for understanding." Mike hurried up the towpath, with Betsy still clutching his arm. Soon Kelly came into view, and Mike halted his footsteps at the sight before him. Stretched out on the quilt, her dark hair fanned out like a pillow, Kelly had fallen asleep. The sketching tablet was in one hand, and a chunk of charcoal was in the other. She looked like an angel. Would she be his angel someday?

13

he following day, Mike was surprised when Kelly's dad entered his store shortly after he'd opened for business.

"Mr. McGregor, how are you feeling this morning?" Mike asked.

"I'll live," came the curt reply.

"I hope the days you spent docked here gave you ample time to rest up and get that cough under control."

Amos coughed and grunted in response. "I'll live, but it looks like we'll be stuck here another day or so, 'cause thanks to you, one of my mules came up lame this mornin'."

Mike frowned. "Really? They both seemed fine yesterday."

"Herman's not fine now. He went and got his leg cut up on a bale of wire you carelessly left layin' around." Kelly's dad leveled Mike with a challenging look.

Feeling a headache coming on, Mike massaged his forehead with his fingertips. "Weren't your mules in their stalls last night?"

"Yeah, in your barn."

"Then I don't understand how one of them could have gotten cut with the wire, which was nowhere near the stalls."

"Guess the door wasn't latched tight and they got out. At least Herman did, for he's the one with the cut leg."

Mike opened his mouth to respond, but Amos rushed on. "You got any liniment for me to put on the poor critter?"

"I'm sure I do." Mike hurried to the area of the store where he kept all the medicinal supplies, and Amos stayed right on his heels. The man seemed grumpier than usual today. Was it because he was so upset about the mule's injury and blamed Mike for the mishap?

Mike had no more than taken the medicine off the shelf, when Amos snatched it out of his hands. The older man stomped up to the counter and demanded, "How much do I owe ya for this?"

"I normally charge a quarter for that liniment, but since you feel the accident was my fault, there'll be no charge," Mike answered as he moved to the other side of the counter. He knew the McGregors weren't financially well off, and now that they couldn't travel because of a lame mule, they would be set back even further.

Amos slapped a quarter down. "I won't be beholdin' to no man, so I'll pay ya what the stuff is worth." He grimaced. "I'm losin' money with each passing day. First I got slowed down when Dorrie was sick and I was tryin' to cook, clean, and steer the boat. Then I came down with the bug and was laid up for a couple of days. Now I've got me a lame mule, and it should never have happened!"

"I'm sorry for your inconvenience, Mr. McGregor," Mike said apologetically.

"Yeah, well, at the rate things are goin', it'll be the end of the week before I can get back up to Mauch Chunk for another load of coal."

"Could you go on ahead with just one mule? I'd be happy to stable Herman until you come back this way."

Amos scowled at Mike. "Hector might be strong enough to pull the boat when it's empty, but not with a load of coal. Don'tcha know anything, Boy?"

Mike clenched his teeth. Even though he didn't know everything about canal boating, he wasn't stupid. Should he defend himself to Kelly's dad or ignore the discourteous remark? After a few seconds deliberation, Mike opted for the second choice. "I hope your mule's leg heals quickly, Mr. McGregor, and I'm sorry about the wire. If you need anything else, please don't hesitate to ask."

Amos coughed, blew his nose on the hanky he'd withdrawn from the pocket of his overalls, and sauntered out the door, slamming it behind him.

Mike sank to the wooden stool behind the counter and shook his head. At least one good thing would come from the McGregors being waylaid another day or two. It would give him a chance to see Kelly again. Yesterday's picnic had been a big disappointment to Mike. First

Betsy invited herself to join them, and then she'd hung on him most of the day. Kelly had fallen asleep while she was waiting for him and Betsy to return from their walk. He'd wakened her when they got back to the picnic site, but Kelly seemed distant after that and said she needed to head for the boat. Mike offered to walk with her, but she handed him her finished picture of two ducks on the water and said she could find her own way. She'd even insisted that Mike see the preacher's daughter safely home.

Mike reached up to scratch the back of his head. He had to let Kelly know he wasn't interested in Betsy. It was Kelly he cared about, and he wanted her to realize that. He just had to figure out how to go about revealing his true feelings without scaring her off.

                              ≥∾

Kelly couldn't believe they were stranded in front of Mike's store yet another day, possibly more. And as she followed Papa's curt instructions to get off the boat and put some medicine on Herman's leg, she shook her head over Papa's refusal to let the mules be stabled in Mike's barn any longer. It wasn't Mike's fault Herman had broken free from his stall and cut his leg on a roll of wire that had been sitting near the barn door. Now Herman and Hector were both tied to a maple tree growing several feet off the towpath, not far from where their boat was docked. Tonight they would be bedded down in the compartment set aside for them in the bow of the boat.

Kelly squatted beside Herman's right front leg and slathered some of the medicine on. "I don't see why I have to do this," she muttered under her breath. "I'd planned to get some drawin' done today, but Papa will probably find more chores for me to do when I return to the boat."

Immediately, Kelly felt a sense of guilt for her selfish thoughts. She knew her dad still wasn't feeling well, and he had a right to get some rest while they were laid over. Trouble was, she wanted to draw. At the rate she was going, she would never have anything to give Mike to try to sell in his store. She had given him the picture of the ducks she'd drawn during yesterday's picnic, but that was all.

Thinking about the picnic caused an ache in Kelly's soul. She didn't understand why Mike had invited her, then asked Becky Nelson to join them.

Well, not asked, exactly, she reminded herself. If Kelly's memory served her right, it was Betsy who had done the asking. Mike only agreed she could accompany them on the picnic. Might could be that he had no real interest in Betsy at all.

"'Course I don't care if he does," she murmured.

Herman brayed, and Hector followed suit, as if in answer to her complaints.

When Kelly stood up, Herman nuzzled her arm with his nose. She chuckled and patted his neck. "You should be good as new in a day or so, Herman the Determined. Then we can be on our way again."

On impulse, Kelly reached into her apron pocket and withdrew the drawing pad and piece of charcoal she often carried with her. She flopped onto the ground and began to sketch the two mules as they grazed on the green grass.

Some time later, she stood up. She had drawn two pictures of Herman and Hector, and now she planned to take them over to Mike's.

When she entered the store, Kelly was pleased to see that Mike had no customers, and he seemed genuinely glad to see her.

"I was sorry to hear about Herman's leg," he said, moving toward Kelly. "Your dad thinks it's my fault because there was a roll of wire by the barn door."

She pursed her lips. "Papa always looks for someone to blame. Don't fret about it, 'cause it sure wasn't your doin'. If anyone's to blame, it's Papa. He's the one who fed and watered the mules last night, so he probably didn't see that the door to their stall was shut tight." She frowned. "Of course, he'd never admit it."

Mike grinned at Kelly, and her stomach did a little flip-flop. She licked her lips and took a step forward. "I . . . uh . . . brought you a couple more drawings."

She held the pictures out to Mike, and he took them. "Thanks, these are nice. I'll get them put on display right away."

"Sure wish they had a little color to 'em. Herman and Hector are brown, not black, but my picture don't show it."

"Maybe you could buy a set of watercolors or oil paints," Mike suggested.

She shook her head. "Don't have enough money for that yet." Kelly knew she needed to save all her money if she was ever going to earn enough to be on her own or open an art gallery.

"Have you considered making your own watercolors?"

Her forehead wrinkled. "How could I do that?"

"I noticed some coffee stains on my tablecloth this morning," Mike said. "Funny thing was, they were all a different shade of brown."

"Hmm . . . guess it all depends on the strength of the coffee how dark the stain might be."

He nodded. "Exactly. So, I was thinkin' maybe you could try using old coffee to paint with. I've got some brushes I could let you have."

Kelly considered his offer carefully. It did sound feasible, but she wouldn't feel right about taking the brushes without paying something for them. If Papa had taught her anything, it was not to accept charity.

"How much would the brushes cost?" she asked Mike.

"I just said I'd be happy to give them to you."

She shook her head. "I either pay, or I don't take the brushes."

He shrugged. "I'll let you have three for a nickel. How's that sound?"

She nodded. "It's a deal."

A few minutes later, Kelly was walking out the door with three small paintbrushes, a jar of cold coffee, and an apple for each mule. Mike had insisted the coffee was a day old and he would only have to throw it out if she didn't accept it. Kelly decided stale coffee didn't have much value, so she agreed to take it off his hands. The apples she paid for.

"Come back tomorrow and let me know how your new watercolors work out," Mike said.

She smiled and called over her shoulder, "I may have more pictures for you in the mornin'."

14

hat night, after Kelly went to her room, she worked with the coffee watercolors. It was the first time she'd ever used a paintbrush, and it took awhile to get the hang of it. But once she did, Kelly found it to be thoroughly enjoyable. In fact, she decided to try a little experiment.

In her bare feet, she crept upstairs to the small kitchen area. She knew her folks were both asleep. She could hear Mama's heavy breathing and Papa's deep snoring.

Kelly lifted the lid from the wooden bin where Mama kept a stash of root vegetables. She pulled out a few carrots, two onions, and a large beet. Next, she heated water in the cast-iron kettle on the cook stove. When it reached the boiling point, she placed her vegetables in three separate bowls and poured scalding water over all. One by one Kelly carried the bowls back to her room. She would let them set overnight, and by tomorrow morning she hoped to have colored water in three different shades.

The following day, Herman's leg was no better, and Papa was fit to be tied.

"I'm losin' money just sittin' here," he hollered as he examined the cut on Herman's leg.

Kelly stood by his side, wishing she had some idea what to say.

"Do you know how many boats I've seen goin' up and down the canal?" he bellowed. "Everyone but me is makin' money this week!"

Kelly thought of the little bit of cash she'd made when Mike paid her for those first few drawings. If Papa were really destitute she would have offered to turn the money over to him. That wasn't the case, though. She knew her dad was tightfisted with his money, and truth be told, he probably had more stashed away than Kelly would ever see in her lifetime. Besides, she didn't want Papa to know she had any money of her own. If he found out, he would most likely demand that she give it all to him—and any future money she made as well.

So Kelly quietly listened to her father's tirade. He would soon calm down. He always did.

"Should I check with Mike Cooper and see if he has any other medicine that might work better on Herman's cut?" she asked when Papa finally quit blustering.

His face turned bright red, and his forehead wrinkled. "I ain't givin' that man one more dime to take care of an injury that he caused in the first place. We'll sit tight another day and see how Herman's doin' come morning." Papa turned and stomped off toward the boat.

Kelly reached up to stroke Herman behind his ear. "He's a stubborn one, that Papa of mine," she mumbled. Truth of the matter, Kelly knew they were losing time and money by waiting for the mule's leg to heal, but didn't Papa realize if he spent a little more on medicine, Herman's leg would probably heal faster? Then they could be on their way to Mauch Chunk and be making money that much sooner. Kelly thought her dad was just being mulish, refusing to see if Mike had any other medicine.

Kelly dipped her hand into the deep apron pocket where she kept her drawing tablet. At least one good thing had happened this morning. She'd gotten up early and painted a couple of pictures, using her new homemade watercolors. The first one was another pose of the mules; only now they were coffee-colored, not black. The second picture was of a sunset, with pink, orange, and yellow hues, all because of her vegetable watercolors. She was proud of her accomplishment and could hardly wait to show the pictures to Mike.

"I think I'll head over to his store right now," Kelly said, giving Hector a pat, so he wouldn't feel left out. The mule brayed and nudged her affectionately. Herman and Hector really were her best friends.

A short time later, Kelly entered Mike's store. He was busy waiting on a customer—Mrs. Harris, one of the lock tenders' wives. Kelly waited patiently over by the candy counter. It was tempting to spend some of her money on more lemon drops, but she reminded herself that she still had a few pieces of candy tucked safely away inside the trunk at the foot of her bed. She would wait until those were gone before she considered buying any more.

"Can I help you with something?" Lost in her thoughts, Kelly hadn't realized Mike had finished with his customer and now stood at her side. She drew in a deep breath as the fresh scent of soap reminded her of Mike's presence. He always smelled so clean and unsullied. His nearness sent unwanted tingles along her spine, and she forced herself to keep from trembling.

"I wanted to see what you thought of these." Kelly held out her drawing tablet to Mike.

He studied the first painting of Herman and Hector, done with coffee water. "Hmm . . . not bad. Not bad at all." Then he turned to the next page, and his mouth fell open. "Kelly, how did you make such beautiful colors?"

She giggled, feeling suddenly self-conscious. "I poured boiling water over some carrots, onions, and a beet; then I let it stand all night. This mornin' I had some colored water to paint with."

Mike grinned from ear to ear. "That's really impressive. I'm proud of you, Kelly."

Proud of me? Had she heard Mike right? In all her seventeen years, Kelly didn't remember anyone ever saying they were proud of anything she'd done. She felt the heat of a blush creep up her neck and flood her entire face. "It was nothin' so special."

"Oh, but it was," Mike insisted. "My idea of using coffee water was okay, and your picture of the mules is good, but you took it even further by comin' up with a way to make more colors." He lifted the drawing tablet. "You've captured a sunset beautifully."

She smiled, basking in his praise. If only Mama and Papa would say things to encourage her, the way Mike did. Mama said very little, and Papa either yelled or criticized.

"I think I'll come up with a better way to display your artwork," Mike announced.

"Oh? What's that?"

"I'm going to make a wooden frame for each of your pictures, and then I'll hang them right there." He pointed to the wall directly behind the counter where he waited on customers. "Nobody will leave my store without first seeing your talented creations."

Talented creations? First Mike had said he was proud of her, and now he'd called her talented. It was almost too much for Kelly to accept. Did he really mean those things, or was he only trying to be nice because he felt sorry for her? She hoped it wasn't the latter, for she didn't want anyone's pity.

"Kelly, did you hear what I said?"

She jerked her head toward Mike. "What did ya say?"

"I asked if you thought framing the pictures would be a good idea."

She nodded. "I suppose so. It's worth a try, if you want to go to all that trouble."

"I like workin' with my hands, so it won't be any trouble at all." Mike looked down at the tablet he still held. "Mind if I take the two colored pictures out now?"

"It's fine by me," she replied, feeling a sense of excitement. "If we stay around here another day or so, maybe I can get a few more drawings done."

He smiled and moved toward the counter. Kelly followed. "That would be great. I hope you do stay around a bit longer—for more reasons than one."

§

Mike felt such exuberance over Kelly's new pictures, done on newsprint, not to mention the news of her staying for another day or so. He'd been asking God to give him the chance to get to know Kelly better, and it looked as if he might get that opportunity. He did feel bad that her father was losing money because of the mule's leg, however. If there was some way he could offer financial assistance, he would, but Mike knew it wouldn't be appreciated. Amos McGregor was a proud man. He'd made that abundantly clear on several occasions.

"Guess I should get goin'," Kelly announced. "Papa left me to tend Herman's leg, and that was some time ago. He'll probably come a-lookin' for me if I don't get back to the boat pretty soon."

Mike carefully removed Kelly's finished pictures and handed her the tablet. "Keep up the good work, and when you get more paintings done, bring them into the store." He chuckled. "If you give me enough, I'll line every wall with your artwork. Then folks won't have any choice but to notice. And if they notice, they're bound to buy."

Kelly snickered, and her face turned crimson. "I like you, Mike Cooper." With that, she turned around and bounded out the door.

Mike flopped down on his wooden stool. "She likes me. Kelly actually said she likes me."

15

It took three days before Herman's leg was well enough so he could walk without limping. Even then, Papa had said at breakfast that they'd be taking it slow and easy. "No use pushin' things," he told Kelly and her mother. "Wouldn't want Herman to reinjure his leg."

As Kelly connected the towline to the mules' harnesses, she felt a sense of sadness wash over her soul. These last few days had been so nice, being in one place all the time, visiting with Mike Cooper whenever she had the chance, and painting pictures. She'd used up all her homemade watercolors and would need to make more soon. Kelly figured as she journeyed up the towpath she might come across some plants, tree bark, or leaves she could steep in hot water to make other colors. It would be an adventure to see how many hues she could come up with.

"You all set?" Papa called from the boat.

Kelly waved in response, her signal that she was ready to go. She'd only taken a few steps when she heard someone holler, "Kelly, hold up a minute, would you?"

She whirled around. Mike Cooper was heading her way, holding something in his hands.

Kelly stopped the mules, but Papa shouted at her to get them going again. She knew she'd better keep on walking or suffer the consequences. "I've gotta go," she announced when Mike caught up to her. "Papa's anxious to head out."

"I'll walk with you a ways," he said.

"What about your store?"

"I haven't opened for the day yet."

Kelly clicked her tongue, and the mules moved forward. Then she turned to face Mike as she moved along. The item he held in his hand was a wooden picture frame, and inside was her sunset watercolor.

"What do you think?" Mike asked as she looked at the piece of artwork.

"You did a fine job makin' that frame."

He laughed. "The frame's nothing compared to the beauty of your picture, but it does show off your work really well, don't you think?"

Kelly nodded but kept on walking. If she stopped, the mules would too.

"When do you think you'll be coming by my store again?" Mike asked.

She shrugged her shoulders. "Can't say for sure. Since Papa lost so much time because of his cough and Herman's leg gettin' cut, he probably won't make any stops that aren't absolutely necessary."

"Guess we could always pray he knocks a few more bars of soap overboard."

Kelly snickered. "With the way things have been goin' these days, Papa would probably expect me to jump in the canal and fetch 'em back out."

Mike reached out and touched Kelly's arm. She felt a jolt with the contact of his fingers and wondered if he had too.

"I'm sorry you have to work so hard, Kelly," he murmured.

She nodded and kept moving forward. "I'm used to it, but someday, when I make enough money of my own, I won't be Papa's slave no more."

"I'm sure he doesn't see you as his slave."

She snorted. "I don't get paid for walkin' the mules. Not one single penny had I ever made 'til you sold my two drawings." She glanced at Mike out of the corner of her eye and noticed his shocked expression.

"That will change," he said with a note of conviction. "By the time you stop at my store again, I'm sure several more of your pictures will be gone."

They were coming to a bend in the canal, and Kelly and the mules would be tromping across the changing bridge soon. Kelly knew it was time to tell Mike good-bye, although she hated to see him go. She was beginning to see Mike Cooper as a friend.

"Guess I'd better head back and open up the store," Mike said, "but I wanted to ask you something before you crossed to the other side."

"Oh? What's that?"

"I was wondering if you've ever accepted Christ as your personal Savior. You know—asked Him to forgive your sins and come live in your heart?"

"I did that when I was twelve years old," she said as a lump formed in her throat. Why was Mike asking about her relationship to God, and why was she getting all choked up over a simple good-bye? She'd be seeing Mike again; she just didn't know when.

Mike took hold of Kelly's hand and gave it a gentle squeeze. She glanced back at the boat, hoping Papa couldn't see what was going on.

"I'm awful glad to hear you're a believer. See you soon, Kelly," he whispered.

"I hope so," Kelly said; then she hurried on.

৯৵

Mike stood watching Kelly until she and the mules disappeared around the bend. She looked so forlorn when they parted. Was she going to miss him as much as he would miss her? He hoped so. These last few days had been wonderful, with her popping into the store a couple times, and the two of them meeting outside on several occasions. Mike felt as though he were beginning to know Kelly better, and he liked what he'd discovered. Not only was the young woman a talented artist, she was clever. She had figured out how to make her own watercolors, and Mike had a hunch she would probably have come up with even more colors by the time he saw her again.

"Sure hope I've sold some of her artwork by then," he muttered as he turned toward his store. "I can't keep buying them myself, and I wouldn't want Kelly to find out about the two I did pay for."

An image of Kelly lying on the patchwork quilt they'd used at the

Sunday picnic flashed across Mike's mind. If Betsy hadn't been there, he might have taken a chance and kissed his sleeping beauty, for he was quickly losing his heart to Kelly McGregor.

ે

Kelly had to hold up the mules at the changing bridge, as two other boats passed and their mules went over. While she waited, she decided to take advantage of the time, so she reached into her apron pocket and pulled out her drawing pad and a stick of charcoal. Kelly had just begun to sketch the boat ahead of her when Reverend Nelson and his daughter came walking up the towpath.

"Good morning," the preacher said. "It's a fine day, wouldn't you say?"

Kelly nodded in reply.

"Daddy and I are walking a stretch of the towpath today," Betsy remarked. "We're calling at people's homes who live near the canal, as well as visiting with those we meet along the way." She stuck out her hand and waved a piece of paper in front of Kelly's face. "We are handing these out too. Would you like one?"

"What is it?" Kelly asked.

"It's a verse of Scripture," Rev. Nelson answered before his daughter could respond.

Kelly took the Bible verse with a mumbled thanks, then stuffed it into her apron pocket. She would look at it later.

"What's that you're drawing?" the pastor asked.

"One of the canal boats."

Reverend Nelson glanced at her tablet and smiled. "It's a good likeness."

Kelly shrugged her shoulders. "I've only just begun."

"Betsy has one of your drawings. It's quite well done, considering what you have to work with."

Kelly's mouth dropped open. Betsy had one of her drawings? But how? A light suddenly dawned. The preacher's daughter must have gone into Mike's store and purchased one of Kelly's pictures. She smiled at Betsy and asked, "Which one did you buy?"

Betsy's pale eyebrows drew together as she frowned. "The picture is of a couple children fishing on the canal, but I didn't buy it."

"You didn't?"

Betsy shook her head. "Mike Cooper gave it to me as a birthday present. A few weeks ago he came over to our house for supper and to help me celebrate. He presented it to me then."

Kelly felt as though someone had punched her in the stomach. If Mike had given one of the drawings away, then he must have bought it himself. Her fingers coiled tightly around the piece of charcoal she still held in her hand. Who had bought the other picture Mike had paid her for? Was it him? He'd led her to believe he'd sold the pictures to some customers who'd come into the store. He hadn't actually said so, but that was the impression she'd gotten from their conversation.

The ground beneath her feet began to rumble, as a steam train lumbered past. Billows of smoke from the burning coal poured into the sky, leaving a dark, sooty trail.

"Guess we'd better be moving on," the preacher said with a wave of his hand.

Kelly only nodded in response. Her heart was hammering in her chest like the *clickety-clack* of the train's wheels against the track.

Just wait until I drop by Mike's store again, she fumed. *I'm gonna give that man a piece of my mind, and that's for certain sure!*

❧

For the rest of the day Kelly fretted about the pictures Mike had supposedly sold. At supper that night she was in a sour mood and didn't feel much like eating, even though Mama had made Irish stew, a favorite with both Kelly and her dad.

"What was that storekeeper doing, walkin' along the towpath with you this mornin'?" Papa asked, sending Kelly a disgruntled look.

She shrugged and switched her focus to the bowl of stew in front of her. "He was showin' me something he made and plans to sell in his store."

"What did he make?" Mama questioned.

Kelly had hoped neither of her parents would question her further.

She didn't want them to know she'd given Mike some of her drawings and paintings to sell in his store. And she sure wasn't about to tell them the storekeeper had been the only person to buy any of her work.

"It was a picture frame," she said, her mind searching for anything she could say to change the subject. She took a bite of stew and smacked her lips. "This is delicious, Mama. Good as always."

Her mother smiled from ear to ear. She was a good cook; there was no denying it. Mama could take a few vegetables and a slab of dried meat and turn it into a nutritious, tasty meal.

"I don't want that storekeeper hangin' around you, Kelly. Is that understood?"

At the sound of her dad's threatening voice, Kelly dropped the spoon, and it landed in her bowl, splashing stew broth all over the oil-cloth table covering.

"You don't have to shout, Amos," Mama said in her usual soft-spoken tone.

"I'll shout whenever I feel like it," he shot back, giving Kelly's mother a mind-your-own-business look.

Mama quickly lowered her gaze, but Kelly, feeling braver than usual, spoke her mind. "Mike and I are just friends. I don't see what harm there is in us havin' a conversation once in awhile."

"Humph!" Papa sputtered. "From what I could see, the two of you was havin' more than a little talk."

So he had seen Mike take her hand. Kelly trembled, but she couldn't let her father know how flustered she felt. She was glad Mama hadn't said anything about her and Mike going on a picnic to-gether, for that would surely get Papa riled.

Mama touched Kelly's arm. "I think your dad is concerned that you'll run off with some man, the way Sarah did."

"You needn't worry about that," Kelly was quick to say. "I don't plan on ever gettin' married." *Besides, Mike Cooper's not interested in me. It's Betsy Nelson he's set his cap for.*

"I'm glad to hear that." Papa tapped his knife along the edge of the table. "Just so you know . . . If I catch that storekeeper with his hands on you again, I'll knock his block off. Is that clear enough?"

Kelly nodded, as her eyes filled with tears. She might be mad as all get-out at Mike, but she couldn't stand to think of him getting beat up by her dad. She would have to make sure Mike never touched her when Papa was around. Not that she wanted him to, of course.

She reached into her pocket for a hanky and found the slip of paper Betsy Nelson had given her instead. Holding it in her lap, so Papa couldn't see it, Kelly silently read the verse of Scripture: *"Jesus said, 'If ye forgive men their trespasses, your heavenly Father will also forgive you.'"* Matthew 6:14

Kelly swallowed hard. She knew she needed to forgive Papa for the way he acted toward her. It sure wouldn't be easy, though.

16

On Thursday morning a sack of mail was delivered to Mike's store, brought in by one of the canal boats. This was a weekly occurrence, as Mike's place of business also served as the area's post office.

While sorting through the pile of letters and packages, Mike discovered one addressed to him. He recognized his brother Alvin's handwriting and quickly tore open the envelope.

Mike hadn't heard from either Alvin or John in several months, so he was anxious to see what the letter had to say:

Dear Mike,

John and me are both fine, and our fishing business is doing right well. I wanted to let you know that I've found myself a girl-friend, and we plan to be married in December, when we'll be done fishing for the season.

Hope things are good for you there at the store.

Your brother,
Alvin

Mike was happy for his brother, but he couldn't help feeling a pang of envy. He wanted so much to have a wife and children, and he wasn't any closer to it now than he had been several weeks before, when he'd prayed earnestly for God to send him a wife. He was still hoping Kelly McGregor might be that woman, but so far she'd given him no indication that she was interested in anything beyond friendship. At least he knew she'd had a personal relationship with Christ, even though she had been in a hurry when he'd asked her, so they couldn't really discuss it.

Mike turned and glanced at the wall directly behind the counter. He'd framed all of Kelly's pictures and hung them there. One had sold yesterday, and the man who'd bought it seemed interested in the others. Kelly had talent, there was no doubt about it, but she was also young and probably insecure when it came to men. Maybe she didn't know how to show her feelings. Maybe she was afraid. Mike had noticed how Amos McGregor often yelled at Kelly and his wife. Kelly might think all men were like her dad.

"I'll go slow with Kelly and win her heart over time," Mike murmured as he continued to study her artwork. "And while I'm waiting, I'll try even harder to get some of these pictures sold."

ða

Papa had kept true to his word and taken it slow and easy on the trip to Mauch Chunk. On a normal run they would have been there by Wednesday night, since they'd left from Mike's store, and it was near the halfway point. Instead, they'd spent Wednesday night outside the small town of Parryville.

They arrived in Mauch Chunk on Thursday afternoon, with Herman doing well and his leg in good shape. Then they loaded the boat with coal from the loading chutes, which descended 250 feet to the river. They spent the night in Mauch Chunk, surrounded by hills that were covered with birch, maple, oak, and wild locust trees.

Now it was Friday, and they were heading back toward the town of Easton to deliver their load. They'd be passing Mike's store either this evening or tomorrow morning, depending on how hard Papa pushed Kelly today. Since Herman was doing well, she suspected they would move faster than they had on Wednesday and Thursday.

"Probably won't be stopping at Mike's store this time," Kelly mumbled. "Sure wish we were, though. I need to talk to him about the picture he gave Betsy Nelson."

As the wind whipped against her long skirt, Kelly glanced up at the darkening sky. They were in for a storm, sure as anything. She hoped it would hold off until they stopped for the night. She hated walking the towpath during a rainstorm.

Hector's ears twitched, as though he sensed the impending danger a torrential downpour could cause—fallen trees, a muddy towpath, rising canal waters. Then there was always the threat of being hit by lightning. Especially with so many trees lining the path. A few years back a young boy leading his dad's mules had been struck by a bolt of lightning and was killed instantly. Such a shame!

Kelly shivered. Just thinking about what was to come made her feel jumpy as a frog. The mules would be harder to handle once the rain started, for she reminded herself that they had no depth perception and hated walking through water, even small puddles. If they came to a stretch of puddles on the path, they would tromp clear around them. There was no fear of the mules jumping into the canal to get cooled off on a hot day either—the way a horse would have done. Kelly's mules liked water for drinking, but that was all.

Forcing her mind off the impending storm, Kelly thought about how glad she was that Papa had chosen mules, not horses, to pull his boats. It was a proven fact that mules, with their brute strength and surefooted agility, were much less skittish and far more reliable than any horse could be. If horses weren't stopped in time, they would keep on pulling until they fell over dead. Mules, if they were overly tired or had fallen sick, would stop in the middle of the path and refuse to budge. A mule ate one-third less food than a horse did as well, making the beast of burden far more economical to own.

By noon the rain began falling. First it arrived in tiny droplets, splattering the end of Kelly's nose. Then the lightning and thunder came, bringing a downpour of chilling rain.

Kelly cupped her hands around her mouth and leaned into the wind. "Are we gonna stop soon?" she hollered to Papa, who stood at the stern of the boat, already dripping wet. He was just getting over a bad cold and shouldn't even be out in this weather.

"Keep movin'!" Papa shouted back to her. "We won't stop unless it gets any worse."

Worse? Kelly didn't see how it could get much worse. Thunder rumbled across the sky, and black clouds hung so low, she felt as if she could reach out and touch them. "I—I'm cold and wet," she yelled, wondering if he could hear her. The wind was howling fiercely, and she could barely hear herself. Then Kelly's straw hat flew off her head, causing long strands of hair to blow across her face. She ran up ahead, retrieved the hat, and pushed it down on her head, hoping it would stay in place.

Papa leaned over the edge of the boat and tossed a jacket over the side. Kelly lunged forward and barely caught it in time. If it had fallen into the canal, it would have been lost forever, as the murky brown water was swirling and gurgling something awful.

Kelly slipped her arms into the oversized wool jacket and buttoned it up to her neck. It helped some to keep out the wind, but she knew it was only a matter of time until the rain leaked through and soaked her clean to the skin.

On and on Kelly and the mules trudged, through the driving rain, pushing against the wind, tromping in and out of mud puddles, murk, and mire. Several times the mules balked and refused to move forward. Kelly coaxed, pushed, pleaded, and pulled, until she finally got them moving again.

By the time Papa signaled her to stop, Kelly felt like a limp dishrag. She glanced around and realized they were directly in front of Mike's store. Lifting her gaze to the thunderous sky, Kelly prayed, "Thank You, God, for keepin' us safe and for givin' Papa the good sense to stop."

"We're stayin' here for the night," Papa shouted. "Help me get the mules on board the boat."

"Can't they bed down in Mike Cooper's barn tonight?" Kelly asked. "I could care for 'em better there."

"Guess it wouldn't hurt for one night," Papa surprised her by saying.

ৡ৶

Mike was about to close up his store, figuring no one in their right mind would be out in this terrible weather, when the door flew open, and Kelly practically fell into the room. She looked like a drowned rat.

Her hair, wet and tangled, hung in her face. Her clothes were soaked with rainwater, and her boots were covered in mud. Her straw hat, pushed far over her forehead, resembled a hunk of soggy cardboard.

Mike grabbed hold of Kelly as a gust of wind pushed her forward. The door slammed shut with so much force that the broom, lying against one wall, toppled over, while several pieces of paper blew off the counter and sailed to the floor.

"Kelly, what are you doin' here?" he questioned.

"We've stopped for the day because of the storm." She leaned into him, and he had the sudden desire to kiss her. Why was it that every time they were together anymore, Mike wanted to find out what her lips would feel like against his own?

He drew in a deep breath and gently stroked her back. "Are you okay? You look miserable."

She pulled away suddenly. "I'm fine, but we were wonderin' if we could stable the mules in your barn tonight."

He nodded. "Of course. I'll put on my jacket and help you get them settled in."

"I can manage," she said in a brisk tone of voice. She'd been so friendly a few minutes ago. What had happened to make her change?

Mike studied Kelly's face. It was pinched, and there were tears streaming down her face. At least he thought they were tears. They might have been raindrops, he supposed.

"Kelly, what's wrong?" Mike touched her arm, and she recoiled as if some pesky insect had bitten her.

As she moved toward the door, her gaze swung to the pictures on the wall.

"How do you like the way I've got your artwork displayed?" he questioned.

She squinted her eyes at him. "How could you, Mike?"

"How could I what?"

"Buy my drawing and give it to Betsy Nelson for her birthday?"

"Her dad invited me to their house for supper to help her celebrate. I wanted to take something, and I thought Betsy would like one of your wonderful charcoal drawings."

She continued to stare at him, and Mike felt his face heat up. Why was she looking at him as though he'd done something wrong? He'd paid her for the picture; same as if someone else had bought it.

"And the other drawing?"

"Huh?"

"You gave me money for two drawings and said you'd sold them both."

The heat Mike felt on his face had now spread to his ears. "I . . . that is . . . I bought both of the pictures," he admitted. "One for Betsy's birthday and the other to hang in my living room."

She shook her head slowly. "I figured as much."

"How did you find out about the picture I gave the preacher's daughter?"

"Reverend Nelson told me when I ran into him and Betsy on the towpath the other day." Kelly bit down on her lower lip, like she might be about to cry. "Why did you lead me to believe you'd sold my pictures, Mike?"

"I did sell them," he defended. "I don't see what difference it makes who bought them."

"It makes a lot of difference," Kelly shouted before she turned toward the front door. "I'm not a poor little girl who needs charity from you or anyone else!"

He couldn't let her leave like this. Not without making her understand he wasn't trying to hurt her. Mike grabbed Kelly's arm and turned her around. "Please forgive me. I never meant to upset you, and I really did want those drawings." He pointed to the wall where her other paintings hung. "I sold one of your watercolors this morning to a man who lives in Walnutport."

She squinted her dark eyes at him. "Really?"

"Yes. He was impressed with your work and said he may be back to buy more."

Kelly's eyes were swimming with tears. "I—I can't believe it."

"It's true. Mr. Porter knows talent when he sees it, and so do I." Mike reached for her hand and gave it a gentle squeeze. "Am I forgiven for misleading you?"

She hesitated a moment, then her lips curved up. "Yes."

"Good. Now will you let me help you stable the mules?"

She nodded.

Mike grabbed his jacket off the wall peg by the door. "You lead one mule, and I'll take the other."

A moment later, they stepped into the driving rain, but Mike paid it no mind. All he could think about was spending the next hour or so in the company of Kelly McGregor.

17

uring the next half hour, Kelly and Mike got the mules fed and bedded down for the night. Kelly was grateful for his help and the loan of the barn. It meant Herman and Hector had a warm, dry place to rest, without cramped quarters, and no bouncing or swaying from the rough waters caused by the storm.

Truth be told, Kelly dreaded going to her own room. It would be hard to sleep with the boat bobbing all over the place. She'd probably have to tie herself in bed in order to keep from being tossed onto the floor.

"I was wondering if you and your folks would like to stay at my place tonight," Mike said, as he rubbed Herman down with an old towel.

"Your place?"

"My house. I've got plenty of room."

Kelly wondered if Mike had been able to read her mind, or was he smart enough to figure out how difficult it would be to spend the night on a boat riding the waves of a storm?

"I'd have to ask Papa and Mama," she said. "They might agree, but I'm not sure."

"Would you prefer it if I asked them instead?"

"That probably would be best. Papa's usually more open to things if it comes from someone other than me."

Mike hung the towel on a nail and moved toward Kelly, who'd been drying Hector off with another piece of heavy cloth. "I take it you and your dad don't get along."

Kelly lowered her gaze to the wooden floor. "I used to think he liked me well enough, but ever since Sarah left, he's been actin' meaner than ever."

Mike's heart clenched. He hated to see the way Kelly's shoulders drooped or hear the resignation in her voice. "Are you afraid of him, Kelly?"

She nodded slowly. "Sometimes."

"Has he ever hit you?"

"Not since I was little. Then it was only a swat on the backside." Kelly's eyes filled with tears, and it was all Mike could do to keep from kissing her. "Papa mostly yells, but sometimes he makes me do things I know are wrong."

"Like what?"

She sucked in her lower lip. "The other day there was a bunch of chickens runnin' around near the towpath. He insisted I grab hold of one and give it to Mama to cook for our supper that night."

Mike drew in a deep breath and let it out in a rush. "But that's stealing. Doesn't your dad know taking things that don't belong to you is breaking one of God's commandments?"

"Papa don't care about God. He thinks Mama is plain silly for readin' her Bible every night."

"What do you think would have happened if you'd refused to do what your dad asked?"

"I don't know, but I didn't think I should find out."

Mike could hardly believe Kelly's dad had asked her to do something so wrong, but it was equally hard to understand why she wouldn't stand up to him. If he wasn't physically abusive, then what kind of hold did the man have on her?

"Does your dad refuse your pay if you don't do what he asks?" Mike questioned.

Kelly planted her hands on her hips. "I told you the other day, Papa has never paid me a single penny for leadin' the mules."

Mike reached up to scratch the side of his head. He'd forgotten about their conversation about Kelly's lack of money. That was why she wanted to sell some of her artwork. And it was one more reason Mike had to help make it happen.

"It's all Sarah's fault for runnin' off with one of the lock tender's sons. She made Papa angry and left me with all the work." Kelly balled her fingers into tight fists, and Mike wondered if she might want to punch someone. He took a few steps back, just in case.

Before he had a chance to respond to her tirade, Kelly announced, "I'm afraid men are all the same, and I ain't never gettin' married, that's for certain sure!"

Mike felt like he'd been kicked in the gut. Never marry? Had he heard her right? If Kelly was dead set against marriage, then what hope did he have of winning her hand? About all he could do was try to be her friend, but he sure wished he could figure out some way to prove to her that all men weren't like her dad.

❧

Kelly felt the heat of embarrassment flood her face. What had possessed her to spout off like that in front of Mike? He'd been helping her with the mules and sure didn't deserve such wrath. She knew she should apologize, but the words stuck in her throat like a wad of chewing gum.

She grabbed a hunk of hay and fed it to Hector. Maybe if she kept her hands busy, she wouldn't have to think about anything else.

"Why don't you finish up with the mules while I go talk to your folks and see if they'd like to spend the night at my place?" Mike suggested.

Kelly nodded. "Sounds good to me."

A few seconds later, she heard the barn door close behind Mike, and she dropped to her knees. "Oh, Lord, I'm sorry for bein' such a grouch. Guess I'm just tired and out of sorts tonight 'cause of the storm and all."

Tears streamed down Kelly's cheeks. Mike thought she was a sinner for taking that chicken. He didn't understand how things were with Papa either. To make matters worse, Mike had been kind to her, and she'd yelled at him in return. What must he think of her now?

"I'm sorry for stealin' the chicken, Lord. Give me the courage to tell Papa no from now on."

Kelly dried her eyes with the backs of her hands and was about to leave the barn when Mike showed up with Mama.

"Where's Papa?" Kelly questioned.

Her mother sighed deeply. "He's bound and determined to stay on the boat tonight. Never mind that it's rockin' back and forth like a bucking mule." She wrinkled her nose. "And now the roof's leaking as well."

"So are you and me gonna stay at Mike's house?" Kelly asked.

"Yes, and it was a very kind offer, wouldn'tcha say?"

Kelly nodded in response and smiled at Mike. "Sorry for snappin' like a turtle."

He winked at her. "Apology accepted."

ॐ

For the next two days, the storm continued, and Papa still refused to leave the boat. He said he might lose it if he did, but Kelly knew the truth. Her dad didn't want to appear needy in front of Mike. He'd rather sit on his vessel and be tossed about like a chunk of wood thrown into a raging river than accept anyone's charity.

Sitting at Mike's kitchen table with her drawing tablet, Kelly thought about a verse of Scripture she'd learned as a child: *The substance of a diligent man is precious—Proverbs 12:27.* Papa was diligent, that was for sure. Too bad he wasn't kinder or more concerned about his family.

The last two nights she and Mama had shared a bed inside a real home, and Kelly found herself wishing even more that she could leave the life of mule driver behind.

"Aren't you gonna eat some breakfast?" Mama asked, pushing a bowl of oatmeal in front of Kelly.

"I will, after I finish this drawing."

Mama leaned forward with her elbows on the table. "What are you makin'?"

"It's a picture of our boat bein' tossed by the rising waters. I took a walk down to the canal this morning so I could see how things were lookin'." Kelly frowned. "The rain hasn't let up one little bit, and I figure God must be awful angry with someone."

Mama looked at Kelly as if she'd taken leave of her senses. "What would make ya say somethin' like that?"

"Doesn't God cause the rain and winds to come whenever He's mad?"

Reaching across the table, Mama took hold of Kelly's hand. "Storms are part of the world we live in, but I don't believe God sends 'em to make us pay for our sins."

"Really?"

Mama nodded. "The Bible tells us in Psalm 34:19, 'Many are the afflictions of the righteous: but the LORD delivereth him out of them all.' Everyone goes through trials, and some of those come in the form of storms, sickness, or other such things. That don't mean we're bein' punished, but we can have the assurance that even though we'll have afflictions, God will deliver us in His time."

Kelly tried to concentrate on her drawing, but Mama's words kept rolling around in her head. *When's my time comin' to be delivered, Lord? When are You gonna give me enough money so I can leave this terrible way of life?*

She grabbed the hunk of charcoal and continued to draw, not wanting to think about her situation. It was bad enough that the storm wasn't letting up and Papa refused to get off the boat. She didn't wish to spend the rest of the day worried about God's direction for her life. If more of her drawings didn't sell soon, she'd have to figure out some other way to make money on her own. When they wintered in Easton, Kelly might get a job in one of the factories. Then she'd have plenty of money, and Papa could find someone else to lead the mules.

A few minutes later the door flew open, and Papa lumbered into the room. Mama jumped up and moved quickly toward him.

"Oh, Amos, it's so good to see you. Can I fix ya a bowl of oatmeal, or maybe some flapjacks?"

He stormed right past Mama as though she hadn't said a word about food. "Stupid weather! It ain't bad enough we lost so much time with sickness and mule problems; now we're stuck here 'til the storm passes by. I'm gettin' sick of sittin' around doin' nothin', and I can't believe my family abandoned me to come get all cozy-like over here at the storekeeper's place!"

Kelly tried to ignore her dad's outburst, but it was hard, especially with him breathing down her neck, as he was now. She could feel his hot breath against her cheek, as he leaned his head close to the table. "What's that you're doin'?" he snarled.

"I'm drawin' a picture of our boat in the storm."

"Humph! Ain't it bad enough I have to endure the torment of bein' tossed around like a cork? Do ya have to rub salt in the wounds by makin' a dumb picture to remind me of my plight?"

Kelly opened her mouth to reply, but Papa jerked the piece of paper right off the table. "This is trash and deserves to be treated as such!" With that, he marched across the room, flung open the door on the wood stove, and tossed Kelly's picture into the fire.

She shot out of her seat, but it was too late. Angry flames of red had already engulfed her precious drawing.

"How could you, Papa?" she cried. "How could you be so cruel?" Kelly rushed from the house, not caring that she wasn't wearing a jacket.

18

$\mathscr{M}$ ike glanced out the store window and was surprised to see Kelly run past. She wasn't wearing a jacket, and the rain was still pouring down. She would be drenched within seconds.

He yanked the door open and hurried out after her. A few minutes later she entered the barn, and Mike was right behind her.

"Kelly, what are you doin' out here without a coat?" he hollered as he followed her into the mules' stall.

She kept her head down, and he could see her shoulders shaking. Mike rushed over to her. "What's wrong? Why are you crying?"

She lifted her gaze to his, and he noticed her dark eyes were filled with tears. He ached to hold her in his arms—to kiss away those tears. He might have, too, if he hadn't been afraid of her response.

"I was working on a drawing of our boat this mornin', and Papa got mad and threw it into the fire," she sobbed.

Mike took hold of Kelly's arms. "Why would he do such a thing?"

"He stormed into your kitchen, yelled about the weather, and said I was rubbin' salt into his wounds by makin' a picture of the boat in the storm. Then he said my picture was trash and deserved to be treated as such. That's when he turned it to ashes." Tears streamed down Kelly's face, and Mike instinctively reached up to wipe them away with the back of his hand.

"I'm so sorry, Kelly. I promise someday things will be better for you."

"How can you say that? Are you able to see into the future and know what's ahead?" she wailed.

Mike shook his head slowly. Kelly was right; he couldn't be sure what the future held for either of them. He wanted things to be better and wished she would allow him to love her and help her. If Kelly were to marry him, Mike would gladly spend the rest of his life taking care of her. If only he felt free to tell her that.

"God loves you, Kelly, and He wants only the best for you."

She glared up at him. "If God loves me so much, then why do I have to work long hours with no pay? And why's Papa so mean?"

"God gives each of us a free will, and your dad is the way he is by his own choosing. We can pray for him and set a good example, but nobody can make him change until he's ready."

Kelly sniffed deeply. "I don't care if he ever changes. All I care about is earnin' enough money to make it on my own. I need that chance, so if you want to pray about somethin', then ask God to help *me*."

Mike's hand rested comfortably on her shoulder. With only a slight pull, she would be close enough for him to kiss. The urge was nearly overwhelming, and he moved away, fighting for control. Kelly had made clear how she felt about marriage. Even if she were attracted to him—and he suspected she was—they had no hope of a future together. He wanted marriage and children so much. All she seemed to care about was drawing pictures and making money so she could support herself. Didn't Kelly realize he was more than willing to care for her needs? As long as he was able to draw breath, Mike would never let his wife or children do without.

"I'll be praying, Kelly," he mumbled. "Praying for both you and your dad."

ᆇ

On Monday of the following week, the rain finally stopped, and the canal waters had receded enough so the McGregors could move on. Kelly felt a deep sense of sadness as she said good-bye to Mike. He truly was her friend, and as much as she hated to admit it, she was attracted to him. She would miss their daily chats as she cared for the mules. She would miss his kind words and caring attitude. As the days of summer continued, she hoped they would stop by his store on a regular basis. Not only to see if any of her paintings had sold, but also so she could spend more time with Mike.

Over the last few days she'd done several more charcoal drawings, always out of Papa's sight, and with Mike's encouragement.

"Get up there," Kelly said as she coaxed the mules to get going. They moved forward, and she turned to wave at Mike one last time. She didn't know why she should feel so sad. She'd see him again, probably on their return trip from Easton.

They'd only traveled a short ways when Papa signaled her to stop. They were between towns, and there were no other boats around. She had a sinking feeling her dad was up to something. Something he'd done a few times before, when he'd lost time due to bad weather or some kind of mishap along the way.

Sure enough, within minutes of their stopping, Papa had begun to shovel coal out of the compartment where it was stored and was dumping it into the canal. He did this to lighten their load, which in turn would help the boat move faster. Of course, it also meant Kelly would be expected to keep the mules moving at a quicker pace.

She shook her head in disgust. "I don't see why Papa has to be so dishonest."

Hector brayed loudly, as though he agreed.

"It's not fair for him to expect the three of us to walk faster," she continued to fume. "It's hard enough to walk at a regular pace, what with the mud and all, but now we'll practically have to run."

Kelly's thoughts took her back to what Mike had told her the other morning in his barn. He'd said they needed to pray for Kelly's dad and set him a good example. That was a tall order—especially since Papa seemed determined to be ornery, and he didn't think twice about cheating someone. She knew from times before that shortly before they arrived in Easton to deliver their load, Papa would wet the coal down, which made it weigh more. Since he was paid by weight and not by the amount, no one would be any the wiser.

She sighed deeply and turned her head away from the canal. There was no use watching what she couldn't prevent happening. Someday maybe she wouldn't have to watch it at all.

ॐ

For the next several weeks, Kelly trudged up and down the towpath between Easton and Mauch Chunk, but they made no stops that weren't absolutely necessary. Papa said they'd lost enough time, and he didn't think they needed to dally. When Mama complained about needing fresh vegetables, Papa solved the problem by turning the tiller over to her. Then he jumped off the boat and helped himself to some carrots and beets growing near the towpath. The garden belonged to someone who lived nearby, but Papa didn't care. He said if the people who'd planted the vegetables so close to the canal didn't want folks helping themselves, they ought to have fenced in their crops.

Kelly had been praying for Papa, like Mike suggested, but it seemed the more she prayed, the worse he became. The effort appeared to be futile, and she had about decided to give up praying or even hoping Papa might ever change.

That morning at breakfast, Mama had asked Papa if they could stop at Mike's store later in the afternoon. She needed more washing soap, some thread, flour for baking, and a few other things she couldn't get by without. After a few choice words, Papa had finally agreed, but now, as they neared the spot in front of Cooper's General Store, Kelly wondered if he might change his mind. His face was a mask of anger, but he signaled her to stop.

She breathed a sigh of relief and halted the mules. At last she could see Mike again and ask if any of her pictures had sold. She didn't have more to give him, as she'd been too busy during the days to draw, and at night she was too tuckered out. At the rate things were going, Kelly doubted she'd ever get the chance to earn enough money to buy any store-bought paint, much less to open an art gallery.

"A dream. That's all it is," she mumbled under her breath a few moments before Mama joined her to head for the store.

క$

Mike stood behind the front counter, praying and hoping Kelly would stop by his store soon. He'd just sold another one of her paintings, and he could hardly wait to tell her the good news. It had been two whole weeks since he'd spoken with her, although he had seen the McGregors' boat go by on several occasions. Each time he'd had customers in the store, or else he would have dashed outside and tried to speak with Kelly—although it probably would have meant running along the towpath as they conversed, for that's pretty much what it looked like Kelly had been doing. Her dad was most likely trying to make up for all the time he'd lost during the storm, but Mike hated to see Kelly being pushed so hard. It wasn't right for a young woman to work from sunup to sunset without getting paid.

Mike was pleasantly surprised when the front door opened and in walked Dorrie and Kelly McGregor. They both looked tired, but Kelly's face showed more than fatigue. Her dark eyes had lost their sparkle, and her shoulders were slumped. She looked defeated.

Mike smiled at the two women. "It's good to see you. Is there something I can help you with?"

Dorrie waved a hand. "Don't trouble yourself. I can get whatever I'm needin'." She marched off in the direction of the sewing notions.

Kelly hung back, and she lifted her gaze to the wall where her artwork was displayed.

"I sold another picture this morning," Mike announced.

"That's good," she said with little feeling. "Sorry I don't have anymore to give you right now. There's been no time for drawin' or paintin' here of late."

"It's all right," he assured her. "I'm sure you'll find some free time soon."

She scowled at him. "Why do you always say things like that?"

"Like what?"

"You try to make me think things are gonna get better when they're not."

"How do you know they're not?"

"I just do, that's all."

Mike blew out his breath. It was obvious nothing he said would penetrate her negative attitude this afternoon. He offered up a quick prayer. *Lord, give me the right words.*

"Would it help if I had a talk with your dad?"

Kelly looked horrified. "Don't you dare! Papa would be furious if he knew I'd been complaining." She squared her shoulders. "I'll be fine, so there's no reason to concern yourself."

"But I am concerned. I'm in—" Mike stopped himself before he blurted out that he was in love with her. He knew it would be the worst thing he could say to Kelly right now. Besides the fact that she was in a sour mood and would probably not appreciate his declaration of love, her mother was in the store and might be listening to his every word.

Mike moved over to the candy counter. "How about a bag of lemon drops? I'm sure you're out of them by now."

Kelly's frown faded, and she joined him at the counter. "Since I sold a painting and have some money comin', I'll take two bags of candy—one lemon drops, and the other horehounds."

"I didn't know you fancied horehounds."

"I don't, but Papa likes 'em. Maybe it'll help put him in a better mood."

So she was trying to set a good example for her dad. That pleased Mike so much. At least one of his prayers was being answered. If Kelly's dad found the Lord, then Kelly might be more receptive to the idea of marriage.

Mike reached into the container of horehound drops with a wooden scoop. "You think you might be stopping over come Sunday?"

She shrugged her shoulders. "If we make it to Mauch Chunk in good time, Papa might be willin' to stop on our way back. Why do you ask?"

"I'd like to take you on another picnic." He grinned at her. "Only this time it'll be just you and me."

She tipped her head to one side. "No Betsy Nelson?"

"Nope."

She smiled for the first time since she'd come into the store. "We'll have to wait and see."

When Mike asked Kelly about going on another picnic, she never expected her family's canal boat would be stopped in front of his store the next Sunday. In fact, they'd arrived the evening before, and Papa had decided to spend the night so he could work on the boat the following morning. He'd accidentally run into one of the other canal boats and put a hole in the bow of his boat. It wasn't a huge hole and was high enough that no water had leaked in, but it still needed to be repaired before it got any worse. Papa would be busy with that all day, which meant Kelly could head off with Mike and probably go unnoticed.

Not wishing to run into Betsy again, Kelly waited until the crowd had dispersed from Reverend Nelson's outdoor preaching service before she walked to Mike's store. They'd talked briefly the night before and had agreed to meet sometime after noon in front of his place.

It was a hot summer day late in the month of August, and Kelly wished she and Mike could go swimming in the canal to get cooled off. She dismissed the idea as quickly as it popped into her mind when she remembered Mike had said he didn't swim well, and she, though able to swim, was afraid of water snakes. They would have to find some other way to find solace from the oppressive heat and humidity.

Mike was waiting for her in front of the store, a picnic basket in one hand and a blanket in the other. "Did you bring along your drawing tablet?" he asked.

She nodded and patted the pocket of her long, gingham skirt.

"I thought we'd have our picnic at the pond behind Zach Miller's house. There's lots of wildflowers growing there, and maybe we can find some to brew into watercolors," he said, offering Kelly a smile that made her skin tingle despite the heat of the day.

"That would be good. Mama's runnin' low on carrots and beets, so I haven't been able to make any colors for a spell, other than the shades I've gotten from leftover coffee and some tree bark."

Mike whistled as they walked up the towpath, heading in the direction of the lock tender's house.

"You seem to be in an awful good mood this afternoon," Kelly noted.

He turned his head and grinned at her. "I'm always in fine spirits on the Lord's day. I looked for you at the preaching service but didn't see you anywhere."

"Mama needed my help with some bakin'." Kelly felt a prick of her conscience. She had helped her mother bake oatmeal bread, but truth be told, that wasn't the real reason she hadn't attended the church service. She didn't want to hear God's Word and be reminded that her prayers weren't being answered where Papa was concerned. Besides, Mama hadn't attended church either, and if she didn't feel the need to go, why should Kelly?

"Sure wish you could have heard the great message the reverend delivered this morning. It was a real inspiration."

"I'm sure it was."

"Summer will be over soon," Mike said, changing the subject. "Won't be long until the leaves begin to turn and drop from the trees."

Kelly nodded, feeling suddenly sad. When fall came, they'd only have a few months left to make coal deliveries. Winter often hit quickly, and Papa always moored the boat for the winter and moved them to Flannigan's Boardinghouse in Easton, where they would live until the spring thaw. That meant Kelly wouldn't be seeing Mike for several months. She would miss his smiling face and their long talks.

A lot could happen in three months. Mike and Betsy might start courting and could even be married by the time they returned to the canal. And Kelly was acutely aware that lots of coal was now being hauled via steam train, which meant fewer boats were working the canals in eastern Pennsylvania. How long would it be before Papa gave up canaling altogether and took a job in the city full-time?

"A lemon drop for your thoughts," Mike said.

"What?"

"I brought along a bag of your favorite candy, and I'd gladly give you one if you're willin' to share your thoughts with me."

She snickered. "I doubt anything I'd be thinkin' would be worth even one lemon drop."

Mike stopped walking and turned to face her. "Don't say that, Kelly. You're a talented, intelligent woman, and I value anything you might have to say."

She pursed her lips. "I'm not sure 'bout my talents, but one thing I do know—I'm not smart. I've only gone through the eighth grade, and that took me longer than most, 'cause I just attended school during the winter months."

"A lack of education doesn't mean you're stupid," Mike said with a note of conviction. "My dad used to say he graduated from the school of life and that all the things he learned helped him become a better man. We grow from our experiences, so if we learn from our mistakes, then we're smart."

Kelly contemplated Mike's words a few seconds. "Hmm . . . I've never thought about it that way before."

"I hope to have a whole passel of kids someday, and when I do, I want to teach them responsibility, so they can work hard and be smart where it really counts."

Kelly wasn't sure she liked the sound of that, but she chose not to comment.

Mike started walking again, and Kelly did as well. Soon they were at the pond behind the Millers' house. Nobody else was around, so Kelly figured they weren't likely to be interrupted, and she might even get some serious drawing done.

৯

Sitting on the blanket next to Kelly, his belly full of fried chicken and buttermilk biscuits, Mike felt content. He could spend the rest of his life with this woman—watching her draw, listening to the hum of her sweet voice, and kissing away all her worries and cares. Should he tell her what he was feeling? Would it scare her off? He drew in a deep breath and plunged ahead. "Kelly, I was wondering—"

"Yes?" she murmured as she continued to draw the outline of a clump of wildflowers.

"Would it be all right if I wrote to you while you're living in the city this winter?"

She turned her head to look at him. Her dark eyes looked ever so serious, but she was smiling. "I'd like that."

"And will you write me in return?" he asked hopefully.

She nodded. "If I'm not kept too busy with my factory job."

"Do you know where you'll be working?"

"Not yet, but I'll be eighteen on January fifth, and I'm gettin' stronger every year. I can probably get a job at most any of the factories. Even the ones where the work is heavy or dangerous."

Mike's heart clenched. "Please don't take a job that might put you in danger. I couldn't stand it if something were to happen to you, Kelly."

She gave him a questioning look.

"I love you, and I—" Mike never finished his sentence. Instead, he took Kelly in his arms and kissed her upturned mouth. Her lips tasted sweet as honey, and it felt so right to hold her.

When Kelly slipped her hands around his neck and returned his kiss, Mike thought he was going to drown in the love he felt for her.

Kelly was the first to pull away. Her face was bright pink, and her eyes were cloudy with obvious emotion. Had she enjoyed the kiss as much as he?

She placed her trembling hands against her rosy cheeks. "I–I think it's time to go."

"But we haven't picked any wildflowers for you to use as watercolors yet," Mike argued.

She stood and dropped her art supplies into the pocket of her skirt. "I shouldn't have let you kiss me. It wasn't right."

Mike jumped to his feet. "It felt right to me."

She hung her head. "It wasn't, and it can never happen again."

Mike's previous elation plummeted clear to his toes. "I'm sorry you didn't enjoy the kiss."

"I did," she surprised him by saying. "But we can never be more than friends, and I don't think friends should go around kissin' each other."

So that's how it was. Kelly only saw him as a friend. Mike felt like a fool. He'd read more into her physical response than there was. He'd decided awhile back to take it slow and easy with Kelly—be sure of her feelings before he made a move. He'd really messed things up, and it was too late to take back the kiss or his declaration of love.

"Forgive me for taking liberties that weren't mine," he said, forcing her to look him in the eye, even though it pained him to see there were tears running down her cheeks.

When she didn't say anything, Mike bent to retrieve the picnic basket and blanket. "I think you're right. It's time to go."

৯৶

All the way back to the boat, Kelly chided herself for being foolish enough to allow Mike to kiss her. Now she'd hurt his feelings. It was obvious by the slump of his shoulders and the silence that covered the distance between them. On the way to the pond he'd been talkative and whistled. Now the only sounds were the call of a dove and the canal waters lapping against the bank.

I was wrong to let him kiss me, but was I wrong to tell him we could only be friends? Should I have let him believe I might feel more for him than friendship? Do I feel more?

Kelly's disconcerting thoughts came to a halt when they rounded the bend where the canal boats could be seen. In the middle of the grassy area between Mike's store and the boats that had stopped for the day, two men were fist fighting. One was Patrick O'Malley. The other was Kelly's dad. Several other men stood on the sidelines, shouting, clapping, and cheering them on. What was the scuffle about, and why wasn't someone trying to stop it?

As though Mike could read her thoughts, he set the picnic basket and blanket on the ground, then stepped forward. "Please, no fighting on the Sabbath. Can't you two men solve your differences without the use of your knuckles?"

Pow! Papa's fist connected on the left side of Patrick's chin. "You stay outa this, Boy!" he shouted at Mike.

Smack! Patrick gave Papa a head butt that sent him sprawling on the grass.

"Stop it! Stop it!" Kelly shouted. Tears were stinging the backs of her eyes, and she felt herself tremble. Why must Papa make such a spectacle of himself? What did Mike and the others who were watching think of her dad?

The men were hitting each other lickety-split now, apparently oblivious to anything that was being said. Closer and closer to the canal they went, and when Papa slammed his fist into Patrick's chest, the man lost his footing and fell over backwards. He grabbed Papa's shirtsleeve, and both men landed in the water with a splash.

Mortified, Kelly covered her face with her hands. How could a day that started out with such promise end on such a sour note?

After the fight was over and the two men settled down, Kelly learned the reason behind the scuffle. It had all started over something as simple as whose boat would be leaving first come Monday morning.

After the way her dad caused such a scene, Kelly didn't think she could show her face to Mike or anyone else without suspecting they were talking behind her back. It was embarrassing the way her dad could fly off the handle and punch a man for no reason at all. Men didn't make a lick of sense!

20

As summer moved into fall, Kelly saw less of Mike. Papa kept them moving, wanting to make as many loads as possible before the bad weather. He refused to stop for anything that wasn't necessary.

It was just as well she wasn't spending time with Mike, Kelly decided as she sat upon Hector's back, bone tired and unable to take another step. After Mike's unexpected kiss the day they'd had a picnic by the Millers' pond, Kelly hadn't wanted to do or say anything that might cause Mike to believe they had anything more than a casual friendship. What if Mike was thinking about marriage? What if he only felt sorry for her because she worked so hard? Kelly wasn't about to marry someone just to get away from Papa.

"I wish I didn't like Mike so much," Kelly murmured against the mule's ear.

❧

It had been a long day, and Mike was about ready to close up his store when Betsy Nelson showed up. She seemed to have such good timing. Mike had just finished going through a stack of mail brought in by the last boat that had come through before dark, and he was feeling lower than the canal waters after a break. He'd gotten another letter from his brother Alvin. This one said his other brother John had also found himself a girlfriend. There was even mention of a double wedding come December.

"Sorry to be coming by so late in the day," Betsy panted, "but Papa's real sick, and I need some medicine to help quiet his cough."

Her cheeks were red, and it was obvious by her heavy breathing that she'd probably run all the way to Mike's store. Mike knew Preacher Nelson didn't own a horse, preferring to make all his calls on foot.

"Come inside, and I'll see what kind of cough syrup I've got left in stock." Mike stepped aside so Betsy could enter, and she followed him to the back of the store.

"I haven't seen you for awhile," Betsy said as Mike handed her a bottle of his best-selling cough syrup.

"I've been kinda busy."

Her eyelids fluttered. "I've missed you."

Mike swallowed hard. Betsy was flirting again, and it made him real nervous. He didn't want to hurt her feelings, but the simple fact was, he didn't love Betsy. Even though Kelly had spurned his kiss, he was hoping someday she would come to love him as much as he did her.

As lonely as Mike was, and as much as he desired a wife, he knew it couldn't be the preacher's daughter. She was too self-centered and a bit short-tempered, which probably meant she wouldn't be a patient mother. Kelly, on the other hand, would make a good wife and mother. It wasn't just her lovely face or long, brown hair that had captured Mike's heart. Kelly had a gentle spirit. He'd witnessed it several times when she tended the mules. If only she seemed more willing.

Maybe I should quit praying for a wife and get a dog instead.

"Mike? Did you hear what I said?"

Betsy's high-pitched voice drove Mike's musings to the back of his mind. "What was that?"

"I said, 'I've missed you.' "

Mike felt his ears begin to warm, which meant they were probably bright red. "Thank you, Betsy. It's nice to know I've been missed."

She looked at him with pleading eyes. No doubt she was hoping he would respond by saying he missed her too. Mike couldn't lie. It wouldn't be right to lead Betsy on.

He moved quickly to the front of the store and placed the bottle of medicine on the counter. "Is there anything else you'll be needin'?"

Betsy's lower lip protruded as she shook her head.

He slipped the bottle into a brown paper sack, took her money, and handed Betsy her purchase. "I hope your dad is feeling better soon. Give him my regards, will you?"

She gave him a curt nod, lifted her head high, and pranced out the door. Mike let out a sigh of relief. At least she hadn't invited him to supper again.

ॐ

The last day of November arrived, and Kelly couldn't believe it was time to leave the Lehigh Navigation System until spring. When Mama said she needed a few things, Papa had agreed to stop by Cooper's General Store. Kelly felt a mixture of relief and anxiety. Even though she wanted the chance to say good-bye, she dreaded seeing Mike again. Ever since the day he'd kissed her, things had been strained between them. She was afraid Mike wanted more from her than she was able to give. He'd said once that he wanted a whole passel of children so he could teach them responsibility. Did he think making children work would make them smart?

"I wonder if he wants kids so he can force 'em to labor with no pay," Kelly fumed to the mules. All the men she knew who put their kids to work paid them little or nothing. It wasn't fair! No wonder Sarah ran away and got married.

" 'Course if Sarah hadn't run off, I wouldn't have been left with all the work. Maybe the two of us could have come up with a plan to make money of our own."

They were in front of Mike's store now, so Kelly secured the mules to a tree while she waited for her parents to get off the boat. A short time later, Mama disembarked.

"Where's Papa?" Kelly asked her mother.

Mama shrugged her shoulders. "He said he thought he'd take a nap while we do our shoppin'. He gave me a list of things he needs and said for us not to take all day."

Kelly followed her mother inside the store. She was glad to see Mike was busy with a customer. At least she wouldn't have to speak with him right away. It would give her time to think of something sensible to say.

Should she ask if he still planned to write her while she was living in Easton? Should she promise to write him in return?

She thought about the paintings she had in her drawing tablet, which she hoped to give Mike before she left. Trouble was, she didn't want Mama to see. Could she find some way of speaking to Mike alone?

As if by divine intervention, the man Mike had been waiting on left the store, and about the same time, Mama decided to go back to the boat. She said something about needing to get Papa's opinion on the material she planned to use for a shirt she'd be making him soon.

Kelly knew she didn't have much time, so when the door closed behind her mother, she moved over to the counter where Mike stood.

"Hello, Kelly," he said, offering her a pleasant smile. "It's good to see you."

She moistened her lips with the tip of her tongue. "We're on our way to Easton for the winter and decided to stop by your store for a few items."

When Mike made no comment, Kelly rushed on before she lost her nerve. "I've got a few more paintings to give you. That is, if you're interested in tryin' to sell them." She reached into her pocket and withdrew the tablet, then placed it on the counter.

Mike thumbed through the pages. "These are great, Kelly. I especially like the one of the two children playing in a pile of fallen leaves."

Kelly smiled. That was her favorite picture too. She'd drawn it in charcoal, then used a mixture of coffee shades, as well as some carrot, onion, and beet water for the colored leaves.

"I've sold a couple more pictures since you were last here," Mike said, reaching into his cash box and producing a few bills, which he handed to Kelly.

"What about your share of the profits?" she asked. "Did ya keep out some of the money?"

Mike gave her a sheepish grin. "I thought with you going to the big city and all, you'd probably need a little extra cash. I'll take my share out of the next batch of pictures I sell."

Kelly was tempted to argue, but the thought of having more

money made her think twice about refusing. She nodded instead and slipped the bills into her pocket.

"When do you think you'll be back?" Mike asked.

"Sometime in March, whenever the ice and snow are gone."

"Is there an address where I can write to you?"

"We'll be staying at Mable Flannigan's Boardinghouse. It's on the corner of Front Street in the eight hundred block."

"And you can write me here at Cooper's General Store, Walnutport, Pennsylvania."

"I'll try to write if there's time." That was all Kelly could promise. She had no idea where she might be working or how many hours she'd be putting in each day.

"Mind if I give you a hug good-bye?" Mike asked. "Just as friends?"

Kelly wasn't sure what to say. She didn't want to encourage Mike, yet she didn't want to be rude either. She guessed one little hug wouldn't hurt. He did say it was just as friends. She nodded and held out her arms.

Mike skirted around the counter and pulled her into an embrace.

Kelly's heart pounded against her chest, and she feared it might burst wide open. What if Mama came back and saw the two of them? What if Mike decided to kiss her again?

Her fears were relieved when Mike pulled away. "Take care, Kelly McGregor. I'll see you next spring."

*W*inter came quickly to the Lehigh Valley, and a thick layer of snow soon covered the ground. Mike missed Kelly terribly, and several times a week he would walk the towpath, as he was now, thinking about her and praying for her safety. He knew she cared for him, but only as a friend. If he just hadn't allowed himself to fall in love with her. If only she loved him in return.

Kelly had been gone a little over a month, and still not one letter had he received. He'd written to her several times, but no response. Was she too busy to write? Had she found a man and fallen in love? All sorts of things flitted through Mike's mind as he trudged along, his boots crunching through the fresh-fallen snow.

God would need to heal his heart if Kelly never returned, because Mike was in love with her, and there didn't seem to be a thing he could do about it.

I shouldn't have let myself fall for her, Lord, he prayed. *What I thought was Your will might have only been my own selfish desires. Maybe You want me to remain single.*

Shivering against the cold, Mike headed back to his house. There was no point in going over this again and again. If Kelly came back to the canal in the spring with a different attitude toward him, Mike would be glad. If she didn't, then he would have to accept it as God's will.

When Mike stepped inside the house a short time later, a blast of warm air hit him in the face. It was a welcome relief from the cold. As he hung his coat on a wall peg, he noticed the calendar hanging nearby. Today was January 5, Kelly's eighteenth birthday. He remembered her mentioning it before she left for the city. He'd sent her a package several days ago and hoped she would receive it on time. Even more than that, Mike hoped she liked the birthday present he'd chosen.

ॐ

Kelly couldn't believe how bad her feet hurt. She was used to walking the towpath every day, but trudging through the hilly city of Easton was an entirely different matter. Papa had insisted Kelly get a job to help with expenses, and she'd been out looking almost every day since they had arrived at the boardinghouse in Easton. No one seemed to be hiring right before Christmas, and after the holidays, she was either told there was no work or that she wasn't qualified for any of the available positions. Kelly kept looking every day, and in the evenings and on weekends, she helped Mama sew and clean their small, three-room flat.

Kelly hated to spend her days looking for work and longed to be with their mules that had been left at Morgan's Stables just outside of town. It wasn't cheap to keep them there, but Papa said they had no choice. Needing money for the mules' care was one of the reasons he'd taken a job at Glendon Iron Furnace, which overlooked the canal and Lehigh Valley Railroad. The work was hard and heavy but pay was better than at many other manual jobs.

Every chance she got, Kelly went to see her animal friends. Today was her eighteenth birthday, and she'd decided to celebrate with a trip to the stables right after breakfast. It might be the only thing special about her birthday, since neither Mama nor Papa had made any mention of it. They'd been sitting around the breakfast table for ten minutes, and no one had said a word about what day it was. Papa had his nose in the Easton newspaper, *The Sunday Call,* and Mama seemed preoccupied with the scrambled eggs on her plate.

Kelly sighed deeply and took a drink from her cup of tea. It didn't matter. She'd never had much of a fuss made on her birthday anyway. Why should this year be any different?

Maybe I'll take some of the money I earned sellin' paintings and buy something today. Kelly grimaced. She knew she should save all her cash for that art gallery she hoped to open some day. Even as the idea popped into her mind, Kelly felt it was futile. She'd only sold a few paintings so far, and even if she sold more, it would take years before she'd have enough to open any kind of gallery. She would need to pay rent for a building, and then there was the cost of all the supplies. It wouldn't be enough to simply sell her paintings and drawings; she'd want to offer her customers the chance to purchase paper, paints, charcoal pencils, and maybe some fancy frames. All that would cost a lot of money. Money Kelly would probably never see in her lifetime.

I may as well give up my dream. If I can find a job in the city, it would probably be best if I stay here and work. Papa can hire a mule driver to take my place. It would serve him right if I never went back to the canal again.

A loud knock drove Kelly's thoughts to the back of her mind. She looked at Papa, then Mama. Neither one seemed interested in answering the door.

Kelly sighed deeply and pushed her chair away from the table. Why was she always expected to do everything? She shuffled across the room, feeling as though she had the weight of the world on her shoulders.

She opened the door and was greeted by their landlord, Mable Flannigan. A heavyset, middle-aged woman with bright red hair and sparking blue eyes, Mable had told them that her husband was killed in the War Between the States, and she'd been on her own ever since. The woman had no children to care for and had opened her home to boarders shortly after the war ended nearly twenty-seven years ago. Kelly always wondered why Mrs. Flannigan had never remarried. Could be that she was still pining for her dead husband, or maybe the woman thought she could get along better without a man.

"This came for you in the mornin's mail," Mrs. Flannigan said, holding out a package wrapped in brown paper.

Kelly's forehead wrinkled. "For me?" She couldn't imagine who would be sending her anything.

The older woman nodded. "It has your name and the address of my boardinghouse right here on the front."

Kelly took the package and studied the handwriting. Her name was there all right, in big, bold letters. Her heart began to pound, and her hands shook when she saw the return address. It was from Mike Cooper.

Remembering her manners, Kelly opened the door wider. "Would ya like to come in and have a cup of coffee or some tea?"

Mrs. Flannigan shook her head. "Thanks, but I'd better not. I've got me some washin' to do today, and it sure won't get done if I lolly-gag over a cup of hot coffee."

The woman turned to go, and Kelly called, "Thanks for deliverin' the package."

A few seconds later, Kelly sat on the sofa, tearing the brown paper away from the box. With trembling hands she lifted the lid. She let out a little gasp when she saw what the box contained. Her eyes feasted on a tin of store-bought watercolor paints, a real artist's tablet, and three brushes in various sizes. There was also a note:

Dear Kelly,

I wanted you to have this paint set for your eighteenth birthday. I only wish I could be with you to help celebrate. I hope you're do-ing all right, and I'm real anxious for you to return to the canal.

Fondly, your friend,
Mike Cooper

P.S. Please write soon.

Kelly sat for several seconds, trying to understand how Mike could have known today was her birthday and relishing in the joy of owning a real set of watercolors, not to mention a store-bought tablet that she'd hadn't put together herself. She would be able to paint any-thing she wanted now, using nearly every shade imaginable.

An image of Mike's friendly face flashed into Kelly's mind. She might have mentioned something to him about her birthday being on January the fifth. The fact that he'd remembered and cared enough to send her a present was almost overwhelming. No one had ever given her a gift like the one she held in her hands.

"Kelly, who was at the door?" Papa hollered from the next room.

She swallowed hard and stood up. Her dad might be mad when

he saw the present Mike had sent her, but she wouldn't lie or hide it from him. While Papa was at work, and after Kelly got home from searching for a job every day, Mama had been reading the Bible out loud, and Kelly had fallen under deep conviction. She'd strayed from God and knew she needed to make things right. It was wrong to lie, or even hide the truth from her parents. It had been a sin to harbor resentment toward Papa, and with the Lord's help, she was doing much better in that regard.

Grasping the box with her birthday present inside, Kelly walked back to the kitchen. "Mrs. Flannigan was at the door with a package for me." Kelly placed the box on the table.

"Who would be sendin' you anything?" Papa asked, his eyebrows drawing together.

"It's from Mike Cooper."

"The storekeeper along the canal?" Mama questioned as she peered into the box.

Kelly nodded. "It's for my birthday." She sank into her chair, wondering when the explosion would come.

Mama pulled the tin of watercolors out of the box and held it up. Papa frowned, but he never said a word. Kelly held her breath.

"What a thoughtful gift," Mama said. "Now you'll be able to paint with real colors instead of makin' colored water out of my vegetables."

Kelly felt her face heat up. So her mother had known all the time that she was taking carrots, beets, and onions out of the bin. Funny thing, Mama had never said a word about it until now.

"Humph!" Papa snorted. "I hope that man don't think his gift is gonna buy him my daughter's hand in marriage."

"Mike and I are just friends, Papa," Kelly was quick to say. She turned to face her dad. "Can I keep it? I promise not to paint when I'm supposed to be workin'."

"You've gotta find a job first," her dad grumbled. "We've been in the city for a whole month already, and not one red cent have you brought in."

"I'll look again on Monday," Kelly promised.

"Why don'tcha try over at the Simon Silk Mill on Bushkill Creek?" Mama suggested. "I hear tell they're lookin' to hire a few people there."

Kelly nodded. "I'll go first thing on Monday morning."

Papa took a long drink from his cup of coffee, wiped his mouth with the back of his hand, and stood up. "I need to get to work."

"But it's Saturday," Mama reminded.

He leveled her with a disgruntled look. "Don'tcha think I know that, Woman? They're operatin' the plant six days a week now, and I volunteered to come in today." His gaze swung over to Kelly. "You can keep the birthday present, but I'd better not find you paintin' when ya should be out lookin' for work."

"Thank you, Papa, and I promise I won't paint until all my chores are done for the day neither." Kelly felt like she could kiss her dad. She didn't, though. Papa had never been very affectionate, and truth be told, until this moment, Kelly had never felt like kissing him.

Papa grunted, grabbed his jacket off the wall peg, and sauntered out the door.

Mama patted Kelly's hand. "Tonight I'm fixin' your favorite supper, in honor of your birthday."

"Hunks-a-go pudding and roast beef?" Kelly asked hopefully.

Mama nodded and grinned. "Might make a chocolate cake for dessert too."

Kelly smiled in return, feeling better than she had in weeks. Today turned out to be a better birthday than she'd ever imagined. Now if she could only find a job.

s Kelly stood in front of the brick building that housed the Simon Silk Mill, she whispered a prayer, petitioning God to give her a job. She didn't know any other kind of work besides leading the mules, but Mama had taught her to sew, and she figured that's what she would be doing if she were hired here. All the other times they'd wintered in Easton, Papa had never demanded Kelly find a job. That was probably because Mama insisted Kelly go to school. She was older now and done with book learning, so it was time to make some money. If only she didn't have to give it all to Papa. If she could keep the money she earned, Kelly would probably have enough to open her art gallery in no time at all. Of course, she didn't think she would have the nerve to tell Papa she wasn't going back to the canal in the spring.

Pushing the door open, Kelly stepped inside the factory and located the main office. She entered the room and told the receptionist she needed a job. Disappointment flooded Kelly's soul when she was told all the positions at the mill had been taken.

Kelly left the office feeling a sense of frustration. What if she never found a job? Papa would be furious and might make her throw out her art supplies. She couldn't let that happen. There had to be something she could do.

Kelly was almost to the front door when she bumped into someone. Her mouth dropped open, and she took a step back. "Sarah?"

The young woman with dark brown hair piled high on her head looked at Kelly as if she'd seen a ghost. "Kelly, is that you?"

"It's me, Sarah. I'm so surprised to see you."

"And I, you," her sister replied.

"Do you work here?"

Sarah nodded. "Have been for the last couple of months. Before that I was home takin' care of little Sam."

"Little Sam?"

"Sam Jr."

"You have a son?" Kelly could hardly believe her sister had a baby they knew nothing about. For that matter, they hadn't heard anything from Sarah since that one letter, telling the family she and Sam had gotten married and were living in New Jersey.

"The baby was born six months ago," Sarah explained. "Sam was workin' at Warren Soapstone, but one day he lost his temper with the boss and got fired. So I had to find work, and he's been home takin' care of the baby ever since."

Kelly stood there for several seconds, studying her sister and trying to let all she'd said sink into her brain. Sarah was dressed in a beige-colored cotton blouse and plain brown skirt covered with a black apron. Her shoulders were slumped, and she looked awful tired.

The fact that Sam Turner would allow his wife to work while he stayed home was one more proof for Kelly that men only used women. Sam was no better than Papa. Sarah had run off with Sam to get away from working, and now she was being forced to support not only herself, but her husband and baby as well. It made Kelly sick to the pit of her stomach.

"Are you and the folks stayin' at the boardinghouse like before?" Sarah's question drove Kelly's thoughts to the back of her mind.

"Yes, we've been there since early December." Kelly gave her sister a hug. "I'm sure Mama and Papa would like to see you and the baby . . . Sam Sr. too."

When Sarah pulled away, tears stood in her dark eyes. "Oh, please don't say anything to the folks about seein' me today."

"Why not?"

"Papa always hated Sam, and when we tried to tell him we were in love and wanted to get married, he blew up and said if we did, he'd punch Sam in the nose."

Kelly flinched at the memory. She'd been there when Papa had gotten all red in the face and shouted at Sam and Sarah. She could understand why her sister might be afraid to confront their dad now.

"I won't say a word," Kelly promised, "but I would sure like to see my nephew. You think there's any way that could be arranged?"

Sarah gave a tired yet sincere smile. "I'd like you to meet little Sam. Mama too, for that matter. Maybe the two of you can come by our apartment sometime soon. Let me talk it over with my husband first, though."

"How will we get in touch with you?"

Sarah looked thoughtful. "Is Papa workin' every day?"

Kelly nodded. "Over at Glendon Iron Furnace, even Saturdays now."

"Then how about if the baby and I come by the boardinghouse next Saturday?"

"That would be great. Should I tell Mama ahead, or do you want to surprise her?"

"Let's make it our little surprise." Sarah squeezed Kelly's arm. "I need to get back up to the second floor where I work on one of the weavin' looms."

Kelly gave her sister another hug. "Sure is good to see you, Sarah."

"Same here." Sarah started for the stairs, and Kelly headed for the front door, feeling more cheerful than she had all morning. Even if she didn't have a job, at least she'd been reunited with her sister. That was something to be grateful for.

ૐ

For the third time that morning, Mike sorted through the stack of mail he'd dumped on the counter after it arrived by canal boat. There was nothing from Kelly. Wasn't she ever going to respond? Had she received his birthday present? Did she like the watercolor set, sketching pad, and paintbrushes, or was she mad at him for giving them to her? If only she'd written a note to let him know the package had arrived.

"I've got to get busy and quit thinkin' about Kelly." Mike slipped each letter into the cubbyholes he'd made for his postal customers. The packages were kept in a box underneath. As local people dropped by the store, he would hand out their mail and be glad he'd taken the time to organize it so well. Any mail that came for the boatmen who were working in the city and wanted their parcels to be held until they returned to the canal was stored safely in a wooden box under the front counter. Most canalers lived in homes nearby, and those, like Amos McGregor, would be getting their mail forwarded to their temporary address during the winter months.

Thinking about Amos caused Mike's mind to wander back to Kelly. Whenever he closed his eyes at night he could see her smiling face, hear her joyous laughter, and feel her sweet lips against his own. Had it been wrong to kiss her? He hadn't thought so at the time, but after she'd pulled away and cooled off toward him, Mike figured he'd done a terrible thing.

"I kept telling myself I would go slow with Kelly, but I moved too fast," Mike moaned. "Why must I always rush ahead of God?" He reached for one of the Bibles he had stacked near the end of the counter and opened it to the Book of Hebrews. He found chapter 10 and read verses 35 and 36: *"Cast not away . . . your confidence, which hath great recompense of reward. For ye have need of patience, that, after ye have done the will of God, ye might receive the promise."*

Mike closed his eyes and quoted from Genesis, chapter 2, verse 18: *"And the LORD God said, It is not good that the man should be alone; I will make him an help meet for him."* He dropped to his knees behind the counter. "Oh, Lord, if I have patience and continue to do Your will, might I receive the promise of an help meet?"

Except for the eerie howling of the wind against the eaves of the store, there was no sound. Patience. Mike knew he needed to be more patient. With God's help he would try, but it wouldn't be easy.

23

On Saturday afternoon Sarah, with baby Sam tucked under one arm, came by the boardinghouse. Kelly was shocked at her sister's haggard appearance. Sarah had looked tired the other day, but it was nothing like this. Puffiness surrounded her sister's red-rimmed eyes, indicating she had been crying. Something was wrong. Kelly could feel it in her bones.

Mama, who hadn't been told about Sarah's surprise visit, rushed to her oldest daughter's side when Kelly stepped away and closed the door. "Sarah!" Mama exclaimed. "I can't believe it's you. Where have you been livin'? How did you know we'd be here?" She reached out to touch the baby's chubby hand. "And who is this cute little fellow?"

Sarah emitted a small laugh, even though her expression was strained. "Too many questions at once, Mama. Can I come in and be seated before I answer each one?"

Mama's hands went to her flushed cheeks. "Yes, yes. Please, let me have your coats, then go into the livin' room and get comfortable."

Sarah turned to Kelly, who so far hadn't uttered a word. "Would ya mind holdin' Sam while I take off my coat?"

Kelly held out her arms to the child, but little Sam buried his head against his mother's chest and whimpered.

"He's a bit shy around strangers," Sarah said. "I'm sure he'll warm up to you soon." She handed the baby over to Kelly despite the child's protests.

Feeling awkward and unsure of herself, Kelly stepped into the living room and took a seat on the sofa. Baby Sam squirmed restlessly, but he didn't cry.

A few minutes later, Sarah and their mother entered the room.

Mama sat beside Kelly on the sofa, and Sarah took a seat in the rocking chair across from them.

"Mama, meet your grandson, Sam Jr.," Sarah announced.

Mama's lips curved into a smile, and she reached out to take the infant from Kelly. He went willingly, obviously drawn to his grandma.

"I can't believe you have a baby, Sarah. How old is he, and why didn't ya write and tell us about him?"

Sarah hung her head, and Kelly noticed tears dripping onto her sister's skirt, leaving dark spots in the gray-colored fabric. "I–I knew you and Papa were angry with me for runnin' off with Sam, so I figured you wouldn't want to know anything about what I was doin'."

Kelly closed her eyes and offered up a prayer on her sister's behalf as she waited for her mother's reply.

Mama's eyes filled with tears, and she hugged the baby to her breast. "I could never turn my back on one of my own, Sarah. I love both my girls." She glanced over at Kelly, who was also close to tears.

"I love you too, Mama," Kelly murmured.

"So do I," Sarah agreed. "Now as to your questions . . . Sam is six months old, and we've all been livin' in a flat across the bridge in Phillipsburg. Up until a few weeks ago, Sam worked at Warren Soapstone, but he got fired for shootin' off his mouth to the boss." Sarah paused and drew in a deep breath. "I've been workin' at the Simon Silk Mill ever since, and Sam *was* takin' care of the baby."

Was? What did Sarah mean by that? Before Kelly could voice the question, her sister rushed on.

"Sam's been drinkin' here of late, and actin' real funny. Last night when I got home from work, he had his bags packed and said he was leavin' me and the baby." Sarah's eyes clouded with fresh tears, and she choked on a sob. "I've got no place to leave Sam Jr. while I'm at work now, and I can't afford to hire a babysitter and pay the rent on my flat too."

"I could watch the baby for you," Kelly spoke up. "I haven't been able to find work anywhere yet, so I have nothin' else to do with my time." *Except paint and dream impossible dreams,* she added mentally.

Sarah shot Mama an imploring look. "Would ya allow Kelly to come live with me?"

"I'm not sure that would set well with your papa." Mama pursed her lips. "Why don't you and the baby move in here with us?"

Sarah glanced around the room. "This is the same place you've always rented from Mable Flannigan, right?"

Their mother nodded.

"Mama, it's so small. There's not nearly enough room for two extra people." She nodded at Kelly. "If you could come stay with me and Sam Jr., I couldn't pay you, but I could offer free room and board. You'd also have a small room, which you'd need to share with the baby."

As sorry as Kelly was to hear the news that Sarah's husband had left, the idea of moving in with her sister sounded rather pleasant. It would give her more time to paint without Papa breathing down her neck or hollering because she still hadn't found a job. She touched her mother's arm gently. "Please, Mama. I'd like to help Sarah out in her time of need."

Mama shrugged her shoulders. "If Papa says it's all right, then I'll agree to it as well."

ॐ

The next few months were like none Kelly had ever known. Much to her surprise, Papa had given permission for her to move in with Sarah. Kelly now spent five days a week taking care of little Sam while Sarah was at work. This gave her some time to use her new watercolor set, since she could paint or draw whenever the baby slept.

Besides babysitting, Kelly cleaned the apartment, did most of the cooking, and even sewed new clothes for her fast-growing nephew. She and little Sam had become good friends, and Kelly discovered she was more capable with children than she'd ever imagined.

As Kelly sat in the rocking chair, trying to get the baby to sleep, she let her mind wander back to the general store outside of Walnutport, along the Lehigh Navigation System. A vision of Mike Cooper flashed into her mind. He was good with children. Kelly had witnessed him giving out free candy to several of the kids who played along the canal and to many who visited his store as well. Mike wanted a whole house-ful of children; he'd told her so.

"I never did write and thank Mike for the birthday gift," Kelly whispered against little Sam's downy blond head. The baby looked a lot like his papa, but Kelly hoped he didn't grow up to be anything like the man. How could Sam Turner have left his wife and child? Just thinking about it made Kelly's blood boil. Was Mike Cooper any different than Papa or Sam? Could he be trusted not to hurt her the way Papa often did or the way Sam had done to Sarah?

Mike had promised to write, and he'd done so several times. He'd also sent her a wonderful present. He might not be the same as other men she knew. Kelly guessed she'd have to make up her mind about Mike when they returned to the canal sometime in March.

She bent her head and kissed the tip of little Sam's nose. "You and your mama might be goin' with us this spring. I don't rightly see how the two of you can stay on here by yourselves." She giggled at the baby's response to her kiss. He'd scrunched up his nose and wiggled his lips, almost as if he was trying to kiss her back.

"Of course, I could always stay on here, I suppose. Papa can't make me return to the canal if I don't want to." Even as the words slipped off her tongue, Kelly knew what she would do when Papa said it was time to return to their boat. She would go along willingly be-cause she missed her mule friends, missed the smell of fresh air, and yes, even missed Mike Cooper.

ॐ

Mike stared at his empty coffee cup. He should clear away the break-fast dishes and get his horse hitched to the buckboard. He was ex-pecting a load of supplies to be delivered to Walnutport today by train, and it would be good if he were there when it came in. Mike knew that Gus Stevens, the man who ran the livery stable next to the train station, would be happy to take the supplies to his place and hold them for him. Gus had done that a time or two, but Mike didn't like to take advantage of the older man's good nature.

With that thought in mind, Mike scooped the dishes off the table and set them in the sink. He'd pour warm water over them and take care of the washing part when he returned from town.

A short time later, Mike climbed into his wagon, clucked to the horse, and headed in the direction of Walnutport. During the first part of the trip, he sang favorite hymns and played his mouth harp. It made the time go quicker and caused Mike to feel a bit closer to his Maker. It also made him feel less lonely.

As the days had turned into weeks, and the weeks into months, Mike's yearning for a wife had not diminished. In fact, he'd been feeling so lonely here of late, he'd actually considered accepting one of Betsy Nelson's frequent supper invitations. The woman was persistent, he'd give her that much. Persistent and pushy. Nothing like Kelly McGregor.

"I've got to quit thinkin' about Kelly," Mike berated himself. "She obviously feels nothing for me. If she did, she would have written by now." Mike wasn't sure he'd ever see Kelly again. For all he knew, she'd decided to stay in the city of Easton. She'd probably found a job and a boyfriend by now. She could even be married.

By the time Mike arrived at his destination, he was sweating worse than his horse. He'd let the gelding run and had enjoyed the exhilarating ride. It helped clear his thinking. Nothing else had mattered but the wind blowing against his face. Tomorrow would be a new day. Another time to reflect on God's will for Mike's life.

24

On Monday morning, the third week of March, the McGregors boarded their boat. The canal was full of water again, and Papa was most anxious to get started hauling coal. Sarah and baby Sam had come along, since Sarah didn't want to stay in Easton by herself and couldn't talk Kelly into staying on. Besides, Mama could use Sarah's help on the boat and would be available to watch the baby whenever Kelly's sister took over walking the mules.

Kelly felt bad that Sarah was returning to the canal she'd hated so much in the past, but it would be nice to have her sister's help, as well as her companionship.

Kelly looked forward to stopping by Mike's store, and she knew they would because Papa had said so. They'd picked up some supplies at Dull's Grocery Store in Easton, but Papa forgot to get a couple of things. Kelly planned to give Mike several more pictures to try to sell, as she'd been able to paint many during her stay in the city. She was also anxious to see whether he'd sold any of her other pieces. Kelly hoped she could continue her friendship with Mike without his expecting anything more. They should arrive at his store sometime tomorrow, late afternoon or early evening.

Kelly pulled the collar of her jacket tightly against her chin as she tromped along the towpath, singing her favorite song, and not even minding the chilly March winds.

"Hunks-a-go pudding and pieces of pie; my mother gave me when I was knee-high. . . . And if you don't believe it, just drop in and see—the hunks-a-go pudding my mother gave me."

&❧

Mike felt better than he had in weeks. He'd had several customers and given away a couple of Bibles to some rough and tumble canalers who were desperately in need of God. Mike had witnessed these two men fighting on more than one occasion, and the fact that they'd willingly taken a Bible gave him hope that others might also be receptive to the gospel.

As Mike washed the store windows with a rag and some diluted ammonia, he thought about Kelly's dad. Now there was a man badly in need of the Lord. Mike had witnessed Amos McGregor's temper several times. If Amos found forgiveness for his sins and turned his life around, maybe Kelly would be more receptive to Mike's attentions. Mike was sure the main reason Kelly was so standoffish was because she was afraid of men.

He glanced at the wall behind his front counter. Only two of Kelly's pictures had sold since she'd left for Easton, and those had both been bought before Christmas. No one had shown any interest in her work since then, even though Mike often pointed the pictures out to his customers, hoping they would take the hint and buy one.

Mike studied the window he'd been washing, checking for any spots or streaks. To his surprise, he noticed Amos McGregor's boat docked out front, and the man was heading toward the store. Trudging alongside of Amos was his wife, Dorrie, Kelly, and another woman carrying a young child.

Mike climbed off his ladder and hurried to the front of the store. Kelly had returned to the canal! He opened the door and greeted his customers with a smile and a sense of excitement. "It's sure nice to see you folks again."

Amos only grunted in reply, but Kelly returned his smile. "It's good to be back," she said.

"And who might this little guy be?" Mike asked, reaching out to clasp the chubby fingers of the little boy who was held by the other young woman.

"That's baby Sam," Kelly said. "In case you don't remember, this is my sister, Sarah. She and Sam Jr. are gonna be livin' with us for awhile."

"Yes, I remember Sarah." Mike nodded and smiled at Kelly's sister. He didn't ask for details. From the pathetic look on Sarah's face, he figured her marriage to Sam Turner was probably over.

"Do you have any soft material I might use for diapers?" Sarah asked. "Sam seems to go through them pretty fast, and I don't have time to be washin' every day."

Mike pointed to the shelf where he kept bolts of material. "I'm sure you'll find something to your liking over there."

Sarah moved away, and her mother followed. Amos was across the room looking at some new shovels Mike had recently gotten in, so apparently Kelly felt free to stare up at her paintings.

Mike positioned himself so he was standing beside Kelly. "How have you been? I've missed you," he whispered.

Her gaze darted from her dad, to the paintings, and back to Mike. "I'm fine, and I've brought you more pictures." She frowned. "But from the looks of it, you still have quite a few of my old ones."

He nodded. "Sorry to say I only sold two while you were gone." He leaned his head close to her ear. "Did you get the birthday present I sent? I'd hoped you would write and let me know."

"Yes, I got the package and put it to good use." Kelly averted his gaze. "Sorry for not writing to say thank you. I kept meaning to write, but I got busy takin' care of little Sam while Sarah went to work each day."

"That's okay. I understand." Mike touched her arm briefly, but then he pulled his hand away. "Do you have the new pictures with you now?"

She nodded, reached into her pocket, retrieved the drawing tablet he'd sent her, and handed it to him. "I was able to make things look more real usin' things you sent me."

Mike thumbed quickly through the tablet. Pictures of row housing, tall buildings, and statues in the city of Easton covered the first pages. There were also some paintings of the bridge that spanned the river between Easton, Pennsylvania, and Phillipsburg, New Jersey, as well as a few pictures of people. They were all done well, and Mike was glad he'd sent Kelly the paint set, even if she hadn't chosen to write and tell him she'd received it. He was even happier that she'd accepted the gift and put it to good use.

"These are wonderful," he said. "Would you mind leaving them with me to try and sell?"

Kelly's eyebrows furrowed. "But you still have most of my other pictures. Why would ya be wantin' more?"

"Because they're good—really good," he asserted. "I've always admired your artwork, and I believe you've actually gotten better."

Her expression turned hopeful. "You really think so?"

"I do."

She pointed to the tablet. "And you think you can sell these?"

"I'd like to try."

She nodded her consent. "Do as you like then."

"Will you be spending the night in the area?" Mike asked.

Kelly opened her mouth, but her dad spoke up before she could say anything. "We'll be headin' on up the canal. Won't be back this way 'til probably late Saturday."

Mike turned his head to the left. He hadn't realized Kelly's dad was standing beside him, holding a shovel in one hand.

"You think you might stay over on Saturday night?"

"Could be," was all Amos said.

Mike smiled to himself. If the McGregors were here on Sunday, then he might get the chance to spend some time alone with Kelly. Even though the weather was still a bit chilly, it was possible that they'd be able to go on another picnic.

&

Kelly left Mike's store with mixed feelings. It was wonderful to see him again, but her spirits had been dampened when he'd told her he'd only sold two pictures during her absence. Mike had given her the money for those paintings as she was on her way out the door. He'd also whispered that he wanted to take her on another picnic and hoped it would be this Sunday, if they were near his store.

"Mind if I walk with you a ways?" Sarah asked, breaking into Kelly's musings. "Sam's ready for a nap, and Mama doesn't need me for anything. I thought the fresh air and exercise might do me some good."

Kelly was always glad for her sister's company. "You wanna be in charge of the mules or just offer me companionship?"

"You can tend the mules," Sarah was quick to say. "I think they like you better than they do me, anyway."

"They're just used to me, that's all." Kelly adjusted the brim of her straw hat, which seemed to have a mind of its own. "Truth be told, I think old Herman kinda likes it when I sing silly canal songs."

"You sing to the mules?"

Kelly nodded. "Guess it's really for me, but if they enjoy it, then that makes it all the better."

Sarah chuckled. It was good to see her smile. She'd been so sad since her husband had run off, and Kelly couldn't blame her. She would be melancholy too if the man she'd married had chosen not to stay around and help out. Sam Turner ought to be tarred and feathered for walking out on his wife and baby. He probably never loved Sarah in the first place. Most likely he only married her just to show her folks that he could take their daughter away.

"Tell me about Mike Cooper," Sarah said.

Kelly jerked her head. "What about him?"

"Have you and him been courtin'?"

"What would make you ask that?"

Sarah gave Kelly a nudge in the ribs with her bony elbow. "He couldn't take his eyes off you the whole time we were in the store." She eyed Kelly curiously. "I'd say it's as plain as the nose on your face that you're smitten with him as well."

What could Kelly say in response? She couldn't deny her feelings for Mike. She enjoyed his company, and he was the best-looking man she'd ever laid eyes on. That didn't mean they were courting, though. And it sure didn't mean she was smitten with him.

"Mike and me have gone on a few picnics, but we're not a courtin' couple," Kelly said, shrugging her shoulders.

"But you'd like to be, right?" her sister prodded.

"We're just friends; nothin' more."

Sarah wiggled her dark eyebrows, then winked. "Whatever you say, little sister. Whatever you say."

$\mathcal{E}$arly Saturday afternoon Mike went outside to help one of the local boatmen load the supplies he had purchased onto his boat. They had no more than placed the last one on deck when Mike saw the McGregors' boat heading their way.

His heart did a little flip-flop. Would they be stopping for the night? Mike stepped onto the towpath, anxious for Kelly to arrive. While he waited, he slicked back his hair, finger-combed his mustache, and made sure his flannel shirt was tucked inside his trousers.

A few minutes later Kelly and her mules were alongside him. The animals brayed and snorted, as if they expected him to give them a handout, as he'd done a few times before.

"Sorry, fellows, but I didn't know you were comin', so there aren't any apples or carrots in my pockets today." Mike gave each mule a pat on its flank, then he turned and smiled at Kelly. "I'm glad you're here. Are you planning to stay overnight?"

She shook her head. "Now that Sarah's here to help, Papa has us movin' twice as fast as before. He says there's no time to waste. Especially when we never know if there's gonna be trouble ahead that might slow us down."

Mike felt his anticipation slip to the toes of his boots. He'd been waiting so long to be with Kelly again, and now they weren't stopping? How was he ever going to tell her what was on his mind if they couldn't spend any time together?

"I'm sorry to hear you're not staying over," he muttered. "I was really hoping we'd be able to go on a picnic tomorrow afternoon."

"Isn't it a mite chilly for a picnic?"

Mike shrugged his shoulders. "I figured we could build a fire and snuggle beneath a blanket if it got too cold."

When Kelly smiled at him, he wanted to take her into his arms and proclaim his intentions. He knew now wasn't the time or the place, so he pulled from his inner strength and took a step back. "When do you think you might be stoppin' long enough so we can spend a few minutes together?"

She turned her palms upwards. "Don't know. That's entirely up to Papa."

Mike groaned. "Guess I'll just have to wait and ask God to give me more patience."

"Get a move on, would ya, Girl?"

Kelly and Mike both turned their heads. Amos McGregor was leaning over the side of the boat, and he wasn't smiling.

"I need to get the mules movin' again," Kelly said to Mike.

He stepped aside but touched her arm as she passed by. "See you soon, Kelly."

"I hope so," she murmured.

ཀ

The next few weeks sped by, as Kelly and Sarah took turns leading the mules, and Papa kept the boat moving as fast as the animals would pull. They stopped only once for supplies, and that was at a store in Mauch Chunk. Kelly was beginning to think she'd never get the chance to see Mike Cooper again or find out if any of her paintings had sold. On days like today, when the sky was cloudy and threatened rain, Kelly's spirits plummeted, and she didn't feel much like praying. All the while they'd been living in Easton, she'd felt closer to God, reading her Bible every day and offering prayers on behalf of her family and her future. It didn't seem as if any of her prayers were going to be answered, and she wondered if she should continue to ask God for things He probably wouldn't provide.

She'd prayed for her sister, and look how that had turned out. She had prayed for Papa's salvation, yet he was still as moody and cantankerous as ever. She'd asked God to allow her to make enough money to support herself and open an art gallery, but that wasn't working out either. So far she'd only made a few dollars, which was a long ways from what she would need. It was an impossible dream, and with each passing day Kelly became more convinced it was never going to happen.

She looked up at the darkening sky and prayed, "Lord, if walkin' the mules is the only job You have in mind for me, then help me learn to be content."

ॐ

It was the end of April before Kelly saw Mike again. They'd arrived in front of his store at dusk on Saturday evening, so Papa decided to stay for the night. Since the next day was Sunday and the boatmen were not allowed to pull their loads up the canal, they would be around for the whole day.

Kelly settled into her bed, feeling a sense of joy she hadn't felt in weeks. Tomorrow she planned to attend the church service on the grassy area in front of Mike's store. Afterward she hoped to see Mike and talk to him about her artwork. She'd managed to do a few more paintings—mostly of little Sam—so she would give those to Mike as well.

Sam was growing so much, and soon he'd be toddling all over the place. Then they would have to be sure he was tied securely to something, or else he might end up falling overboard. Canal life could be dangerous, and precautions had to be taken in order to protect everyone on board. Even the mules needed safeguarding from bad weather, insects, freak accidents, and fatigue.

Kelly closed her eyes and drew in a deep breath as she snuggled into her feather pillow. She fell asleep dreaming about Mike Cooper.

ॐ

The following day brought sunshine and blue skies. It was perfect spring weather, and Kelly had invited her sister and mother to join her for the church service that had just begun. Mama said she'd better stay on the boat with Papa, but Sarah left the baby behind with her parents and joined Kelly.

The two young women spread a blanket on the grass and took a seat just as Betsy Nelson began playing her zither, while her father led those who had gathered in singing "Holy Spirit, Light Divine."

Kelly lifted her voice with the others. The first verse spoke to her heart:

Holy Spirit, Light divine,
Shine upon this heart of mine.
Chase the shades of night away;
Turn my darkness into day.

The song gave Kelly exactly what she needed. A reminder that only God could turn her darkness into day. As difficult as it was, she knew she needed to keep praying and trusting Him to answer her prayers.

Kelly felt her sister's nudge in the ribs. "Psst . . . look who's watchin' you."

Kelly turned her head and noticed Mike sitting on a wooden box several feet away. He grinned and nodded at her, and she smiled in return.

"I told you he likes you."

Kelly put her fingers to her lips. "Shh . . . someone might hear."

Sarah snickered, but she stopped talking and began to sing. Kelly did the same.

A short time later, the preacher gave his message from the Book of Romans.

" 'For we know that all things work together for good to them that love God, to them who are the called according to his purpose,' " Rev. Nelson read in his booming voice.

All things. For them that love God and are called according to His purpose. Kelly was sure that meant her. The preacher was saying all things in her life would work together for good because she loved God. Surely He wanted to give her good things. The question was, would those good things be what she'd been praying for?

Kelly hadn't realized the service was over until Sarah touched her arm. "You gonna sit there all day, or did ya plan to go speak to that storekeeper who hasn't taken his eyes off you since we sat down?"

Kelly wrinkled her nose. "You're makin' that up."

"Am not." Sarah stood up. "I'd better get back to the boat and check on little Sam. Got any messages you want me to give the folks?"

Kelly got to her feet as well. "What makes you think I'm not re-turnin' to the boat with you?"

"Call it a hunch." Sarah bent down and grabbed the blanket. She gave it a good shake, then folded it and tucked it under Kelly's arm. "Should I tell Mama you won't be joinin' us for the noon meal?"

Kelly felt her face heat up. Was Sarah able to read her mind these days?

"Well, I . . . uh . . . thought I might speak to Mike about my paintings. See if any more have sold."

"And if he invites you to join him for lunch?"

Kelly chewed on her lower lip. "You think I should say yes?"

Sarah swatted Kelly's arm playfully. "Of course, silly."

"What about the folks? Shouldn't I check with them first?"

"Leave that up to me."

"Okay, then. If I don't return to the boat in the next half hour, you can figure I'm havin' a picnic lunch with Mike. He did mention wan-tin' to do that the last time we talked."

Sarah gave Kelly a quick hug, hoisted her long skirt, and trudged off in the direction of the boat. Kelly turned toward the spot where Mike had been sitting, but disappointment flooded her soul when she realized he was gone. With a deep sigh, she whirled around and headed the same way Sarah had gone. There was no point in sticking around now.

Kelly had only taken a few steps when she felt someone touch her shoulder. She whirled around, and her throat closed with emotion. Mike was standing so close she could feel his warm breath on her neck. She stared up at him, her heart thumping hard like the mules' hooves plodding along the hard-packed trail.

"Kelly." Mike's voice was soft and sweet.

She slid her tongue across her lower lip, feeling jittery as a june bug. "I came to hear the preaching."

"Reverend Nelson delivered a good message today, didn't he?"

Kelly nodded in response. It was hard to speak. Hard to think with him standing there watching her every move.

"Can you join me for a picnic?" Mike asked. "It will only take me a few minutes to throw something in the picnic basket, and it's the perfect day for it, don't you think?"

"Yes, yes, it is," she replied, glad she'd found her voice again.

"Then you'll join me?"

"I'd be happy to. Is there anything I can bring?"

"Just a hearty appetite and that blanket you're holding."

Kelly glanced down at the woolen covering still tucked under her arm. Sarah must have given it to her because she'd been pretty certain Mike would be taking her on a picnic. "Where should I meet you?"

"How about at the pond by the lock tender's house again? That way you won't have to worry about anyone seeing us walk there together."

Kelly knew Mike was probably referring to her dad, and he was right. It would be much better if Papa didn't know she was going on a picnic with the storekeeper.

"Okay, I'll head there now, and maybe even get a bit of sketching done while I'm waitin' for you."

Mike winked at her. "See you soon then."

"Yes, soon."

26

*T*he warmth of the sun beating down on her head and shoulders felt like healing balm as Kelly reclined on her blanket a few feet from the pond. She always enjoyed springtime, with its gentle breezes, pleasantly warm temperatures, and flowers blooming abundantly along the towpath. Summer would be here soon, and that meant hot, humid days, which made it more difficult to walk the mules. So she would enjoy each day of spring, and try to be content when the sweltering days of summer came upon them.

"Are you taking a nap?"

Kelly bolted upright at the sound of Mike's voice. "I . . . uh . . . was just resting and enjoyin' the warmth of the sun."

He took a seat beside her and placed the picnic basket in the center of the blanket. "It's a beautiful Lord's day, isn't it?"

She nodded and smiled.

"I hope you're hungry, because I packed us a big lunch."

Kelly eyed the basket curiously. "What did ya fix?"

Mike opened the lid and withdrew a loaf of bread, along with a hunk of cheese and some roast beef slices. "For sandwiches," he announced.

Kelly licked her lips as her mouth began to water. She hadn't realized how hungry she was until she saw the food.

"I also brought some canned peaches, a bottle of goat's milk, and a chocolate cake for dessert."

"Where did you get all this?" Surely the man hadn't baked the cake and bread, canned the peaches, and milked a goat. When would he have had the time? Papa always said cooking and baking were women's work, although he had been forced to do some of it when Mama had taken sick last year.

Mike fingered his mustache as a smile spread across his face. "I must confess, I bought the bread and cake from Mrs. Harris, the lock tender's wife. I often buy her baked goods and sell them in my store. The peaches came from Mrs. Wilson, who lives in Walnutport."

"And the goat's milk?"

He wiggled his eyebrows. "I recently traded one of my customers a couple of kerosene lamps for the goat."

"Couldn't they have paid for the lamps, or were you actually wantin' a goat?"

He chuckled. "Truth of the matter, they didn't have any cash, and even though I offered them credit, they preferred to do a bit of bartering." He poured some of the goat's milk into a cup and handed it to Kelly. "I enjoy animals, so Henrietta is a nice addition to the little barnyard family I adopted this winter."

"Your barnyard family? How many other animals do you have?"

"Besides Blaze, my horse, and Henrietta the goat, I also own a cat, a dozen chickens, and I'm thinkin' about getting a pig or two."

Kelly shook her head. "Sounds like a lot of work to me."

"Maybe so, but a man can get lonely living all by himself, and taking care of the critters gives me something to do when I'm not minding the store."

Kelly was about to take a sip of her goat's milk, when Mike took hold of her hand. "Shall we pray?"

"Of course."

After Mike's simple prayer, he sliced the bread and handed Kelly a plate with a hunk of cheese, some meat, and two thick pieces of bread. She made quick work out of eating it, savoring every bite.

When they finished their sandwiches, Mike opened the jar of peaches and placed two chunks on each of their plates.

"Don't you ever get lonely walking the towpath by yourself?"

"I'm not really alone," Kelly replied. "Herman and Hector are good company, and of course, now that Sarah's back, she sometimes walks with me."

His eyebrows drew together. "Mind if I ask where Sarah's husband is?"

Kelly felt her stomach tighten. She didn't want to think of the way Sam had run off and left his family, much less talk about it.

"I guess it's none of my business," Mike said, before she could make a reply. "Forget I even asked."

Kelly reached out and touched the sleeve of his shirt. "It's all right. Others will no doubt be askin', so I may as well start by telling you the facts." She swallowed hard, searching for the right words. "Shortly after we arrived in Easton, I ran into my sister at the Simon Silk Mill, where I'd gone looking for a job."

Mike nodded but didn't say anything.

"That day Sarah told me Sam had lost his job at Warren Soapstone. Said it was because he'd gotten mad at his boss and talked back." Kelly paused a moment and was surprised when Mike reached for her hand. She didn't pull it away. It felt good, and his hand was warm and comforting.

"Sarah said Sam had been staying home with the baby while she worked," Kelly continued. "I invited her to drop by the boardinghouse where we were staying, so Mama and me could meet Sam Jr."

"And did she stop by?" Mike asked.

"Yes, the next Saturday. But as soon as I laid eyes on my sister, I knew somethin' was wrong."

"What happened?"

"She said Sam up and left her, which meant she had no one to watch the baby." Kelly's eyes filled with tears, just thinking about how terribly her sister had been treated. "I agreed to move in with Sarah and watch the little guy while she was at work."

"So that's how you were able to get so many paintings done." Mike squeezed Kelly's hand. "That was a fine thing you did, agreeing to help care for your sister's child." He frowned. "I'm sorry to hear Sam Turner couldn't face up to his responsibilities. Guess maybe he wasn't ready to be a husband or father."

Kelly snorted. "I'd say most men aren't ready."

"That's not true," Mike said, shaking his head. "I'm more than ready. Have been for a couple of years." He eyed Kelly in a curious sort of way. What was he thinking? Why was he smiling at her like that?

She didn't know what to say, so she withdrew her hand and popped a hunk of peach into her mouth.

"Ever since my folks passed away, I've felt an emptiness in my heart," Mike went on to say. "And after Alvin and John left home to start up their fishin' business in New Jersey, I've had a hankering for a wife and a houseful of kids." He stared down at his plate. "I've been praying for some time that God would give me a Christian wife, and later some children who'd take over the store some day." His gaze lifted to her face, and she swallowed hard. "I feel confident that God has answered my prayer and sent the perfect woman for my needs."

Kelly's heart began to pound. Surely Mike couldn't mean her. He must be referring to someone else . . . maybe Betsy Nelson, the preacher's daughter. It was obvious that the woman had eyes for Mike. Maybe the two of them had begun courting while Kelly was away for the winter months.

"I think the preacher's daughter would make any man a fine wife," Kelly mumbled.

"The preacher's daughter?" Mike's furrowed brows showed his obvious confusion.

"Betsy Nelson. I believe she likes you."

Mike set his plate on the blanket, then took hold of Kelly's and did the same with it. He leaned forward, placed his hands on her shoulders, and kissed her lips so tenderly she thought she might swoon. When the kiss ended, he whispered, "It's you I plan to marry, and it has been all along."

Kelly's mouth dropped open, but before she could find her voice, he spoke again. "Ever since that day you and your folks came into my store so you could buy a pair of boots, I've had an interest in you. I thought you might feel the same."

"I–I—" she sputtered.

"We can be married by Preacher Nelson whenever you feel ready," Mike continued, as though the matter was entirely settled. "I'm hoping we can start a family right away, and—"

Kelly jumped up so quickly she knocked over the jar still half-full of peaches. "I won't be anyone's wife!" she shouted. "Especially not someone who only wants a woman so he can have children he can put to work and never pay!"

Mike scrambled to his feet, but before he had a chance to say one word, she turned on her heel and bounded away, not even caring that she'd left her blanket behind.

ॐ

Mike stood staring at Kelly's retreating form and feeling like his breath had been snatched away. What had gone wrong? What had he said to upset her so?

Taking in a deep breath of air, Mike tried to sort out his tangled emotions. Kelly had to be the one for him. After all, she'd appeared at his store last year only moments after his prayer for a wife. He'd thought they'd been drawing closer with each time they spent alone. She'd allowed him to kiss her. Had Kelly really believed he was interested in Betsy Nelson? And what had she meant by shouting that she didn't want to be anyone's wife—especially not someone who only wanted a woman so he could have children he could put to work and never pay?

"I would never do such a thing," Mike muttered. "I can't imagine why she would think so either."

An image of Amos McGregor popped into Mike's mind. The man was a tyrant, and he remembered Kelly saying on several occasions that her dad had refused to pay her any money for leading the mules. That was the reason her sister, Sarah, had run off with Sam Turner a couple years ago.

Mike slapped the side of his head and moaned. "How could I have been so stupid and insensitive? I should have realized Kelly might misunderstand my intentions."

He closed his eyes and lifted his face toward the sky. "Father in heaven, please guide me. I love Kelly, and I thought by her actions she might have come to love me now. Help me convince her, Lord."

$$\textbf{27}$$

$\mathcal{K}$elly knew her face must be red and tear-stained, and she also knew her parents would want to know where she'd gone after the church service. She couldn't face anyone now or answer any questions. She just wanted to be alone in her room, to cry and sort out her feelings.

Kelly climbed onto the boat and hurried to her bedroom, relieved that nobody was in sight. They were probably all taking naps, which is what Mama and Papa usually did on a Sunday afternoon.

She flung the door of her room open and flopped onto the bed, hoping she too might be able to nap. But sleep eluded her as she thought about the things that had transpired on her picnic with Mike.

Did the man really expect her to marry him and bear his children, just so they could work in his store? Mike hadn't really said it would be without pay, but then she'd run off so fast there hadn't been a chance for him to say anything more. Maybe she should have asked him to explain his intentions. Maybe she should have admitted that she'd come to care for him in a special way.

A fresh set of tears coursed down Kelly's cheeks, and she sniffed deeply while she swiped at them with the back of her hand. *I can never tell Mike how he makes me feel. If I did, he would think I wanted to get married and raise his children. I won't marry a man just to get away from Papa's mean temper or the hard work I'm expected to do. I want the opportunity to support myself. I need the chance to prove I can make money of my own.*

She squeezed her eyes shut. "Dear God, please show me what to do. Help me learn to be content with my life, and help me forget how much I enjoyed Mike's kiss."

ॐ

For the next several weeks, Kelly avoided Mike's store. Even when they stopped for supplies, she stayed outside with the mules. She couldn't face Mike. He probably thought she was an idiot for running out on their picnic, and it was too difficult for her to explain the way she'd been thinking. She was pretty sure she loved him, but she couldn't give in to her feelings. No way did she want to end up like Mama, who had to endure Papa's harsh tongue and controlling ways. Nor did Kelly wish to be like her sister, raising a baby alone and continuing to work for their father with no pay.

Today was hotter than usual, especially since it was only the end of May. Kelly looked longingly at the canal as she plodded along the towpath, wishing she could stop and take a dip in the cooling waters. Even though she was leery of water moccasins, Kelly would have set her fears aside and gone swimming if they'd stopped for any length of time.

A short time later, Kelly's wish was granted. A long line of boats waited at the lock just a short way past Mike's store. No telling how long they might be held up. Kelly decided she would take off her boots and go wading. No point in getting her whole body wet when all she needed was a bit of chilly water on her legs to get cooled off.

She made sure both mules had been given a drink of water, then secured them to a nearby tree. She thought about asking Sarah to join her in the water, but the baby was down for a nap, and Sarah and Mama had taken advantage of the stop and begun washing clothes.

Kelly plunked herself on the ground, slipped off her boots and socks, and then stood up again. It was time to get cooled off.

ॐ

Mike closed the door behind a group of tourists from New York who were traveling by boat up the canal. They'd dropped by his store in search of food supplies, but to his surprise, they'd been favorably impressed with Kelly's artwork. So much so that Mike had sold all of

Kelly's paintings, and two of the travelers had asked if he would be getting anymore, saying they would stop by the store on their return trip.

Mike promised to try to get more, but after the customers left he wondered how it would be possible. He hadn't seen Kelly since their picnic, when he'd been dumb enough to announce that he wanted to make her his wife. Her folks had stopped by a couple of times, but Kelly never came inside.

He'd been tempted to seek her out, but after a time of prayer, Mike decided to leave their relationship in God's hands. He had tried to take control of the matter before, and it only left him with an ache in his heart. From now on he'd let God decide if Kelly McGregor was meant for him. If she showed an interest, he would know she was the one. If not, then he needed to move on with his life. Maybe it wasn't meant for him to have a wife.

Feeling a headache coming on, Mike closed his store a bit early and went outside for some air. He hoped it would be fresher than what was inside his store on this hot, muggy day. Even though Mike had never learned to swim well and couldn't do much more than dive in the water and paddle back to the lock, today seemed like the perfect day for getting wet. Wearing only a pair of trousers he'd rolled up to the knees, Mike jumped into the canal near the stop gate.

ॐ

With her skirt held up, Kelly plodded back and forth along the bank by the lock tender's house. Several swimmers had been there earlier, but most had gone for the day. It would be awhile until Papa was ready to go, as there had been a break in the lock and all the boats were still held up. Kelly decided to take advantage of this free time to get some sketching done. She'd left her drawing tablet on the grass next to her boots and was about to reclaim it when she noticed Mike Cooper in the water. He dove from one dock, then crossed the gates and grabbed hold of the dock on the other side. She was surprised to see him, as she remembered Mike saying once that he wasn't a good swimmer and didn't go into the canal very often.

Kelly stood still, watching in fascination as Mike took another dive. She waited for him to resurface on the other side, but he didn't come up where he should have.

A sense of alarm shot through her body when she noticed small bubbles on top of the water. They seemed to be coming from a large roll of moss about ten feet above the gates. With no thought for her own safety, Kelly jerked off her skirt, and wearing only her white pantalets and cotton blouse, she dove into the water and swam toward the spot where she'd seen the bubbles. Her scream echoed over the water. "Hold on, Mike! I'm comin'!"

A few seconds later, Kelly dove under the water and spotted Mike, thrashing about while he tried to free his hands and feet from the twisted moss. Visions of them both being drowned flashed through her mind as Kelly tried to untangle the mess. Mike wouldn't hold still. He was obviously in a state of panic. At one point, he grabbed Kelly around the neck, nearly choking her to death.

Her lungs began to burn, and she knew she needed air quickly. Desperation surged within. Her insides felt as if they would burst. She knew they were in a tough spot, so she sent up a prayer and did the only thing that came to mind.

Pop! Kelly smacked Mike right in the nose. Blood shot out in every direction, but Mike loosened his grip on her neck. Using all her strength and inner resolve, Kelly managed to get his hands and feet free from the moss, and she kicked her way to the surface, pulling Mike along.

When Mike's face cleared the water, she breathed a sigh of relief. Gasping for breath, Kelly propelled them through the murky water, until at last they were both on the shore. Mike lay there, white as a sheet, and Kelly worried that he might be dead. She rolled him over and began to push down on his back. A short time later, he started coughing and sputtering.

A great sense of relief flooded Kelly's soul. She grabbed hold of the skirt she'd left on the grass, ripped off a piece, and held it against Mike's bleeding nose. How close she'd come to losing the man she loved. The realization sent shivers up Kelly's spine, and she trembled and let out a little sob.

Mike opened his eyes and stared up at her, a look of confusion on his face. "What happened? Where am I?"

"You were trapped in a wad of moss," she rasped. "I'm awful sorry, but I had to punch you in the nose to get you to stop fightin'."

He blinked several times. "You hit me?"

She nodded. "Sorry, but I didn't know what else to do."

Mike reached up and touched her hand where she held the piece of material against his nose. "Is it broken?"

She pulled the cloth back and studied the damage. "I don't think so. The bleedin' seems to be almost stopped."

"You saved my life."

"I guess I did, but it was God who gave me the strength to do it."

He clutched her hand. "Why would you do that if you don't care about me?"

She frowned. "Who says I don't care?"

"Do you?" Mike's eyes were seeking, his voice imploring her to tell the truth.

Kelly's heart was beating so hard she thought it might burst wide open. She'd been fighting her feelings for Mike all these months, yet seeing him almost drown made her realize she wouldn't know what to do if he wasn't part of her life. But was love enough? If she were to marry Mike, would he expect her and their children to work for free at his store?

"Kelly, my love," Mike murmured. "You're the answer to my prayers."

"You were prayin' someone would find you in the moss and save your life?"

He laughed, coughed, and tried to sit up.

"You'd better lie still a few more minutes," she instructed. "That was quite an ordeal you came through."

"I'm okay," he insisted as he pulled himself to a sitting position in front of her.

"Are you sure?"

"I'm sure about one thing."

"What's that?"

He pulled her into his arms. "I'm sure I love you, and I believe God brought us together. Will you marry me, Kelly McGregor?"

Before Kelly could answer, Mike leaned over and kissed her

upturned mouth. When the kiss was over, he said, "I promise never to treat you harshly, and I won't ask you or any children we may be blessed with to work for free. If you help me run the store, you'll earn half the money, same as me. If our kids help out, they'll get paid something too."

She opened her mouth, but he cut her off. "There's more."

"More?" she echoed.

He nodded. "This morning a group of tourists came by the store, and they bought the rest of your paintings."

"All of them?"

"Yes, and they said they'd be stopping by the store on their return trip to New York, so if you have any more pictures, they'll probably buy those as well."

Kelly could hardly believe it. All her pictures sold? It was too much to digest at once. And Mike asking her to be his wife and help run the store, agreeing to give her half of what they made? She pinched herself on the arm.

"What are you doing?" Mike asked with a little scowl.

"Makin' sure I'm not dreaming."

He kissed her again. "Does this feel like a dream?"

She nodded and giggled. "It sure does."

"Kelly, I've been thinking that I could add on to the store. Make a sort of gallery for you to paint and display your pictures. Maybe you could sell some art supplies to customers as well."

Her mouth fell open. She'd been dreaming about an art gallery for such a long time, and it didn't seem possible that her dream could be realized if she married Mike. "I'd love to have my own art gallery," she murmured, "but I won't marry you for that reason."

"You won't? Does that mean you don't love me?"

Mike's dejected expression was almost her undoing, and Kelly placed both her hands on his bare shoulders. "I do love you, and I will marry you, but not because of the promise of a gallery."

"What then?"

"I'll agree to become your wife for one reason and only one." Kelly leaned over and gently kissed the tip of Mike's nose. "I love you, Mike

Cooper—with all my heart and soul. This is finally my chance for real happiness, and I'm not about to let it go."

Mike looked upwards and closed his eyes. "Thank You, Lord, for such a special woman."

ℰPILOGUE

*I*t was a pleasant morning on the last Saturday of September. So much had happened in the last four months that Kelly could hardly believe it. From her spot in front of an easel, she glanced across the room where her husband of three months stood waiting on a customer.

Mike must have guessed Kelly was watching him, for he looked over at her and winked.

She smiled and lifted her hand in response. Being married to Mike was better than she ever could have imagined. Not only was he a kind, Christian man, but he'd been true to his word and had added onto the store so Kelly could have her art gallery. Whenever she wasn't helping him in the store, she painted pictures, always adding a verse of Scripture above her signature. This was Kelly's way of telling others about God, who had been so good to her and the family.

Sam Turner had returned to the canal a few weeks ago, apologizing to Sarah and begging her to give him the chance to prove his love for her. Rather than going back to the city, the couple and the baby were living with Sam's parents. Sam assisted his dad with the lock chores, and Sarah helped her mother-in-law make bread and other baked goods, which they sold to many of the boaters who came through. They'd also begun to take in some washing, since many of the boatmen were either single or didn't bring their wives along to care for that need.

Kelly had finally seen the seashore along the coast of New Jersey, where Mike's brothers lived. They'd gone there for their honeymoon, and she'd been able to meet Alvin, John, and their wives.

The most surprising thing that had happened in the last few

months was the change that had come over Kelly's dad. He'd accepted one of Reverend Nelson's cards with a Bible verse written on it, and Papa's heart was beginning to change. Not only was he no longer so ill-tempered, but Papa had given money to Kelly and Sarah, saying they'd both worked hard and deserved it. Since neither of them was available to work for him any longer, their dad had willingly hired two young men—one to drive the mules, the other to help steer the boat. Kelly figured if she kept praying, in time Papa would turn his life completely over to the Lord.

When the front door opened and Betsy Nelson walked in, Kelly smiled and waved. What had happened in the life of the preacher's daughter was the biggest surprise of all.

"That's a beautiful sunset you're working on," Betsy said, stepping up beside Kelly.

"Thanks. Would ya like to have it?"

Betsy shook her head. "I'm afraid where I'm going, there will be no use for pretty pictures."

Kelly nodded, knowing Betsy was talking about South America, where she'd recently decided to go as a missionary. "No, I suppose not."

"I'm leaving tomorrow morning for Easton, and then I'll ride the train to New York. From there I'll board a boat for South America," Betsy said.

"Everyone will miss your zither playin' on Sunday mornings," Kelly commented.

Betsy gave her a quick hug. "Thanks, but I'll be back someday, and when I return, I expect you and Mike will have a whole houseful of little ones."

Kelly smiled and placed one hand against her stomach. In about eight months the first of the Cooper children would make an appearance, and she couldn't wait to become a mother. God had given her a wonderful, Christian man to share the rest of her life with, and she knew he would be an amazing father.

As soon as Betsy and the other customer left, Mike moved across the room and took Kelly into his arms. "I sure love you, Mrs. Cooper."

"And I love you," she murmured against his chest.

Mike bent his head to capture her lips, and Kelly thanked the Lord for giving her the chance to find such happiness. She could hardly wait to see what the future held for Cooper's General Store on the Lehigh Canal.

ُ◈

Recipe for Hunks-a-Go Pudding

Make a batter with the following ingredients:

1 cup flour
1 tsp. salt
1 cup milk
2 eggs

Pour the batter into hot grease left over from cooked roast beef. Cover with a lid and cook on top of the stove until done.

Surrendered Heart

by Jeri Odell

———————

For Adam & Melissa:
May God always find your hearts surrendered
to Him, and may He bless your May 28 wedding day
with His presence and His love.

And for Anna W. & Elise Y.:
Thanks for being two special teenagers and
encouraging me to tell Isabel's story.
I hope you enjoy her tale.

September 1883

*S*tanding in line before boarding the train, Isabel Fairchild raised her gaze, taking in the foggy San Francisco sky. Her pulse raced. *I'm leaving! I'm actually leaving!* At last, she was free. Free to find her way in the world. Free to find independence and adventure. Free from marrying a man her father deemed good for her. A man less exciting than milk toast. No, she would never be Mrs. Horace A. Peabody, no matter how much her father desired the match.

She couldn't help smiling. At the top of the steps, she paused and turned, taking one last gander at the city of her birth. Isabel sucked in a deep breath, savoring the moist sea air. "I will not miss this place," she whispered. "I will not miss a family who cannot accept me for who I am." *Well, perhaps I shall miss them a little.*

"Miss, I need your ticket." The conductor held out his hand. "You're holding up the procession."

"Yes, please." Several people behind her, also waiting, agreed.

Isabel flashed her most charming smile at the crowd following her and at the railroad employee—the smile that worked on all men. "I'm so sorry, sir." She riffled through her satchel and handed him her ticket. "I longed for one last peek because I'll never be back. I didn't mean you any trouble." She tilted her head toward the right, just so.

The conductor's annoyed expression melted away. "Why, you're no trouble at all, miss." He tipped his hat, and she moved forward into the train car. Securing a window seat, Isabel shoved her satchel underneath. She brought very little with her, since she'd sneaked out of the house. After all, this was the beginning of a new life, and she wanted all things new, including her clothes.

"Excuse me, ma'am, is this seat taken?"

"Why, no, and I'd be honored if you used it." Isabel held the full skirt of her dress close so the older gentleman could settle in beside her.

"Name's Ronald Tripp, ma'am." He removed his hat and nodded his head.

"Nice meeting you, Mr. Tripp. I'm Miss Isabel Fairchild."

"Where are you headed, Miss Fairchild?"

Something about his keen eyes made Isabel uncomfortable, so she kept her answer short. "Arizona."

"Me, too." He nodded his silver head. "Going to Phoenix, myself. How about you?"

"No, not Phoenix." Isabel pulled her bag out and dug through for the letter she'd written her family. Perhaps if she were reading, this man would let her alone. She unfolded the letter and reread her words for about the tenth time.

Dearest Mother and Father,

I'm writing so you will know I am safe and en route to Tombstone, Arizona. I've accepted a respectable job there.

She doubted her family would consider a dancer in a saloon respectable, so she didn't mention what she'd be doing. Her parents didn't understand her sense of adventure. Didn't understand her at all. Only knew they wanted her to be more like her sister Magdalene. The harder they tried to push, the more she rebelled and chose to be different.

I do love you both and hope you realize I can't possibly marry Mr. Peabody. Nor can I be Magdalene or Gabrielle. There must be more of life than what they've settled for.

Isabel breathed out a wistful sigh. "Although for the chance of becoming Mrs. Chandler Alexandre, I'd have settled for the same."

"I beg your pardon, miss?" Mr. Tripp appeared confused, and his question brought Isabel out of her reminiscing.

"Sorry. I'm thinking aloud." Isabel refolded the letter and tucked it back into the envelope.

"Running from a love gone wrong?"

"Something like that." Isabel stuck the envelope into the pocket of her suit coat.

"Did he marry someone else?"

"None other than my sister."

"Oh, dear girl, what a painful loss."

Isabel nodded. "No man had ever even been interested in Magdalene. I never thought of her as competition."

"Poor lass." Mr. Tripp patted Isabel's hand in a grandfather-like gesture. "Hearts do heal. Time, you need time. You'll meet another."

"There is only one Chandler."

"Ah, too true, but somewhere out there is a lad even better than him. More suited for you. I'm sure 'tis true."

Isabel gazed into his kind gray eyes and smiled. She lifted her chin. "I've given up on love. Life is too short not to live every day. I shall sing and dance and find a wonderful adventure."

"How is your family feelin' about this adventure of yours?"

"They don't know yet. Won't until they get this letter." She patted her pocket. "Why, do you know my father wished I'd marry some man twice my age? But I'll have none of his silliness! This is my life, and I'll not accept Horace A. Peabody as my betrothed!"

"I see your quandary, but fathers, more often than not, fancy the best for their young lassies."

A tiny stab of guilt pricked Isabel's conscience. She'd gotten pretty wild. Her father hoped marrying a respectable man would rein her in. "True enough. He does desire the best for me. We can't agree on what that is, so I took control of my life and am doing this my way."

"I hope things work out and you find the life you're searching for." He set his hat back on his head and rose. "I'm in need of a little rest. The seat behind us is now empty, so I'll be laying myself down."

Isabel smiled. "Good day, Mr. Tripp."

"And good day to you, Miss Fairchild."

Isabel focused her gaze out the window. Her family did want the best for her. She'd embarrassed them with her flirtatious ways, but it was all so harmless. She loved a good party, loved dancing and singing, but so what? And yes, she'd kissed more men than any young woman should have, but again, so what? A little innocent kissing never hurt anyone. She enjoyed men's attention, but what woman didn't?

Isabel glanced back over her seat at Mr. Tripp, wondering if he'd fallen asleep, but the seat sat empty. She considered asking his opinion about kissing without commitment. She shrugged. At his age, he'd side with her father.

ès

Slade Stanfield first noticed the girl with the fiery curls when he waited in line for the train. Something about her tall, slender frame caught a man's eye; something about the graceful, confident way she carried herself held a man's attention; and something about those large, emerald eyes as they gazed over the city sparked a man's interest. Therefore, he planned on avoiding her like a moldy batch of hay, but alas, he boarded last and one seat had remained—the one across the aisle from her.

Certain she wore the latest style, Slade wondered why any sane person would have such an outlandish hat. What woman in her right mind wanted a bird's nest perched on her head? Some old codger had settled in alongside her. The aged fellow got her talking, and Slade learned a lot. Not that he condoned eavesdropping. He couldn't help it; they were an arm's length away. He didn't care to know a thing about her or the details of her life. He shouldn't think about her anyway. No matter how appealing or interesting Miss Isabel Fairchild might be, he'd committed himself to Susannah; he had no room in his life for another woman.

Thoughts of Susannah brought a pang of regret. Would he ever find a suitable companion for her? He'd hoped this trip up the coast to San Francisco would have been fruitful, but the only women interested in being a lame woman's companion were elderly types. He searched for a young woman who'd share a friendship with Susannah. Two years and still no one. He shook his head in frustration and returned to eavesdropping on Miss Fairchild and her problems—then he didn't think about his own.

When the old guy decided on a nap, so did Slade. This went on for hours—talking, napping, eating, listening. When he awoke this time, the conductor announced they were pulling into Los Angeles.

Miss Fairchild stretched and yawned across the aisle. Their gazes met. She smiled, and he knew any man was clay in her hands. Earlier he'd shaken his head at the way she'd used her beauty for manipulating the conductor. Now he realized how effortlessly he could fall under her spell. She knew how to look at a man.

As the train slowed, Miss Fairchild reached under the seat for her bag. "My satchel is gone!" Panic laced each word. Next thing he knew, she was crawling on her hands and knees, frantically searching. She checked under the seat in front of her. "Have you seen my bag?" She glanced in Slade's direction. "Perhaps it slid to your side of the train."

Slade doubted the plausibility of such an event transpiring, but he checked under his own seat, the one in front of him, and the one behind him. He found no bag.

The confident, controlled Miss Fairchild seemed terrified. "What will I do? My money, my ticket for Tombstone, everything I own is gone." She sank onto the cushioned seat. "I have nothing except the clothes on my back."

Her fearful expression left Slade feeling concerned; after all, an honorable man didn't abandon a lady in distress. "Let's search the whole car." It had almost emptied out by now. "We'll start at the front. You take your side, and I'll take mine." He offered his hand and helped her up, surprised by the jolt of electricity shooting through him at her touch.

He wished he could assure her they'd find the missing luggage, but in all honesty, he doubted they would. That Mr. Tripp fellow probably absconded with Miss Fairchild's belongings. Maybe this was some kind of scam, and they were in it together. He glanced at her pale, worried face as she checked yet another row. *Why is trust so difficult for me? Maybe she's telling the truth. Or maybe she'll be asking for a loan,* his cynical side argued.

Miss Fairchild's face grew more anxious as they searched under seat after seat with no luck. At the back of the car, she appeared near tears but raised her chin, drawing in a determined breath. She was a fighter—that he knew for certain.

"Let me help you find the conductor. We'll see what he advises." Slade took her arm, leading her down the steps. *Don't think about how she smells like the lilac growing down by the barn. Don't think about how fragile and forlorn she all of a sudden seems. Most of all, don't think about those moist green eyes, harboring unshed tears. . . .* Once on the ground, he quickly released her and took a step back. Glancing down the track and then up, he spotted the conductor near the front of the train, speaking with the engineer.

"There he is." Miss Fairchild hiked up her skirts and ran in the opposite direction. "Mr. Tripp, stop! You've got my bag."

Slade spotted the older man, and, sure enough, he carried the satchel Miss Fairchild had boarded with. Slade caught up with her. "Go tell the conductor what has transpired here today." Before she'd had time to respond, he sprinted after the old codger.

Mr. Tripp ducked around another train. Slade cut between cars. He stopped, his breathing ragged. Slade searched in every direction, but the man had vanished. Slade jogged up and down, hunting between the various trains. *How can a man evaporate?* Then he searched the depot, but the man had disappeared into thin air. Discouraged, Slade sought out Miss Fairchild, dreading giving her the bad news.

He found her standing near the depot entrance, looking regal and every bit a lady. "Did you catch him?" she asked in a desperate tone.

"No, I'm sorry. I didn't." Slade took another glimpse in each direction.

The conductor approached. "I'm sorry, miss. We searched every train. He isn't to be found."

She swallowed hard. "Can the railroad replace my ticket?"

The conductor shook his head. "Only if you pay for another one."

Isabel took a deep breath. She placed her hand on the conductor's arm. "Surely an important man such as yourself could do something." She licked her lips and tilted her head to the right. "I'm just asking one tiny little favor." Holding her thumb and forefinger about an inch apart, she illustrated what a tiny bit of help she requested.

She had the poor man right where she wanted him. He patted the hand perched on his arm. "I'll go check and see what I can do."

Isabel batted her eyes, long lashes making the action all the more appealing. "Thank you so much. I'm certain a man in your position can take care of this for me."

With his chest puffed out so that he resembled a strutting rooster, he tipped his hat and walked toward the station.

Miss Fairchild turned toward Slade, her green eyes assessing him—eyes a man could drown in. Laying her hand on his arm, she said, "We've not been properly introduced."

Her touch sped up the beat of his heart. "Name's Stanfield. Slade Stanfield." Pulling away from her, he removed his hat and ducked his head.

"It's a pleasure to meet you, Mr. Stanfield. I'm Isabel Fairchild." She stretched out her arm, expecting him to kiss her hand. Well, he had news for her; he'd not be clay in her hands like that foolish conductor. Besides, he needed his wits about him, and being near her shattered them, so he ignored her outstretched arm and searched the area one last time, still not seeing any sign of Mr. Tripp.

"Anyway," Miss Fairchild recovered quickly from his rejection, "I cannot thank you enough for all your kindness toward me."

The conductor reappeared, making a response to Miss Fairchild avoidable. Slade knew by his sheepish look, he'd failed to fulfill Miss Fairchild's request.

"Miss, I'm so sorry, but nothing can be done by the railroad. According to the station agent, you were responsible to see to your own belongings." He kept his eyes focused on the hat in his hands rather than look at her when he delivered the news.

Miss Fairchild stomped her slender foot. "If you did not allow thieves and scoundrels to ride your railroad, this never would have happened! I am now penniless, and you have not heard the last of me!"

The poor man backed a step away with each word she spat at him. "I must get to my train. It's due to leave soon." He turned and bolted.

"Can you believe that man had the audacity to imply this is somehow my fault? How could I have known that Mr. Tripp was a less than honorable man?" Isabel shone her brightest smile on him. "Mr. Stanfield, you seem like a kind and reasonable man. A gentleman who wouldn't possibly leave a lady stranded in Los Angeles with no money and no belongings."

She wasn't about to play him for a fool. "Miss Fairchild—"

"Please, you must call me Isabel."

Her hand was back on his arm, wreaking havoc with his senses. *Don't think about how soft her skin is. Don't think about the fear in her eyes. Don't think about her at all.*

"Slade—may I call you Slade?"

"You don't need to call me anything. In five minutes, I'll be on the train to San Diego, and we will never lay eyes on one another again." The words came out sounding as harsh as he'd intended, and they affected Miss Fairchild. Her confidence eroded some, and she removed her hand from his arm. He was thankful for that. Now maybe he could think clearly.

"I'm sorry to have offended you." Her chin quivered, and tears pooled in her eyes. "I only hoped you'd loan me the money to get to Arizona. I would have repaid you in full, plus interest. Forgive my intrusion on your time."

With those words, Isabel Fairchild walked away. Only Slade couldn't help but notice the slump of her shoulders and the defeat in her step.

Maybe I should loan her the money, but then again, maybe it's all a scam. Maybe I could offer her a job. After all, I need a companion for Susannah. But with this intense attraction to her, that might not be such a good idea, and what if she really is a crook? If she's a crook, she won't take the job. She'll find someone to give her cash.

All the good sense he'd ever possessed melted away when he thought of what might happen to her if he left her there—what she might be forced to do to earn her passage. But having Isabel Fairchild underfoot day in and day out could wear a man down. With either decision, he wasn't sure he could live with himself.

❧

"I will not cry. I will not cry. I will not cry." Isabel sauntered toward the train station like a woman without a care in the world, whispering the reminder with each step. Taking deep breaths, she attempted to squelch the fear that rose inside. What if no one would help her? Had she lost her ability to get a man to do her bidding?

I'll sit down and compose myself. I'll find someone to loan me the money. I will not let my plans go by the wayside because of one man. Oh, that Slade Stanfield. She'd never met a man immune to her charms until this year. Now, she'd met two. First Chandler and now Slade. Well, she'd not give him another thought. She reached for the depot door handle.

"Miss Fairchild! Isabel."

Well, well, well, he wasn't immune to her after all! She fought a smug smile. It wouldn't do at all for him to see her gloat. Instead, she adopted a sad and forlorn expression before turning to face him.

He hustled toward her. "Miss Fairchild, I cannot offer you money, but I can, however, offer you a job."

"A job? A respectable job?" What might he be suggesting?

"Much more respectable than a dance-hall girl."

"How dare you condemn me?" He sounded just like her father. "I may want to dance and sing, but it's not as though I'd work in a brothel. I have my standards."

"I'm sorry. I didn't mean to insult you. Come sit with me inside, and we'll discuss my proposition."

Proposition? She didn't like the sound of that at all. After she settled her skirts, her bustle, and herself onto the bench, Slade joined her.

"Miss Fairchild, I have a lame sister who is begging me to hire a companion about her age. I've searched the whole state of California but have yet to find someone suitable."

"And you find me suitable?" Isabel doubted that.

"Let's just say I find you in need of a job, so I'm offering you one, if you are willing to accept to my terms."

"What terms?" Would he expect her to be his mistress? She fidgeted with one of the large buttons on her suit coat.

"You come with me to my ranch in San Diego and live there for six months—"

Isabel shot up off the train station bench. She spun to face him, arms crossed in vexation. "Mr. Stanfield, I will not live on your ranch and be your mistress for six months." Her voice was louder than she'd intended, and several people turned to stare.

2

*S*lade jumped up off the bench. "Miss Fairchild, I assure you I have no interest in you except as a companion for my younger sister."

His rejection stung. Isabel was used to having men respond to her in a more positive light.

"And even in that capacity, you are probably a bad choice." His words poured out in a clipped, exasperated tone. "Now will you please sit down and refrain from further outbursts?"

Both returned to their previous spots on the seat. How could he say she'd be a bad choice as a companion? And how did he find her so unappealing? Looking at his grim expression, she refrained from asking.

"Miss Fairchild, I am offering you a six-month stint at my ranch as my lame sister's companion. She's very lonely. At the end of that time, I will pay your passage to Tombstone and give you a small stipend to boot."

Isabel chewed her bottom lip and weighed her options. This was only a minor setback. Maybe even an unplanned adventure. Yes, in six months she'd be back on course, boarding a train for Tombstone, *or maybe I should find someone else to loan me the money.* She glanced around the station. Every man was with a lady or a family. She didn't see anyone traveling alone with whom she could flirt, charm, and borrow money from. Her gaze returned to Slade. His slate gray eyes stared into her soul, and she squirmed under his scrutiny.

"You think you can find a better offer?" He, too, glanced around the room and rose. "Your decision." He shrugged one shoulder as if he couldn't care less which one she made.

The panic and fear returned. "Wait. I'll go with you for six months."

She held out her hand to seal the deal, just the way she'd seen her father do. Her father. She reached in her pocket and pulled out the letter to her parents. "Will you loan me the postage for this? You can deduct it from my pay at the end of the six months."

Slade reached for the envelope and nodded. "Wait here." He made his way to the station agent behind the counter. He exchanged cash for her ticket and left the envelope with the man as well, then returned to Isabel. "Our train leaves soon." Slade offered her his arm; Isabel accepted it, and he led her to the correct line. "I paid the man extra for mailing your letter."

"Thank you."

"Isabel, I want you to understand a few things." His bleak expression tied her stomach in knots. "You must abide by my rules since you'll be living under my roof for the next six months."

Her father had said those same words to her. She was running from rules to freedom, and now she was right back where she started. "What are your rules?"

He placed his hand on the small of her back, propelling her forward with the rest of the line and sending goose bumps up her spine at the same time. "Neither you nor my sister may leave the house at any time unless accompanied."

"Why?"

"Isabel, I don't owe you an explanation. You work for me—therefore, you abide by my rules." The pulse in his jaw throbbed, and Isabel knew this must be a heated subject.

They'd reached the front of the line and climbed the steps into the train car. Slade handed the conductor their tickets and led Isabel to the nearest empty bench. He waited for her to situate herself next to the window before he settled beside her.

"My sister will most likely adore you. She's a sweet girl who's wishing for a friend. I expect you to show the utmost integrity when dealing with her. She doesn't need to know your sole ambition is to dance for men in some outlaw-infested town."

Isabel bristled at his description. "If your opinion of me is so low, why would you offer me the job of your sister's caretaker? And for your information, I happen to come from a well-known and upstanding Christian family."

"Isabel, coming from a Christian family doesn't make you a Christian. It doesn't even mean you live by your family's moral code. It only means you grew up going to church and have probably had some exposure to the Bible."

Now she was incensed. "I will have you know my father read us the Bible every night before we knelt for prayer." *But he pressed too hard for me to believe the words. Made me that much more resistant.* The train jerked forward and Isabel's heart sank. *What have I done? I'm committed to this man for six months.*

"Mr. Stanfield, I have no choice but to honor your wishes for the next six months as long as they are not illegal or immoral. After that time, I assure you I will be gone as fast as possible. Until then, we must tolerate each other, but you have no right making assumptions about me or my family."

"I agree, Miss Fairchild. I'd prefer that my sister not know there is tension between us. As for assumptions, time will tell—time will tell." The sure line of his mouth made Isabel desire to wipe the smug expression off his chiseled face.

"Then perhaps you must treat me with kindness instead of disdain."

"And perhaps you will learn respect for authority and submission to rules."

They sat together in silence, watching the miles roll by, and Isabel wondered if she'd just made a deal she'd live to regret. Well, even so, she'd not let him ruin six good months of her life. She'd just make the best of this, she would.

੨≫

Neither spoke again until the train stopped. Isabel spent the ride looking out the window, and Slade was sure she wished she'd been more careful with her things. Then she wouldn't be in this grand mess and neither would he. If Slade could stay angry with her for the duration, he might be able to avoid dealing with his attraction to her, and staying angry seemed plausible since she constantly irritated him.

Somehow, someway he must keep his distance. Being near her made him ache, ache with wanting things he could never have. Things like a wife, children, even just a life . . .

"My buckboard is at the livery stable. We'll have to walk over there." He took her arm and guided her off the train. He wasn't about to let her out of his sight.

"Surely, you don't expect me to walk. Wouldn't a gentleman allow me to wait here? That is, if you are a gentleman." She raised her brow in a silent challenge, and he knew she hoped to goad him into giving in.

He grasped her elbow in determination. "I think I'd like you by my side, if you don't mind." He led her out of the stuffy station into a sunny San Diego day.

Isabel stopped. "And if I do mind?"

His anger flared. "Isabel, you were bought and paid for, and for the next six months, I hope you'll remember that."

She raised her chin. "A bond servant?"

"If you must view it that way, then yes. You are mine until you work off your debt." He cringed inwardly at his cold, heartless words. "You have no rights except any I choose to give you. Now come on. Time's wasting." He tugged on her arm, but she remained firmly planted.

"You don't trust me."

"No, I don't." *Why should I?*

Isabel stomped her foot. "I am an honest and honorable person. I may be wilder than my family approves of, wilder than you think is proper, but I do have integrity. You paid my passage, and I gave you my word. That should be enough."

He knew he'd offended her—again. "It's not, Isabel. I don't even know you. How can I trust your word?" *And trust is always an issue for me. Trusting people, trusting God . . .*

"So for the next six months, are you going to handcuff me to yourself so I don't escape?" She folded her arms across her midsection.

He sighed, bent his head back, and stared into the sky. *Lord, I*

*realize You continually try to show me, reminding me I have no control. I
simply never learn the lesson, do I?*

"Okay, Isabel. I'm about to find out if you are a woman of your
word." He walked away, leaving her standing in the middle of the
road, a determined angle to her chin. Would she still be there when he
returned with the buckboard? He wasn't sure, but something about
her passionate declaration convinced him she would, and even if she
weren't, maybe her leaving would be best. She was on his mind too
often, even though he'd only known her a short while.

Upon his return, Slade spotted Isabel on the bench in front of the
train station. A part of him felt relieved. At least she was a woman of
her word. Maybe he could trust her with Susannah, after all. Just
maybe . . .

Isabel smiled when he stopped the buckboard in front of the depot. Oh, that smile. "Surprised?" she asked, tilting her head in that
coy way of hers.

"A little." His heart softened toward her as the tiniest seed of trust
planted itself there. He climbed down and lifted her up by her tiny
waist. Her mouth, mere inches from his, beckoned for his attention.
He swallowed hard the urge to kiss her and instead walked around the
horses to the other side and climbed up next to her on the hard
wooden seat, putting as much distance between them as he could.

"This is my first ride on a buckboard."

"They aren't known for comfort. You may be disappointed."

"Doubtful. It's a new adventure."

"Ah, Miss Fairchild, the girl that is always in search of an adventure."

She smiled up at him, and her green eyes danced with mischief
and excitement. At that moment, he realized Isabel Fairchild didn't
just live life—she embraced it. Maybe he could learn a thing or two
from her. His life had become pretty mundane and ordinary. He'd lost
his zest.

"I've decided to make this whole six months an adventure. After
all, I've never lived on a ranch or helped a lame girl. So this will all be
new and exciting for me."

Slade bridled at her declaration. He wanted to lecture her that being lame wasn't any sort of adventure and ranch life was more hard work than anything, but he figured he'd been hard enough on her this trip. She'd figure out soon enough how wrong she was. "I need to stop at a couple of places and load up on supplies. First, we'll stop at the hardware store and then the grocers."

A couple of hours later, the buckboard was loaded to overflowing, and they were on their way. Isabel noticed every detail of her surroundings, often asking questions or making observations.

"Where is your ranch located?"

"North of San Diego. It's set in the most beautiful valley this side of heaven." His voice echoed his love for the place.

"What's it like living on a ranch?"

"You, Miss Fairchild, will have to wait and live the adventure for yourself."

She nodded her agreement. "Where is all the green? Why is the whole world yellow and brown?"

"It's the color of September, and September is a time for waiting. Waiting for the rains to bring new grass, waiting between harvesting the corn and planting the oats, waiting for spring to bring a new batch of wildflowers. Even the livestock are waiting for their young to be born."

"In September I start waiting for Thanksgiving and Christmas, for parties and dances."

He grinned and shook his head. "There are no parties and dances out here, Isabel," he warned. "Just a lot of hard work."

"Then we'll make our own party, Mr. Stanfield." She seemed determined not to let him discourage her. "How about you, Mr. Stanfield? What are you waiting for?"

For you, Isabel. I've waited my whole life for you or someone like you, but it's no longer meant to be. How could he go on with his life when he'd robbed Susannah of the chance to go on with hers? "I'm not waiting for anything, Miss Fairchild. I have all I need, all I want."

"Then I'd say you're a lucky man. Few can make those claims."

Few indeed. The horses plodded up the narrow, winding road, working hard pulling the weighty wagon behind them. "If you look back over your shoulder, you get a clear view of the ocean." He took his own advice and glanced back at the panoramic scene. The ocean and sky blended together into a horizon of blue.

"It's beautiful. Makes me feel all wistful inside." She had a faraway, dreamy appearance on her beguiling face. They passed a herdsman. "Why does that man have his cattle grazing along the road outside the fence?"

"Saving hay is money in the bank to a rancher. By utilizing the food nature provides along the roadway, he can save his hay for another day. Out here, a man counts on the seasons and cycles of life. He knows them well." *Those are the only things a man can count on, not people—sometimes not even God.* Slade hated himself for doubting God's goodness, but where had He been when Susannah lost her leg? Where was God when Slade begged Him to heal his sister just hours before the doctor amputated her leg? Where was He today when Slade was being tortured by old dreams he'd long ago buried?

Just before they crested the hill, Slade asked, "Are you ready for your first glimpse of my home—Rancho San Miguel?" He reined the horses to a stop and pointed. "There is the roof of the house down between the sycamore trees and the live oaks. Do you see it over near the river?"

Isabel nodded, not sure what she expected, but certainly nothing so grand. Something about this valley Slade called home tugged her heartstrings. The serene and peaceful place invited her to come, come find what she'd spent her whole life searching for.

No, I won't find it here. I can't find it here. This isn't at all what I want or need. Isabel closed her mind to the possibility. Instead, she focused on her surroundings, drinking in every detail. Wild tobacco and goldenrod grew along the fence. Ground squirrels scampered about, ducking in and out of their burrows.

As the buckboard creaked its way down the path, Isabel squirmed. The jolting and hard seat had grown tiresome. She focused on the house, coming into clear sight now as they descended into the valley.

Slade must have sensed her studying his home. "Looks nothing like San Francisco's three-story, fancy wooden homes, does it?"

"No." The single story had a low, wide veranda. It was made of adobe, which complemented the red tile roof. Ten arches opened the wide porch to the outside world. "But I like it. It's quite charming. It reminds me of the Spanish haciendas I've seen in books."

Slade smiled, and her stomach reacted with a tingling sensation. His gray eyes warmed her. Sometimes his gaze held anger, but sometimes, like this moment, he seemed to admire her. This was the Slade she preferred, not the cool, distant one.

"We'll stop at the house first, and I'll introduce you to Susannah."

Isabel nodded, attempting to swallow her apprehension. She'd never been around lame people before. She wasn't sure how to act. Not always known for her decorum, what if she blurted out something insensitive?

3

*S*lade, you're home!" A petite brunette hobbled toward them from one of the archways off the front porch. Slade ran to her, forgetting about Isabel or helping her down from the wagon. He hugged his sister tight, and her carved staff fell forgotten to the ground.

"Susannah, I finally found a companion. Come, I want you to meet Miss Isabel Fairchild." For the first time since Isabel had met him, Slade's smile lit his eyes, and the genuine pleasure he experienced was for his sister.

Slade swung Susannah into his arms and carried her to the buckboard, depositing her next to it so she could hold the wooden side for support. She grinned up at Isabel, still sitting on the inflexible wooden seat. "Isabel, how kind of you to come."

Isabel immediately liked the black-haired beauty with her striking violet eyes and dimples so like her brother's. The old wood of the buckboard creaked beneath her feet when Isabel stood. Slade lifted her down, his strong hands cradling her waist. He was quite handsome now that his sister's presence had erased his brooding expression. His nearness caused Isabel's heart to trip over itself. Must be the excitement of her new adventure, for surely it wasn't his touch; she didn't even like the man, nor he her.

As soon as Slade released her, Isabel turned to his sister. "So good to meet you, Susannah."

"Thank you. I feel exactly the same, and I love your outfit. Is it the very latest style?" Susannah glanced down at her plain cotton skirt and smiled. "We're not much for fashion out this way." She held her skirt out on one side and laughed.

"I saved all my money to buy this. I wanted to travel in style."

Susannah's brows drew together. "To come to our ranch?"

Great. How do I respond to that? Isabel glanced at Slade, not sure how much to reveal.

"Isabel was actually headed to Arizona when we met. She decided to take a detour and visit the ranch for a few months."

"Only a few months?" Susannah's disappointment was evident.

"Yes. I have a job to get to—"

"Let's not worry about when she'll leave, but enjoy her while she's here." Slade interrupted Isabel—probably afraid she'd say too much. "Why don't you show Isabel the house? She can stay in the room next to yours and will need to borrow some of your things for the duration. Her satchel was stolen."

"Oh, how terrible. You have nothing?" Susannah's forehead crinkled in concern.

"Nothing but this dress, and it seems quite useless on a ranch."

Susannah giggled. "Oh, Isabel, it will be wonderful to have someone to share with. My closet is filled, but I have nothing as grand as your one dress. Now, if you'll stand on my left side and allow me to cling to your arm, I will hobble alongside you. My left leg was amputated just below the knee, and I have a wooden one to replace it, but I still need to lean heavily on someone or something in order to walk."

Susannah's acceptance of her injury made Isabel feel at ease, too. She squeezed between Susannah and the wagon, and Susannah grasped Isabel's upper arm in a tight hold.

Slade tipped his hat. "I'll see you ladies at dinner. Behave, and stay out of trouble." Isabel knew the warning was for her benefit. He climbed back up onto the wagon and tapped the reins against the horses' haunches. The wagon lurched forward toward the barn.

Slowly, Isabel and Susannah tottered toward the house. Isabel stooped to pick up the staff and carried it in her free hand.

"I can't wait for you to meet Mama. You'll take such a load off of her. She's worn out, trying to take care of everything a ranch wife takes care of and care for me as well. Oh, Isabel, I prayed so hard for you." Susannah stopped at the arched opening and hugged her. "You have no idea how grateful I am you came." She loosened her hold, and they continued their slow pace across the long, wide porch.

No one had ever expressed gratitude for Isabel before, and Susannah's attitude brought a lump to her throat. She'd always been the youngest sister everyone shooed away, the younger daughter underfoot and in the way, but here she mattered. Here she could make a difference.

Isabel opened a massive, carved wooden door, and they entered the foyer of the house. The outside walls were almost a foot thick. "This place is a fortress," she commented as they moved across the tile floor.

"Adobe keeps the house cooler in the summer, warmer in the winter," Susannah informed her. They passed through a sitting room and out onto another porch. "As you can see, the house is a U-shape, and every room has a door leading out onto this inner court." Susannah pointed to the wing on the left. "Those are all the bedrooms, and over here . . . ," she said, looking to the right, "is the kitchen, dining hall, parlor, smoking room, and game room."

Isabel took in the grandeur of the place. The portico ran along all three sides of the house and rested on huge pillars covered by various types of vines. Huge bowls swung by rope from the roof, holding other varieties of flora.

"My mother loves plants and flowers."

Isabel nodded. "I've never seen such large pots." Red clay vessels lined the walls.

"They are actually watering jars made by the Indians, but Mother fills them with her favorite things. These porches are where we live life. Nobody chooses indoors unless the weather forces us to. Mother does all her kitchen work except the actual cooking over there at those tables. Often we sleep on the porches, especially in the hottest days of summer." The love and pride Susannah had for her home shone through her words and expressions.

A small woman came through one of the doors to the right. Her brown skin revealed her Spanish ancestry. "Mama, look who Slade has brought for me! This is Isabel Fairchild, and she'll be visiting with us a few months."

Mrs. Stanfield nodded her gray head and laid her armful of vegetables on a nearby worktable and approached them. "Only a few months?" With eyes black as night, she eyeballed Isabel up and down. "Surely not! My son needs a wife, and you appear strong, able to bear many sons."

Isabel's mouth dropped open. "No, Mrs. Stanfield. I'm only here as a companion for Susannah."

"You misunderstood, *mija*. He has promised me he'd search for a wife. He is a man of his word, a man of honor. He will court you, and you can be his wife as well as Susannah's companion. This will be best, *si?*"

"See?"

"It means yes in Spanish," Susannah whispered.

"Yes. I mean no. No! I will not marry your son. He doesn't even like me. He wouldn't want me—I guarantee you that. And while I'm sure he's nice enough, he's not what I want, either. I mean—" What had she gotten herself into?

Isabel gazed helplessly to Susannah, who only shrugged her shoulders. "My mother is a very determined woman. She's afraid if Slade doesn't soon marry and produce heirs, our family will lose Rancho San Miguel. Besides, then you and I could be sisters, and you wouldn't have to leave, not ever."

Susannah's hopeful face made Isabel want to scream, "But I want to leave!" Slade hadn't mentioned anything about needing or desiring a wife. And truth be told, she wasn't exactly wifely. A companion for his lame sister was a difficult enough job for Isabel. Had she been brought here under false pretenses? Panic rose within, and she fought the urge to take flight.

"Why don't you show me to my room? I think I'd like to rid myself of this dress." The corset suddenly felt like it was cutting her in half. "May I borrow something less constraining?"

Susannah nodded.

"Excuse us, please, Mrs. Stanfield."

"*Si.* Supper will be ready shortly."

"Your room is the second door. Mine is the first," Susannah explained.

Once in her room, Isabel handed Susannah her cane.

Susannah moved toward the doorway. "I'll return shortly with a change of clothing."

Isabel removed the plaid suit coat, draping it across a chair in the corner. She unpinned the hat, wishing her red curls didn't insist on popping out every chance they got. She carefully set the hat on her bureau, letting her long, thick mane fall over her shoulders and back. Suddenly very tired from the trip and worried about the next six months, she laid across the bed, wishing she'd never come.

"Isabel, it's me." Her door swung open and Susannah appeared with an almost new outfit. "Look, I brought you split skirt, a bandana, and even a hat! Aren't they perfect?"

Perfect wouldn't have been the way Isabel chose to describe the wide-legged denim trousers that could almost pass for a skirt.

"You can ride in these. All the ranch women own a pair."

She couldn't disappoint Susannah. "As you said, these will be perfect." She took the offering.

"Meet me in the kitchen once you're dressed." Susannah closed the door behind her.

Isabel shed her long bodice and plaid skirt. She removed the slip, large bustle, and tight corset, and slipped into the blouse and culottes. Pulling the front of her hair up and pinning it in place, Isabel left the back long and free. Following the porch toward the west wing, she stopped short.

"Mother, I am not going to marry Isabel Fairchild!" Slade's voice carried to where Isabel quickly dashed behind a tall, treelike plant in one of the many clay pots. His mother must have approached him with her marriage nonsense, too.

"You promised, *mijo.*" Isabel noted the desperation in the woman's voice.

"I promised I'd consider the idea. I have and decided against it, but even if I changed my mind, Isabel Fairchild is not a candidate." Why did that bother her? He certainly was no candidate, either.

"She is pretty," Mrs. Stanfield insisted.

"She is tolerable, I suppose, but not tempting to me in the least. There is no beauty in her character, and should I ever marry, I must insist on a woman of strong character. Beautiful inside and out." Now his words stung, leaving Isabel's pride wounded.

"You must marry! What will happen to our land otherwise? My parents and grandparents worked hard for this *rancho.* You cannot throw that gift away by producing no heir. You gave your word."

Susannah was right—their mother was determined.

"Mother, I promised if and when Susannah is married, then and only then would I consider matrimony for myself."

Isabel heard Susannah shuffling toward her and knew she must come out of hiding before she got caught listening in on a conversation she wasn't part of. Lifting her chin, Isabel sauntered like a woman without a care in the world toward Slade and his mother.

ॐ

"You have not heard the end of this from me," his mother informed Slade on her way back into the kitchen.

He knew she'd not let it go, not as long as Isabel was here to remind her of his perceived need for a wife. And speaking of Isabel, Slade swallowed the interest he felt as she neared. She moved with grace, and her hair swung free and loose down her back. He rose. *Tolerable, but not tempting What a liar I am. She nearly drives me out of my mind, she's so beautiful, but it wouldn't do to let Mother in on that secret. She'd have a preacher here so fast, I wouldn't know what hit me. And, honestly, I do doubt her character. What sort of woman of sensibility and integrity heads for Tombstone?*

He nodded toward Isabel. "Now you look more like a *ranchero,* senorita."

Isabel spun around, showing off the full effect of her new outfit. "And I'm fit for horseback riding."

"Oh, yes!"

At Susannah's voice, Isabel swung around; Susannah approached from behind her. "Riding a horse is—" Susannah stopped, looking like a girl who'd lost her best friend. "It was . . . was my favorite thing to do in the entire world."

Before the accident, Slade reminded himself.

"I don't know how to ride. I only spoke in jest," Isabel assured Susannah.

"Slade can teach you! He's a wonderful teacher and rider."

Slade planned to spend little to no time with Isabel, so Susannah's suggestion didn't sit well with him. "I have things to catch up on around here. No time for frivolous activity." He hated the disappointment his words brought to his sister's face. So much of her life these past three years had been disappointing.

"I thought September was a time for waiting." Isabel raised one brow in challenge, throwing his words back at him.

"The livestock and earth are waiting. The rancher is mending fences, painting barns, catching up on chores."

"I'll help you paint so you'll have more time to teach me to ride." She tilted her head and smiled a most pleasing smile, but her charm wouldn't sway him.

Spoiled and used to getting your own way, are you? "Miss Fairchild, may I remind you—your sole purpose here is Susannah, not riding or painting."

"Oh, Slade, please," Susannah begged. "I could sit and watch. It would bring me great pleasure. I haven't been to the barn since . . . Please, do it for me."

Susannah, however, could easily sway him. He knew he'd give in to her. "Fine." Isabel wore a satisfied smile when he turned to her. "Tomorrow will be your first lesson."

"Can we go to the barn this evening after dinner? I long for the smell of the horses and hay. I long to leave these walls," Susannah pleaded.

"Why haven't you gone to the barn?" Isabel asked Susannah as they both sank into the chairs around the table where Slade sat.

Susannah glanced at him, and he fought the guilt assailing him. "It's for your own safety."

Isabel chewed her lip and frowned. "You force her to stay cooped up in the house?"

"It's for the best," Susannah assured her. "I know he's only protecting me."

"You haven't left this house since your accident?" Isabel's tone reflected both amazement and disapproval.

"This is family business," Slade informed her, not wanting this particular conversation to continue.

Isabel smiled, shaking her head. "And I'm not family, so you'd like me to keep quiet, wouldn't you, Mr. Stanfield?" The color rose in her cheeks and she stood. "Keeping her locked up here is inhuman. No wonder the poor girl is lonely and needs a companion. She is not an animal to be caged!"

Slade rose, equal to the confrontation. "Miss Fairchild, as I've already said, this matter is of no concern of yours. I do what is best for my sister."

Isabel's hands were balled into fists. "By bringing me here as her companion, you've made this my business! How can staying within ten feet of the house be best?"

Slade's voice rose. "It's safer!"

Isabel paced across the width of the porch and spun to face him. "The roof could fall on her head."

Mrs. Stanfield carried a plate of hot food from the kitchen. She placed it on the table. "She is right, Slade. You know the truth here." His mother laid her hand on his chest over his heart. "You can't control everything in Susannah's life—only God can."

Slade glimpsed Susannah's hopeful eyes. "Fine." He sighed. "I'll take you and Miss Fairchild down to the barn after we finish supper." He settled back into his chair, and Isabel returned to hers. She might have won this battle, but she wouldn't win the war. Susannah lost one limb because he'd been careless with her; he wasn't about to let something worse happen if he could stop it.

Susannah reached over and squeezed his hand. "Thank you," she whispered just before her mother said grace. After the *amen,* she promised, "I'll be careful."

Slade determined to set Miss Fairchild straight after dinner. There'd be no more usurping his authority!

৵

Isabel decided they needed a change of topic to help break the tension. "Mrs. Stanfield, the meal is delicious." The spiced beef with cabbage had a unique flavor. "I think the beans are my favorite. I have never had anything like them."

"They are *frijoles* and so dear to my people's hearts. My grandmother taught me to cook them as a young girl."

"Mama mostly cooks the old recipes from Mexico," Susannah informed her. "And nobody cooks like her. She's teaching me. Maybe we can teach you, too."

"Maybe." Isabel peeked over at Slade. By the set of his jaw, she doubted she'd be here long enough to learn much of anything.

After dinner, Slade carried Susannah down near the barn; Isabel trailed behind. He lowered her to a bale of hay near a fenced riding area. "I'll be right back."

Susannah rotated and faced her. "This is where they break the wild colts and the very spot I learned to ride. At three, my papa brought me down here and placed me on my first pony."

"Well, well, well, hello there, Susannah, miss."

Isabel twisted and found one very handsome cowboy grinning at them. He removed his hat. "Name's Dusty, ma'am." He glowed golden from his sun-bronzed skin to his blond hair and light brown eyes. The admiration in his gaze renewed her confidence. This was the kind of attention she was used to.

Isabel returned his grin and was certain approval seeped from her eyes as well. "Hello there, Dusty. It's a great pleasure to meet you." Isabel extended her hand, which he cooperatively reached for and kissed. *Here is a man who knows how to treat a lady, unlike Slade Stanfield.* "I'm Isabel Fairchild."

"Well, Miss Isabel Fairchild, I assure you the pleasure is all mine." He bowed from the waist, still holding her hand. "And Miss Susannah, how good to see you. I've missed you."

"Dusty, I believe there is work to be done—work you're being paid to do." Slade walked toward them, leading a horse, a disapproving scowl plastered on his face.

$\mathcal{T}$'m done for the night, Mr. Stanfield." Dusty placed his hat on his head and sent an amused expression in Isabel's direction. He waltzed over and settled on the hay next to Susannah. "Think I'll just sit here a spell and keep Miss Susannah company." He all but dared Slade to make him leave.

Slade gritted his teeth. "Are you going to ride or stand there?" he snapped at Isabel.

"Ride, of course." She grinned and moved to the horse. Slade liked being in control of all things, and Dusty's appearance had ruffled his plan. Roughly, Slade lifted her into the saddle. He led the horse to the arena. She waited until Dusty and Susannah were out of earshot. "Another bond servant?"

He glared up at her. "He tends to be lazy."

"And that gives you the right to be rude?"

"I wasn't rude. I'm growing tired of insolent employees usurping my authority." Isabel knew he had directed the remark at her. "And," he continued, "I'd appreciate you keeping your opinions regarding my sister to yourself."

"I may not be able to do that," Isabel answered honestly.

"Then I may not be able to keep you here for six months." Slade stopped the horse on the other side of the ring and faced her.

"You are a dictator and a bully, aren't you?"

"If I have to be. Now do you want to ride this mare or not?"

Oh, the man infuriated her. She wanted to stomp her foot and yell but was afraid of scaring the horse. "Yes."

Slade went through the paces of teaching her to stop, go, and turn in both directions. All the while, he kept a close eye on Dusty and

Susannah. Their chatter and laughter seemed only to goad him into a worse mood. After Isabel practiced each command several times, Slade had her ride to the gate; he lifted her down before opening it.

Isabel looked at the horse for the first time. She had kind eyes, unlike her owner.

"Slade, she's a beautiful little mare. When did you get her?" Susannah asked. Dusty had assisted her in walking to where they stood; she clung to his arm.

"Don't let her size fool you," Dusty said. He lifted Susannah into the saddle recently vacated by Isabel. "She's small but a powerful runner."

Susannah patted the dapple-gray neck. Pure pleasure radiated from her face.

Isabel peeked at Slade; he appeared near the boiling point. "What's her name?" Isabel asked, rubbing the velvet-soft nose.

"Lady," Dusty answered

"It suits her," Susannah proclaimed.

"She should be running in that race two months from now." Dusty absently stroked her head.

"What race?" both Isabel and Susannah asked simultaneously.

"Enough chatter. It's time to rub this mare down and put her away." Slade unceremoniously pulled Susannah off the horse and plopped her back on the bale of hay. Then grabbing the reins from Dusty, he led the mare toward the barn.

The three of them stared after him. "I'm so sorry. I don't know what's gotten into my brother. He's never rude."

Never rude? That was news to Isabel.

Susannah now stood, holding on to the fence for support. "Please, Dusty, tell us about this race."

"Oh, you know, the annual event at the Ochoa ranch." Dusty walked over and brought Susannah closer to him and Isabel.

Susannah let out a sigh filled with longing. "I have missed that! Isabel you must go. Perhaps Dusty might escort you."

Susannah glanced at Dusty, and Isabel glanced at the barn, knowing full well Slade would forbid her attending. "What is the Ochoa ranch and this race? Tell me about it." Sounded like an adventure, indeed.

"All the ranchers from around the area gather at the Ochoas' place for a picnic and horse racing." Dusty dug the toe of his boot into the ground. "Wish Slade would let me race Lady. On a short sprint, I don't think a horse in southern California could beat her."

"I remember those days at the Ochoas'. We'd get up before dawn to get an early start. I could hardly sleep the night before. Oh, Isabel, there were so many people, so much excitement. There'd be dancing and singing, horse races and buggy races." Susannah's face lit with her memories. "I wish Slade wasn't so determined to protect me from all of life."

An idea formed. "Dusty, if I can secure Mrs. Stanfield's approval, would you chaperone the three of us to this big event?"

A momentary fear crossed his face. "I don't know, Miss Fairchild. Mr. Stanfield might have my hide for that."

Isabel tilted her head to the right, just so, batted her eyes in a pleading manner, and laid her hand on his arm. "Why I'd be so obliged, I'd dance every dance with only you." Isabel watched the inner war Dusty fought play out across his face. The promise of dancing every dance with him worked in her favor. He wanted to say yes, but she knew he feared risking the fury of Mr. Stanfield.

"I need this job, ma'am."

Isabel raised her brows—one step ahead of Dusty in working this out to everyone's advantage, everyone, that is, except Slade Stanfield. "Perhaps Mrs. Stanfield will order you to take us. There won't be a thing he can do about that, now will there?"

"Isabel, I don't want to hurt or upset Slade. He's a dear brother and always has my best first and foremost in his mind."

"Well then, he'll be agreeable if you need a change of scene, some fresh air, and sunshine, now won't he?"

"I'm not sure my mother would go against Slade's wishes." Susannah's forehead creased in worry.

Isabel patted her hand. "I think she made her feelings clear earlier at supper. She doesn't believe Slade has the right to keep you prisoner in your own home, either."

Isabel watched Slade walk toward them from the barn. His bowed legs testified to his life on the range. He wore his hat pulled low on his brow, making his eyes shadowed. Why was he such a stubborn man when it came to his sister? Didn't he know bad things could happen anywhere, even inside the house?

Isabel whispered, "Let's say nothing more until I speak to your mother. I will honor whatever she says." *But I may use a little persuasion first.*

Susannah nodded, and all three looked toward Slade. His brooding presence cast a gloom on their conversation. "Ladies, it's time to return to the house." He swept Susannah into his arms and dismissed Dusty with a look.

Isabel lagged behind. "I promise I'll do nothing that might risk your good standing here at the ranch," she whispered. "It was very good to meet you, Mr . . ." Isabel spoke loudly for Slade's benefit.

"Mr. Thomas."

She smiled and nodded. "Lovely to meet you, Mr. Thomas." To ensure his future loyalty, she stood on tiptoe and kissed his cheek.

Slade had stopped and was waiting for her. He shot daggers at her with his gaze. She hadn't intended for him to see the kiss, but he had. His wrath was all too evident. She even spotted disappointment in Susannah's eyes.

Oh, well. Isabel tossed her hair and walked right past them. For the first time in her life, she'd found a purpose, something more important than herself. Susannah—kind, loving Susannah—needed her to break down the prison walls Slade had so carefully erected. And while Isabel was on this ranch, she'd spend all her time and energy finding ways to do just that.

She entered the house through the front door, holding it open for Slade and Susannah. "I'm exhausted. If you'll both excuse me, I shall retire to my room. Good night." She marched straight to her room. Tomorrow morning, she'd help Mrs. Stanfield with breakfast, and they'd have a talk about that son of hers.

❧

Slade couldn't get out of his mind the picture of Isabel kissing Dusty weeks ago. The woman had been here only a couple of months and had caused more trouble than a loose bull with a bee on his back. Why did it bother him so much? He liked her less each day, so why did he care? Susannah. She must be the reason. After all, she looked up to Isabel, and he didn't want her copying Isabel's unladylike behavior.

They'd learned to avoid each other well, though. He'd changed his habits, making sure Isabel was finished with her breakfast before he came in from his chores to have his. They saw each other only on Sundays when the family went to church and at dinner, and that was a quiet affair. When he walked into a room, everyone seemed to choose silence.

He came through the back of the house and into the kitchen. "Morning, Mama." He kissed her cheek.

"Morning, Slade." She handed him a plate of ham and eggs, which he carried to the porch. She brought out a pan of warm biscuits and took the chair across from his. He knew immediately they were about to embark on a serious conversation by the determined set of her jaw.

"Next week is the annual Ochoa party."

Slade laid his fork down, dreading her next words.

"Dusty will escort Susannah, Isabel, and myself, unless you'd like the honor."

"How did that woman talk you into this?" He rose from his chair, scraping it across the tile. "You know how I feel about keeping Susannah safe." He ran a hand through his hair.

"Please sit down, Slade, and we will discuss this without anger."

He honored his mother's wishes and returned to his seat. "How can you expect me not to be angry? She went behind my back."

"Going to you would be hopeless, would it not?" His mother had that knowing glint in her eye.

He nodded.

"Slade, it is time. Susannah is a vibrant young woman. You cannot keep her locked away forever. I allowed it for a while, thinking it would help you cope, but it hasn't. You must forgive yourself; Susannah has. Why can't you?"

Slade didn't know the answer. All he knew was his sister—his dearly loved sister—had lost her leg due to his careless behavior. How could a man forgive himself for such an offense? He couldn't, but at least he'd stay nearby and try to prevent anything else from harming her. Pushing his barely eaten breakfast away, he stood and returned his hat to his head. "I'll take you."

His mother nodded, sadness in her eyes. He hated knowing he was the reason.

"I'm going to get back to work. I'll see you at noon."

Fuming, he decided to hunt down Isabel and give her a piece of his mind, but he found Susannah instead, snuggled in a comfortable chair with her Bible. "Where is Isabel?"

"While I do my study, she enjoys a morning walk." Susannah closed her Bible and laid it in her lap. "Mama told you, didn't she?"

"Yes, and I will be there with you." He removed his hat again and twirled it on his finger.

"Please don't be angry. I so appreciate all you do for me." Susannah smiled, but in her eyes resided the same sorrow he'd seen in his mother's. "You are the best brother a girl could ask for, and I'm glad you'll be attending the party with us. Oh, Slade, I do so miss things such as this. Please understand, if you keep me locked in this house too much longer, I shall simply go crazy."

"And please understand, Susannah, if anything else happened to you, I could not live with myself." He gripped his hat so tight the brim crumpled.

"God is in control. What He allows in our lives, we must accept as His will."

"How can it be His will for a beautiful, young girl to lose a leg? Was it also His will that her brother behave in a careless manner?"

"Slade, we were just having fun. I in no way hold you responsible. I've assured you of this countless times. God could have prevented my leg from being crushed, but He allowed it. He has His reasons. I know not what they are, but I trust Him implicitly. He loves me and has my best in mind."

"But I was responsible, and I'm not nearly as charitable as you, my dear sister."

Susannah's expression bore resignation. "I pray you will learn to be charitable to yourself and to all people I love, even Isabel."

Slade scoffed.

"I fear that will never happen." Isabel's voice came from behind him.

"Miss Fairchild, you are just the person I wished to see."

"That surprises me." He'd come to expect her frankness.

"May I speak to you alone?" He held his temper in check, not wanting Susannah to witness his ire.

"If you must." Isabel glanced in Susannah's direction.

Susannah smiled her encouragement, then turned her gaze to Slade. "Remember the charity we just spoke of?" she whispered. "Now might be a good time to employ it."

Slade had no intention of being charitable to Miss Fairchild. She deserved no such treatment. She'd come uninvited into his life and turned his world upside down. Now he would give her the verbal lashing she so deserved, but if his wrath frightened her, she hid it well.

Slade held the door for Isabel. "Have you walked down to the river yet?"

"No, not yet."

He set off in an easterly direction. "I'm surprised, given your propensity toward adventure. Of course it's ill advised for a young woman to walk to the river alone, but that would certainly be all the more reason for you to insist on doing it. Would it not?"

"Why don't you speak what's on your mind, Mr. Stanfield, instead of playing word games filled with sarcasm."

He'd planned to wait until they were well away from the house and barn before they started their verbal sparring. "You know good and well what's on my mind."

"The warm air smells of mountain lilac and wild mustard. How can you walk through this beautiful valley and not be infatuated with all you see and smell and hear?"

Her question caught Slade completely unaware.

Isabel spun around, arms extended wide, eyes raised to the sky. "How can you breathe in all the smells of this ranch and not want Susannah to have the same privilege? How can you not see the hills and want her to climb them? See the horses and not want her to ride them? See the river and not want her to swim?"

Isabel stopped and looked deep into his soul. Tears brimmed in her eyes. "Susannah sings your praises and believes you to be the most wonderful man on the face of the earth, but I believe you to be the most selfish." She resumed her walk toward the river.

Slade grabbed her arm; she stopped and faced him. With her jaw clenched, she was ready for a fight.

"Do you see my barn over there?"

Isabel nodded, clearly confused by his response.

"That barn isn't big enough to hold all the guilt I have over Susannah, so I don't need your help making me feel worse. And I don't need you reminding me of all the things she can't do, all the things in life she's missing out on." Slade swallowed, hoping to loosen the lump growing in his throat.

Isabel pulled her arm from his grip and rubbed the spot where his hand had been. "Slade, I'm not trying to make you feel worse—only to help you see the possibilities. I want you to permit me to open up the world to her, and I want you to quit being so ridiculous and over-protective. You haven't allowed her to live since the accident. She merely exists locked away in that house all the time." The passion in her eyes testified to how strongly Isabel felt about Susannah's having a chance for normalcy, but she didn't understand. *Maybe it's me who refuses to understand.*

Slade rubbed the back of his neck and sighed. "Do you know how Susannah lost her leg?"

Isabel shook her head.

He began to walk again, not wanting her peering into his face as he tried to make her see reason. "I was responsible. We entered the buggy race at the Ochoas'. I hated losing, and we were in second. I took the turn too fast because I wanted the prize." He kept his face turned from her, not wanting to see pity in her eyes.

"Even so, Susannah has no bitterness regarding the accident. She told me she grieved, accepted it, and now she'd like to move on. When will you let that happen? When will you accept it and move on?"

"I was reckless, and now my sister can't walk, let alone climb hills." He looked around at all the hills they'd once climbed together as children. His heart clenched at the reality. "How does someone forgive himself for such an atrocity?"

Isabel stopped, and he followed suit, though he didn't turn face her. He kept his eyes on the brown and yellow earth beneath his feet.

"I don't know, Slade. I don't know." She laid a hand on his arm. "I only know locking her away isn't the answer." Her hushed tone carried compassion and tenderness.

"I don't want anything to hurt her, not ever again."

"Neither do I. Neither does your mother." Isabel moved around in front of him and took hold of his hands. "But none of us has that sort of control over another's life. People we love get hurt. I don't know why, but I've lived long enough to know it is so."

All his anger had faded, and what Isabel said almost made sense. His well-meaning plan to keep Susannah safe and to control her environment was being blown to bits by one determined, fiery-haired woman. He made the mistake of looking up into those green eyes, and he forgot how much he disliked her, forgot how headstrong she was, and forgot everything except her lips. Those he couldn't forget, and he inched his way toward them.

5

*J*sabel's heart pounded so hard, she no longer even heard the rushing of the river. *Slade's going to kiss me.* Shocked both by the fact that he would and how much she wanted him to, she anticipated their lips meeting. When he laid his palm against her cheek, she closed her eyes. His kiss—long, slow, and so very wonderful—was like none other. It wasn't playful, or pretend, or just for fun.

When it ended, he rested his forehead against hers. One hand still held hers and the other lay against her cheek. He traced her lips with his thumb. "Isabel," he whispered.

She saw remorse in his eyes. "Please, no regrets." Feeling vulnerable, she twisted away from him, wrapping her arms around her waist. "It was, after all, just a kiss. No obligations, no expectations," she said, pretending it was so. For some reason the kiss mattered very much to her, but she'd not let him know that. "I've been kissed by at least a dozen boys."

"Have you ever been kissed by a man, Isabel?" His tone was thick and husky. He pulled her back into his arms, wrapping her in his embrace and sliding his hand through her hair. Gently his lips met hers. *No, I've never been kissed by a man before, not until now.* He settled that question once and for all time. His was the kiss of a man, and she kissed him back with the kiss of a woman.

She'd not let him know how deeply he affected her. Lightly, she said, "I think not, but if you'd like to practice, I have no objection to helping you learn. You, Mr. Stanfield, might one day learn to kiss like a man."

He laughed, shaking his head and lingering there holding her, burying his face in her hair. Isabel laid her cheek against his chest, feeling content for the first time in a very long while. She loved the steady beat of his heart and the deep roots he had in this land. She loved the way he cared for his mother and sister, even if he went about it utterly and completely wrong. She loved being here on this ranch and investing in Susannah's life. She loved kissing him, and if doing so would make her stay more delightsome, then so be it.

The thought of kissing this man often seemed pleasing, indeed. Just to prove it, she pulled his head toward her for another try. Their third kiss was short and lighthearted, but nonetheless sweet.

He released her and took her hand. They followed the river for a ways, both obviously contemplating the tenderness they'd shared. He'd surprised her and shown a vulnerable side. Her heart surprised her with all the new feelings churning inside. *How can I help him and Susannah both? They need me.* No one had ever needed Isabel, and it was certainly a grand feeling.

Too soon he dropped her hand, and Isabel sensed his distress over their kisses. *"She is tolerable, I suppose, but not tempting to me in the least."* His words to his mother returned to her. No wonder he felt remorse. *"There is no beauty in her character."* He didn't even like her. *"I must insist on a woman of strong character. Beautiful inside and out."* Nor did he consider her pretty—inside or out.

Isabel watched a hummingbird whiz around the wild tobacco blossoms, wondering how she could handle this ordeal with the least embarrassment. She couldn't bear his rejection. A woodpecker hammered a tree trunk, and she understood his frustration. Reaching Slade's heart would prove as impossible as making a hole in a tree with her head.

The worst part was that this really hurt. He mattered to her. His opinion mattered.

る

Slade had known his attraction to Isabel was strong, but what had he done? Kissing her, touching her, holding her only made his plight twice as difficult. His life was no longer his own; he'd devoted it to Susannah's well-being. How could he fall in love when Susannah never would? Every possible suitor fled after she'd been injured. Apparently, no man wanted a wife with a wooden leg. It was because of his carelessness that she'd be a spinster. He could not allow himself to have what she never would.

"Slade." Isabel's voice broke into his thoughts.

"Umm?" he asked absentmindedly, still brooding over his dilemma.

"I fear I've given you the wrong impression." She stopped and turned to face him. "I'm not interested in you as a beau." Isabel was nothing if not frank.

"I see." Though he knew this was for the best, disappointment settled in his heart.

"I did, however, enjoy the kisses." Pleasure filled her face. "Though they still need some work," she teased. "Sadly though, I won't be able to help you in that capacity."

"You won't?" More disappointment instead of relief.

"You see, I find myself quite fond of Dusty."

"Dusty?" The man's name brought a pang of jealousy.

"So for me to accept your affection would be most inappropriate. Would you not agree?"

They had arrived back at the barn. He paused at the door. "Yes, most inappropriate." Slade tipped his hat. "I'll be sure and act in a more gentlemanly manner in the future. Good day, Miss Fairchild."

Slade was now over an hour behind on his work. He grabbed the pitchfork. *Dusty!*

Wait! Maybe Dusty was the solution to all Slade's problems. Isabel wasn't ready to settle down and get serious with anyone, so if he could convince Dusty to spend a little brotherly time with her, she'd be occupied and less likely to wreak havoc on Slade's own emotions. Sure, Dusty was his answer. Slade saddled up and searched for his foreman. He found him in the north field, running new fence line.

"I need a little help from you." Slade swung down off his saddle.

"Sure, boss. What's up?" Dusty straightened and gave his crew the sign to take a five-minute break.

"I'd like you to court Miss Fairchild."

Dusty raised his brows. "Miss Fairchild?"

"You can help me keep an eye on her, keep her in line, and keep my mother from pestering me as well."

"In line?"

"She's a wild one that Isabel. I don't want that sort of influence rubbing off on Susannah. I thought having a beau might tame her some."

"You want me to be Miss Fairchild's beau?" Dusty shook his head. "I don't know, Mr. Stanfield. That doesn't seem too honest."

Dusty's words pricked Slade's conscience; he, however, ignored the jab.

"You'll be spending a little time in the company of one mighty pretty woman. Maybe you'll decide you like her; maybe you won't."

"And what's this about your mother?"

"She has some idea Isabel would be a good wife for me."

Dusty cocked his head. "As you said, she's one pretty lady. You could do worse."

Slade lost his patience. "Will you or not?" he demanded.

"What about Miss Susannah? Isn't Miss Fairchild her companion?"

"Take her along."

Dusty's face lit up. "Two pretty ladies I can handle." He shook Slade's hand. "You've got yourself a deal there, boss."

❧

Trudging from the barn toward the house, Isabel didn't feel as relieved as she'd hoped. Truthfully, she felt downright deceitful. Why had she deceived Slade? She shook her head, disgusted with herself. *Only to save face and spare my pride.* Somehow, she'd convinced herself that rejecting him before he could reject her was the best thing to do. Now she felt ashamed.

"Isabel, is everything satisfactory?" Susannah waited for her on the front veranda, her voice anxious.

"Fine." Isabel forced a smile and swallowed, hoping to dislodge her displeasure with herself.

"Come sit with me." Susannah patted the wooden bench next to where she sat. "Did Slade say something to upset you?"

Isabel stared at the hands in her lap. "No. He was the perfect . . ." *Kisser?* "Gentleman." She didn't want to be interviewed by Susannah just now. Much too vulnerable, she might let her feelings slip. Taking a deep breath, Isabel jumped to her feet. "I'm certain we need some fresh air and sunshine. A walk will lift my glum and brighten your pale face."

"But Slade won't allow that." Susannah pulled herself to a stand, leaning on her cane.

"He and I had a talk—" But she couldn't remember exactly how the discussion ended. Untrue, she did remember exactly how it ended— with a few heart-stopping kisses. But she couldn't remember the decision they'd reached. "Anyway, he didn't dispute the fact that you, my dear, need a life." Isabel smiled. "So today your life shall begin!"

"Oh, Isabel, thank you."

Isabel took the cane in her left hand and extended her right for Susannah.

"Walking with me, you might not go far," Susannah warned as they crossed the porch.

"How far doesn't matter. Just enjoy the day."

"I will. Let's walk toward the pond. It was always my favorite place."

"The pond it shall be."

"Isabel, tell me about you. Why are you going to Arizona? Why do you never speak of your family? Are you running from something?"

Moving over the dead stubble of grass at a snail's pace, Isabel took her time forming her answer. Slade had warned her not to shock Susannah with the truth of who she was, but there was enough pretense between her and Slade; she'd not deceive Susannah, too. "Not from something, but hopefully to something."

"What do you mean?"

"I'm the youngest of three girls—"

"You have sisters! I've always wished for sisters." Susannah's exuberance made Isabel smile.

"And I have always wished for a brother."

"Mine is truly wonderful, but it's still not the same. We can't giggle together and share clothes."

Isabel laughed. "No, Slade would look pretty silly in this split skirt you loaned me."

"And he has no interest in hair or embroidery."

Isabel crinkled her nose. "I confess, embroidery bores me to tears."

Susannah giggled. "What do you enjoy, Isabel?"

"Sewing. I've made my sisters several dresses. I love hair and fashion. I've tried drawing but am not very good. I wished to be musical, but that talent escaped me as well. The awful truth is there isn't much I'm very good at."

"That cannot be true."

"I feel certain your brother would agree. I enjoy the frivolities of life—parties, dancing, the theater. I'm not much good on a place like this." Isabel spread her shawl near the edge of the pond and helped Susannah lower herself onto it.

Susannah took Isabel's hand. "You've been good for me. I'm quite indebted. I haven't seen this pond in three years. Do you know what a gift you've given me? And as for Slade, I wish you could have known him before—" She let go of Isabel's hand and pointed to her leg. "Before this." Susannah smiled, remembering. "He was so much like you, Isabel, filled with laughter and merriment. So alive, so jovial. There was nothing we didn't try at least once, much to Mama's chagrin."

Isabel imagined Slade enjoying life instead of brooding. "I would very much have liked knowing that Slade." *I already very much like knowing this one.* Though she ached for him. "If only he could forgive himself."

"I pray for that every day." Susannah untied her shoe and kicked it off.

"My father has a strong faith like yours. I've never really understood." Isabel followed Susannah's lead, ridding herself of shoes and stockings as well. "When I was ten, his bank closed down, and he sold our beautiful mansion to help return some of the depositors' money. He bought a small cottage for the family and became a fisherman. His main reason was to get me and my two sisters away from the influences of society and give us a simpler and more God-focused upbringing. He'd surrendered his life to God a couple of years before all that happened. He changed so much and wanted each of us to change as well."

"He sounds like a man of integrity."

Isabel nodded, and a wave of longing washed over her. How she'd love to see her family again. The desire caught her by surprise.

"Will you help me up? I cannot be this close to that water and not wade in, letting my foot enjoy the cool wetness."

Isabel jumped up and pulled Susannah to her feet. They shuffled to the water's edge. Isabel curled her toes in the damp sand. She pulled her riding skirt up to her knees. Susannah lifted her skirt and tied it up, exposing part of her thigh. They both laughed.

"Good thing there are no men around."

Isabel waited until Susannah had a firm hold on her. Then they waded out until the water circled their knees. Susannah had much difficulty between the water, the sand, and her wooden leg. Finally, she gave up and fell forward into the pond, catching herself with her hands. She splashed Isabel. "Swimming will be much easier than trudging through all this."

Isabel splashed her back, waded farther out, and dove in. She swam out toward the center. The pond was chilly but a pleasant relief from the heat of the day. Isabel was surprised by the cold San Diego mornings and the dry, hot afternoons. She shook the water from her face and found Susannah right next to her.

"Is it safe for you to be out this far?"

"As safe as it is for you." Susannah's face shone. "Swimming is easier than walking."

They swam together back to the shore. Both laid on their backs in the shallow water, staring up at the sky. "You still never told me about your family. We got as far as two sisters."

"Gabrielle and Magdalene."

"Tell me about them."

"Magdalene and her husband, Chandler, run an orphanage. I once fancied myself in love with him, but he chose Magdalene—sweet, plain, God-fearing Magdalene." *Everything I'm not.* "Gabrielle is married to a fisherman. Slade would like her because she *is* beautiful inside and out."

"Why do you say Slade would like her?" Susannah grabbed her arm. "Are we moving?"

"I think we are. Let's just lie here and float for a while. Hang on to me, and we'll swim back when we grow tired."

"Now back to Slade."

Isabel hoped Susannah would forget, but she hadn't. "I just heard him comment to your mother once that the only kind of woman he'd be interested in was one of character—beautiful inside and out. Gabrielle is."

"So are you, Isabel." Susannah spoke softly, barely above the splashing of the waves.

"My parents don't think so. I disappoint them often with my choices, so I have given up." Isabel felt the pain their displeasure always brought.

"Is that why you left?"

"That and the fact my father arranged a marriage for me." Isabel paused, remembering. "I don't want you to think badly of them. My parents are good people, but they don't understand me, nor I them. It felt like I never measured up to the person they hoped I'd be. Never measured up to the people my sisters are. The type of person my parents and Slade would admire."

"Do you want him to admire you?"

Isabel swatted at a mosquito. "Doesn't everyone enjoy being well thought of?"

"I suppose they do. You know, Isabel, Mama's right. You'd be a perfect wife for Slade."

Isabel smiled. *Slade would be perfect for me.* "I have grand plans, Susannah, and they don't include a husband. Besides, I just confessed to you how useless I'd be on a place like this."

"These grand plans, what do they include?"

৯

"Susannah! Isabel!" Slade yelled at the top of his voice. Both startled and swam toward shore.

"What were they doing out there floating all the way on the other side of the pond?" he asked his mother.

"Enjoying life. Something you never do anymore," she responded.

"Hiring her was the biggest mistake of my life." Slade paced the shoreline. "She's too adventuresome, too much like I used to be. She'll end up getting Susannah killed."

His mother grabbed his arm, forcing him to stop and look into her eyes. "Would you rather her die a prisoner, *Mijo?*"

"Neither," he snapped. "I'm firing Miss Fairchild. She can earn her passage to Arizona somewhere else."

His mother dropped his arm. "You can't fire her for being determined to give your sister a second chance at life."

"No, but I can fire her for disobeying a direct order." Hands on his hips, he waited at the water's edge.

"A direct order? Is this the military?"

"Why are they swimming so slowly?" Slade unbuttoned his outer shirt.

"I'm sure they are resting for a moment. Susannah's had no exertion in three years. Her endurance must be low."

He handed his mother his shirt.

"What are you doing?"

"Getting ready to save one or both of them," he informed her, removing his boots.

"Slade, they'll get back to shore just fine without you, and you are not firing Isabel."

He faced his mother, clenching his fists. "She can't grasp the reality of Susannah's limitations. A young woman with a missing leg can't live a normal life! Am I the only person to understand this fact?"

"Slade, the only thing preventing me from living a normal life is you!"

Slade spun to face the pond. His heart broke watching his once virile sister crawling through the mud, unable to walk from the pond on two legs. He lifted her wet, soggy body from the ground and held her close. "Are you crying?"

"Yes."

Slade caught a glimpse of Mama and Miss Fairchild out of the corner of his eye. They walked together toward the house, both solemn with their heads hanging down. "Were you afraid? Is that why you're crying?"

Susannah punched his chest—hard—with her right hand while clinging to him with her left. "I can't do this anymore. I can't remain locked up. You have to let me have a life!" She fell into him, sobbing, and if he hadn't already been wet from holding her, she'd have soaked him with her tears.

He held Susannah and let her cry, feeling angrier than ever with Isabel. He resented her interference, resented his attraction to her, but most of all, he resented the rift she'd caused between him and Susannah. They never argued, and she'd not been angry with him for years, not until today.

"Susannah—"

"Don't say it, Slade. Do not tell me this is for my best!" She raised her head and lifted her gaze to his. "This is for *your* best, not mine. You want to keep me locked away safe and sound, so you don't worry. You have no regard for me or my needs."

Her teary eyes and accusations stabbed his heart with grief. Isabel must have put those ideas in her head. He remembered her words from this morning. *Susannah sings your praises and believes you to be the most wonderful man on the face of the earth, but I believe you to be the most selfish.*

"Until recently—until Isabel filled your mind with her thoughts— you were content." Slade carried Susannah to a nearby log. He retrieved her shoe, then sat down next to her.

"Resigned, not content. There is a world of difference." Her expression pleaded for understanding. "I can't go back." She crossed her arms in determined fashion. "Now that I've been away from the house, I cannot return to the confinement you wish me to live in. I cannot."

Slade rose from the log and paced a few feet away. Facing her, he said, "Now I fear I must resign myself to yours and Isabel's escapades. Isabel's stubborn refusal to submit to my authority as her boss has rubbed off on you and Mother. I have no alternative but to grudgingly give you your way."

A huge smile curved Susannah's lips. "Please don't be mad. I promise to be careful."

"Promise me you'll never leave the house again without Mother knowing the exact direction you shall take."

"I promise. Thank you, Slade. Thank you."

He lifted Susannah and carried her home. He had not the patience to spend the time needed for her to walk. When they arrived, he deposited her in her room for a change of clothes.

He knocked on Miss Fairchild's door. This was the second time in one day he'd searched her out for a talking-to, only this one wouldn't end with a kiss. He'd guarantee that.

Isabel swung her door open. Her hair was down, still damp and curling wildly. He swallowed and looked away, staring at some spot beyond her. For some reason, her hair and eyes intrigued him most.

"May we talk?"

"Two summons in one day?" Isabel raised a brow and followed him to the front porch. He motioned for her to sit on the wooden bench.

"If it were my decision alone, you'd be packing your bag to leave at this very moment, but, for some reason unknown to me, my mother and sister insist on your continuing here."

Isabel bit her bottom lip, and he knew she fought her frank nature.

"If you ever leave this house with my sister again and don't let my mother know exactly where you'll be, I will put you on the next train, no matter how much they disagree. Do you understand?"

"Tell me, Slade, what bothers you the most—that I enjoy life or that you've forgotten how? I'm very sorry. I never intended to frighten you or your mother. Now if you'll excuse me, I promised to help in the kitchen."

What bothered him most? Just about everything about Isabel bothered him.

6

The day of the races came, and Isabel climbed out of bed before sunrise. She heard Susannah's peg leg against the floor and knew she was up as well. Isabel braided her hair and carefully dressed in a real cowgirl outfit. It was the first time she'd worn honest-to-goodness men's trousers, chaps, a shirt, and vest. She tied a bandana around her neck and slid a hat low on her brow just the way Slade did. For the finishing touch, she pulled her braids forward so they hung down in the front.

Looking in the mirror, she smiled at the final result, pleased with her new appearance. *What will Slade think?* Why did she waste so much time contemplating him and wishing? She hadn't seen him since the pond incident and knew he intentionally avoided her. The friendship with his mother and sister continued, and she was growing to love them both. If only she and Slade could find some neutral territory on which to build a friendship.

She blew out her lamp and grabbed the Levi jacket Susannah had loaned her. Stopping by Susannah's room, she offered her an arm out to the buckboard. As they walked across the porch, she realized how much she'd grown to love this place—the house, the ranch, her and Susannah's daily visit to the pond. She had four months left to enjoy it, but she feared upon leaving, she'd miss this place and the people very much. Even Slade. Mostly Slade.

He lifted his mother, then Susannah, and then Isabel into the back of the wagon. His large hands spanning her waist was enough to give her heart a jolt. He didn't comment on how she looked, but his eyes seemed pleased nonetheless. She smiled at him, and he gave her a tiny nod to acknowledge he'd noticed.

"I filled the back of the wagon with straw to make your ride more comfortable," Slade stated to no one in particular.

"Good morning, ladies." Dusty rode up on Lady, grinning. "Slade's going to let me race her in the quarter mile today." He dismounted and tied the mare to the back of the wagon, hopping up on the seat next to Slade.

Slade signaled the team and the wagon jerked forward.

"We're off!" Susannah could barely contain her excitement.

"Isabel, this day is a custom passed down from the time my grandfather and his best friend, Jose Ochoa, got land grants from the Mexican government for two parcels of land beside each other." Mrs. Stanfield's eyes lit up as she remembered. "It comes from old Spanish times in California when the ranch owners invited the whole country-side to come and feast. It has been a great and wonderful event in my family since before my birth. You won't find anything like it in the whole world, except here in California."

Isabel enjoyed hearing Mrs. Stanfield reminisce while Slade drove the wagon over the sun-browned hills to the next valley. The Ochoa ranch had whitewashed fences and large, rolling pastures filled with mares and yearlings. They were nearly the first to arrive since they lived the closest, but several families were there who had come the night before.

Slade parked the buckboard and unhitched the horses while Dusty retrieved Lady and led her to a grassy spot under a shady tree and tied her there. He removed her saddle and patted her on the rump before leaving her. He lifted both Stanfield women from the wagon first, commenting on how beautiful each looked on this won-derful autumn day.

"Miss Fairchild." He reached for her, but his hands around her didn't affect her the way Slade's nearness did.

"Would you take a walk with me?" she asked.

He shrugged. "Sure." He held out his arm and she threaded hers through his.

Isabel licked her lips, feeling guilty about her plan. "I wondered if you and I could pretend to . . . well, sort of be courting?" She felt her face grow hot at the request.

Dusty stopped and faced Isabel. "What are you up to now?"

"Now?"

"Well, didn't you scheme your way into getting the whole family here today? Not that I don't appreciate it." He smiled and tapped the end of her nose with his forefinger.

Scheme? He made her sound conniving and underhanded. *Well, isn't that just what I am?* Isabel let out a long, slow breath. "Now I'm up to convincing Mrs. Stanfield and Susannah that I'm not the right girl for Slade."

He chuckled and raised a brow. "You and Slade?"

Why was the idea so funny? "Yes, me and Slade," Isabel snapped. "Will you help me or not?"

"Sure." He tucked her hand in the crook of his arm and led her down to admire the yearlings and two year olds. "Slade is watching us. Is that what you want?"

Isabel sighed again and leaned on the fence, admiring all the beautiful colts prancing around. They seemed to sense the excitement of the day. "I don't know. I suppose."

Dusty eyed her with frank appraisal. "Are you trying to convince the Stanfield women you're the wrong girl or convince Slade you're the right girl by making him jealous?"

"Maybe a little of both," Isabel confessed.

"You like him?" Dusty clearly wondered why.

"Sometimes, but he has no interest in me."

"None? I find that hard to believe. You're a beautiful woman, Isabel."

She grinned at his compliment. "Slade doesn't think so. I overheard him telling his mother as much. I've tried flirting and pouring on the charm, but he remains distant and unmoved."

Dusty frowned. "Isabel, what intrigues you—the man or the conquest?"

She raised her eyes heavenward. "Frankly, both. He's the first man I couldn't interest, even for a brief period of time. I guess my pride is hurt. And he needs me."

"How so?"

"He needs to learn to relax and have fun. I'm just the girl to teach him."

"Maybe he's more interested than you think. He can't seem to quit watching us."

"Probably just grateful I'm not bothering him."

"I don't know. He's a pretty complicated character. He's so serious, and you're so carefree. You two are like oil and water. Are you sure he's what you want?" Dusty placed a boot toe up on the fence.

"Not forever, but while I'm here. He's constant, stable, unchanging." She rattled off his attributes that drew her to him.

"Unbending?"

"That, too, but maybe I can teach him to live again." A colt meandered over to them, and Isabel scratched the gray foal behind the ears. "How long have you known him?"

"I've worked at the ranch four years. Why?" A bay strode up to them and Dusty stroked its neck.

"So you knew him before?"

"The accident? Yes. He was a different man back then."

"I've heard. Any special women friends?" She tried to sound casual, but failed.

"None that I remember. Music's started. Shall we dance, Miss Fairchild?" He held out his arm and she accepted it. They strolled back toward the growing crowd.

"Hey, how long are we going to be courting, anyway?"

"Not long, why?"

He led her to the dance line. "I have my eye on another little filly."

The music started, and the gentlemen bowed. Isabel spotted Slade and Susannah, both watching her and Dusty. They spent the next hour responding to the square dancer's calls.

ॐ

"I figured out a way we can waltz, Susannah," Slade told her. "I've been working on an idea for square dancing, but I haven't come up with one yet."

Susannah grinned up at him. "I think both are equally impossible, but it's pure joy just to watch. Thank you for bringing us. Isabel is having the time of her life."

"Yes, it appears so. I think she's sweet on Dusty." He hated the fact that it bothered him and the fact he'd instigated it.

"And you're sweet on her?"

Slade sneered. "Me? Isabel? I think not."

"You never take your eyes off her." Susannah gave him that same knowing look his mother often used.

"You are imagining things. Isabel Fairchild is the last woman on earth I'd be interested in. She's impulsive—"

"And you, my dear brother, are too rigid. Perhaps you could balance one another the way God intended."

"She does love life," he admitted grudgingly. Watching her with Dusty pained him. He wanted to be the one swinging her around the dance floor, but why? A million things about her annoyed him, but they were the same qualities he admired. Her wit, her determination, her passion for Susannah.

"If she intrigues you, why do you treat her with such disdain? You constantly make your disapproval of her obvious."

"I do disapprove of her choices with you, but she disapproves of me just as much."

"Because of the choices you make on my behalf." Susannah chuckled. "Honestly, without me, the two of you would be perfect together."

"Neither of us would want to be without you. We both love you and want the best for you."

"You just don't agree on what that is."

"Exactly."

Finally the square dancing ended and the waltzing began. Slade grabbed Susannah's hand. "Come on. We'll show them how it's done."

Susannah pulled her hand out of his grasp. "No. I can't dance. I'll make a spectacle of myself and you."

"I've got it all figured out." He took her hand again and pulled her to her feet. "Trust me."

She rolled her eyes. "That's amusing coming from you. When is the last time you trusted someone?"

He only smiled at her and stopped on the edge of the floor. "Put your feet on top of mine."

"I thought the object when dancing was to keep one's feet off of one's partner." Susannah laughed but did as he asked.

"In most cases it is." Slade slowly waltzed to the music, carefully holding Susannah, keeping her steady. "But you are allowed."

Slade watched Isabel and Dusty across the room, laughing, talking, dancing. *Why is she under my skin? I don't even like her. Well, not much anyway.* But he did like her. Worse, he admired the tenacious way she fought for Susannah, even though he didn't agree with her ideas. And he admired the way she was willing to lose her job by fighting against something she believed an atrocity. As he observed her, he had a hard time remembering somewhere inside lurked a dance-hall girl. He couldn't picture her in that lifestyle.

At the start of the third dance, Dusty and Isabel drifted in their direction. "Mr. Stanfield, I'd like to cut in if you don't mind."

He stared at Dusty. What if he did mind? Could he trust him to be careful with Susannah? *Trust. There's that word again.* Slade carefully handed over his sister and took Isabel into his arms. He kept one eye on Susannah, worried about her being embarrassed.

"Shouldn't a gentleman pretend to be thrilled about his partner, even if it's untrue?"

Slade focused on those pools of emerald. "I'm sorry, Isabel. It's not you. This is Susannah's first social event since the accident. I'm concerned."

Her expression was compassionate, caring. "I understand. Dusty's concerned, too. I think she'll be fine."

Slade took one last gander; Susannah laughed, her face glowed, and she seemed completely comfortable with Dusty. "Guess I can trust Dusty to take care of her." He relaxed and floated through several songs with Isabel in his arms. With every breath, he inhaled the scent of lilac.

"Shall we take a break?" he asked, having lost all track of Dusty and Susannah.

"Yes, some punch would be nice," Isabel agreed. "They are over there in the shade." She'd caught him frantically searching. "You are worse than a mother bear." Isabel joined Dusty and Susannah while Slade obtained their drinks.

Slade returned with four small cups. "They are serving lunch—barbeque beef and Mexican beans—down at the tables under the grove of trees. Shall we?" he asked, offering his arm to Susannah.

"We shall. Dusty, why don't you and Isabel join us?"

Slade wasn't certain he wished to watch the happy couple, but he had no choice. He seated Susannah at a table, where Isabel joined her. He and Dusty went to get the food.

"Mr. Stanfield," Dusty began, then hesitated. "I've been giving Miss Fairchild the attention you asked me to, but what about Susannah, sir?"

"What about her?" Slade piled the barbeque beef onto his plate.

"I've heard several young men express interest in her. When will you allow callers?"

Slade nearly dropped his food. "Not for a while yet. We must see if she can keep up the pace of this normal life she's chosen." Slade felt certain all this business would take its toll, and Susannah would return to her subdued and protected lifestyle.

❧

"Isabel, what are your feelings for Dusty?" Susannah asked the moment the men were out of earshot.

Isabel shrugged. "He's very nice." Something in Susannah's eager expression made her ask, "What are your feelings for Dusty?"

Susannah blushed. "He used to call on me back before . . ."

Isabel squeezed Susannah's hand. "I'm not competition, if that's what you're asking. I'm gently letting your mother know I'm not interested in Slade by allowing her to think I am interested in Dusty. He's in on my scheme, and he's no more interested in me than I am in him."

Slade and Dusty returned. Dusty carried a plate for Isabel, but nothing for himself.

"Why aren't you eating?" she questioned.

"The races will start soon. I must excuse myself and go warm up Lady."

Isabel could barely eat as the preparations for the first race began.

In a small ring, Dusty led Lady, and the mare seemed to anticipate what lay ahead. She was dancing and snorting and tossing her head high.

"Do you think she'll win?" Isabel asked.

"She has as good a chance as any. Dusty's a good rider. Are you going to finish your lunch?" Slade asked.

"I can't. I'm too excited."

He gathered their three plates.

When he returned, he said, "Let's go sit on the grass over there." He assisted Susannah to a spot where they could all see well.

A bell rang, and all the riders for the first race gathered at the starting line. Spectators lined both sides of the track from beginning to end. Slade chose a spot near the end so they could all watch Lady cross the finish line first. Dusty struggled to make Lady stand still.

Someone shot a gun. The crowd shouted. The horses darted across the line and stretched their beautiful legs out and ran. Isabel's heart beat hard and fast. Lady sprinted out ahead. Isabel screamed and jumped. Slade was next to her, doing some yelling of his own. By the time Lady and Dusty crossed over the line, the horse was a full length ahead of the competition.

Slade grabbed Isabel, and they hugged while hopping up and down and shouting. "She won, Slade, she won!"

Slade pick up Susannah, and they ran down to congratulate Dusty. He and Slade patted each other's backs. Then Dusty hugged Susannah and Isabel.

"I have great news," he told Isabel when the excitement died down and they'd all hugged and patted Lady. "Mr. Ochoa offered to lend me his buggy for the race, and you, Miss Isabel, can be my partner."

"No, Isabel." Slade's voice came from behind her. "You can't do it. I will not allow you to!"

She whirled around and faced him. On the tip of her tongue was, *Slade Stanfield, I will not permit you to run my life the way you run Susannah's!* However, the terror in his eyes, the fear on Susannah's pale face stopped her.

Dusty hung his head. "I'm sorry, Mr. Stanfield, Susannah. I didn't mean to bring up any painful memories. If you'll excuse me, I'll inform Mr. Ochoa that we won't be needing a buggy after all."

"No, wait." Susannah stepped forward and grabbed Isabel's hand. Then she faced her brother. "Slade, we can't give in to our fear. It isn't right."

They all stood in a little cluster. Slade pale, staring at the ground. Dusty seemingly wishing he'd never mentioned the buggy race, and Susannah fighting the fear and digging deep for courage. Isabel studied each of their faces, and for the first time in her life was willing to forgo her desire for the good of someone else, for the good of people she cared about.

"Don't worry. Neither Dusty nor I mind backing out on Mr. Ochoa's offer."

Slade raised his gaze to meet hers. She saw surprise, gratitude, maybe even admiration. Her heart soared. That was enough for her. She smiled, both at him and at herself. Maybe she'd changed and had grown up some. Maybe her father would even be proud of her.

Slade cleared his throat. "Susannah's right. Please don't change your plans on our account."

$$7$$

Isabel glanced from Slade's blanched face to Dusty's sorrowful eyes and back to Slade. "We don't need to race." She tried to lighten the moment. "We'll have a lot more fun spending the afternoon with you and Susannah." Isabel glanced over at Susannah; she leaned on Lady for support. "What do you say? Ready for more dancing?"

Susannah pasted a smile on her lips. "No. I apologize for my—our—reaction. You must race. Isabel, you are always in search of an adventure, and the buggy race is a great one. Momentarily, I panicked, but I'm fine. You must do it. Don't you agree, Slade?"

He cleared his throat and looked out over the horizon. "Know there are risks. Seems every year someone gets hurt. Susannah, however, has sustained the worst injuries so far."

A knot of anticipation developed in Isabel's midsection. She did ache to race. "What do you think?" she asked Dusty.

He stared at Susannah for a long time.

"Do it," Susannah whispered.

"All right." Dusty looked at Isabel. "You coming?"

She licked her dry lips. Her heart pounded. "I'm coming."

Susannah reached for Dusty, grabbing his arm. "Be careful."

He took her hand and squeezed. "I will," he promised. Dropping Susannah's hand, he offered his arm to Isabel.

"Hold on tight, Isabel," Susannah cautioned.

Isabel took Dusty's arm. "Guaranteed." She laughed. "My knuckles will be white from my death grip."

Slade said nothing as they walked away, but his expression told her he battled many emotions resulting from events three years ago.

Dusty led Isabel to the Ochoa barn. The large building smelled of hay and horses. Mr. Ochoa helped them harness a two-year-old sorrel filly to a two-wheel buggy. Isabel stroked the mare's velvet nose while the men adjusted straps and hooks.

"This gig is a new model and more lightweight than those built even ten years ago," Mr. Ochoa told Dusty. "The weight factor is an advantage. This cart won last year, though a different horse pulled it."

They led the small mare out of the barn. Her coat gleamed in the sunshine. Dusty patted her neck. "You're a pretty one, little girl."

"Her name's Henrietta." Mr. Ochoa straightened the reins and checked the harness one last time. "You're ready to go." He shook Dusty's hand. "Good luck." Then he tipped his hat in Isabel's direction. "Ma'am." He walked off toward the food.

"Henrietta? Who would name such a beautiful horse Henrietta?"

Dusty grinned at Isabel and shook his head.

"Mr. Ochoa," they said in unison.

Dusty lifted Isabel up into the gig and climbed in after her. "We are set up in one mighty fine rig, Miss Isabel. I think you and I will go home winners today." Dusty tapped the reins on Henrietta's haunches, and the mare pranced forward. He guided her to the spot where all the buggies gathered for the start of the first race.

Excitement coursed through Isabel, and she could hardly wait for the race to begin. She surveyed each of the other five teams that had entered various sizes and shapes of buggies. Theirs was the smallest and sleekest. Her hopes surged. "We're going to win. I just know," she whispered to Dusty.

He nodded and lined up at the starting line, holding the reins tight to keep Henrietta in her rightful spot. He spoke softly to the mare, trying to calm her.

Isabel spotted Slade, Susannah, and Mrs. Stanfield on a rise not far from the start and finish line. Feeling torn once again between her desire to experience the race and their pain, she smiled and waved. Only Susannah returned the gesture. Maybe this would help Slade realize the futility of worry.

"Are you holding on tight?" Dusty asked, keeping his eyes straight ahead.

"Yes." With not much to hold on to, Isabel tightened her grip. One hand wrapped around the gig frame and the other held tight to the edge of the seat between her and Dusty. Her hands were sweaty, and her grip was slippery at best.

Out of the corner of her eye, Isabel saw the starter raise the gun. She clutched harder to her anchors. The gun fired. Henrietta lurched forward. The gig followed. Isabel's head jerked back at the impact, then whipped forward. The wind stung her eyes, and she squinted, glimpsing rocks and trees as they flew by.

Her braids blew behind her, hitting against her back from time to time. Her hands ached from her tense grasp, but most incredible was her sense of almost flying. Isabel was moving faster than she ever had. "This is wonderful!" she yelled at Dusty, not certain he even heard. Between the wind in their ears and the hoof beats of six horses, the noise level was deafening.

Isabel looked around, trying to measure their lead. Henrietta led the pack but barely. The six racers were in a cluster, all sticking together and keeping the same pace. "We're winning!" Her competitive nature kicked into gear. "Can't she go any faster? They could catch us in a heartbeat."

Again, Dusty made no response. He kept his focus straight ahead.

Isabel caught sight of a black horse coming up on Dusty's side of the gig. With each breath, the horse moved closer to taking the lead. Isabel dug her fingers into the seat. They were so close, she knew Dusty could reach over and touch the horse if he chose to.

They hit a rut in the road. The gig bounced, and Isabel flew up off the seat. She lost her hold with one hand. Smacking back down on the seat, she clutched at the front edge once again. Her heart pounded and her mouth went dry. The black horse's nose was even with Henrietta's neck. Glancing back, Isabel felt fear wrap itself around her.

"They're too close!" she screamed.

In slow motion, Isabel watched the scene play out. The wheel of the passing buggy caught their wheel. Their buggy flew up in the air. Isabel shrieked. Unable to hold on, she shot through the air like a bullet. Sickened by the sound of crashing metal and squealing horses, she tried to focus her eyes on the noise. She hit the unrelenting ground in a heap. Her head jerked back. Something hard and sharp caught the back of her skull. The world spun, and a black void threatened to sweep her away.

Isabel tried to stay alert. She fought to open her eyes, but they wouldn't cooperate. Her head throbbed, and she felt warm liquid oozing down her neck. She tried to move, but her body refused to oblige. Her head hurt so badly. She gave up trying and welcomed the black fog that enveloped her.

ॐ

"No! Not Isabel," Slade yelled. He took off running. "Not Isabel. Please, God, not her, too." His boots pounded against the dirt. The sight of tangled buggies, flying bodies, and downed horses stuck in the forefront of his mind. The memories of three years before blended with the current happenings. By the time he reached the wreck, his whole body trembled with fear.

Mr. Ochoa and many others were digging through the debris of bent metal and broken harnesses to free hurt people beneath. As Slade neared the scene, he spotted Isabel. She'd been thrown away from the mess and lay off on the outside edge of the track. Her still form squeezed his heart with dread.

He didn't stop running until he'd reached her. Kneeling beside her, he checked her neck for a pulse. A sigh of gratefulness escaped his lips when he found the strong, steady beat.

"Isabel," he whispered. No response. He doubted he'd hear her anyway over the pounding of his heart and the loudness of his own heavy breaths.

He checked her arms and legs for breaks. Apparently, she was in one piece, but he noticed her head lay against a rock. Gently, he lifted it and felt for bumps. A huge knot protruded, and he felt blood dripping onto his hand. He removed the scarf from around her neck and tied it around her head to stop the bleeding.

"Lord, please heal Isabel. Don't let her have life-changing injuries from this like Susannah does."

Laying his palm against her ashen cheek, feelings of love over-whelmed him. He'd tried so hard, yet in spite of all his efforts not to, he'd fallen in love with Isabel Fairchild. "Lord, help me. I promised You I'd not fall in love for Susannah's sake. Now what do I do?"

He tenderly scooped Isabel into his arms; her auburn braids hung down and swung back and forth with each step he took.

"She all right?" Mr. Ochoa asked.

"Unconscious, but I think she'll be fine. Her head hit a rock."

"Why don't you lay her here and go get your buckboard? I'll have one of the women keep an eye on her."

Slade didn't want to leave her, didn't want her out of his sight, but he knew the suggestion was best. Gently, he placed Isabel on a soft mound of dirt. He carefully arranged her arms until she looked com-fortable. "Don't go anywhere, Isabel. I'll be right back." He placed a kiss on her forehead.

"Any casualties?"

"Just my mare, Henrietta. Dusty is in pretty bad shape."

Dusty. In his panic over Isabel, he'd forgotten all about Dusty.

"Apparently he was trampled by a couple of horses and run over by a couple of buggies. His legs took the brunt of it. Both appear bro-ken."

A sense of duty came over Slade. "Will you stay with her? Dusty's my foreman. I better have a look."

Mr. Ochoa nodded. As Slade moved toward the crowd of people, he heard the man yell, "Margarita, come sit with this woman."

Slade found Dusty. Doc Christiansen was with him. Susannah held one of Dusty's hands, and his mother held the other. Bloodied and bruised, Dusty was thankfully conscious.

"Isabel?" Dusty rasped out her name.

Slade knew talking pained him. "She's fine." *At least I hope she is.* He didn't want Dusty feeling worse than he already was.

Susannah had been crying, and his mother appeared scared stiff.

"What's the prognosis, Doc?"

"Both legs are broken. He's bruised. I'm trying to splint him good, and then we'll haul him up to the Ochoas' house. Ramon said he's welcome to stay here as long as he needs to. I think it will be a few days before he's making the trek back to your place. Miss Susannah volunteered to stay and care for him."

Slade frowned at his sister. She could barely take care of herself. How had she gotten down here anyway? Why did she run to Dusty and not Isabel? Slade didn't take time to ponder these questions further. "I'm going to get the buckboard and pick up Isabel. Doc, when you're done here, would you mind taking a look at the woman over there?" He pointed to Isabel's still form.

Doc nodded.

Slade jogged back toward the Ochoas' barn area, where he'd parked the buckboard. *Why did I let her and Dusty race? Why didn't I stop them?* He wrestled with God every step of the way, asking a million questions. God remained silent through the whole interrogation.

Slade rushed through hitching up the horses and returned to Isabel as quickly as possible. Doc knelt beside her. "She's bruised and sore and has a big goose egg on her noggin, but I think she'll be up and about in a few days."

As Slade drew closer, he realized Isabel's eyes were open. His heart swelled with relief. He ached to take her into his arms but couldn't. He'd promised himself and God. His love for Isabel must remain unacknowledged.

Doc helped her drink a few sips of water. "I think she's ready to make the trip back to your place." Doc rose. "Travel slow, and try to avoid jolts as much as you can. Her headache is pretty intense."

Slade nodded and stooped next to her. Isabel touched Slade's cheek. "Doc told me about Dusty," she whispered. Tears gathered in her eyes. "Please forgive me for wanting to race. It's my fault he's hurt. I'm so very sorry."

He took her hand in a tight clasp. "It's no one's fault, Isabel." *Except maybe God's.* "You ready?"

"I don't think I can get up."

Slade laughed. "Always Miss Independent. I planned on carrying you."

Isabel smiled. "Please be careful. Every inch of my body hurts."

Slade lifted her, and she groaned. He stopped moving and stood still for a moment. Then he took small, careful steps. When he reached the wagon, he laid her across the back. Then he climbed in and situated her in the center of the straw.

"I'll be back as soon as I find my mother and Susannah."

Isabel touched his cheek again. "Thank you."

He kissed her hand. "You're welcome."

❧

Susannah knew Slade would fight her decision to stay with Dusty, so she mentally prepared herself for the battle. She'd suspected that she loved him even before her accident. She'd had many callers, but he was the one she wished for and thought about.

After her accident, she hadn't wished to see anyone, especially not him. How could he ever want a woman who wasn't whole? He'd tried to visit several times, but Slade had chased him off. Then, she'd been grateful, but once she worked through her grief and accepted this as God's plan for her life, she felt differently. She did want Dusty to call, yet he'd given up long ago. However, not one day passed that thoughts of Dusty didn't slip into her mind and heart.

The evening when she, Slade, and Isabel had run into Dusty down by the barn, all the emotions Susannah had carefully tucked out of sight hit her with the force of a train. She loved him still. Now, seeing him broken and battered tore at her until she wondered if her heart was literally bleeding. She must tell him how she felt. He had to know.

What if he has no such feelings for me? What if he really is attracted to Isabel?

No, I'll not give in to this fear. If he chooses Isabel, he chooses Isabel, but I'll not be a coward and avoid speaking the truth to him.

Slade approached. "Dusty, I have to get Isabel back to the ranch." Slade squatted next to the injured man. "Doc says you need to stay here for a few days. I'll be back for you when Doc sends word."

Dusty nodded.

"Ladies, are you ready?" He looked at Susannah in his pointed way.

Dusty's hand tightened around hers. The action warmed her heart.

"Susannah." Dusty ground out her name through tremendous pain. "Stay."

She looked at Slade. He looked at Mother. Mother rose and nodded. She kissed each of Susannah's cheeks. Mother smiled in her knowing way and walked with Slade back to the buckboard.

Doc and several of Mr. Ochoa's hired hands lifted Dusty onto a board and then into the back of a wagon. Doc then lifted Susannah up, where she settled next to Dusty, holding his hand for support. How she wished she'd allowed him close to her after her accident. How awful he must have felt when she shut him out.

❧

"Mama, is there something between Susannah and Dusty?" Slade asked on their walk to the buckboard.

"No, *mijo*, they are *amigos*. Only good friends. At least that is Susannah's belief. What about you and Isabel? You run to her like a man in love."

"I'm responsible for her while she's in my employ. Concern drove me, not love."

He lifted his mother into the back of the buckboard where she could keep an eye on Isabel. He held the horses to a slow pace, carefully avoiding the ruts and potholes along the way. Occasionally, Isabel groaned. The creaking of the wagon and the plodding of the horses weren't enough to keep his mind off his growing feelings for her.

Thoughts of her infiltrated his mind during the journey home. Her laughter echoed through his memory. Visions of her sopping wet, stepping up from the pond. Teaching her to ride. Holding her close. Dancing with her. Kissing her. And kissing her again. He attempted to rein in the wayward thoughts, but all he could think of was Isabel. Witty, charming Isabel. Fun-loving, adventurous Isabel. He'd almost lost her today, and the thought nearly killed him, but she wasn't his to have, wasn't his to love.

Arriving home, he stopped the buckboard in front of the house. His mother helped him as he carefully lifted Isabel from the straw-filled wagon and carried her into the house. Isabel winced with pain, and unshed tears filled her eyes. Her breathing was ragged.

"Lay her on the settee," his mother instructed. "I'll clean her up and help her into her night clothes before I turn down her bed."

He did as directed. "I'll take care of the horses and then help you settle her into bed." Unable to help himself, he placed an angel-soft kiss on Isabel's forehead. Her startled, pain-filled gaze met his. Her eyes, filled with questions he couldn't answer, probed his face.

"I'll be back," he promised, wishing he could say more yet knowing there was nothing he could freely say—not today, not ever.

Isabel barely nodded and closed her eyes. How he wished he could take her pain and make it his own. Truth be known, it was already his own.

8

I know this hurts, Isabel, but I have to get you out of these dirty, bloody clothes and clean you up so I can get you into bed."

Isabel groaned as Mrs. Stanfield sat her up to remove the vest and clean the wound on the back of her head. "Never . . . hurt so . . . before."

"You're pretty banged up, but at least nothing is broken."

"Why, God . . ."

"Isabel, God didn't do this to you just like God didn't amputate Susannah's leg. We live in a fallen world. We take risks and bad results sometimes occur."

Isabel's father would have responded the same way if he'd been there. He often said, "God uses pain to get our attention, but He doesn't cause the pain." *But if He's God, couldn't He stop the pain?* How did Susannah manage joy and peace in the midst of her daily trial? Isabel felt neither of those emotions.

Mrs. Stanfield unbuttoned Isabel's blouse and helped her into a clean flannel gown. The nights were now pretty chilly. By the time she was done, tears streamed down Isabel's cheeks from the intense pain that every movement brought.

"Your whole body is bruised. I don't mean to hurt you. There's no other way." Mrs. Stanfield laid pillows on the settee, and Isabel leaned back against them. "I'll go start dinner. In the meantime, you just rest here. I'll have to have Slade lift you into bed a little later."

Isabel closed her eyes. Slade. He confused her. Her emotions around him confused her. Today he was so tender, so gentle. His eyes bore her pain, but then she'd heard what he'd said to his mother. *I'm*

responsible for her while she's in my employ. Concern drove me, not love.
Maybe the feelings she stirred in him were nothing more than concern, but the feelings he stirred in her ran much deeper.

"Isabel?"

She must have dozed off. Slade's voice speaking her name awakened her. His warm breath caressed her cheek. She'd been dreaming of him, and when she opened her eyes, Slade's face was mere inches from hers. Her heart beat faster. Moving her arm caused her to wince, but she had to touch his face and make sure he was real. She ran her fingers over his whiskered cheek. Slowly, very slowly, she traced his jaw line down to his strong chin.

His breath left his body in a whoosh. "Isabel." He turned his head and kissed her palm. "I'm so glad you're alive."

"Me, too." Her words came out in a moan.

He threaded his fingers through hers.

Isabel bit her bottom lip.

"I'm hurting you. I'm sorry." Slade laid her arm across her stomach and ran his hand over his hair. "All I could think about was how much I wanted you to see the ranch in the springtime. It's my favorite time of year and more beautiful than you can imagine."

Isabel focused on his warm eyes.

"Close your eyes and picture every shade of green imaginable. Can you see the fields covered in velvet soft grass?"

Isabel knew the beauty would take her breath away, but since talking hurt, she only listened.

"The hills are covered with wildflowers. Newborn colts and calves fill the pastures." Slade's voice carried a smile. "I want you to be here, Isabel, and share all this with me."

Isabel opened her eyes and forced a smile, a tiny one, but a smile nonetheless.

"You want that, too. I can tell, so we have to get you well."

"Mmm," she groaned her agreement.

"Have you ever seen a cow give birth?"

She turned her head an inch or so to the left and then back.

"No? Well in some ways birth is a cruel thing. Usually the calves fall into the world headfirst. Being limber, they are almost always fine, but can you imagine having your first meeting with the earth be such a hard blow?"

She blinked twice.

"I understand. One blink for yes and two for no."

She blinked again—once.

"Then the momma cow faces her calf with this lovesick look in her eyes. She makes a strange rumbling, moaning sound—partly triumphant, partly anxious—as she waits for her baby to stand for the first time." Slade chuckled. "Picture a damp calf trying to stand on stick-thin legs, usually very wobbly legs that appear too long for the rest of its body. You have to be here for that, Isabel, and for the birth of the colts, too."

She blinked once. "Love . . . ranch?"

"Do I love this ranch?"

Another blink.

A faraway expression settled on his face. "I love everything about this ranch—the land, the livestock, the memories, the stories."

"Stories . . ."

"You want me to tell the stories?"

She blinked once. Blinking was about the only activity that didn't hurt.

"My great-grandfather Miguel Sanchez received a land grant from the Mexican government. He was given Rancho San Miguel, and his closest friend, Jose Ochoa, received the parcel next to ours."

Isabel blinked once. She remembered his mother telling her that this morning.

"My great-grandparents had many daughters—a dozen—before they finally had a son. The son, my grandfather, the sole heir to the *rancho*, married Jose Ochoa's youngest daughter. They loved each other deeply and worked the land together but had much difficulty producing a living heir. My mother was born in their old age—much like Isaac being born to Abraham and Sarah—but of course my grandparents weren't in their nineties. They were almost forty.

"They thought the sun rose and set in my mother's eyes. When she was sixteen, they carefully arranged a marriage for her with a man from back East. He had the maturity and education to take the ranch far. My father was a good man, a kind man. Sadly, he and my mother faced the same struggles her parents had regarding children.

"They were married nearly twenty years before I came along. My father put my mother to bed the minute they knew I was on the way, and he hired servants to wait on her until I arrived. He did the same thing with Susannah. My mother was thirty-five when she had me and thirty-nine when Susannah came. My father was already fifty and only lived until I was ten.

"He gave Susannah and me a love for books, music, and knowledge. My mother gave us a love for the land, the Lord, and family."

Mrs. Stanfield entered, carrying a bowl of soup. "Are you hungry, *mija?*"

Isabel blinked once.

"She says she's starved," Slade answered for her.

Mrs. Stanfield gave her son a puzzled frown.

"One blink is yes, two is no."

"*Si.*" She handed Slade the soup and a spoon. "Do you mind? I need to finish the rest of our supper."

He'd never fed anyone before. With great care, he spooned the warm liquid into Isabel's slightly opened mouth. She ate slowly, closing her eyes and resting between bites. Somehow caring for her brought out even more feelings of tenderness. What was he going to do about Isabel Fairchild?

❧

Hard pressed to believe a week had passed, yet feeling every weary minute of the past seven days, Susannah laid her cheek against Dusty's forehead. Sure enough, his fever had finally broken. She let out a sigh of relief and rubbed the back of her neck. Today would mark a turning point in his recovery; the breaking of a fever always did.

Doc kept him pretty doped up on strong pain medication, hoping to keep him still as possible and give the bones a chance to mend. Both Dusty's legs were wrapped in splints, and Doc had wrapped his ribs as well. He had two black eyes and bruises over every part of his body that Susannah could see.

Doc came into the Ochoas' parlor. They'd turned it into a makeshift hospital room for Dusty. "How's my patient today?"

"Better. Fever's gone."

Doc's bushy brows drew together in a frown. He laid the back of his hand against Susannah's forehead. "You don't look so good yourself. You feeling all right?"

She let out another sigh. "Just weary."

"You've been a fine nurse, feeding and caring for my patient."

"It feels good to be useful again. Three years is a long time not to be."

Doc nodded. "I hope this proves to you and that bullheaded brother of yours that you are a whole person. Losing a leg doesn't mean you can't live a normal life. Why, you could even be a wife and mother if you chose."

"A wife?" She glanced at Dusty. "And a mother?" Hope bubbled up inside. "How?"

Doc chuckled. "I'm guessing you're asking how you could run a household."

"Yes. I fed Dusty, but the Ochoas' cook prepared the food."

"You'd be surprised what you could do if your mother and Slade would give you half a chance. I'm certain you could run a home as efficiently as any other woman. It may take you awhile longer, but you're more than capable."

Emotion welled up in her, and she threw her arms around Doc's sizeable middle. "Thank you," she whispered. "You have no idea the gift you've given me."

Doc chuckled and hugged her back. "You're welcome. Now, let's take a look at my patient." He checked Dusty over, and Dusty winced and groaned. "I'd like to see how he does without these." Doc pointed at the pain medication. "If he can handle the discomfort, I may send you two back to your ranch in a day or so."

Susannah nodded and grinned. It would be good to be home.

"I'll stop by in the morning."

"Bye, Doc."

When the door closed, Susannah took her chair next to Dusty. She laid her hand on his. "Did you hear?" she whispered. "Doc says I can be a wife and a mother! But do you think anybody would really want me?" Somehow she'd let her mother and Slade convince her she was doomed to the life of an invalid, but now she knew better.

Lord, You know my feelings for Dusty. Could he feel the same toward me? If marriage is in Your plans for me, I ask that You would fill his heart with love just for me.

ℜ

Slade had barely seen Isabel the past week. He worked from before sunup until long after sundown to keep up with both his and Dusty's jobs. He missed his foreman more than he'd thought possible. He missed Isabel, too, but knew staying away was best for both of them. He'd seen too many questions in her eyes, and she was frank enough to ask.

His good sense had returned, and he knew there was no room in his future for Isabel. He had to take care of Susannah and now probably Dusty, as well. The man had been loyal to them for four years and had no family. Slade felt responsible.

The sun had yet to rise over the eastern mountains, and he had more work than daylight hours. Opening the barn doors, he was greeted by the horses' neighs and snorts. Daisy mooed. Slade headed for the straw shed and collided with Isabel. He grabbed her upper arms to keep her from falling, and she cried out in a painful yelp.

"What are you doing out here?" he demanded, his tone gruff and annoyed. As soon as her stance steadied, he moved away from her.

Her pain-filled expression changed into one of hurt. "I thought I'd help you out until Dusty's back on his feet."

He scoffed. Seeing her, accidentally touching her, left him vulnerable, so he forced an arrogant, uncaring attitude. "What do you know about ranching? What do you know about work for that matter?"

Isabel raised her chin, and he noted the determination in her eyes. "I know your mother, your grandmother, and your great-grandmother all worked on this ranch. I may not know anything about ranching or work, but I'm willing to learn. Now, if you'll excuse me, I'll ask your mother to show me some chores I can do to help out."

All he needed was his mother involved. "Fine, Isabel. You want to work; I'll give you work." He'd give her so much work, she'd quit the first day. Bumping into her fifty times a day was the last thing he needed or wanted.

"I'm volunteering to help you out. You don't have to be rude. Your mother's worried about you working sixteen-hour days. I offered to assist you for her peace of mind."

"I thought you were still in bed, nursing aches and pains." He led her to the stall inside the big old building.

"I'm still sore in some spots, like the bruise on my upper arm, but a week does a lot for a battered body."

He wished he could tell her how thankful he was that she'd healed, but what good would it do either of them to be kind to one another? Caring would only make their inevitable good-bye harder. He'd make her glad she was leaving in less than four months, glad to see the last of him.

"The horses spend the daylight hours in the south pasture. About four in the afternoon, they have to be rounded up and led in here. They each have their own stall where they spend the night."

Isabel nodded, and he knew from her expressive face that she wondered how in the world she'd round up ten horses and get them safely into the barn. He'd leave her to solve the problem herself. He didn't want her back out there tomorrow.

"Morning starts before dawn on a ranch. First thing you do is feed the horses fresh hay. While they are eating, you milk the cows." He led her toward the straw shed, grabbing two pitchforks on the way out the barn door.

"Where do I get the hay?"

"I'm taking you there now." He showed her where the hay was stored. "You feed them the hay." He pointed to his left. Then pointing to the right, he added, "And use the straw to line the stalls after you clean them out." Slade handed her a pitchfork. He stabbed his into the hay pile and walked away carrying a breakfast-sized portion. He paused after a few steps, waiting for Isabel to do the same.

Sticking her pitchfork in the pile, she raised it, but most of the hay fell off. She tried again with the same result. Sighing, she gave it another shot, stabbing harder. This time she pulled up a fair amount of hay. Slade nodded his approval and led the way back to the hungry horses.

He carried his hay all the way to the last stall where Buck waited, then chucked the horse's breakfast over the fence. Isabel crept around the corner, trying hard to keep the hay balanced at the end of the pitchfork. Her face reflected ardent concentration.

"Go ahead and throw yours over the first stall to the big black gelding."

Isabel paused, looking at the five-foot fence and back at the hay perched precariously on the end of the long-handled tool. "You want me to throw the hay up and over the fence."

Slade nodded and moved toward her. "There's a feed trough—"

Isabel gripped the handle tighter, rotated, and swung. The hay flew up and plopped back down all over her.

"In the corner." Slade finished his sentence with peals of laughter.

Isabel had hay everywhere except in the feed trough. She joined him in his laughter, then picked hay off her clothes and out of her hair while Slade used the pitchfork to clean up the hay and feed the gelding. They returned to the shed for another round. Slade fed seven horses to Isabel's three. He chuckled. This job alone would take her hours.

Next, Slade led her to Daisy. He grabbed the pail, sat Isabel on the stool, and guided her through the milking process. He held her hands as they pulled the teats. Once the milk started flowing, he let Isabel do the work unassisted, although she struggled to milk as competently on her own. He had to put some distance between them. *Don't think about her smooth hands and velvety skin. Don't think about how good it would feel to wrap her in your arms. Just don't think!*

Once Isabel finished the milking, they visited the chicken coop for the day's egg supply. "After you have the milk and eggs, you carry both buckets up to the house to my mother." Slade carried the milk and let Isabel carry the eggs.

"Isn't it nice to have a helper, Slade?" his mother asked as he entered the kitchen.

He wanted to point out he was already running almost an hour behind but couldn't bring himself to be any ruder than he already had been.

"I think, so far, I've been more of a nuisance than a help," Isabel admitted.

Slade's mother took the pail of eggs and patted her arm. "At least you're trying. That's more than most women would do, isn't it, Slade?"

"It sure is." She had him there. Few women would even attempt what Isabel had tried to learn in one day. He grudgingly admired her tenacity. "We still have quite a few chores left. Let's go."

Isabel followed him back outside. "What's next?" she asked.

"We move the horses to the south pasture. They should have finished their breakfast by now." Once in the barn, he showed Isabel where the halters and lead ropes were stored. He helped her do the first one, then she waited while he caught a second horse. They led them together to the pasture and turned them lose.

"Why do you feed them if they'll be out on the pasture all day?" Isabel asked on their way back to the barn for two more horses.

"I only give them about half their daily food supply. The other half they get out here. When the fields are green, I let them get all their food on their own, but rations are harder to come by this time of year."

Slade caught his second horse and waited while Isabel fought with the halter. She finally got it buckled, and they walked back out to the pasture.

"Thanksgiving is next week," she commented idly, but somehow Slade knew this conversation had a purpose.

"Mmm," was his sole response.

"I saw in the newspaper that on Thursday, November 29—Thanksgiving evening—there is a grand ball in Armory Hall."

He knew she planned on roping him into taking her. "No, Isabel."

"No, there isn't a ball?" she asked in innocence, batting her eyes.

"No, there might be a ball, but no one from this *ranchero* is attending."

"Slade, it's only $1.50 per couple, including supper. Your mother would get a much-deserved day off."

She was trying to ply him with guilt about how hard his mother worked. Make him think this was all for Mother's benefit.

"Is that the whole reason you're out here helping—because you hoped to shame me into letting you have your way?" Slade was angry.

"No. One has nothing to do with the other."

Slade doubted her but said nothing more.

After helping Isabel clean out the first stall, Slade left her to clean the rest of the stalls and the water troughs. Next she'd put out fresh straw and carry in fresh water. Those jobs would consume most of the rest of the day. He was thankful she'd be out of his way. He would not take her to any dances or hold her again. He would not!

$\mathcal{D}$ usty had been alert for the past two days, but Susannah's courage abandoned her. She'd planned on sharing her feelings with him, but he seemed different now, more distant and pensive.

"Slade's coming to get us this morning."

Dusty nodded but said nothing.

"I'm more than ready to get back home. I'm certain you are, too."

"I have no home, Susannah." Pain resonated through his declaration.

"Of course you do. Rancho San Miguel is your home as well."

"No, Rancho San Miguel was where I worked. It was never my home." His words left knife-sharp imprints on her heart. "I'm going to write my aunt in Kansas and see if I can stay with her. I've saved a little money over the years, so I can buy myself a one-way ticket."

Susannah wrapped her arm around her midsection and limped to the window, leaning heavily on her cane. Tears blurred her vision. All the words she had planned on saying to Dusty would now never be spoken. All the love in her heart would never be returned. Dusty would leave and never know. He'd never know.

The parlor door burst open, and Slade walked in. "Good morning!"

Susannah swiped at her eyes before facing him. She only nodded to acknowledge him, fairly certain words wouldn't squeeze past the lump in her throat.

Dusty said nothing at all.

Mr. Ochoa and several of his sons entered. They helped Slade move Dusty from the bed onto a board. Then they loaded him into the straw-filled wagon. Susannah followed behind them, and Slade lifted her onto the seat next to where he'd sit.

No one spoke all the way home.

ॐ

Slade wondered what had happened at the Ochoas'; both Susannah and Dusty brooded and were uncharacteristically quiet. A couple of Mr. Ochoa's sons met him at the ranch to help unload Dusty. Mother had readied the guest room next to Slade's room. Once they had him in the bed, Dusty asked Slade to stay. Slade thanked everyone, and Mama and the Ochoas left.

"Would you shut the door? I'd like our conversation kept private between us."

Slade nodded and obliged.

Dusty shared his plans to return to his aunt's in Kansas. He gave Slade her information and asked him to send a telegram.

"I'm happy to do whatever you need." Slade settled into the chair at the side of the bed. "But you know, I was thinking about your loyalty to me and the ranch. I appreciate you and all your hard work. You're welcome to stay. We planned on caring for you and nursing you back to health. Then I thought you might want to discuss buying a little piece of the land for yourself. Someday, you'll yearn for a wife and young ones all your own."

Dusty looked away but not before Slade saw the pain in his eyes. He couldn't help but wonder if Dusty was in love with Isabel.

Slade rose. "You think about my offer. If you still want me to send the telegraph, say the word. But know we will care for you for as long as it takes."

"Send it." Dusty still had his face turned away, and his voice carried deep emotional pain.

"I'll take care of it in the morning."

Dusty was running from something or someone. Slade just wasn't sure who or what.

Slade headed out the door to unhook the team of horses from the buckboard. The trip to the Ochoas' had cost him a precious day of fence mending. Tomorrow he'd have to ride into town for Dusty. Isabel had taken over many of the daily chores. He didn't know what he'd do without her, and he didn't want to feel that way. He didn't think she'd stick with it, but she had. He shook his head. She'd moved into his life, then his head, and now his heart.

&

Isabel knew the minute Susannah hobbled into the house that she'd been crying. While the men took Dusty into his room, Isabel followed Susannah into hers.

"I missed you. Do you mind if I come in for a visit?" Isabel stood in the doorway.

"I'm afraid I won't be good company, but you're welcome to join me as long as you don't expect interesting conversation."

Isabel closed the door and situated herself on Susannah's settee. Susannah sat on the edge of her bed, appearing exhausted. "Why don't I come back later, after you've had a chance to rest?" Isabel rose.

"No, don't leave." Tears streamed down Susannah's cheeks. Isabel moved over next to her on the bed and wrapped her in a hug. She wasn't sure what to say or do, so she simply held Susannah and let her cry.

After many minutes, Susannah said, "Dusty's leaving." More tears fell as she told Isabel the Kansas story.

"Susannah, are you in love with Dusty?"

She nodded and wiped her tears on a lace handkerchief.

"Does he know? Have you told him?"

"I planned on at least dropping a few hints. The way he held me and looked at me and treated me when we waltzed led me to believe he felt something, too, but since the buggy wreck, he's barely said three words to me." Susannah limped the length of her room.

"I know he's probably dealing with grief, just like I did when I lost my leg, but he won't even talk to me. I've tried."

"I'll go talk to him, see what I can find out."

Panic filled Susannah's face. "Please don't tell him how I feel. I couldn't bear the embarrassment if he thought I was in here pining away for him."

"I'll show the utmost restraint." Isabel patted the bed. "You lie down for a nap. We'll talk again when you awaken."

Susannah lay across the bed, and Isabel covered her with a light quilt.

Isabel knocked on Dusty's door. When he answered, she opened it and stood in the doorway. "I just wanted to say hello. See how you are feeling."

"How do you think I'm feeling, Isabel? I can't walk, can't work. I'm worthless."

A knot of tears formed in Isabel's throat. She hadn't thought about how hard this might be on a man. "Dusty, please don't say such things. You're still the same wonderful man. This accident is a temporary setback."

Dusty shut his eyes. "Please shut the door. I prefer to be alone."

Isabel did as he asked. She went to her room and cried. This was the first time in her life she recalled feeling other people's pain so intensely. She cried for Dusty and Susannah and over the hardships in their lives. "God, if You are there, if Your are who my parents believe Your are, please heal the hurts of my two friends. Please touch their lives and bring hope."

Glad she had chores to do to keep her mind occupied, Isabel washed her face and headed down toward the barn. "I wonder why life turns out the way it does," she commented to Lady as she led the mare back to a stall filled with fresh straw and clean water. She rubbed the horse between her eyes and kissed her velvet nose. "Someday, I hope to own a horse just like you."

She turned and ran into Slade. Heat rushed into Isabel's cheeks. He'd not only caught her talking to a horse, but kissing her!

Slade lifted an amused brow.

"Tomorrow I'm going to town to send Dusty's aunt a telegram and pick up the Thanksgiving supplies. Do you think you can handle everything around here?"

"I think I can. Would you mail another letter for me? I need to inform my family that I never made it to Arizona."

"Just a temporary setback," Slade reminded her.

"Maybe." She doubted she'd ever make Arizona. No longer even sure she wanted to, Isabel thought she might return home next spring and make things right with her family.

§✦

Thanksgiving arrived the following week, but it seemed no one felt very thankful. The house was glum, and Slade had no idea how to reach Dusty, or Susannah, for that matter. Isabel spent more and more time outdoors. She'd take hours brushing the horses and caring for them. The woman never ceased to amaze him. He smiled just thinking of her.

When Mama called them in for dinner, he and Isabel walked back to the house together. She seemed content, and working in the sun had darkened her skin a few shades. He saw a few new freckles across her nose, and she had a healthy glow about her.

"I love this time of year—the briskness in the air," Isabel commented, raising her face to the sky.

"Me, too," he agreed.

When they got to the house, Mama and Susannah had Dusty at the table, though he didn't appear any too happy to be there. They'd put him in the wheelchair Susannah had used.

"Today," Mama announced, "we'll eat in the dining room." She wheeled Dusty in there, and they all followed.

As they gathered round the food-laden table, Isabel asked, "Can we each take a minute to share what we're thankful for? It's an old tradition back home."

Dusty's scowl said he wanted no part of any such nonsense, but Mama agreed. "I'm thankful for my Lord Jesus Christ and for a son and daughter who fill my life with blessings. I'm thankful for Isabel and Dusty, who share our hearts and lives." She looked to Slade. "*Mijo?*"

"I'm thankful for each of you and this *ranchero.*" He turned to Susannah, who sat to his left.

"For life," was all she said.

She looked across at Isabel.

"I'm thankful for Slade, who didn't leave me stranded in Los Angeles." She glanced at him, a smile gracing her lips. As usual, whenever she looked at him, his heart banged against his ribs. "And I'm thankful for you, Mrs. Stanfield. You've been like a mother to me—both kind and loving. I'm thankful for you, Susannah, and your friendship, and Dusty, I'm so grateful you are alive and sitting at this table with all of us."

Jealousy crept into Slade's heart. He'd suspected there was something between Isabel and Dusty, but Isabel's words brought it out in the open. No more denying their mutual attraction.

Everyone waited for Dusty's response. He finally looked up. "I think I'll pass." Bitterness laced each word.

They finished the meal in silence. Apparently, no one knew how to respond to Dusty.

ஜ

The following two weeks passed in near silence. Dusty brooded. Susannah grieved over lost love. Isabel and Slade both worked themselves to exhaustion. She'd taken on a few new chores as she got faster and more efficient. Ranch work wore her out but fulfilled her, too. She loved the animals, and every day presented some new adventure.

On this day, she rode Lady out to where Slade worked in the far north pasture. His mother had sent Isabel with a picnic lunch. She planned to talk Slade into allowing Susannah to attend the Christmas ball. Susannah needed to see there were other possibilities, other available men.

Isabel followed Mrs. Stanfield's directions and finally found Slade. He mended fences. Lady neighed at Blacky, causing Slade to notice her approach. He stood and waited.

"Your mother sent me with your lunch," she hollered, still a ways off.

"Good. I'm feeling hungry and dreaded the ride back to the ranch." He took the basket containing their food and the blanket for them to sit on.

Isabel slid off and tethered Lady near Blacky.

"Bless my mother's heart." Slade spread out the blanket and then the food.

"Fried chicken, potato salad, even some chocolate cake," Isabel informed him.

"And fresh lemonade. All my favorites."

Isabel joined Slade on the blanket. "The ride out here is beautiful. I love this ranch more all the time."

Slade smiled. "Me, too. There's not another place on earth I'd rather live or die." He bit into a fresh, warm tortilla.

"You're lucky."

Slade nodded. "Isabel, I can't thank you enough for all your help. I'll pay you Dusty's wage, and you'll earn your passage to Arizona even quicker."

Isabel's heart dropped at the reminder that her life on the ranch was temporary. "If you don't mind, I'd like to stay for my full six months."

"Suit yourself," Slade said, but he acted like he'd prefer she leave sooner.

"Why don't you have ranch hands like Mr. Ochoa?"

"We've had a couple of lean years, so I had to let everybody go except Dusty. I hire grub-line workers during the branding season and for the cattle drive, but since this year has been much more prosperous, I'll hire a few regulars in the spring. Also, the Ochoa ranch is much larger than ours."

"I thought he got a land grant the same as your great-grandfather." Isabel speared a bite of potato salad.

"He bought up more land as time passed."

"Oh." Isabel bit into a chicken leg. "Did Dusty ever hear back from his aunt?"

"Yes, but she's failing herself and can't take care of him."

"The poor man has no one."

"He'd have us if he wanted, but he doesn't seem to." Slade wiped his greasy fingers on a cloth his mother had enclosed.

"He's having a difficult time accepting his injury. I've tried to talk to him, and so have your mother and Susannah. No one can get him to respond. I feel just awful. I wish he'd let someone help him."

Slade cocked his head, and his brows drew together. Isabel saw the questions in his eyes, but he didn't say anything.

She laid down her picked-clean chicken bone. "What? What are you thinking?"

Slade stretched his legs out and propped himself on one elbow. "I just expected you to be more torn up over Dusty."

"I do feel awful." Isabel shrugged.

"I thought you were in love with him." Slade shook his head.

"You have the right emotion, but the wrong girl. Susannah is the one pining for Dusty."

He sat up straight. "Susannah? My little sister, Susannah?" The thought of her being in love apparently stunned him.

Isabel laughed. "Yes, Susannah. She's a grown woman, Slade. Did you think she'd never fall in love?"

"No." He relaxed a little. "In her condition, how can she care for a home and a man?"

Isabel rose to her knees and brought out the chocolate cake. "Because she's lame?"

Slade nodded.

"Doc told her you and Mrs. Stanfield have limited her abilities."

At the hurt expression on Slade's face, Isabel regretted so carelessly blurting out the truth. "I'm sorry. I didn't mean that quite the way it sounded." Isabel took a deep breath and tried again. "Doc believes Susannah is more than capable of becoming a wife and even a mother."

"He told you this?" Slade accepted the cake from Isabel.

"No, but he told Susannah." Isabel tasted the moist chocolate treat and thought she'd gone to heaven. The cake melted in her mouth. "Your mother is by far the best cook I've ever known."

Slade smiled. "That she is. Now back to Susannah. What have my mother and I done to limit her?"

"You do everything for her and protect her so much, she'll never meet a man who might love her. Doc encouraged her to become independent, to take care of herself."

From Slade's thoughtful expression, Isabel knew he weighed her words.

"And speaking of meeting men. There is a Christmas ball. . . ."

"You never give up, do you?" He looked annoyed.

"Slade, it's for Susannah. Don't you want her to live as normal a life as possible?"

10

id Slade want Susannah to live as normal as possible? Truth be known, he ached for that, yet the thought also terrified him. If Susannah met someone and married, maybe there'd be a chance for him and Isabel. He gazed into the green eyes studying him, and his heart ached—ached to touch her, to hold her, to tell her he loved her. He did love her. The observation startled him. He loved Isabel Fairchild. He grinned at the revelation.

"What's so funny?" she asked.

"Life. Life is funny." Slade leaned back on one elbow and stared at the blue sky. "My goal was to protect her and keep her safe, but I've realized I can't do that. Only God can." He leaned up on one elbow. "You deserve the credit for that revelation." He reached for Isabel's hand and squeezed. "Thank you, Isabel, for not giving up until I saw the truth."

Isabel's mouth dropped open at Slade's confession.

"Now, tell me about this ball," Slade encouraged.

Her whole face lit up. She really was beautiful. "The Grand Christmas Ball is at the Horton House on Christmas evening. It's more expensive than the Thanksgiving ball, though. For $2.50, a couple can dance the night away and eat supper."

"If I bought two tickets—one for my mother and Susannah, the other for you and me—would you allow me to escort you?"

Her eyes glowed. "You want to escort me?" she asked, astounded.

"Yes." Slade rose to his feet and offered Isabel a hand. His heart hammered in his ears when she put her hand in his. They faced one another. In Isabel's eyes resided all the longing he felt. Placing a hand on each side of her face, he drew her lips to his.

The awe on her face made him smile. He felt exactly the same way. "I think I've now been kissed by a man," Isabel whispered.

He kissed her forehead. "Maybe you should go back home so I can get back to work. I find you a bit of a distraction."

Isabel grinned. "It's taken you long enough. You've been distracting me since I first arrived here. See you back at the house." She started cleaning up their lunch mess, and Slade retrieved Lady. He helped Isabel into the saddle and handed her the blanket and basket.

Slade returned to work with a grin on his face. Maybe things would work out for Isabel and him. Just maybe.

ક≫

Isabel rushed home, wanting to tell Susannah the news, hoping to give her friend something to look forward to. She tethered Lady outside the house and ran inside.

"A Christmas ball? I don't think so. Thank you anyway, Isabel. Besides, who would dance with me?"

"Susannah, the fact that Dusty's aunt is failing hasn't changed his mind about leaving us as soon as he can travel and make plans. You need to get on with your life, and I guarantee you a missing leg won't stop men from requesting a spin around the floor with you. You're a beautiful woman, Susannah."

A tear slithered down Susannah's cheek. "I love him. It's not that easy. I don't want to meet someone else. I want him to get over his brooding and figure out he loves me, too."

"I'm sorry." Isabel hugged Susannah. "I'm being selfish and thoughtless. Of course you aren't ready to go dancing. I'll tell Slade it's too soon. He can escort me to another dance sometime, maybe in the spring."

Susannah pulled back and met Isabel's gaze. "Slade invited you to the ball?"

"I suggested the ball to divert your attention. Once he agreed, he asked me." Isabel knew her smile went from ear to ear.

"Oh, Isabel, I dreamed of this happening." Susannah hugged her. "Of course, we'll go. I don't want Slade to miss his evening with you."

Susannah smiled for the first time in weeks. "Let's search my closet for two party dresses."

"Are you certain?" Isabel asked, concerned with Susannah's well-being.

"Indeed I am. Oh, Isabel, if Slade asked for your hand, would you give it?" Susannah clutched Isabel's arm, and they proceeded to Susannah's closet.

Isabel hesitated. Dare she put her feelings to words? "I think I would. I love the ranch, you, your mother, the animals. I find ranch life is a daily adventure."

Susannah's face reflected disappointment. "What about Slade, Isabel? Do you love him?"

"I love kissing him." She giggled.

"I know many people grow to love one another later, but, Isabel, I must know if you care for Slade even a little." Susannah sat on her bed, no longer interested in dresses.

Isabel grew serious. "I care for him very much. So much it scares me."

Susannah sighed. "I'm glad. I'd be saddened if that weren't the case." Susannah went back over to the closet and dug through the garments, pulling out several dresses. Sadly, they were all too short for Isabel, who towered over Susannah by many inches.

"Perhaps I'll wear my traveling clothes." She tried not to sound disappointed.

"You said you sew. Why don't you make something?"

"Perhaps I will. Now if you'll excuse me, I have an errand to take care of this afternoon. I'll be back by supper." Isabel headed outside, climbed back up on Lady, and rode to the Ochoa ranch.

"Good day," one of Mr. Ochoa's sons greeted her.

"Hello. May I speak to your father?"

He nodded. "Come into the house, and I'll get him for you."

Isabel took a seat on a horsehair sofa in the parlor and waited. She hoped her plan would work.

"Miss Fairchild, what a pleasant surprise. What can I do for you?"

"I'm here on an errand of mercy. Miss Stanfield has agreed to attend the Grand Christmas Ball, and I hope to ensure her dance card is full."

He frowned. "I'm a married man."

Isabel giggled and rose. "I wasn't thinking of you as much as your sons and your ranch hands."

Mr. Ochoa blushed.

"I hoped you'd *encourage* them to make sure she danced every dance."

He grinned. "I will do so. How thoughtful of you to watch out for your friend."

"Thank you, sir. I will most appreciate your help in this delicate matter. And you may wish to mention that in order for her to dance, she must stand on the gentleman's feet."

"I will take care of it. Might I offer you some refreshment before you leave?"

"Thank you, yes."

After a cool drink of water, Isabel rode back over the ridge to Rancho San Miguel. When she returned, she found Slade doing her evening chores.

"Where have you been?" He was furious.

"I rode over to the Ochoas'."

"Isabel, do you remember me requesting that you not leave the house without letting someone know where you are?"

Isabel nodded. "I'm sorry. Susannah knew—"

"Susannah knew you had an errand to take care of. Not which direction you went. What if something had happened? What if your horse threw you? No one would know where to begin to look, and what business could you possibly have at the Ochoa ranch?" Was Slade jealous?

"I rode over to request dance partners for your sister—to make sure she'd be busy all evening. Help take her mind off Dusty."

"Isabel, you can't just traipse off to the next ranch and order the hands to dance with my sister. Do you know how humiliated she'd be?"

"I didn't think—"

"That's the problem. You never think."

"No, I never do, especially when I let you kiss me." Isabel unsaddled and rubbed down Lady, boiling all the while. Then she helped

Slade finish her chores but never said a word to him. How dare he act so bossy!

On the way back to the house after they'd finished, Slade stopped. "I'm sorry, Isabel. I was worried, and I don't like the idea of you making deals with a bunch of cowpokes."

"You're forgiven, and I didn't make any deals with *cowpokes*. I only asked Mr. Ochoa if he could make certain Susannah's dance card was full. It seemed the right thing at the moment."

ೋ

The following week at breakfast, Slade announced, "We're all going to town today." Then he looked pointedly at Isabel. "I've done the morning chores already."

"Why are we going to town?" Mother asked.

"Because we all need a break from the routine and because Marston's is having a winter clearance, and I know two young ladies who have no gowns to wear to the ball."

Slade enjoyed the delight on Isabel and Susannah's faces. They looked at each other and squealed. Dusty, on the other hand, mumbled something under his breath.

"Don't worry, we won't leave you behind. I've built a ramp so we can roll your wheelchair right up into the buckboard. Wouldn't dream of leaving you out of the fun."

Dusty wanted no part of their outing; the expression on his face made his stance clear. However, both Slade and his mother had learned a thing or two in the past three years, or at least the past three months with Isabel around. They knew Dusty needed to keep living, even though he didn't want to, so they insisted he go along.

The five of them loaded into the buckboard for a day in town. Isabel tried to get some singing going, but no one cooperated. Finally, she gave up and they made the trip in silence.

"Marston's is our first stop. While you ladies shop, Dusty and I will pick up some supplies. Then we'll pick you up and go to the Bandini House in the Cosmopolitan Hotel for some dinner."

All three of the women's faces lit up, and Slade chuckled, pleased to have pleased them. After dropping them off, he and Dusty headed for the general store. Mama had given him a list to fill. While the grocer handled the list, Slade rolled Dusty over to the café for a cup of coffee.

"How are you doing?" Slade asked after he'd taken a sip of the hot liquid.

"Fine." Dusty sipped his coffee. "I'm just fine."

"When you asked me about letting men court Susannah, who were you referring to?"

Dusty blanched. "Doesn't matter now. That man's gone."

Slade nodded and studied Dusty's bitter countenance. "You were the man, weren't you?"

Dusty glared into Slade's eyes. "Why are you doing this? Is your goal to kick a man when he's down?"

Slade ignored the comment and the anger. "If you'd have asked, I'd have said yes. If you asked now, I would still grant my permission."

Dusty attempted a laugh, but an embittered sound was all that came out. "Yeah, I was the one interested, but I didn't ask because I had nothing to offer the boss's sister. I have even less now."

Slade hurt for the guy. A man couldn't go to a woman empty-handed.

"I offered to sell you a piece of land."

"What if I never walk again? Doc says at best I'll limp. What if I can never work?" Dusty stared at his coffee, refusing to let Slade see the pain in his eyes. But the pain in Dusty's voice, Slade could never miss.

Slade decided to blurt out the truth. Maybe, just maybe, it would knock some sense into his friend. "Susannah fancies herself in love with you."

Dusty's head jerked up, and Slade saw the tiniest glimmer of hope on his face. "Did she say so?"

"She said so to Isabel."

Dusty took a long, slow swig of his coffee. "I've loved her since before she got hurt." His voice reverberated with pain. "But she was always the boss's sister, and I was always just a ranch hand."

What do I say, God? How do I reach him? "I've never been class conscious. You're a hardworking man. That's enough for me."

"What if I can never work again? I can't even take care of myself, much less a wife."

"I understand." And the sad part was, he did. A man had a code of honor to live by. Part of that honor was providing for family. "I just wanted you to know the truth."

"I appreciate that and all you've done for me. At least now I have a reason to work hard to get out of this chair." Dusty almost smiled. "And now I understand why Susannah treats me like I have the plague. She doesn't think I care, but I do." He drained his coffee cup. "She's the reason I never moved on to another ranch. I kept hoping someday I'd find a way to offer her more than just my heart.

"Then when she got hurt . . ." His cracked with emotion. "I couldn't leave."

Slade remembered how almost daily Dusty had inquired about Susannah. Several times, he'd paid a visit, but Susannah never wanted visitors. Now the puzzle pieces fit together into a clear picture.

"When you're ready, I have a piece of land to sell you and a sister who loves you." Slade never expected this day to come, and he was overwhelmed with gratitude to the Lord.

Dusty nodded, and Slade knew he, too, was deeply moved by God's goodness.

Slade rose and wheeled Dusty back to the general store. After loading their supplies and pushing Dusty up the ramp into the buckboard, Slade returned to Marston's for the women. They waited outside, chattering like magpies. A smile settled on Slade's lips. Today, all seemed right with the world.

&

Isabel and Susannah had their dresses wrapped in paper so Slade couldn't see them until the night of the ball. They wanted to surprise him. This was the first time in the past month Susannah had shown any enthusiasm for life, and Isabel knew going to the ball had been a good choice.

While they waited in front of the store for Slade, they talked about the fashions they'd seen. Even Mrs. Stanfield had bought a new dress for the ball. "Times like these, I miss your father so much," she commented to Susannah.

"I miss him, too, Mama. Someday, I pray God will give me a man who'll love me as much as Papa loved you."

"And someday He will, *mija*."

Isabel hoped that someday would be soon and the man would be Dusty. She couldn't help hoping a little for herself and Slade, too. Every time they made progress, something came along and knocked them backwards. Just thinking about him caused her heart to pitter-patter.

Slade pulled up on the buckboard. His eyes met hers, her heart jolted, and she smiled wide. *I love you, Slade Stanfield. I hope you figure out soon that you love me back.*

Slade climbed down and helped the women into the wagon. First, he laid their dresses on top of the supplies, then he assisted his mother onto the bench up front with him and helped Susannah and Isabel to get in the back with Dusty. His and Isabel's gazes were like magnets, constantly drawn to each other.

Once she settled in the back, Isabel noticed Dusty watching Susannah. Something had changed. A tiny chunk of his self-made armor seemed to be missing. His face appeared more vulnerable and less bitter. Isabel smiled to herself. Maybe he and Slade had had a talk.

The Bandini House was on the bottom floor of the Cosmopolitan Hotel. The hotel was one of only a few two-story buildings in San Diego. It was a wooden building with a balcony all the way around the second floor. "This looks more like it belongs in San Francisco than here," Isabel commented.

Slade agreed. "It's not even adobe."

Though the restaurant was crowded, the group was able to find a table for five. Isabel knew Dusty hated the stares and always kept his gaze on the floor. *Dear Lord, please give him his life back.* Isabel found herself praying more and more. *Does that mean I believe?* Yes, she knew she believed in God, always had. It was the personal relationship she really didn't understand. Her mother said God longed to be Isabel's best friend. How did one become best friends with God? Isabel would ask Susannah sometime when they were alone.

Mrs. Stanfield took the end seat, and Dusty and Slade faced Susannah and Isabel. After they ordered, they talked about the ranch and the ball. Even Dusty said a couple of things. Susannah smiled at Isabel, a hopeful expression on her face.

They all arrived home after a full day, tired but happy.

ॐ

"Susannah, would you take a walk with me?"

Susannah's heart stopped beating, then sped up double time. She turned to face Dusty as Slade rolled him down from the buckboard, wondering if she'd heard him right.

He watched her with expectancy.

She swallowed. "Did you ask me to . . . ?"

Dusty nodded. "Walk with me."

Slade rolled the wheelchair over to her, and she grasped the handles.

"Where are we walking?" she asked.

"Not far."

"That's a relief," she joked. "It's close to sundown." They must have made quite a pair, him in his chair and her limping along behind him. "The good thing about you being in this chair is I don't have to use my cane."

"That's the only good thing. Let's stop under the big oak there." They'd only gone a few hundred feet from the house.

After parking Dusty to face her, Susannah sat on the bench Mama had had Slade build. This was where Mama came every morning to meet with the Lord.

"Susannah, I'd like to escort you to the Christmas ball." Dusty grinned, looking a little shy. "Of course, you realize I won't be able to actually dance with you."

She reached for his hand. "Dancing doesn't matter to me. I'd rather be with you."

"Then I'll take that as a yes."

"A definite yes."

Dusty raised his head toward the sky. "Susannah, how did you learn to accept your accident? How can you always be so cheerful and happy?"

"I read the book of Job over and over. Each time, God did a little more work on my heart until I could say with Job, 'Though He slay me—yet will I praise Him.'"

"It's hard to feel like praising when my whole life is gone."

Susannah felt a lump tightening her throat. "I know." She lowered her head so he wouldn't see tears building in her eyes. "Believe me, I know. But I learned the more I praise Him, the more I want to." Susannah raised her gaze and saw the tears in Dusty's eyes as well. Hers spilled over and trailed down her cheeks.

"I wish I wanted to, but I feel so mad at God. Why? Why did this happen?" Dusty balled up his fist and pounded it into the open palm of his other hand.

"I don't know, but I do know that I appreciate God more than I ever have. I know Him better because, in my pain, I sought Him out."

"Were you ever mad?"

"Oh, yes. At first I was so mad I never wanted to see another human being or talk to God ever again."

"I came to see you many times, but you always turned me away." His quiet words brought her gaze to his face, his handsome, strong face.

"I wish I hadn't," she responded honestly. "Why did you keep coming? No one else bothered."

"Don't you know?"

She shook her head.

"I was once in love with you."

"Oh." His words settled into her heart like an anchor settles into the ocean—heavy and hard. *Was once* not *am still*. Once she lost her leg, he probably lost his interest.

Slade and Isabel approached from the barn, where they had finished evening chores. After a greeting, Slade pushed Dusty back to the house, and Susannah leaned on Isabel for support. She was glad they'd prevented her from responding to Dusty. She had no idea what to say.

11

*S*lade waited with his mother and Dusty on the front veranda for Isabel and Susannah. All three dressed in finery.
They had celebrated Christmas by sharing their favorite
Christmas stories and eating a huge breakfast. No gifts were exchanged, but tonight was Slade's gift to each of them.

When the front door finally opened and Dusty and Slade caught
their first glimpses of Susannah and Isabel, there was a collective gasp.
Both women were so beautiful—Isabel in her Christmas green silk
gown and Susannah in her red velvet one. Isabel's hair was swept up
in a bun on the crown of her head, while ringlets cascaded down her
back. Susannah's hair was styled in a similar manner.

"Ladies," Slade announced, offering them each an arm, "your carriage awaits." He surprised them by borrowing one of the Ochoas'
nicest coaches.

Isabel smiled up at him, making the surprise all the more worthwhile. "Oh, Slade, it's beautiful."

"And so elegant," Susannah added.

Slade helped each of them into the coach and then returned for
his mother in her midnight blue gown. After she settled in across from
the girls, Slade lifted Dusty into the closed carriage. Then he climbed
in and shut the door.

"I've arranged for two drivers. One for us and one for the buckboard carrying your chair. Doc says a couple more weeks and you can
start using those legs."

"I hope they still remember how to work." Though Dusty's comment sounded offhanded, Slade knew the man wrestled with fear—fear

he'd never walk or work again. Fear he'd never have anything to offer Susannah.

"They'll work. I've just got a feeling," Isabel stated.

Isabel never let life get her down. Slade loved that about her. Come to think of it, he'd been finding lots to love about her and less and less to dislike. He'd convinced himself Isabel wasn't really a dance-hall girl at heart. She was searching for herself, and he believed she'd found her place here at the ranch.

The girls spent the ride to town chatting about their favorite dances. Slade had worried no one would dance with Susannah, even though Isabel had tried to ensure that didn't happen. However, since Dusty asked to escort her, that didn't seem to matter so much. Slade guessed that if Susannah didn't dance once, she'd be happy as a lark in Dusty's company.

Once they arrived at the Horton House, they were directed to the dining hall, where dinner would be served before the ball began. Slade pushed Dusty into the room, while his mother and Isabel gave Susannah the support she needed.

"All the tables seat eight, sir," a servant informed Slade. "So other guests will be joining your party."

Slade nodded and pulled out a chair for Susannah and one for his mother. Lastly, he seated Isabel next to him and rolled Dusty up between Isabel and Susannah. The man who seated them removed the extra chair Dusty wouldn't need.

As the room filled up, three single gentlemen were seated at the Stanfield table. They showered attention on Susannah and Isabel. Slade glanced at Dusty and knew he felt possessive, too. Isabel made a point of drawing Slade into the conversation. She laid her hand on his arm, letting everyone know they were together. He appreciated the tactful way she handled the situation.

"Susannah, you and Dusty must forget trying to be alone tonight," Isabel said out of the blue. Both Susannah and Dusty appeared dumbfounded.

Slade chuckled, knowing she had insured the other three men knew the ladies at this table were spoken for.

"Aren't they the most handsome couple?" Isabel asked the man on his mother's right.

The man nodded his agreement. Dusty and Susannah both turned five shades of red. Mrs. Stanfield nodded at Isabel, apparently appreciating her shrewdness. Slade patted Isabel's hand, which still lay on his arm.

"Thank you," he whispered in her ear. "Susannah's rather protected life hasn't prepared her to handle all situations."

Isabel endowed him with her smile. "Protected life? Not Susannah."

"Point taken," he agreed.

After dinner, guests at each table were guided to the grand ballroom. Mrs. Stanfield went first, with Susannah leaning heavily on her for support. Isabel followed, and Slade trailed behind, pushing Dusty. The three men brought up the rear. The moment the three fellows noticed Susannah's limp, they commented a little too loudly, "No wonder she's with a lame fellow."

Another one laughed and said, "Why would two cripples pay money to go to a dance?"

Slade noticed Dusty tense. He tried to walk faster so they'd not have to hear anymore comments, but following Susannah made moving fast impossible.

"What if she'd been available and one of us got stuck with her all night?"

"Seems a little underhanded to sit at a table and look normal."

Slade spun around. "I suggest you all be quiet, or we will have to take this discussion outside."

"Your wheelchair friend coming, too?" one of them asked.

Mr. Ochoa stepped up. "Slade, is everything all right?"

"These men are mocking Susannah."

"Susannah? My cousin's daughter, Susannah? I think not." Mr. Ochoa signaled some of his men, and they helped the loudmouths out the door.

Slade knew the encounter had affected Dusty badly. How helpless he must have felt, unable to defend the woman he cared about. Slade wished he could change the facts, but truth was, he couldn't. All he could do was let the incident go.

è

Isabel hoped Susannah hadn't heard the rude comments, but the expression on her pretty face denied Isabel's wish. "Don't worry. You're with the man you'd choose above all others, so who cares what they think?"

"I know you're right." Susannah raised her chin. "They can't ruin tonight for me."

"Good for you!"

Almost the minute they arrived in the ballroom, men swarmed around Susannah, asking her to dance. She appeared overwhelmed by the attention and looked to Dusty for the answer to her plight. He shrugged his shoulders, helpless to whisk her away from it all. Isabel realized this line of men was her doing. Now she wished she hadn't been so overzealous.

"Go ahead," Dusty said. "I obviously can't dance with you. One of us might as well enjoy themselves." The bitterness was back in his voice.

One of Mr. Ochoa's sons helped Susannah plant her feet on his and whirled off with her.

"Dusty, I'm sorry. This is my fault," Isabel confessed, feeling horrible. This was his second big blow tonight. "Once I convinced Susannah to attend the ball, I rode to the Ochoa ranch to line up a full dance card for her. I had no idea you'd offer to escort her. Had I, I'd never have meddled."

"This is a good reminder, Isabel. I have no business courting a woman. I can't even take care of myself, let alone protect Susannah." Dusty shook his head, sinking back into sullenness.

Isabel, Slade, and Mrs. Stanfield sat with Dusty for several songs while Susannah was passed from partner to partner. Isabel sighed her frustration. Watching Susannah laugh and enjoy herself did nothing to improve Dusty's mood.

"You don't have to sit here with me," Dusty said. "Frankly, I'd rather be alone, so if you don't mind, why don't you go dance or something?"

Slade stood and held out his hand to Isabel. She accepted. The orchestra played a slow waltz, so she slipped into his arms, and they glided across the floor. Mrs. Stanfield went to find some of her quilting friends.

"You know what I realized tonight?" Slade asked once they'd put some distance between themselves and Dusty.

"What's that?"

"Trying to control other people's lives always ends in disaster."

Isabel beamed at him. "Like the awkward situation I created tonight?"

"And like the problems I made during the past three years. I was foolish to think I could protect Susannah from all the hurts of life."

Isabel glanced back at Dusty. "I wish we could erase the hurt tonight has heaped on him."

"Me, too." Slade let out a long, slow breath. "At least she's having a good time."

Susannah's face glowed from pleasure and exertion.

"Mr. Ochoa certainly lived up to my request."

"Thank you for doing this for her." Slade spun Isabel around.

"Even though the plan blew up in Dusty's face?"

"I know you meant well, and I'm grateful." Slade stopped. "Do you want to get some air out on the balcony?"

"Some air would be nice." She sensed he wanted to tell her something important.

They spent a few moments in silence, enjoying the stars and the crisp night air. Finally, Slade turned her to face him. "Isabel, I've been wrong about many things—most things when it comes down to it. Would you forgive me?"

"For what? For loving your sister and doing what you thought best? There's nothing to forgive, at least not from me. Maybe Susannah might feel differently. I don't know."

"I was more thinking about the way I treated you and reacted to your suggestions."

"I forgave you long ago. I knew you only wanted your idea of the best for Susannah."

Slade's eyes darkened a shade. "I realize now you were a godsend. We all needed you, Isabel, but me even more than Susannah." He ran his fingers through her ringlets. "I'm so grateful for everything you've done for her benefit, even the line of men waiting to dance with her tonight." He kissed her cheek. "Thank you, Isabel."

Feeling choked up, Isabel replied, "You're welcome," but her voice sounded squeaky.

"Look at her, dancing and enjoying this wonderful, enchanted evening. You did this for her."

Isabel smiled, and a tear trickled down her cheek. She'd never received such high praise before, and, frankly, the words sounded wonderful. The deep appreciation Slade felt for her made her heart swell with love for him. All of her life, she'd longed for something, and tonight she realized it was gratitude and appreciation.

Her family loved her, but she'd always been the youngest one, the one in the way. Her mother and father had one another, and Gabrielle and Magdalene, who were close in age, had been close friends for years. Isabel had been so much younger and had no one who needed or appreciated her until now.

"Isabel, are you still planning that trip to Arizona?" The urgency in Slade's voice drew her attention back to him.

She shook her head, recognizing that her earlier plans simply grew from her search for men's admiration. Now she only wanted one man's admiration. And the way he looked at her, she believed she had it.

Slade bent his head to kiss her, tenderly holding her face in his hands. "I love you, Isabel."

Her heart nearly jumped out of her chest, and her knees felt weak. "You do?" She knew he thought highly of her and that she loved him, but she had no idea that he loved her.

"I do, and now that you've been kissed by a man, I plan to be the only man who ever kisses you again. Will you marry me?"

Stunned, Isabel's mouth dropped open. "Oh, Slade, yes! A million times, yes!"

She hugged him and rained quick kisses across his cheek.

He laughed. "That was another thing I failed to control—the love growing in my heart for you since about day one." He kissed her nose.

"I'm glad you gave up on the whole idea of trying to control life."

"Me, too. Now let's go keep Dusty company."

"Slade, can we wait to share our happiness until Dusty and Susannah figure out theirs?"

"That was my plan," he said as they reentered the hall.

&

As they approached Dusty, Slade watched Susannah go up to him. The scowl on Dusty's face caused Slade's steps to slow. Dusty turned his chair and rolled away from Susannah and out another doorway.

"Maybe I should talk to him."

"I'll go console Susannah." Isabel pulled back on his arm. "Don't forget that I love you." She grinned, and her dimples danced across her cheeks.

"I won't." And he wouldn't. Slade was grateful to the Lord for Isabel. *The Lord.* He'd forgotten all about Him when it came to Isabel. What had he just gone and done? He'd asked Isabel to marry him without seeking God's leading. His stomach tightened up into a giant knot of worry. He hadn't prayed about marrying her; he hadn't prayed about much lately. Not much at all. "God," he whispered, "I'm sorry. We'll have to work this out later. Right now, I have another problem to address. Give me Your wisdom to share with Dusty."

Slade found Dusty all alone on a small porch. He knew the man had been crying by the redness of his eyes. His heart ached for Dusty, yet he didn't know what to say or do. "I thought I might find you out here." Not wishing to embarrass his friend, Slade made a point to avoid looking at him. Instead, he stared up at the moon.

"I made a huge mistake, Slade. I can't court Susannah or even think about marriage." Dusty's voice was flatter than one of Mama's tortillas.

"But you love her," Slade argued.

"That's not enough. I would become an anchor around her neck. She'd grow to hate me."

"Somehow I doubt that." Slade spoke quietly.

"Look at me, Slade! Look at me."

He did as Dusty asked.

"I'm half a man with no way to protect myself, let alone Susannah. Sometimes love isn't enough."

"I think love would be enough for Susannah." Slade knew he was fighting an already lost battle.

"Well, it's not enough for me. I'll be leaving the ranch as soon as I can manage a little better on my own."

Slade closed his eyes. Was God giving him a way out with Isabel? If Susannah wasn't getting married, neither could he. He'd made a promise. "Where will you go?"

"Doesn't matter. I just have to go. Please don't say anything about this to Susannah."

Slade nodded his agreement. What a mess their lives were in. Soon, there would be four brokenhearted people with hopes dashed and dreams lying dead at their feet. Once again, he and Susannah would be alone.

ેૹ

"Isabel, am I wrong to dance and enjoy myself?" Susannah asked.

"Not since Dusty told you to go ahead. Problem is, he's hurting. How do you think he feels not being able to dance with you himself?" Isabel led Susannah out onto the balcony where Slade had just proposed.

"I know how he feels! But if he had the chance to dance for the second time in years, I'd encourage him." Susannah's face scrunched in frustration. "I'd plead with him to go and enjoy."

Isabel shivered and wrapped her arms around her middle. "Would you have right after the accident, while you were still in your—what did you call it—grieving period?"

Susannah's face registered how true Isabel's words rang. "Maybe not," she admitted.

"Probably not?" Isabel asked.

"You're right, Isabel. I've been thoughtless. How much he must hurt watching me with other men. Please take me to him this minute. I must apologize at once."

Isabel guided Susannah to the door she'd seen Slade exit. They found the two men alone and in the midst of a serious conversation.

"Can we interrupt? Susannah has something she wishes to say to Dusty."

Both men waited expectantly, but Isabel spotted the worry in Slade's eyes.

"Maybe Slade and I should wait inside."

"No, it's all right if you hear." Susannah still clung to Isabel's arm. "Dusty, please forgive my thoughtless behavior tonight. I never considered your feelings. And I'm now undergoing deep regret for dancing the night away and ignoring you. This newfound freedom went to my head. Will you forgive me?"

"The truth is your choices tonight only served to make my decision easier. I had no business inviting you here tonight. I have no business courting at all." Dusty rolled his chair back into the ballroom.

Susannah's face puckered, and Isabel ached for the both of them. After all, she knew the joy of loving and being loved. She'd yearned for Dusty and Susannah to share what she and Slade had, but apparently it wasn't meant to happen.

"I think it's time for us to go home," Slade said. "I'll take Susannah and get the driver to bring the carriage around front. Why don't you round up my mother and Dusty?" He whisked Susannah into his arms and went around the outside of the hall rather than going back inside.

Several minutes passed before Isabel found Mrs. Stanfield. They went together and collected Dusty. The carriage ride home was dismal, indeed.

12

$\mathcal{T}$he following morning, Isabel was carrying a pail of milk and a pail of eggs when she finally spotted Slade riding in from the east. Quickening her pace, she rushed toward the house, handing Mrs. Stanfield the pails and hurrying back out the door. She longed to see Slade this morning, feel his arms around her, and make certain last night wasn't a dream.

She found him down by the barn, loosening Blacky's cinch so both horse and rider could eat before they headed out on another task. "Good morning!"

The expression on Slade's face stopped her midstep. "What's wrong?" Maybe she had dreamed the proposal because Slade Stanfield didn't resemble a man in love. Rather, he looked like a man with a big problem. Isabel's stomach suddenly felt sick.

"We need to talk." His grim words caused even more apprehension.

He motioned for her to sit down on an old tree stump. Since her legs were shaky, she welcomed the invitation. Running his hand down the back of his head, Slade paced a few steps away and then came back to face her. Finally, he kneeled in front of her.

"Isabel, the things I said last night—"

"You didn't mean them," she accused, jumping up and putting distance between them. Fighting tears, she stood stiff with her back to Slade.

He came to her and turned her around, raising her chin with his hand until their eyes met. "I did mean them. I meant every word. I do love you."

She swallowed hard. "But?"

"I can't marry you, Isabel."

She pulled her lips together in a tight line and closed her eyes. Her heart suddenly weighed a hundred pounds. Nodding her head, she pulled away from him, fighting the tears.

"Wait, Isabel. Please, let me explain."

She paused and looked back at him. One tear slid out, then another.

He came to her again and roughly pulled her into his arms. She laid her head against his chest, and the tears flowed unchecked. She loved him so much, and now he didn't want her, either. No one had ever wanted her, not really. Her parents loved her but always wanted to change her into her sisters. They didn't want Isabel just as she was. Neither did Slade.

"Isabel, I promised myself and God I'd not marry until Susannah did. How can I take things from life that she no longer can? Especially since I'm responsible for her condition."

Isabel raised her head to look at him. His eyes glistened with unshed tears, and the pain on his face resembled the anguish in her heart. She wanted to argue with him, but his jaw was set in determination. She'd not win.

"What about Dusty? I thought he cared about Susannah."

"Barring a miracle, he's leaving as soon as he can figure a way to take care of himself. Last night made him conclude he is in no position to care for himself, let alone another." Slade led Isabel to an oak, and they sat, leaning back against the trunk.

Isabel let out a sigh. "Does Susannah know?"

"Not yet. I think Dusty should tell her, so I'm minding my own business." Slade swatted at a gnat.

"She might marry someone, someday. We can wait."

"I can't ask you to wait. What if she never marries, Isabel? You shouldn't throw away your chance for a family on a maybe." Slade took her hand in his. "I've thought about this from every angle. I don't know what else to do except to set you free." He squeezed her hand.

"Do you mind if I finish out my six months? Maybe in the three I have left, Susannah will meet someone else, and we won't have to say good-bye."

Slade kissed her hand. "There is also the matter of God."

"God?"

"Isabel, I'm not sure exactly where you stand with Him."

Isabel frowned. "I believe in God."

"I know you do, but do you have a relationship with Him?"

"I talk to Him . . . occasionally." She pulled her hand free. "If you don't want to marry me, just say so. Don't blame God." Isabel jumped up and ran until she reached the house. She sneaked into her room, and lying across her bed, she let her pain pour out. Susannah must have heard the muffled sobs, for a few minutes later, she knocked softly on Isabel's door.

"Isabel, can I come in?" she asked softly from the porch.

"Go away, Susannah. Please go away."

Susannah ignored the request and entered. "I can't just leave you here. Please tell me what's wrong. How can I help?"

Isabel sat up. "Can you make your brother love me? Can you give him the desire to spend the rest of his life with me? No, I think not, so you can't help."

Susannah shuffled across the room and sat on the bed. In a soft voice, barely above a whisper, she said, "No more than you can make Dusty fall in love with me. No more than you can make Dusty wish to spend all his days with me." By then Susannah cried, too. "We are quite a pair, Isabel, quite a pair, indeed."

Isabel hugged Susannah. "I'm sorry. I forgot you're hurting, too."

"We are both heartbroken women heading for spinsterhood because the men we've given our hearts to don't want them," Susannah said.

Isabel laughed and cried at the same time. "Spinsterhood?"

"I don't know about you, but I will never see another man. I don't want to hurt like this again. Slade was right to keep me locked away. I should have stayed under lock and key, then I'd not hurt so much."

Isabel's hope plummeted with each of Susannah's words. There was no hope she'd marry anytime soon, which made Slade unavailable. Besides, with his new excuse, he'd probably have no interest in Isabel even if Susannah were happily married. Isabel blew out a long, slow breath. The honest truth was that Slade didn't want her. He'd acted impulsively and now regretted his actions, so he'd made up some excuse and blamed God.

Did she want to stay here anymore? She thought of Susannah, Mrs. Stanfield, Dusty, Slade, even the horses. Yes, she'd stay and finish her six months. With nowhere else to go, she'd have time to figure out where to go from here. She'd probably go home.

Lord, I'm so sorry I hurt Isabel. Please forgive me and enable her to forgive me. I thank You for bringing her into my life, even if it's only for six months. Knowing her has changed me. Loving her has changed me. Forgive me, Father, for not consulting You about my love for Isabel. Forgive me for the years of doubt and silence. Lord, my heart echoes the father in the Bible—help my unbelief. Help me to trust You. In Your Son's precious name I pray, amen.

≈

The next six weeks passed in stony silence. Isabel avoided Slade. Susannah avoided Dusty. Slade and Dusty were solemn and seldom spoke. Finally, Isabel could take no more. Even though she'd only been at the ranch for five months, she had to leave. Staying another month would be simply impossible.

"I'm riding to town today," Isabel announced to Susannah. "Would you like to come along?"

Susannah's eyes brightened. She laid her brush down on her bureau. "I don't know. What will Slade say?"

"He'll probably say no. I wasn't asking. He told me to let your mother know of any outings you and I take, so I plan to tell her after he's long gone."

Susannah grabbed her cane and moved toward Isabel. "I do want to go. I haven't ridden in such a long time." She moved her head in a defiant gesture. "I'm so tired of the miserable silence resonating through this house. For the past six weeks—ever since the Christmas ball—neither Dusty nor Slade ever say a word. You, Mama, and I carry on useless prattle, but we're only trying to cover the obvious quiet."

Isabel bobbed her head in concurrence. "I'll see you at breakfast." She, too, was sick of the silence, the brooding, and her own broken heart. Seeing Slade daily made her plight worse. That's why she'd decided to leave.

She hurried back to Susannah's room. "Please don't mention our plans yet. Also, bring a coat. The temperature is running about sixty degrees this week." She'd miss this drier, warmer climate when she returned to San Francisco.

"All right. I'll see you in the kitchen."

After breakfast, Isabel hurried through her chores, thinking this might be one of the last days she spent with the horses. She wanted to cry but wouldn't. As soon as she finished her chores, she saddled Lady for herself and Flaxie—a small, flax-colored mare—for Susannah. Flaxie had been Susannah's horse before the accident. Then she put the other horses back in their stalls so Slade wouldn't have to later.

Isabel led both horses up to the house. Susannah waited on the front veranda, dressed in some of her old riding clothes. "I'll let your mother know we're taking a ride in a southwesterly direction." Isabel winked. "Let's get you on the horse in case she decides to come out. That way we look all ready, and she'll have fewer doubts."

Isabel took Susannah's jacket and tied it behind the saddle. "I know Slade says you always mount on the left, but today we're doing things a little differently."

Susannah laughed. "It would be hard to mount on the left with a wooden stump for the bottom half of my left leg."

"My thinking exactly."

Susannah grabbed the saddle horn and jumped, jamming her right foot into the stirrup. Isabel held on to her for support. Susannah threw her left leg over the saddle and looked like a pro in no time.

"You'll have to teach me how to do that jump. Makes you look like a cowgirl from way back." Isabel handed Susannah Flaxie's reins.

"I am a cowgirl from way back. I've been riding since I turned three. And it feels good to be on a horse again. Thank you, Isabel."

"And thank you for accompanying me. I'll be right back."

Isabel went through the front door and straight to the kitchen. Mrs. Stanfield spent a good deal of time there each day. Grabbing two apples, she said, "Susannah and I are going for a ride." She turned to leave.

"Where, *mija?* You know Slade will want to know."

"We thought we'd head off in the direction of San Diego."

"*Sí.* Don't go too far. I think rain may fall later today."

Isabel had noticed the overcast sky but hadn't thought too much about it. It rained here far less often than it did in San Francisco. "I did pack a lunch, so we will be home before supper."

Mrs. Stanfield looked worried but said nothing.

Isabel headed out the door, avoiding any other questions Mrs. Stanfield might ask.

She tossed an apple up to Susannah and mounted Lady. They rode at a leisurely pace, both chomping on their apples.

"Why are we going to San Diego?"

Isabel had dreaded this question but knew it would come sooner or later. "I plan on sending a telegram to my father, asking him to send me a ticket so I can go home."

Susannah made a disappointed clicking sound with her tongue. "Oh, Isabel, I don't want you to leave."

"I have to." Tears sprang into her eyes. "It's past time for me to go."

"Will you ever come back?" Susannah's voice resounded with disappointment and sorrow.

"No. I'll never come back." The words sounded more emotionally charged than she had intended. Her heart couldn't endure coming back. Her heart couldn't bear seeing Slade again. "But we can write." Isabel tried to sound positive, as if her leaving was a good thing, a right thing. "Maybe you can come to San Francisco one day for a visit."

"Maybe. I wish I could go with you now and get away from Dusty. I'm glad he moved out of the house and back into the bunkhouse. At least I don't have to see him every day." Susannah patted Flaxie's neck. "You know the worst part? I know he loves me. I know we could have a wonderful life, but he's too prideful and stubborn to see that. All he can see is his wheelchair."

"Your brother's not much different. He told me he loves me, but he can't marry me because of God. I think it takes a lot of nerve to blame God. A lot of nerve."

Susannah got real quiet. Finally she asked, "Isabel, tell me about your relationship with God."

"Why do you and Slade keep speaking of a *relationship*—just like my parents used to? How do you have a relationship with an invisible God?"

"That's the amazing part." Excitement filled Susannah's tone. "The God of the entire universe, the maker of heaven and earth yearns to have a relationship with each one of us." Susannah held up her index finger. "The first step is realizing you are a sinner in need of a Savior."

"But I'm not that bad. I've never murdered anybody or anything."

"Have you ever lied?"

Guilt stabbed Isabel's heart as she remembered misleading Mrs. Stanfield just that morning.

"Or cheated or treated somebody badly?"

More memories surfaced. She'd treated her own sister pretty badly when she wanted Chandler for herself and he chose Magdalene. Isabel nodded, hoping Susannah wouldn't think less of her because she'd done a few rotten things.

"To a holy God, sin is sin. It doesn't have to be murder or stealing. Even something as seemingly innocent as gossip is very offensive to Him."

Gossip—add another transgression to her list. She and Josephine, a friend from back home, had not only gossiped about Magdalene, they had slandered her. Isabel felt warm. All this soul-searching brought a nauseous feeling over her. "You're right. I am a sinner."

"And the wages of sin is death," Susannah spoke softly, reverently.

"But the gift of God is eternal life through Christ Jesus our Lord." Isabel finished the verse for her. "My father taught me that as a little girl. Only today, it somehow makes more sense than ever before."

Susannah looked like she might cry. "I'm glad, Isabel."

"So how does one make Christ her Savior?"

Susannah grinned an ear-to-ear, my-oh-my-am-I-happy kind of grin. "It's easy. You ask. You admit to Him you've sinned, even name the ones that come to mind. Then, you ask forgiveness for your sins. Invite Jesus to come into your life as your Lord and Savior. That's when the relationship starts."

"And what happens if I never ask?"

Susannah's face took on a serious, frightened look. "Upon your death, you are sent to hell because you didn't accept Christ's love and payment for your sins. He died on the cross in your place, but you must accept the gift."

"By inviting Him to forgive me and come into my life?" Isabel wanted to be certain she understood.

"Exactly! Then you get a relationship with God, and you get to spend eternity with Him in heaven."

"Instead of hell without Him?"

"Do you want to do that, Isabel—invite God into your heart and life?"

Her pulse raced, and she knew now was the time. She licked her suddenly dry lips. "I do." The girls stopped their horses side by side. Susannah reached for Isabel's hand. "Do you want me to help you?"

Isabel smiled at Susannah, loving her all the more. "No. I think I understand." She closed her eyes and bowed her head. "Lord God, it's me, Isabel. After all these years, what my father has said about You makes sense. I am a sinner." Emotion choked her words. "And You are the Savior, so today I ask You to come. . . ." Isabel swallowed hard and wiped tears from her cheeks. "Come and forgive me. Come and save me. Come have a relationship with me." Isabel felt warmth and peace wash over her. "I thank You in Jesus' name, Amen."

Both she and Susannah cried happy tears. "Now you and I will spend eternity together, Isabel, even if we never see each other again on this earth. Maybe my mansion will even be next to yours."

"My own mansion? I've heard about that but never personalized the thought before." Isabel smiled.

"On streets of gold."

What more could she want? "Speaking of streets . . ." Isabel stopped Lady on the outskirts of town. "Do you know the way to the telegraph office?"

Susannah said, "Follow me."

A couple of turns and they were there. Susannah waited with the horses while Isabel went inside. Susannah didn't want to make a spectacle of herself getting off and on Flaxie. She also loaned Isabel the money to pay for the telegram.

Isabel dictated her message to the worker. "Want to come home.

Stop. Please send a train ticket. Stop. In care of Slade Stanfield San Diego, California. Stop. Accepted Christ today. Stop. Love and miss you. Stop. Isabel." She paid the man. The thought of leaving Slade, Susannah, the ranch—all the people and things she'd grown to love— broke her heart. "But for him, I know it's best," she whispered on her way out the door.

"We'd better hurry, Isabel. The sky toward the ranch looks dark."

Isabel jumped on Lady. "Let's go," she hollered. The wind had picked up and lifted her hat off her head. She chased it down the street, finally retrieving it. She might need it to keep the rain off her head. Pushing the hat down low, she remounted Lady. They took off in a gallop toward the ranch.

ও

"I think it's going to rain," Slade said to Dusty, staring up at the sky. "Maybe we should call it a day and get back early."

Dusty sniffed. "Yeah, smells like rain for certain."

"Thanks for helping me with the fencing today. Having you riding Buck and stretching the wire was a huge time saver," Slade commented as he gathered up his tools and packed them in his saddlebags.

"It's the least I can do. Feels good to get out of the bunkhouse and do something useful."

Slade mounted Blacky. He'd hoped his plan to help Dusty feel needed wouldn't backfire, and it hadn't. "Have you been following Doc's orders and exercising your legs every day?" he asked.

"Yeah. My legs are getting a little stronger each day, but they still won't hold me up. I don't know how Susannah does it. The crutches rub sores under my arms, but I guess even sores beat riding around in a wheelchair."

Big wet drops fell from the sky. "We'd better hurry, or we'll be soaked. Can you gallop?"

Dusty nodded, and both men set out in a gallop toward home. Slade hopped off his horse and opened the barn door. Dusty rode through, and Slade led Blacky in. The drops falling on the roof made a loud, thudding noise.

"That's some downpour," Slade commented, helping Dusty off his mount and handing him his crutches.

While Dusty rubbed down his horse, Slade took the saddle and carried it over to the rack. He prayed today would go a long way in building Dusty's belief and confidence that he was still a capable cowhand.

As Slade led Dusty's gelding to his stall, he noticed Lady was missing from hers. "Flaxie is missing, too."

"What?" Dusty asked from the front of the barn where he was rubbing down Blacky.

"Lady and Flaxie are missing." Slade felt panic rising up from his stomach. "You wait here. I'm going to run to the house. I'll be back."

Slade ran as fast as his legs would carry him and was still soaked to the bone when he reached the house. He opened the front door and yelled, not wanting to track water and mud all over. "Mama."

Her worried face confirmed his suspicions even before she said anything. "*Mijo*, are the girls back?"

Slade shook his head. "Where did they go?"

"For a ride—toward town."

Slade shook his head. Did he go look for them or hope they were safe? He'd never been patient at waiting. "I'll go search for them."

"Be careful. I'll pray, *mijo*."

He kissed Mama's cheek.

"Wait. I'll grab coats and blankets."

"I'll stop for them on my way out." Slade ran back to the barn.

13

"ou can't go out in this," Dusty yelled above the rain pelting the roof.

"I have to. I can't risk leaving them out there in this." Slade grabbed Blacky's bridle and headed to his stall.

"Then I'm going with you." Dusty hobbled behind him with Buck's bridle.

Slade wanted to say no, but the man had been stripped of so much of his dignity the past few months, all Slade could do was nod in agreement. Slade carried Dusty's saddle to him and they hurried to get their horses ready. "Just when I'm finally convinced Isabel has been right all along, this happens," Slade yelled as he tightened his cinch.

"Right about what?"

"Susannah deserving a normal life. I give her a little freedom, and look what happens." Slade helped Dusty into his saddle and opened the barn door, and they rode out into the pouring rain.

Mama stood on the veranda with coats and blankets. Slade shoved the blankets into his saddlebags, grabbed a coat for himself, and handed one to Dusty.

"I imagine they took the main road. We'll have to take it slow. This mud is slick."

Dusty kept his head ducked against the rain, but he gave Slade a quick nod.

Rain dripped into Slade's eyes and slammed against his face, but he'd not give up until he found the girls.

God, is this Your way of teaching me to trust You? He thought back to his request a few weeks ago that God heal his unbelief. Was this some sort of test?

"In the four years I've been here, I've never seen it rain like this." Dusty shouted to be heard.

"Me, either." That worried him. How long until the normally dry gullies filled with water and ran out over the road, making continuing impossible?

Lord, please hold Susannah and Isabel in Your righteous right hand. Please keep them safe. I admit only You can provide safety and protection. Though I thought I could keep Susannah out of harm's way, I now know that job belongs to You, not me. Forgive me for trying to take Your role in my sister's life.

Again, I ask You to forgive my three years of anger. I surrender my future, Susannah's future, and Isabel's future to You—the God of the universe. Please use this to draw Isabel to You. I ask for their safety in Jesus' name, amen.

Peace settled on Slade. He knew whatever happened, God was in control.

At the bottom of the hill, a wash filled with water ran across the road, wiping the roadbed away.

"It looks deep," Dusty commented.

Slade didn't want to believe it was, so he dismounted and used a tree branch to gauge. The water was several feet deep and ran at quite a pace. Slade knew it would be foolish to attempt to cross. They might end up stuck out in the weather for days.

Trust, his heart kept saying. He bowed his head. *I'm helpless, Lord. I trust You to work Your good and perfect will in this situation.*

"We'll have to go back. No use us being stranded, too." Slade hopped on Blacky and they returned to the ranch.

"I'm dropping you at the house. This mud is too slick for you and your crutches. I'll take the horses down."

Once in the barn, Slade dropped to his knees and prayed again.

Mama had hot bowls of soup ready when Slade finally returned to the house. He changed into dry clothes and joined Dusty at the table.

"I must speak with both of you," she informed Slade and Dusty. "I have watched you both destroy the love you have for Susannah and Isabel."

Slade glanced at Dusty. He looked as guilty as Slade felt.

"I say nothing. Now I must speak. Love is a gift. How will you feel if they don't come back alive?" Mama stood at the end of the table, her arms crossed.

"Devastated," Slade answered.

"You both let your male pride get in the way. Do you love Susannah?" she asked Dusty.

"I do." His quiet voice was self-condemning.

"Then why are you not married? Or at least courting? Because of a few rude men and a bruised ego, you walk away from this good and perfect gift from God's hand?" Mama shook her head in disapproval.

Dusty cleared his throat. "I have no way to provide for her, no way to protect her. Both of those responsibilities are given to a man with regard to his wife and family, by God Himself."

"When you marry Susannah, we become your family. Families look out for each other and fight battles together. We would help until you are well enough to take over."

Dusty hung his head. "I have nothing to offer her, no home, no possessions—nothing."

"And if she never returns, will that still matter? What will your regrets be?"

Slade felt for Dusty and knew his own reckoning with his mama was coming.

Dusty raised his gaze and met Mama's reproachful look. "I'll regret hurting her, driving her away, and not making her my wife."

"*Si.*" Mama wore a satisfied expression on her face. "And you, Slade—"

"I told you I'd not marry until Susannah did." He wouldn't let her run over him the way she'd just done to Dusty.

"That is now taken care of."

"And I'm not sure about Isabel's relationship with God."

"Did you ask her?" Mama drew her brows together.

"She believes but doesn't understand the relationship part."

"She will soon. I've been praying."

Slade envied his mother's faith.

"If anything happens to either of them, both Dusty and I will be heartsick. Isabel is as important to me as Susannah." He smiled. "I'm taken with her, and yes, I have told her I love her."

"And you know, in spite of this disaster, she is correct?"

"Yes, Mama, I know. I've already repented. I had no right to keep Susannah locked up these three years. I just pray I'll have the chance to tell her how sorry I am." Slade stared at his soup, which had long since cooled.

"Because her leg is missing doesn't mean she can't live a normal life just like you and me."

Slade nodded. "I promised God at the first opportunity, I'll make things right with Susannah."

"And never interfere in her life again?" Mama stared straight into his soul.

"Never."

"Since we have this worked out, you may both eat now." Mama moved toward the kitchen. "Don't forget to pray."

ॐ

The girls galloped for a little ways, but soon rain pelted them in the face, and they had to slow down. The rain fell harder, and soon they were soaked. Isabel shivered.

"We have to get out of this. We'll end up with pneumonia," Susannah shouted over the deafening roar of the wind and rain. "There's an old shack along here somewhere, if nobody tore it down. Pray, Isabel. Pray we'll find it."

Isabel searched the horizon but didn't see a shack. They rode awhile longer, taking turns praying aloud and begging God to provide a way out.

"There it is!" Susannah hollered and pointed northeast. They rode toward the rundown hut. "I hope that it's still abandoned."

"Sure looks it." If not for the storm, Isabel wouldn't take money to enter the old shack. She climbed down and opened the door. Her hand quivered with fear at what she might find inside or what might find her. She returned to Susannah a minute later. "Since it doesn't have a porch, and the floors are dirt, let's take the horses in with us."

"A horse in the house?"

Isabel chuckled at the thought, feeling much better now that they'd found cover. She led Lady inside. Susannah waited just outside the door. Isabel helped her dismount and led Flaxie in. Susannah held on to the wall and hobbled in on her own. Isabel tended the horses, and Susannah checked out the two rooms.

"Someone must use this place occasionally and keep it stocked. There's wood in the fireplace all ready to burn and canned goods in the cupboard."

Isabel wanted to cry with joy. "Thank You, Lord. Now we can warm up and dry out our clothes." She placed the saddles in the corner and laid the saddle blankets out in the other room so they could dry out of the way. By the time Isabel was done, Susannah had a fire going in the fireplace.

Both girls huddled on the floor in front of the blaze. Isabel began to warm from the outside in. "You said earlier that the first step to a relationship with God was inviting Christ into my life. What comes next?"

"That is the only thing required for forgiveness and eternity, but the Bible says we need to get baptized. It's a public declaration of our new life in Christ and follows right after salvation. But to know God like you know a friend, you talk to Him daily through prayer and you listen to Him daily by reading His Word."

"Do all Christians do that?"

"No. Some only think about God on Sunday, but He wants to be closer to us than that. He wants us to come to Him every day."

"I hope I'll do what He wants." Isabel walked to the window. "The rain has let up a little. I'm going to the shed beside the house. Maybe more firewood is stored in there."

"Be careful."

"I will." Isabel opened the door and ran out into the rain. She'd almost dried out, and now she'd be soaked again. She ran to the shed and tugged on the door. After three tries, it finally opened. Not only were there piles of wood, there was a pile of hay. She made several trips back and forth, carrying armloads of wood and then armloads of hay. She didn't plan to go back outside anytime soon, so she brought in enough for at least the next day. While she took care of this, Susannah opened jars of canned peaches for them. Isabel was so hungry that she'd have eaten just about anything. Well, not anything.

"Why do you think this place is here and so well stocked?"

"I remember Slade said this little place used to be the main house on a small ranch. When the couple grew too old to manage it, a neighboring ranch bought them out. That happens a lot out here. The Ochoa place is at least twice its original size. Anyway, if I have the story straight, this is now part of the biggest ranch in the area. They most likely use this when they are out mending fences."

"And get caught in the rain." Isabel laughed. "In spite of it all, I feel wonderful. I feel lucky—"

"Not luck, Isabel, but God."

Isabel smiled. She had a lot to learn. "All right, I feel God, not luck, took care of us, and somehow I feel lighter than I have in years."

Susannah hugged her. "You're glowing. You won't have to tell anyone what happened; they'll know just by looking."

৯৯

Two days later, the rains had stopped, but the creeks all ran high. Slade couldn't wait any longer. He'd take his chances with the water, but he couldn't chance Susannah and Isabel dying while they waited for him.

He and Dusty rode to the Ochoas'. Several men volunteered to help in the search. Slade mapped out a plan and assigned each man a few square miles. "Look under every rock. Check every possibility. Don't stop until you've searched every inch of your area." Slade handed each pair of men their map.

He and Dusty kept to the road and the areas running along each side. They'd burned most of their daylight hours. Dusk fell.

"Slade, I see smoke." He pointed at the hut.

Hope rose. Slade squeezed Blacky with his legs, and the horse broke into a canter. "Anybody could have found cover in that shack. Let's just pray it's them."

The door flew open before he dismounted. Isabel ran to him. He jumped off his horse and Isabel landed in his arms. "Slade," she sobbed and held on to him with all her might.

He kissed the top of her head and held her just as tight.

Out of the corner of his eye, he watched Dusty use his arm strength and lower himself to the ground right at the front door. He grabbed the door for support. Susannah stood in the doorway, tears streaking down her face. Dusty reached for her. She fell into his arms. He kissed her cheeks, her lips, her forehead.

Isabel turned, and together she and Slade watched the event unfold.

"I love you, Susannah. I need you. Please say you'll be my wife."

Susannah wrapped her arms around his neck. "Just try to get rid of me."

Dusty wiped her tears away with his thumbs, and then he bent his head for one very long kiss.

Isabel blushed. "Slade, I'm sorry. You were right all along. Susannah doesn't need adventure. She needs safety. I promised God I'd quit meddling in your family."

"You promised God?" Slade barely dared to breathe, waiting for Isabel's answer.

Isabel's smile shamed the sun. "I now have a relationship with Jesus. I asked Him to come into my life as my Lord and Savior."

"Oh, Isabel." He pulled her back into his embrace, his heart overflowing with joy. God had removed all the obstacles.

"Slade?"

"Mmm?" He never wanted to quit holding her.

"Can you forgive me? I mean truly forgive me."

"Of course I can, Isabel." He pulled back and gazed into her eyes.

"I do have good news for you."

He smiled. "More good news?"

"I'm going home."

His heart felt like it dropped out of his chest. "To San Francisco?"

"It's time. I need to make things right with my family. I figured you'd be thrilled. Now you can run your sister's life any way you want."

"I'll miss you." His heart already hurt.

"And I'll miss all of you. You've become like a second family to me."

He noticed she lumped him in with the rest of the family. Isabel must have realized she wasn't in love with him after all. He'd lost her, and he had no one to blame but himself.

"Guess we should start home." Slade didn't wish to talk more about her leaving. "Where are the horses?"

Isabel giggled. "In the house."

Slade shook his head. With Isabel, one never knew. Ah, but he knew—knew he loved her, knew he'd miss her, knew his heart would never heal. But she seemed sure of her plans. He'd not try to convince her to stay. He'd respect her decision, even if it killed him inside.

"Isabel, will you forgive me for hurting you and for not listening more readily to your suggestions about Susannah?"

"I do, and you're forgiven." Her eyes were serene, and he knew she'd found peace.

When they walked into the cabin, Dusty and Susannah were still kissing. Slade cleared his throat, and they both looked over at him.

Slade picked up his baby sister and twirled her around.

"I'm getting married," she declared.

"I know." Slade grinned. "I've spent a lot of time with this fellow the past few days. He's in love with you."

Susannah gazed at Dusty. "And I with him."

"Before we leave, I want you to know how sorry I am for holding you prisoner these past few years." He hugged Susannah tight.

"I know you did it because you love me and wanted to protect me."

"Now you have someone else to protect you, so I'll stay out of your life." He kissed her cheek. "Let's head for Rancho San Miguel. I know one mother who'll be glad to see you both."

14

They stopped by the Ochoa ranch on the way home. Mr. Ochoa fired off his gun three times to signal the men to stop the search. Then he led them inside, offering tea or coffee. After all Mr. Ochoa had done to help Slade, Isabel knew Slade felt obligated to visit, so the four of them sat in the parlor, sipping tea with Mr. Ochoa.

"I sent a man to town today." Mr. Ochoa opened the newspaper dated Thursday, February 7, 1884. "Most severe wind and rain storm ever seen in San Diego," he read. Looking up over the paper and the top of his spectacles, he said, "You girls are lucky to be alive."

"Not luck, sir," Isabel stated.

"God," she and Susannah said in unison and then giggled.

He frowned and continued reading. "The town has suffered considerable damage, especially the railroad."

"The railroad?" He'd caught Isabel's interest.

"Washouts are reported, and at least one bridge is gone." Isabel's heart sank. *How will I get home?*

"Many roads are gone, as well, and the telegraph lines are down."

Isabel's eyes burned. Her father might never have received her telegram.

"Seems it will take months before everything is repaired and up and working again."

Months? Isabel glanced at Slade. He watched her. How could she stay here for months? She had to get away; her heart couldn't take much more.

"Isabel, you don't look well. Perhaps we should get you home." Slade rose. "Thank you for all your kindness and hospitality, sir.

We most appreciate it, but we need to get these ladies home and rested up."

Mr. Ochoa escorted them out and bid them good day.

Dusty and Susannah talked the entire ride home, so Isabel was able to be quiet. *Now what, God? Please get me out of here.* She almost felt like she'd smother if she couldn't get away.

"Isabel." Slade rode up next to Lady. "You appeared quite upset by the news, especially regarding the railroad and telegraph lines."

She stared off at the horizon, not wanting to look into his face, the face she loved. "I sent my father a telegram on Tuesday, requesting he send me a ticket home." She chewed on her bottom lip, fighting the desire to give in to fatigue and disappointment. "Now, I don't know if he received my note, but even if he did, the tracks won't be passable for several months." Her words cracked with emotion.

"You want to go home really badly, don't you?" His tone carried sadness, but she'd not think about that or hope his feelings might have changed. He didn't want her. He'd made that much clear to her on more than one occasion.

"I do. I'd leave tomorrow if I could." She blinked, fighting the impending tears.

"What about Susannah's wedding? I know she'd like you here for that."

A wedding was the last thing Isabel wished to attend. "Well, she'll probably get her desire since the train isn't running." She almost sounded bitter.

Slade didn't say anything, and they rode the rest of the way in silence.

They stopped at the house first. Mrs. Stanfield cried and hugged them all about ten times each.

"Dusty and Susannah wish to speak to you in private, Mama, so Isabel and I will take the horses down to the barn." Slade led two of the mounts, and Isabel led the other two. "You look weary. Why don't you let me take care of them, and you can return to the house for some rest?"

"I don't wish to interrupt your mother, Susannah, and Dusty. Besides, I enjoy spending time with Lady."

Slade accepted her answer. He finished unsaddling the other three and gave each horse a good rubdown. She did the same with Lady, only she felt like she moved in slow motion. She'd gotten little sleep either night and now felt tired beyond words.

They left the barn together. "Isabel, if you're really in such a hurry to go home, I'll buy you a ticket on a stage."

She stopped and burst into tears, covering her face with her hands.

Slade took her into his arms. "Are you sure you want to leave?"

"You have no idea how much." She laid her head against his chest and listened to the steady beat of his heart. *I have to get away from you, Slade. I have to escape. My heart is broken into a million pieces and needs time to heal.*

For several minutes, Slade held her. For several minutes, she reveled in his touch. "I'll take you tomorrow to catch the stage." His voice was low and controlled.

"Thank you."

ल

Slade ached to kiss her, but he wouldn't. Instead, he'd hold her as long as she needed.

I love you, Isabel. How am I ever going to let you go? What happened to my plan to ask for your hand in marriage?

He knew what had happened. Her announcement that she was going home happened. The words not only left him stunned and silent, but they also sent his heart reeling in pain.

Finally, Isabel pulled out of his embrace and wiped her tears with her palms. If only she knew how dirty her face was. All she did was rearrange the grime. Even so, she was beautiful to him. He wanted to memorize each feature so he'd never forget that face—her eyes, her smile, her dimples.

When they arrived at the house, Isabel said, "I think I'd love to rest. Will you excuse me?"

Slade proceeded to the kitchen, certain his mother and sister sat around the worktable planning a wedding. They didn't disappoint him.

"Where's Isabel?" his mother asked.

He explained.

"Will we have another family wedding soon?" Susannah asked.

Slade wondered if he could say the words aloud without giving away the depth of his pain. "Isabel is returning to San Francisco tomorrow."

They stared at him. He walked away before they could probe. The only day in his life Slade remembered feeling this bad was the day his father died. Today, his and Isabel's future died. She'd never be his wife, never bear his children. And he'd never hold her again.

ε

Slade went to the barn in the predawn hours the next morning so he and Isabel could get an early start. The sun had just begun to lighten the sky. As soon as he opened the door, he heard a strange sound. He followed the noise, discovering Isabel sobbing into Lady's neck. Did he stay? Did he go?

Frozen in indecision, he heard her say, "I'm so sad to leave you. You have no idea how much I'll miss you."

She'd miss a horse but not him? For some reason, that really bothered him. He turned to slip away unnoticed when he heard Isabel call to him.

"Slade." She wiped her eyes with the sleeve of her shirt. "I was telling Lady good-bye."

"I'm sorry. I didn't mean to interrupt."

She glanced back at Lady. "Do you mind if I go ahead and do the chores one last time?" She sounded as if she'd really miss her routine.

"Not if you really want to." He shrugged.

"I do. I love this ranch and all the little jobs that come with it." They walked together to the straw shed. "I grew up in the city, and we never had animals. I had no idea how much I'd grow to love them."

Then stay, Isabel. Stay. Slade's gaze rose to the sky. "Maybe you should marry a man with some land so you can have animals of your own."

"Maybe I should." She grabbed the pitchfork.

"Do you want me to milk Daisy and collect the eggs?"

Her eyes glistened with extra moisture. She shook her head. "No." She smiled slightly. "You must think I'm silly, but I want to do it all one last time."

"No, not silly, just sentimental." He touched her cheek. "I'll get the buckboard ready."

"Wait. Would you mind if we rode the horses instead?"

"Not if that's what you want. As soon as Blacky and Lady finish eating, I'll saddle them while you finish your chores."

"Thank you." She rose up on tiptoe and kissed his cheek. "For everything. You're almost like the brother I never had."

Brother? He certainly didn't consider her a sister. No, there was nothing brotherly about the feelings he had for Isabel. Nothing brotherly at all.

Slade went back up to the house. Susannah met him at the door. "I can't find Isabel."

"She's down at the barn doing her chores." At Susannah's disapproving expression, Slade said, "She wanted to. Not my idea or suggestion. I went down to do them myself, but she insisted she had to do them one last time."

Susannah shook her head. "What does that tell you?"

Slade lifted his brows, not certain what it told him. "That she likes caring for animals?"

Susannah sighed in exasperation. "No. She doesn't want to leave."

"She doesn't?"

"Of course not." Susannah put her hand on her hip; the other held her cane.

"Susannah, I asked her if she was certain she wanted to leave. She said yes. Not maybe. Not sort of, but yes!"

"Did you ask her to stay?" Mama questioned from the doorway.

"No! She can't wait to get home. Almost panicked when she thought she might be stuck here a few months." His voice rose both in pitch and in volume. "Don't you understand? She can't wait to get away from me."

There. He'd stated the truth. Isabel Fairchild loved the ranch, the animals, even the chores. She loved Mama, Susannah, even Dusty. He was the one she didn't love.

Slade strode to the barn. He planned on saddling the horses and waiting outside until Isabel was ready to leave. He refused to take any more badgering questions from those two women!

ও

Isabel took her time feeding each horse, rubbing their noses, talking to them. She cried a few tears, too, but tried to leave each one with a positive memory of her. Then she milked Daisy, carrying on a conversation with her all the while. She talked to each hen while collecting eggs. Then she carried the milk and eggs to the house.

She went around back and into the kitchen, hoping she'd not run into anyone. She didn't want Mrs. Stanfield or Susannah asking too many questions. Slade's raised voice carried to her. *Why is he so angry?* She froze and listened.

"No! She can't wait to get home. Almost panicked when she thought she might be stuck here a few months." His voice rose both in pitch and in volume. "Don't you understand? She can't wait to get away from me."

Isabel felt like Slade had punched her. Is that what he thought? She slipped out the back door and ran through the grove of trees to the barn and into Lady's stall. Out of breath, she asked the mare, "What should I do?"

In a sense, Slade was right. She was leaving because of him. Every word he said was true, but not because she hated him. She loved him. "I'll just let him believe the worst." She put Lady's halter on and led the horse to the hitching rail. "I don't want him to know I'm pining."

One by one, Isabel led the horses to the pasture while she cleaned their stalls. After cleaning the water troughs and laying fresh straw, she returned to the pasture to watch them. Slade already had both horses saddled and was fixing a gate.

"I'll go say my good-byes, and we can leave."

He nodded but didn't follow her. She knocked on the bunkhouse door. Dusty stepped out onto the porch, relying very little on his crutches.

"I like seeing you standing on your own two feet." She smiled.

"Me, too. I think I'll make an almost complete recovery." His eyes probed her face.

"No more buggy racing."

Dusty laughed. "I'm not planning on any, and I fear my bride would have my hide."

Isabel giggled along with him. Then she got serious. "You take care of her."

Dusty nodded. "And you take care of yourself." He pulled her into a tight hug. "I'll miss you, Isabel. You kind of turned this place upside down for a while."

The tears were coming, and Isabel didn't want to cry. She dug for strength. She leaned up and kissed his cheek. "I'll remember you always." Turning away quickly, she strode toward the house.

She heard Dusty say, "And I'll remember you."

But she didn't turn or acknowledge his words. Instead, she took deep breaths and whispered, "I will not cry. I will not cry. I will not cry."

Finding Mrs. Stanfield in the kitchen, she gave the woman a quick hug, hoping to avoid any questions or an emotional scene. After the hug, Mrs. Stanfield put her hands on Isabel's shoulders. "Many thanks, *mija*." She kissed each cheek. Isabel noticed the tears in her eyes.

"Many thanks to you. My stay with your family was lovely. I will never forget you." Isabel wiped away a couple of determined tears. No matter how fast she blinked, they insisted on escaping.

She found Susannah in the garden on her knees, getting the soil ready for spring planting. "Thanks to you I am now allowed to play in the dirt."

They both laughed.

Susannah struggled to stand up. Isabel reached down to help her.

"No, let me do it. Tomorrow you won't be here to help, so I need to do this by myself."

Isabel took a step back to give her room. After four tries, Susannah managed to stand and get her cane situated. With a dirt smudge on her cheek and dirt under her fingernails, she was quite the sight.

"I wish you'd stay."

"I can't. I have a deal to make with you, though. I'll trade you this riding outfit for my traveling suit you liked so much."

Susannah's face lit up.

"You'll need to have it altered. I'm sure it's too long for you, but I won't be needing it."

Susannah nodded and looked toward the barn. "Isabel," she choked out.

"Let's not cry." Isabel blinked back more tears. "I know how you feel, and you know how I feel."

Susannah wasn't very good at this. Her face puckered up, and the tears ran freely down her cheeks. "I can't help it. I'm losing a friend and the only sister I've ever had."

Isabel lost her battle with the tears. She hugged Susannah. "I will miss you. You are so dear to me. Please write to me and tell me of your life."

"And you write and tell me of yours."

Just don't tell me of Slade's. I won't be able to bear the news when he someday marries another. Isabel stepped back. "I must go. Will you take Lady carrots every now and again? She's come to expect them."

Susannah nodded, her nose red and her face blotchy. Isabel walked a few steps away and then ran back. "I love you, Susannah." She hugged her tight again and then ran toward Slade and the horses.

§❧

Slade watched Isabel in the garden with Susannah. He couldn't hear what they said, but the scene played out painfully before him. He knew they both cried, and he nearly cried along with them. He was ready for this day to be over, not that he desired Isabel to leave, but he was ready for his heart to start healing.

Isabel stopped halfway between the garden and the barn. He busied himself with the horses, keeping one eye on her. She removed a lace hanky from her pocket and wiped the moisture from her cheeks and eyes. Raising her chin, she sauntered the rest of the way to the barn.

"I'm ready." Her voice was composed and calm. He handed her

Lady's reins, and Isabel mounted. He hopped on Blacky, and they rode past the house and toward the road. Isabel sat ramrod straight, and he knew she tried not to look at Susannah on the veranda, crying in Dusty's arms, and she tried not to look at Mama waving her good-bye next to them. She almost made it but then gave in and turned to wave.

Slade gave her a few minutes of quiet to compose herself. Then he asked, "What are your plans when you get back to San Francisco?"

She chuckled. "I owe a lot of people apologies. I guess I'll start with those."

Slade admired the changes in Isabel. She'd grown into a woman of integrity. "And then?"

She stared into his eyes for several seconds. "And then . . . I don't know."

She had no plans, yet such an urgency to get home. Another reason to believe she couldn't stand him. "Will you marry Horace A. Peabody?"

"I'm surprised you remembered. No, I don't think I'll ever marry. Paul says it's good to be single."

She was quoting Scripture! "But you once said yes to my proposal."

He glimpsed pain on her face for one brief moment. "That was before I put God in charge of my life. Now I have to do what He says, so it's a good thing you changed your mind. We'd have both made a huge mistake."

Her words cut into his heart. *It's a good thing you changed your mind.* But he'd changed his mind for reasons that no longer existed. If only he hadn't run ahead of God in the first place, he wouldn't be in this predicament now. He'd be asking for the first time, and maybe, just maybe, she'd have said yes.

We'd have both made a huge mistake. How did she go from loving him to considering him a huge mistake? He rubbed the back of his neck, realizing he'd never understand God's fairer creatures. And knowing he yearned to understand Isabel and discover what went wrong between them.

15

*S*uddenly, the events of Christmas night popped into Slade's mind. He'd been on the balcony with Isabel during the ball, staring into her mesmerizing emerald eyes. *"I realize now you were a godsend. We all needed you, Isabel, but me even more than Susannah. I'm so grateful for everything you've done for her benefit."*

He'd touched her deeply. He knew at that moment he never wanted her to leave. Then he'd kissed her, tenderly holding her face in his hands. *"I love you, Isabel."*

He smiled, remembering her shocked expression. *"You do?"* she'd asked.

"I do," he'd assured her. Then he'd blurted out a proposal. Without thinking, without praying.

Isabel's mouth had dropped open. *"Oh, Slade, yes! A million times, yes!"*

Almost immediately, he'd known he'd made a grave error. The next morning he'd attempted to right his wrong. He recalled the apprehension in her expression. *"Isabel, the things I said last night—"*

"You didn't mean them," she'd accused.

"I did mean them. I meant every word. I do love you." And he had—still did, for that matter. He'd not lied, but he had failed to consult the Lord.

Then he'd uttered the words that brought pain to her face and tears to her eyes. *"I can't marry you, Isabel."* When she'd turned to leave, he'd tried explaining, talking his way out, but looking back, each word condemned him more. No wonder Isabel had wanted to leave as soon as possible.

When he'd reminded her of his promise to God to not marry

until Susannah was married, Isabel had been so understanding, even offering to wait. She had been willing to wait for him no matter how long it took, and now she couldn't wait to get away from him. One of life's ironies.

He'd informed her that he couldn't ask her to wait. But on reflection, he realized he had sounded like a man with too many excuses, a man who didn't really love her. They'd barely spoken since.

And I wonder why the girl desperately wants to escape me? Thinking back, I want to escape me.

The seriousness of sin struck Slade's heart. Sin didn't simply hurt the one sinning; it also affected everyone that person loved. Because Slade had not sought God first, Isabel had been deeply hurt. The consequences of sin were far reaching. Not only had Isabel been affected, but he'd also ruined their chance for a future because now she could barely stand him.

Lord, I'm so sorry. I'm so sorry. The weight of his sorrow was breaking his heart.

ૐ

Much to Isabel's relief, Slade had finally quit talking, but his brooding silence drove her to distraction. Besides, conversation kept her from thinking, and she'd rather not think. "This is beautiful country, isn't it?"

Surprise etched itself on Slade's face. "None prettier."

"I love southern California. I'd not know that if I'd made it to Arizona. Guess I owe Mr. Tripp a debt of gratitude." She laughed at such an absurd notion.

"But you missed your great dance-hall adventure," Slade reminded her.

Isabel scanned the hills and valleys. "I think in response to my father's pleas, God intervened and gave me a different adventure."

"You enjoyed ranch life, didn't you?"

Isabel smiled at him. "I can't begin to tell you how much. You and Susannah are so lucky—" She quickly changed her word choice. "So blessed to have this legacy."

"What about you, Isabel? What's your legacy?"

She thought about his question before giving an answer. "My legacy is a father and mother who love the Lord. Father gave up a career in banking to become a fisherman because he and my mother saw the effect money and high society were having on their three daughters. They made a huge sacrifice for our sakes."

"That's a rich legacy. And in a few days, you'll be home."

"That I will." She felt some apprehension. She'd never fit in well before. Why did she think she would now? *I'm not going there to fit in. I'm leaving to get away from Slade.*

"You don't seem very excited to be going home," Slade commented.

"I'll be happy to see my family again and make things right with them, but I'll miss all of you and Lady."

Slade stopped his horse. "We're here," he said quietly.

She hadn't noticed, but they'd reached the stage depot. Her throat grew tight. She pulled her lips together, hoping they'd dam the emotions welling within. This was it. Good-bye. She'd never be in this city or be with Slade again.

He dismounted and handed her Blacky's reins. "I'll go purchase your ticket."

She nodded, gazing in each direction to imprint this place forever in her heart.

&

Slade stood in line and bought the ticket. He swallowed, then swallowed again, trying to dislodge the lump threatening to choke him. Stopping at the edge of the street, he studied Isabel. She'd gotten off her horse and nuzzled Lady's nose. He couldn't see her face but was fairly certain the tears fell. She kissed the small star on Lady's head, and Slade wished leaving him were as difficult.

He cleared his throat and handed Isabel her ticket. "We were almost late. They are ready to board now, so you need to get in that line." He pointed to several people with bags and tickets. Handing her an envelope, he said, "This is for you."

She opened it, saw the money inside, and started to protest.

"You earned every cent." He closed her hand around the envelope. The contact brought a stronger ache inside him. "And you'll need money to eat along the road."

"Thank you, Slade." She kissed his cheek and ran for the line.

Slade touched his face, still feeling the imprint of her lips. Absently rubbing Lady's nose, he watched Isabel. Her head was bent forward, and she kept wiping her face with her lace handkerchief. *Lord, please get her safely home.* He'd wait here until she boarded.

The stage driver opened the door, and one by one the line of people were swallowed up into the coach. Soon Isabel, too, would be out of sight.

Ask her to stay. Slade couldn't rid himself of the impression. *Ask her to stay.* He tied Lady and Blacky to a nearby hitching post and ran the short distance. He stopped a few feet from the coach. Isabel had just handed her ticket to the driver.

"Don't leave."

She paused, her foot on the first step.

"Isabel, please don't leave."

She turned. Their eyes met. He saw the hesitation on her face.

"I love you."

Biting her bottom lip and with fear in her eyes, she stared at him.

He moved toward her, taking her hand in his. He led her a few steps away from the stage. "I can't imagine my life without you in it."

She didn't trust him not to change his mind again. He could see it in the battle of emotions warring on her face.

"I'm sorry. I know I hurt you so deeply. Will you give me another chance? I'll spend the rest of my life making this up to you."

Her bottom lip quivered.

"I love you." He said it again.

She swallowed hard.

"I need you."

Squeezing her eyes shut, he knew she fought more tears.

"I'm sorry, Isabel. It's unfair of me to pressure you like this." His voice quivered. "I just had to try." He kissed her forehead. "God be with you." When he turned toward the horses, she grabbed hold of his arm.

"What if tomorrow comes, and you don't want me anymore?"

He gazed into the teary eyes of the woman he loved with all his heart. "I promise I will want you every tomorrow for the rest of our lives." He drew her into his embrace and held her tight in his arms. "Take a chance on me, Isabel."

She sniffed.

"Take a chance that I'm the great adventure God has planned for your life."

She raised her head and looked into his eyes. Holding her face between his hands, he kissed her, praying all the tenderness, all the love, all the hope would be transmitted to her. Her dazed gaze when the kiss ended spurred him on. He had to find the right words. She yearned to stay; he knew that much.

"If I'd not run ahead of God, if I'd waited for His plan and His timing, I'd never have hurt you. Sin does that, Isabel. Sin hurts innocent people. I loved you so much, so I just said what my heart felt. That was what got me into trouble." He paused. "Even if you still choose to leave, please forgive me."

"I'm not leaving, Slade, and I do forgive you." Her smile nearly undid him.

He closed his eyes and drew her against his chest, thanking God for His faithfulness. "Will you marry me, Isabel?"

"I will marry you, Slade." Her words carried a smile.

They kissed again.

He took her hand, and they walked back toward the horses. "You need to know, I always wanted you and loved you. I never changed my mind about those things."

"I realize that now, but I assumed you couldn't wait to get rid of me. I thought the happiest day of your life would be sending me home. After all, I seemed to cause you trouble no matter which way I turned."

Slade chuckled. "That you did, Miss Fairchild. That you did. But your perception is so far from the truth. Your leaving was killing me inside. I guess we should have been more honest about what we were thinking and feeling. Maybe things between us wouldn't have been so confused."

He untied Lady's reins and handed them to Isabel. She wrapped her arms around the mare's neck. "I'm back," she whispered near the horse's ear.

"Exactly why did you decide to leave? Because you thought I wanted you to?"

Isabel shook her head. "Because I loved you so much I couldn't bear to stay."

He closed his eyes and savored her words. Groaning, he pulled her to him. "Tell me again, Isabel."

She drew her brows together. "Tell you what?"

"Tell me you love me. You've never said it before."

She smiled, her playful, dimpled smile. "I love you, Slade Stanfield. I love you!" She turned to a couple passing by. "I love this man."

They smiled and nodded and obviously thought she was touched.

She held his head and stared deep into his eyes. "I love you. Today, tomorrow, and forever." She sealed her promise with a kiss.

*E*PILOGUE

A month later in the Stanfields' church in San Diego, Isabel Fairchild and Susannah Stanfield walked down the aisle toward the men they loved. Both were dressed in beautiful gowns of white, Susannah in her mother's gown and Isabel in a borrowed one. Isabel thought of the marriage supper of the lamb she'd just read about in her Bible. After reading that text, the rich symbolism of her wedding meant so much more.

They moved slowly toward Slade and Dusty. Today, Susannah floated more than she limped.

At the sight of Slade, Isabel's heart leaped. He smiled, and she smiled back. *I thank You, Lord, for Slade. He not only loves me, but he appreciates me.*

When they reached the end of the aisle, Dusty took Susannah's arm and lifted her up the steps. Slade threaded Isabel's arm through his, and they joined Dusty and Susannah at the top of the steps. The love in Slade's eyes, the look on his face made Isabel's heart melt into a puddle of devotion. She hoped he never quit gazing at her with that delight in his expression.

The minister stood before them and talked about the covenant of marriage—a vow made before God. He spoke of the seriousness of the commitment they made not only to each other, but also to God Himself. And then he said the words she'd longed to hear. "Do you, Isabel Fairchild, take this man . . . ?" She did. A thousand times she did. After Slade, Susannah, and Dusty each took their turn, the minister said, "I pronounce you, Slade and Isabel, and you, Dusty and Susannah, man and wife. You may kiss your brides."

Slowly, carefully, Slade lifted the veil. His eyes told her he cherished her. Inch by inch, he moved closer for the kiss. At last, his lips touched hers and ignited a longing within her to know him in every way. To truly be his wife.

"I have a surprise for you, Isabel," he told her on their way back down the aisle. "I'm taking you to San Francisco next week."

She stopped. Dusty and Susannah ran into them from behind. "San Francisco? To see my family?"

"Mr. Ochoa lent me a couple of men to help Dusty keep things running while we're gone."

She hugged him tight, thanking God again for this thoughtful husband of hers.

The following week they took the stage to Los Angeles, where they caught the train up the coast to San Francisco. They planned on surprising her family, so they arrived in the city on Saturday and spent the night in a hotel. Isabel knew that after church Gabrielle and Magdalene would bring their families to share Sunday dinner with Mother and Father. They'd each take a dish, and Isabel's nieces and nephews would be running all over the place, playing loudly. It had become tradition. Her heart longed to see each of them.

After she and Slade attended church, they paid a visit to the little cottage by the sea. Bobby ran to her first, giving her a hug. Then he ran to the house, shouting, "Aunt Izzy is home." Within seconds, the entire family surrounded Isabel and Slade.

After hugs and tears, Isabel introduced them to Slade. Then she proceeded to tell them the whole story of the last five months of her life. When she got to the best part, inviting Christ into her life, she looked her two sisters and her parents each in the eye and asked forgiveness. After more tears, they spent the day celebrating Isabel and Slade's marriage.

The entire family seemed to like him, especially Isabel's father. Slade liked them, too. Isabel could tell. But more important, Slade liked her, loved her, valued her, appreciated her, and adored her. And she felt the same about him. How glad she was she'd surrendered to the Lord and to this man's love. Life had never looked or felt better. Her adventure had just begun, and it had started with a surrendered heart.

Some Trust in Horses

by Sally Krueger

To my daughter, Caitlin,
who loves animals,
with all my love

1

$\mathcal{T}$he little foal struggled to stand up, fighting as much against its own gangly legs as against gravity. Hannah breathed a sigh of relief. The foal wasn't breathing properly when it was born that morning, and by the time Garth, its owner, had found Hannah, the foal was almost gone. Hannah had quickly pulled her suction equipment out of her saddlebags, found the clogged mucous, and dislodged it.

"Thanks, Han, old chap! I really don't know what I'd do without you."

Hannah looked up into Garth's handsome, smiling face. She smiled back quickly and started packing up her equipment. She always felt awkward with Garth, and she wanted to make her getaway before he started teasing her. He seemed to think it was hugely funny that a woman should be a vet, and she was easy prey because she was always too tongue-tied and shy with him to fire back some witty comment and deflect her embarrassment. She used to think she preferred the company of animals to people, but Garth was making her feel that it was merely that she was less afraid of animals than of people.

Hannah threw the bags over the rump of her horse, Kindye, and turned around to say good-bye. Garth was pulling some bills out of his pocket. Her fee. She reached out and took it.

"Thanks, Mr. Whitehead." She pulled her hat out of the back pocket of her trousers, stuffed the money in, and plastered her hat over her frizzy blond thatch of hair.

"How many times do I have to tell you, Han, old chap, call me Garth. Until I get the hang of raising horses in this African veldt, you and I will be seeing a lot of each other. If the tsetse flies or the lions or

447

the snakes don't get them, the heat or the diseases will! That is, unless you help me out!"

Hannah could feel it coming. She turned and mounted Kindye and whistled for Simba, her dog. The big golden lab came bounding out good-naturedly from behind the stables. Garth continued.

"Not that I mind, of course. Working with a woman vet is a rare treat, even if she does wear trousers and the ugliest hat I've ever seen. I'd hire you, Han, even if you weren't the only vet within a hundred miles." He laughed delightedly at his little joke. Hannah knew that every unmarried woman in Kikuru would give her eyeteeth to be laughing with the rich, blue-eyed horse breeder and racer, but she couldn't wait to get away.

She ducked her head and tried to smile back. "I have another call to make before lunch," she lied. Giving Kindye a slight nudge with her heel, she trotted quickly down the jacaranda-lined driveway and out onto the dusty road that led into town.

Out on the road, Hannah slowed Kindye to a walk. She was in no rush to get home to Mother. The heat of the African noon made the dust in the air shimmer and shine, but there was a telltale breeze. Hannah looked upward just as a huge black cloud covered the sun. Suddenly, she could hear the rain thundering behind her, galloping like the giant herds of wildebeest out on the plains, swooping down onto her from over the hill that stood behind Garth's farm. She urged Kindye into a gallop to reach the nearest thorn tree beside the road. The tabletop branches were thin, thorny, and almost useless as shelter from the rain, but she and the animals waited anyway.

Peering through the torrent, Hannah could already see that sunshine was swallowing up the tail of the storm. Steam rose off the dusty grassland in its wake, sucked upwards into the blue sky. Soon the sunshine reached Hannah's thorn tree, but the rain still fell. *A monkey's wedding,* thought Hannah, remembering the old expression her father had used, and how she and her father would race out of the house to be part of the wedding. Hannah had always looked up into the tall trees that surrounded their house to see if she could see the monkeys getting married. Her father laughed and said, "One day, Han, one day!"

But the years since he had died had slowed and stretched out, long and cheerless. Even taking over his practice hadn't really helped the pain in the way she had hoped it would. But over the years the aching void he had left in her heart had crusted over and left a scar. Maybe it was because of Mother. But that was another story. Hannah shook her head. Time to be getting on. She whistled for Simba and they stepped out into the road, which was now a torrent of red, steaming, muddy water.

Up ahead, a clutch of little totos played and splashed in the stream, and quickly their black skins turned as red as the mud they played in. Their mothers, walking along the road with baskets of vegetables on their heads, laughed and chattered together, enjoying the brief reprieve from the heat and dust.

"*Jambo,* memsahib," they chorused as Hannah rode past. She smiled down at them and envied them for their easy, friendly ways, and their children and their homes. What she wouldn't give for that. But the only hope she had of marriage was, as her mother never failed to make abundantly clear, with Charles Montague. She shuddered. Not that he wouldn't be a good catch and a good husband, in his own way, but she just couldn't bring herself to encourage him. And he would insist she give up her practice and join the proper social circles. How much of herself would she be willing to sacrifice for marriage? And why did getting married have to be such an unpleasant business? She had always dreamed and read that it was a wonderful and romantic experience, not merely the least of several unhappy alternatives.

Hannah sighed. She was twenty-five years old this year. Mother was getting very difficult to put off much longer. She was practically courting Charles for her. She would have to make up her mind soon. It was too bad that Charles couldn't be more like Garth. The thought caught Hannah by surprise. Garth always made her feel like running away, but something about him made her think about him on the lonely evenings and long rides through the countryside. She never gave Charles a thought if she could help it.

She rode alone along the outskirts of Kikuru, where she and her mother lived in a lovely Spanish-style house with a red tile roof and a courtyard in the center. She turned into a tree-lined driveway with an old worn sign that Hannah no longer saw. "Dr. Butler's Veterinary Clinic," it read. Her father had been Dr. Butler and had built the clinic at the corner where the driveway and the road met. Hannah rode past the neat concrete building with the corrugated iron roof glinting in the midday sun. The house was just visible through a bushy forest of brush that sheltered it from the road.

As Hannah came through the trees, she glimpsed her mother waiting for her, as usual, on the veranda where they always took their lunch. But today there was someone else there too. Hannah's heart sank. Surely it couldn't be Charles Montague. Mother hadn't said anything about him coming for lunch. But as Hannah rode a little closer, she realized it was indeed Charles. Simba suddenly noticed him too and ran up onto the veranda barking and growling. Simba had never liked Charles, and no matter how many times he came to visit, she always barked at him as if she had never seen him before. Unkindly, Hannah hesitated before calling her back. Poor Charles, try as he might, could never quite disguise his fear of large dogs. He stood up quickly and put his chair between himself and Simba. Reluctantly, Hannah called her.

"Simba, Simba, come!" Simba turned slowly around, giving one last growl over her shoulder before returning to where Hannah was just dismounting and handing Kindye over to the syce to take to the stable.

"Hannah Butler!" Mrs. Butler's shrill voice accosted Hannah as she started up the stairs of the veranda. "What have you been doing? You're dripping wet! Charles has been so good to pay us a call and you turn up looking like something the cat dragged in. It is bad enough you insisting on dressing like a shenzi old farmer, but you're soaked to the skin! Go and change at once!"

"Mother, I got caught in the downpour. It couldn't be helped. Hello, Charles. If you'll excuse me for a moment. Simba, stay!"

"Well, hurry up! Juma has the food ready and it's getting cold."

Hannah shot Charles a grim smile as she walked around the table to the door. Simba lay down, careful to keep one eye cocked open in case Charles moved. To her disappointment, he only sat gingerly back down and kept one eye on her as well.

Hannah suddenly felt tired. She really didn't feel like having lunch with Charles. He probably wanted to invite her to some profoundly dull function at the Kikuru Club and she would have to turn him down, then she would have to face her mother's fury. Maybe it would just be easier to accept whatever invitation he was going to spring on her. She sighed. No, that would only encourage him to invite her again. She changed into a clean white shirt and new pair of khaki trousers. She knew her mother would be expecting her to be in a dress, but she had work to do after lunch.

Charles Montague always had this disquieting effect on her. Whenever she gave him any thought, she could only conclude that he was a very nice person, and she should be pleased that he took an interest in her. But when she was actually in his presence, she had the most perverse inclination not to have anything to do with him. She could barely muster enough civility to turn him down politely. She just didn't understand what came over her. Surely every woman didn't go through this kind of conflict when a man invited her to go somewhere with him. She had never read about it in any books. She didn't really know anyone she could ask such a personal question of, either. The closest person she had to a friend was Fiona Brown, but she wouldn't really be able to ask her about that sort of thing.

Hannah finished dragging a comb through her damp hair. It didn't take very long. Her hair was short and just sprang back into its usual unruly yellow curls the minute the comb let it go. Hannah glanced at herself in the mirror, shrugged, and headed out to the veranda.

As she opened the door, Charles eagerly sprang up to pull out her chair for her. Simba immediately sat up and growled.

"Down, Simba. Thank you, Charles," said Hannah, feeling her mother's disapproving glare on her clothes.

Juma followed Hannah onto the veranda with a tray of steaming platters. Hannah had tried for years to persuade her mother to serve something cold for lunch on such hot, muggy days, but she may as well have tried to move a mountain. Mrs. Butler's routines, of which a hot luncheon was the centerpiece, were her bulwark against the uncivilizing effects of Africa on her family. The further Hannah strayed from conventional womanly behavior, the more strictly Mrs. Butler's routines were enforced.

Everyone helped themselves to slices of tender roast beef and mounds of creamy mashed potatoes, then poured hot, thick gravy over them. Vegetables consisted of peas and carrots dripping with dollops of melted butter. In the heat of the African midday, it was ridiculous. It put her in a bad mood. She decided to take the bull by the horns and find out what Charles had come for.

"Well, Charles, it's lovely to have such an unexpected visit from you," she began, sounding as buttery as the peas. "What brings you out this way?"

Unfortunately, poor Charles had just taken a bite of beef. Hannah smiled sweetly and watched him swallow it almost whole before answering. He was a tall, pale man with a long face and a very upper-class beak of a nose. He had long arms with long, delicate fingers. Hannah thought he would have looked perfectly at home eating roast beef and drinking brandy in a club in London, rather than out here in the fierce sunlight and rough-and-tumble of the African colonies. But, he was, like Garth Whitehead, a younger son, and had been sent out to make his fortune in Africa. He was working for the British government as a district commissioner, and Hannah predicted he would soon be able to go home and find work in the civil service in England, where he would live happily ever after telling stories of grand adventures in darkest Africa to his grandchildren.

He cleared his throat and looked pleadingly at Hannah from under his long, pale eyelashes. "Miss Butler. Hannah." Hannah, unkindly, didn't respond. He carried on anyway. "I know you are interested in the horse races and Garth Whitehead—you know him, don't you?" Hannah nodded, suddenly interested. "Well, Garth has reserved a box at the Kikuru Cup Races in two weeks, and he's invited a group of us to join him watching his horses race from the box with him. I would like to invite you to join me in Garth's box, as my guest." He stopped speaking and waited for Hannah's reply.

Hannah found herself involuntarily smiling at him as she paused with a forkful of vegetables halfway up to her mouth. "Why, Mr. Montague, that sounds very nice. I'd love to watch the races with you from

Mr. Whitehead's box. How nice of you to think of inviting me." Hannah popped her food into her mouth and felt as shocked with herself for accepting as Charles did that she had accepted.

Mrs. Butler was ecstatic. "What a grand plan! I'm so thrilled you've invited Hannah to go with you. And in Mr. Whitehead's box too. Aren't you thrilled, Hannah? I'm going with the Fitzhughs myself. It is going to be such an exciting day. Everyone who is anyone will be there, don't you know, Hannah?"

Hannah already regretted accepting Charles's invitation, but she couldn't figure out what on earth had possessed her to do so. Now she had two weeks of her mother's planning and scheming to look forward to, and surely that was far worse than her temper when Hannah insisted on saying no to Charles.

"But I only have one small request, Mr. Montague—"

"Hannah, you must call me Charles. I insist upon it!"

"Alright then, Charles, there is just one thing I must ask. I am obligated to look in on Mr. Whitehead's horses before the races. I need to be sure that they are all in good running condition, so if you don't mind, I'll have to meet you there."

"No, not at all. That will—"

"Hannah! You can't be serious!" Mrs. Butler's voice pierced the conversation like a machete. "You can't possibly mean that you are going to work, and in a filthy stable, no less, when you have been invited to watch the races in a box with Charles Montague. I won't allow it; I simply will not!"

"Oh, it really is alright with me, Mrs.—" Poor Charles gallantly tried to come to her rescue, but Mrs. Butler cut him off.

"It is most certainly not alright! She will smell like a horse! And how on earth will she wear the right clothes if she has to go traipsing around a stable checking the undersides of sweaty horses like some common syce. I won't have it, Hannah Butler; I won't." Mrs. Butler's voice was like the high-pitched whistle of the train. Charles was turning pink with embarrassment at the scene he had inadvertently caused. Hannah was livid.

"Mother! How dare you speak to me this way in front of Mr. Mon—I mean—Charles. Stop it. Now." Hannah hissed the command between her teeth, and her mother was so taken aback by her daughter's fury she stopped herself just as she was about to let another barrage go.

"We'll discuss this later," Hannah said, glaring her down and then smiling grimly at Charles. "Thank you very much for inviting me. Now, let's see," she searched desperately for another topic. "Have you heard any news from Europe lately? I hear there is quite a bit of talk of war. I don't believe it will actually come to that, do you, Charles?"

Charles looked immensely relieved, "Yes, some people are saying that a war is inevitable. The Balkans are very unstable, I hear." And so he chattered on about war and rumors of war. Hannah listened with interest. He really was a very nice and interesting man. She heartily wished she could fall helplessly in love with him. Everything would be so easy then.

When lunch was over, Charles took his leave of the two women, looking gratefully at Hannah as she held Simba's collar while she shook his hand. Mrs. Butler looked grim and the instant that Charles had ridden behind the trees at the end of the lawn, she turned on her daughter.

"How dare you speak to me that way, young lady! Who do you think you are? I simply will not allow myself to be treated so rudely by my own daughter. And to think that Charles Montague asks you to sit with him in Garth Whitehead's box at the Kikuru Cup Races and you actually tell him that you have to go and fuss over horses! Horses!" Mrs. Butler was spluttering and turning purple.

"It is 1914, Mother. The twentieth century. There is more to life than just catching a man. We women will have the right to vote someday soon, and we can support ourselves and earn our own livings. We don't have to depend on a man for everything anymore. You should be proud of me. Daddy would be if he were here."

"Your father did you more harm than good with all those modern, newfangled ideas of his. He was just disappointed because you weren't a boy, that's all, and he tried to pretend you were. And I never had a chance with you, the way your father spoiled you."

This line of conversation always made Hannah furious, and her mother knew it. That's why she said it. "Daddy did not wish I was a boy. He told me so!" Hannah retorted, her fair skin turning pink with repressed rage as she watched her mother nod knowingly.

"Of course, dear, if he said so," her mother said sweetly, "but now it is time you behaved in a more ladylike manner. You will tell Garth Whitehead that you are otherwise engaged on the day of the races. His horses will be just fine. If they aren't, it will be too late to do anything about it anyway."

Hannah was suddenly tired. No matter what started it, they always ended up in the same old arguments. Her fury had abated now, and she just wanted to go back to work. She couldn't really believe she had actually accepted Charles's invitation anyway, and the price she was paying to have done so was already getting too high.

"I have to go to work now, Mother. I promised Jack Osbourne that I would come and look at one of his cows. He is afraid it has foot-and-mouth disease. Come on, Simba." Hannah pulled her hat out of her pocket and crammed it over her hair, which had frizzed up like cotton candy after the storm. She went around to the back of the house where the stable was. The syce had Kindye already saddled, and Hannah set off over the field behind the stable, taking the shortcut to the Osbourne farm.

It felt very nice to be out in the open air. She rode past the compound where the African people who worked on the Osbourne place had their huts, neatly enclosed by a stick fence. Through the fence she could see Rosie, her old ayah, sitting outside her son's hut. She waved, but Rosie was old and quite blind now, so she didn't see Hannah. Several little totos did, though, and came running over the field toward her. She waved them away, shouting, "*Mimi nakwenda* Bwana Osbourne. I'm going to Osbourne's!" They stopped and watched her ride away. Perhaps she would stop in and visit Rosie on the way back if it wasn't late. She could always tell Rosie everything. And she still was angry with her mother, so it would be nice to tell someone about it. *After all,* Hannah thought, *I would actually like to be married the way Mother wants, but I just feel so . . . so trapped.* She just couldn't suddenly metamorphose, like a butterfly, into one of those feminine women with the swishing silk skirts and soft feathery hats. And if she did, she could no longer work as a vet. How could she suddenly give it all up?

Even if she did try, it was too late to change. *In fact,* she thought, *it has been too late to change all my life.*

The laughing face of Garth Whitehead flashed into her mind and before she thought about what she was doing, she suddenly wished she could change. It was a breath-catching, heart-stopping moment of wishing, and Hannah quickly shook it off. But it left her shaken.

ৡ

Rosie had been with the Butlers since Hannah was born and had looked after her until she had gone to England for her veterinary training. She lived with her son's family, now out in the village behind the Butler place, but Hannah still visited her often.

Hannah could see Rosie still sitting on a stool outside her round thatch hut watching a gaggle of totos playing with the rim of an old bicycle wheel. They were pushing it with a stick to see how long they could keep it rolling upright. The totos noticed Hannah when she interrupted a couple of hens scratching in the dirt, who cackled and flapped off indignantly, waking a couple of shenzi dogs lying in the shade. The dogs reluctantly barked and growled. The totos buzzed around her like a cloud of flies.

"Memsahib, memsahib, *tikki, tikki.*" They always begged her for the little coins that could buy the smallest piece of sugar cane or licorice, and she only encouraged them by handing out some every time she came. Rosie was smiling as she walked slowly and stiffly out to meet Hannah. They walked out toward a pair of thorn trees where they could see a bit of shade.

"What's the matter, missie?" Rosie asked, looking at Hannah slumped dejectedly against the dry, rough trunk of the tree.

"Oh, nothing really, I'm just hot, I suppose." Hannah sighed. Rosie knew better. She waited.

"Bwana Whitehead's black mare delivered a filly this morning. It had mucous in the air passage so he called me in to clear it. Poor little thing; I was almost too late." Hannah paused; Rosie waited. It was a comfortable silence. Hannah sometimes thought she loved Rosie more for her silences than anything she said. Hannah took her time to try to think through what she needed to tell Rosie, but then remembered that telling Rosie was almost the same thing as thinking it through for herself.

"Bwana Whitehead," she hesitated. "Garth," she whispered, trying out his name out loud. She could tell Rosie was watching her closely. She wished she didn't have such fair skin. She could feel a warm flush of emotion rising up her throat. "Garth likes to tease me about being a woman. And a vet. Usually, I hate being teased. I still do, but, well, I felt differently all of a sudden." Suddenly, Hannah's thoughts that had started as a few free-falling raindrops gathered themselves into a flash flood, pouring out of control down a dry, empty streambed.

"I often help him with his horses, you know, Rosie. He grew up in London and he really doesn't know a thing about animals, or even farming, especially in Africa. I know he wouldn't be able to manage without me. Perhaps that's the reason he teases me; he feels a little embarrassed needing me the way he does. What do you think, Rosie?"

Rosie opened her mouth to reply, but Hannah's flood was rushing too fast to be diverted. "Anyway, Rosie, today, when I was standing there next to him watching the little horse struggling to live, I felt suddenly that we really did perhaps have a bit of a bond, only I knew he was going to tease me the way he always does, so I rushed away as soon as I could. I wish I were different, Rosie. I wish I weren't so shy and I could just tease him right back. But I get so tongue-tied. And then I turn a ghastly shade of red, and my hair is so uncontrollable I'm sure a decent hat would never stay on my head. So I always run away as quickly as I can."

Hannah paused for a moment. "But today as I left I really, really wished that I were different. And I honestly think that maybe he likes me. Maybe not the way he would one of the ladies at the Kikuru Country Club that Mother wants me to be like. But perhaps in a certain kind of way. After all, Rosie, you know he really couldn't handle those horses properly without my help."

Hannah stopped suddenly. Floods in Africa disappear as quickly as they come. But there was one more thing. "And now I have accepted an invitation to watch the races with Charles Montague from Garth's box. I wish Charles Montague were a little more like Garth— he is very nice, nice and dull." Hannah sighed discontentedly.

Rosie sat silently, waiting to be sure Hannah had really finished. Hannah watched her worn, wrinkled, kindly face anxiously. The the years had carved out the hollows in her cheeks, but her lips were still as full and wide as they must have been when she was twenty. And her eyes, though deep and dark, glittered and twinkled with as much intelligence and life as they ever had. Hannah watched her eyes, knowing from her lifetime of experience that she would only get the faintest hint from them of what was going on in that ancient mind. Hannah was a little nervous when she saw them softening and then even pitying her.

"What, Rosie? What are you thinking?" she blurted, suddenly impatient.

"You are right, missie, he couldn't do without your help. My cousin's son is a houseboy at Bwana Whitehead's, and he knows how things go over there. I hear things from his mother about Bwana Whitehead. He doesn't know much about animals, and he doesn't know much about this country."

"Yes, Rosie, that is true." Hannah was impatient for Rosie to get to the point, and her attitude was evident in her tone of voice. Instantly she stopped herself. "I'm sorry to sound so rude. I really don't know what has come over me today, Rosie." She caught a glimpse of pity in Rosie's eyes again, but she waited. Impatiently.

"My cousin," Rosie continued thoughtfully, "does not have a very high opinion of Bwana Whitehead. She says he drinks too much and gets angry, then he doesn't always pay her son his wages on payday. She says her son doesn't like working there."

"Well, Rosie, lots of people drink a little too much now and then. I've never known Bwana Whitehead not to pay me my fees. Is your cousin's son a reliable worker? Perhaps Bwana Whitehead is not entirely satisfied with him."

Rosie's eyes flashed an angry response to Hannah, but she said, "Missie, I think my cousin's boy is a hard worker. But if I were you, I would be very careful about becoming friends with Bwana Whitehead. My cousin tells me things about him. He is not a good man, missie."

Hannah felt frustrated. It was a silly idea to come and talk to Rosie about something she obviously knew nothing about. How could she? She was an African. What on earth could she be expected to know about the European culture? "I have to go now, Rosie," she said, going over and fetching Kindye from where she was grazing on a nearby patch of green grass. "Thanks for your advice. I'll keep it in mind." Passing through the little clutches of totos and chickens and a dog or two, Hannah whistled to Simba, who was lying in the shade with the other dogs.

As she rode down the dusty cart track in the late afternoon sunshine, Hannah thought about Garth. Now that she had actually spoken about him out loud to another human being, even if it was only to Rosie who didn't really understand, she found that her thoughts were bolder and more insistent. She couldn't just squeeze down the feelings of longing and hope that he had roused in her as she left his farm this morning. He needed help. He needed her help in particular. And if she could help him, who knows what that would do for him. After all, he might realize that those fancy ladies who spent their nights dancing and gossiping at the Kikuru Country Club were not what he wanted after all. Perhaps he would finally see that what he really wanted was a woman like her. A woman who knew Africa and how to live and thrive here. Perhaps he would realize that he needed her.

The hot, dusty field was no longer there for Hannah. In her mind's eye she and Garth were out riding up in the hills she could see through the haze on the horizon. Garth had settled down, and he now spent all his time with her. A good woman was all he needed, everyone would say. Who would have thought that Hannah Butler, the vet, would be the one to rescue him? Hannah Butler, I mean Hannah Whitehead, of all people, they would say. Well, I always thought there was more to her than met the eye, someone would point out. Hannah smiled, lost and happy in her daydreams.

But when she reached home the dreams vanished like the rain in the desert and she fell back into her old thoughts, and nothing good seemed possible anymore. She was just the vet—plain, but useful. Nothing more.

2

*H*annah woke the next morning with Garth Whitehead on her mind. She remembered her silly daydreams from the day before and blushed to herself. But she could, perhaps even should, go over to his place and check on the little filly. It would be a nice gesture. Her heart fluttered a little at the thought of looking up into his face again so soon. Would he be able to tell what she had been daydreaming about? Of course not. She really was going balmy. The bright morning sun was already pouring in through the curtains, making everything look ordinary and matter-of-fact. All her fantasies withered and slunk away in the clear, sensible first light of day.

Hannah quickly threw off her covers and pulled the mosquito netting surrounding her bed out of her way. She had work to do. She had worked hard to become a vet, and she wasn't going to throw it all away now. She'd go out to the clinic and see who was there first, then in the hard glare of the midmorning she'd decide whether or not to go over to Garth's.

After breakfast, Hannah and Simba walked down to the clinic. Her father had finished building it just before he died, so it was quite modern and well equipped, especially considering this was East Africa. Hannah noticed the usual assortment of goats and a couple of cows, all with Africans holding onto them by ropes. But as she got closer she saw that they were all gathered around someone who was standing near the door. He was a tall, clean-cut man dressed in the white settler's uniform of a white shirt and khaki shorts. He and the Africans surrounding him were all looking down at an animal that must have quite an unusual problem, judging by the amount of interest they were showing it. "*Jambo! Nini shauri?* What's the fuss about?" Hannah called.

The Africans moved aside and the tall man walked toward Hannah. She tried to remember where she had seen him before, but she couldn't place him. She thought she knew everyone around here, so he must be new.

"*Jambo*, Miss Butler," he held out his hand and smiled timidly at Hannah. She shook his hand.

"I'm sorry; have we met before?" she answered.

"Oh, please forgive me for not introducing myself." The man flushed, turning nearly the color of his red hair. "I'm Dan Williams. I am the teacher at the mission school over by Limaru." Hannah smiled and thought how different he was from Garth. Garth would never look so flustered and awkward at the mere prospect of introducing himself.

"What is it I can do for you this morning, Mr. Williams? Or should I call you Reverend Williams?" Hannah found herself replying to him confidently and professionally, the way she would have liked to be able to speak to Garth.

"Oh, my, no!" He blushed and looked down at his dusty boots. "I'm just a teacher. It's that one of my students, you see . . ." He stopped and looked around.

"Mr. Williams!" Hannah spoke quickly, suddenly embarrassed for him. "I'm a vet. Not a doctor. I don't treat students."

"Oh, my goodness, how silly of me. It's not the student I want you to look at; I didn't mean that at all. It's that the student brought me an animal, an elephant, actually. It's the elephant, Miss Butler." At this point a little toto appeared beside Mr. Williams, pulling on a rope. Then a snaky gray trunk suddenly curled around Mr. Williams's knee. He bent down and brushed it away awkwardly and let the little calf elephant come between him and the toto.

Hannah knelt down on the ground and put out her hand. "My goodness, isn't she lovely!" she breathed. "She must only be a few weeks old. Where did you find her?"

The elephant put its trunk out and touched Hannah's hand. Her little gray ears flapped nervously out on the sides of her head, like the wings of an enormous bird. But her small, clear eyes peered curiously out from the wrinkly folds of the skin on her little face. Hannah caressed her trunk carefully with her fingers. *It's so alive and soft, just like a real baby,* she thought.

Dan Williams was kneeling down beside the little elephant now, his arm draped protectively over its back. He was smiling, and Hannah was touched by how gently he whispered into the creature's ear.

"Sophie, this is Miss Butler." Hannah noticed that his awkwardness had vanished as he spoke with the elephant. He turned to look at Hannah and said shyly, "I call her Sophie, because she looks so wise and so old, and Sophie means wisdom."

"That suits her," Hannah said, smiling at the little creature that was now reaching forward with her trunk to touch Hannah's face. "Where did you get her?"

"Pindanny," he nodded at the toto on the other side of Sophie who looked to be about ten or eleven years old. "Pindanny is one of the students in my school. He found her crying beside the body of her mother, who had been shot by a farmer. The farmer was apparently trying to frighten off a herd of elephants that was raiding his mealies. He didn't realize that he had actually hit one of them until he came back a few hours later to check the damage to his crop. He had Pindanny here with him and when he raised his rifle to shoot the baby, Pindanny rushed over and begged him to give him the baby." Dan smiled over at Pindanny. "You always were too softhearted, weren't you?"

"Anyway, Pindanny had no way of keeping Sophie, so he brought her to school and asked me if I would like her. I didn't have the heart to send her back to the bush to be supper for some local lions, so here she is."

"Well, I've never had an elephant for a patient before. What is it you need me to do for her?"

Dan Williams stood up and Hannah noticed his shyness return as he did. "I'm not terribly sure," he spoke uncertainly. "Well, in the couple of days since Pindanny brought her to me, well, she seems to be losing weight. I don't really know anything about baby elephants, and well, I don't know if I am feeding her the right things, really. I heard you were the nearest vet, even though you are a bit of a distance, and I wondered if you're not too busy if you could give me a bit of a hand with her." Hannah got to her feet, but Dan wasn't finished yet.

"This is a bit awkward, I'm afraid, but I don't have much of a salary and I couldn't really afford to pay you for your time, at least not what you probably ask for a fee." He stopped speaking and looked down at his boots. Hannah felt embarrassed for him. What an awkward fellow he was. No wonder he was a missionary. He probably didn't feel comfortable with ordinary society. Well, she supposed, they did have that in common. Suddenly she felt generous.

"That's all right, I don't mind helping you out with Sophie. In fact, I'm sure it will be my pleasure to get to know her too."

Dan smiled with relief. "Oh, thank you very much, Miss Butler! I am terribly grateful."

"There's just one thing, though. I've got rather a busy morning ahead of me by the looks of all these people. Perhaps you wouldn't mind waiting for me to get to them first. Then I could take a few minutes to look at Sophie without rushing so much."

"Oh, of course, by all means!" Dan said quickly, pulling Sophie off to one side. "Is there somewhere I could wait for you?" Hannah showed him to a small shaded porch on the side of the building and called for some water for Sophie.

•

It was almost noon by the time Hannah had finished in the clinic. She felt bad that she had kept Dan Williams waiting for so long. At about eleven o'clock she had impulsively sent out word to him to invite him to lunch. She shuddered at the thought of what her mother would say to her inviting a poor missionary over, but she couldn't keep him waiting so long without offering him a meal.

So at lunchtime she and Dan walked up the road to the house with Sophie and Simba trailing along behind them. Simba was not at all sure about this elephant that her mistress had so inexplicably befriended. It smelled too much like a wild animal for her to be sure about it, and she kept her distance. Sophie, on the other hand, behaved just like a naughty toddler, frolicking along, trying to tease the sedate old dog into playing with her and paying no attention to the warning growls that Simba emitted whenever Sophie got too close.

Dan had lost none of his awkwardness, and Hannah found it quite a novelty to be the one to be trying to put someone else at ease. She commented on Sophie's playful attempts to attract Simba's attention.

"I do hope I'm not inconveniencing you by imposing on you for lunch, Miss Butler," he worried.

"Not at all," Hannah replied, "I would not have invited you if it was inconvenient. Besides, I sent word to Mother to expect you."

Dan looked dismayed. "Oh, my, I didn't realize I would be imposing on your mother as well! Perhaps I should just be on my way. I wouldn't want to be any trouble; after all, you are so kind as to give me some advice about Sophie. That's more than—"

"Mr. Williams!" Hannah interrupted him. He reminded her of the antelope she would catch grazing in the fields early in the morning. They would look at her in fear, torn between flight and food. "Mr. Williams, my mother loves to have guests. She often complains about how lonely she is, especially since my father passed away." She stopped. Now it was her turn to be embarrassed. Why was it that she still felt it necessary to bring her father into conversations?

"Oh, I'm awfully sorry to hear that," Dan was saying. "I can see I am intruding on you and your mother at a difficult time. I really won't stay. I'm terribly sorry I have been so terribly rude." His face was beet red, and Hannah felt a sudden surge of sympathy for him. "In fact, I'm sure Sophie will come around just fine. Please accept my condolences." Already he had turned and was reaching out to steer Sophie back in the direction they had come.

Now Hannah felt stupid. She put her hand on Dan's arm, "Mr. Williams, we have a misunderstanding. My father died five years ago. It was silly of me to mention it. I'm just used to speaking to people who know us. Please stay for lunch. I want you to. Besides, I would worry about Sophie if you just left with her like this."

Dan stopped and looked down at Hannah. For an instant the shyness in his eyes gave way to comprehension. They understood each other. Dan nodded. And then the shyness returned. They walked on together. The Butler house was in view, its red roof twinkling in the sunshine. But Hannah could already see the midday rain shower boiling up in the sky beyond.

"Look," she said, pointing the clouds out to Dan, "we'd better be quick."

They walked on more quickly, but Sophie was enjoying all the new sights and smells. She kept stopping and making little charges into the grass alongside the road. At one point she startled a flock of guinea fowl and gave herself as much of a fright as she gave them. Dan and Hannah laughed. She reminded Hannah of a huge kitten.

As they were watching Sophie, the wind roared through the treetops and swept down onto them. Within seconds huge drops of rain hurled themselves into the dry red dust of the road and then the heavens opened. Dan and Hannah were already running; even Sophie was running.

"Oh, Miss Butler, I'm awfully sorry," Dan was shouting through the curtain of rain, as if he had accidentally ripped the clouds open himself. He was pulling off his jacket and Hannah suddenly felt herself sheltered underneath it as they scurried along. She could feel Dan's breathing beside her as they ran, and she looked up just in time to catch the look of shock on her mother's face as she stood on the veranda watching them. They must be a sight, she realized, running in the rain, two people under one coat with a baby elephant charging along behind them.

They stormed up the steps, laughing gleefully. They stopped short. The laughter drained out of their faces as Mrs. Butler stood before them. Hannah realized what fun she had had, if only for a second. She didn't think she even remembered how to laugh.

But Sophie was carefully coming up the steps and Dan was looking startled and fearful. Hannah called out to Juma to bring a bowl of milk. Then she introduced Dan to her mother.

"I–I–I'm terribly sorry to be such an imposition, M–M–M–Mrs. Butler," stammered Dan.

"Oh, nonsense," Mrs. Butler brushed him off. "One more person isn't such a difficulty." She was looking him up and down as if he were a scrawny chicken being sold to her by the butcher. "I hear you are that missionary schoolteacher out by Limaru. They don't pay you much for being a missionary, do they? But then what have you got to spend your money on anyway, out in the bush where you live? Besides, you missionaries aren't allowed to do much besides teach the blacks anyway. Sit down. I wouldn't want it to be said that I didn't feed a man of the cloth when he came begging, would I?"

Dan took his seat, looking horrified. *Poor man,* thought Hannah.

"Mother! Let Mr. Williams at least wash up before he eats. He's soaking wet too."

She took Dan inside. They could have been in an English country gentleman's home, if they didn't look out the windows. Mrs. Butler let absolutely nothing into the house that could possibly be said to be African. There were the English oak table and Queen Anne chairs, not to mention the bone china, handpainted, set out on the oak sideboard. And then a lovely old grand piano took up fully a half of the drawing room. The wooden floors had intricately woven Persian rugs placed between the pieces of furniture, and Dan carefully stepped around them so he wouldn't get mud on anything.

Hannah showed him into a room with lacy curtains and a china washbasin steaming with hot water. It was set on a small table with a lace tablecloth and a white towel beside it.

"Here you are," she said, "I'll just wash up in the kitchen. We always eat on the veranda. You know your way." Before Dan could apologize again, she was gone.

When Hannah came out of the kitchen, she could hear her mother talking excitedly outside on the veranda. *Good,* she thought, *she's at least trying to make Mr. Williams feel welcome.* But suddenly she caught the sound of a deep, familiar laugh and her heart missed a beat. Garth!

She hurried through the drawing room and outside. Dan was sitting at the table looking as though he was trying to squeeze himself into the most insignificant place he could find. Mrs. Butler was standing on the top step of the veranda, where the dripping of the rain off the roof was just about over, and in front of her was Garth, still mounted on his horse. They were both laughing at something on the front lawn, and when Hannah looked out, there was Sophie. Sophie had found a small puddle and was pulling water up from it into her trunk and trying to spray herself. Hannah laughed and rushed right past Dan to stand next to her mother.

"Han, old chap!" called Garth when he saw her. Hannah blushed and her mother looked at her with shock, as if Hannah had particularly asked Garth to refer to her as "old chap."

"I just popped over to thank you for coming to save my little filly yesterday," Garth went on, oblivious to the women's discomfort. "As I was saying to your mother, there is nothing like having a vet with a woman's touch, especially when it comes to delivering babies!

"I see you have another type of baby on your hands today!" Garth nodded at Sophie.

"Yes, isn't she sweet," said Hannah quickly, anxious to change the subject and use Sophie to make a good impression on Garth. "Mr. Williams, the missionary teacher at Limaru, brought her here this morning to see if I could help him decide on the best diet for her." She spoke about Dan as if he weren't there, justifying it by thinking that he was just too shy to be drawn into the conversation anyway.

Garth glanced at Dan, and Mrs. Butler quickly stepped back to show him the table. "Mr. Whitehead, please stay for lunch with us. We have plenty, as we were already expecting Mr. Williams. It would be such a pleasure for us poor women to have a man such as yourself for company. We really don't have much opportunity to entertain gentlemen." Hannah wanted to sink through the flagstone floor of the veranda at her mother's shameless speech, but she looked anxiously up at Garth, begging him with her eyes.

Garth smiled benevolently, enjoying the flattery, but he shook his head. "Thank you anyway, Mrs. Butler, but I have a lot to do, so I must pass up a visit today. As you must have heard, I have two horses entered in the Kikuru Cup Stakes next week and I have my work cut out just to get them ready." He nodded at Hannah. "I'll be expecting you to be there, of course, to make sure they are both in tiptop condition to run." Hannah blushed with pleasure at his attention, and Garth tipped his hat to her and spurred his horse.

Mrs. Butler and Hannah turned back to the lunch table. Mrs. Butler sat down angrily. Without even a glance at Dan, she launched into a tirade.

"There you are, Hannah Butler! What did I tell you! If you had the decency to even wear a simple dress, perhaps Mr. Whitehead might— just might—mind you, consider staying to have lunch with us. But what do you expect a man to do when a woman doesn't even bother to dress properly? And did you hear what he called you! I don't believe I have ever been so humiliated in my entire life! Old chap! Old *chap!*" Hannah cringed as Mrs. Butler's voice rose to a piercing squeal.

Looking furtively at Dan from under her lashes, Hannah was startled to see a look of sympathy and warmth from him in return. She looked back at her mother. Mrs. Butler was drawing a deep, shaky breath to illustrate just how upsetting this whole thing had been for her.

"Mother!" hissed Hannah, "please, we have a guest." Mrs. Butler glanced over at Dan as if she only just noticed him.

"Yes, well, of course," she said, collecting herself again. "But really, Hannah, you do try me so."

There was silence for a few moments while Juma brought in the lunch dishes. Hannah lifted up her fork.

"Mr. Williams, would you be so kind as to give thanks for the meal?" Mrs. Butler said, and Hannah quickly put down her fork. They never said grace. What was her mother doing now?

"Father in heaven," began Dan, his head bowed, "thank You for this delicious food that You have blessed us with today. And thank You for the hospitality of Mrs. Butler and Miss Butler. Also, Lord God, I thank You for the generosity of Miss Butler. I pray You would give her guidance and wisdom and bless her in all her future endeavors. We pray to You in the name of Jesus Christ. Amen." He looked up and picked up his fork.

Hannah stared at him. She had never heard anyone speak to God in the familiar "You," as though He were actually living in the modern world with them. And to pray about such an earthy thing as an animal. She loved animals, too. After all, she was a vet. But to pray about them. At a meal. She picked up her fork again. Dan noticed her looking at him and glanced shyly at her. She looked away. *Funny,* she thought, *he didn't seem so shy when he prayed.*

Mrs. Butler was speaking. "Mr. Williams, surely it is your Christian belief that a woman should not wear men's clothing. I would appreciate hearing your opinion on that subject."

Dan stared at her. His face turned painfully red, and Hannah stopped feeling embarrassed about her mother and began to feel angry instead, but Dan managed to compose himself.

"Mrs. Butler, I don't like to judge other people by their appearance. But when a person becomes a Christian, I believe that the Lord makes them into a new creation. At that time He will make it clear to them if they are dressing inappropriately. Of course, modesty is always a virtue, whether one is a Christian or not." He fell silent.

"Hmph," said Mrs. Butler.

Hannah was curious. She had been to church, of course, although it had been a few years since she had attended regularly, she had to admit. But the old church that the Butlers sporadically attended didn't talk about God in nearly the same way Dan Williams did. At church God was spoken to only in the most old-fashioned language, Thees and Thous, and Hannah had never gotten even the slightest impression that God had any interest in speaking directly to people today. Especially not about things like someone's clothing, or animals. He merely disapproved if you did not do what you were supposed to do.

Mrs. Butler realized that Dan Williams was not going to be of much use as an ally against her daughter, so she reverted to ignoring him. Turning to Hannah, she resumed her usual topic of conversation. "Looks do make a world of difference to men, you know." She glanced at Dan. "Well, of course, not to a man like you, Mr. Williams, but then Hannah couldn't marry a missionary, and one as poor as a church mouse, no doubt."

Hannah knew that once her mother got going on this topic there was very little that could stop her. It was mortifying that she should carry on like this in front of Dan Williams, but luckily he was nobody important. Hannah had devised the best way to get through mealtimes many long years ago. She put her head down and ate as quickly as she could.

"Mrs. Worthington-Smyth called this morning," Mrs. Butler began. "You remember Mrs. Worthington-Smyth, don't you, Hannah? She is down from Nairobi visiting her daughter, Fiona, Jim Brown's wife. All she could do was complain about her son-in-law. She says he spends too much money on horses and gambling and poor Fiona has barely a dress to her name. He chums around with Garth Whitehead, you know, and those Whiteheads have money to burn, but Jim Brown is just not part of that social class and he shouldn't be pretending he is." Mrs. Butler passed Hannah a plate of roast beef and then handed her the gravy boat, all the while talking nonstop, not expecting a reply.

"Nevertheless, Harriet, I tell her, at least your daughter is married and associating with the proper class of people. You should be thankful for small mercies. I am the one who has more to worry about with Hannah. She doesn't even wear a dress. And a vet, mind you. I have to put up with far more than you do, Harriet, I tell her; I doubt Hannah will ever marry." She paused and took a deep breath. Hannah braced for the attack.

"Hannah, it is a disgrace the way you shame me so in front of my friends with your outlandish ways. Why can't you give up this veterinary nonsense and behave like a proper woman? You are twenty-five years old and it is time to grow up.

"I would just like to know how much longer you expect me to put up with this? I am the laughingstock of our circle. I can hear them whispering behind my back that I can't even bring up my daughter properly. Of course, I blame your dear father for much of it. He gave in to you far too much and there wasn't a thing I could do to stop him. But it's been five years since he passed on, and it's high time you put all his nonsense behind you and listened to me."

Hannah watched her pause for breath. Once or twice when she had been in her teens and still thought it was possible to change people, she had attempted to argue with her mother. But it hadn't even made the smallest dent in the convictions etched in the stony tablet of Mrs. Butler's heart.

Today there was Sophie to think on. She had no idea at what age young elephants were weaned from their mother's milk. She suspected they were quite old when they were. That would mean that the milk of the elephant would have to be extremely nutritious to keep such a creature healthy. Probably Dan had been feeding her cow's milk. She had lots of energy, but you could tell that she was quite thin.

Mrs. Butler was still talking when Hannah looked up from her empty plate. Mr. Williams was still eating, but since he had had no opportunity to talk with his meal, he too was almost finished. Mrs. Butler had hardly touched hers.

"Mother, I must get back to work, and Mr. Williams has a long trip ahead of him." Hannah glanced over and saw Dan rushing to eat his last few bites of mashed potato. "We still have to talk about Sophie's diet, too, so if you will excuse us, we must be off."

She stood up just as Dan popped the last mouthful in, and he hastily wiped his mouth and stood up too.

They walked back down the road to the clinic, talking about the various things Dan could try feeding Sophie. Sophie was walking along quietly beside them, tired from the long day she had had. Dan kept his hand on her head, stroking her ears now and then. Sophie moved her head around so he could scratch the parts she found itchy, and Hannah noticed how gently and thoughtfully Dan took her hints.

After Hannah had written down all the instructions and suggestions she had for Sophie's care, they stood in front of the clinic to say good-bye. Hannah knelt down and stroked Sophie on the trunk. Sophie reached up to touch Hannah's face.

"She's really taken to you," Dan was saying. "You have quite a way with animals. It is a gift."

Hannah stood up, blushing at the compliment. "Well, I am a vet, after all. Please send me a note to let me know how Sophie does with her new diet."

"I will," Dan replied, and they shook hands. "I am very grateful for your help, Miss Butler. Good-bye." He turned and left.

Hannah stood and watched the tall, awkward man and the small, gangly elephant calf disappear together into the haze of the afternoon. *It is a pity,* she thought, *that I can't be as relaxed and easy with Garth as I was with Dan Williams today.* She walked slowly back to the stables and whistled for Simba. She was going to head out on the calls she had this afternoon.

As she walked, she wondered. Maybe her mother was right. Perhaps she should try a little harder to look nice. What harm could there be in that? But an involuntary shudder shook her spine at the mere thought of trying to socialize with the women from the Kikuru Country Club. She pulled her hat down lower to shield her eyes from the unrelenting midday glare.

Then there was Rosie. She knew Rosie had other ways of helping a woman attract a man. She remembered what Rosie thought of Garth Whitehead. But perhaps, somehow, she could convince Rosie that she was mistaken about Garth and get her to give her a charm to get him to pay the right kind of attention to her. She knew a lot of the African women came to Rosie for help with a variety of problems, and she knew many times something actually worked for them.

There was definitely much that she couldn't explain about African medicine. Some people called it witchcraft, but Hannah didn't want anything quite that serious from Rosie. She just wanted one of those harmless little charms or potions that Rosie liked to do for her family when they needed a little extra help. And that was what she needed— a little extra help.

Ever since she had been a little girl, she had loved to sit outside the kitchen door where Rosie and the other Africans who worked for the Butlers would gather to eat and gossip. She would sit, leaning against the wall as quiet and unobtrusive as the little lizards that slipped in and out of the house every day. She always pricked up her ears and listened carefully when Rosie was giving someone advice about a problem with a cow or a husband or a sickness, or any of the little things that plague everyday life. The most intriguing thing to Hannah was the way the prescriptions often worked.

Of course Hannah had learned a more scientific worldview and rarely thought any more about Rosie and her old wives' tricks. But in the back of her mind she remembered that there were times when the African methods for healing illnesses did seem to work. Often this could be attributed to knowledge about the healing properties of a particular plant, or even to the patient's own desire to recover, but there were enough unexplainable cases to make Hannah wonder about how much she really learned about the scientific nature of the world.

She hadn't been a terribly faithful churchgoer ever in her life. She couldn't reconcile the power of prayer to her scientific worldview either. But then, she had never really known anyone personally who had been healed from anything through prayer, while she had seen Rosie's remedies work with her own eyes. Nevertheless, there were an awful lot of people in the world, Christian and African, who were claiming that there was more going on in this life than you could see with the naked eye. She thought of her friend, Fiona Brown, and now there was Dan Williams, too.

As she rode over the hot, dusty road to the farm where she had been heading, and looked over the grassy fields to the west, she could make out the cluster of trees and the white walls of the house in the center of them of the Whitehead Farm. What harm would there be in trying to get Rosie to get up one of her charms to make Garth fall in love with her? She had nothing to lose by doing that, did she? After all, if Fiona and Dan prayed to their God, how different was what Rosie did from praying, really? And as she made this decision to ask Rosie for her help, Hannah felt a strange sense of foreboding in her heart. In fact, she felt strangely ashamed of her decision, and the memory of Dan praying over Sophie at the lunch table slipped into her thoughts, but she quickly brushed it away. She was coming up to the farm now anyway. Already the dogs had noticed their arrival and were barking and running out to meet them. The hair on Simba's back stood straight up.

It certainly would be nice to have a little help, Hannah thought as she headed out to the barns behind the farmhouse. She remembered Dan's prayer for her. He spoke as though God were his personal friend, someone who actually took an active interest in his life. She wondered if God existed, and if He did exist, was He like Dan Williams said He was? Maybe one day she would have a chance to ask him about it. But here she was at the barn. Time to get to work.

3

*H*annah drank the smell of the stables into her soul. The memory of her father was nearest to her in the earthy smell of horses, and she could almost see his familiar face through the steam rising from their sleek, shiny flanks in the cool morning sunshine. She and her Dad were out early, her little hand tightly held by her father's rough, wrinkled one, keeping her out of the way of the horses' swishing tails and deadly hooves. She never knew exactly where they were; the stables of all the farms they traveled to blended together into her memory. *If Father is in heaven,* she thought, *he would be caring for God's horses now, keeping them fit for racing over the high hills of heaven, hooves and manes flying ecstatically, glistening in the sunshine.*

When the minister spoke at her father's funeral of the mansion that was being prepared for those whom God would be taking to heaven, she thought of the stables with their labyrinth of rooms and the warm, comfortable welcome she always felt there.

A horse snorted and stamped its hooves impatiently and jerked Hannah into the present. It was the morning of the Kikuru Cup and the stables were already buzzing with activity. Stableboys led horses in and out of the stalls. Owners dressed in their Sunday best stalked through the halls, delicately avoiding steaming piles of dung. She saw the odd lady here and there, her filmy skirts carefully pulled just up to the ankles by small, white-gloved hands. Hannah noticed two of them making their way down to the far end of the stables where Garth's horses were being brushed by a couple of syces. She followed them. Despite the fact that she had taken special care with her appearance this morning, putting on her best trousers and a crisp white blouse rather than her usual khaki shirt and slacks, she felt uncouth and ugly behind these two ladies tripping so comically through the dirt and hay of the stable hall. She thought she recognized Leticia Charlesworth, one of Garth's lady friends whom she had seen once or twice at his place in the last couple of weeks. Sure enough, it was her. When they came to the Whitehead stalls, the women stopped.

"Yoo-hoo, Garth," Leticia called out, waving a lace handkerchief over her head. Garth stepped out from behind King, his black stallion, and waved at them. But just as he did, he caught sight of Hannah in the background.

"Han, old chap, there you are!" He left the horse and came striding up the hall, tipping his hat at the ladies as he brushed by them. "I've been waiting for you. Come, I'd like you to take a look at King's fetlock. I'm sure it's nothing to worry about, but nevertheless, I'd like your opinion."

He took Hannah by the elbow and tipped his hat again to the ladies as he steered her past them. Hannah floated along, attached to reality only by the feel of his hand touching her arm. As they bent down, side by side, to look at the small bump on the horse's leg, Hannah was barely able to keep her eyes focused as her mind took in the concern in Garth's voice and the way he looked at her face, trying to read her opinion as she made it up. She was vaguely aware of the two young ladies who were standing out by King's stable door whispering to each other as they never took their eyes off Garth. But for Hannah the whole scene was wrapped in the warm, welcoming scent of the morning stables, adding romance and familiarity to the warmth in her heart.

She and Garth rose together to stand next to the beautiful, shining black horse, and Garth looked into her eyes with his own filled with care and worry. Hannah knew then that she was in love with him. The two ladies still stood in the background, silent now, like lovely lifeless dolls, but Garth looked only at her. She was real and alive. She was the one who held the key to his happiness, his horses. She was the one he was interested in.

"I think it is just an insect bite, Garth," she said softly, using his name for the first time, watching the relief flood his face. "I'll put something on it, which may help the swelling a little, and I'm sure he'll be ready to run this afternoon."

"I was terrified he had injured it. I'm so relieved, I could kiss you!" And without missing a beat, he put his hands on Hannah's shoulders and bent down and kissed her lightly on the lips. Hannah stood still. The soft touch of his lips on hers created a rushing flood of emotion that raced through her body. She thought for a moment that it would knock her to the floor. She could still feel his lips on hers and his breath and his eyes and his hands.

He was laughing now. "Now, now, Han, you look as though you're about to slap my face for taking liberties. But really, you'll forgive me, won't you? I couldn't help myself. Come, let's get going and fix King's leg. Where's your bag?"

Still speechless, Hannah bent down and picked up her black bag. She rummaged around until she found what she needed. Meanwhile, Garth walked over to the two women and started to chat with them. Hannah could hear them laughing and talking above her as she worked on King, but it was all so far away now. When she was done, she stood up.

"There you are, King, you'll be fine." Hannah spoke aloud to catch Garth's attention. Immediately, he turned around.

"Han, old chap, you know Leticia Charlesworth, don't you?" Hannah nodded. So did Leticia. "And I'd like to introduce you to her cousin, just arrived from England. Felicity, this is Hannah Butler, my vet and right-hand woman." The two ladies tittered and Felicity mumbled something appropriate, but already Hannah was blushing with shame. She was such a bumbling fool in the company of women like this. How could she possibly think Garth saw anything but a useful vet in her?

"Well, we're off to the races!" announced Garth, stepping out of the stall and offering the two ladies his arms. "Cheerio, Han, thanks a million!" Then he paused and looked back over his shoulder. "Oh, I almost forgot; I'll be seeing you later! Montague told me you'd be joining us in the box! See you then, Han, old chap. Cheers!" And they were gone.

Hannah, the syce, and the jockey were left in the stall. One of his hired people was all she was to him. Hannah blushed with embarrassment at the thought of how she had felt only minutes ago. Quickly, she packed up her bag and slipped away down the hall and out into the fresh air, where she found Simba faithfully waiting for her at the door.

"Hannah, I've been looking for you!" Hannah looked up to find Fiona and Jim Brown coming towards her. She had known Fiona since they had been to school together, and she was grateful for Fiona's faithfulness in keeping up their friendship. She had been a bridesmaid at Fiona's wedding when she had married Jim Brown, a local farmer. Fiona's mother had been horrified by her daughter's choice of a husband, thinking he was socially far beneath her. But lately Jim had been trying to improve his social standing to suit his mother-in-law, and had been seen often in the company of Garth Whitehead at the Kikuru Country Club.

"The races are about to begin, Hannah!" Fiona said, taking Hannah by the arm. "Charles told me you were coming to Garth's box with him. I hope Garth doesn't have you slaving away doing something for him! Jim says you've been practically running the stables for him these days."

"Oh, no, not really!" said Hannah, blushing far more furiously than the compliment warranted. She noticed Jim glance curiously at her, but in a moment they were swept along by the crowds surging around the track. Hannah excused herself, explaining that she had to change before she met Charles.

A little while later she made her way up to Garth's box at the top of the grandstand. He was ensconced up there, still in animated conversation with Leticia and Felicity. But Charles Montague, who had been anxiously watching for Hannah, had already seen her and was rushing over to greet her. Hannah forced herself to smile at him.

"Hannah, why, you look lovely this morning!" he beamed at her while he took in the rather old-fashioned navy blue dress she was wearing with the white sailor's collar and white buttons down the side of the straight skirt. It wasn't the height of fashion, but it was crisp and clean looking. Mrs. Butler had insisted that Hannah buy a small white hat to wear with it, as well as white shoes. Hannah suddenly felt shy being surveyed with such obvious satisfaction. For an instant she had the feeling she was a racehorse being looked over by a prospective buyer, but she shook the feeling away and smiled back at Charles. After all, if she was going to try to be a part of this crowd, it would not be her skill as a vet, nor would it be her intelligent conversation that would attract people. It would be the way she looked. She would just have to get used to being looked over like so much horseflesh and try to feel grateful when she was approved.

"Come along, my dear," said Charles, taking her by the elbow and leading her fussily over to the chairs he had saved for the two of them. "The races are about to start and I'm so frightfully glad you've arrived in time. It is so exciting to be able to cheer on Garth's horses. I do hope they win." He leaned confidentially over her as he pulled out her chair for her and whispered, "I've placed a small wager on each of his horses to win. Of course knowing that you personally are his veterinarian, I feel my wager is quite safe!" He laughed gleefully at his very small joke and Hannah smiled vaguely. She was grateful to see that they were seated next to Fiona and Jim Brown. Quickly, she turned to greet them. But as she did, Garth suddenly noticed her arrival.

"There you two are!" he said, shaking Charles's hand and smiling approvingly at Hannah's dress before looking at her face. "And you brought Han with you! Good! Good!" He pulled out another chair and sat down next to Jim. Within seconds the two men were engaged in an intense conversation about the quality of the other horses in the race. Hannah wished she could strike up a few words with Fiona to avoid listening to Charles, but Fiona was concentrating on her husband's conversation.

Hannah was surprised to notice how unhappy Fiona looked. She was watching Jim with a kind of sullen resentment. Jim, on the other hand, turned to her now and then with a bright smile and asked her how she would like to make some good money today on the races.

"Cheer up, darling, Garth and I know what we're doing. We'll be coming out ahead of the game after today. We simply can't lose. Not today—not against this bush-league competition." Then he turned to Garth with another morsel of gossip he had picked up that morning from one of the syces he had been talking to. Fiona pursed her lips and glared at Garth angrily for a moment before he glanced her way. She quickly looked down at the track where the horses in the first race were being led to the gates. Beside Hannah, Charles was rummaging through his program, making exclamatory noises here and there and asking Hannah if she knew this or that horse.

"Are you feeling alright?" Hannah said impulsively to Fiona. Fiona looked up, surprised, as if she hadn't noticed Hannah's presence until now.

"Oh. Yes. Thank you," she responded automatically.

"Don't you like the races?" Hannah tried again. Why on earth was Fiona suddenly behaving so strangely?

"Yes. I mean, no. Jim does. Not me." She stopped. Then added. "I like horses. It's just the betting I don't like. It seems like a waste of money to me."

Jim caught the last few words and turned to Fiona. "Now, darling, don't start that again." There was an edge to his voice. Garth leaped to the rescue.

"Don't you be worrying your pretty little head about that, my dear. Jim and I have everything under control. And Hannah here is keeping the horses in tiptop condition, aren't you, Han, old chap?" His quick glance at Hannah brought the tidal wave rushing to her face in a flood of color. But no one noticed and he continued to address Fiona.

"You must realize, my dear, that farming in this infernal country is far more of a gamble than betting on the odd horse race. If you need a little bit of pin money here and there, there is no easier way to get some than a good old-fashioned horse race. Now, my dear, don't be giving your poor husband a hard time over it. He's only doing it for your sake, you know. And you must let a man have his fun now and then."

He turned away from Fiona and back to Jim with an air of having dealt with the problem in a professional way. Fiona was sullen. Hannah was suddenly swamped again by the waves flooding her thoughts with Garth's kiss.

"Hannah! There you are at last! I was afraid you might be late!" Hannah looked up, dismayed to see her mother leaning precariously over the railings that separated the box from the regular stands. "Goodness me, Mr. Whitehead, I didn't mean to interrupt. I just noticed my daughter. Hello, Jim, Fiona. I saw your poor mother the other day, Fiona. Mr. Whitehead, it is such a pleasure to see you again. I do hope you'll drop by again for a visit when you are able to stay longer." She turned to Fiona. "He's such a busy man, you know!

"Have you heard the latest news from home? There are rumors of war against the kaiser. Oh dear, what shall we do if there is war? I am so frightfully worried. Aren't you worried, Mr. Whitehead? Will you go and fight?"

Garth glanced at Jim. Hannah thought she detected a look of mutual irritation pass between the two men, and she felt like sliding under her chair with embarrassment at her mother. But there was no escape now.

"I've been hearing those rumors for years, Mrs. Butler," Garth was saying. "I really don't think it will amount to much. We are far too civilized to stoop to shooting each other in this, the twentieth century. And if those Huns are barbaric enough to start a war, I'm sure we'll put them in their place in short order. We won't even know about the war here in Africa until it is all over. At least I certainly hope that is the case, because I have better things to do than risk my life in a ridiculous war in Europe." The grandstands were filling up rapidly now with the crowds.

"Harriet, dear, there you are. I'm so sorry we're late." Hannah looked up with relief to see Maureen Fitzhugh bustling between the rows of benches to reach her mother.

Garth and Jim stood up and nodded politely. Garth looked at Mrs. Butler. "It has been lovely chatting with you," he said, smiling at her insincerely. Hannah cringed at the tone of Garth's voice. It would be so much easier to fit in with Garth's crowd if her mother were less embarrassing. No wonder she was such a social failure. Mrs. Butler was making her way away from the box, and Hannah suddenly felt the overwhelming need to get away also. But there was no escape.

Instead, she shrank within herself while Charles put his arm possessively around her shoulders and began pointing out the various horses he knew who were starting to line up near the starting gates.

Hannah only had eyes for the magnificent black King. He was prancing and tossing his head in anxious anticipation of his run, the energy in his sleek black body barely held in check by the tiny jockey perched precariously on his back.

All of a sudden the gates swung open, and King burst out onto the track. As if he were sailing with the wind, he slid into first place next to the railing. On her left, Garth, Leticia, and Felicity were shouting and cheering, enjoying themselves immensely. But Jim was as tense as a lion stalking its prey.

"Come on, King, keep it up. Run for me, King, you can win this one." He spoke quietly and intensely, as though he and King were the only two beings at the track. Beside him, Fiona sat silent and grim.

King sailed gracefully and easily over the finish line, and Hannah leaped up to join the cheering crowd. Leticia and Felicity were kissing congratulations on Garth's cheek, even as he shook hands with everybody within reach, including Hannah.

Glancing behind her for a moment, Hannah noticed that Jim slumped back into his chair, exhausted with relief, before rising to shake Garth's hand. Fiona just smiled, her face tight but relieved. For an instant they were a stark contrast to the happy crowd around them, but quickly they adjusted their expressions to fit in.

"Thanks for everything! I don't know where I would be without you, Han. I must run!" Garth bent over and kissed her cheek, and he was gone. They all sat back down to watch the presentation of the cup.

"Would you like to join me this evening for the victory party at the club, Hannah?" Hannah turned, startled for a moment. She had completely forgotten about Charles.

"Oh, yes, thank you. That would be lovely," she replied without thinking as she watched Garth wend his way down through the hands reaching out of the crowd to congratulate him. Instantly Hannah regretted her words, but she couldn't call them back.

Most of the evening she stood next to Charles, who escorted her chivalrously around the room making small talk with all the right people. But Hannah always had one eye on Garth, and in her heart of hearts it was Garth she was standing beside, even as she watched him chat and laugh with his guests. Leticia and Felicity were always one step away from him, ready to bask in his smile whenever he turned in their direction. Hannah watched and wished. It was a long, long evening.

Late that night Hannah was at last in her own bed alone with her thoughts and too tired to sleep. She lay and listened to the distant night noises of insects buzzing, faraway grunts and calls of the animals, and the myriad of birds that filled the night. The mosquito net over her bed rippled in the wind like a ghostly veil, and inside, her mind moved and danced between fantastic dreams and longings.

Garth was elusive, but never far from her mind. She remembered the way he made her feel as though she were the most important person in the world to him one minute, and the next he hardly realized that she existed. But there was one thing she did know for certain: If Garth Whitehead ever should decide that he wanted her, she would be his. She wouldn't even give it a second thought. She would be gone. But until then, if that day should ever come, she must keep her feelings to herself. Could she possibly do that? She dreamed of his surprise and joy to find that it was she that he really loved and that she had always loved him.

Far off in the distance a lion roared. She shuddered and was catapulted out of her dreams of Garth. Her thoughts moved to Jim and Fiona. Something was very wrong. She felt bad about Fiona. Fiona had always been a good friend to her, but she never really worked much at being a good friend in return. Perhaps she should try to change. Perhaps Fiona could use someone to talk to. She would go out and have tea with her in a couple of days. Of course Fiona was one of those people who was terribly involved in the church, and she likely had many friends. *But still,* Hannah thought, *she has been a good friend and if she is unhappy, it is only a kindness to go and visit her, even if she does have other church friends.*

And that brought her mind to Dan. She wondered how Sophie was doing on her new diet. She wished she could talk to Garth freely and easily the way she talked with Dan. But then, Dan wasn't Garth. At last she drifted to sleep.

4

T he next few weeks Hannah only saw Garth occasionally. The horse racing season was over, and he didn't need her help as much anymore. He had done fairly well at the Kikuru Cup, but King's win was his only first-place finish. She heard rumors from Rosie that there were wild parties at his house, and once she had met him in town. He had Leticia with him. Hannah had been shopping for groceries in the little duka when the two of them had walked in, arm in arm.

"Han, old chap!" Garth had called to her as the storekeeper was tallying up her bill. "How are you? Lettie, you remember Han, don't you?"

"Yes, of course, we met at the horse races. Hello, Han," Leticia answered, smiling casually at her. Hannah knew from the way she used Garth's nickname for her that they were close friends.

Hannah tried to tell herself that it was inevitable that Garth would fall for someone like Leticia. After all, even as she had fallen in love with him she had known she had no hope of ever having her love returned. Still, it didn't make it any less painful. She braced herself for the day she would hear news of his engagement to Leticia.

૪૭

She had gone over to Fiona's one day after the races. Fiona greeted her kindly enough and invited her into the little farmhouse for tea. Hannah had always liked Fiona's little house. It was so unlike the way her mother kept their house. Fiona tried to be a part of Africa. There was no ceiling inside and the thatched roof was visible as well as the supporting beams in the roof. It was cool and comfortable, with more air circulating in the heat of the day. The furniture they sat upon was a mixture, with African hides strung over frames and lovely polished English end tables scattered here and there. The whitewashed walls were incongruously decorated with English prints and Jim's hunting trophies, and there was a large wildebeest skin rug on the floor. It was a newlywed's home: bachelor furniture mixed with elegant wedding presents.

Fiona served tea and little gingerbread biscuits on beautiful English china decorated with delicate pink roses.

"It is lovely to see you, Hannah," Fiona began politely. "I hope you've been well lately. I feel very remiss that I haven't been over to see you and your mother for so long. How is your mother?"

"She's very well, thank you," replied Hannah, wondering how to break through Fiona's polite chatter. It wasn't at all like the warm, genuine friendliness she was used to from Fiona. They chatted on for a few minutes about their respective mothers and their mothers' health. Hannah sipped her tea and nibbled on her biscuit. This was exactly the sort of conversation she detested. She decided she would have to be the one to initiate a more personal subject.

"F–Fiona," she began, stammering a little, "I am worried that you are not feeling quite well. I hope there is nothing wrong."

Fiona looked surprised and then smiled genuinely for the first time that afternoon. She reached out and took Hannah by the hand. "Thank you for inquiring, Hannah. You are a kind friend, but I really can't discuss my troubles with anyone, although I wish with all my heart I were free to do so. It would lift the burden so much just to be able to talk, but pray for me when you remember, Hannah. I would be grateful for that."

"I will," Hannah mumbled, blushing at the idea of praying. Since she had made an effort to come to this point with Fiona, she decided she must try one more time to help her.

"I hope there is nothing the matter between you and Jim. I know I am the last person who would be of any help to you if there was, but I would do anything within my power to help if you would only feel free to call on me."

The pained look on Fiona's face told Hannah she was right in her guess, but Fiona quickly hid it behind a falsely cheerful smile.

"Thank you so much for your concern, Hannah. It is a comfort to me to know you care about my troubles. I must only ask you to pray that I may have the strength to face everything." Fiona was clearly determined not to discuss her situation, so Hannah didn't press her any more about it. They spoke about the weather and the prices that farmers could be expected to receive for their crops this year. Fiona had lost her sparkle and enthusiasm for life, and Hannah could see that it was an effort for her just to keep the conversation going. As soon as she had finished her tea, Hannah stood up.

"Thank you for the tea, Fiona. I'd better be getting back to work."

"I thank you for coming to see me, Hannah," Fiona said as they walked together out onto the little veranda made by the overhanging thatch of the roof. "It means more than you know that you care about me enough to come and see me. I can only ask you to pray for me. And Jim also."

Hannah took her hat out of her back pocket and plastered it over her blond head. "I will, Fiona," she mumbled shyly—glad, yet embarrassed, that Fiona assumed that she prayed. And she did, later that night as she pulled her mosquito net around her bed. "Lord, God, please help Fiona. Amen."

કે

"I don't care whether she has an animal in there or not! Let me through!" It was Mrs. Butler's voice. What on earth was she doing here at the clinic? Hannah braced herself, and the next instant Mrs. Butler burst into the room where Hannah was just bandaging up a large dog's leg.

"Hannah, have you heard the news! We're at war! Oh, dear, I just had to rush down and let you know. What is the world coming to! The news was sent over the wireless this morning. Everyone who is able to fight is asked to do his duty for the king and sign up. What a terrible, terrible day this is! War!"

Hannah opened her mouth to respond, but Mrs. Butler didn't wait.

"I am going into town to see if I can find out some news. I know the Fitzhughs have a son at home in Ireland. I must go and see Maureen. Oh, Hannah, this is the first time in my life that I am grateful you weren't a boy. Good-bye!" She rushed out the door. Hannah was left staring into the soft brown eyes of the large black Labrador on her table. She shook her head and stroked his, glad as always that she spent her days with animals, not people.

She wondered if Garth had heard the news yet. He had said he wouldn't be risking his life in a war, but perhaps now that war was a reality, he would change his mind. After all, one did have a duty to defend one's country, and Garth would surely want to join the cause. She wished she were the one who would be seeing him off to war. He would look so handsome in a uniform, and she would stand on the platform with all the other women, waving good-bye as the train pulled away from the station, tears streaming down her face, and Garth would dream of coming home to her.

Daydreams. Her whole life was daydreams now that she had fallen in love with Garth. She had to admit that they were incredibly unfulfilling. She lifted the dog gently down onto the floor, then reached into her pocket and gave him a biscuit. She led him limping, but wagging his tail gratefully, out to the waiting room, where his master was waiting for him.

৯

On Sunday, Mrs. Butler, who had not heard much more news about the war in Europe, was nevertheless still in a terrible uproar about the whole situation. She decided to go to church to pray for the boys who would be off to fight. She insisted that Hannah go with her, and so Hannah found herself sitting uncomfortably in a pew in the second to last row of St. Bartholomew's Church, where she and her mother very occasionally attended. As the choir marched up the center aisle following the altar boy with the cross, Hannah made a quick inventory of the people in the pews in front of her. It wasn't easy to tell who everyone was from the back, and it was made a little more difficult by the fact that the church was as full as at Christmas and Easter services. Everyone must have had the same idea as her mother. She thought she recognized Jack Osbourne and his wife Mary, who had the farm next door to she and her mother. She also thought she saw Fiona Brown, but her husband, Jim, didn't appear to be with her. Mr. and Mrs. Fitzhugh slipped sheepishly into the pew next to Hannah and her mother. They were late and came in after the choir. Mrs. Butler nodded a greeting.

The church service proceeded like clockwork. Hannah followed the prayers in the prayer book and sang the hymns in the hymnal. Everything was beautiful, solemn, and ordered. It made her wonder about Dan Williams. How did his informal prayers fit into this kind of a service? And whose prayers did God listen to? Did He find Dan's prayers too familiar? After all, He was, assuming He existed at all, the God of the entire universe, and a small, personal prayer from nobody in particular in the middle of Africa was probably beneath His dignity.

Hannah's thoughts wandered to Sophie. She wondered if she were doing well on her new diet. She really ought to send Dan a note asking about Sophie. She resolved to do so that very afternoon. Perhaps she would even invite Dan over for tea. After all, she had enjoyed his company, and an afternoon of not being alone with her mother, especially in the excitable condition she was in these days, was always a good thing.

When at last the choir filed out and the congregation followed, Hannah found herself walking outside into the heat of the day next to Fiona Brown. They greeted each other warmly and one after the other they shook Reverend Cosgrove's hand. Then they were standing together in the churchyard. "Warm weather, isn't it?" Fiona said politely.

"It certainly is," agreed Hannah. They stood in silence for a minute. A guilty thought slipped quickly into Hannah's mind. Before she let herself think it through, she spoke it aloud.

"I was just wondering how Mr. Whitehead is doing? Have you seen him lately?" Hannah felt shameless, but she knew if he were engaged, Fiona would mention it. A shadow crossed Fiona's face. Hannah held her breath.

"He's very well, I'm sure, although I can't say I've seen much of him recently," she responded with a chill in her voice. "Jim sees him much more than I do. If you'll excuse me, I really must be going." She smiled the same falsely cheerful smile that Hannah had seen when she had been to tea. "Good afternoon, Hannah." And quickly she turned and walked away.

Hannah stared after her, hurt and surprised, but a minute later a familiar voice rang out behind her.

"Miss Butler, Hannah, I've finally caught up with you!" Hannah's heart sank even lower as she steeled herself and turned to face Charles Montague.

"Good morning, Mr. Montague," she replied stiffly. She hadn't seen him since the day of the races. He had driven her home after the victory party at the club and asked if he could call on her again, but she mentioned that she was very busy at the moment. After that, he had sent word to her several times asking to call, but she had managed to avoid him, until now.

"Miss Butler, I have terrible news for you. I am going home to join up and defend my country against the dreaded Hun." He paused, waiting for Hannah to absorb the import of this tremendous announcement. When Hannah merely nodded, he tried to clarify his point.

"I am leaving at the earliest possible moment. There is a ship leaving Mombasa next week and I have secured a passage on it. Of course we will not see each other again until the war is over. I trust it will be over by Christmas. Nevertheless, I would be grateful if you would consent to correspond with me. I know that to receive letters from you whilst I am on the field will sustain me in my loneliness. Of course, with my family connections I don't expect to be one of the foot soldiers. But I would look forward to your letters, and of course, you will have mine in return."

Hannah fixed her smile rigidly. Fortunately, her mother had just finished speaking with the Fitzhughs when she spotted Hannah and Charles.

"Oh, Mr. Montague, how lovely to see you. Isn't this news of the war a dreadful shock? You are going home, of course, a man of your standing and family would be anxious to do his duty." Charles nodded and opened his mouth to reply, but Mrs. Butler took no notice. "I do hope you won't forget all about those of us here in Africa who will be praying for you and for the country. You will write to us," she nodded toward Hannah, "won't you, Mr. Montague? We will be so anxious to hear how you are." She stopped to take a breath. Charles seized the moment.

"Of course I am going, Mrs. Butler, and Hannah and I have agreed to correspond whilst I am away."

"Oh, Mr. Montague, we will look forward to your letters. We are very grateful that an important personage such as yourself should think of us, aren't we, Hannah, dear?" Hannah nodded dumbly and Charles took advantage of the lull to make his escape. Tipping his hat, he announced to Hannah that he would call on her to take his leave, and much to Hannah's relief he slipped away through the dispersing congregation.

Mrs. Butler and Hannah made their way out of the churchyard to their waiting buggy. Jolting home along the rutted road, Hannah slipped away into her daydreams again. It was becoming a serious habit with her these days, especially when she didn't want to think about other things, such as Charles Montague, for instance.

She drifted into a future where she and Garth were married, or at least engaged. He was grateful to her for rescuing him from his wild ways. Hannah pictured Felicity and Leticia watching wistfully as she and Garth swept by them on the street, arm in arm and so engrossed in each other that they hardly noticed who was around them. Garth would decline invitations from the crowd who partied every weekend at the country club because he and Hannah had better things to do. They had his horses to care for and meals to enjoy together and quiet evenings talking together. Hannah could just imagine the warm joy of his caresses, his kisses, and the things he would whisper in her ear about how much more wonderful it was to be with her than with anyone else. *Oh, the blissfulness of it all,* Hannah sighed to herself, *if only it could be true.* If only she could wish hard enough to make it happen.

The buggy came around the bend and the red tile roof of her home glinted in the morning sunshine. It was still another good hour before lunch would be served. Hannah couldn't face the thought of spending it with her mother, listening to the local gossip. There was only one person she would like to talk about, and there was little chance that her mother would have heard anything about him. Her friends didn't associate with anyone in his circle. She decided to pop over to visit Rosie before lunch. Perhaps Rosie's cousin would have passed on some news.

Rosie was sitting outside her hut as usual. The compound was as full as ever, with dogs and chickens and totos running in and out of the huts. Together she and Rosie walked out towards the shade of their thorn trees, chatting for a few minutes about Rosie's family. At last Hannah decided she must plunge in.

"How is your cousin getting on at Bwana Whitehead's these days?" She tried to make her voice sound casual, but Rosie wasn't fooled for a minute. Rosie turned to face Hannah.

"Memsahib, Bwana Whitehead is bad news. He is only interested in parties and spending money and women. You are not interested in him, are you?"

Hannah picked a twig sticking out of the tree behind her. She tried to explain her feelings in a positive light. "I spend quite a lot of time with him during the racing season, you know, Rosie. He loves horses and so do I. We spend time talking and planning for the races, and he really values my opinions. He listens to me and he needs my help. We have a friendship and I see a side of him that other people don't. He is kind and gentle and thoughtful. Other people only see the social, outgoing, partying side of him. But there is much more to him than just that. I know because I have seen it, Rosie." She paused, took a deep breath, and plunged on. "I remember the charms you give people when they need some help, Rosie. I want to try one."

Hannah looked anxiously into Rosie's deep, dark eyes. She could never fathom what was going on in her mind. She would just have to wait for her to tell her, and Rosie was never in much of a hurry. She lived in African time, not rushed, scheduled European time. Hannah sighed impatiently and waited.

At last Rosie took a deep breath. "It doesn't help you if you don't believe, memsahib."

"How can I believe if I don't have a chance to try it?"

There was a pause, and Rosie shook her head. But when she looked up at Hannah, she was smiling. "Alright, missie, you can try. Perhaps it will help you."

"Thank you for your help, Rosie," Hannah said, falling into step with her as they headed out into the sunshine toward the shamba. Rosie went inside the dark hut and returned with a small cowrie shell that she had strung on a leather thong. It was a beautiful shell of golden brown with black stripes along the edge where it curled outward.

Hannah took it and thanked Rosie as she tied it around her neck and tucked it inside her shirt. A heavy and unhappy feeling overcame Hannah as she left the shamba. She walked slowly, her head hanging down and her feet dragging in the dusty path. She suddenly felt very, very tired.

Because she wasn't paying any attention to where she was going, she was startled by the sudden trumpet of an elephant right in front of her. She nearly jumped out of her skin, and it took her a couple of startled seconds to see Sophie, the baby elephant, come running toward her along the path.

"Oh, my goodness, Sophie, what are you doing here? You frightened the daylights out of me!" Hannah bent down to scratch her behind her ears. Sophie moved her head from side to side like a cat being stroked. Hannah had to laugh at her. "Sophie, you silly little thing! You are an elephant, for crying out loud, not a kitten. You'll be purring for me any minute if you keep this behavior up." Sophie reached up and caressed Hannah's face with the end of her trunk.

Suddenly Hannah felt better. This was reality—warm, healthy, living reality. The little shell still felt a bit strange around her neck, but it had warmed to the temperature of her skin and it was easier to ignore. Perhaps she would throw it away. It was, after all, in comparison to the reality of life before her, a silly thing to believe in. Her life was looking after animals, not chasing after dreams that could never come true. Hannah stood up with a lighter heart. The red tile roof of the house was visible along the path up ahead, and Hannah and Sophie walked together under the shady trees. Hannah was glad to know that

Dan would be on the veranda with her mother and she wouldn't have to face lunch alone with her.

Dan was indeed on the veranda, but Mrs. Butler was nowhere to be seen. Dan stood up when he saw Hannah and Sophie appear through the trees at the bottom of the garden.

"Good afternoon, Mr. Williams," said Hannah as she came striding up the lawn. "It is so nice to see you again. I see Sophie is looking well too!"

"Y–yes, sh–she is," stuttered Dan, turning red with the embarrassment of having to speak. "It is th–th–thanks to the new diet you gave her. It seems to agree with her. I really appreciate it, Miss Butler." His face was crimson by now and Hannah had to laugh to herself. Why did she feel so glad to see him? He was, after all, so inept and shy.

"We are just about to sit down to lunch. I hope Mother's invited you to stay." she said confidently.

"Oh, yes, she did, but I didn't mean to intrude. I went to the early service this morning so that I could get here and back with Sophie before dark. I really didn't intend to be here for lunch, but your mother was kind enough to invite me to stay. She said she had to go inside, though." Dan rushed headlong through this speech.

"Well, it was very nice of you to come and visit. I am so glad to be able to see Sophie for myself. It seems as though she hasn't forgotten me," Hannah replied.

"Oh, yes, but I did have another reason for coming to see you—at least, I think I do—but I find that it might be too much trouble for you now that I think about it."

Suddenly the door opened and Mrs. Butler swept out onto the veranda. "Oh, there you are, Hannah! What on earth were you doing? I had all the servants looking everywhere for you!" Mrs. Butler didn't bother with Hannah's reply before plunging onward. "As you see, Mr. Williams is here with that elephant of his again. I felt it only polite, considering we hadn't dined yet, to invite him to stay." She shot him a withering glare, as if the impudence of calling on people at mealtimes was more than she could possibly bear.

Dan fell right into the trap, visibly withering and barely able to get out an abject apology. "I'm s–s–so t-terribly sorry for the dreadful inconvenience, Mrs. Butler. I don't need to stay for lunch, I only came for a word with Miss, Doctor, Miss, but—"

"Nonsense!" interrupted Mrs. Butler impatiently. "What kind of people do you think we are that we can't offer a simple meal to a man of the cloth?"

"Mother!" Hannah felt it was time for her to put a stop to Dan's suffering. "Let's all just sit down and eat something." She marched up to the table and sat firmly down in her chair. Her mother and Dan followed.

"Please say the blessing, Mr. Williams," said Mrs. Butler in a businesslike fashion.

"Thank You, Lord Jesus, for the hospitality and graciousness of Mrs. Butler and her daughter. Thank You for the food You have set before us. May it serve to make us strong to enable us to serve You day by day. In the name of Jesus Christ, we pray. Amen."

Hannah raised her eyes and looked at Dan, whose eyes were still closed as though he were not quite finished praying. One day she might actually talk to him about his view of God and ask him why his faith was so different from what she saw at church. But not today. She thought of Rosie and the charm around her neck. There were still some things she needed to sort out about what she truly believed in.

"Well, Mr. Williams," began Mrs. Butler as soon as lunch was finished being served, "I suppose you have heard all the news about the war out there on that mission of yours."

"Yes, indeed," mumbled Dan, who had unfortunately been caught with a mouthful of ham. He swallowed quickly and painfully. "That's why I came to talk to your daughter today, despite it being terribly rude of me to intrude like this."

"Yes, of course, news of that import must get through to even the remotest parts of this dark continent. I myself was absolutely shattered when I heard the dreadful story. I was struck dumb, literally struck dumb. Mind you, so were all the rest of our circle, weren't they, Hannah?" Hannah was glad she was only the partial recipient of the lunch hour tirade. Dan glanced over at her like a cornered animal, and Hannah wondered if he would ever venture to visit them again.

"You must know our esteemed Reverend Cosgrove?" Dan nodded,

his mouth unfortunately full again, but it didn't matter. Mrs. Butler went on to give a blow-by-blow account of the morning's sermon.

Hannah looked out and watched Sophie tasting the trees at the edge of the lawn. She hoped her mother wouldn't notice, but she needn't have worried. Mrs. Butler had barely paused to take a breath in the last ten minutes. Her ham and potato salad lay almost untouched. Dan was already finished and pushing a lone potato around his plate trying to pretend he hadn't really wolfed down his meal so fast. Hannah finished her lunch and nodded to Juma, who was standing by the door. Juma came and took away their plates. Mrs. Butler waved hers away also, commenting how it was impossible for her to eat much of anything at a time like this. Juma brought little bowls of custard for each of them and when they were finished, Mrs. Butler stood up, announcing that she was extremely tired and would lie down.

"I didn't expect guests this afternoon and I planned to rest, so you will excuse me, if you don't mind," she announced. Dan blushed and stood up so suddenly his chair fell over backwards. Mrs. Butler glared quickly at Hannah while Dan rushed back to retrieve his chair from the floor.

"Th–thank you so much for you hospitality, Mrs. Butler, I do appre—"

"Don't mention it," Mrs. Butler cut him off and swept back through the door into the house.

Dan sank down into his chair and Hannah heard him suppress a sigh of relief. She felt so sorry for him and her guilty feelings were exacerbated by her use of him as a foil for her mother this afternoon. She apologized for Mrs. Butler's rudeness. "She hasn't much patience with anyone from a lower social sphere than herself," Hannah explained.

Dan didn't respond. They sat in silence for a few minutes watching Sophie, who was now rolling on the grass, rubbing her back into the ground and making funny little grunting noises.

"She's such a sweet little creature," Hannah broke the silence. "It must be a great joy for you to have her."

"Yes, I have enjoyed her immensely," replied Dan. He looked shyly at Hannah, who smiled pleasantly back at him. Why was it so easy for her to feel at ease with this man while Garth Whitehead threw her into a state of nerves the likes of which she had never experienced before? *Probably because I'm in love with Garth, while I'm not in love with Dan,* she decided.

"I want to talk to you about Sophie, actually," Dan was saying. There was a long pause.

"Please, go on," Hannah prompted.

"It's because of the war."

"Oh no, not the war again!" Hannah groaned. "If I hear any more about that blessed war, I'll just scream!"

"Oh dear, I'm terribly sorry, I didn't mean to bring it up. Perhaps this visit was not a very good plan, Miss Butler." Dan started to push his chair out. Quickly, without thinking what she was doing, Hannah reached out and put her hand on his arm to stop him.

"No, I didn't mean it; please stay! I was just grumbling because of my mother."

Dan stopped instantly, looked at her hand, and turned brilliantly red. Hannah quickly removed it. "Go on, please; what did you need to ask me?"

Dan took a deep breath. "I feel it is my duty to enlist in the army, Miss Butler, and to serve my country in its time of need. I am going to return to England."

"Oh!" Hannah was taken aback. She had never pictured Dan as a soldier; he was so timid. "What will you do with your mission? What will you do with Sophie?" she blurted in surprise.

"Yes, that is the difficulty. Sophie, I mean, not the mission. I work with Reverend MacRae. He is an elderly gentleman and past the age of soldiering. He will gladly hold the fort, as he puts it, until I am back. But he doesn't want the trouble of Sophie. He thinks wild animals belong in the wild, not in a mission station. So I was wondering," Dan paused and took a deep breath as if to steel himself for the worst, "I was just thinking that you might consider, if it wouldn't be too much trouble, looking after her for me while I am gone. Please don't feel obligated to say yes, if it would be too much of an inconvenience. I wouldn't be at all offended, and I would understand completely." He stopped speaking suddenly and looked desperately at Hannah.

Hannah wanted to reach out and touch his arm again, but instead she just nodded. "Of course, I will. I would love to look after her! It would be my pleasure!" Hannah watched the relief well up in Dan's eyes.

"Oh, Miss Butler, thank you very much! Are you sure it wouldn't be too much trouble for you? They do say we'll be home by Christmas. Of course, it may take longer, but not much longer, I'm sure."

"Don't worry, Mr. Williams, she'll be welcome here as long as you are away. My only worry is for you. What if something should happen to you? War is a dangerous business, or so I've heard."

"Yes, I've heard that too." He smiled ruefully. "But I must do my duty for my God and my country, come what may. I am ready to die. Sophie is the only creature I would leave here on this earth with regret. Yet if anything should happen to me, perhaps you would be so kind as to keep her until she is old enough to return to the wild. I realize it is a lot to request, Miss Butler, but I don't know what else I could do. I must trust that our Lord knows what will be best for us. After all, not a sparrow dies without Him knowing and caring, so I'm sure Sophie's life is safe in His hands also." *And your life, too,* Hannah added to herself.

But there was one thing she must clarify before this agreement went much further. "There is only one thing, Mr. Williams. It is just that my faith in God is not at all like yours. Although I admire your faith and your convictions very much, I find that I do not have the same faith in the Lord's control of the outcome of our lives that you do. I hope that will not be a difficulty for you in leaving Sophie with me should anything happen to you. I would probably just raise her as best as I could and release her into the wild again. What God would have to do with it, I wouldn't know."

"Yes, I have sensed that you are not a Christian, Miss Butler, at least not yet. Nevertheless, you are a compassionate and kind person, and you have a love of nature and God's creatures. Even if you don't yet know God, He knows you and loves you. I'm sure one day you will love Him in return."

Hannah felt skeptical about this. He didn't know that she was wearing a magic charm. It made her feel a little ashamed. Perhaps if he did know, he wouldn't trust her with Sophie. But she tried to put the thought out of her mind.

"Then I'm sure everything will be fine. Sophie will stay with me and you'll be home by Christmas. It's a bargain!"

She put out her hand, and Dan took it, smiling warmly. "Thank you so much, Miss Butler. You have no idea how much this means to me to have you looking after Sophie while I am gone. The war will be much easier for me knowing that she is in such good hands."

Hannah and Dan rose from the table and walked down the steps of the veranda. Sophie came charging over to greet them, and they bent down to play with her. Dan and Sophie wrestled and tumbled on the grass for a moment while Hannah watched, entranced. What kind of a man was this who was so awkward and shy with people, yet wasn't afraid to look like a fool playing on the grass with a baby elephant? The handsome face of Garth popped into her mind, and she couldn't imagine him even thinking of behaving so foolishly. But, on the other hand, Dan was a kind man, even if he was rather embarrassingly fanatic about that faith of his, not to mention a bit of a fool over this little elephant. Perhaps if it weren't for that faith issue—but no, she was in love with Garth and always would be.

5

*H*annah was busy making rounds the following morning, but her mind was elsewhere, as usual. She was with Garth in the distant, misty, unreal future. Mechanically, she went through the motions of her business and was surprised when she was handed a note on a folded piece of familiar fresh white paper. She unfolded it, her heart suddenly pounding in her ears.

"Han, old chap," she read, "King has gone off his feed. Could you please come and look at him as soon as possible? Yours, Garth."

She told the young farmer who was with her that his cow had mastitis and explained the treatment as quickly as she could. She rushed out to Kindye and galloped down the road, leaving a cloud of dust to settle slowly in her wake.

She heard Garth before she saw him, ranting and raving at his horseboy for not telling him soon enough about the horse's trouble. Hannah dismounted and walked quickly into the stables. As her eyes adjusted from the brightness outside, she could hear the boy trying to explain.

"But, Bwana, you were not home last night. We waited for you and sent a toto to fetch you at the country club, but no one there knew where you were."

"Well, then, you should have looked harder!" Garth whirled around and saw Hannah standing in the entrance. "Hannah! There you are. These ignorant Africans have let King get sick. I think he's got blackwater. I hope we're not too late to save him. Come here and tell me what you think can be done."

Hannah's eyes were adjusted to the darkness now, and she could see into King's stall. He had already gone down and was lying panting on the straw. Once a horse was down, there was very little she could do but watch him die. She should have been called in much sooner. She looked at Garth's face. It wasn't the anger in it that took her aback. It was the grayness of the skin and his bloodshot eyes. His hair was unbrushed and his shirt was rumpled and unbuttoned. He looked ghastly. She glanced at the unfortunate horseboy, who was trying to sidle out of the stall under the cover of Hannah's arrival. He looked pleadingly back at her and she nodded quickly, letting him go.

Turning back to Garth, she asked, "How long has he been down? Was he alright yesterday?"

Garth pressed his fingertips to the sides of his temples and groaned. "I don't know." He spoke through clenched teeth. "I wasn't here and those blithering idiots I pay to be horseboys didn't even try to get hold of me. Anyone could have told them I was at Lord Dunbar's over at Lake Navasha, but did they have the sense to ask anyone? It appears not."

Hannah glanced around. The horseboy had disappeared. She bent over and stroked King's mane. Already his breathing had become shallower. He wouldn't last long now. "Why didn't they call me if they couldn't find you?" she asked.

"They said I had given them instructions not to call you unless it was serious. I didn't want to be paying unnecessary fees every time one of the horses sneezed. But no matter how much I explain things to these oafs, they just don't understand horses. They are the most thickheaded, unteachable lot of dunderheads I have ever come across. Why I ever thought Africa was the land of the future, I'll never know. I must have been out of my mind to try to make a living here. I tell you, Hannah, they have driven me to drink."

Hannah doubted it. Even with the sympathy she felt for him, she knew better than that. She knelt down beside King and stroked his huge face, his sensitive ears, and whispered to him comfortingly. Garth paced back and forth, complaining. About three-quarters of an hour later, King finally stopped breathing.

Hannah put her head down and rested it on his mane for a moment. What a magnificent creature he had been. She thought of him pounding around the track just a few short weeks ago, his muscles rippling, his hooves flying, and his huge head straining and pushing forward, willing his body to fly faster. If any creature could be invincible, King was. Yet death had managed to overcome him so easily, so quickly, so irretrievably. He had been powerless.

When Hannah raised her head, she found Garth kneeling beside her. He had come over so quietly, she hadn't noticed. She looked into his eyes and saw tears spill over onto his cheeks. Quickly he covered his eyes with his hand, and they knelt silently together over the great animal's body, and for a moment Hannah thought Garth could have been praying. But she knew better than that, though Dan would have prayed at a time like this. She remembered how he had prayed for Sophie's health. He believed God loved animals. *Please take King's soul to be with You, God, if he does indeed have one.* Hannah whispered the prayer in her heart.

As she prayed, she heard Garth standing up. She struggled stiffly to her feet also. She was cramped with kneeling for so long and with the tension of watching a great creature die. She felt shy to look up into Garth's face again and encounter his grief, but he spoke in a matter-of-fact voice.

"Let's go inside and get some coffee. I could use a cup, and I'd be grateful for your company also." Hannah felt her heart leap into her throat. He had actually asked her to be with him at a time like this. She must mean something to him. She looked up at him, but his face only betrayed a grim resignation. He had managed to master his feelings so quickly.

"Thanks, a coffee would be lovely." She smiled back. She really was getting a little better at talking to him. Perhaps it was the practice she was getting chatting with Dan.

They walked back to Garth's house together. It was a beautiful old place he had bought from one of the founding families of Kikuru. It had a quiet, wide veranda with vines hanging down from the roof and bright-tissue bougainvilleas growing up to meet them. Hannah realized that for all the times she had been to Garth's place, this was the first time she had ever been into his home. The veranda was set comfortably with wicker furniture, but they walked right inside through the large wooden front doors and into a wide, dark room with shiny parquet floors. The furniture inside was definitely bachelor style. The chairs were animal hides strung over wooden frames, the kind you could buy at the bazaar in Nairobi. There were a couple of African drums made of skin tightly stretched over a cylinder and secured with strings pulling painfully downward. There was an elephant foot, stuffed and used as a footstool. Hannah thought of Sophie's feet waving wildly as she rolled on the grass with Dan and winced at the thought of cutting them off. An assortment of wild game trophies, mainly bucks, with horns of various configurations, decorated the walls. Scattered between the hunting trophies were horse rosette ribbons, the only color in the room. But Garth didn't linger here either.

They marched out of the lounge and through a dining room, whose main feature was a heavy oak sideboard stacked with bottles and crystal glasses. From the dining room they went into the kitchen. The cook was sitting on a stool chatting with one of the farm bibis, who was leaning against a door that led outside to the yard. An old dog lay at his feet and only raised its head sleepily when Garth and Hannah entered. The cook stood slowly up.

"*Jambo,* Bwana," he said, looking at Hannah curiously.

"Kamau, get us some coffee on the veranda, will you?" Garth spoke in Swahili, then turned and steered Hannah back into the dining room and through another door to a room with a washstand and washbasin in it. "Would you like to wash up a bit? I'll meet you out on the veranda. I'm just going to get something for this infernal headache I have."

Hannah washed and made her way outside again. There were two wicker chairs with comfortable cushions and a table between them. The table had a pile of books and papers on them. This was obviously where Garth spent most of his time when he was at home. Hannah sat in one of the chairs and looked out at the view. The house was set a little bit up the hill on one side of the valley, and it looked out over the river meandering into town, and the dark green trees interspersed with red tile and silver tin roofs of Kikuru. Beyond the town misty, blue-green hills faded into the dusty blue sky.

After a few minutes, Garth still hadn't appeared, and Hannah looked at the books piled beside her on the table. They were mainly about raising horses, which didn't surprise her much. On the bottom of the pile a letter stuck out as if it had been stuffed under the books to keep it from blowing away in the breeze. "With much love and worry from your Mother," the letter announced in a spidery handwriting. *Of course Garth has a mother,* Hannah thought, surprised because she had never thought of her before. It was common knowledge that he received money from home, and she supposed that of course it must come, at least partly, from his mother.

The house was quiet. Hannah wondered how long Garth would take to find something for his headache. She leaned over the table a little. She thought she'd just look at the last sentence of the letter. Maybe it would tell why his mother was worried about Garth. She felt her face flushing with guilt, but her curiosity was too much for her. She had to at least glance.

"War or no war, I'll be arriving on the next boat to see for myself what you're up to," the letter said. Reading it was so easy. She could just be looking at it by accident. After all, the letter was right out in the open. Hannah leaned over a little more.

"I need to be certain you are not gambling it away," the line above that read, and, "Even here in England I hear rumors about your wild adventures and extravagant ways." This was too much temptation for Hannah to resist. Garth was nowhere nearby. Hannah peered into the dark window of the lounge behind her. All was quiet. She leaned over a little more. There were only three or four lines left sticking out from under the books that she hadn't read.

"You are, after all, thirty-five years old and it is high time you learned how to be responsible. I am on the point of insisting you find a nice quiet girl and settle down to have a family before I send you any more money."

The door burst open and Garth came out carrying a tray of coffee things. Hannah jerked herself quickly back into her chair. She fiddled distractedly with her hat that she had in her lap, not daring to look up at Garth in case he noticed how red her face was and read the guilt in her eyes. But he wasn't paying any attention. His black mood prevented him from noticing anything but his own inconveniences.

"Kamau is one of the laziest, most useless Africans on the whole estate. I can't imagine what Lady Higgins-Smythe thought she was doing when she recommended him to me when I bought the house. If I had any sense, I'd fire the old coot on the spot. But I don't have time to go chasing around after another useless African and then train him on top of that! Cream?" He handed Hannah a china cup and then a dainty pitcher of cream when she nodded.

"I don't know what I'm doing out here in this barbarous country, anyway," he continued after taking a large gulp of his own coffee. "I thought perhaps I needed a new start where no one knew me and I could make my way on my own. But really, I don't know how anyone is supposed to cope with this place. I should have gone out to Australia instead. There would have been less to cope with. They know how to handle their natives down there." There was an uncomfortable silence while Garth brooded on the unfairness of Africa.

"Well," Hannah started. She hesitated, but reminding herself that he had just lost his best horse and he had told her he needed her company, she plunged in. "I for one am glad you chose Africa." Garth swallowed the coffee he had just sipped and looked at her in surprise. Hannah suddenly felt her old shyness overwhelm her, and she looked down at her hat in her lap.

"Why, Han, old chap, thank you. I didn't know . . ." Hannah could feel his eyes looking at her with a new kind of curiosity. "I'll be . . . !" she heard him say a mild curse more to himself than her, and she glanced quickly up at him. He was smiling at her.

"You know, Han, it has been a hard row to hoe here, what with sick horses and deadly diseases and useless Africans. You know more than anyone how hard it has been. You've been here with me through thick and thin, helping with the horses and the Africans and the racing and everything. I couldn't have come this far without your help, you know."

Hannah twisted her hat around and around in her hands and blushed hideously. She had jumped into water that was far, far too deep for her. One part of her wanted to leap up and run to the stables where she had left Kindye. The other part forced her to stay. This was what she had been wishing and begging for all these past weeks. She must stick it out no matter how she felt, and she felt embarrassed beyond belief.

Garth was saying nice things to her, but somehow she had imagined it would feel different. Warmer and friendlier, perhaps. Suddenly Garth reached over the table, moved the books out of the way, and took her hand out of her lap. She looked up at him. Nothing was different. He was smiling at her the way he always did, half teasing, half serious. But now he was actually holding her hand. "Thank you, Han, old ch—" He stopped himself midword. "I shouldn't call you that, should I? It really isn't very flattering. I'll have to think of a new name for you. Just give me some time and I'll come up with one!"

This was too much for Hannah. Her shyness overcame her desire. She couldn't banter back and forth with him; in fact, she could hardly say a word. "I must go now, Garth." At least she had managed to say his name. She pulled her hand away and without looking at him, she fled off the veranda and across the lawn.

"Han, what about your coffee? You haven't even touched it." But she was running like a frightened gazelle. "Bye, Han! I'll call on you next week if you don't mind." She was fleeing too desperately to turn around. She jumped onto Kindye and galloped home as if her life depended on it.

For once she was glad to see her mother sitting on the veranda waiting for her. As soon as she caught sight of Hannah, she ordered lunch. By the time Hannah had given Kindye to the syce and washed up, lunch dishes were on the table waiting to be served. Mrs. Butler had a whole morning full of information that she had heard from Harriet Fitzhugh, who had called in for coffee. Hannah sat and picked at her meal in grateful silence, nodding at the appropriate pauses while the news of Kikuru and the war in Europe flowed harmlessly over her head.

ૐ

Hannah spent that week in a state of turmoil. She didn't sleep well at night. It was too difficult to stop her mind from going over and over the conversation she and Garth had had. When she had exhausted herself replaying every detail and nuance, she imagined how it would be when he came to call on her. She would be wearing a dress, of course. Maybe her green one with the white collar. It was either that or the navy blue one that she always wore to church. But that was too severe; besides, she had worn it to the races. No, it would be the green one, and Garth would look at her with admiration in his eyes the way she had seen him look at Felicity or Leticia that day at the race. He would take her hand in his and raise it to his lips, and she would look up into his eyes. . . .

These daydreams attacked her mind with vengeance now. She could hardly think of anything else. In her heart of hearts she knew that Garth broke hearts the way elephants broke trees, leaving them bare and torn as they went on to greener younger ones just further on. But the more she dreamed of him, the less she remembered what she knew about him. She fingered the little shell she wore around her neck and wished she could live in her daydreams forever.

The week stretched slowly on. Each afternoon, Hannah rode eagerly home from her office, looking for a sign that Garth would be there calling on her. Would she see his horse tied up at the veranda? Would he be sitting having a drink with Mother? Perhaps there would be a message telling when to expect him. Hannah had her green dress ironed and waiting. But the days went by and no one came.

On Friday a letter from Charles came for her. Hannah opened the letter absentmindedly, vaguely wondering why he would write to her so soon. Surely he couldn't have left Mombasa yet. With little interest, she began to read the letter.

My dear Hannah,

I am awaiting the departure of my ship, which has been delayed for a few days due to the possibility of submarines being in the vicinity, although I personally feel this is very unlikely.

It has, however, made me realize how fleeting life can be, especially during times of war. I therefore decided I must write to you and declare my intentions. In case I do not reach England safely, I would like you to know that I have the highest regard for you. I fear that I may even be in love with you. If you have any feelings for me at all (I rather hope that you do), I would be most grateful if you would let me know. It would make my separation from you almost bearable if you were to inform me that I may live in hope of a

happy reunion after the war. In short, Hannah, I am asking you to
consider being my wife. You need not decide right away, I only ask
that you tell me if there is any hope that you can love me. I look
forward to hearing from you at your earliest possible convenience.

With deepest regards,
Charles

Hannah quickly folded the letter. Her first thought was that she must not let her mother see this. Mrs. Butler was sitting opposite her at the table, watching her read the letter with great interest. Hannah knew her mother felt she must take charge of Hannah's relationship with Charles, since Hannah herself was so incapable of doing it properly.

"Well, Hannah, what did he say? Why did he write so soon? He must be very interested in keeping in touch with you to write so soon. What did he say?"

"Nothing," Hannah lied. "He was delayed in Mombasa because of a submarine scare and he was just passing the time in writing letters, that's all." But Hannah's telltale cheeks were pink, and Mrs. Butler obviously wasn't satisfied.

"Give it to me to see, dear. A man doesn't write to a woman just to pass time. I know far more about these things than you do. Let me see the letter." She held out her hand, but Hannah knew she would have no peace if her mother knew that Charles had proposed to her. She must not let her have it.

❧

On Sunday she wore the green dress to church with her mother, who complained that it was too frivolous to wear to the Lord's house. Hannah ignored her and looked out instead for Fiona. But Fiona wasn't there. They rode home together in the buggy discussing which men were heading back to England to sign up. War was declared, but there was no fighting as of yet. Just armies gathering around Europe. The world seemed to be holding its breath. Garth wouldn't be going, Hannah knew. She wondered if his mother would be arriving soon. She had hoped to find out from Fiona.

When they drove up the track to their house, Hannah's heart leaped. There on the veranda stood a man. Garth!

No, it wasn't Garth. Hannah glanced sheepishly at her mother to see if she had noticed the sudden joy in her face when she had seen the man. But her mother hadn't noticed him yet. *It must be Dan,* Hannah thought as they approached. She felt angry and betrayed. Why did he have to come today of all days? And right at lunchtime, of course! What if Garth arrived and he was there? She must find a way to get rid of him.

"Mother, look, Mr. Williams is on the veranda. Do you really think we need to invite him to lunch with us again?" Hannah felt mean-spirited and unkind. Really, she did like Dan Williams, but he was just so . . . so . . . inconvenient.

Mrs. Butler glanced at her daughter in mild surprise. "I thought you enjoyed Mr. Williams's company. But it wouldn't upset me just to mention that I am not feeling well. After all, he could at least send us word ahead of time if he wants to show up on our doorstep every Sunday." The syce pulled the horse to a halt in front of the veranda, and Dan stepped forward to hand Mrs. Butler and Hannah down.

"Good afternoon, Mr. Williams," said Mrs. Butler firmly as she alighted on the ground. "I am afraid I am not well this afternoon," she began. But Dan was looking up at Hannah in the buggy. He reached up to take her hand, and as he did so she looked down into his eyes. There was the look she had been imagining in Garth's eyes all week. His eyes followed her as she stepped down and just before he let go of her hand, he whispered, "You—you—look so nice today, Miss Butler." Then he turned hopelessly red and stared at the ground.

Mrs. Butler was still speaking. "So, Mr. Williams, if you don't mind excusing us today, we will have to dine alone."

"I am terribly sorry to intrude, Mrs. Butler. I–I—just mentioned last week to Miss Butler that I would be bringing Sophie over before I shipped out. She very kindly offered to look after her for me. I'll just leave her here and be on my way, if you would be so good as to excuse me."

"Oh, dear, I didn't expect you would be leaving so soon, Mr.

Williams!" Hannah interrupted. "I thought it would be a matter of weeks, not a matter of days!"

"I'm terribly sorry, I should have explained more carefully. Please forgive me. If it is inconvenient for me to leave Sophie with you, I will take her back with me and leave her at my mission. It was frightfully remiss of me not to explain to you exactly when I was leaving. There is a merchant freighter shipping out of Mombasa for Southampton in three days. I have managed to secure a berth on it as I am anxious to get back and enlist as soon as I possibly can."

"Oh, don't worry about Sophie, she's very welcome to stay with me," Hannah explained quickly to save Dan from any more apologies. Secretly she wondered how he was planning to fight for his country when he could barely face her without crumbling with fear. A man like Garth, on the other hand, she could see marching handsomely and confidently off to war with Charles Montague, but of course Garth wasn't going unless it was absolutely necessary. She found herself admiring Dan, but quickly she pushed the thought away. Garth would probably be coming over any minute. After all, he had probably been waiting all week to come over on Sunday when she wasn't working. She must get rid of Dan.

Suddenly Sophie noticed that Hannah was there and she ambled up to say hello. "Hello, Sophie," said Hannah, stroking her between the eyes. "I hope you're going to be happy here. We'll take very good care of you until your master gets home from fighting in the war." She turned to Dan. "Come around to the stables with me and we'll settle Sophie in before you head home. You must be anxious to get back. I suppose you have a lot to do before you leave." She felt mean and unkind again. It was amazing what the expectation of a visit from Garth could drive her to. She knew it would be hard for Dan to say good-bye to Sophie, and it was very selfish of her to make him do it so quickly. But Dan followed her gratefully to the stables.

She picked her way carefully over the hay and the dirt of the stable floor because she hadn't wanted to change from church. She led Sophie into a clean, empty stall and called a stableboy to cover the floor with straw. She discussed Sophie's feeding arrangements with the syce, and she and Dan headed back toward the farmhouse. Hannah was relieved to see that there was no sign of either Garth or his horse yet.

When they reached the front lawn, Dan knelt down to say good-bye to the little elephant. She thought he was bending down to play with her, and she put her trunk around his neck and pulled him onto the grass. "Oh, Sophie girl, I'll miss you so much," Dan said as they rolled together. "You be a good girl now until I get back for you. Don't cause any trouble for Hannah . . . Miss Butler, I mean." He buried his face in Sophie's ear so that Hannah couldn't see his embarrassment. But he didn't take it out. Sophie lay panting on the grass and when Dan finally looked up, Hannah was touched and ashamed to see that his eyes were filled with tears.

He stood up and reached shyly out to shake Hannah's hand. He had the musty smell of elephant on him and he didn't meet Hannah's eyes. "Thank you, Miss Butler; it means so much to me, all you are do-ing for Sophie."

"Please, it will be my pleasure to have her. We'll get along just fine, won't we, Sophie?" Sophie was trying to pull Dan back down onto the grass with her trunk.

"Would it be alright if I wrote to you now and then, Miss Butler? I am afraid I will miss everything so much and it would be awfully good of you if you could write back to me now and then with news of So-phie, if it wouldn't be too much trouble."

"Of course, I'd be happy to write and tell you all Sophie's news. And it would be good to hear from you too," she added quickly as an afterthought. After all, the poor man was going off to war.

"Good-bye, Miss Butler. Good-bye, Sophie girl." Dan turned and quickly strode down the driveway. Sophie started to follow him, but Hannah stopped her. She bent down and held her around the neck. Dan turned and looked quickly over his shoulder, and Hannah saw him take out a handkerchief and blow his nose. Sadly, she led Sophie back to the house.

6

*T*he little elephant was distraught when Dan left. She kept trying to run down the driveway as if he were waiting just around the corner for her. Hannah's heart went out to her, so she sat with her on the stoop and comforted her all afternoon. She scratched behind Sophie's ears and stroked her between her eyes and down her wrinkly trunk. Whenever she took her hands away, Sophie made a break for the driveway to follow the sad figure of Dan walking alone and lonely. But Hannah's eyes were also searching the driveway. She was sure any minute Garth would appear riding tall and confidently around the bend, handsome and smiling.

Sophie spent a miserable night in the stable, and Hannah could hear her trumpeting forlornly all through the night. The next day, Sophie followed Hannah everywhere, much to the delight of everyone who brought animals to Hannah's clinic. Sophie was quite a little celebrity by the end of the day. All the attention did her good, and she seemed a little happier by the time the two of them trudged up the driveway in the long evening shadows. Hannah had her hand slung companionably over Sophie's short wrinkly neck. Sophie no longer whimpered and tried to run away down the driveway. She seemed to accept Hannah as a reasonable substitute for Dan and as long as Hannah was nearby, she was content.

Hannah took her straight to the stables and fed her her supper. She could tell Sophie was exhausted from her wakeful night and her busy day. She closed her into the little stall, and Sophie barely complained before she was quiet and, Hannah assumed, asleep.

It was dark when Hannah reached the farmhouse.

"I had supper without you," called Mrs. Butler from the veranda where she sat with a small lamp flickering bravely against the huge dark night.

"Good," said Hannah, "I was just getting Sophie settled. I'll go and eat, then I'm turning in. I didn't get much sleep last night."

Hannah was grateful for her tiredness. The thought of Garth flicked across her mind as she dropped her head on her soft welcoming pillow, and she wondered what he was doing tonight. But she had hardly given him a thought all day because she had had her hands and mind full with Sophie. She was asleep before she gave him another thought.

ॐ

Sophie and Hannah became inseparable as the weeks passed. The little elephant grew happy and playful again. Children would come down from the compounds of the surrounding farms just to see her and play with her, and Sophie lapped up all the attention like it was ice cream, but only as long as Hannah was nearby. She always had one eye on her, and the minute Hannah went out of sight, Sophie stopped whatever she was doing and slipped away after her. Hannah got so used to her being underfoot that she hardly noticed her anymore when she was working.

The only one who didn't fall in love with Sophie was Simba. Simba didn't appreciate being followed around by an elephant. Hannah was sure she felt it was beneath her dignity to be trailed by such a shuffling, baggy-skinned, long-nosed creature. Every time Sophie passed near her, Simba would give a low growl so Hannah could see just how unfair it was for her to be forced to mingle with such an unhorselike little thing. Sophie, unfortunately, thought it was some sort of a game, and she lifted her trunk and trumpeted gleefully into Simba's face. Simba would get up and turn her back to her in disgust. "Simba, you ridiculous old thing," Hannah would exclaim. "You're just jealous of a silly elephant!"

Garth did finally come to see Hannah. She was trudging home from delivering a calf late one afternoon, dirty and weary. Sophie, who was following along behind Kindye, was the first to notice him cantering up from behind them. She trumpeted a friendly greeting, and Hannah turned to see him. While her heart jumped with joy for a moment, her stomach sank as she realized what she looked like. Quickly, she pulled her hat down over her damp, greasy hair and wiped her forehead and cheeks with her sleeve because she could feel the dirt and grime that had settled on her face as she worked on the cow. She wiped her hands on her trousers just as Garth caught up to her.

"Han, old chap, long time no see. What have you been doing with yourself these days? Working too hard as usual, I suspect." Hannah blushed as his eyes took in her appearance and he seemed to laugh inwardly. Then he turned to look at Sophie. "I heard rumors about this little addition to your family. What a little charmer she is, too!" Sophie was giving Garth a good once-over with her trunk. He took it as a compliment, of course.

"Yes," Hannah said, "I am looking after Sophie for a friend who is over in England joining up." Did he not realize that he had promised to call on her? Had he completely forgotten everything that had happened on the afternoon King died?

"You are the serious one, aren't you, Han? Joining up, you say. Well, if they ever start anything over there it may be worth it, but from what I hear they're just shouting insults at each other over the trench lines. Some war!" He snorted. "I have better things to do.

"Are you going to be able to help me with the horses this season, Han? I am still devastated without King, but Raj, my three-year-old, is looking awfully well these days. You really must come and have a look at him for yourself. I think you'll be impressed."

"Certainly, if you want me to," Hannah replied, giving Kindye a little kick to move her along. She couldn't believe how Garth could have forgotten their last conversation so easily. He was behaving as if nothing at all had passed between them. And she had been living all these last few weeks on the memory of that conversation—eating, drinking, and dreaming it. Garth followed along cheerfully, oblivious to Hannah's moody reply.

"Wonderful! I am really hoping to have a good season. My mother's coming over on the next boat, you know, and I am determined to impress her. But I am going to need your help to do that. What do you say you drop by tomorrow to have a look at Raj run? Surely you can spare a few minutes from your busy day. These old farmers can deliver their own calves for once in their lives. I need you more than they do." Garth chatted on, quite unaware of Hannah's silence. They came around the bend in the driveway in view of the house and Mrs. Butler on the veranda. Garth reined in his horse.

"Well, I'll be off then, Han, old chap. It's been lovely to chat with you again. See you tomorrow morning!" He turned his horse and clattered off, leaving Hannah and Sophie staring after him. Hannah turned back to the house. Unfortunately, her mother had witnessed the whole scene.

"Hannah Butler, look at you! You look absolutely hideous! How could you possibly leave someone's house looking like that? No wonder Mr. Whitehead didn't come up to the house. He was probably embarrassed to be seen in public with you. You did invite him in, didn't you? Didn't you?"

"He had to go," Hannah mumbled as she handed Kindye off to the syce. She patted Sophie on the rump, so she dutifully trotted off after the syce to get her dinner. Feeling humiliated, Hannah pulled her hat off and slipped past her mother and into the house.

"There's a letter for you," she heard her mother say just before the door slammed behind her. Hannah looked up and there on the mantelpiece a white envelope stood out in the gloom of the shadowy room. *It's from Dan,* she thought as she tore it open. She felt a sliver of gladness pierce her black mood. "It's funny how Dan always manages to appear just when I'm feeling my worst," she said to herself as she walked slowly through the house to her room, reading as she went. He wrote in a fast, confident script, quite unlike how Hannah would have imagined from his stuttering speech.

Dear Hannah,

I have arrived safely in England and everyone here is gearing up for the war, although not much is happening yet. I will be shipping out to France tomorrow and I just wanted to drop you a line before I left.

I miss Africa more than I thought possible. England seems so small and tame and crowded in comparison to our beautiful wild landscapes and huge dramatic skies. I have been thinking of you often and wondering how Sophie is getting along also.

Hannah cringed a little, realizing how little she had been thinking of Dan, her mind being so full of Garth.

I am praying that you are both well and that Sophie is not being too much trouble to you. I thank God every day for your gracious willingness to help me out with her. I know she takes a lot of looking after! Thank you, Hannah.

If you don't mind my writing to you about myself, I am doing fine in every way, except for a severe case of homesickness. But should God see fit to spare me from death, I will be home as soon as the war is over. Otherwise I will also be home, with Him. I often think heaven must look like Africa in some ways, but of course without the disease and the sickness and suffering, not to mention war.

I hope I am not imposing on your good will too much, but I would be grateful if I may write to you about my feelings and experiences over here. I feel quite alone. I have come to love Africa in my years of work out there and I miss it very much. I miss little Sophie also, and if I may be so bold as to say so I do miss walking over to visit you and the enjoyable conversations we had. If you do manage to find the time now and then, I would be deeply grateful if you could send me a note to let me know how Sophie is.

I must go now. I am praying for a quick, merciful end to this war, and I am always thanking God for your friendship and care for God's little creature, Sophie.

In Christ's Love,
Dan

By the time Hannah had finished reading the letter, she was sitting on the edge of her bed. She put her head into her hands and prayed, "Dear God, I know You don't hear from me often, if You exist at all, but I do pray that You would be so kind as to spare Dan's life in the war and bring him safely back to his beloved Africa. He believes in

You, and although I don't know what I believe about You, if You are there, please keep Dan safe. Thank You. Amen."

She sighed deeply and raised her head. Dan himself was like Africa. He always brought such a wide-open perspective to her small, narrow thoughts. Here she had been so depressed about Garth seeing her look so dirty after he hadn't even come to visit her when he said he would. But Dan was thinking about life and death, war and peace. About Africa and elephants. About her kindness to him, not her appearance. Why couldn't Garth be more like Dan? She shook the thought out of her head. Garth was so much more exciting and charming than Dan. How could she possibly want him to be different?

But she would write back to Dan. After all, they were friends, she did enjoy his company, and he was feeling so homesick. Besides, she needed to tell him that Sophie was doing very well and he needn't worry about her.

"Hannah, hurry up; your supper is getting cold," her mother's voice drifted through the house. Hannah quickly cleaned up and went out to the veranda, where her supper was waiting for her.

She wrote to Dan that very evening and went to bed early. She wanted to get up early in the morning because she was determined that she would go to Garth's house looking her very best.

When Hannah left the house in the morning, her blond hair shone in the clean morning sunshine. She had a clean white shirt and clean trousers, and she looked and felt as fresh as the morning itself. But in Africa even the most beautiful morning can turn into a hot and dusty midday in a matter of minutes.

She had left Sophie behind, bellowing forlornly in the stables with the syce. But she didn't want Sophie frightening Garth's horses. Besides, it was high time Sophie learned that she couldn't go everywhere with her.

Garth was already out in the paddock and the horses were just about ready for their run.

"Aha, Han, old chap, there you are! Just in time, too. I want you to take a look at Raj and tell me what you think of him. I have high hopes for this horse. He may even be as good as King was."

Raj's jockey took him around the paddock several times. When he stopped running, Raj whinnied with impatience and tossed his mane in the air, prancing and stepping nervously. But as soon as he was allowed to run, a look of concentration and intensity came into his eyes and he took off like a rocket, hooves thundering and nostrils flaring. Hannah was impressed.

She looked up at Garth, who was standing at the fence next to her with his hands in his pockets and his cap pulled low over his handsome face. "I think he will do very well, Garth," she said shyly, still awkward about saying his name out loud.

Garth took his eyes off the horse and looked down at Hannah, as if he had only just noticed her. His eyes strayed from her face, down her blouse and trousers, and back up to her face. Hannah blushed. It was gratifying to see the look of appreciation in Garth's eyes when they met hers again, but it was also strangely humiliating to be surveyed like so much horseflesh.

"Well, thank you, Hannah," he said in his most charming voice, and Hannah's heart stopped beating. Garth put his arm around her shoulders and looked out at the horse on the far side of the paddock. "He is a fine runner, isn't he?"

Hannah nodded. "He is indeed," she breathed, too overcome to trust her voice to anything more than a faint whisper. They stood watching Raj come closer and closer along the fence. Like a locomotive at full speed, he roared by. The dust settled over the two of them, and Hannah felt a shiver of pleasure go through Garth's arm over her shoulder. Suddenly, he bent down and kissed her on her lips.

"Hey, you two, what's this kanoodling in broad daylight!" A voice boomed out from behind them, and Hannah turned as if she had just been caught with her hand in the till. But Garth laughed out loud as if he were caught kissing people every day.

"Jim! You old renegade, you! How dare you come creeping up on us like that? I'm liable to turn and shoot you like a thief if you do that to me again." The two men laughed and Jim dismounted from his horse and shook Garth's hand. Hannah then noticed that Fiona was riding along just behind him. But Fiona wasn't laughing. In fact, she looked positively angry as she glared at her husband and Garth.

"Hello, Garth, Hannah," she said without smiling. Hannah smiled up at her and felt a fountain of blood rushing into her face. Fiona dismounted and walked over to the fence. The four of them stood in silence, watching Raj race around the paddock.

"Very nice," Jim said to Garth. The two of them talked about the race coming up next month. Hannah listened as well as she could, but her mind couldn't stop replaying the kiss. Over and over she lived it: the closeness of Garth's eyes looking into hers, the warmth of his lips on hers, the feel of his fingers on her face, and most of all the elation that surged through her body in response to his touch.

Gradually, she sensed something going on around her. Fiona was speaking, arguing. Her harsh voice penetrated into Hannah's consciousness.

"Jim, we simply cannot afford to bet on these horses anymore, and I don't care how good you two think they are. There are always better horses, or the horse stumbles, or the jockey doesn't run him properly, or something. You are driving us into the poorhouse with this gambling of yours. And Garth too. I know you are losing money, Garth. Don't you think I don't hear things! But you have your mother's money to bail you out and we have nothing!" She stopped speaking abruptly, as though she would break down if she said anything else.

"Now, now, darling, you're working yourself into a terrible state about nothing. I'm not putting all our money on Garth's horses, just a little. And Raj is a sure bet. Just look at him. He's magnificent!" Jim tried to put his arm around his wife's shoulders, but she shook him off and turned to face Hannah.

"Hannah, you know what it's like. Surely you can tell him that animals cannot be relied upon. Anything can happen at the last minute, you must know that. Tell him!"

Hannah was dismayed. How could she get into an argument between a husband and wife? How could she take sides with someone against Garth? She couldn't. She stared helplessly at Fiona, watching as the look in Fiona's eyes turned from pleading to contempt to rage.

"So, you're in this too! I might have known. You know he's just playing along with you, don't you, Hannah? I saw him kissing you when we rode up here. Don't be fooled. He doesn't mean anything. He only cares about himself and his precious money. He goes through women as quickly as he goes through money. He doesn't care whose women or whose money, just as long as he gets what he wants. And he's even got Jim charmed into giving him whatever he wants. Be warned, Hannah Butler!" She marched over to her horse and rode away down the road, leaving Garth, Jim, and Hannah staring after her in shocked silence.

"Well!" said Garth as soon as she had disappeared from sight. "Women!" He turned back to the paddock where his jockey had just dismounted and was rubbing down Raj. "So, do you think we have a chance at the cup next month?"

"I don't think there is another horse in the country that could touch him," Jim responded, as though carrying on a conversation after his wife had just stormed off was the most natural thing in the world to him.

Hannah felt ill. She was fighting off the horrible thought that Fiona might be right about Garth. But of course, Fiona was really angry at her own husband. After all, Jim wasn't as well off as Garth was, and he probably wasn't as clever or as charming as Garth. She probably just found it easier to blame Garth for their problems instead of blaming her own husband.

No, she couldn't blame Garth for Jim's faults. That wasn't fair. And Garth didn't even have the advantage of having a wife to love him. No wonder he invested his whole life in his horses. Hannah understood that feeling. Of course, it wasn't very nice of Garth to have said what he did when Fiona left, but she couldn't really blame him after what Fiona had said about him.

Having settled this in her mind, Hannah turned her attention to the men's conversation. But they were so engrossed in arguing about the merits and faults of the competing horses, they had forgotten she was there. They wandered off toward the stables, and Garth didn't even look over his shoulder to see if she was coming along.

The morning sun had moved up overhead. The air was shimmering over the paddock. Dust seeped into Hannah's skin, and she felt hot and muggy. Her hair was plastered onto her forehead, and she wished she had brought her hat. Vanity—it was all very well in the morning, but it didn't leave a person much protection in the heat of the day. She walked over to where Kindye was grazing on some grass under a thorn tree. She should get back to work, and Sophie didn't like to be left alone for too long.

But as soon as she was on the lonely road home, her mind returned to Garth's kiss. *It's worth living for,* she decided, *no matter what Fiona says.*

Mrs. Butler was waiting anxiously for Hannah on the veranda when she rode up to the house. She gleefully presented her with a letter from Charles. Hannah took it, wondering what he was going to spring on her now, and how she would ever prevent her mother from finding out about his proposal? She opened the letter with nervous fingers.

Dear Hannah,

My regiment is still undergoing training exercises in England. It seems to take so terribly long. However, I hear terrible rumors of the conditions in trenches in Europe. And they say the Germans are using gas! I shudder to think that it is true!

I hope you received my last letter and have given some thought to your feelings for me. I look so forward to hearing from you to know whether I might dare to hope. I pray that the powers that be will protect me from any permanent injury so that I may return to you after the war as a suitable husband for you. And I pray also that the war will be over soon, but I fear it may last longer than we all thought.

With my highest regards,
Charles

Hannah looked up from the letter into the excited face of her mother eagerly watching her from across the lunch table.

"Well, what did he say? How is he, and is the war going to be over soon? Did he say anything about his feelings for you? A man doesn't write so often unless he has feelings, you know, my dear. I know these things. Tell me; what did he say?"

Hannah sighed and prepared a careful white lie for her mother. "He is still engaged in training, Mother, so he has time to write, that's all. But he feels that the war may last longer than we thought it would, and he hears rumors that the Germans are using gas on the soldiers in the trenches."

She sat back, pleased to see the horror on her mother's face at the mention of gas. That would distract her from prying into Charles's feelings for her.

る

"The British Army has begun fighting in Europe!" Mrs. Butler was reading the morning paper agitatedly at the breakfast table a few days later. "The Germans have invaded Belgium, and they are pushing their way into France!"

"Oh dear!" replied Hannah, sitting down. "I hope Dan will be alright." But Hannah's mind was far away from Europe and Dan. Her inner thoughts were only of Garth, but she had no intention of discussing them with her mother, so she listened with one ear as her mother read her the news.

The racing season would be starting again soon, and Hannah wanted to make sure Garth had Raj on the best possible diet. She thought she would pop over to his place after she had finished at the clinic that morning. Absentmindedly, she pushed her chair out from the table and excused herself. Her mother stopped in midsentence to look at her, but then she continued reading as though Hannah were still there.

It is a strange thing, Hannah thought to herself as she walked down the driveway with Sophie following happily along behind her, *how two women can live together in the same house and have absolutely no idea what is going on in the mind or the heart of the other one.* She shuddered at the thought of sharing her inmost thoughts with her mother. *Well, perhaps it's just as well.*

Sophie followed her to Garth's later that morning. She caused quite a sensation in the stables. The syces and stable-boys all wanted to see her and touch her. Hannah found herself thinking of Dan as she explained Sophie to them. Perhaps he was already involved in the fighting. She stroked Sophie behind her ears and bent her head forward and whispered a prayer that Dan's God would be gracious enough to keep him safe and bring him home soon, for Sophie's sake.

Garth came striding into the stable and stopped short at the sight of Sophie. Remembering that he had seen her at Hannah's, he laughed and stroked her trunk. Hannah straightened up and put out her hand.

"Good morning, Garth," she said, blushing warmly. He took her hand and greeted her with a peck on the cheek.

"Han, old chap, what brings you here?" He appeared not to notice her red face, nor did he seem to remember the kiss from the day before.

"Well," Hannah stumbled over her words, "I just . . . well . . . it seems that I ought to make sure that Raj's diet is adequate for all the training he is going to do for the upcoming races."

"But of course, my dear; I'll just let you speak to the syce about that. I have to run. Did I tell you my mother is coming out to visit me? I hear she'll be arriving on the day before the Kikuru Cup. What timing! I think I'll throw a party for her arrival and introduce her to the neighbors after the race. You'll come, of course?"

"Y–yes, if you like." Hannah couldn't believe her ears. It had actually happened at last. He had invited her to a party at his house. She was suddenly overwhelmed with shyness. How would she manage it? She had always been so terribly awkward at social do's. She pulled her hat down over her eyes.

"Of course I like! And bring your mother along too. I'll send out formal invitations as soon as I'm organized. Here's Jomo! Tell him exactly what you think Raj should be eating. I must run. Cheerio!" And he turned and was gone.

Hannah had to make an enormous effort to control her thoughts. They had flown out the door with Garth, and she could hardly rein them in so that she could focus on Raj's diet. There was so much else to think through. She was actually invited to one of Garth's parties. That said something about how he felt about her. And what about what she would wear and how she would behave, and whether Garth would pay attention to her in front of all his friends, even his mother? Raj's diet was so hard to think about at a time like this. It was only with a supreme effort that she was able to pull herself together and do her job.

ও

"Hello, Hannah; you're late again." Hannah's mother was sitting at the table on the veranda when Hannah wandered dreamily up the driveway, still lost in daydreams of Garth and trailed by Sophie. "There's a letter here for you from that Dan Williams fellow. I completely forgot to give it to you this morning. I was so upset about the news from Europe."

"Thanks," Hannah said, taking it and absentmindedly opening it. "Garth Whitehead has invited us to a party at his house on the day of the Kikuru Cup. His mother will be here then and he is throwing a party to welcome her."

"Oh, my goodness gracious me!" Mrs. Butler let her knife and fork fall onto her plate with a clatter. "What will you wear? You have nothing at all. Nothing whatsoever! We must go to Nairobi. And everything I have is old and tired. I'll have to have something made as well.

"Oh, my goodness! Imagine, an invitation to one of Garth Whitehead's parties. It must be because I invited him for lunch when you brought him over to see the horses. He finally realizes that despite your rough appearance, we are people of quality. Oh, dear, there is so much to do, and so little time to do it!" Mrs. Butler began fanning herself distractedly with her napkin.

Hannah looked down at the letter she was holding.

Dear Hannah,

I was so gratified to get your letter yesterday while I was here in France. You have no idea how much it cheered me up to hear how well you and Sophie are getting along. I could almost smell the African air in between the pages.

I am writing to you from what they call a trench. We live like moles in the ground here, and every time it rains we are waist deep in mud. But the worst of it is the incoming shellfire and rumors of soldiers being gassed in the trenches. We fire at the Germans and they retaliate. Day and night it goes on, and you never know when your particular section of the trench will be hit.

There isn't much chance of surviving if you take a direct hit, but so far God has graciously spared my life. Just yesterday, I had a very close call. I was sitting with my unit playing cards to pass the time when suddenly I had an overwhelming urge to walk. My comrades thought I was balmy, but I couldn't sit still. I got up and made my way through the trench towards where the next unit was holding the line, when suddenly I heard the whistle of incoming fire. I turned just in time to see the spot where my friends had been sitting take a direct hit. Rushing back to where I was only moments ago, all I found were the stumps of my comrades' legs. I dropped to my knees and prayed. I only hope that I will be worthy to serve God in whatever capacity He has spared my life for. I don't deserve to be alive today.

Hannah looked up with unseeing eyes. Her mother was still chattering excitedly about the upcoming party. Or was it the raging war in Europe? Whatever it was, it didn't really matter to her as long as she could be in a state of alarm over it. Hannah wasn't listening anyway. She wondered if Garth would decide to return to England to serve his country now that things were getting so serious. She thought of the stumps of Dan's friends' legs and hoped Garth wouldn't be so foolish as to risk his life unnecessarily. After all, Dan had God protecting him. Who would protect Garth?

ಹಿ

The weeks passed with excruciating slowness. Hannah and her mother made the necessary trips to Nairobi, and Hannah was fitted for a gorgeous brown silk dress with an off-the-shoulder bodice and a full skirt. The color complimented her hair and brought out its red highlights while the style emphasized her thin waist, so the dressmaker explained. Hannah hardly recognized herself when she finally tried on the finished product. It literally took her breath away to see herself standing in the looking glass, tall and willowy and feminine. She could sweep Garth off his feet in a dress like this. And right then and there while staring at her own image, she made a vow.

I will get him. Whatever it takes, that is what I will do. The highest mountain; I'll climb it. The deepest river; I'll swim it. The wildest animal; I'll tame it. Garth Whitehead, you don't stand even the ghost of a chance. Come what may, you will be mine! She smiled sweetly at herself, then turned away to change back into her old clothes.

When Hannah arrived home that day, there were letters from Charles and Dan. She opened Charles's letter first. Charles wrote to her regularly. Every letter he wrote to her seemed to give him more confidence that she must accept his proposal. She evaded the issue in her return letters.

She had been writing regularly to Dan to keep him updated on Sophie's growth and antics. She liked to tell him how Sophie followed her nearly everywhere she went these days. All the farmers that she visited expected Sophie now, and they loved to talk to her and treat her with little tidbits that they would save when they knew Hannah would be coming.

Hannah opened Dan's letter. It was short. All it said was that he was too tired to write much. They were in Belgium, near the city of Ypres, and the fighting was brutal and unrelenting.

We still get mail now and then, and the letters I get from you give me the strength to go on. Thank you, and please pray for me and all the soldiers. We are hanging on by only a thread these days. If I don't come home again, thank you for taking such good care of Sophie. It gives me immense comfort to know she is in your capable hands. My prayers are with you.

With love from Dan

Hannah hung her head after she had read the letters. If either of them knew how very little she thought of them these days, she would be so ashamed. She dutifully wrote each week, but other than that, Dan Williams and Charles Montague barely crossed her mind. "Oh, Lord God," she prayed with a guilty heart, "please look after Dan and Charles and all the men fighting in the Great War. Help them to victory quickly. And please bring Dan safely back to Africa, which he loves so much." She folded the letter. She didn't mention Charles's return. There would be terribly awkward scenes when he got back. She wanted to pray that he would somehow stay in England forever, but she didn't know if that was the right kind of prayer to pray. Luckily, Dan was different, although lately she had caught herself thinking that if she didn't know better, she could imagine that Dan had feelings for her. But she quickly put the thought out of her mind. Perhaps she would be with Garth by the time Dan came back.

She was seeing a lot of Garth these days. It was the racing season, and Garth was racing his horses in several different places around the country. Hannah kept his horses in "fighting trim" as he called it, so she was often over at his place overseeing their feed and exercise as well as their general health. The weeks breezed happily past for Hannah. No matter where Garth spent his evenings, she knew he would be spending his days with her and his beloved horses.

7

y the time the day of the Kikuru Cup finally dawned, Hannah had fingered the little cowrie shell around her neck that Rosie had given her almost bare. She kept it with her wherever she went, and every time she thought about Garth, she touched it. She hadn't seen much of Garth in the last few days. He had been busy preparing for his mother's arrival, so he usually just left a message with his syce for Hannah. She had seen Jim and Fiona at the farm a few times, but Fiona deliberately avoided her. Usually, though, Jim came alone and often Hannah saw him and Garth out in the field watching and analyzing the horses Garth would be entering along with Raj. *Garth's so busy,* Hannah decided to herself. *Once the race is over, he'll be able to devote more time to his personal life. Besides, when he sees me at the party, I know he'll notice how well I look in my new dress.* She touched the shell around her neck and wished with all her heart for her dreams to come true. And today was the day they might be closer than they ever could be again to coming true.

She had decided to spend the whole day with Garth's horses, making sure everything went perfectly for them; then she would slip away just before the last race so she could spend a little extra time getting ready for the party.

Hannah arrived at the racetrack early, but already the excitement was electrifying the air. The horses could feel it, and they were stamping and snorting impatiently in their stalls. Syces and owners bickered and shouted out orders, and stableboys scurried and scampered between the horses, carrying buckets and saddles and all the assorted gear needed for a horse race. Flags and streamers were all over everything, and people were arriving in their best clothes and most elaborate hats. Even one or two motor cars could be heard chugging around the place.

Hannah scanned the scene looking, as always, for Garth. She was surprised to see him near the stands with a woman on his arm. Her heart sank. For a moment she had the urge to turn and flee. It would be better not to know. But they turned to face her, and Hannah saw the woman was older than Garth. Of course, it was his mother! How could she have forgotten the whole reason for his party? She sighed out loud with relief. Garth caught sight of her and waved.

"Han, old chap, there you are!" Hannah waved shyly back and broke out in her usual furious blush. "Han, this is my mother, Lady Eunice Whitehead. Mother, Hannah Butler, vet." Lady Whitehead nodded politely at Hannah, and Hannah mumbled something about how pleased she was to meet her. She could tell that Garth's mother didn't miss much. She couldn't have missed Hannah's blushing when Garth spoke to her, and Hannah thought she detected her smiling to herself, perhaps with the knowledge that Hannah was in love with her son. But Lady Whitehead had a nice warm smile, and she seemed genuinely interested in the fact that Hannah was a vet.

"Dr. Butler, my son has told me all about you. You have been an invaluable help to him as he has learned about farming this untamed country. I am grateful to you for all you have done for him."

"Oh, I'm sure he would have done just as well without me," Hannah said as she reached to pull her hat down, quite forgetting that she had not brought it. Her hand waved about awkwardly for a minute before she shoved it quickly into her pocket. "Did you have a good trip over?" Hannah asked, glad she had thought of the polite question the visitor is always asked.

"Yes, thank you. The weather held very nicely for us for the entire trip, but we were rather concerned about submarines. There were some very near to us, and there are rumors that we will be blockaded."

"Oh, dear," Hannah replied. The art of starting polite conversations was still so new to her that she hadn't mastered the technique of continuing the conversation. There was an awkward silence for a moment, but Garth spoke up.

"Come, Mother, Han; let's go and look in on the horses."

They went to the stable, where Garth showed his mother his horses and then took her back to her place in the viewing gallery. Hannah stayed in the stables. She felt nervous on Garth's behalf. She could tell that he was anxious to do well in front of his mother. She fingered the amulet and made her usual wishes that Garth would fall in love with her and that his horses would do well.

Raj was Garth's highest hope, and he raced at the end of the day. Hannah was surprised at how quickly the time came. The other two fillies that Garth entered had finished a respectable third and fourth. Hannah supervised as Raj was saddled up and taken out to warm up. She kept waiting for Garth to come and see how his horse was doing, but he only popped down for a moment to make sure that Hannah was there. When he saw she had everything under control, he said he must rush back to be with his mother. Hannah was surprised. Usually he paid much closer attention to his horses.

Hannah watched Raj race from a high point just beside the stables. She hardly dared go any closer because she didn't want her nerves to seep out onto the track and spoil the race for Raj. She could see Garth sitting in a box next to his mother across the field. There didn't seem to be anyone else with them, and Hannah was relieved about that.

Suddenly the gates flew open and the horses thundered out onto the track. She found Raj and was relieved to see he was running beautifully. The jockey hardly had to touch him to make him go, but there was another tall bay horse that was keeping up with him. As the two horses pulled away from the crowd, Raj strained to pull ahead of the bay, but he couldn't get away from him.

They roared around the backstretch, where Hannah could see them closely. The two jockeys were glancing at each other and whipping the horses, but neither could pull away from the other. They came to the last corner. Raj was straining and struggling. The bay began ever so slowly to pull in front of Raj. The jockey was frantic, but nothing he could do could make Raj faster. The bay had more stamina. He had more to give down the final stretch. He didn't even look winded. The race was over. Hannah turned away before Raj crossed the line.

Poor Garth, he was counting on this race so much. Hannah felt so bad for him. He had been convinced that Raj would win and he probably had a lot of money riding on the result. She hung her head and walked slowly back to the stables, where she sat and waited for Raj to be brought in. She wondered if Garth would come too.

When the doors burst open and Raj was brought into his stall, Garth was leading him.

"Han, old chap! Here you are! I've been looking everywhere for you!"

Hannah stared disbelievingly at Garth. He didn't even look concerned about Raj's second-place finish.

"I'm sorry Raj didn't win, Garth. I know it would have meant so much to you if he had." Hannah spoke with as much sympathy as she felt, but Garth just laughed merrily.

"Oh, well, these things will happen. We just didn't count on that beautiful bay, Baron, being as good as he was. But don't worry, we'll get him at the next race, won't we, Raj?" He patted Raj's neck as though Raj was more upset than he was. Hannah didn't know what to say. All the words of condolence that she had been rehearsing seemed suddenly inappropriate.

"Well, you are coming to my party tonight, aren't you, Han? I'm counting on you being there, you know."

"Yes . . . yes, of course," Hannah stammered.

"Good, now, don't be late; I'll be looking out for you!" Garth bent over as he said this and kissed Hannah on the cheek. Before Hannah recovered, he was gone.

She walked over to Raj, who was dejectedly nibbling at some straw on his floor.

"What happened, Raj? Was he just too fast for you? It's alright; you just need a little more training and you'll be beating them all." She stroked Raj's soft nose and he snuffled appreciatively.

"Why doesn't Garth care about it, Raj?" She spoke her thoughts aloud to the horse, "What has gotten into him now? I thought he was going to live or die by the results of this race." Raj just snorted into Hannah's ear.

She gave him a hug and headed off to find Kindye. She had better get home. There was a lot to do before the party tonight if she was going to look her absolute best. Garth's words and kiss came into her mind, and she thrilled at the thought that he was actually looking forward to seeing her tonight. Rosie's magic must be working. She put her hand to her throat to touch the shell and reassure herself.

Sophie was pacing back and forth in her pen when Hannah returned home. She wasn't used to being left at home all day, and clearly she didn't appreciate it. She lifted her trunk and let out an indignant bellow when she saw Hannah.

"Sophie, are you cross with me for leaving you for so long? I'm sorry; I just had to go and help Garth at the track today. Come on, out you come." Hannah opened Sophie's gate and the little elephant trotted out onto the grass. The two of them walked back to the house together. Mrs. Butler was still at the racetrack, and Hannah was grateful for the peace and quiet. But there was someone talking to the servants at the back door when Hannah got there.

"Memsahib!" A young man turned from the door and approached Hannah with a worried look on his face. "I am here with a message from Bwana Osbourne. One of the cows is having difficulty delivering her calf and he wants you to come right away! If you please, memsahib."

Hannah let her shoulders droop visibly and sighed loudly. She wanted to say, "I am busy today," but even as she tried to think of an excuse, she knew that she couldn't just leave the farmer in the lurch with a dead calf and head out to a party where everybody in town would see her.

"Alright, let's go. But I must hurry. I have to get back as quickly as possible." She strode off to the stable to retrieve poor Kindye. Sophie trotted happily along behind her.

"Sophie, you have to stay at home. I'm in too much of a hurry to take you with me, and you'll just be in the way. Kamau!" The syce appeared from the stable. "Saddle Kindye up for me again, will you? I have to help Bwana Osbourne with a difficult delivery. I'll be back as soon as I can, but I need you to take care of Sophie for me or she will follow me. Put her back in her pen."

Within five minutes Hannah was galloping down the driveway to the clinic to pick up her equipment. She could hear Sophie trumpeting furiously behind her as Kamau restrained her and tried to lead her to her pen. "Rotten cattle," she muttered angrily to herself. "The one day in the entire year when I want to have an evening to myself to go out, they have to have a crisis. I should have known."

She was still in a bad mood when she arrived at the Osbourne farm. Luckily it was not too far from the clinic, and she made good time taking a shortcut across two cow pastures and a coffee field. But the cow was in pain. The calf was breech and there was nothing Jack had been able to do to get it out. Hannah knelt quickly down behind the poor cow and tried her best to deliver the calf with the equipment she had brought along. It seemed to take forever. Hannah was dirty and grimy, not to mention tired, hungry, and very grumpy by the time they got the calf out. It was dead, and the mother was almost dead too. Hannah hurriedly gave Jack instructions for looking after his cow, and jumped up onto Kindye and galloped home.

It was already getting dark and she still had to bathe and wash her hair, not to mention dress and try to put on a little makeup without looking obvious about it. Why, oh why, couldn't she just have had a few minutes to herself to get ready? Garth would be waiting for her tonight. He seemed anxious to see her. If she was ever going to catch him, tonight was the night. Her stomach filled with collywobbles just at the remembrance of Garth's words in the stable this afternoon. "Now or never, Hannah Butler." She said the words out loud as she rushed to the stables.

Kamau came running out to meet her. "Memsahib, memsahib! Sophie ran away. I tried to catch her, but I couldn't keep up. I have sent five totos out to look for her, but she was determined to follow you and I just couldn't keep her back."

Hannah was livid—would nothing go right today? "Well, find her!" she ordered. "I can't help you. I have to go to Bwana Whitehead's now. I don't care how many totos you sent out. You find her. I'm busy tonight and I can't help you."

"But, memsahib!" Kamau protested. "She will not listen to anyone else but you! She won't come unless you call her."

"Well then, she'll have to stay out all night. I am not going to ruin an evening I've been looking forward to for weeks because of a silly animal that won't behave herself. Now, has Memsahib Butler told you to hitch up the buggy?"

"*Ndio,*" Kamau nodded his head and slunk off to the stable. Hannah strode angrily back to the house. Sophie was really turning out to be quite an inconvenience, running off like this on the one night when Hannah couldn't go and find her. Not to mention all the letter writing to Dan to reassure him she was doing fine. Really, how she got herself into this silly arrangement was beyond her. Next time she wrote to Dan she would . . . come to think of it, Hannah suddenly realized it had been several weeks since she had heard from him. A little twinge of worry crossed her mind. She hoped nothing had happened to him. But as quickly as the thought came, she brushed it away; she had other things, very important things, to think about tonight. She would worry about Dan, and for that matter, Sophie, tomorrow. Tonight was her night. She wasn't going to let anything spoil that.

"At last, here you are. Do you realize we are expected at the Whiteheads' in less than an hour!" Mrs. Butler was pacing back and forth impatiently in the lounge. For a moment Hannah had the impression of a ship under full sail. Her mother was swathed from head to toe in pink, her favorite color, from her large, flat hat with the sweeping black ostrich feather and the swirling gauze, to the full chiffon skirt boiling about her ankles as she swept around to face her daughter.

"Don't start, Mother!" Hannah said angrily, and her mother stopped in midturn, stunned for a moment by Hannah's uncharacteristic rudeness.

"Good heavens! How dare you speak to me like that!"

"Mother, I'm in a hurry." Hannah's voice was flat and cold. She strode past her and off to her room.

"Well, I never!" Mrs. Butler commented to the swinging door Hannah had just disappeared through.

The Hannah who reappeared through the door again nearly an hour later was a sight to behold. Her white, strong shoulders rose majestically out of the swath of silk that surrounded her and came together under a beautiful cameo brooch in the center of her bosom. Her hair sparkled like gold where the sun had bleached the topmost curls, and her cheeks were rosy and warm from the sunshine and her own excitement. The bronze silk of her skirt shimmered and gleamed like molten metal as she moved through the room. Even Mrs. Butler was rendered speechless at the sight, and the two of them went out onto the veranda and climbed up onto the waiting buggy.

"Have you found Sophie yet?" Hannah asked, knowing the answer.

"*Hapana,* memsahib," he shook his head and looked worried.

Hannah squelched the flutter of apprehension she felt at the look on his face and flicked the reins. Sophie wasn't stupid. She would find her way home. She would most likely be home before Hannah. *Besides,* Hannah thought as they jogged down the road, *this is my night, my only night, and I intend to make the most of it. I have every right to have one evening of fun in my life and I have no reason to feel guilty about Sophie. If the totos don't find her, she'll surely find her own way back.*

But when Hannah and her mother pulled the buggy up in front of Garth's house, all her bravado shrank and shriveled away to nothing. She looked at all the carriages and horses milling about the driveway. Music rolled out of the open windows and lights poured out into the darkness. Ladies flitted elegantly in and out of the lighted rooms, and the sound of laughter wrapped the whole scene up like silk ribbon. She felt weak with nervousness. Where was Garth? How would she ever find him among all these people? And what if he had forgotten about their conversation that afternoon?

"Well, let's go in; we're late enough as it is." Mrs. Butler's harsh voice jolted Hannah into action. She threw the reins down to a waiting syce and stepped carefully down from the buggy. Then she reached up to hand her mother down. The two of them ascended the veranda steps and hesitated. Even Mrs. Butler suddenly seemed daunted by the scene before her. Hannah felt panic rising in her breast, but just as she thought she would have to slip away and pretend she never came, Garth's familiar "Han, old chap!" reached out and stopped her.

Garth himself stepped out onto the veranda to greet them, but the second he saw Hannah he stopped dead in his tracks. Hannah felt his eyes take in her dress and her shoulders, her neck and her cheeks, and finally reach her eyes. They looked at each other for a long moment, and Hannah saw admiration and pleasure in his look. This was new to her. No one had ever looked at her that way, except perhaps Dan, but then that didn't really count. As she smiled at Garth, the thought of Dan brought that flicker of worry to her mind for a moment, but it was too distant a thing compared to the reality of Garth smiling like this at her and offering her his arm to escort her inside.

She took a deep breath and slipped her arm through his. Neither she nor Garth even remembered Mrs. Butler, who followed them inside, but it didn't matter because Mrs. Butler was glad enough that it was her daughter who was going into the party like Cinderella with her prince. Like magic, the music started up just as they entered the door, and Garth turned to Hannah.

"May I have this dance, Miss Butler?"

Hannah couldn't speak. Even she hadn't dared to imagine that the evening would start off like this. But Garth didn't bother with her answer. Before she could gather herself together, he had gathered her into his arms and they were waltzing around and around the dance floor.

"You look exquisite tonight," Garth was breathing the words into her ear. Hannah felt herself blush with pleasure right from the top of her head down to her bare shoulders. "Thank you." She could barely bring herself to speak. The sound of her own everyday voice might break this breathtaking spell. The last thing she had done before she left her room that evening was to sew Rosie's shell into the bodice of her dress. She could feel it now, pressing into her soft flesh just above her heart. It surely was magic.

"I'm so glad you came." There was the whisper again. "I was worried when you were late."

Luckily, just as Hannah was trying to bring herself to reply, the music died away and the swirling couples drifted away. Garth drew Hannah to him in an imperceptible hug before he let her go.

"Come," he said, looking warmly down at her, "I'd like you to meet my mother."

"I met her this afternoon at the races. Remember?"

"Oh, yes, of course. Well, she mentioned what a nice and interesting person you are, so I thought I'd take you to see her again, if you don't mind."

"No, of course I'd love to see her."

Lady Whitehead was sitting on a couch speaking to a cluster of women scattered about her on assorted chairs.

"Mother!" said Garth, marching boldly into their midst. "Do you remember Hannah Butler? You met this afternoon at the track."

"Oh, yes, of course I remember. It is my pleasure, Miss Butler. Do sit down and join us. Garth, fetch the young lady some punch. You would like some punch, wouldn't you, Miss Butler?"

Hannah nodded and sat down on the chair Garth had drawn up for her. Lady Whitehead was dressed in black, but she had a soft, blue wool shawl drawn cozily about her, giving her a warm and gentle appearance. *Almost fragile,* Hannah thought. But there was a sense of determination about her, especially in her eyes. Hannah remembered that from this morning. No wonder Garth paid so much attention to her opinions.

Garth returned promptly with a glass of punch for Hannah, but he didn't stay. Hannah was left with the panicky thought that she was expected to entertain Lady Whitehead. But her fears were groundless because Lady Whitehead was a very gracious and skilled conversationalist. She put Hannah at ease quickly and easily by admiring her chosen profession and stating that if she had her way, women would be allowed much more freedom in choosing their own life's work. Then she asked Hannah all about her work, her life as a child in Africa, and how she liked it here now.

Hannah found herself chatting easily and without shyness with Lady Whitehead. Out of the corner of her eye, she caught Garth watching her sometimes, but there were also a few times she noticed him dancing with several of the more glamorous young women.

Hannah stayed with Lady Whitehead until dinner was served. Garth came over to escort his mother into the dining room and to Hannah's surprise and consternation, he offered her his other arm. Hannah took it shyly, and immediately she felt the glares of several of the other ladies boring into her bare back. It was an uncomfortable sensation, but she was also quite gratified to see the surprised look on her mother's face as she swept past her on Garth's arm with Lady Whitehead on the other side.

Garth seated himself next to Hannah at dinner. She was grateful to him for refraining from referring to her as "old chap" all evening. But even as she watched him chat with and smile at the other guests, she couldn't help wondering why Raj's second-place finish that afternoon didn't seem to have affected his mood at all.

She noticed Jim and Fiona sitting further down the table. They were too far away to speak to, although Fiona smiled grimly at Hannah when she saw her seated next to Garth. Jim looked particularly miserable. He hardly made any effort to speak to the other people around him, and Hannah even thought she saw Fiona nudge him sharply to make him pay attention to something someone was telling him. *Fiona is laughing awfully loudly and shrilly,* Hannah thought. But she didn't have a chance to watch them any more because Garth was speaking to her. Every time he said anything to her, it was as though they were the only two people at the table.

"Do you like my mother?" he asked her quietly when the others around them were involved in a loud discussion about how long they felt the war would last.

"Yes, of course. She is a very nice person. I enjoyed speaking to her very much." Hannah was surprised that he cared about her opinion of his mother.

A few minutes later he leaned toward her and asked, "Do you think this pheasant is properly cooked? I told my cook that it had to be well done, but I have so much trouble with the help, as you know from what happened to King. Still, I wouldn't want anyone to become ill."

Hannah stopped chewing. With all the excitement, she had hardly noticed what she was eating, but she nodded quickly. "Yes, it is very nicely cooked."

When the creme caramel was served later in the evening, Garth leaned over again. "You dance very well. I would be honored if you would save a few dances for me after the meal."

Hannah looked at him in surprise. Then she looked shyly down at her plate and said, "I'm sure I won't be booked at all. It would be very nice to dance with you."

"Well, I wouldn't count on your being free. You do look very lovely tonight, and I think there are quite a few young men who have noticed that fact."

Hannah didn't know what to say in response to this. Finally she blurted out the question on her mind all evening. "Garth, aren't you feeling badly about Raj not winning the race this afternoon? I know you were counting so much on him winning."

Garth laughed. *A little hollow,* Hannah thought. "Well, I would have liked him to win, that's true, but there is only so much one can do to make it happen. Still, he's a good little horse, and I'm sure there will be many other chances for him to win. And if you keep helping me the way you have been, I know we can make a winning team." Again, Hannah didn't know how to respond. This evening was turning out to be altogether unpredictable.

"I think we do very well together. We can only get better, don't you agree, Hannah?" Hannah looked up at Garth in dismay. How could she answer questions like this? What was he getting at? But Garth was looking at her with a very serious, intense look in his eyes. Again Hannah felt as though there were only the two of them at the table. She nodded her agreement, and Garth's face relaxed into a smile.

When dinner was finished and all the guests were slowly filtering back into the lounge, Garth took Hannah by the hand and led her onto the dance floor. As they whirled around and around, Hannah found the time to wonder why this was so easy. If she had known how easy it was to have Garth Whitehead pay attention to her, she should have tried it ages ago. But she had the distinct feeling that she was missing something here. The evening was not hers to seize the way she had planned; it was Garth's. It was under his control. She felt the shell pressing into her breast. Perhaps that was it. It was neither her nor Garth, but Rosie's magic. However, as she thought about it, now that she was living in the reality of dancing with Garth, floating and flying around the room in his arms, the magic shell was really just a silly, insignificant thing compared to reality. She wished for a moment that she could slip it out of her dress and throw it away.

The music was dying and Garth took her elbow and steered her to where the band was stationed. He whispered something into the leader's ear and in a few minutes the music started again. This time the music was slow and romantic. Hannah felt her breath taken away as Garth took her into his arms again, pulled her close, and lay his cheek next to hers. She hardly dared breathe. Her heart was beating so hard, he must feel it. But he said nothing. Not until the end of the dance.

"Come, Hannah, let's walk in the garden." He took her by the hand and led her out onto the veranda.

Hannah was overwhelmed. She could only register sensations in her mind. She felt the strength and control in Garth's hand over hers, and the sensation of smiling and nodding at other guests as she wove through them behind Garth. When they stepped out onto the veranda, she felt the music and chatter die away behind her as the door closed. She stepped into a dark, cool world of sweet perfume mingled with the faint smokiness of distant fires. The buzzing, chirping, and gentle cooing of the evening insects and birds wrapped around her. As Garth took her in his arms, his nearness and the familiar musky scent of his cologne blotted out everything else around her.

In a minute he drew away from her, and she felt his hand reach for her face and lift it up to his own. Then the touch of his lips on hers sent a thrill of joy throughout her body, and there was nothing else left in Hannah's world except that feeling for a long time. Later, he drew away. Hannah could feel the cool, quiet African night envelope her again, and she saw a blanket of stars swirling above Garth's head. Garth was speaking to her, but his words were only sounds, the tone husky and the feeling pure joy. Her mind didn't take them in. She smiled back and he bent to kiss her again. And after he kissed her, she heard his words at last.

"Hannah, will you marry me? We've known each other a long time and we would make a good team, don't you think?"

Hannah was startled. She stepped backwards and turned away from him, his kiss still imprinted on her lips and his words swirling through her mind. She felt his hands on her shoulders and his voice sounded in her ear.

"Please marry me, Hannah. You and I belong together." His voice had a coaxing note to it, the way he would speak to a balky colt. As he spoke the words, all the romance of the evening fell away, and Han-

nah's mind kicked into motion. This was the moment she had been
dreaming of all these months. It was actually here. Yet the idea of actually making the dream into a reality suddenly, without warning, trans-
formed it into a nightmare—all the people who would have to be told,
what they would say, her life with Garth, parties, races, new dresses,
and teas. What would happen to her life? Would he love her alone?
The thought sliced like a cold knife into her mind. Inexplicably, Dan's
face appeared and she wished she could talk to him.

But Garth was twisting her around to face him and again he kissed
her, hard and demandingly, making her feel powerless. When he was
finished, she said, "Yes, I will."

8

*H*annah woke early the following morning after only a few hours of sleep. She lay still for a moment trying to remember what had happened the night before that gave her a feeling of dread. And then it broke through her mind like a flash flood, roaring down the dry but peaceful stream that her life had been so far and uprooting everything in its path. She had actually agreed to marry Garth, she remembered, but it hadn't quite turned out the way she dreamed it would. At first it was nice, when only the two of them knew and he was kissing her and holding her in his arms. But then, they had gone inside and he had announced that he had to say something. He had stood up on the platform where the band was playing and pulled her up there after him. Hannah had cringed with embarrassment at the stunned looks on the faces of all his guests. She had tried to smile bravely back into their faces, but she had wanted to run. This wasn't at all what it was supposed to feel like.

"Friends," Garth had begun, pulling Hannah towards him and putting his arm around her waist. There was a shocked silence and Hannah had continued to smile bravely into it. "Friends, this is the happiest day of my life. Hannah Butler—I think you all know Hannah—has done me the great honor of agreeing to marry me." Hannah felt rather than heard the guests gasp, but someone had begun to clap. It was her mother. Gradually the rest of the group took the cue and clapped too. Garth held up his hand. "Thank you, thank you. I had a case of champagne saved in the icebox just in case I would have the pleasure of celebrating my engagement . . . our engagement here tonight. I hardly dared to hope, and yet my prayers have been answered. Please join me in a toast, everyone." He jumped down to the floor and handed Hannah down after him. Instantly Hannah had been surrounded by a throng of guests. Some shook her by the hand, but most of them kissed her politely on the cheek and offered their best wishes.

"Well, well, this is a surprise. Who would have thought our Garth would ever settle down. All the best to you, my dear."

"My, aren't you the sly one, stealing Garth right out from under our noses. But I do wish you both much happiness."

"My word, you certainly took us all by surprise, Hannah Butler. Who would have thought you of all people . . . But let me congratulate you both."

"So, how long have you been keeping this little secret? You certainly had everyone completely baffled!"

"What a shock, I mean, surprise . . ."

"I had no idea . . ."

"When did this all happen?"

And on it went. Hannah's smile was plastered to her face, but it was getting very tattered and tired, she remembered, before everyone finally began to drift home. She had begun to think the night would go on forever. Garth flitted around making sure the champagne kept flowing and stopped beside Hannah now and then to accept someone or another's heartfelt congratulations.

As she lay there in the morning watching her curtains twitch with the early morning breeze, Hannah recalled that only Lady Whitehead hadn't seemed very surprised. She hadn't seemed very pleased, either, come to think of it. She started out well, but . . .

"Hannah, my dear, I can't imagine a nicer girl than you marrying my son."

"Thank you, Lady Whitehead," Hannah had replied, looking up just in time to see Garth smiling approvingly across the room at them.

"Garth never told me you and he were romantically involved."

"Yes, I know; it is a bit sudden." Hannah felt herself blushing. "But we have known each other a long time, Lady Whitehead. We work together very closely with Garth's horses."

"Ah, I see. You love him, then?"

"Yes . . . yes, of course."

"Well, my dear, I hate to be less than thrilled for you and Garth, but please understand; I think you are a fine girl. It is just my son's motives that I worry about."

"Lady Whitehead . . . are you trying to tell me he doesn't love me?" Hannah had felt anger rising. How dare this lady who had only been in the country for a few days tell her how her son felt about her!

Lady Whitehead had taken Hannah's hands in her own. "No, no, my dear. I didn't mean to upset you. It is only because I really do like you, even though we've only just met. It is Garth I am worried about. He can be so fickle sometimes, you know, and I don't want anything to be amiss. Just promise me you won't let him rush you into this. Take your time and make sure that he loves you as much as you deserve."

"I'm sure he does, Lady Whitehead."

"That's good, my dear. But, nevertheless, don't rush into it." With that, she had bent and kissed Hannah on the cheek. Garth had come over and put his arm around Hannah again, which she had been grateful for.

Looking back on that conversation, Hannah still couldn't make much sense of it. She would have understood if Lady Whitehead had been angry with Garth for marrying someone beneath him. After all, that would have been true. But to suggest that Garth didn't really love her? Now that she thought about it in the clear and harsh light of the morning, the idea gave her a very strange, sickly sensation in the pit of her stomach. She wished she could just ride over to his house right now and ask him about it. It was always a comfort to know that no matter how badly she felt about Garth when she was not with him, he had the knack of banishing all those thoughts just by his mere presence with her. Soon she would be with him forever and the worrying thoughts would be gone. Forever.

As she lay there thinking, Hannah heard Kerioki bringing the morning tea. First he took a tray to her mother's room; a few minutes later, she heard the door close and a soft knock on her own door.

"Come in, Kerioki," Hannah said, sitting up.

Kerioki came in and put the tray down on the bedside table.

"Memsahib, I have a message from Rosie for you this morning."

"Yes, what is it?"

"Memsahib, Rosie wants to come to see you this morning."

"Thank you, Kerioki. Tell Rosie to come to me after breakfast. And tell her not to worry; I know what I am doing." Hannah was fairly certain Rosie must have heard the news.

"*Ndio,* 'sahib," Kerioki nodded and slipped out the door.

Hannah sipped her tea thoughtfully. The strange fear in the pit of her stomach had returned. *But that's just because of Rosie's message,* she thought. It was so frustrating to be tossed about by every whim of her feelings. But of course that would all change once she and Garth were actually married.

After they were married, would Garth expect her to give up her practice? She knew he would still want to give the parties and they would spend a lot of time at the club. Of course when he was married, he would have a wife and perhaps soon there would be children, reasons enough to stay at home. She hoped her company would be reason enough for Garth. She sighed. Why were there so many undercurrents in her thoughts this morning? After all, surely it was the happiest morning of her life, and she wasn't happy enough. There must be something wrong with her.

She looked out of her window, between her blowing curtains. And then it dawned on her. Sophie! Where was Sophie? Usually she waited for Hannah on the lawn in the mornings. She must have come back last night. Maybe she was just tired out from all her adventures and was not eating her breakfast as quickly as usual. Hannah jumped up and threw her dressing gown around her shoulders.

"Kerioki! Kerioki!" She rushed down the hall to the kitchen and burst through the door. Kerioki and the cook and a toto were sitting at the kitchen table while sausages and bacon sizzled gently on the stove behind them. They looked up in surprise when they saw Hannah, but they did not smile. Hannah hardly noticed.

"Kerioki, where's Sophie? She came back last night, didn't she?"

Kerioki stood up, looking confused and unhappy. "I–I don't know, memsahib. Perhaps the syce would know. You must ask him, I think."

Hannah looked at the cook and the toto. They were both staring at her with inscrutable expressions on their faces. Hannah whirled around and stormed out of the door. Striding down the hall to return to her room and get dressed, she almost bumped into her mother just coming out of her own room.

"Hannah, what are you doing up so early? You had such a night last night, you should be getting some beauty sleep. You can just tell those farmers at that clinic of yours that they will have to wait. You have a wedding to plan! There is so much to do! Oh, my goodness, I can't believe this is happening to us!"

Mrs. Butler's face was flushed with excitement and she obviously hadn't slept much either. She took Hannah by the elbow and steered her to her room.

"You simply must go back to bed, my dear. I will take care of everything. You get your rest. You want to look your best for your fiancé and if I do say so, you look like an absolute fright this morning!"

"Mother!" Hannah turned to face her when they got to her room. "Do you know where Sophie is? I haven't seen her this morning. I must go out to the stables and check that she is alright."

"Oh, for heaven's sake, Hannah Butler! You have other matters to consider now. You are engaged to Garth Whitehead! Don't worry about that creature. You shouldn't have said you would take her on. Now you are going to have to get rid of her. You cannot possibly take her to the Whiteheads' with you, and I cannot have her here with me. You'll just have to write and tell Mr. Williams that due to unforeseen circumstances, you cannot keep her for him. He will have to make other arrangements.

"Now, come along, there is a lot to do, but first you must get rested in case Garth calls on us today. It simply would not do to have him regretting what he has done if he sees you looking like this. Now, off you go. I'll send Kerioki in with some breakfast later."

Suddenly there was a commotion outside and the sound of footsteps on the veranda. "Oh, no! He's here already! Get dressed at once!" Mrs. Butler shrieked as she shoved Hannah into her bedroom and slammed the door behind her.

Hannah heard a sharp rap on the door as she threw on her usual trousers and white blouse. What was he doing here so early? Could he have regretted last night and come to call it off? The thoughts panicked Hannah as she tried to slap some water on her face and drag her brush through her hair. She could hear her mother's footsteps coming down the hall. She fought off the impulse to climb out of her window and run away. How would she face the town if he called the engagement off? The humiliation would be unbearable. She must run. The door burst open and Mrs. Butler stood there, looking angry.

"Jack Osbourne is here to see you. If he wants you to go over to his place at this hour of the morning, you just tell him you can't. You are engaged now, Hannah, and you have far more urgent duties to consider than someone's sick cattle!"

Hannah sighed with relief. So it wasn't Garth. "It's alright, Mother. I am still the vet." She strode confidently down the hall.

Jack was standing in the lounge holding his hat in both his hands, twisting it around and around. He looked about as comfortable as a zebra in a lion's den.

"Jack! What can I do for you this morning?" Hannah put her hand out to shake his.

He didn't answer her question. "Miss Butler, I have very bad news for you. I am terribly sorry, but I shot your pet elephant last night. A herd had gone through my maize two nights ago, and I thought they had come back to finish it off. I saw the elephant standing in the field, eating, and I assumed that where you see one elephant, there are more. So I shot it, just to warn the others off, you know. But there were no others and when I went out there this morning, I realized it was the little elephant you are boarding for that missionary chap who went off to war. I'm terribly sorry, Miss Butler. If there's anything I can do to make amends . . ."

Hannah stared at him in disbelief. His voice trailed off as he looked into her face and the two of them stood silently for a moment.

"I'm awfully sorry. It was an accident," Jack stammered, looking as if he would take off with fright at any moment.

At that moment, Mrs. Butler bustled importantly into the room. "Hannah, have you told Mr. Osbourne your wonderful news? Jim, if you haven't heard already, congratulations are in order for my daughter. She became engaged last night! To Mr. Garth Whitehead! I'm sure she won't be keeping up her veterinary practice now that she is engaged, will you, Hannah, my dear?"

Jack stepped hesitantly forward and shook Hannah's hand again. "Congratulations, Miss Butler. And again, I'm awfully sorry." Then he turned and fled.

Mrs. Butler stared at the door, then turned to Hannah. "What on earth was that all about? What does he mean that he's sorry? Sorry!"

Hannah sank into the nearest chair and put her head into her hands and began to cry.

"Well, I never!" said her mother angrily. "What an unbelievably rude man! That is what you get for associating with the lower classes, who have absolutely no manners whatsoever! But at least we can take comfort in knowing it won't last much longer. Soon you'll be keeping a far better class of company. And not a moment too soon, I say!

"Come now, Hannah, there's no need to be so upset about it. You are just a little overwrought with all the excitement, and everything happening so suddenly. You just lie down in your room for a few minutes." She tried to urge Hannah out of her chair by taking her by the elbow, but Hannah shook her off.

"Mother! He came to tell me that he accidentally shot Sophie last night. Sophie is dead, Mother. What will I do now? And how will I tell Dan?" She burst into a renewed bout of sobbing.

Mrs. Butler stood looking at her daughter with confusion. "Well, my dear, it is rather a tragedy," she began when Hannah had calmed down slightly, "but wasn't I just telling you a few minutes ago that you would have to get rid of the creature anyway, now that you're engaged? So it is for the best. You'll get over it. You have much bigger fish to fry now. Come along, my dear, pull yourself together and go and lie down. I wouldn't wonder if your fiancé didn't come over to see you this morning. I know what young men who are in love are like. They have absolutely no idea what an engagement entails if you are a woman. But he mustn't see you looking like this."

Hannah looked up incredulously at her mother and caught sight of Rosie standing behind her in the doorway. She could tell by the stricken look on Rosie's face that she had been there long enough to have heard what happened to Sophie.

"Oh, Rosie, thank goodness you're here!" Hannah stood up and went over to her. "What am I going to do, Rosie? Sophie's dead. What will I tell Dan?"

Rosie steered Hannah toward her bedroom. "Your mother is right, Miss Hannah; you must come with me and lie down." She led Hannah to her room as though she were still a little girl. It felt good to feel her strong arms guiding her down the hall. Rosie tucked her back into her bed and drew the curtains shut.

"We'll talk this afternoon. You rest now. You are very tired."

Hannah lay in the filtered daylight. How would she explain to Dan that she had left Sophie and gone off to a party at Garth's without even bothering to make sure Sophie was home safely? It would only have taken her a few minutes to have made sure Sophie was secure in her boma. After all, she should have known that Sophie would try to follow her. And now, because of her own selfish carelessness, Sophie was dead. Automatically, she reached for the shell around her neck. She had put it back on the leather thong when she took off her dress last night. As she touched the warm, smooth shell, the whole idea of magic, of making Garth fall in love with her against his own natural desires, seemed repulsive beyond belief. What if there were such a thing as magic? What if it had actually worked for her and that was the only reason Garth was marrying her? What if it was an evil thing? Dan would say it was evil. At the very least it was profoundly selfish and manipulative, the opposite of what Dan said God was. He said God was unselfish, loving, and giving. A feeling of repulsion and loathing for the thing around her neck rose in Hannah's throat and she yanked so hard on it that it broke off. She could feel a stinging welt around her neck as the leather broke against her skin, but she felt relief to be rid of it. She got out of bed, pulled open her curtain, and hurled the thing away, not even waiting to see where it landed. Then slowly she crawled back into her bed and prayed.

"Oh God, please forgive me. Please let Dan forgive me, too, God. I'm so sorry." Hannah said the words aloud into her pillow. Over and over again she repeated them and gradually her shock subsided and she began to think.

She found herself thinking of Dan and how he prayed. She

remembered how sure he seemed that God loved him and how he said that God loved her too. If God had loved her, surely He wouldn't any longer, not after what she had done.

But then who is forgiveness for if not for people that you love? She wished she knew more about forgiveness. She wished she had thought more about the old Sunday school stories about Jesus dying on the cross.

"Oh, Jesus, please, please forgive me for this. And make Dan forgive me too," she prayed aloud again.

৯৬

She felt better when she awoke a few hours later. She heard lunch being carried out onto the veranda, and she realized she was hungry. Then she remembered Sophie. Sorrow and guilt overwhelmed her. She heard footsteps coming down the hall. Her stomach knotted as her door opened quietly.

"Oh, good, you're awake." It was her mother. "Lunch is ready. And Garth sent over a message to invite us both for tea this afternoon. He said his mother was looking forward to getting to know us better.

"Just think; I haven't a decent thing to wear and neither have you, but there's not a thing we can do about it until we can get up to Nairobi to do some shopping. Oh, Hannah, you should have warned me that you were thinking of becoming engaged and we could have been prepared. This is such an embarrassment—actually to be invited to tea with Lady Whitehead and on such dreadfully short notice!"

"I'll be there in a minute, Mother," Hannah said, wearily getting out of bed. Her hunger had vanished. Tea with Lady Whitehead and her mother and Garth. It didn't bear thinking about. As she tried to push the thought out of her mind, she had a vision of her whole future: an endless round of tea parties, cocktail parties, dinner parties, and dances whirlpooling off into the distance, sucking her deeper and deeper until she died. She shook her head to free herself from the horrible thought. "It must be because I feel so awful about losing Sophie that I have become so morbid. I am actually engaged to be married to Garth Whitehead. This is the happiest day of my life. I must remember that." And with that thought held resolutely before her, Hannah marched out to the veranda.

However, eating turned out to be an entirely different matter. The cold roast beef and the jellied braun set out at the table turned her stomach. And there was a letter on the table waiting for her. It bore an English stamp, not a European one, and for a moment Hannah dared to hope it wasn't from Dan. But she recognized his handwriting on the envelope.

"There, now you can write back to that young man and apologize for losing his elephant and at the same time mention that you are engaged to Mr. Whitehead. It will be good to have done with him. I didn't really like him at all, the way he trailed around after you whenever he had a chance. I was almost beginning to think he was in love with you. But you write to him directly and explain."

Hannah tore open the envelope with trembling hands and began to read.

Dear Hannah,

I am writing to you from a hospital in England. I took a shell to the legs and seem to be full of shrapnel. My left leg can be repaired quite easily with a bit of minor surgery, but it is still touch and go for my right leg. I am thankful to God, because I am one of the lucky ones who escaped the shelling with my life. But it looks as though I will be out of commission and will have to be sent home. I miss Africa terribly, as you know, as well as Sophie, and of course, you too. I hope to come out on the very first ship as soon as I am well enough to travel. Please pray that the Lord will be gracious enough to save my leg for me so that I may be able to continue my work. And give my love to Sophie. I am so grateful to you for taking care of her for me. God willing, I'll be home soon.

In Christ's love,
Dan

Silently, Hannah put the letter back into the envelope, but Mrs. Butler had recognized the handwriting.

"Well, how is your Mr. Williams?" Mrs. Butler began as soon as she saw Hannah was finished reading the letter. But she didn't wait for Hannah's answer. "You and Garth could well be married by the time the war is over! Of course, we must set the date right away. I'm sure all the Whitehead family in England need to be notified and given enough time to attend, if they should choose to. And then there are our own relations . . ."

Hannah wasn't listening. She pushed her chair out from the table and put on her old hat.

"Hannah, come back! You haven't touched your lunch!" But Hannah just kept walking. She wanted to go over to the Osbourne place and arrange to bury Sophie.

9

The days after her engagement turned out just as Hannah had feared. She hardly had time for her practice at all with all the shopping and partying. Everyone assumed she would be giving it up anyway after she was married, and she didn't have the courage yet to tell them that she didn't plan to. But the wedding, much to Mrs. Butler's consternation, was not going to be imminent. Lady Whitehead had had them over to tea on the first day, the day Sophie had died, and suggested again to Hannah and her mother that a long engagement would be a good idea. It would give Hannah time to think through her decision, she said, and then there was also the problem of the war. Garth had agreed, saying that he didn't want to rush Hannah into anything. He had wanted her to take all the time she needed to be sure.

"But, she is sure!" Mrs. Butler had protested. "Aren't you Hannah, dear?"

But Hannah had smiled gratefully up at Garth, and Lady Whitehead had inquired whether Mrs. Butler had seen the gardens. She had not and so the two of them went for a tour, leaving Hannah and Garth together on the patio.

In Garth's shining presence, all the qualms Hannah had felt about marrying him dried up to nothing, and she basked in the pleasure of his attention.

"Well, Han, old chap," he said smiling at her as he reached over to take her hand in his, "this is quite a situation we've gotten ourselves into, isn't it?" Then he bent over the table and kissed her. "I hope you aren't having second thoughts."

"Oh, no, of course not!" Hannah replied, only remembering the happiness she felt when they were together. He kissed her again.

"I've been thinking, Hannah," he spoke again. The suddenly serious tone in his voice sent a fearful shiver down Hannah's spine. "Jim and I have been talking about a safari company for quite a while, and I think I will go along with his idea. There is a lot of money to be made off people who want to be taken out on safari to bag some big game. Trophy hunters generally can afford to pay a pretty price to get what they want." Hannah looked silently up into his blue eyes. She knew what was coming next, but she didn't want to hurry it, so she waited.

"So you see, Han, old chap, it would be a bit awkward having a new wife and to be off on safari all the time. I was just thinking that perhaps we could prolong our engagement for a little while longer than I first thought, just until Jim and I get the business up and running. Then, of course, I wouldn't need to be out on safari all the time. Jim and I could alternate and we could both spend more time at home with our wives."

NO! NO! NO! Hannah's mind screamed. *He is putting me off. I must fight for him.* She had come so close; she couldn't let him go now. She forced herself to think. What could she say? Jim was the answer.

"But what about Jim? What will Jim do with his farm if he is on safari all the time? And Fiona? What will Fiona do?" She knew she was speaking too fast and her voice sounded high-pitched and desperate. Garth smiled. She could see he already had thought that through.

"Hannah, Hannah, you sound so upset. Don't worry, my dearest, it is only temporary." Hannah could feel her face turning red with rage at the patronizing tone of his voice, but his next words made her forget her anger.

"And really, I am doing it all to help Jim and Fiona out. Didn't you know that they have lost their farm? It seems that Jim had lost quite a bit of money on the horse races this season and he had to put his farm up for sale to pay the debts off. They are moving into town, so Jim will need to find some other work. This will be the perfect opportunity for him to support Fiona and rebuild his life. I really am doing it as a favor for him. It is important to make absolutely sure the business is a complete success, for his sake. And Fiona's too."

Hannah was speechless. She had had no idea that Fiona and Jim were in such trouble. She thought back to the day Fiona had asked her to pray for her and how she had prayed once and then never given it another thought. The rest of what Garth said washed over her like a rainstorm. She just trudged on through it until Garth kissed her goodbye and she and her mother drove home.

She hadn't even really spoken to Fiona for such a long time. She wondered if she could do anything to make amends for how much she had neglected the only real friend she had ever had.

Mrs. Butler chatted gaily on about the wonders of Garth's home and the charms of his mother as they bumped over the red, dusty roads. Hannah could see a storm building on the horizon, but she thought if she urged Kindye into a trot, they would be home in time.

She couldn't stop thinking about Fiona. It was the first time in weeks that she had really been able to think of anyone but Garth, only this time she felt very guilty and ashamed. Would Fiona be able to forgive her if she went and spoke to her and apologized for having been so self-centered?

By the time they reached home, just as the first furious drops of rain were lashing the treetops, she had made up her mind that she must at least visit Fiona and apologize. If Fiona were able to forgive her, then she would try to think of how she could help her. But Fiona was in the midst of moving, according to Garth. She would have to wait a week or two until she had settled into her new home. This would give Hannah time to think through how she would approach Fiona.

In the days that followed, Hannah lived for the moments when she and Garth were alone together and he was touching her and looking into her eyes and reassuring her that everything was going to be wonderful after they were married, but they must wait. But in between those moments there were the parties and the shopping and the teas, and these in turn had to be fitted around Hannah's practice delivering calves, repairing wounds, and caring for sick horses. Hannah wondered if she saw less of Garth now than she did before they had become engaged. He never asked her to go to the stables and look at his horses anymore. In fact, he didn't seem to have the same degree of interest that he used to have in racing. These days, all he seemed to talk about with his friends was safaris and big-game hunting. That was where all the money was to be made, they all said. He and Jim were planning a big safari soon, as soon as they felt safe enough to travel. And once the war was over, they would start a safari company and make lots of money. And of course, the war would surely be over soon. *But the news from Europe is not very encouraging,* Hannah thought.

Hannah found herself thinking of Sophie every time they spoke of safaris. She hated to think of Garth, her own husband, stalking and shooting elephants. Every time they shot an elephant, she would remember Sophie being shot. She knew this was a silly thing, but she was finding it hard to get over Sophie's death. It had taken her two weeks to get up the courage to write to Dan and confess to letting her run away and be killed. But she felt better when she had done it because she hadn't tried to hide her own role in Sophie's death. She had asked Dan to forgive her, but she couldn't bring herself to tell him about her engagement. She would tell him in person, she decided, when he finally came back, and that might not be for a long time. Meanwhile, she missed the little elephant trotting around after her wherever she went.

At the interminable dinner parties that she now went to with Garth, she often found herself wishing she were out in the stables settling Sophie in for the evening. She tried to behave with grace and good humor, but Garth's friends really had very little in common with her. At first they were very condescending, saying things like, "Well, Miss Butler. You are a vet, I believe. How nice. Garth must have relied on you to help him a lot with his horses."

Or, "I suppose being so 'horsey' as you are, you and Garth must have quite a lot to talk about. Isn't that so romantic?"

Or, "My dear, we were all so shocked to hear that Garth had finally become engaged. How on earth did you manage to snare him? You must have a secret weapon." The ladies would exchange knowing looks across the table at each other, and Hannah wouldn't know how to reply. She counted the hours until Garth would drive her home in his buggy.

One evening when she and Garth were at the Kikuru Club and Garth had rushed off to talk to some gentlemen, she was looking over the ladies present to see whom she could approach when she noticed Leticia. Her heart sank. Leticia had been in South Africa visiting relatives, so she hadn't seen her since before her engagement. Just as she was about to duck quickly behind a potted palm, Leticia caught her eye. Hannah winced and braced herself as Leticia made her way over to her, looking grimly cheerful in a beautiful cream silk dress that had far too many little fashionable touches in the cut of the sleeves and the scoop of the neckline ever to have been bought in Nairobi.

"Congratulations, Miss Butler. I hear you and Garth are engaged." Leticia's voice had a very slight edge of anger to it, Hannah thought, but then none of Garth's lady friends had been exactly overjoyed at his engagement.

"Yes," Hannah replied, "we've been engaged for nearly a month now."

"Oh, really? I have just arrived from South Africa, where I was visiting my mother, so I only just heard. I must say I was quite surprised. I thought you looked after his horses." Leticia spoke to Hannah as though she were an upstart of a servant, marrying her master. This was by far the rudest treatment she had received yet, and she blushed with anger and embarrassment.

"Hannah, I was hoping to find you here tonight!" Hannah turned to see who was speaking. To her relief she looked into the warm face of Fiona Brown.

"Oh, Fiona," she gasped, "I'm so sorry. I heard about—" Suddenly she remembered that Leticia was there and probably didn't know Fiona's situation. She stopped.

Fiona took Hannah by the elbow and looked at Leticia. "Excuse me, Miss Charlesworth, but I must just borrow Miss Butler for a moment," and she steered Hannah away. Hannah silently complied, not knowing what to make of Fiona's new friendliness.

"Hannah," she said when they were alone, "I feel awful about my behavior towards you lately. Please forgive me for being so rude and unfriendly. I must apologize to you. I have been unforgivably rude to you since you and Garth became engaged and it was completely uncalled for. I was angry with Garth because I thought he was the one who was leading my husband astray and making him spend all our money on the horse races. And I lumped you in with my feelings about Garth. I hope you'll forgive me."

Hannah blushed to the roots of her hair. "Oh, Fiona, don't mention it, please; it is I who has behaved rudely toward you. I had no idea you and Jim were encountering such difficulties, and I haven't been a friend to you at all. I have only been thinking of myself. I am so sorry, Fiona."

Impulsively, Fiona reached forward and hugged her. "You must come and see me in my new home, Hannah," she said as they walked over to sit together and talk.

Hannah hardly noticed the evening fly by, even though she hadn't seen much of Garth. And then he sent her home with his syce, rather than driving her home himself. He kissed her good-bye as he handed her up into the buggy, and she was bouncing along the road in the moonlight without Garth.

Secretly she felt grateful for the reprieve. She was getting very weary, with work during the day and being out late two or three nights a week. And there was so much to worry about all the time, as her mother made clear. She must buy clothes and shoes and all sorts of bits and pieces to complement them. Mrs. Butler dragged her up to Nairobi several times for shopping sprees. These days were exhausting and long, although Hannah did enjoy the new clothes. She surprised herself with this discovery. She had never been interested in clothes before, but now she began to like the looks of herself in beautiful colors and fabrics. She had to admit she also liked the effect her new appearance had on Garth and the other men in his circle. This was a new feeling for Hannah.

But during the next few weeks, when Hannah seemed slightly tired, Garth often sent her home before him with the syce. She would try to insist that she was having a lovely time and would wait for him, but he wouldn't hear of it. She looked peaked, he would say, or something similar, as he walked her out to the waiting buggy and kissed her goodnight. Hannah thought the ordeal of the dinner parties wasn't really worth it for a quick peck on the cheek at the end of the evening.

One morning Hannah was having a late breakfast because she had arrived home exhausted, and alone with the syce, after one of the dinner parties. As she pushed the sliced mango around her plate, grateful that there was no animal emergency to have to deal with, she decided that the time had come to go and see Garth. The times they were alone together were further and fewer between. She simply must tell him that she really was finding that the parties were not enjoyable anymore if she had to go home alone.

She was absorbed in this thought when a toto came riding up the driveway. She stood up to see what he wanted, and he handed her a letter. She took it absentmindedly, giving him a sixpence for his trouble, expecting it would be another call for her to go to a sick animal. She gasped audibly as she read.

Dear Hannah,

I am back at last. Although I still have both my legs, it was a rough trip over. I am afraid that I am not feeling terribly well, yet, but I would love to see Sophie. Of course, I am looking forward to seeing you too, but perhaps the excitement would be a bit much for me just yet. If you would be so kind as to send Sophie over for a visit, or even to stay here, depending on how much you will miss her, I would be most grateful and I'm sure it would help to speed my recovery.

Yours as always,
Dan

"Dan's back. He hasn't heard. My letter was too late." She spoke out loud.

"Oh, well, if that's all it is," replied Mrs. Butler, who had come out to see who had arrived. "I thought it was something serious. You look like you've seen a ghost. Anyway, as I was saying last night about long engagements . . ."

Hannah wasn't listening. "I'll have to go and see him myself," she said.

"Yes, of course you will," Mrs. Butler responded. "You and Garth are the ones who have to set the date before anything else can really be done."

Hannah gave her mother a puzzled look and excused herself. She would go and see Dan right away. The less time she gave herself to think about it, the better. She sent a toto out to the stable with a message for the syce to saddle up Kindye at once.

The ride to Dan's was long and stressful. Hannah lived over and over again the moments after she heard of Sophie's death. She tried out different ways of telling Dan, sometimes confessing outright that it was all her fault, and other times making it sound as if it was only an unavoidable accident. By the time she came over the hill and saw the mission station in the valley below, nestled comfortably by a stream, surrounded by stately old thorn trees, she was in a state of utter turmoil. She reined Kindye in for a moment and tried to collect her thoughts. Why, oh why, hadn't she written sooner? None of this would be happening if she had. Just then a dog down at the station noticed the strange horse up on the hill and started barking. There was no turning back now. Hannah nudged Kindye and they headed downward.

She was surprised that Dan didn't come out to meet her. One of the schoolchildren came out instead and took Kindye. "Bwana's in the house," he explained, nodding toward the door of the little tin-roofed building off to the side of the large schoolhouse. Hannah took a deep breath to steady her nerves and went over to knock on the door. But the door was open.

"Hello," she called out hesitantly, peering into the gloom inside. There was a creaking noise, and as her eyes adjusted to the darkness, she saw a figure moving slowly towards her in a wheelchair.

"Hannah! What are you doing here? Did you bring Sophie with you?" The voice was thin and colorless and for a moment Hannah didn't recognize it as Dan's. She stood in the doorway, staring in horror.

"What happened? You never told me!" she blurted out.

"There was a war, Hannah. These things happen in a war, you know." Hannah was speechless. There was emotion to the voice now, but it was bitter and sarcastic. "I wanted you to send Sophie over, not to come yourself. Now, you see why."

There were a few moments of complete silence while Hannah tried to take in the sight before her. Dan's legs were thin and useless in the chair, but the most horrifying thing was the huge scar across his face. It sliced right from his chin, over the lips and up the right cheek to the temple, just missing the eye. "I'm so sorry, Dan," she managed to whisper.

Dan shrugged, "Don't be. I'll live."

"Sophie's dead," she blurted out quickly in case she gave in to the overwhelming urge she was feeling to turn and flee.

"What? Why didn't you tell me? When? How? What do you mean, dead?"

"I did tell you, Dan, but you must have left England before my letter arrived. I'm sorry, Dan, please forgive me. It was my fault. I accidentally let her follow me to Osbourne's and he thought she was a wild elephant and shot her. She was getting so big, you see. It was a terrible mistake. Please forgive me, Dan. I'm so sorry."

Dan's voice was cold and distant. "Come in here, Hannah, and sit down. Explain what happened to me again; I don't quite understand."

Hannah came inside and repeated the whole story of Sophie's death. She sat at a small table opposite Dan, and he listened in total silence. The longer he was quiet, the more Hannah talked, desperate to get some kind of reaction from him, but he just stared at her while she babbled away. Finally, realizing how ridiculous she sounded repeating herself over and over again, she said, "That is the whole story, Dan. It was my fault. Please forgive me."

"There is just one thing I don't understand," replied Dan. "Why didn't you go and look for her if you knew she was missing?"

Hannah realized with a sinking feeling that she had been carefully avoiding mention of Garth, who was in fact the whole reason for her behavior on that day. She took a long, shuddering breath and plunged in.

"I was invited to a party at Garth Whitehead's house. His mother had just arrived from England, and he had invited me to meet her." Dan stared at her, as if there should be more to the story than that. "He asked me to marry him. We are engaged," she added lamely.

"Ah," replied Dan. "Well, thank you for coming. And congratulations on your engagement. I hope you'll be very happy. Good-bye." He turned his chair around and wheeled through a door on the far side of the room. Hannah stared after him for a moment. She could feel hot emotion rising up inside her, and she suddenly turned and rushed outside to find Kindye before she erupted into a rush of tears.

Hannah's ride back from the mission station was as unseeing as her ride out. At first she was blinded by the tears streaming down her face. The picture of Dan—broken, scarred, and ugly in the small, dark hut waiting for Sophie—made her weep with sorrow. But the cold harshness of his voice had shocked her more, and then she wept for what the war had done to his mind and heart. Finally she remembered his abrupt dismissal of her and how he refused to answer her when she begged him for forgiveness, and she became angry. Furious even. He was a Christian, wasn't he? She wept tears of humiliation and frustration. What was the good of being a Christian if you treated people this way?

But as she got closer to home, she began to feel calmer. Her emotions were spent and she was drained. Her mind began to function again. She had heard reports of the terrible suffering the soldiers were experiencing in the war. How could she know what Dan had been put through over there in those trenches, watching his friends die and being in danger of dying every minute himself? And then to be wounded the way he was. How would he be able to carry on with his life's work and live in Africa when he couldn't even walk? And the scar across his face made him look hideous. Of course he wouldn't behave like the old Dan she used to know. How could he?

And then to find out so suddenly about Sophie. She remembered how devastated she had been when Sophie died, and she hadn't even been through a war. She couldn't expect Dan to take it well. She should have realized that. And to have to face her seeing him in the condition he was in would be humiliating for him. She should have understood that he didn't want to see her or he would have invited her over with Sophie. Any man would be embarrassed to be seen in such an incapacitated condition, especially a man who was used to being so independent.

Suddenly, she felt a twinge of guilt. It took her a couple of minutes to work out what was causing it. Dan was upset about her marrying Garth. She should have realized that he was beginning to have feelings for her by the way he wrote to her, but she was so preoccupied with Garth she didn't want to admit it to herself. Deep down she must have known; after all, that was why she didn't want to talk about why she had failed to look for Sophie when she knew she was missing. It was only when she told him about her engagement that he turned and left.

But as soon as Hannah had thought this through, she became angry. After all, she had a right to become engaged if she chose. She had never given Dan any kind of encouragement. They were just friends; she had never thought of him in any other way. He had no right to be upset about her engagement; in fact, he should be happy for her. Her anger acted on her like a bucket of cold water. All of a sudden she felt better. She was not the one at fault here. Dan was.

And what about his Christian duty to forgive her when she asked him to? What was the use of all this high-flown talk about forgiving one another if you only did it when you felt like it? She had apologized for what happened to Sophie, and after all, how was she to know that old Jack Osbourne would shoot her? It was, at least partly, just an accident, and Dan didn't have any right to treat her so contemptuously. So much for Christianity. Perhaps Rosie's magic charms worked better anyhow. After all, she was engaged now, even if it didn't bring her as much happiness as she thought it would.

By the time Hannah arrived back at the house, she was starving. It was well past lunchtime, so she would have to go around to the kitchen to see if there was anything in the pantry. Then she would head down to the clinic to see if anyone needed seeing to. Dan Williams was old news now. She was sorry for him, with all his injuries, but he was no longer any of her concern. And neither was that useless faith and prayer business that he used to be so proud of.

10

Mrs. Butler met Hannah at the door in a state of high anxiety. "Good gracious, Hannah, where have you been? Don't you realize it is Garth's going-away party tonight? And look at the state you're in, filthy and tired and sunburnt! He will be gone for three months. The very least you could do is to look nice for him before he goes."

"Mother, there is plenty of time to get ready. And I really don't feel much like going anyway. There will be so many people there and I honestly don't feel like smiling and simpering all night." Hannah spoke without thinking.

"Hannah Butler! I really don't know what a man like Garth Whitehead sees in you, but since he sees something, you'd better at least try your best to fit in with his friends. They are the best of what little good society we have here and you simply must make an effort.

"And I think you and Garth should set a date for the wedding before he leaves. Lady Whitehead and I both need to know when to tell people to expect to come. I want you to mention it to him tonight. He won't be leaving for two more days, so you can make some sort of decision before then if you get him thinking seriously tonight. I want you to do that for me."

Hannah sighed and went through to the kitchen to ask that some hot water be prepared for her. This endless round of parties was turning out to be more work than running her veterinary practice. *But at least Garth will be gone in a couple of days and I'll have some peace,* she thought.

As she bathed and washed her hair for the evening, she found herself descending into a blacker and blacker mood. At first she decided that it was Dan's reaction to the news of Sophie that was upsetting her—that, and the fact that Garth was going to be gone for three months. But the more she thought about her life these days, the more she realized it was more than that. She was feeling frustrated that she was being pressured by her mother into setting a date for the wedding. Surely it wasn't supposed to be this way. The prospective groom shouldn't be avoiding the wedding, should he?

Her hair was still wet and she was still in her housecoat, but she was feeling so low at the thought of Garth avoiding the wedding that she sank down onto her bed and lay without moving. As she thought about it, she realized Garth wasn't just advoiding the wedding he was advoiding her, too. She could hardly remember the last time they had had any time alone together. The only time she saw him these days was at parties, endless parties. And she usually went home with her mother. What had she gotten herself involved in? Her wildest dreams had become reality and they were turning out to be nightmares.

There was a rap on the door. "Hannah? Are you nearly ready?" Mrs. Butler's voice jarred her peace.

"Yes, give me a few more minutes, Mother. It won't matter if we are late."

Hannah sighed and dutifully swung her feet to the floor and began to brush out her hair. Her mother was right. She wasn't as pretty or bubbly as all the other girls Garth knew. What did he see in her? At first she thought it was because they both loved horses, but they hardly spent any time with his horses anymore. Garth seemed to have lost interest in racing. All he thought about now was safaris and making money. Maybe he had lost interest in her too. The thought sent a chill through her heart. Being engaged to Garth wasn't turning out to be the joy she had thought it would be, but perhaps it was her fault. Perhaps if she could just try a little harder to be like the other girls, then Garth would remember how he had loved her and things would go back to the way they were at the beginning. Yes, she decided, setting her face like flint, she would try harder. She wished she hadn't thrown away the cowrie shell Rosie had given her.

Later that evening when Hannah and Mrs. Butler arrived at the Whiteheads', the twinkling lights and the music and all the horses and surreys lined up outside the stately old place sent a shaft of fear into Hannah's heart. Surely, this was not where she belonged. She was much more at home in the stables, with the animals. She wanted to turn and run, but it was far too late for that now. She had to face what she had gotten herself into.

As she ascended the steps up to the veranda with her mother on her arm, she caught a glimpse of Garth chatting with some ladies in front of the window. They were all laughing and giggling. Hannah could tell that Garth was teasing the prettiest one about something by the way she blushed and nodded her head so that the ringlets that framed her pink cheeks bobbed up and down. Garth smiled indulgently down at her and Hannah wondered if he had ever looked at her that way. She doubted it.

As they entered the room, Lady Whitehead spotted them and came over to greet them. "Hannah, my dear, and Florence. How lovely to see you. May I take your shawls? Juma, please fetch the ladies a glass of wine." She linked her arms through both of theirs and drew them into the party. Hannah glanced over her shoulder. Garth was still talking to the group of ladies. He hadn't noticed that she had arrived. This was so very unlike the first party he had invited her to, where he had proposed. What had she done to let things go so far wrong?

"Hannah! How are you?" Hannah turned and saw Fiona Brown smiling beside her.

"Oh, hello, Fiona. It's nice to see you. You are looking very well."

"Thank you, Hannah." She smiled warmly and Hannah was grateful that Fiona was her friend.

Mrs. Butler had moved on to another group of guests once Fiona had begun to converse with Hannah. But in the moment of silence that followed, a familiar voice cut through the rest of the party buzz. Hannah looked up to find that Leticia was standing a few feet away with her back to them, regaling a group of her friends with something she felt strongly about.

"Yes, it simply wouldn't do to have your fiancée working out in the stables amongst all the animals and the dirt and what have you. I can't imagine what Garth thought he was doing! Well, I hope they will be very happy." She glanced significantly over at Garth, who was animatedly chatting with another group of ladies.

Hannah wished she could crawl under a couch and hide. She was never very good at playing the games that other women played with each other. She suddenly felt overwhelmed with longing for Sophie, and tears came to her eyes. Luckily, Leticia was sweeping off in the direction of Garth and his group of ladies. Hannah took two or three steps backwards as if she had been hit and fortunately bumped into a settee, where she sank down gratefully. Fiona, looking concerned, quickly sat down beside her. Hannah wished she would go away so she could be alone for a moment, but Fiona's voice was sympathetic when she spoke.

"Never mind Leticia, Hannah. She is only jealous. After all, Garth is quite a catch, or so people think."

Hannah was grateful for the kind tone of Fiona's voice, but she was too overcome to say anything. She sat quietly for a moment, then looked up and saw Garth, who finally looked her way. He excused himself and came over to greet her.

"Hannah, my dear. You slipped in without my noticing." He bent over and kissed her on the cheek. "Hello, Fiona! How are you?" Fiona merely nodded in response, but Garth didn't seem to be offended.

"What's the matter, Hannah? Your eyes are rather bloodshot and your face is all red. Did you drive too fast and catch a bit too much wind? Perhaps you'd better retire to the powder room for a few minutes and fix up your face. You wouldn't want people to see you looking so disheveled.

"Leticia, how are you?" Garth suddenly caught sight of Leticia as she sidled back over to Hannah's side. "I haven't seen you for ages. My, my you're looking even lovelier than I remember!" He bent over and whispered into Hannah's ear. "Just pop over to the bedroom for a few minutes and powder your nose." Without missing a beat, he straightened up and took Leticia's arm. "Let me fetch you a glass of wine."

Hannah looked after him in horror.

"Come with me, Hannah." It was Fiona. She took Hannah's elbow and steered her out of the room and into the garden. "Let's walk out here for a few minutes until you feel better," she said as they stepped onto the soft dewy grass of the front lawn. Although the sounds of the party bubbled away behind them, Hannah was immensely grateful for the quietness of the garden.

"Thank you, Fiona," she whispered. They walked along the edge of the lawn in silence. A few tree frogs croaked in the night air and cicadas buzzed lazily around them. There was the odd bird that dared compete with the noise of the party, and a guest's horse whinnied impatiently now and then, but to Hannah it was blessed silence.

After they had made a complete circuit of the lawn and were about to start another one, Hannah's emotions became too powerful to contain any longer. She felt she must tell someone what she had been thinking. There was no one else but Fiona. It was a humiliating admission, but she simply felt she must tell someone, and Fiona understood trouble.

"Fiona, I must tell you something," Hannah blurted out suddenly. Fiona looked at her and Hannah was grateful to see that she didn't look shocked, only sympathetic. "Fiona, I think I have made a terrible mistake by becoming engaged to Garth." She sighed audibly. Just saying the thought aloud lifted a huge burden from her shoulders. She waited for Fiona's reply, but there was only silence as the two of them followed their first set of footprints around the wet lawn. The silence stretched out for a long time, and Hannah thought she had made another mistake in speaking aloud when finally Fiona responded.

"Hannah, I have been praying for you." This was not the response Hannah was waiting for. The picture of Dan rolling angrily out the door in his wheelchair that morning flashed into Hannah's mind at the mention of prayer. Hannah groaned aloud.

"I'm sorry, Hannah, I didn't mean to offend you," Fiona said. "Only there is something I learned about only last week and I feel very uncertain about whether or not I should mention it to you. And I prayed for some guidance." She paused. Hannah didn't have anything to say. She didn't feel she could handle any more emotionally wrenching news today, but she had a sinking feeling that it would be better to find out and get it over with.

Fiona continued, "Anyway, after seeing how things are for you tonight, I feel that perhaps the Lord is leading me to say something, if you don't mind." She waited for Hannah to reply.

"Go on," Hannah said reluctantly and steeled herself to listen.

"Jim and Garth were talking about the safari business that they are starting up. I was writing letters in the bedroom and the house was very quiet, so I overheard their conversation. It seems that Lady Whitehead had told Garth that she wouldn't support his gambling any longer and that he had to settle down and get married or she would withhold his allowance."

Hannah blushed with shame. Even though she hadn't admitted it even to herself, she hadn't really forgotten the letter from his mother she had seen on Garth's table that day long ago. So, Garth did have an ulterior motive in marrying her. How could she have been so unbelievably stupid and naïve?

"Anyway, Hannah," Fiona went on, "I feel just awful telling you this. I know it is none of my business, but I hate to see you hurt and humiliated in front of people like Leticia, so I just want you to know that Garth told Jim that he was only going to stay engaged to you for as long as his mother was visiting and once she was gone he would break it off with you. By then he and Jim thought they would be making enough with their safari business, so if Lady Whitehead cut Garth off it wouldn't matter."

Fiona was speaking quickly now, rushing to get everything out in the open before Hannah could react. "I'm so sorry, Hannah, but I know how difficult it is to be married to a non-Christian man, and so I just wanted to save you some awful heartache. I hope you won't hold this against me."

Hannah was still thinking about the letter. They came to a bench in a dark corner of the garden, and Hannah sat heavily down. She was having so much trouble even finding the energy to stand up this evening. "I know, Fiona," she said, putting her head into her hands. "I've known all along, but I was just too stupid and vain to admit it."

Fiona put her arm around Hannah's shoulders. "I'm so sorry, Hannah," she said softly. As they sat there in the evening quietness and coolness, Hannah knew what she must do. She was grateful to have Fiona there because she wouldn't be able to back out of her plan once she had told someone.

"I read a letter that Garth had left out from his mother," she began. Fiona listened quietly. "It was ages ago, before Garth asked me to marry him, but I chose not to think about it. It was very stupid of me, but you know how Garth is. He can make you feel like you are the only person who exists for him, and I got caught in his spell. Actually, I chose to think that he was caught in mine." Hannah laughed bitterly at the thought of how she had tried to capture Garth with the magic shell. She had been caught in her own web.

"Thank you, Fiona. You are a real friend to me, and now I know what I must do." Hannah stood up. The heaviness that had weighed her down like a stone all night was slowly lifting and a sense of resolve energized her mind. Fiona stood up too. Together they walked towards the party, making a new path of wet footprints right across the middle of the lawn and up the steps of the veranda.

Hannah spotted Garth regaling a group of friends with stories of adventure and fortune to be had in the world of big-game hunting. Mrs. Butler caught sight of Hannah as she strode towards the center of the room.

"Hannah, there you are. Where have you been? I've been looking everywhere for you. Lady Whitehead wants to ask you about—"

"Not now, Mother! I have to speak to Garth."

Mrs. Butler dropped away from her daughter's side, but she looked after her nervously.

"Garth, I need to speak to you. Now." Hannah announced as she approached the group. He turned and looked at her, irritated with the intrusion.

"Hannah, I'm in the middle of a story, if you don't mind. And look at your shoes. What are you doing trekking all that wet grass in here?"

Hannah noticed Leticia, who was standing next to Garth, smirking with amusement at the scene she was creating. Steel entered her mind.

"Garth, I need to speak to you now," she repeated.

Garth turned and faced her again, but this time he was angry. Mrs.

Butler rushed up and tugged on Hannah's elbow. "Hannah, what do you think you are doing? Come away. Behave yourself."

Hannah shook her mother off. "Fine, Garth, if you won't talk to me alone, we'll talk here. I am breaking off our engagement. I know you have never intended to marry me. You don't even have time to speak to me in private anymore."

There was a collective gasp and Mrs. Butler shrieked. Garth stepped forward and put his hands on Hannah's shoulders. "Come now, Han, old chap, you're just overwrought. I'm sorry; I have been awfully preoccupied these days, and I admit I have shamefully neglected you. But there is no need to be so upset. Come with me; we'll just go to my study and sort it all out." He slipped one arm around Hannah's shoulder and tried to lead her towards the door, but she planted her feet like a balky colt.

"No, Garth, there is nothing to sort out. I know you are only engaged to me because of your mother. I know what you are up to. Now let go of me. I'm going home."

Garth stepped back, his face darkening with fury. "How dare you stand here in my home and accuse me like this in front of my guests." His voice cut like glass and his lips were pulled tightly back against his teeth. Hannah suddenly felt afraid, but she turned away to leave.

She had taken only one step when her shoulder was wrenched backwards and she was spun around to face Garth's raging anger.

"You little strumpet! You are the one that used me. You followed me around like a little puppy, begging me to pay attention to you, begging me to kiss you, and practically throwing yourself at me. I didn't notice you showing any reluctance to marry me, and now you have the audacity to use me like this in front of my mother and my guests. You are the one who has treated me shamefully." He suddenly turned to face the horrified guests. "She has used me, I tell you!"

Lady Whitehead was galvanized into action. "Garth, be quiet this instant!" Her voice wasn't loud, but the conviction with which she spoke silenced her son. He looked at her for a moment, stunned, and then turned tail and fled out of the front door.

This was the cue for Mrs. Butler to let out another shriek and faint dramatically into the surprised arms of a young man standing behind her. Hannah glanced at her mother, then back into the still-smirking face of Leticia. That was the last straw. She followed Garth to the door, where he had brushed rudely past Fiona.

"Fiona, would you be so kind as to give me a lift home?" Hannah was surprised at the strength and confidence of her own voice.

"By all means," Fiona answered, and the two of them walked arm in arm down the steps of the veranda, out into the warm welcome of the frogs and insects and away from the shock and disdain behind them.

11

$\mathcal{H}$ ow could you embarrass me like that, in front of Lady Whitehead, in front of all my friends, everybody who is anybody in this town!" Mrs. Butler shrieked as she burst into Hannah's room, catching her daughter as she slipped into bed. Her face was red with rage. Hannah faced her with a cold calmness.

"Mother, he was using me. Using me for money. Doesn't that make you angry?" Hannah suddenly saw her mother as a self-centered, fearful, lonely woman, not the raging, awe-inspiring, powerful woman she had feared for so long. She was amazed at herself for being so blind for all these years.

"I don't care!" spluttered Mrs. Butler, still livid. "I don't care what he was doing. You had no right to wash your dirty laundry in front of everyone in town. There are other ways to deal with men like that, and if you weren't so incorrigible, you would have seen that you could have used him in return. What did you think? He was put on Earth to cater to your whims?"

Her newfound ability to see through her mother gave Hannah an advantage. "Mother," she said firmly, "I will not be used like that. I doubt there was anyone else in that room who was surprised at what I said except you and me. And I don't need anything Garth Whitehead has. I am perfectly capable of supporting us both with my work."

"You are the most selfish child in the world! What do you think it is like for me to have to live with a spinster daughter and no grandchildren and, worst of all, absolutely no social standing whatsoever? What do you think it is like for me? Have you ever given a thought to the feelings of your poor mother? Or do you only think of yourself? What did I ever do wrong when I raised you? I should have stood up to your father. He spoiled you. Spoiled you completely, and now I have to suffer the consequences!" She turned and stormed out, slamming Hannah's door so hard the mirror on the back of it came crashing down.

Hannah went over to pick up the mirror. There was a large crack down the length of it, but it hadn't shattered. Automatically, her mother's voice came to mind, "It's bad luck to break a mirror."

"Luck. Magic." Hannah spoke the words aloud. It seemed that all her life she had been surrounded by superstition. It was bad luck to have been used so badly by Garth, but she had tried to lure him to her with magic. Everything was an illusion with one of them trying to control the other without the other one knowing. What a dishonest, unfair way to treat each other. How could she have mistaken it for love?

Dan's face slipped uninvited into her mind, as it did so often. Dan was the one who spoke of love. He seemed to think he knew what love was about. It was about God and prayer. But God didn't answer her prayers, so how could He love her?

Hannah crawled into bed again. She went on puzzling it out in her mind as she lay there in the darkness. If God had answered her prayer, she wouldn't have had to go to Rosie. She wouldn't have become engaged to Garth and she wouldn't have been used so shamefully by him.

And what about Sophie? If she hadn't just prayed for her, then gone rushing off to Garth's, Sophie might still be alive. Could she really expect God to answer her prayers when her own actions didn't correspond to what she was praying for? Perhaps she had been mistaken about God. Perhaps she should have been paying more attention to what she thought were unanswered prayers instead of being so intent on getting her own way by whatever means she could come up with. Perhaps it was time to change the way she thought about things. And with that in mind, Hannah fell into a deep and exhausted sleep.

She was awakened abruptly in the morning by a loud knock at her door. Without waiting for a reply, her mother strode in. She was still in her dressing gown and carried an envelope in her hand.

"This just arrived from Lady Whitehead for you. Open it." Mrs.

Butler's voice was cold and angry this morning, but she was obviously overcome with curiosity.

Hannah struggled to sit up and wake up, trying to remember everything that had happened the night before. She took the letter from her mother's hand and tore it open.

My dear Hannah,

I am writing to tell you how sorry I am to be losing you as a future daughter-in-law. I am deeply sorry for the way my son has treated you. I was rather afraid that that may be the case, which is why I encouraged you to take your time with the engagement. However, I confess I didn't want to admit to myself that he would do such a thing and I hoped that you and he were in love. You would have made a wonderful wife for him if he had treated you well, and I am sorry to lose you.

I will be returning home to England as soon as I can secure a passage on a ship. I wish you all the best of luck in your future.

Yours sincerely,
Lady Whitehead

Hannah silently handed the letter to her mother, who had been waiting impatiently for her to read it. Mrs. Butler took it, read it, and threw it down on Hannah's bed. Snorting angrily, she stalked out of the room. Hannah lay back down with a sigh.

Later, after breakfasting in silence with her mother, Hannah walked to the clinic feeling lighter and more content than she had for a long time. She would throw herself into her work, she decided. That had been the way she had dealt with the difficulties in her life up until now, and it had worked fairly well. There would be only one thing different and that would be that she would stay away from superstition. That was what had gotten her into trouble, and she would keep away from it.

The morning light slanted through the trees onto the damp, dewy road. Everything felt fresh and new, like the dawning of a new world. Birds were singing loudly, and Hannah felt it had been ages since she had heard them. Her mind had been so filled with Garth—first the all-consuming daydreams, then counting the hours when she would see him, wondering what he was thinking, analyzing how he had treated her the night before, and wondering how he would treat her that night. It was such a relief to be a part of the real world again—to feel the morning sun, listen to the birds, and look forward to a day of doing something worthwhile.

But as she drew closer to the clinic, she felt a certain emptiness. She still missed Sophie. She felt badly that Dan was so angry with her. If only she could go back to the way things were before she had become involved with Garth. She had spoiled so much. Or rather, she had let him spoil things for her.

She hadn't been long at the clinic before a note arrived for her. It was from Fiona, asking her to meet her for lunch in town, and at noon Hannah duly set out for the Kikuru teahouse where Fiona suggested they meet. Fiona was there, waiting at a table, when Hannah arrived. She rose excitedly when she saw her.

"Hannah, how are you today? I'm so glad you could come!"

Hannah pulled off her hat as she went over to Fiona's table, and wished she had gone home first and dressed up a little more. Fiona had on a light blue cotton dress and a small straw hat with a blue ribbon around it, and she looked so young and fresh. But it was too late to change now. *Besides,* she reminded herself, *I no longer need to impress anyone.* Nevertheless, she could feel a hostile glare boring into her from behind. Glancing up, she caught the image of Leticia in a mirror behind Fiona. She hadn't noticed her when she came in, sitting by the window staring at her with a look of amused contempt. Hannah focused her eyes on Fiona's welcoming face.

"Hello, Fiona. Thank you for inviting me. I'm afraid I didn't have time to go home to change into something nicer."

"Good heavens, this isn't Nairobi. Sit down and relax!"

Hannah sat down gratefully, and they ordered some sandwiches for lunch.

"I'm so glad you could come to lunch with me," began Fiona, leaning forward to speak to Hannah quietly. "I was worried about you after last night, and I just wanted to be sure you are alright."

"Yes, I'm just fine, thanks," Hannah replied. "I feel better than I have in weeks. I am very grateful to you for telling me what you knew about Garth. I only feel embarrassed to have been so gullible. I really made an awful fool of myself in front of all of Kikuru."

"I'm sorry it happened like that, Hannah. But you know, I admire you for facing up to it the way you did. And Garth deserved to be shown up like that in front of all his friends for what he did to you. He should be ashamed of himself."

The waiter brought cucumber sandwiches and set them in front of Hannah and Fiona. Hannah looked down at the little crustless triangles, nestled between a sprig of parsley and a couple of slices of tomato. She was starving and these ladylike little morsels would hardly keep her going for an hour. She wished she had ordered the plate of roast beef, but it had seemed so unladylike at the time. Still, she would have to get over trying to be ladylike at meals while working at a man's job all day. She sighed and started slowly, trying to make the sandwiches last.

"I do love to come here for lunch," Fiona was saying. "They make the most delicious sandwiches. The bread is so light and fresh and their pastries are just delicious, don't you think?"

Hannah was caught with her mouth full, but she nodded and finally managed to say, "I don't really know. It has been such a long time since I have taken lunch in town."

"Oh, dear, we'll have to do this more often then," Fiona responded, but Hannah could tell that her eyes were following someone else behind her. She winced, guessing who it may be.

"Hannah Butler!" came Leticia's shrill voice, and Hannah knew she had been right. "Well, I see you are out on the town already. Your broken heart heals very quickly, doesn't it?" Leticia's smile was brittle and icy.

"Leticia, I don't think you have any right to judge Hannah's actions," Fiona spoke up angrily. Leticia glared at her.

"Fiona Brown! Why, I didn't notice you. Is Hannah unable to speak for herself, poor thing?"

Sarcasm dripped off Leticia's words like icicles, and Hannah turned crimson with rage. She stood up, knocking her chair down and drawing the attention of everyone in the cafe.

"Why don't you marry him, Leticia? You would be just what he deserves." Hannah surprised herself with the vehemence of her voice, and obviously she must have surprised Leticia too. There was a pin-dropping silence while everyone waited for Leticia to reply. Leticia's face turned pink and then white.

"You are obviously upset because he was losing interest in you. I can assure you, if I had wanted to marry him, he wouldn't have lost interest in me." She spun around and swept out the door. The waiter scurried around the tables and set Hannah's chair up again. Hannah sat down, feeling the eyes of everyone in the room on her back, but in a minute the buzz of voices resumed like ripples of water in a pool covering the spot where a stone had just landed. Fiona reached out and took Hannah's hand.

"Well done, Hannah. You put her in her place. I didn't know you were so good at that sort of thing!" Hannah was surprised to hear a note of admiration in Fiona's voice.

"Neither did I," she replied, "but she had the last word."

"Never mind. She is not the kind of person you would choose for a friend, so I wouldn't worry about her opinion." Fiona paused, and Hannah could tell she wanted to say something else. "I was wondering, Hannah, if you would be interested in joining some of us at the church. We meet once a week to pray for our soldiers in Europe, and we also put together boxes of food and clothes to send to the soldiers in the trenches."

Fiona rushed on, speaking quickly to get all her thoughts out before Hannah could say no. "I notice that you and your mother come to church quite often these days, and I also hear that you and Dan Williams at the mission station are friends, so I thought maybe you would like to join us in doing church work. I thought it would be a good way for us to become better friends; that is, if you would like to become better friends with me." She stopped speaking suddenly and looked anxiously at Hannah.

Hannah was silent. There was something she wasn't quite sure about, and she wanted to ask Fiona. But it was an awkward question.

"Well, that sounds like a good cause," Hannah said haltingly, "only—well, I don't know if I would fit in properly. You say you pray for the men every week. I'm not sure about praying, you see. I haven't done that sort of thing before very much and I don't know if I . . . well, I'm just not sure . . ."

"Oh, Hannah, I don't mean to offend you," Fiona jumped in quickly. "I know we don't know each other very well. Perhaps I should tell you a little about myself first.

"When I came to live in Kikuru three years ago after Jim and I were married, I began to attend the church here. I never really gave much thought to my faith before, but I didn't know anyone here and the people I met at church were very welcoming and friendly. I joined the ladies' prayer group and I learned that Jesus had died for my sins. I could pray to Him and He would hear my prayers.

"At first I didn't know how important that was that I could pray, but as you know, my marriage to Jim has had its difficulties with him spending all his money on horses and racing. I turned to Jesus and asked Him to help me. And He did. I could feel His presence with us when we had no money. Always something would turn up to prevent us from starving. Even though we had to sell our farm to pay Jim's debts, Jim got work as a farm manager out on the Suffolk Estate. That was a real answer to prayer, and we will be able to start afresh. I think Jim was really shaken to his foundations when he lost the farm. I know I was. It has made him pay attention to God." Fiona paused and looked down at her plate, and when she looked up again, Hannah could see that her face was flushed with pleasure.

"I learned last week that we are expecting a baby. We had been hoping for news like this ever since we were married and we were beginning to worry that we would never be able to have a family. Jim was so happy. I don't think I had ever seen him so happy since we got married. I really think God is answering my prayers for Jim and he will become a Christian through all this.

"Then yesterday when he learned Garth's reasons for becoming engaged to you, I think his friendship with Garth was quite shaken. Last night after we drove you home, he was very concerned for you and actually, it was he who suggested I ask you to join our ladies' prayer group.

"Anyway, Hannah, please excuse me for telling you all these personal things, but I thought we might become friends and you may be interested in Christian things."

Hannah was thinking hard. Everything was happening so quickly. Everywhere she turned, she was being met by Christians who wanted her to pray and trust in Jesus. She was beginning to feel that she should trust, but there were still some things she didn't really understand. She didn't know if she really was able to tell anyone about them. It was still too new to put into her own words yet.

"I am so happy to hear you are expecting a baby," she said at last, buying herself a few more moments.

"Thank you. I am grateful to God for giving me such news at such a time."

"Fiona, it is so strange that you are asking me to join the prayer group. It seems to me that everywhere I turn these days, I am meeting up with God, or at least someone who wants to tell me about Him."

Fiona smiled broadly. "He is trying to reach you, and is already working in your life, Hannah."

"Well, I'm not terribly certain that is true, Fiona. There are some things that I have done and I don't think He is very pleased with me." As she spoke to Fiona, Hannah began to feel the need to tell her about Sophie. There was no one who knew but Dan, and he was so angry. It would be such a relief to tell someone who understood what had happened to Sophie. She blurted out the whole story while Fiona sat quietly and listened. Then she came to the part where she had tried to ask Dan to forgive her.

"He just turned and wheeled his chair out of the room," she explained, and suddenly Hannah felt her eyes filling with tears. It was not the part about Sophie that was making her cry anymore, but suddenly she realized what Dan meant to her. "He won't forgive me, Fiona, and how can I know that God will forgive me if he won't? I know I was wrong and I did pray for forgiveness, but I don't feel that anyone has forgiven me. And I haven't forgiven myself either, especially when I learned that Garth was just using me, and Sophie died for nothing!" Hannah's voice choked and she took her napkin and wiped her eyes.

Fiona reached over the table to take her hand again. "Hannah, I'm so sorry. I'm so sorry about Sophie and about Dan too. But Dan is only a man. He is not God; remember that. Even if Dan hasn't forgiven you, remember that God does forgive you." She reached into her bag and brought out a tiny Bible, worn and frayed around the edges. Hannah wondered how she could possibly read such tiny print, but Fiona flipped the little book open to a page and began to read. "If we confess our sins, he is faithful and just to forgive us our sins." She paused and looked at Hannah. "You confessed to God what happened to Sophie, Hannah, so you can be certain God has forgiven you. The only unforgiven sins are unconfessed ones."

"But Dan is a Christian. Aren't Christians supposed to forgive?" Hannah asked.

"Yes, they are, but Christians aren't always perfect. I am surprised that Dan treated you that way, Hannah. I have always heard the most wonderful things about him and the work he is doing. All I can think of is that the war was very hard on him, and he isn't quite himself yet. You know there is terrible suffering over there in the trenches. Men come back broken in body and in spirit. Perhaps something very bad happened to Dan and he is having trouble coping with it. That is why I believe it is so important that we pray for the poor men who are over in Europe fighting to end war forever."

"Yes, perhaps you are right," Hannah replied slowly, "but if God has forgiven me, then why don't I feel as though He has? I don't feel that He has even heard me."

"Hannah, it is not the way you feel that is important. It is what God says that is important. God cares about how you feel, but you can't go around making decisions based on feelings. You make decisions based on God's Word and then God takes care of your feelings. Think about what happened with Garth. Garth used your feelings to trap you. You must use a more reliable guide than your feelings to live your life. And you are forgiven by God; your feelings will come around later.

"Perhaps it would be helpful to you for us to meet together now and then to study the Bible so you understand what God is saying to you."

Hannah nodded. Their sandwiches were finished and the waiter had taken away their plates. Fiona paid the bill. "My treat," she explained.

"Jim is not gambling anymore, so I can afford a few little things now." She smiled and took Hannah by the elbow as they left the cafe. It was almost empty now, Hannah noticed gratefully, thinking of her meeting with Leticia.

The two women parted on the street after making arrangements for Hannah to come to Fiona and Jim's new home in town the following evening.

As Hannah rode slowly back to the clinic, she thought over what Fiona had said. Perhaps she was right about Dan. After all, he had suffered and he had seen others die horribly in the trenches. Her heart went out to him. She wished she had been a little kinder and more patient with him when she had told him about Sophie. She remembered his smiling blue eyes looking down at her before he had gone off to war and tears came to her eyes again. She let them flow down her cheeks, making dirty wet tracks in her skin as they mingled with the dust from the road.

"Oh Lord, if You have really forgiven me for letting Sophie die, please let Dan forgive me too. I love him, Lord." She caught her breath at the words she had prayed. She had told God about what she felt for Dan before she had even admitted it to herself. But it was too late for Dan now. Even if he managed to forgive her, how could he ever come to like or respect her again after what she had done? Not only had she neglected Sophie, but she had chased after Garth so shamelessly. Kindye turned the corner and the clinic came into view. Hannah pulled a dirty handkerchief out of her pocket and wiped her face. It was time to face the rest of her life.

12

*T*he days followed each other more quickly than Hannah dared to hope. She had plunged herself into her work, visiting sick animals on farms and seeing others in her clinic from morning to night. She spent a lot of time at Fiona and Jim's as well. Jim had joined her and Fiona in the little Bible studies that Fiona was doing for her to help her learn the basic truths of her new faith. She could see the happiness radiating around the couple as they bent over the table reading and talking with her, and her heart felt full with both joy for them and sorrow that she wouldn't see Dan again, that he hadn't forgiven her, that she hadn't treated him kindly when she had had the chance. But she tried hard not to think about him.

She tried to avoid her mother as much as she could. Mrs. Butler hadn't forgiven her either, but that was only to be expected. Surprisingly, Lady Whitehead had been very understanding. She had called in for tea a few days after the fateful party, just the day before she left on her way back to England. Mrs. Butler had apologized so profusely for her daughter's behavior that Lady Whitehead had hardly been able to get a word in edgewise as they sat drinking tea on the veranda. Hannah had wanted to jump up and shout at her mother to be quiet, but Lady Whitehead had looked over and given her a kindly but knowing look.

When at last Mrs. Butler paused for breath, Lady Whitehead addressed Hannah, "My dear Hannah, I have enjoyed getting to know you these last few months and I am terribly sorry about how abominably Garth has treated you." Mrs. Butler gasped in horror, but Lady Whitehead quickly continued.

"I'm afraid it was partly my fault, and I just want to apologize to you personally. As you know, Garth and I have had our differences, but I was hoping he would settle down. However, it was wrong of me to try to bribe him into doing so. My only regret is that he isn't good enough to fall in love with a sensible young woman like yourself. I know you would have made him a wonderful wife, and my wish is that one day you will make some other lucky young man very happy." She put her teacup down on the table in front of her.

"Oh, dear Lady Whitehead! How could you say such a thing! Garth is a wonderful young man. A little bit wild, but he will settle down soon." Mrs. Butler was bubbling over herself trying to mend unbroken fences between Hannah and Lady Whitehead, but Lady Whitehead simply smiled warmly at Hannah and picked up her sunshade.

"I must go, Mrs. Butler," she interrupted. "I have so much packing to see to before my train leaves tomorrow. Thank you so much for tea." She turned to Hannah and bent forward to kiss her cheek. "Good-bye, my dear; all the best to you in your future." And she slipped away down the steps and into her waiting surrey before Mrs. Butler could catch her breath. By the time she turned to face her daughter, Hannah had slipped inside and gone to her own bedroom to get ready to go back to work.

Two Sunday afternoons later Hannah was just finishing her lunch with her mother after they had come back from church. Hannah was debating her afternoon's activities in her mind. She wished God hadn't decreed that people should rest on the Sabbath. That meant a whole afternoon of her mother's company. She wanted to go to the clinic and work. Perhaps a farmer would have an emergency and she would have to attend to it, but that wasn't likely. She was just deciding that she would go out to the stables and saddle Kindye up for a ride when she caught sight of a figure riding up the driveway. *Oh, thank goodness,* she thought. *Someone needs a vet.* But she didn't recognize the figure. She waited until he came fully into view from out of the trees, and when she saw Dan Williams riding slowly up to the veranda she blinked with surprise. Her heart stopped beating for an instant, and she thought she must be imagining the sight. But Mrs. Butler wasn't.

"Good heavens, it's that missionary man again! I thought he had gone off to fight in the war. What is he doing here? I hope he doesn't have another elephant to foist upon you."

Hannah ran out to meet him, but then stopped short a few yards away, remembering how it had been the last time she saw him.

"Hannah!" he said, and she smiled with relief. Then she noticed the crutches strapped across his back like a gun. Awkwardly, he climbed down from his horse and transferred himself to the crutches. Hannah wanted desperately to help him, but she was still afraid he would be angry with her.

"Hannah, I'm so glad you are here. Would you mind walking with me for a few minutes? I need to speak to you alone, if you don't mind." Hannah was taken aback. His voice was not the way she remembered, stuttering and shy. He spoke with a calm determination. She walked over to his side, and they started slowly across the lawn. Mrs. Butler was calling out from the veranda.

"Hannah, where are you going? Hannah!" But to Hannah, she might have been a million miles away; she only heard Dan.

"Hannah," he was saying. He was trying to look into her face, but it was her turn to be shy, and she kept her eyes on the lawn at their feet. "Hannah, I behaved very, very badly when you came to see me a few weeks ago. I would like to apologize to you. It was shameful of me to treat you that way. Please accept my deepest apology. I am sorry, Hannah."

They reached a path that wound through the trees at the bottom of the garden. It was too narrow for them to walk side by side with Dan on his crutches, so Hannah paused. Dan glanced quickly back at the house, where Mrs. Butler was standing on the veranda, her hands on her hips, watching them angrily. He nodded to the path, indicating that Hannah go first. Tentatively, Hannah began walking into the cool, soft shade of the huge trees. The cool air soothed her hot, red face, and she was relieved that Dan could no longer try to catch her eye. But the silence between them was heavy, and it was Dan who broke it again.

"Hannah," the authority in his voice stopped her in her tracks, and she turned to look at him. "Hannah, I don't deserve it after the way I treated you, but I feel so ashamed of losing your friendship that way after all you did for me while I was gone. Your letters meant so much to me and I don't deserve your forgiveness, but I need to know if you will accept my sincere apology for the way I behaved."

"Oh, Dan, of course I accept your apology! It is I who needs to apologize to you for letting Sophie get away. It is I who needs to be forgiven by you!" The smile that Hannah saw forming in Dan's eyes drew her forward. She reached out to touch his arm, but instantly his eyes became as hard as glass, and Hannah pulled away as if she had touched a live coal. She turned away and walked quickly down the path, glad it was so narrow. She could hear Dan hurrying along behind her on his crutches.

"Hannah! Wait!" She stopped, but she didn't turn around. "Hannah, I must go now." His voice was still as hard as that last look in his eyes, and Hannah cringed as he spoke. "I am grateful to you for looking after Sophie and I have only thanks and gratitude to you for all you did so graciously. Thank you for accepting my apology, Hannah. Now before I go, I just want to offer you and your fiancé my best wishes, and may God bless you richly in your marriage. Good-bye, Hannah." How could he not know that she was no longer engaged! She turned to face him, but he was already heading away from her.

"Dan!" He kept going, and she realized her voice had only been a whisper. She ran after him and caught his arm. "Dan, I broke off the engagement weeks ago, after I saw you." He turned and looked at her. She couldn't read the new look in his eyes. She had never seen anyone look that way at her before, but it had a powerful effect on her. She wanted to laugh and cry at the same time.

"Hannah," his voice was shy and hesitant again, the way she remembered from before he went to war.

"Yes, Dan," she was still whispering.

"If I put my crutches down, will you take my arm and help me to walk without them?"

"Yes, Dan." And she took his arm and felt his weight bear down on her, but she stood firm and they took a step down the path.

"Hannah, I'm going to learn to walk again." He spoke slowly, his concentration on taking one step and then another. Hannah could feel his breath in her hair and she moved closer to support him more. She couldn't speak; the feel of his presence so close to her overwhelmed her. It was a far deeper and more intimate sensation than she ever remembered when she was near Garth. She suddenly realized Dan wasn't so much concentrating on walking; he was concentrating on her. She caught her breath, and she knew Dan had noticed. He stopped and turned, putting his hands on her shoulders.

"Hannah, I have another confession." He looked deeply into her eyes, but this time she couldn't turn away and hide; she was transfixed. "Hannah, I have fallen in love with you. You needn't answer me yet, but I need to know if I could ever hope that one day you might love me too. I have prayed and prayed that the Lord would help me to look upon you as just a dear friend, and I thought your engagement was my answer from Him. But now you are free and I cannot help myself from asking if there would ever be any hope for me. Of course, Hannah, you understand that if you take me into your life, you also take Jesus into your life too. If you can't have us both, then there is no hope for me." After such a long speech he stopped suddenly, hope and fear mingled together in his face.

Hannah could hardly take it in. After all these weeks trying to believe that he didn't even want her as a friend, now he was saying that he loved her. And looking into his face, she knew it was the truth. "I love Jesus, Dan. He is how I have managed to live through the last weeks." Dan was still watching her, hope a little stronger than fear now. But Hannah couldn't find words for anything else. She looked into his eyes, and they didn't need words anymore. He let his arms slip around her shoulders. Ever so slowly his lips touched hers, and time stood still for both of them.